CONTENTS

Foreword	By Eric Peters	
Introduction	The Bead Game	
Chapter 1		The Call
2		Waldzell
3		Apprenticeship
4		Two Orders
5		The Mission
6		Magister Ludi
7		In Office
8		The Two Poles
9		A Conversation
10		Preparations
11		The Circular Letter
12		The Legend

Joseph Knecht's Posthumous Writings

  I. *The Poetic Fragments from Knecht's Student Days.*

 II. *Three Incarnations:*

    i. *The Rainmaker.*

   ii. *The Father Confessor.*

  iii. *The Indian Incarnation.*

FOREWORD

LAST YEAR, following close upon the award of the Goethe-Preis, the Nobel Prize for Literature was bestowed upon Hermann Hesse. It was as if the World of Letters had suddenly awakened to the importance of this German-Swiss poet who is not only the author of numerous arresting and distinguished books, but was a prophet who had foreseen the world cataclysms of the last three decades and whose Cassandra-voice had been drowned in the clamour of conflicting national interests and ideologies.

Hesse, perhaps in greater measure even than Thomas Mann—another outspoken critic of Nazi Germany—inherited his full share of that *"Innerlichkeit"* which the latter recently described as the most obstinate trait of the German character. But, unlike the majority of his fellow-countrymen, he has been fully alive to this spiritual "Third Column," and ready to combat those tendencies to sadism and masochism, to pseudo-mysticism and an unhealthy preoccupation with pain and death which are its concomitants. Indeed his books bear eloquent testimony to the intensity of this writer's struggle to avoid the slippery slope that leads in the last resort to Prussianism, to Nazi fanaticism and all the horrors of Buchenwald and Belsen.

Born in the little Swabian town of Calw seventy years ago, Hermann Hesse came of mixed stock: Esthonian-Baltic on his father's, French-Swiss on his mother's side. Both families were actively concerned with missionary work, with which the young Hermann, too, was made to occupy himself. From early manhood on he travelled widely, ultimately settling in Switzerland, of which country he has become a naturalised citizen.

Already at the time of the 1914–1918 war Hesse's "unpatriotic" attitude incurred the censure of the powers-that-were in Germany, who regarded him as an apostate. His collection of poems, *Musik des Einsamen*, which he had completed in 1914 but which was not published until two years later, shows that he spoke a very different language from that of the warmongers. As early as October of that year—that is, two months after the outbreak of war—an essay of his entitled *O Freunde, nicht diese Töne!* was published in the *Neue Zürcher Zeitung*, in which he deplored the Gadarene stampede to disaster.

No, Hesse knew only too well that a man's—particularly a poet's—bitterest struggle is within himself, *"weil er den Feind in eigenem Busen trägt"*—because he bears the enemy within his own breast. His battles were not fought on the bloody fields of Flanders but in the quiet of his own room. Every one of his writings, over a period of half-a-century, has been devoted to the faithful delineation of this inner conflict which, he felt, would serve at once as a warning and an inspiration to his fellow-men. With laudable integrity and a high degree of self-dedication he has sought to unravel the skeins of a convoluted, not to say psychopathic personality, not from exhibitionism or a desire for sensationalism, but because he believed himself one who was destined *"allen zur Freude zu schaffen und nur sich selber nicht zur Lust"*— only to create joy and only to bring himself no pleasure.

Hermann Hesse first came to the notice of the reading public, when at the age of twenty-four, his *Hinterlassene Schriften und Gedichte Hermann Lauschers*, an autobiographical novel of refreshing candour but still immature and somewhat tentative, saw the light. Already in this early book his tendency to self-probing and introspection was evident: *"Ich muss Menschen sehen, Wagen fahren hören . . . auch sehne ich mich danach, Nächte in kleinen Weinschenken zu verbringen, mit gemeinen Mädchen gemeine Gespräche zu führen, Billard spielen und tausend Nichtigkeiten, zu treiben, die"*—and here comes the telling phrase— *"ich mir selber als tausend Gründe dieses Jammergefühls aufzählen kann, dass ich ohne Gründe und Betäubung nicht länger erträge"*—I must see men, hear the sound of passing cars . . . I long, too, to pass my time in little wine taverns, to have loose talk with loose girls, play billiards and do a thousand trifling things which I can enumerate to myself as a thousand reasons for this feeling of despair, which I could no longer bear without reasons and without narcotics.

His first collection of poems appeared a year later; these, too, followed traditional lines—the Swabian tradition of Hölderlin and Mörike, melodious, bucolic and wistfully romantic.

In *Peter Camenzind* (1904) we first encounter a character who is to reappear in many guises in this author's work: the wanderer—how often we meet him in the lyrics! —forever on the move, seeking the farther side of the rainbow, trailing the bluebird, but taking pleasures by the wayside as and when they offer. This Peter Camenzind, and Knulp, the quizzical hero of a trilogy of short tales published in 1915, are still, however, lighthearted and gay, brushing aside, even if they are not wholly oblivious of the antinomies of human existence which torture the later Hesse.

Unterm Rad (1906) and *Unterwegs* (1915) continue the autobiographical sequence, but it is not until the appearance in 1919 of *Demian* that we find Hesse exposing his innermost soul to the searching beam of pitiless self-analysis. It is significant that in this instance the author adopts the pseudonym "Emil Sinclair" who, it will be remembered, was Hölderlin's closest friend. This unabashed and uninhibited book first introduces the Eva—or *Urmutter-Motiv*, the idea of an eternal Lilith-like figure from whom we all spring, and to whom we yearn to return. Of this presence, which re-appears in many subsequent books, sometimes as the poet's own mother, sometimes as the combined image of all the women he has known, the dying Goldmund says to his friend Narziss (in a later work): *"Ich kann mich von dem Gedanken nicht trennen, dass statt des Todes mit der Sense es meine Mutter sein wird, die mich wieder zu sich nimmt und in das Nichstein und in die Unschuld zurückführt"*—I cannot rid myself of the thought that instead of Death with his scythe, it will be my mother who takes me to herself once more and leads me back into non-existence and innocence.

Klingsor's Letzter Sommer also came out in 1919 and besides the title story, a knowledgeable analysis of the painter's attitude to life, contains a short and tender little study, *Kinderseele*—based on a childhood experience of the poet's—and that relentless tale *Klein und Wagner*. In the last-named story the antinomy between the spirit and the flesh becomes so intolerable that the defaulting official,

Klein, having burned all his boats, comes in the end to welcome death by drowning. The death and transfiguration of Klein is a magnificent feat of imaginative writing.

Following a visit to India, Hesse wrote what is perhaps his most lyrical and contemplative book, *Siddartha* (1923). It is a prose poem on Eastern mysticism, wherein Siddartha's final summing-up comes very close to the kernel of Christ's teaching—universal love; nearer, indeed, than to that of Buddha, in whose time the story is set. Siddartha refuses to become a disciple of Gotama for, he says, true belief cannot be learned from another, however inspired—*"Nein, keine Lehre konnte ein wahrhaft Suchender annehmen, einer, der wahrhaft finden wollte"*—No, a true seeker can accept no doctrine, one who really wishes to find truth—but must be sought the hard way, through experience and suffering.

But *Siddartha* proves to be no more than a temporary lull in the poet's tempestuous pilgrimage. Two years after that entertaining psychological self-study *Kurgast*, in which Hesse focusses his sardonic eye upon the fads and foibles of the invalids at a well-known watering-place, the storm breaks out with renewed fury in *Der Steppenwolf*, published in 1927. Here Hesse identifies himself with one, Harry Haller, the "Wolf of the Steppes," who rebels against the safe, dull existence of the bourgeois citizen, while envying him his ostrich-like peace of mind. As Hermine, who is by way of being the personification of Haller's destiny, remarks: *"Wer heute leben und seines Lebens froh werden will, der darf kein Mensch sein wie du und ich. Wer statt Gedudel Musik, statt Vergnügen Freude, statt Geld Seele, statt Betrieb echte Arbeit, statt Spielerei echte Leidenschaft verlangt, fur den ist diese hubsche Welt keine Heimat"*— Who to-day wishes to live and have joy of his life must not be one like you or I. For he who demands music instead of tootling, enjoyment instead of pleasure, a soul instead of gold, real work instead of activity, true passion instead of dalliance, this pretty world is no homeland.

The dichotomy of the spiritual and the worldly man is handled at length, but with more deliberation and calm, in *Narziss und Goldmund* (1930). Here is elaborated the theme, which Hesse doubtless derived from Dostoievski, of redemption through sin: the theory that for *l'homme moyen sensuel* a state of grace can be attained only by plunging through the torrent of sensuality and emotional unrestraint, not by attempting to skirt or by-pass it. Asceticism, at least for a man of Goldmund's calibre, will always be an evasion: will never lead to spiritual calm, to the greater understanding. Only by running the gauntlet of evil—if necessary to the point of suicide—and coming out the farther side, as a soul purged and purified by suffering, as a phœnix re-arisen, is true enlightenment to be found.

Finally we arrive, by a logical progression, at Hesse's most substantial work, *Das Glasperlenspiel*, that superb philosophical romance which, ably translated by my friend Mervyn Savill, it is my pleasure and privilege to introduce to English-speaking readers. This book, first published in its entirety in 1945, represents an attempt on the author's part to formulate an ideal design for living. Whilst he indulges in neither the Gallic fantastication of Noel Delvaux nor the macabre invention of Maurice Richardson, Hesse takes us, as they have done in some of their shorter tales, into a future where a very different order of society from our own obtains. He invents, and describes in fascinating detail, an aristocratic hierarchy of intellectuals who form the so-called Castalian Order, in which is incorporated the faculty of the *Glasperlenspieler*—a beautiful German word the full quality of which the literal English translation "Bead-Players" fails to convey. Members of the Order must seek to co-ordinate all the arts and sciences into a whole which transcends the sum of the constituent parts; something akin to what Robert Bridges, I presume, had in mind, when in "The Testament of Beauty" he wrote of the "accord of Sense, Instinct, Reason and Spirit."

For those who attain to proficiency in it the *Glasperlenspiel* is raised to the level of a mystic rite, in which acutest mental awareness is coupled with a Yoga-like discipline of meditation. Music—in particular the "pure" music of Bach—and mathematics are the foundation stones upon which the whole complicated structure is erected. The book is a *tour de force* in which vision is offset by meticulous analysis, fantasy balanced by sound argument.

Yet, even here the antinomy is not resolved. Representing as it does the Greek tragic concept of life, the implications of

which ultimately drove Nietzsche out of his mind, the problem is indeed insoluble. As A. R. Orage has said, in his short
summary of the latter's philosophy: "Life . . . is the spectacle
of the eternal play and conflict of two mutually opposing
principles: Dionysos ever escaping the forms that Apollo is
ever creating for him. And it is just this unceasing conflict
that is the essence of life itself; life *is* conflict. . . . The drama
of life is thus a perpetual movement towards a climax that
never comes."

Whereas Hesse makes his hero, Joseph Knecht, sum up
the *Glasperlenspiel* as follows: "The Game, as I interpret
it, encompasses the player at the conclusion of his meditation
in the same way as the surface of a sphere encloses its centre,
and leaves him with the feeling of having resolved the
fortuitous and chaotic world into one that is symmetrical
and harmonious"—yet the Castalian Order does not in the
last resort satisfy him as an answer to the problem of *how to
live*. This interpretation gives us a clue to the symbolical
meaning of the *Glasperlenspiel*—the idea of macrocosmos
and microcosmos—but the conflict remains. It is brilliantly
expounded in the battle of wits between Knecht and
Designori, the extra-mural student who, in his heart,
despises the "unworldliness" of the Castalians; and it leads
to the former's ultimate renunciation of the Order after he
has attained to its highest office, that of *Magister Ludi*.
This duologue, and the beautiful conclusion of the life-story
of Josef Knecht, where he witnesses for the last time the
sunrise in the mountain retreat with his pupil-to-be,
Designori's son, are the highlights of this impressive work.
One is a distillation of wise thoughts, the other a brilliant
evocation of atmosphere and scene.

Death and suicide, actual or projected, are much in
evidence in Hesse's works. Not only does Klein, the deserting
civil servant, actually drown himself, but book after book
contains characters who are obsessed by thoughts of self-
destruction. Such an obsession is, as Kretschmer and others
have pointed out, characteristic of the German romantic
temperament, which tends towards the manic-depressive.
To quote Thomas Mann: "Romanticism bears in its heart the
germ of morbidity, as the rose bears the worm; its innermost
character is seduction, seduction to death." Nor is Hesse

unaware of his own schizophrenic proclivities, those same unresolved conflicts of the inner man which had sent his Swabian antecedent Hölderlin, as well as Nietzsche, to the madhouse. Writing of Novalis, that self-consuming flame, he says: "He stands in mortal peril who subordinates his senses all too exclusively to the asceticism of the spirit." It is Hesse's remarkable capacity to pull back into the world of light and air, of lakes, mountains and streams, of browsing cattle and singing children, of men and women going about their daily duties and indulging in simple pleasures, that has prevented him from hurtling into the abyss which must many a time have gaped at his feet.

Though with each successive book he seems to have been approaching nearer and nearer to what Josef Knecht in one of his poems describes as *"die heilige Mitte,"* Hesse, like all seekers after truth, is still—at the biblical age—faced with the Eternal Paradox. Hermann Lauscher, lifting his face to the skies, is transformed into Peter Camenzind; he, in turn, falls Lucifer-like into the pit of Demian, only to emerge once again in the guise of the "Steppenwolf" to fight his battles anew. Narziss and Goldmund are but the obverse and reverse of the same human coin, and the *Morgenlandfahrt* leads to the magic circle of the *Glasperlenspiel.* As Hesse, with the courage born of desperation, proclaims: *"Allein das Paradoxe muss immer wieder gewagt, das an sich unmögliche muss immer neu unternommen werden."*

ERIC PETERS

July, 1947

To the Eastern Wayfarers

THE BEAD GAME

*An attempt at a comprehensive introduction to its history
. . . non entia enim licet quodammodo levibusque hominibus
facilius atque incuriosius verbis reddere quam entia, verumtamen
pio diligentique rerum scriptori plane aliter res se habet: nihil
tamen repugnat ne verbis illustretur, at nihil adeo necesse est
ante hominum oculos proponere ut certas quasdam res, quas esse
neque demonstrari neque probari potest, quae contra eo ipso,
quod pii diligentesque viri illas quasi ut entia tractant, enti
nascendique facultati paululum appropinquant.*

ALBERTUS SECUNDUS: *tract. de cristall.
spirit. ed Clangor et Collof. lib.* 1, *cap.* 28.

In Joseph Knecht's holograph translation:—
*. . . then in certain cases and for irresponsible men it may be that
non-existent things can be described more easily and with less
responsibility in words than the existent, and therefore the
reverse applies for pious and scholarly historians: for nothing
destroys description so much as words, and yet there is nothing
more necessary than to place before the eyes of men certain things
the existence of which is neither provable nor probable, but which,
for this very reason, pious and scholarly men treat to a certain
extent as existent in order that they may be led a step further
towards their being and their becoming.*

IT IS OUR intention in this book to collate the small
amount of biographical material that we have been able to
gather together concerning Joseph Knecht, or Magister
Ludi Josephus III as he was known in the archives of the
Bead Game. We are not blind to the fact that this attempt is,
or appears to be, to a certain extent in contradiction to the
laws and customs which dominate our spiritual life. For, in

actual fact, is not the extinction of the individual—the most
perfect absorption possible of the individual in the hierarchy
of "the pedagogy" and of science—one of the cardinal
principles of our spiritual life? This principle has also, as a
result of long tradition, been so widely realised that to-day it
is uncommonly difficult—in many cases quite impossible—to
discover biological and psychological details of individuals
who have served the hierarchy in the most outstanding
manner; in very many cases their actual names can no longer
be recorded with certainty. Again, it is one of the characteristics of the spiritual life of our province that its hierarchic
organisation has taken anonymity as its ideal, and that this
ideal has very nearly been realised.

If, in spite of this, we have persisted in our attempt to
establish to some degree the life of the Magister Ludi
Josephus III, and tried to give some indication as to his
personality, we believe that we have done so, not from any
personal cult or in disobedience to the customs, but on the
contrary with the sole object of rendering a service to truth
and science.

There is an ancient axiom, which runs: the more bitterly
and acutely we formulate a thesis, the more irresistibly it
clamours for the antithesis.

We approve and revere the thought which underlies the
anonymity of our authorities and of our spiritual life. A
glimpse into the antecedents of the latter, *viz.* into the
development of the Bead Game, shows us irrefutably that
every stage of development, consolidation, change or
essential deviation, whether it be considered progressive or
conservative, invariably conjures up not its single and actual
originator but the person who carried out the change and
who became the instrument of transformation and perfection.

One thing is certain: what we to-day understand by
"personality" is very different from that which biographers
and historians of earlier times understood by it. For them,
namely for the authors of those periods—authors who possessed an unveiled penchant for biography—it appears, one
might almost say, that the important ingredients of a
personality were deviation, abnormality and originality—
often to the point of pathology—whereas we of to-day only
speak of personalities when we meet with men who are beyond

all originalities and peculiarities and who have succeeded in achieving the most perfect possible self-identification with the general, and in rendering the most perfect possible service to the supra-personal.

When we examine this more closely, we see that this concept was already known to Antiquity—the figure of the "Sage" or "Perfect One" for example in Ancient China, and the ideal of the Socratic doctrine of virtue, can hardly be distinguished from our modern ideal. Many great spiritual organisations, too, such as the Roman Church in its mightiest epochs, knew similar fundamental truths, and many of its greatest figures, *vide* St. Thomas Aquinas, appear to us like early Greek sculptures, classical representatives of types rather than individuals. Nevertheless, in the days before the reformation of our spiritual life, which began in the twentieth century and whose heirs we are, that true ancient ideal very nearly disappeared. We are amazed when we find related in detail in the biographies of those times how many relatives the hero had, or what scars and blemishes remained to him from childhood and adolescence, his struggles for recognition and his love aspirations. To-day we are disinterested in the pathology, family history, urges, digestion or sleeping moments of a hero; not even his spiritual antecedents, his education through favourite studies, reading material, etc., are of much importance to us. For us the only hero worthy of especial interest is he who, by nature and education, has found himself capable—capable almost to perfection—of allowing his person to enter into its hierarchic function without losing the strong fresh urge which is worthy of admiration and which goes to make up the savour and value of the individual. And if conflicts ensue between the individual and the hierarchy, we see in them a yardstick wherewith to measure the greatness of his personality. The less we approve of rebels whom envy and passion drive to break with law and order, the more estimable to us is the memorial of their sacrifice, of their real tragedy.

Now, in the case of these heroes, these really exemplary men, an interest in the person, the names, appearances and gestures seems to us permissible and natural, for we see also in the most perfect hierarchy, in the smoothest-running of organisations, by no means a machine pieced together out of dead and disjointed parts, but a living body, created of parts and quickened with organs, each possessing its own nature and freedom and participating in the miracle of life. In this spirit we have taken the trouble to gather intelligence of the life of the Magister Ludi, Joseph Knecht, and specifically everything which he himself wrote, inasmuch as several manuscripts have become available which we consider to be worth reading.

Everything that we have to tell of Knecht's person and life is certainly partly or fully known by the fellow members of his Order, *i.e.*, to the players of the Bead Game, and on account of this our book is not intended for that circle alone but has been written in the hope that it will reach the intelligent lay reader.

For that first mentioned narrow circle our book would need no introduction or commentary, but because we wish the life and writings of our hero to reach the reader outside the Order, and so as to facilitate the reader who lacks previous knowledge of the subject, we are constrained to the somewhat difficult task of prefacing our book with a small popular introduction into the meaning and history of the Bead Game. We should like to stress that we intend this introduction to be of a popular nature, and to point out that it makes no claim to clarify any questions under discussion within the Order itself upon the problems of the game and its history. For an objective portrayal of that subject the time has not yet arrived.

Should a complete history and theory of the Bead Game be expected of us, we would submit that even authors more worthy and capable than ourselves are not in the position to furnish such a compendium. This task remains for future epochs, always providing that the sources as well as the necessary spiritual premises shall not in the meantime have been lost. Even less should this be considered a manual of the Bead Game, for such a manual will never be written. One only learns the playing rules of this game of games in the usual prescribed ways—the result of many years' experience—and none of the initiated could have the least possible interest in making its rules easier of acquisition.

These rules, the symbols and grammar of the Game, represent a type of highly developed, secret language, in which several sciences and arts, in particular mathematics and music (not to forget the theory of music), play their part, and which are capable of expressing the contents and results of nearly all the sciences and of placing them in relation to each other. The Bead Game is also a device that comprises the complete contents and values of our culture; it plays with them as, in the springtime of the arts, a painter may have toyed with the colours on his palette. All that mankind, in creative periods, has produced in the field of beliefs, elevated thoughts and works of art, all that the ensuing periods have furnished in scholarly observation and concept and consolidated into intellectual property, will be utilised by the Bead Game adept. He will play upon this colossal material of spiritual worth as an organist plays upon the organ. This specific organ, however, is of incredible perfection; its keyboards and pedals register the entire cosmos, its stops are almost innumerable, and in theory this instrument allows the entire spiritual world to be reproduced in play. The keyboards, pedals and register are static, and to their number and arrangement changes and attempts towards perfection are only possible in theory; the enrichment of the playing speech by the inclusion of new content is submitted to the strongest imaginable control of the grand master. As opposed to this static structure, or, to continue in our previous metaphor, within the complicated mechanism of this giant organ, a whole world of possibilities and combinations is presented to the individual player, so that in a thousand rigidly executed performances the eventuality that even two of them could be superficially similar remains outside the bounds of possibility. Even should it happen that two players were to make, as the subject of their playing, the same choice of themes, these two performances could, according to the mode of thinking, character, mood and virtuosity of the player, appear and devolve entirely differently.

It lies ultimately at the discretion of the historian as to how far back he will trace the beginning and antecedents of the Bead Game; for, as in the case of every great idea, it has in actual fact no beginning but has always been in existence fundamentally. We find it as an idea, a presentiment and a desired image, already represented in many early ages, as for example in Pythagoras, in the later stages of antique culture, in hellenistico-gnostic circles no less than in ancient China;

we find it again at the zenith of Arabo-Moorish spiritual life, and the traces lead further through scholasticism and humanism to the mathematical academies of the seventeenth and eighteenth centuries, to the romantic philosophers, and to the runes of Novalis' magical dreams.

At the root of every spiritual movement towards the ideal goal of an Universitas Litterarum, every platonic academy, every spiritual élite, each attempt at approximation between the exact and freer sciences, each essay at reconciliation between science and art or between science and religion, lay this eternal idea, which for us has taken shape in the Bead Game. Spirits like Abelard, Leibnitz and Hegel undoubtedly visualised this need to capture the spiritual universe in concentric systems, to unite the living beauty of art and the spiritual by means of the magic formulary strength of exact disciplines. In that age, in which music and mathematics experienced an almost contemporary classicism, the alliances and fecundations between the two disciplines were of frequent occurrence. Two centuries earlier we find phrases in the same vein in the works of Nicholas of Cusa, such as the following: "The spirit adjusts itself to the potentiality in order to measure everything in the manner of the potentiality and of the absolute necessity, so that it may measure everything in the manner of unity and simplicity—as God does—and of the necessity for interconnection in order to measure everything in respect of its existence. Furthermore, the spirit also measures symbolically, through comparison, as in the case when it uses numbers and geometrical figures and applies them metaphorically." In parenthesis, it is not this particular thought alone of the Cusan which already points towards our Bead Game, and which conforms to and originates from a similar trend of imaginative power as the conception of the Game; in his writings there are many, many similar assonances. The pleasure which he took too, in mathematics, and his capacity and joy in making use of figures and axioms of Euclidian geometry as intelligible similes in theologico-philosophical ideas, seems to stand very near to the mentality of our Game. At times even, his style of Latin—his vocabulary is more often than not composed of words of his own invention, which does not, however, prevent it from being understood by a Latin scholar—resembles the resilient plasticity of the mode of speech used in the Bead Game.

To no less a degree—as the maxim which heads our treatise shows—does Albertus Secundus belong among the forefathers of the Bead Game. And we postulate, without actually being able to prove it by citations, that the idea of the Game was possessed by those learned musicians of the sixteenth, seventeenth and eighteenth centuries, whose musical compositions were based upon mathematical speculations.

Here and there in ancient literatures we come across legends of wise and magical games, devised by scholars, monks and enlightened princes, and played for example in the form of chess games, the figures and boards of which had extraordinary significances. And those accounts, fairy tales and sagas from the springtime of all cultures, in which music, far in advance of all the other pure arts, is accredited with a soul and an inquisitorial power over people, raising it to the status of a secret regent or code of laws for men and their states, are common knowledge.

The concept of an ideal heavenly life for men under the hegemony of music plays its rôle from most ancient China to the sagas of the Greeks. The Bead Game is also most intimately connected with this cult for music (". . . the occult power of song salutes us here below in eternal transmutations."—Novalis).

If we recognise also the idea of the Game as eternal and as having been in existence and active long before its materialisation, then its materialisation in the form in which we know it must have had its distinct history. We shall now endeavour to give a short account of its most important stages.

The spiritual movement, the fruits of which, among many others, were the foundation of the Order and the Bead Game, had its origins in an historical period which, as a result of the exhaustive researches of the literary historian Plinius Ziegenhals, bears the name coined by him of "the Age of the Digest." Such names are pretty but dangerous, and always bring with them the temptation to criticise unjustly the life of man in past ages. For the "Age of the Digest" was likewise by no means lacking in the spiritual and was not for one instant poor in spirit. According to Ziegenhals, however, it seems that it had little idea as to what to undertake with its spirit, or rather did not know how to direct it within the economics of life and State to conform with position and function.

To be frank, we know this period very imperfectly, although it was the soil from which nearly everything grew that went towards the creation of our spiritual life. It was—again according to Ziegenhals—to an especial degree "bourgeois," and a period which idolised an all-round individualism. If, in order to give some indication of its atmosphere, we quote certain features from Ziegenhals' portrayal of it, we at least know for certain that these features are neither false nor particularly exaggerated or ill drawn, for in his monumental investigation he has illustrated them profusely with innumerable literary and other documentations.

We throw in our lot with this scholar who until now has been the only man to give earnest consideration to the "Age of the Digest," not forgetting however that it is ridiculous and insane to raise one's eyebrows at the errors or immoralities of bygone days.

The development of intellectual life in Europe from the end of the Middle Ages onwards appears to have had two major tendencies: firstly, the liberation of thought and belief from all authoritative influence, *i.e.*, the struggle of the intellect, that felt itself sovereign and mature against the supremacy of the Roman Church; and secondly, the secret but passionate quest for a legitimisation of this freedom within the framework of a new, self-inspired but adequate authority.

As a generalisation one can almost say that, by and large, the spirit won this often remarkable and inconsistent struggle between two goals diametrically opposed in principle.

As to whether the gain outweighed the countless sacrifices, and whether the present arrangement of our intellectual life is wholly adequate and will be able to last long enough to enable us to judge whether all the suffering, the frustrations and abnormalities, from heresy trials and the stake to the fate of many "geniuses" who died in a madhouse or had recourse to suicide, justified the sacrifice, we are not permitted to ask.

That is past history. Whether it were good, or whether it were better had it never happened, or whether we can understand its "sense," is of no importance whatsoever.

At all events those struggles for the freedom of the spirit took place, and even in that late "Age of the Digest" resulted in the spirit enjoying an unheard of freedom, which it found intolerable inasmuch as it had completely thrown off the tutelage of the church and to a great extent that of the state. It had not, however, been able to find a true self-formulated and respected code, a true new authority and legitimacy.

The examples of degradation, venality and self-abandonment of the spirit during that age of which Ziegenhals writes are at times quite astounding.

We must confess that we are not in a position to define clearly those phenomena which have caused us to dub that age "the Age of the Digest."

It appears that these "digests" or "*feuilletons*" were produced by the million as a particularly favourite component of the daily press, represented the staple diet of the culture-thirsty reader, gave information or rather "chattered" upon a thousand-and-one subjects of knowledge and, it would appear, often brought pleasure to the creators of this tabloid wisdom. At least Ziegenhals insists that he has unearthed countless writings of this nature which, inasmuch as they are quite incomprehensible, he is inclined to classify as persiflage on the part of the authors.

It is possible that a preponderance of irony and self-irony was infused into these mass-produced articles, for which, in order to make them comprehensible, the key must again be found. The perpetrators of these trifles were partly members of the editorial staffs of newspapers and partly writers, some of whom even bore the title of poet. Many of them, however, seem to have belonged to the scholar class and to have been university professors by calling. The favourite subjects for their theses were anecdotes from the lives of famous men and women and their exchange of letters. They bore such titles as "Friedrich Nietzsche and Women's Fashions in 1870," or "The favourite dishes of the composer Rossini," or "The rôle of the lap dog in the lives of great courtesans," and similar fripperies.

In addition to these, semi-historical essays upon subjects topical among the well-to-do, such as "The alchemical dream of making gold artificially down the ages" or "Attempts to influence the weather by physico-chemical

means," were very popular. Scores of similar subjects were
much in demand. When we study Ziegenhals' list of titles of
these lucubrations we feel less hostile towards the men who
gulped them down avidly as their daily dope than to the
authors of good repute and education who "prostituted"
themselves to this plethora of worthless interests.

The term which Ziegenhals uses admirably describes the
contemporary relationship of man to the machine.

Again, a particularly beloved feature was one which took
the form of questions upon topical subjects put to well-known
personalities (Ziegenhals devotes a whole chapter to this),
in which we may read for example the utterances of famous
chemists and piano virtuosi upon the political situation,
popular actors, dancers, athletes, aviators and even poets
upon the advantages and disadvantages of bachelorhood or
upon the hypothetical causes of a financial crisis, etc., etc.
It was simply a question of bringing together a well-known
name and a popular subject. We can read some occasionally
striking examples in Ziegenhals' "magnum opus" in which
he cites many scores of them. As we have already mentioned,
all this industrious activity was probably tempered with a
goodly proportion of irony, but apparently too, there was in
it something demonic—an irony of despair—although we
find it hard to credit this. By the great majority, who at that
time must have been particularly keen on reading, all these
grotesque things were undoubtedly accepted in earnestness
and good faith.

Whenever a famous picture changed hands, a valuable
manuscript came under the hammer, an old castle burned to
the ground, or the bearer of an old and noble name found
himself embroiled in a scandal, the reader would learn in
many thousands of *feuilletons* not only the facts, but would be
presented on the same day—or at the latest the following
day—with a mass of anecdotic, historical, psychological,
erotic and other matter on the particular slogan or topical
event. Every daily occurrence was the target for a flood of
zealous verbiage, and the collection, sifting and classification
of all this information bore the unmistakable mark of hurried
and irresponsible mass-production.

In addition to this it appears that there were certain games
that went with the *feuilleton*, games which intrigued the

reading public and which had been born of their over-consumption of scientific fodder. A long footnote in Ziegenhals' book explains in detail the amazing subject of "The Crossword Puzzle."

Thousands and thousands of men who, for the most part, were engaged in serious work, and whose lives were extremely precarious, used to sit in their leisure hours poring over squares and crosses made from letters whose gaps they had to fill in according to certain fixed rules of the game. We must try to prevent ourselves from seeing only the laughable and insane aspect of this, and forbear from mockery.

These men, with their childish puzzle games and their theses on culture, were in actual fact in no way harmless children or playful Arcadians: on the contrary they lived anxiously in the midst of political, economic and moral turbulence and earthquakes, had carried out a series of hideous wars, both foreign and civil, and their small cultural games were not simply charming and meaningless infantilities, but represented a deep need to escape into a world of harmless phantasy and to shut their eyes to their forebodings of disaster.

They learned with persistence to drive motor cars, to play complicated card games, and devoted themselves dreamily to the solution of their crossword puzzles, for they stood almost defenceless in the face of death, fear, pain and hunger, spiritually unadvised and no longer able to find consolation in the Church. They, who read so many theses and listened to so many lectures, allowed themselves neither the time nor the energy to fortify themselves against their stark fear, to struggle against their inherent dread of death, and lived in trembling, believing in no to-morrow.

Lectures were also given, and we must mention these briefly as a more aristocratic variety of the *feuilleton*. They were written by specialists as well as by intellectual footpads from among the bourgeoisie of that epoch who were still attached to the ancient idea of culture before it had been robbed of all meaning. These lectures and articles were not in the nature of inaugural speeches written under special provocation, but were turned out in a wild spirit of competition in almost inconceivable numbers. The dweller in a medium sized town, or his wife, could hear once a week—in

large towns practically every evening—lectures instructing
them theoretically in some subject; lectures on art, poets,
scholars, pioneers or world travellers, during which the
audience remained purely passive; lectures which presumed
some knowledge of the subject, some previous culture, some
preparedness and eligibility which in the majority of cases
was lacking.

There would be witty, entertaining and temperamental
discourses on some such subject as Goethe, who would be
pictured in a blue frock coat leaving his post-chaise to seduce
some girl from Strasbourg or Wetzlar; or perhaps on Arabic
culture, in which a host of fashionable clichés would be
bandied about like dice from a shaker and at which everyone
would be delighted if he or she recognised a single one of
them. One could hear lectures upon writers whose works one
had never read and which no one had the slightest inclination
to read. These would be accompanied by lantern slides and,
as in the case of the *feuilletons*, one would be obliged to
struggle through a spate of fragmentary knowledge and of
isolated cultural values which had been emasculated of all
purport. In short, one was confronted at close quarters by
that appalling evaluation of the spoken word which primarily
called forth in small secret circles that heroic-ascetic counter
movement that was soon to come into the open, grow
powerful and represent the rise of a new discipline and
respect for the intellect.

The uncertainty and artificiality of the intellectual life of
that period—which nevertheless in many respects showed
pluck and greatness—we of to-day explain as symptoms of
that terror which befell the spirit as it suddenly found itself at
the end of an age of apparent victory and prosperity facing
the void; of a great material distress, a period of political
unrest and war storms, and of a mistrust that had sprung up
overnight in oneself, in one's own strength and dignity—in
one's very existence.

Parallel to these, however, in that period of disastrous
foreboding, there arose many high intellectual achievements,
including the beginnings of that science of music whose
grateful heirs we are to-day.

Although it is easy enough to fit at random sections of the
past gracefully and intelligibly into world history, it is

impossible for any particular age to assess its own position within the general picture; thus at that time, as the result of a rapid decline in the intellectual claims and achievements to a very modest level, a terrible uncertainty and despair was born, particularly among the intellectuals.

For it was suddenly discovered (a fact which had been divined here and there ever since Nietzsche) that the youth and creative period of our culture had passed, and that old age and twilight had set in. This sudden realisation, universally felt and quite bluntly stated by some, may account for the numerous disturbing signs of the time—the sterile mechanisation of life, the sharp decline in morality, the lack of belief among the people and the spuriousness of their art. As in the marvellous Chinese fairy tale, the "music of the decline" had sounded. Like the sustained bass note of an organ it had endured for decades, seeped in the form of corruption into the schools, newspapers and academies, driven the majority of those critics and historians who could still be taken seriously into a state of melancholia and insanity, run wild in all the arts and appeared in the open in the form of a savage and dilettante overproduction.

There were different modes of behaviour in the face of this enemy, who had appeared and who could not be charmed away. One could realise the bitter truth in silence and bear it stoically, as many of the noblest did; one could try to banish it with lies, and this attitude presented the literary protagonists of the "theory of decline" with many comfortable weapons of attack. On the other hand, those who took up the fight against these warning prophets were listened to by the bourgeoisie, whom they influenced, because the idea that the culture which but yesterday they had thought to possess, and of which they had been so inordinately proud, was extinct, that their beloved art and culture should be no longer true art and culture, seemed to them no less impertinent and intolerable than the sudden gold inflation and the threat to their capital through revolution.

In addition to this there was still the cynical attitude which could be used as a defence against the great premonition of disaster. One went to dances, and declared that every care for the future was but old men's folly; one sang good-humoured ditties on the approaching end of art, science and language;

one admitted with a certain suicidal voluptuousness in that
feuilleton world, which one had built oneself out of paper, to a
complete demoralisation of the spirit and an inflation of ideas,
and acted with cynical weariness or bacchanalian frenzy as
though one were witnessing not only the decline of art, the
spirit, morals and probity, but the end of Europe and
"the world."

Among the good a quiet and gloomy pessimism reigned:
the evil were malicious. A certain reconstruction of the
superannuated, a certain rearrangement of the world and of
morality through politics and war must take place before
culture would be capable of a true self-contemplation and a
new system.

Already in the heyday of the *feuilletonistes* there had existed
small and isolated groups who were determined to remain
true to the spirit, and to use all their strength, to rescue a
nucleus of good tradition, discipline, method and intellectual
conscience from this period.

As far as we can recognise these events to-day, it seems
that the process of self-scrutiny, consciousness and conscious
resistance to decay fell into two groups. The culture conscience
of the scholars took flight into research and methods of
instruction in musical history—for this science had reached
a very high pitch. In the midst of the *feuilleton* world two
seminaries, which had already become famous, nurtured a
healthy and scientific technique. And, as though Destiny had
wished to recognise and encourage the efforts of this small
brave cohort at the height of this melancholy era, that
wondrous miracle—a coincidence in itself, but which
appeared as a sign from heaven—occurred. It was no less than
the re-discovery of eleven MSS. of Johannes Sebastian Bach,
which had once been in the possession of his son Friedemann.

A second point of resistance against degeneration was the
League of Eastern Wayfarers, whose brothers cultivated a
spiritual rather than an intellectual discipline, and fostered
piety and reverence. From this direction came our present-day
form of spiritual culture and also the important impulses of
the Bead Game, especially on the contemplative side.

The Eastern Wayfarers also played their part in the new
enquiry into the essence of our culture, and into the possibility of its continuation—not so much through scientific and

analytical achievement as through their tranquil capacity to penetrate into remote ages and cultural conditions by means of their ancient occult practices.

There were for example among them musicians and singers who, we are assured, possessed the faculty of performing music of earlier ages in all the perfection of its original purity. They would play, for example, a piece of music dating from 1600 or 1650 as though all later refinements, fashions and virtuosities were still unknown. This was something unheard of in those days when the quest for dynamism and climax dominated all playing of music and where the music itself was almost forgotten, eclipsed by the performance and "conception" of the conductor.

It has been recorded that the audience at times remained completely bewildered, but at times listened attentively and were then under the impression that they had heard real music for the first time in their lives, as when an orchestra of the Eastern Wayfarers performed for the first time in public a suite from the time of Handel without *crescendi* and *diminuendi* and with all the ingenuousness and modesty of another age and world.

One member of the League built, in the great hall between Bremgarten and Morbio, a Bach organ exactly as Johannes Sebastian Bach would have built for himself had he possessed the means and possibilities of doing so. The builder of this organ, conforming to the ruling custom of the Order, preserved his anonymity by styling himself Silbermann—the name of an eighteenth century predecessor.

We have touched here upon the sources from which our present day concepts of culture were born. One of the most important of these was the youngest of the sciences, the History of Music and Musical Aesthetics—a swiftly successful improvement upon mathematics. Here, too, came a drop of precious oil from the wisdom of the Eastern Wayfarers in closest connection with the new form and inner meaning of music—that serene, resigned and courageous attitude towards the problem of the age of culture.

It would be useless to speak of this at length in our introduction, as these facts are universally known. The most important features of this new attitude—or rather this new system in the process of culture—were a very far reaching renunciation in the matter of producing new works of art, the gradual release of the spiritual from mundane activities and— no less important, and the finest blossom of them all—the Bead Game.

The increasing interest in the science of music which set in shortly after 1900—and therefore at the height of the Age of the Digest—had the greatest influence imaginable upon the origins of the Game. We who have inherited this science believe that we know better, and in a certain sense understand better, the music of the great creative centuries, especially the seventeenth and eighteenth, than did the people of earlier epochs (those of classical music itself included).

We, the descendants, have quite a different relationship to classical music than had the men of the creative centuries; our spiritual reverence for true music, which is not always sufficiently free from resigned melancholy, is completely different from the wonderful, naïve pleasure taken in the music-making of those periods—periods we are inclined to envy as fortunate if we happen to forget the condition and fate in which that very music of theirs was born.

For generations now we have not considered—as was the case during practically the whole of the twentieth century— philosophy or poetry, but rather mathematics and music to be the great lasting achievement of that period of culture which lies between the end of the Middle Ages and our own.

Since, at least by and large, we have renounced creative competition with those generations, since we have also denied that cult for the supremacy of harmony and pure sensual dynamism in music, which from Beethoven and the early romantics onwards dominated the practice of music throughout two centuries, we believe—in our own fashion naturally, our uncreative, epigonal but reverential fashion— that we see the picture of that culture whose heirs we are in a purer and more correct light.

We no longer possess the sybaritic lust for production of those days. It is for us an almost unimaginable miracle how the fifteenth and sixteenth centuries could have maintained their musical style for so long in unchanging purity, how it is almost impossible to discover anything really bad in the mass material that was composed during those centuries, how the eighteenth century, when degeneration had set in, could still produce that pyrotechnic display of styles, fashions and schools—vivid, magnificent and self-conscious.

But we do believe that we have understood the secret, the spirit, the virtue and the purity of those generations in that which we to-day call classical music, and which we have adopted as a prototype.

We have little or no interest to-day for example in theology and the ecclesiastical culture of the eighteenth century or for the philosophy of the Age of Reason, but we see in the cantatas, passions and preludes of Bach the ultimate sublimation of Christian culture.

Moreover, the relationship of our culture to music still presents an age-old and seemly pattern, to which the Bead Game pays great reverence.

In the fabulous China of the "old Kings" we recall that music was accorded a leading rôle in the life of court and state. The well-being of music was almost identified with culture and morality—even with the kingdom itself. The master of music had to keep strict watch over the preservation and the keeping pure of the "old harmonies."

Were music to degenerate, then it was a sure sign of the collapse of government and state. The poets told terrifying fairy tales of forbidden, diabolical and infernal harmonies—for example the tones Ch'eng Shang and Ch'eng Tze, the "Music of Decline." When these blasphemous notes were played in the King's Hall, the Heavens grew dark, the walls rocked and collapsed and both Prince and Kingdom came to grief.

In preference to citations from the old authors, we will quote here a few passages from the chapter on music in Lü Bu We's "Spring and Autumn."

"The origin of music lies far back in the past. It sprang from the Measure and had its roots in the Unit. The Unit gave birth to two poles, which in turn gave birth to the powers of darkness and light.

"When the world is at peace, when all things are at rest and all follow their leader in their transformations, then music can be perfected. When envy and passion do not take false courses, then music can be consummate.

"Perfect music has its cause: it rises out of balance.

Balance springs from the good, and good springs from the meaning of the world. Therefore it is only possible to have a discussion on the subject of music with a man who has recognised world significance.

"Music is based upon the harmony of heaven and earth, upon the union of the sombre and the bright.

"The decaying state and the men who are ripe for destruction cannot of course do without music, but their music is not serene. Therefore the more intoxicating the music, the more melancholy do men become, the more menaced the land, the deeper the degradation of the Prince. In this way, the essence of music, too, becomes lost.

"That which all pious princes appreciated in music was serenity. The tyrants Hia and Chow Sin created intoxicating music: they found powerful tones beautiful, and mass effects of interest. They hankered after new and curious effects of harmony, and after tones such as no human ear had ever heard. They sought to outbid each other and to surpass measure and aim.

"The cause of the downfall of the Ch'u State lay in the fact that they discovered ecstatic music. Intoxicating as such music may be, it is in truth far removed from the essence of pure music, and for this reason is not serene. When music is not serene the people murmur and life becomes discordant, all of which is the result of the essence of music having been misunderstood since it was composed solely of intoxicating harmonic effects.

"Therefore the music of a well-ordained age is tranquil and serene, and the government commensurate: the music of a restless age excitable and ferocious, and its government unstable. The music of a decaying state is sentimental and sad, and its government is in danger."

The phrases of this Chinaman shows us clearly enough the origins and the true, almost forgotten, significance of music.

Music, like the dance and all exercises of art, was in prehistoric times an instrument of magic—one of the oldest and most legitimate instruments of magic. Beginning with rhythm (hand-clapping, foot-stamping, beating of wood upon wood—the earliest art of the drum), it was a powerful and proven method of bringing a number of men into the same mood—unifying their breathing, their heart beats and their state of courage—of encouraging men to invocation and the conjuring up of the eternal powers, to the dance, to wrestling, to the war train and to sacred occasions. And music, this primal, pure and age-old mighty being, this spell, has endured far longer than any of the other arts. One has only to remember the many utterances of historians and poets, from the Greeks to Goethe's novels. In practice the march and the dance have never lost their meaning. But let us return to our original theme.

As regards the origins of the Bead Game, we will confine ourselves to outlining the most important and essential details. It apparently originated simultaneously in Germany and in England, and was in use in both countries in those narrow circles of music teachers and musicians who worked and studied in the new seminaries of musical theory.

If we compare the preliminary condition of the Game with that of later developments and with those of the present day, it is precisely as though we were to compare a musical score of pre-1500 with its primitive notes, which were not even divided into bars, to a score of the eighteenth or even the nineteenth century with its confusing superfluity of abbreviations for dynamics, tempi, phrasing, etc., which often makes the printing of such a score a difficult technical problem.

In the beginning the Game was no more than a witty form of practice in harmony and combination among students and musicians. As we have already mentioned, it was played both in England and in Germany before it was "discovered" and given a name by the musical academy of Cologne. It has retained this original name for many generations, although to-day the Game has no longer anything to do with beads.

The latter were used by their inventor, Bastian Perrot of Calw—a rather eccentric though intelligent and sociable musical theoretician—to take the place of letters, numbers, notes or other graphic symbols. Perrot, who, incidentally, has left us a treatise on "The Rise and Decline of Counterpoint," discovered that the Game was moderately well developed in the Rhenish seminary and in use among the students. They used to call out to each other in the abbreviated formulas of their science favourite motifs or opening phrases from the classical composers, to which the one addressed had to reply

with the continuation of the piece, or better still in a higher or
lower key or with a counter theme.

This was an exercise in memory and improvisation (even
if not theoretically in formulas, then in practice on the
cembalo with the flute, lute and voices) similar to that which
might once have been used by eager music and counterpoint
pupils of Schütz, Pachelbel and Bach.

Sebastian Perrot was a friend of the handicrafts, a man who
with his own hands had built many pianos and clavichords
after the pattern of the ancients, who in all probability
belonged to the League of Eastern Wayfarers and of whom
legend relates that he could play the violin in the original
mode—an art which had been forgotten since 1800—with a
high arched bow and hand-regulated spring tension. This
Perrot constructed for himself, upon the model of a simple
abacus for children, a frame with a dozen wires across it upon
which he could string glass beads of different sizes, shapes
and colours.

The wires represented the lines of the music, the beads the
note values, etc., etc. With his beads he built up musical
citations or invented themes, which he varied, transposed and
developed, reversed or opposed to each other.

From the technical point of view this was of course a
triviality, but it delighted the students, was copied, and
became fashionable also in England. For many years this
game of musical exercises was played in this graceful
primitive manner.

And thus, as is often the case, a lasting and important
organisation took its name from a transitory incident. The
development which ensued from the students' game and
from Perrot's bead-strung wires still bears to-day the
popular name of "The Bead Game."

Two or three decades later the Game seems to have fallen
out of favour with the musical students and to have been
taken over by the mathematicians: for a long time one of the
outstanding features in the history of the Game is the fact
that it was immediately seized upon, used and developed by
that particular science, which at the time was undergoing a
prosperous renascence.

In the hands of the mathematicians the Game was brought
to a high standard of flexibility and capacity for sublimation,

and had achieved something in the nature of a consciousness
of itself and of its own possibilities. This characteristic found
its parallel in the contemporary culture-consciousness which
had weathered the great crisis and which, as Plinius
Ziegenhals remarks, "with modest pride found itself in the
rôle of belonging to a late culture corresponding somewhat to
the late antique and to the Hellenistic-Alexandrian age."

So much for Ziegenhals. We shall now endeavour to
establish and bring our concise history of the Bead Game
to a close.

Having been transferred from the musical to the mathematical seminaries (a change which took place somewhat
more rapidly in France and England than in Germany) the
Game reached a point of development where it could express
certain mathematical symbols and abbreviations. The players
would serve each other, to their mutual development, with
those abstract formulas, and enact before each other the
combinations and permutations of their respective sciences.
This mathematical-astronomical game of formulas demanded
great attention, awareness and concentration. Among
mathematicians, to be considered a good bead-player was
tantamount to being a good mathematician.

Gradually the Game was adopted or imitated by nearly all
the sciences, *i.e.*, adapted to their particular provinces—and
this applied especially to classical philology and logic.

The analytical study of works of music reached the point
where musical themes were transformed into physico-
mathematical formulas. Not long after this philologists began
to work on the same lines, and to measure word pictures in
the same way as the physicists measured the manifestations
of nature: this brought the analysis of pictorial art into line
with the long standing relationship between architecture and
mathematics. Abstract formulas, relationships, analogies and
correspondences were now discovered among those which
had already been gained by following these paths.

Each science which made use of this game devised for its
own ends a game of speech composed of formulas, abbreviations and possible combinations, and these games of serial
formulas and formulary dialogues were everywhere greatly
appreciated among the élite of intellectual youth. The game
was not simply an exercise or a recreation, but a concentrated

self-acknowledged spiritual discipline. The mathematicians in particular used it with a kind of ascetic and athletic virtuosity and formal rigidity, finding in it an enjoyment which helped them to lighten the intellectual renunciation of mundane pleasures and activities which was then in force.

The Bead Game contributed largely towards the complete victory over the "Feuilletons" and the newly awakened joy which had been aroused by some of the most exact exercises of the intellect, for which we have to thank the birth of a new spiritual discipline of monastic rigour.

The world had changed. "The Age of the Digest" can be compared to a degenerate plant which had spent its seed in hypertrophied luxuriance, and the ensuing correctives to a drastic cutting back of the plant to its very roots.

Young men who wished to devote themselves to intellectual studies no longer understood by this a vague browsing in a college, where the residue of a once superior culture was debited to them by famous and loquacious professors: they were obliged to study ever more earnestly and methodically as once the engineers and polytechnicians had been forced to do.

They had a steep path to climb, had to purify and heighten their brain capacity by mathematics and Aristotelian-scholastic exercises, and in addition to this learn to renounce all that which generations of teachers had held to be worth while striving for—quick and easy moneymaking, fame and public honours, praise from the newspapers, marriage with the daughters of bankers and industrialists, pampering and luxury in their material lives. Authors of large editions with Nobel prizes and charming country houses, great doctors with knighthoods and liveried flunkeys, academicians with rich wives and brilliant salons, analytical chemists with high positions in industry, philosophers with feuilleton factories and floral tributes—all these figures had disappeared, and have not reappeared to this day.

There were still of course gifted young men to whom these figures of the past appeared enviable and worthy of emulation, but the paths to public recognition, wealth, fame and luxury no longer led through the lecture halls, seminaries and doctorates. The intellectual occupations which had previously sunk to their lowest depths and become bankrupt in the eyes of the world had now regained a fanatical sense of devotion to the spirit. Talents who strove more after fame or comfort were forced to turn their backs upon intellectuality, which had become boorish, and look for professions which had been abandoned to mere good living and the earning of money.

It would take too long in this introduction to describe the manner in which the spirit after its purification took its place in the state.

It had soon been discovered that a few generations had sufficed to produce a lax and conscienceless spiritual discipline which was also materially damaging to practical life; that ability and responsibility in all the higher professions—even in the technical—had become increasingly rare, so that the care for culture in State and people, *i.e.*, education as a whole, had become more and more the monopoly of the intellectuals. As a result of this, in nearly all the countries of Europe to-day which do not remain under the control of the Roman church, it is in the hands of that anonymous Order whose members are recruited from among the élite of the intellectuals.

However galling to public opinion the power and alleged arrogance of this caste may at times have been, and however many times individuals may have revolted against it, this leadership still remains unimpaired. Not only does it retain its integrity, and hold to its renunciation of all other goods and advantages except those of the intellect, but it preserves that presentiment—which has long since become common knowledge—of the necessity for this strong school in order that civilisation may survive.

Now we know or sense that if thought be no longer pure and alert, and respect for the spirit no longer valid, then ships and motor cars no longer run correctly; all authority and validity totter, for the slide rule of the engineer, for mathematics, banks and stock exchanges alike—and ultimately chaos ensues.

It was long enough in any case before the knowledge began to dawn that the externals of civilisation, technics, industry, business, etc., also required a common basis of spiritual morality and probity.

At that time the Bead Game lacked the capacity for universality and had not been elevated above the Faculties. The astronomers, students of Greek, Latin, scholastics and

music played their well regulated and spiritual games, but
for each Faculty it had its own particular discipline, variations,
speech and set of rules. This state of affairs lasted for half-a-
century before the initial spanning of these bridges was
accomplished. The reason for this lag was undoubtedly more
formal than technical: the means of bridging the gaps were
to be found, but hand-in-hand with the strong morality of
the new-born spirituality went a puritanical horror of
"ἀλλοτρια," of intermingling disciplines and categories,
and a deep and justifiable horror of a recidivism of frivolity
and the feuilleton.

The action of a single man brought the Bead Game almost
instantaneously to a realisation of its potentialities, and
therewith to the threshold of an universal capacity for
development. And once again it was the conjunction with
music that caused this progress.

A Swiss music teacher, who was at the same time a fanatical
lover of mathematics, gave a new twist to the Game, thus
opening the way towards its highest expansion. The
bourgeois name of this man cannot be revealed, for in his age
the cult of the individual no longer existed in intellectual
circles. In the history of the Bead Game he was known as
Lusor (vice: Joculator) Basiliensis. His discovery, like any
other, was entirely the result of personal achievement and
grace, but did not spring from a private need and urge alone:
it was actuated by a far stronger driving power. Among the
intellectuals of his time there was everywhere to be found a
passionate desire for a possible mode of expression for their
new thought-content. There was a yearning for philosophy
and for synthesis. They had found the erstwhile happiness of
pure withdrawal into their discipline to be inadequate. Here
and there a teacher broke away from the bonds of specialisation and tried to storm the citadel of the universal. A new
alphabet was envisaged and also a new symbolic speech, in
which it would be possible to determine and differentiate new
spiritual experiences. A particularly strong proof of this is
given by the manuscript of a Parisian scholar of the time
which bore the title "A Warning Cry from China."

The author of this work, who was scorned by his contemporaries as a kind of Don Quixote—we may mention that
he was an acknowledged authority on his subject, Chinese

philology—pointed out the danger in which science and spiritual care stood, in spite of the courageous behaviour on the part of their leaders, should they refuse to build up an international speech of symbols which, similar to the Chinese script, would allow of the most complicated idea without eliminating personal fantasy and invention being expressed graphically, and which would be comprehensible to every scholar throughout the world.

The most important step towards the fulfilment of this aim had been contrived by Joculator Basiliensis. He had invented for the Bead Game the basis of a new speech, namely, a mixture of symbols and formulas in which music and mathematics played an equal part, and in which it was possible to combine astronomical and musical formulas under a common denominator. Even if development remained unrestricted, the basis of all the later history of our worthy Game was postulated by this unknown man from Basle.

The Bead Game, once the entertainment perquisite of, alternately, mathematician, philologist and musician, now attracted more and more true intellectuals into its sphere of influence. Many of the old academies and lodges—and in particular the ancient League of Eastern Wayfarers—gave him their support. Even a few of the Catholic Orders sensed in it a new breath of the spirit, and allowed themselves to succumb to its charm. In certain Benedictine monasteries so much sympathy was shown to the Game that the question now arose—one which had often cropped up before—and became acute, as to whether the Game was to be tolerated, supported or forbidden by the Church and the Curia.

After Joculator's outstanding discovery the Game rapidly developed into what it still is to-day—the totality of the spiritual and the musical, the sublime cult, the Unio Mystica of all the separate limbs of the Universitas Litterarum. In our life it has assumed in part the rôle of art and in part that of speculative philosophy. It was, for example, in the time of Plinius Ziegenhals, having been the yearned for ideal of many a perspicacious spirit, christened with the name which originated in the "Age of the Digest," namely "The Magic Theatre."

Although, since its origin, the Bead Game had advanced in technique, by its infinite embracing of material and by the

spiritual claims of the player, into a high art and science, in
the time of Joculator it still lacked something vital. Until then
the Game had been an arrangement, a grouping and opposing
of concentrated performances from many fields of thought and
from the beautiful, a quick self-reminder of timeless values
and forms, a short virtuoso flight through the realms of the
spirit. Gradually, but considerably later, from the spiritual
inventory of its educational essence—particularly from the
customs and usages of the Eastern Wayfarers—the concept
of contemplation had entered into the game. The fault became
apparent that the players, without any other virtues than
prodigious memories, could become gifted and brilliant performers with the power to bluff and confuse the participants
by the rapid variations of their countless performances. This
virtuosity fell gradually more and more under a ban, and
contemplation became a far more important factor in the
game. It became in fact the predominant requisite both for the
spectators and for the listeners in each game. This was the
natural reaction against religiosity. Now it was no longer a
question of following the sequence of ideas and the whole
spiritual mosaic of the game intellectually, with rapid attention and practised memory, but of giving to it a deeper and
more soulful devotion. According to each sign which the
leader conjured up, a quiet, rigid contemplation would be
observed as to the constituents, origin and meaning of the
symbol, compelling each of the players to vivify the content
of the symbol intensively and organically.

The technique and exercise of contemplation attracted all
the members of the Orders and playing guilds of the élite
schools where the greatest care was devoted to the art of
contemplation and meditation. In this manner the hieroglyphics of the Game were prevented from degeneration into
simple letters.

Until then the Bead Game had, despite its popularity,
remained a purely private exercise among scholars. It could
be played singly, by two, three or more people, and especially
ingenious, well-composed and successful Games were sometimes given publicity, circulated from land to land and
admired or criticised. But now the Game began to take on a
new function and to become in the nature of a public festival.
Even to-day the private Game is open to everyone and is

practised eagerly by young people, but the Bead Game is now primarily an occasion for public festivity. These public Games take place in all parts of the world under the leadership of the few superior Masters who in each land hold the position of Ludi Magister or Master of the Game, who have the respectful obedience of the guests and the strict attention of the listeners. Some of these Games last for days and weeks on end, and while such a Game is in progress all the players and listeners live according to certain precepts, which also regulate their sleeping hours—an ascetic and selfless life of absolute contemplation, similar to the rigid life of penance as practised by the participants in one of the exercises of St. Ignatius.

There is little more to add. This Game of games, under the changing hegemony of now this, now that, science or art, has developed into a kind of universal speech, through the medium of which the players are enabled to express values in lucid symbols and to place them in relation to each other. The Game has always stood in close relationship to music, and is generally played according to musical or mathematical rules. One, two or three themes are chosen, played and varied, and these undergo quite a different fate from that, say, of the theme of a fugue or a concert piece. A Game can originate, for example, from a given astronomical configuration, a theme from a Bach fugue, a phrase of Leibnitz or from the Upanishads, and the fundamental idea awakened can, according to the intention and talent of the player, either proceed further and be built up or enriched through assonances to relative concepts. While a moderate beginner can, through these symbols formulate, parallels between a piece of classical music and the formula of a natural law, the adept and Master of the Game can lead the opening theme into the freedom of boundless combinations.

For a long time a certain school of players loved to develop the correlation, opposition and infinite harmonic consummations between two antagonistic themes or ideas, such as law and freedom, or individuality and community. Great value was laid upon the capacity to conduct both themes or theses in an equitable and impartial manner, and from theses and antitheses to develop the purest possible syntheses. Apart from certain genial exceptions, Games with negative, sceptical or discordant issues were generally disliked, and a t times actually forbidden; and this was in deep harmony with the sense which, in its heights, the Game had gained for the players.

It represented a select, symbolical form of the quest for perfection, a sublime alchemy, a self-approach to the inherent spirit beyond all images and pluralities—and thus to God.

Just as the pious thinkers of earlier ages portrayed the animal world as a leading to God and saw the multiplicity of the world of phenomena first perfected in heavenly unity and conceived to an end, so in similar manner the figures and formulas of the Bead Game constructed, made music and philosophised in an universal speech composed from all the arts and sciences and striving towards perfection, pure being and reality. "Realisation" was a favourite expression of the players, and they considered the accomplishment of this to be the path from becoming to being, from the possible to the real.

At this juncture we should like to refer the reader back to the passage we have quoted from Nicholas of Cusa.

Furthermore, the expressions of Christian theology, insofar as they were classic in form and appeared to be of general cultural benefit, were naturally incorporated in the symbolic speech of the Game. One of the major canons of faith, a biblical text, a phrase from one of the Church Fathers, could be as easily and concisely expressed and accepted within the Game as a geometrical axiom or a melody of Mozart.

It is hardly an exaggeration to say that, for the narrow circle of genuine bead-players, the Game was almost synonymous with a church service inasmuch as it contained its own theology.

In their mutual struggle for survival in the midst of un-spiritual world powers, both the bead-players and the Roman Church became so much aware of their mutual interdependence that they did not dare to force matters to an issue, although many incidents could have been found to warrant this, for intellectual probity and the genuine urge for a clearer and less equivocal formulation might have driven both these powers to the point of a schism.

It never happened. Rome was content to regard the Game alternately with benevolence and rejection: many of the congregations and members of the high and highest clergy were among the most gifted of the players. Moreover the Game, since its public inauguration and the appointment of a Magister Ludi, stood under the protection of the Order and of the pedagogy, towards both of which bodies Rome was politeness and courtesy itself. Pope Pius XV, who as a cardinal had been an ardent player, did not only renounce it for ever—as his predecessors had done—upon assuming the triple crown, but instigated proceedings against the Game. At that time it was in danger of being placed on the Catholic Index. But the Pope died before this occurred and a much read biography of this not insignificant figure describes his relationship to the Bead Game as a deep passion which, as a Pope, he knew how to dominate, but unfortunately in a hostile manner.

By its public organisation the Game, which had previously been freely practised by individuals and clubs, and which had long since been regarded favourably by the authorities, spread to France and England. Other countries quickly followed suit. In every country there was now a Games commission and a chief leader with the appointed title of Ludi Magister. There were also official Games and spiritual festivals under the personal leadership of the Master.

The Magister Ludi naturally remained anonymous, as was customary for all the high and highest functionaries of culture: apart from a few of his intimates, no one knew his personal name.

Only the great official Games for which the Ludi Magister was personally responsible could make use of the official and international broadcasting apparatuses such as the radio, etc., etc.

Apart from leading the public Games, the duties of the Magister included the promotion of players and schools of playing. His most important task was to watch over the development of the Game.

The world commission of Magisters from all countries made the final decision as to the acceptance of new symbols and formulas (an eventuality which hardly ever occurs to-day) as to the expansion of the Game, certain modifications of the rules and the advisability or indispensability of possible new fields for development.

If one considers the Game as a type of world speech for

intellectuals, then the Games commissions of all countries under the ægis of their respective Magisters, in their totality, may be compared to an academy watching over the duration, development and purification of this speech.

Each Land Commission possesses archives of the Game, *i.e.*, a catalogue of the proven and admissible symbols and keys, whose number has reached a higher figure than that of the old Chinese ideographs.

In general the final examination for advanced scholars of the élite school was considered as sufficient preliminary education for a bead-player, but an exceptional mastery of one of the leading sciences or of music was and still is tacitly presumed.

To become a member of the Games Commission, or even Ludi Magister, was the dream of nearly every fifteen-year-old in the élite schools.

But already among the candidates for the doctorate only a small percentage had the serious ambition to serve the furtherance of the Bead Game in an active capacity. As a result, all these amateurs of the Game practised meditation and the art of the Game industriously, and comprised that innermost circle of adoring and devoted participants in the public Games who gave to them a festive character and prevented them from becoming mere degenerate and decorative performances.

The Magister Ludi is considered by these actual players and amateurs as a prince, a high priest—almost a God.

For the independent player, however, and even for the Magister, the Bead Game is primarily a making of music, somewhat in the sense of that phrase which Joseph Knecht once uttered upon the essence of classical music: "We consider classical music to be the essence and epitome of our culture because it is its most lucid, characteristic gesture and utterance. In this music we possess the heritage of antiquity and Christianity, a spirit of serener and more courageous piety, an unsurpassed knightly morality. For a code of morals, in the last analysis, means that classic gesture of culture—an amalgamated image of human behaviour in the form of a gesture.

"Much music was composed between 1500 and 1800; style and means of expression were highly varied, but the spirit—nay more, the morality—is everywhere the same.

"Human behaviour, the expression of which is music, is everywhere the same: it rests on the same type of knowledge of life and strives for the same type of superiority to co-incidence. The gestures of classical music signify knowledge of the human tragedy, acceptance of man's destiny, courage and serenity.

"Whether it be in the grace of a Handel or a Couperin minuet, the over-tender sublimated gesture of sensuality as in many of the Italians or in Mozart, the tranquil prepared-ness for death as in Bach, it is nevertheless always a courage in the face of death, a courtliness, possessing within it a sound of superhuman laughter, of immortal serenity. Thus should it ring too in our Bead Game, and in our whole life, actions and suffering."

These words were transcribed by one of Knecht's pupils, and with them we bring our study of the Bead Game to a close.

Chapter One

THE CALL

WE KNOW NOTHING of Joseph Knecht's origins. Like
many other élite pupils he had either lost his parents at an
early age or else been taken from them owing to their
unfavourable circumstances and adopted by the pedagogy.
In any event he was spared that conflict between the élite
school and the home which burdened the youth of so many
young men of his kind—the parents often threw difficulties in
the way of their entering the Order, which in many cases
turned highly talented young men into complex and problem
characters.

Knecht was one of those lucky ones who seem to have been
predestined for Castalia and the Order, and for entrance into
the service of the pedagogy. Although he was left by no means
in ignorance of the problems of the spiritual life, he was at
least permitted to experience the innate tragedy of that life of
consecration to the spirit without any personal bitterness.

It is not so much this tragedy which has inspired us to
devote our searching study into the personality of Joseph
Knecht: it is far more on account of the tranquil, serene—we
might also add, radiant—manner in which he accomplished
his destiny and developed his talents and vocation.

Like every man of significance he had his δαιμόνιον and
his *Amor fati*, but the latter appears to us to have been
singularly free from gloom or fanaticism. Admittedly we
know nothing of his inner life, nor shall we forget that
history, however much sobriety, goodwill and objectivity we
bring to bear in the writing of it, still remains invention, and
that fiction is its third dimension.

Thus, to choose a broad example, we have no idea as to
whether Johannes Sebastian Bach or Wolfgang Amadeus
Mozart actually lived on a serene or on a troubled plane.
Mozart has for us that peculiarly moving and endearing
grace of the infant prodigy, while Bach has an edifying,
consoling resignation to the inevitability of suffering and
death, which he saw as God's paternal will. We do not learn

this from their biographies or from the recorded facts of their private lives, but solely from their musical works.

Furthermore, in the case of Bach, whose biography we know and whose portrait we can reconstruct from his music, we involuntarily take into consideration his posthumous destiny: in our fantasy we allow him to a certain extent to have known already while he was alive—allow him to have smiled in silence about it—that his whole work was to be forgotten immediately after his death and his manuscripts destroyed as rubbish; that instead of himself one of his sons would achieve success and become "the great Bach"; that his work was to be revived in the midst of the misunderstandings and barbarities of the Digest Age, etc., etc.'

And similarly, we are inclined in romantic fashion to attribute to a still living, flourishing Mozart at the zenith of his power a knowledge of his security in the hands of posterity, a notice as it were in advance, of his immortality after death.

Where an authority is available, the historian cannot do otherwise than deal with the life of his subject as two inseparable halves of a living unit. This we do with Mozart, Bach and also with Knecht, although the latter belongs to our comparatively uneventful era, and has left behind him no "works" in the sense that the other two masters have done.

When we attempt to describe Knecht's life, we also attempt to assess his significance. As an historian we must deeply regret that nearly all true and authentic information is lacking in respect of the latter part of his life, but the very fact that this last period has become shrouded in legend has given courage to our undertaking.

We have accepted these legends and approve them, irrespective of whether they are pious romances or not. Just as we know nothing of Knecht's birth and descent, so we know nothing of his end. We have, however, not the least justification for accepting his end as having been anything but a coincidence.

We see his life, as far as it is known, as a series of clear gradations, and if we are prepared in our speculations to accept the legend of his death, we do so because all that the legend tells us seems to correspond perfectly with the

previous stages of his life. We even admit that the flight of
this life into the realms of legend seems to us organically
correct, just as the continued existence of a star which has
disappeared out of sight and which for us has "declined"
raises no scruples of faith.

In the world in which the author of this book as well as its
reader lives, Joseph Knecht achieved and attained the highest
that can be conceived, inasmuch as, in the rôle of Magister
Ludi, he was the leader and shining example of all spiritual
striving and culture.

He administered and increased our inherited spiritual
legacy in an exemplary manner. He was the high priest of a
temple which is sacred to us all. But he did not simply achieve
the post of a Magister—the highest peak of our hierarchy—
by natural disposition: he surpassed and outgrew it in a
dimension which we can only try with respect to imagine.
For this very reason it seems to us perfectly seemly and in
accordance with his life that his biography, too, should have
overstepped the usual dimensions and finally have crossed
over into the legendary.

We accept the miraculous aspect of this fact and rejoice in
the miracle without wishing to stress the point too much.
As far as Knecht's life remains history—and this is up to a
certain definite day—we wish to treat it as such, and have
taken pains to repeat the tradition accurately in the light of
our own research.

Of his early childhood, that is to say of the time prior to
his entering the élite school, we know only one small detail.
This detail is however important and of symbolical significance, for it reveals the first great moving of the spirit within
him. It is characteristic of the man that this first call did not
come from the direction of science but from that of music.

For this biographical trifle, as for nearly all the memories
of Knecht's personal life, we must thank the jottings of a
pupil, one of his genuine admirers, who wrote down many
of the axioms and stories of his great teacher.

Knecht must have been about twelve or thirteen at the
time and was a pupil in the grammar school of Berolfingen, a
small town which stands on the borders of the Zaberwald.
He was also probably born in that town.

The boy had for a long time been a boarder in the grammar school, and had already been recommended two or three times by the teachers—and most earnestly by the music teacher—for admittance to the élite school. He himself knew nothing of this, and up to the time had had no relations either with the élite school or with the masters of the higher pedagogy.

He was informed one day by his music teacher, from whom he was learning the violin and the lute, that the Music Master would soon be coming to Berolfingen to examine the pupils in music. He told Joseph that he must practise hard and not bring discredit upon his teacher. This news disturbed the boy greatly, for naturally he knew the identity of this particular Music Master. He knew that it would not be one of the routine school inspectors who put in an appearance twice a year from one of the higher departments of education, but one of the twelve demi-gods, one of the twelve highest leaders of those most worthy authorities, and one of the foremost figures in the musical affairs of the land. In short, the Music Master himself, the "Magister Musicæ" in person, was coming to Berolfingen!

There was perhaps only one figure more fabulous and mysterious in the whole world, and that was the Master of the Bead Game.

Knecht was filled with an overwhelming fear and shyness at the announcement of this visit. He envisaged the man alternately as a king, a magician, one of the twelve apostles and one of the legendary great artists of classical times— someone in the nature of Michael Prætorius, Claudio Monteverdi, J. J. Froberger or Johannes Sebastian Bach. His joy was as deep as his terror at the thought of the moment when this great star should appear.

That one of the demi-gods and archangels, that one of the mysterious and omnipotent regents of the spiritual world should appear in the flesh in the grammar school of this insignificant hamlet, that he himself would see him—that the master might even address him, test him, blame or praise him—was a prodigious event, almost in the nature of a miracle or heavenly apparition.

In addition to this, as his teacher assured him, this was the first time for many decades that a "Magister Musicæ" had paid a personal visit to the town and the little grammar school.

The boy pictured the coming event in a host of varied images. Above all he dreamed of a great public festival and a reception such as he had once seen when the new burgomaster had taken office, with brass bands and beflagged streets. He thought that there might possibly be a firework display, and his comrades nourished the same ideas and hopes.

His joy of anticipation was marred by only one thought— that he might perhaps approach too near this great man, and be scolded for his playing and his answers, which would be intolerable. But there was a certain sweetness in his tormenting fear, and he admitted to himself in secret that he found the whole anticipated festivity with flags and fireworks less magnificent, exciting and important than the fact that he, the small Joseph Knecht, would be seeing the Master at close quarters—that it was a little on his account that he would be paying this visit to Berolfingen, for he was coming to test them in music and his music teacher had told him that he too would be examined.

But again, perhaps this would not be the case. It was hardly credible that the Master should have nothing better to do than to examine small boys on the violin. He would in all probability wish to see and hear the older and more advanced pupils.

Such were the thoughts with which Joseph awaited the great day, which at last arrived and began with a disappointment. No music rang out in the streets, no flags and garlands hung from the houses, and, as on ordinary days, they had to take their books and notebooks to their usual classes. Even in the classroom itself there were no signs of decoration or festivity. The lesson began, and the teacher was wearing his everyday coat: there was no speech, no word about the great guest of honour.

In the second or third hour of lessons, however, it came; there was a knock at the door, and a school waiter entered. He greeted the teacher and informed him that in a quarter-of-an-hour the pupil Joseph Knecht was to appear before the Music Master. Furthermore, the boy was to take care that his hair was properly combed, and that his hands and fingernails were clean.

Knecht grew pale with terror, stumbled from the classroom, and ran up to the dormitory. He put away his books, washed his hands and combed his hair; then in fear and trembling took his violin case and with a constriction in his throat made his way to the music classrooms, which were in the out-buildings.

An excited comrade met him on the steps, and led him into the practice-rooms with the words: "You're to wait here until you are called."

Joseph did not have long to wait, although it seemed to him an eternity. He was not sent for: a man simply entered the room. A very old man—it seemed to him at first—a rather small white-haired man with a beautiful serene face and penetrating, twinkling blue eyes whose gaze might have terrified had it not also possessed a tranquil and imperturbable serenity, neither smiling nor laughing.

He gave the boy his hand and nodded to him, saying as he sat down carefully at the old practice piano: "So you are Joseph Knecht? Your teacher seems very pleased with you. I think he likes you very much. Come, let us make a little music together."

Knecht had already taken his violin from its case. The old man struck an A. The boy attuned his instrument, and then looked questioningly and timidly at the Master.

"What would you like to play most?" asked the old man.

Joseph could not answer because he was awestruck before this Master, this man whose like he had never encountered in his life. He took up his music-book, and handed it shyly to the Master.

"No," said the old man. "I want you to play from memory, not to repeat a practice exercise. Something simple that you know by heart—perhaps a song that you like very much."

Knecht was confused, and at the same time enchanted, by this man's face and eyes. He was speechless, and most ashamed of his embarrassment, but still could not manage to utter a word. The Master did not insist, but struck the first notes of a melody with his finger, looked enquiringly at the boy, who nodded and immediately repeated the tune. He was pleased, for it was one of the old songs that was often sung in the school.

"Once more!" said the Master.

Knecht repeated the melody, and the old man now added the second part. The old song now rang out through the little practice-room in two voices.

"Once more!"

Knecht played again and the Master played the second part, and then added a third. The old song now rang out through the room in the three voices.

"Once more!" And the Master repeated the three parts.

"A beautiful song!" he said gently. "Play it again in the tenor!"

Knecht obeyed. The Master gave him the opening notes, and then commenced playing the three other parts together. Time after time the old man said: "Once more!" and each time the words rang out more contentedly. Knecht played the melody in the tenor part, and was always accompanied by the three contra voices. They repeated the song many times, and no prompting was necessary any longer. With each repetition the song grew richer in embellishments and variations. The notes echoed joyfully through the cool little room, bathed in the early morning sunlight.

At last the old man stopped. "Is that enough?" he asked.

Knecht shook his head, and began to play once more. The old man added the three voices, and now the complex harmony followed a clear course, with the voices corresponding, sporting and playing around each other in serene arcs and figures. They had both become oblivious of everything save the music, and gave themselves up to the beautiful related lines and figures of the melody they were creating. They made music, swaying softly and obeying the baton of an invisible conductor, until at last, as the melody came to an end once more, the Master turned to the boy and said: "Did you enjoy that, Joseph?"

Grateful and transfigured, Knecht looked at him. He was radiant, but still could find no word to say.

"Do you know by any chance what a fugue is?" the Master went on.

Joseph looked puzzled. He had heard fugues, but had never been taught the art.

"Good," said the Master. "Then I will show you. You will understand it more quickly if we compose a fugue oùrselves. So! The first essential to a fugue is a theme. We will not look very far for one: we will take it from our song."

He played a short phrase, a fragment of the song's melody. It sounded strange, cut out thus from the tune without head or tail. He repeated the theme and developed it. Next came the first entrance; the second entrance changed the fifth into a fourth, the third repeated the first an octave higher, as did the fourth the second; and finally, with a phrase in the dominant key, the exposition came to a close. The second composition was a freer modulation in variant keys, and the third had a change into the minor, returning to the major.

The boy watched the skilled white fingers of the musician, saw the development lightly reflected in his attentive face while his eyes rested beneath half-closed lids. His heart was filled with reverence and with love for the Master. His ear became attuned to the fugue, and it seemed to him as though he were hearing music for the first time in his life. He divined the spirit behind the melodies, the felicitous harmony of law and freedom, of service and rule; he praised and surrendered to this spirit and to this Master, and saw in those moments his own life and the whole world accompanied by music, ordered and given meaning. And when the playing came to an end, he stared at the object of his admiration—the magician and king who was still bent with half-closed eyelids over the notes, his face shining from within—not knowing whether to shout for joy or to weep because the music had ceased.

The old man raised himself slowly from the piano stool, looked at him earnestly with his calm blue eyes and said in an incredibly friendly voice: "In no way is it easier for two men to become friends than in making sweet music. It is a beautiful thing, and I hope that you and I will remain friends, Joseph. Perhaps you, too, will learn how to compose fugues."

He held out his hand to Joseph, and made towards the door; but just as he was about to leave, he turned round and said farewell with a look and a polite little nod of the head.

Many years later Knecht related to one of his own students that, as he had left the music room, he had found the town and the world far more transformed and enchanted than if it had been decorated with flags and flowers, or if there had been fireworks and bands playing.

Joseph had experienced his first call, which one may rightly term a sacrament—a vision, an inviting revelation of the ideal world, which had hitherto been dormant in his young soul and of which he had a knowledge partly from hearsay and partly in the form of fiery dreams. This world had only existed in the far distance—in the past and in the future—but now it was there and active, radiant, and it sent messengers, apostles and ambassadors—men like this old Music Master, who, by the way, as Joseph later discovered, was not so particularly old.

And from this world there had come a warning and a call to him through this venerable messenger, to the little grammar school pupil. This then was the significance of his experience, although it was some weeks before he really knew and was fully convinced that the magic occurrence corresponded exactly to the events of the real world; that the call was not merely a happiness and a warning in his own soul and conscience, but also a gift and a warning from the earthly powers.

For after a time it could no longer be concealed that the Music Master's visit had been neither an accident nor in the nature of a routine school inspection. Knecht's name, as a result of his teacher's reports, had already for some considerable time stood on the list of scholars who were considered possible candidates for the élite school or who had been recommended to the highest authorities. As the boy Knecht had not been praised for his progress in the general curriculum alone, but in particular by his music teacher, the Magister Musicæ had taken it upon himself, and had spared a few hours in the course of an official journey, to visit Berolfingen and see the boy. For him it was not so much a question of prowess in his school subjects or in his musical execution—he left that to the testimony of his teacher (in whose study he had spent a whole hour)—but a question of whether this boy possessed the intrinsic material necessary

to become a musician in the highest sense of the word—
enthusiasm, self-discipline, reverence and service to the cult.

In general, teachers in the public grammar schools were
very free with their recommendations of pupils for the élite
school, and these were usually inspired by some hope of
personal reward or other similar ulterior motive. Often, too,
a teacher with lack of perspicacity would recommend some
favourite pupil who had little merit beyond being industrious,
ambitious and clever in his behaviour towards the teacher.

This particular type was held in especial abhorrence by the
Music Master, who had a sharp eye for seeing whether the
candidate realised that it was a question of his future and of
his career or not; and woe betide the pupil who confronted
him too adroitly, consciously or cleverly, or who tried to
flatter him: he would very often be dismissed abruptly before
the examination had started.

The pupil Knecht had pleased the old Music Master
exceedingly, and he thought of the boy with pleasure as he
continued on his journey. He had made no notes or remarks in
his book, but had borne away with him the memory of a fresh
and modest youngster. On his return home he wrote Knecht's
name with his own hand on the list of scholars who had been
personally examined by a member of the higher pedagogy
and who had been found worthy of acceptance.

Joseph had at times heard this list spoken of in very
equivocal tones. To the grammar schoolboys it was generally
known as "The Golden Book," although it was often dis-
respectfully referred to as "the lickspittle's catalogue."

Whenever one of the teachers had occasion to mention this
list, were it only to warn a pupil that an oaf like himself could
never aspire to the honour of seeing his name upon it, a
certain pomposity, respect and bumbledom would creep into
his voice. But when the pupils spoke of the "lickspittle's
catalogue," they did so mostly in a saucy manner with a
rather exaggerated indifference. Once Joseph had heard a
comrade say: "I myself don't give a tinker's curse for their
stupid 'lickspittle's catalogue.' A real fellow never gets on it,
you can be certain. The teachers only send in the names of all
the worst swots and toadies!"

For Joseph a remarkable phase now followed upon this

event. At first he had no idea that he now actually belonged to the "electi," to the "flos juventatis" as the élite scholars were known within the Order. He gave no thought at all to the practical results and the discernible effects of this event upon his destiny and everyday life, and although for his teacher he was now a distinguished and transitory guest, he himself experienced his call only as an occurrence which had taken place within himself.

Despite this it was a sharp incursion into his own life. If, too, that marvellous hour with the master had filled his heart and given rise to some premonition, it was by very virtue of that experience that for him yesterday was now separated from to-day, the past from the present and the future, in the same way as one who has been awakened from a dream and who, on finding himself awake in the same surroundings as he had seen in his dream, can no longer doubt that he really *is* awake.

There are many different varieties and forms of "call," but the kernel and meaning of the event are always the same. The soul becomes awakened, so that inner dreams and premonitions are suddenly replaced by a summons from without, and a fragment of reality is found to exist and comes into play.

In Knecht's case the fragment of reality had been the figure of the Master. The now remote, awe-inspiring, half-godlike figure of the Magister Musicæ—an archangel from the highest heavens with omniscient blue eyes—had appeared in the flesh, had sat on a little stool at the practice piano, made music with Joseph—wonderful music—shown him, almost without words, what music really meant, had blessed him and departed once more.

As to the possible results, Knecht was at first not capable of conceiving, because he was occupied and over-filled with the immediate inner echo of the event. Just as a young plant, which has previously developed with hesitant calm, suddenly begins to breathe and grow as if in a wondrous hour it has become aware of the laws that govern it, and now strives inwardly for their fulfilment, so the boy, once he had felt the touch of the Magister's hand, began quickly and avidly to gather and brace his strength, feeling new tensions, new harmonies between himself and the world, able at times to solve problems in music, Latin and mathematics far beyond his years, and as a result to feel himself capable of any achievement, could at other times forget everything in dreams—in a new found softness and devotion—listen to the wind and the rain, stare at the flowers or into the running streams, understanding nothing, surmising all, a prey to sympathy, curiosity and the will to understand, torn from his own self and drawn towards another—to the world, to secret and sacrament, to the bittersweet game of appearances.

Thus, beginning from within and developing towards the union and confirmation of the inner with the external, the call of Joseph Knecht had been fulfilled in perfect purity: he had passed through all its stages and tasted of all its joys and fears. Undisturbed by sudden revelations and indiscretions. the noble event had transpired, the typical youth and early history of that noble spirit had burgeoned; in harmony and moderation the inner and external had worked and grown up together.

At the end of this development, when at last Joseph had realised his position and external fate, when the teachers had begun to treat him as a colleague—almost as an honoured guest whose departure is expected at any moment—and he had begun to be half-admired or envied by his fellow scholars, half-avoided, half-tormented, mocked and hated by a few rivals, more and more separated from and abandoned by former friends, a similar process of separation and isolation had already long since taken place within himself. It was due to this inward change that the teachers seemed now no longer superiors but comrades, that erstwhile friends might have been travelling companions who had been left behind on the journey, that he now found himself in his school and town no longer in the right place and among his own kind, and that everything had died and become unreal—a provisional halting place, a worn out and unseemly cloak. And this outgrowing of a formerly harmonious and beloved homeland, this sloughing of a life form that no longer represented or belonged to him, this intermittent feeling of supreme happiness and radiant self-awareness, denoting the interrupted life of one about to depart—one who had been called away—became at last a torture, a pressure and a suffering that he could at times scarce endure, for everything seemed to have been withdrawn from him without his being quite convinced as to whether it were actually he who had been abandoned or whether he had not brought upon himself this dying away and estrangement in his beloved familiar world through ambition, immoderacy, arrogance, inconstancy and lack of love.

Among the pangs that a true call brings in its wake, these are the bitterest.

Whoever receives the call not only receives a reward and a command but takes upon himself something in the nature of an obligation, just as in the case of the soldier who is raised from the ranks and promoted to officer, this promotion is paid for more dearly by virtue of a feeling of guilt—a guilty conscience towards his former comrades.

Knecht, however, was allowed to develop undisturbed and in complete innocence. When at last the headmaster informed him of his distinction, of his forthcoming acceptance into the élite school, he was momentarily surprised, but realised almost immediately that this fact had been known to him intuitively all along and that he had been anxiously awaiting its confirmation.

For the first time he was aware that for the past weeks the words "electus" or "chosen boy" had been flung at him frequently, almost as a term of derision. He had only half understood its significance, and had never attributed it to anything except contempt. He had felt that he should never have been called "electus," but rather "one who in his arrogance might have put on the airs of an 'electus'."

He had frequently suffered under these outbursts of hostility and estrangement between himself and his companions, for in actual fact he had never considered himself as an "electus." The call was for him not a promotion but an inner warning and an encouragement. But then, had he not, in spite of everything, always known and surmised it—felt it a hundred times? Now the time was at hand. His bliss was now confirmed and legitimised, and his sufferings had not been in vain. The old cloak, which had become outmoded and outworn, could now be discarded for a new one, which lay at his disposal.

With his entrance into the élite school, Knecht's life was transplanted on to another plane. This was the first decisive step in his development.

It is by no means inevitable that the entrance of all élite scholars into the school corresponds with the realisation of a call. That happy condition is a question of exceptional grace, or, to put it plainly, of luck. But the candidate whom this good fortune overtakes will inevitably possess a plus quantity in life, as is the case of all who have been granted particularly felicitous gifts of body and soul. The majority of the élite school boys—in fact nearly all of them—considered their acceptance as a great piece of fortune, and a distinction of which they were very proud. Many of them, too, had passionately desired this distinction for a long time in advance. But the change over from the normal country schools to the Schools of Castalia entailed more difficulties than the chosen ones had expected and brought disappointment to many of them. The transition period for every pupil who had been happy and beloved in his own home was above all a difficult time of farewell and renunciation. It often happened, therefore, particularly during the first two years in the élite school, that there were a high number of dismissals, not from lack of talent and industriousness but because of the incapacity of the scholar to reconcile himself to the monastic life of a boarder, and more especially to the idea that for the future he would be forced to sever all ties with family and country and know no allegiance and respect other than to the Order.

Then from time to time there were scholars for whom, on the other hand, the release from the tyranny of home or from a school where they had been unhappy had been the main object of their striving for acceptance into the élite school. These scholars, who had been freed from a stern father or some unpleasant teacher, breathed freely for a while, but had counted upon so many impossible alterations in their lives that disappointment soon set in.

Neither could the actual "lickspittles," model pupils or pedants endure for long in Castalia: not that they were unfitted for the studies, but because in the élite schools learning and certificates did not suffice and educational and musical aims were the objectives, which proved insuperable obstacles to them.

There was, however, always room for every variety of talent within the ramifications of the four large élite schools, with their innumerable secondary establishments and branch institutions. An assiduous mathematician or philologist, if he really possessed the seeds of true scholarship, had no reason to fear his lack of musical or philosophical talents.

There were at times in Castalia strong tendencies towards the cultivation of pure, sober, specialised sciences, and the pioneers of these trends were not only critically and scornfully opposed to the "dreamers," but had frequently within their own circles banished and abjured everything musical, particularly the Bead Game.

As Knecht's life, in so far as we know it, was passed entirely in Castalia—in that most tranquil and serene province of our mountainous country, which has often been referred to by the Goethean phrase "the pedagogic province" —we shall, at the risk of tiring our reader with long familiar details, and as briefly as possible, outline the structure of that famous country and its schools.

These schools, or élite schools as they are called, are a wise and elastic system of selection, by means of which the authorities (a so-called "Council of Studies" composed of twenty Councillors, ten of whom belong to the Pedagogy and ten to the Order) can see to it that the cream of the talented youth from every branch and school of the land is attracted to the Order and to all the important offices of education and learning.

The many secondary schools, gymnasia, etc., whether humanistic or scientific (both natural and technical) are preparatory schools for more than ninety per cent. of the youth of our country. These serve for the so-called "free vocations," and end with matriculation for the high school, where there is a scheduled curriculum for each subject.

This is the normal course of study for our students, which is common knowledge. These schools are extremely strict in their requirements, and eliminate the untalented as far as possible. Parallel or superior to these schools runs the system of the élite schools, where the talent and character of the most outstanding students will be put to the test. Access to them is not the result of examination, but the élite scholars are chosen by the personal judgment of their own teachers and recommended to the Castalian authorities. An eleven or twelve-year-old-boy will one day be approached by his teacher and told to reflect carefully whether or not he feels himself called, and considers himself a suitable candidate for entrance. Should his answer, after a seemly period, be in the affirmative, and subject also to the unconditional agreement of both parents, he will be accepted by one of the élite schools as a probationer.

The directors and head teachers of these élite schools are members of the "Pedagogy," which body determines all the curricula and controls all the intellectual organisations of the country. Once a boy is accepted as an élite scholar, it is no longer a question of his studying for a specialist or money-making career, unless he fails in one of the subjects and be returned to the grammar school: he is destined for recruitment into the Order and hierarchy of the academic authorities, which embrace careers from school teacher to the highest officials, *viz.*, the twelve academic directors or "Masters" and the "Ludi Magister" or Master of the Bead Game. The majority finish their last courses in the élite schools at the age of between twenty-two and twenty-five with their admission into the Order. From this moment on all the cultural establishments and research institutes of the Order and of the pedagogy, including the organisations of the Bead Game, lie open to them: the élite universities, the libraries, archives, laboratories, etc., are reserved for their use.

Any scholar who, during his school years, has shown a special aptitude for some subject such as languages, philosophy or mathematics, will immediately be allocated to that particular Faculty in the higher stages of the élite schools which offers the best outlet for his talents. The majority of these scholars finish as professional teachers in the public and high schools and remain, even should they leave Castalia, life members of the Order. This imposes upon them the need to maintain a strict distance between themselves and the "grammar scholars" (who have not been educated in the élite schools) and, unless they secede from the Order, they can never enter the "free" professions, such as doctor, lawyer, technician, etc., but must submit for the rest of their lives to the rules of the Order, which entail among other things celibacy and total lack of possessions. The common people call them, with a mixture of derision and respect, the "Mandarins."

In this manner the majority of the élite scholars find their ultimate destinies. A free choice of studies of indefinite duration is reserved for the very small remainder, the cream of the Castalian schools—a contemplative, painstaking and intellectual life. Many of these highly talented scholars who, on account of some defect of character or other ground such as physical debility, are not suited to the teaching profession or to a responsible position in the upper or lower pedagogies, continue to study, to research or collect data for the rest of their lives, destined for the most part to works of pure scholarship as pensioners of the authorities. Some of them are appointed advisers to the Dictionary Commission, or to archives, libraries, etc., while others pursue learning under the device of "Art for Art's sake." Many of them have devoted their lives to very abstruse and curious subjects. We may cite as examples the famous Ludovicus Crudelis, who in the course of thirty years' work translated all the extant Ancient Egyptian texts into both Greek and Sanscrit, or that eccentric Chattus Calvensis II, who left a four folio holograph manuscript on the "Pronunciation of the Latin tongue in the Universities of Southern Italy at the end of the Twelfth Century." This work was planned as the first part of a "History of the Pronunciation of Latin from the Twelfth to the Sixteenth Centuries," but despite its thousand sheets of manuscript has remained a fragment and has never been completed.

It is quite understandable that many jests have been made at the expense of this type of pure scholarship, but its actual value for future generations of scientists and for the public cannot possibly be calculated. Nevertheless science, to as great an extent as did art in former times, on occasions needs a certain extensive field, and a research worker may amass knowledge, in some subject which interests no one apart from himself, capable of rendering the highest services to his contemporary colleagues, in the form of, say, a dictionary or an archive. As far as it is possible, these scholarly works are printed. The scholars themselves are left in almost complete freedom to indulge in their studies and interests, and it never occurs to them that many of their works may not prove of any immediate use to the community as a whole, and must seem to the layman like so many extravagant futilities.

Many of the scholars are laughed at because of the nature of their work, but none of them is ever blamed or deprived of his privileges. The fact that they are also respected by the public and not merely tolerated, even though much fun is poked at them, is accounted for by the price which they have to pay for their intellectual freedom.

They are granted many privileges, including a modest allowance of food, clothing and lodging, the use of many magnificent libraries, collections and laboratories, but in exchange for these they have to renounce not only good living, marriage and family, but live as in a monkish community, cut off from the activities of the world, knowing no personal possessions, titles or honours, obliged to content themselves with an extremely simple existence.

Should one of them choose to waste his life in deciphering some old inscription, he is entirely free to do so—he is even given every assistance—but should he lay claim to luxury, elegant clothes, money or fame, he meets with intransigent sanctions. Should he find such tastes to be indispensable, he will return to the "world" in early youth and become a professional teacher or private tutor, journalist, etc., or else marry and look for some such style of life more compatible with his tastes.

On the day that the boy Joseph Knecht said farewell to Berolfingen, his music teacher accompanied him to the station. The parting made him sad, and his heart sank a little. He felt alone and unsure of himself as he watched the white-washed, stepped gable of the old town castle disappear from view. Many scholars before him had taken this departure with less fortitude, and had broken down and wept. Joseph, however, was already living more in his destination than in Berolfingen, and easily withstood this ordeal. It was not a long journey. He had been posted to the school at Eschholz, of which he had already seen pictures in the headmaster's study.

Eschholz was the largest and newest school establishment in Castalia. The buildings were all modern, and there was no town in the vicinity—only a small village-like settlement close set with trees. Behind this settlement the establishment spread out wide, flat and tranquil; in design it was a large, spacious quadrangle, in the middle of which five mammoth trees raised their dark cubes to the sky in the form of the five spots on a dice. This colossal square was laid partly with sand and partly with grass lawns, and only broken up by two great swimming pools with running water, to which broad, low steps led down. At the entrance to this sunny square stood the school house—the only high building of the establishment— with its two wings, each of which had a five-columned entrance hall.

All the remaining buildings, enclosing the square on three sides without a break, were low, flat and devoid of ornament. They were separated into equal sections, each of which possessed a porch and a flight of steps leading on to the square. Pots of flowers stood at most of the porch entrances.

As was the custom in Castalia, Joseph was not received by a school servant on his arrival, and led before the headmaster or a group of teachers, but was met by a comrade, an attractive well-built boy dressed in blue linen overalls and a few years older than himself. He put out his hand, and said: "I am Hubertus, the head boy of Hellas House, where you will live, and it is my duty to welcome you and show you round. You are not expected to attend classes until to-morrow, so we have plenty of time to see everything and you will soon feel at home.

"I hope, for the first few days until you settle down, that you will regard me as your friend and mentor, and also as your protector in case you should be molested by any of the other boys—many of them think that a new boy must always be tormented a little. It won't be so bad, I can assure you. Now I will take you to Hellas House, so that you can see where you are going to live."

This was how Hubertus, the house prefect, who had been appointed mentor to Joseph, greeted the newcomer. In actual fact, he took the trouble to carry out his duties well: it was nearly always a source of amusement to the seniors to play this rôle, and were a fifteen-year-old boy to take pains to fascinate one two years his junior with an amiable note of easy condescension and cameraderie, it would always prove successful. Joseph was treated by his mentor for the first few days entirely as a guest who might have been leaving on the following day, and whom one wished to bear away with him a good impression of the house and host.

He was taken to his dormitory, which he was to share with two other boys, given rusks and a glass of fruit cordial, and shown Hellas House—one of the dormitories of the great quadrangle—shown where to hang his towel in the open-air bath, and in which corner he was allowed to grow plants should he so wish. He was also taken to the launderer in the wash-house, who gave him a pair of blue linen overalls to his measure. From the first moment the boy took kindly to his new home, and found pleasure in Hubertus' manner; he felt hardly a trace of embarrassment, although the elder boy had been for some years an inmate of Castalia and was naturally something of a demi-god in his eyes.

Hubertus' occasional little mannerisms and showing off attracted him, as when, for example, he wove a complicated Greek quotation into his conversation only to excuse himself immediately, as he remembered that the new boy would obviously not understand—and who would have dreamed of asking such a thing of him, anyway?

Furthermore, the life of a boarder was not new to Knecht: he adapted himself to Eschholz without effort. We have no record of any important occurrences during his four year stay at this school, and he could not have been there at the time of the appalling fire. His testimonials, as far as we have been able to discover, show him as having received the highest marks in music and Latin, while in mathematics and Greek he was well above the average. In the "House register" we find from time to time such entries as :"*Ingenium valde capax, studia non angusta, mores probantur*" or "*Ingenium felix et profectuum avidissimum, moribus placet officiosis.*" As regards the punishments he received, we cannot be certain, as the punishment book, like so many others, was destroyed in the

great fire. A fellow pupil insisted at a later date that Knecht
was only punished once during his four years at Eschholz for
cutting the weekly excursion, and because he obstinately
refused to betray the name of a boy who had done something
forbidden. The anecdote sounds plausible, for Knecht was
without doubt a loyal comrade and never subservient to his
superiors. However, the fact that he was really only punished
once in four years seems to exceed the bounds of probability.

Because we are so ill-furnished with a documentation of
Knecht's early élite school life, we have inserted here a
passage from one of his later lectures on the Bead Game.
Actually no original manuscripts exist of these lectures for
beginners, and one of his pupils typed this excerpt from an
impromptu speech.

Knecht was speaking on analogies and associations in the
Bead Game, and had differentiated between "legitimate" or
objective, and "private" or subjective, associations. He said:
"In order to give you an example of these private associations, which do not lose their private value although they are
forbidden in the Bead Game, I will tell you a similar
association from my schooldays. I was about fourteen years
old, and it was in early spring—February or March, I think—
when a comrade invited me to go for a walk with him one
afternoon in order to cut some elder sticks, which he wished
to use as conduits for a little water mill that he was construct-
ing. We set out, and it must have been a very lovely day
either in reality or in my imagination, for this little experience
has remained in my memory. The earth was damp but
innocent of snow, and there was already a profusion of green
near the waterfalls. There were buds on the bare branches,
and the first catkins had already taken on a vestige of colour.
The air was full of odours—odours pregnant with life and
contradiction—the odour of moist earth, decaying leaves and
young shoots, and at each moment I expected to see the first
violet—although it was still too early. We found the elder
trees, which had tiny buds·but no leaves, and as I cut off a
twig an overpowering bitter-sweet scent assailed me, which
seemed to be the epitome, quintessence and potential of all
the perfumes of spring. I was quite captivated by it. I smelt
my knife, my fingers and the elder twig, and found that it was

the sap that smelt so strong and irresistible. We did not mention it, but my companion, too, smelt his stick long and thoughtfully, for the odour had also made an impression upon him.

"Now this experience possesses its own magic, and is the essence of my experience: the approach of spring, simply by my crossing the damp plangent meadow, by the perfume of the earth and the buds which I had found potent and pleasurable, had now become concentrated and increased, as a physical expression and symbol, in the fortissimo of the elder scent. Perhaps I should never have forgotten this scent even had this little experience remained my own, but, far more than that, every future encounter with this scent throughout my life should immediately have awakened the memory of that first experience because I had experienced the scent consciously. But now a second factor comes into play. In my piano teacher's study I had discovered an old score which greatly attracted me—it was a volume of Schubert's songs. I had glanced through them one day when I had been obliged to wait for a long time for the teacher, and at my request he had lent them to me for a few days.

"In my leisure hours I lived completely in the joy of my discovery, for I had previously known nothing of Schubert and was immediately enchanted by him. And I now discovered —on the day of the elder tree episode or perhaps on the following day—Schubert's "The Soft Airs have Awakened," and the first chords of the piano accompaniment came to me like a sudden recognition, for these chords seemed to carry with them exactly the aroma of the young elder—so strong, so concentrated, so full of early spring! From that moment onwards the association: early spring—elder perfume— Schubert chords has been permanent and absolutely valid, and with the striking of the chords I immediately and positively smell the sharp plant odour. and the two together represent early spring.

"In this private association I possess something very beautiful, something that I would not forego for anything in the world. But the association, that convulsion of two sensual experiences in the thought 'early spring,' is my private affair. It can be imparted, of course, as I have just related it to you, but it cannot be translated.

"I can make you understand my association, but I cannot convert it for a single one of you into a valid symbol or into a mechanism which will react at call and take exactly the same course."

One of Knecht's fellow scholars, who later became chief archivist of the Bead Game, used to insist that Knecht was on the whole an unobtrusive although merry boy. At times when making music his face would assume a wonderful expression of contemplation or happy ecstasy, although he seldom showed any energy or passion except at the rhythmic ball game, which he loved.

Sometimes, however, this healthy and friendly boy would draw attention to himself and arouse scorn or anxiety, particularly when certain of the lower boys had been expelled —a not uncommon occurrence.

When it happened for the first time that a classmate who had failed, either in his lessons or in games, did not appear on the following day, and it was rumoured that he was not ill but had been dismissed—that he had left not to return—Knecht was not only sad but completely distracted for several days.

He himself admitted later, years later: "Each time a scholar was expelled from Eschholz and left us, I felt as though someone had died. Should anyone have questioned me as to why I mourned, I should have replied that it was out of pity for the unfortunate who had ruined his future through carelessness and indolence, and perhaps, too, out of fear—fear that one day the same thing might happen to myself. Only after I had experienced the same thing many times, and knew that the possibility of the same fate overtaking me was out of the question, did I begin to look into the question a little more deeply. At last I came to regard the expulsion of an 'electus' no longer as a misfortune or a punishment, for I knew then that in many cases the dismissed boy had been delighted to return home. At last I felt that it was not only to justice and punishment that a reckless fellow could fall a victim, but that the 'world' outside, from which all the 'electi' had once come, had not by any means ceased to exist as it had appeared to me, but on the contrary, was a very great reality and full of attraction for many, and that it lured and finally recaptured them. And perhaps this was not only the case for individuals but for everyone; perhaps it was not the weaker and inferior that the outside world attracted, and the apparent relapse which they had suffered was no disgrace and hardship but a leap forward and a brave deed; and perhaps it was we who remained steadfastly at Eschholz who were the weaklings and cowards."

We shall see that this thought became very real to Knecht at a later date.

One of Joseph's greatest joys had been to see the old Music Master again. The old man came two or three times each month to Eschholz to visit and inspect the music classes; he was also very friendly with one of the teachers, whose guest he would be for several days. On one occasion he presided in person at the final rehearsals of a performance of a Monteverdi vesper.

Above all he kept a close watch on the more talented among the music pupils, and Knecht was one of those whom he graced with a paternal friendship. From time to time he would sit for an hour with Joseph in one of the practice rooms and play through with him the works of his favourite composers or a classic example from one of the old composition manuals.

"To build a canon with the Music Master, or to hear him reduce a badly constructed one *ad absurdum*, often had a solemnity or a matchless vivacity, so that at times one could hardly hold back the tears and at others hardly refrain from laughing. One left a music lesson with this Master as though one had come from a bath and a massage. "

As Knecht's schooldays at Eschholz drew to a close—he was to be transferred, together with about a dozen other scholars of his grade, to a higher school—the headmaster addressed his customary speech to these candidates, in which he recapitulated for their benefit the significance and laws of the Castalian schools, outlining briefly in the name of the Order the path at the end of which they themselves would have the right to enter the Order.

This solemn occasion was in the nature of a festivity which the school always offered to its promoted boys, during which they were treated as guests by their schoolfellows and teachers, and a well-rehearsed musical performance was staged. This year it was a great cantata of the seventeenth century, and the Music Master himself came to hear the performers.

On the way to the festooned dining hall, after the headmaster's speech, Knecht approached the Music Master with a question. "The headmaster," he said, "has just explained to us what takes place in the ordinary schools and high schools outside Castalia. He told us also that the scholars there prepare in universities for the 'free vocations.' These, as far as I can see, are to a great extent vocations of which we here in Castalia are ignorant. What am I to infer by this? Why then do they call those vocations 'free'? And why are we Castalians debarred from them?"

The Magister Musicæ took the boy aside, and stood with him under one of the mammoth trees. An almost cunning smile brought out the little wrinkles around his eyes as he replied: "You, my young friend, bear the name of Knecht, which means in German a serf or thrall, and this is perhaps why the word 'free' has such a pleasant ring for you. But do not take it too seriously in this instance! When the non-Castalians speak of 'free vocations' the words have perhaps an earnest, somewhat pathetic ring. But in our mouths they are meant ironically. The freedom of those vocations lies only in the fact that the learners have chosen them themselves. That gives an illusion of freedom, although in most cases the choice lies less with the pupil than with his family, and many a father would rather bite out his tongue than really allow his son to choose a career for himself. But perhaps that is a slander: let us overrule this objection! Freedom, then, is confined to this single act of choosing a vocation. After this, freedom comes to an end. Already in his studies in the high school, the doctor, lawyer or technician is constrained to a rigid curriculum, ending in a series of examinations. Should he graduate successfully, he receives a certificate which allows him to practise his vocation once more in apparent freedom. But he then becomes a slave to the lower powers, dependent upon success, money, ambition and desire for fame, and the regard in which men hold him or do not hold him. He must attend elections, earn money and participate in the ruthless struggles of caste, family, political parties and the newspapers. In return he has the freedom to become successful and well-to-do, hated by the unsuccessful or vice-versa. The reverse applies to the élite scholar and eventual member of the Order. He 'chooses' no vocation. He does not consider himself a better judge of his talents than his teacher. He allows himself—within the hierarchy—to be placed in that position or in that function which his superiors elect for him. Provided that the reverse does not altogether apply, and the characteristics, gifts and faults of the pupil compel the teacher to appoint him to a particular position.

"In the midst of this apparent bondage, each 'electus' enjoys the greatest possible freedom after his first course. While the man of the 'free' vocations must undergo an education in his speciality, a narrow and rigid curriculum with rigid examinations, the 'electus,' as soon as he begins to study independently, enjoys so wide a freedom that many of them spend their whole lives at the most abstruse and often almost foolish studies of their own choice, and no one interferes with them unless their morals degenerate. He who is suited to be a teacher will become a teacher, an educator will become an educator or a translator a translator, each discovering his own place in which to serve and be free in his service. And, furthermore, he is released for his lifetime from that 'freedom' of vocation which entails such terrible slavery. He knows nothing of the struggle for money, fame and rank; he knows no political parties, no strife between individual and official, between private and public, and no dependence upon success. You see now, my son, that when we speak of 'free vocations' the word 'free' has a somewhat jocular interpretation."

The departure from Eschholz was an important milestone in Knecht's life. If until then he had had a happy childhood and had lived in a system and harmony almost devoid of problems, a period of conflicts and difficulties of development now began for him. He was about seventeen years old when he was informed that he would be transferred with a group of his classmates to a higher grade school. For a short while the main and most vital topic of conversation had been their respective destinations: according to the tradition, each boy would be told where he was to be sent during the last days before his departure, and the interval between the end of term feast and his leavetaking was a holiday.

During these holidays a wonderful and important event

took place for Knecht: the Music Master had invited him, while on a walking tour, to be his guest for a few days. This was a great and singular honour. Early one morning Knecht wandered, in company with another scholar—for he still belonged to Eschholz and it was against the rules for boys to travel alone—towards the forest and the mountains. After a three-hour climb through the shady trees they reached an open spur, and saw Eschholz lying below them, small and clearly visible in the plain. It was easily recognisable by the dark mass of its five giant trees, the grass-sown quadrangle with the swimming pools, the tall school house, administration buildings and little village. The famous Eschholz! Both the youths stopped and looked down. Many of us remember this enchanting view, and it was not very different from what it still is to-day, for the buildings have been faithfully restored to their original form since the great fire, and three of the giant trees have survived the destruction. They saw their school lying there below, their home for so many years to which they must now soon say farewell, and both of them felt a pang in their hearts.

"I do not think," said Joseph's companion, "that I have ever before realised how beautiful it is. Yes, it may be that I am seeing it for the first time now that I am leaving, and have to say goodbye to it."

"You are quite right," replied Knecht. "I feel the same as you do. But even when we leave here we shall never really have left Eschholz. The only ones who have left it for ever are boys like Otto, for example, who used to compose such wonderful Latin limericks, or Charlemagne, who could swim so long under water, and many others I could name. I have not thought about them for a long time now, but at this moment I recall them all. You may laugh at me, but those fallen ones have something imposing for me despite everything, just as the apostate angel Lucifer has a certain grandeur.

"They may perhaps have done wrong—they certainly have done wrong!—but all the same they have done something, completed something; they have dared to take a leap forward, and that requires courage. We others have been patient, and industrious, and intelligent, but we have done nothing, and we have not taken any leaps."

"Oh! I don't know," observed his friend. "Some of them

neither did nor dared anything at all, but simply went on the loose until they were expelled. But perhaps I have not quite understood you. What actually do you mean by a leap?"

"I mean, the power to be independent. Taking things seriously. In fact—the leap! I personally have no desire to leap backwards into my former country and mode of life. They do not interest me, and I have almost forgotten them. But I do wish, when the time comes—and it will be necessary —to free myself, and to be able to leap not merely back into something inferior but forwards and upwards."

"Well, we are on our way. Eschholz was a stage, and the next one will be higher, and eventually—the Order awaits us."

"Yes, but I didn't mean that exactly. But let us push forward, *amice!* It is so marvellous to wander, and it will make me gay again. We have become quite melancholy."

In this mood, and with these words—which that comrade has left to us—the stormy period of Knecht's youth was foreshadowed.

The boys were en route for two days before they arrived at Monteport in the hills, a former monastery, where the Music Master dwelt, and was holding a course for conductors.

Knecht's friend was given a room in the inn, and a small cell in the Master's house had been reserved for Knecht himself. He had hardly unpacked his knapsack and washed himself when his host appeared.

The worthy man held out his hand to the youth, sat down on a little stool and closed his eyes for a few minutes, as he always did when he was tired. Opening them again, he said in a friendly tone: "You must forgive me: I am a bad host. You have walked a long way and must be very tired, and to tell you the truth, so am I, for I have had a very full day. But if you are not sleepy, I would like to spend an hour with you in my room. You can stay here for two days, and to-morrow you can bring your friend to dine with me, but unfortunately I have not very much time to spare for you, and we must see how we can arrange the few hours I *can* spend with you to the best advantage. Shall we begin straight away?"

He led Knecht into a large vaulted cell, which was bare except for an old piano and two stools. They sat down.

"You will soon be entering a new grade," the Master

began, "and you will be learning all manner of new things, some of which are very fine indeed. You will also begin to dabble in the Bead Game. That is good and important, but there is something even more important still—you will learn to meditate. All the students learn it apparently, but it cannot always be controlled. I wish you to learn it correctly and well —as well as you have learnt music. Everything else will come of itself. Therefore, I want to you give the first two or three lessons in person, and that is the reason why I have invited you here. To-day, to-morrow and the next day we will attempt an hour of meditation to music. You shall now have a glass of milk, so that you will not be disturbed by hunger or thirst: we shall have our evening meal later."

There was a knock at the door, and a servant brought in a glass of milk.

"Drink slowly—very slowly," he warned. "Take your time, and don't talk."

Knecht did as he was bid, and drank the cool milk very slowly. The old man sat down opposite him and closed his eyes once more. His face looked very old but friendly, as though he had plunged into his own thoughts like a tired man into a hot bath. Peace radiated from him, and Knecht felt this and was calmed in turn.

The Master then turned round on his stool and placed his hands upon the keys. He played a theme and developed it: it seemed to be a piece from some Italian master. He explained to his guest that he should follow the course of this music as though it were a dance, like an uninterrupted sequence of balanced exercises, a suite of smaller or larger steps from the centre of a symmetrical axis, and to pay no attention to anything except the figure which these steps produced. He played the bars again, reflected upon them in silence, repeated them and remained sitting there quite still with his hands on his knees and eyes half-closed, recalling and considering the music within himself. The pupil, too, listened to it inwardly, began to see fragments of the staves as though moving, pacing, dancing and swaying, and sought to recognise the movements and read them like the line of a bird's flight. They became confused and vanished again, and he was obliged to start afresh, for his concentration had left him for a space; he found himself in a void looking around him with embarrassment. He observed the quiet, immersed face of the Master, swaying, pale in the twilight. Then he once more entered that spiritual space whence he had slipped, heard the music echo within it, saw the notes pacing, the staves begin their movement, saw and meditated upon the dancing feet of the Invisible. . . .

A long time seemed to have passed before he was conscious once more of the room, before he felt the stool and matting-covered floor beneath him, and saw the twilight, which had deepened, through the windows. He felt that someone was watching him, and as he looked up he saw the eyes of the Music Master regarding him intently. The Master gave him an almost imperceptible nod, played the last variation of the Italian piece *pianissimo* with one finger, and then stood up.

"Remain seated here!" he said. "I will come back again. Look for the music once more within yourself, and pay attention to the figures. But do not strain: it is only a game. And if you fall asleep at it, it won't do you any harm."

He left the room, for he still had some work to do which he had not completed, despite a full day, and moreover it was neither an easy nor a pleasant task, such as he might have wished for. It was a question of one of the pupils of his class for conductors, a talented but vain and overbearing man, to whom he felt he must speak, pointing out his improper conduct and faults, with as much care as superiority and as much love as authority. He sighed. Why could not an ultimate solution be found by which recognisable faults could be banished? One was forced over and over again to struggle against the same failings, and to exterminate the same weeds! Talents without character, virtuosity without a feeling for the hierarchy, such as had dominated the musical life of the "Age of the Digest," had been rotted out and finished with in the musical renaissance, but had now started to sprout and bloom again.

When he returned from this task to take supper with Joseph, he found the boy calm, but happy and no longer tired.

"It was wonderful," said Joseph dreamily. "The music entirely disappeared and became transformed."

"Let its rhythm sway within you," said the Master, leading him into a small room where bread and fruit were laid upon a table.

They ate together, and the Master proposed that he should attend the course for conductors for a little while on the following day. Before he retired and showed his guest to his cell, he said: "You have seen something of meditation, and the music appeared to you as a figure. If it amuses you, try and write it down."

Knecht found a sheet of paper and pencils lying on the table in his cell, and before he went to sleep tried to draw the figures into which the music had been transformed. He drew a line, and then short branch lines from it diagonally in rhythmical intervals, until it reminded him somewhat of the pattern of leaves on a twig. He was not content with this, but felt a desire to try again and again. At last he bent the lines of his drawing into a circle, from which the branches radiated like a garland of flowers. After this he lay down and fell asleep.

He dreamed that he was standing once more on that spur above the forest, where he had rested with his comrade a few days before and had seen his beloved Eschholz lying there below: but the right angles of the school buildings began to change to an ellipse, and then gradually to a circle—a garland which began to turn slowly and increase in speed until at last in a mad whirl it burst asunder in a shower of sparkling stars.

On awakening he remembered nothing of this dream, but when the Master, during their morning stroll, asked him whether he had dreamed or not he felt for the moment that he must have experienced something unpleasant or exciting during the night. He reflected, recalled the dream, and was amazed at its innocence as he related it. The Master listened with great attention.

"Should one pay attention to dreams?" asked Joseph. "Can one explain them?"

The Master looked him in the eyes, and answered firmly: "We should pay attention to everything, for everything can be explained."

A few paces farther on he enquired paternally: "Which school would you prefer to enter now, Joseph?"

Knecht reddened, but answered quickly and softly: "Waldzell, I think."

The Master nodded his head. "I thought as much. You know the old tag, then: '*Gignit autem artificiosam* . . .'?"

Still blushing, Joseph completed the phrase, which was well-known to every scholar: " '*Gignit autem artificiosam lusorum gentem Cella Silvestris*'." (In English: "But Waldzell produces the artists of the Bead Game.")

"That is probably your path, Joseph," the old man said, looking at him affectionately. "But you know that everyone is not in favour of the Bead Game. They say that it is a substitute for the arts, and that the players are belletrists who cannot be regarded as being actually inspired but only as artists of free fantasy and dilletantism. But you will see how much truth there is in that. Perhaps you have already formed your own conclusions about the Bead Game, and have placed greater confidence in it than one would credit you with, or again, perhaps you have done nothing of the kind. One thing is certain: the Game is not without its dangers. And for this very reason we love it, for we only send the weaker ones upon safe paths. But you must never forget what I have so often told you: our object is to discern opposites correctly, in considering them primarily as opposites but eventually as poles of a single unit. This applies also to the Bead Game. Those of an artistic bent are enamoured of the game because it allows them to give free reign to their fantasy: the rigid technical scientists despise it, as do musicians, because for them that degree of strong discipline is lacking which they can attain in the special branches of their science. Good. You will get to know these antitheses, and will in time discern that they are not objective but subjective, and that, for example, an artistic dreamer does not avoid pure mathematics or logic because he has recognised and found it contradictory, but because his leanings are instinctively elsewhere. You can recognise with certainty the smaller souls by such instinctive and violent leanings or aversions. In actual fact, in great souls and superior intellects these passions do not exist. Each of us is only a man, only an essay, a traveller. He should be travelling, however, towards perfection, striving for the centre and not for the periphery. Mark well: one can be a strict logician or grammarian and yet be full of fantasy and music. One can be a musician or a bead-player, and yet be devoted to law and order. The man whom we take as our ideal and try to emulate should be able at all times to exchange his art or science for any other, should allow the most crystal clear logic to radiate from his Bead Game and display the most creative fantasy in grammar. That is how we should be, and we should be prepared at any moment to be transferred to another post without opposition or allowing ourselves to become confused."

"I think I understand," said Joseph. "But are not those who have such strong preferences and aversions the more passionate natures, and the others, on the contrary, the more tranquil and gentle?"

"This would seem to be the case, and yet it is not so," said the Master with a smile. "In order to be capable of everything and just to everyone, one certainly does not need to have a deficiency in spiritual strength, drive and warmth. On the contrary, a super-abundance of these characteristics is necessary. What you term passion is not spiritual strength, but friction between the soul and the outside world. There, where violent passion rules, you will not find a plus quantity of strength, desire and striving, because it is turned towards a restricted and false goal, which accounts for the tension and sultriness of the atmosphere. Whoever directs the highest power of yearning towards the centre, towards true being, towards the perfect, seems outwardly more peaceful than the passionate man because the flame of his ardour is not always apparent, and perhaps because he does not rave in argument and does not always scourge the poorer in spirit. But I tell you he will inevitably glow and burn with ardour!"

"Ah! If only one could really know!" cried Knecht. "If only there were a doctrime—something in which one could believe! Everything is so contradictory, and there is no certainty: everything can be explained and then re-explained in the opposite manner. One can interpret the whole of world history as development and progress, and yet, on the other hand, one can just as well see in it nothing but decline and insanity. Is there no truth then, is there no true and valid doctrine?"

The Master had never before heard Joseph speak with such violence. They walked on a little further in silence.

"Yes, there is truth, my dear boy," he said at last. "But the doctrine that you desire, the absolute, perfect, comprehensive and instructive doctrine, does not exist. You should not yearn for this, my friend, but only for self-perfection. The Godhead is in *yourself*, not in theories and in books. Truth must be lived, not taught. Prepare yourself for your conflict, Joseph Knecht, for I see that it has already begun."

Joseph was seeing his beloved Master for the first time at his daily work, and although he had only been given a glimpse into a small part of the latter's daily activities this gave him cause for great admiration. The thing that won him over most was the fact that the Master had accepted him so intimately, and had invited him in the midst of his work, that this harassed man, who often looked so weary, could spare precious time for him—and not only time! If his initiation into the art of meditation had made so deep and lasting an impression upon him, it was, as he was later able to judge, not as the result of a particularly fine or unusual technique, but on account of the personality and example of the Master. The teachers who instructed him in meditation during the course of the following years gave him more directions and more precise tuition, controlled him more sharply, put more questions to him and were more apt to correct him. The Music Master, confident of his power over the youth, had hardly spoken at all and had taught him practically nothing: he had confined himself to the main principles and their practical illustration.

Knecht observed how old and exhausted the Master sometimes looked, how he would suddenly withdraw into himself, his eyes half closed, and then look up at him after a while, so tranquil, serene and friendly, yet strong; and nothing could have convinced him more profoundly of the way to the source —of the way from unrest to tranquillity. Whatever the Master had to say on the subject, Knecht learned during a short walk or at meal times.

We know that on that visit Knecht received his first indications and inklings of the Bead Game, although we are in possession of no actual documents.

He was impressed, too, by the fact that his host could spare time for his comrade, so that the latter should not feel that he was in the way. The old man seemed to think of everything.

The short stay in Monteport, his three hours of meditation, his attendance at the course for conductors, and the few conversations with the Master himself, had meant a great deal to Knecht. The Master had certainly chosen the most

effective moment to tackle his pupil. The primary object of
his invitation had been to render the boy susceptible to
meditation, but no less important, the invitation was in itself
a sign that Joseph had been noticed and that great things
were expected of him. It was in fact the second stage of his
call. He had been granted an insight into his new surroundings, and if one of the twelve Magisters summoned a pupil so
closely at this stage, it did not signify a personal benevolence
alone. Whatever a Magister did was always supra-personal.

On leaving Monteport each of the boys received a little
present. Joseph was given a score of two Bach choral preludes,
and his friend an elegant pocket edition of Horace.

As Knecht was leaving, the Master said to him: "In a few
days from now you will learn to which school you have been
allocated. I shall be going there less frequently than to
Eschholz, but we shall be seeing each other again if my health
remains good. If you wish to do so, you can write me a letter
once a year, giving me details in particular of your musical
studies. Criticisms of your new teachers are not forbidden,
but I warn you I shall not lay very much store by them. I hope
you realise that great things await you. Our Castalia must
not merely be a choice selection of talent, but must above all
be a hierarchy, an edifice, in which every stone takes its
meaning from the whole. There is no path leading away from
this whole, and whosoever rises higher and is given greater
tasks will be proportionately less free and will have more
responsibility. Until we meet again then, my young friend . . .
It has been a great pleasure to have had you here!"

The two boys set out for Eschholz. Both of them were
calmer and more talkative than they had been on the outward
journey. The few days, with the change of air and new
scenery, the contact with another mode of life, had intrigued
them, made them more independent of Eschholz, freed them
from their valedictory mood and made them doubly curious
as to their change and future.

Many times, as they rested in the forest or sat perched
high above one of the gorges near Monteport, they took their
wooden flutes from their pockets and played duets.

When they reached that spur above Eschholz with the
view of the school and its giant trees, it seemed to both of

them that their previous conversation already lay far in the past and that things had taken on a new aspect. They did not speak of this, and were a little ashamed of their former feelings and words, which had been so quickly outmoded and rendered meaningless.

On the following day in Eschholz they learned their fate. Knecht had been posted to Waldzell.

Chapter Two

WALDZELL

"BUT WALDZELL produces the artists of the Bead Game," runs the old tag concerning this famous school.

Among the Castalian schools of the second and third grades Waldzell was noted chiefly for its music. If the other schools had an outspoken predilection for a specific science— Keuperheim for ancient philology, Porta for Aristotelian and scholastic thought and Planvaste for mathematics—Waldzell had by tradition a tendency towards universality and a closer alliance between science and the arts, the highest symbol of which was the Bead Game.

As in the other schools, this was by no means taught officially as a compulsory faculty, but the Waldzellian students devoted their private studies almost without exception to the Game, for the little town was also the home of the official Bead Game and its organisation. Here also were to be found the halls for the ceremonial games, the gigantic archives with their officials and libraries and the residence of the Ludi Magister.

Even though these institutions were completely independent and the school in no way affiliated to them, their spirit nevertheless ruled the school, and something of the inspiration of the public Games hung in the air of the place.

The little town was very proud of sheltering not only a school but also the Game: the townspeople called the scholars "students," but the guests and members of the Game College were known as "Lusors"—a corruption of "Lusores."

In addition to this, Waldzell was the smallest of the
Castalian schools, the number of pupils rarely exceeding sixty,
a fact which made it appear unusual and aristocratic, eclectic,
and harbouring only the very cream of the élite. During the
last decades, too, many Magisters and several Ludi Magisters
had been produced from this worthy school.

In any case, the fame and splendour of Waldzell was
uncontested. Here and there the opinion was voiced that the
Waldzellians were conceited intellectuals and pampered
princes, useless for anything apart from the Bead Game. At
times, in several of the other schools, harsh and bitter words
were current with regard to them, but the acerbity of these
jests and criticisms show clearly that they were based on
jealousy and envy.

When all was said and done admission to Waldzell denoted
a certain mark of distinction. Joseph Knecht was by no means
unaware of this, and although not ambitious in the vulgar
sense of the word, he accepted the distinction with pride
and joy.

He arrived on foot in Waldzell in company with several
companions. Filled with great expectations, and in all
preparedness, he strode through the South Gate, to be
immediately captivated and enchanted by the ancient brown
roofed hamlet and the imposing former Cistercian monastery
which now housed the school.

As soon as he had changed his clothes and taken his first
meal in the buttery, he went out on a tour of exploration of
his new home. He discovered the footpath which led over the
ruins of the old town walls to the river, remained standing on
the arched bridge listening to the roar of the mill race, and
then skirted the cemetery by the lime avenue until he saw and
recognised, behind its high hedge, the Vicus Lusorum, the
little auxiliary town of the bead-players with its feast halls
archives, classrooms, guest and instructors' houses.

He saw a man emerging from one of the buildings attired
in his Bead Game costume, and thought that he must be one
of the legendary "Lusores"—perhaps the Magister Ludi
himself.

Knecht felt the powerful magic of this atmosphere, for
everything here seemed old, venerable, hallowed and
saturated with tradition: he felt that he was a little nearer to

the centre of things than in Eschholz. As he left the Vicus Lusorum he felt, too, another magic, less venerable perhaps, but no less exciting—the magic of the little town, that particle of the profane world with its bustle and trade, its dogs and children, the odours of booths and workshops with bearded merchants and fat women behind the counters, the playing and screaming children and the mocking glances of the girls.

Much of this reminded him of a far distant world, of Berolfingen, which he had thought completely to have forgotten. But now deep layers of his soul responded once more to the scenes, the noises and the odours. A less tranquil but far richer and gayer world than Eschholz seemed to await him here.

The school was of course an exact continuation of the Eschholz pattern, even though the curriculum contained a few new subjects. The only real innovation was the exercises in meditation, of which the Music Master had already given him a foretaste.

He entered into these with good will, but saw in them at first no more than a pleasant and relaxing game. Only somewhat later, we imagine, did he recognise their true value.

The headmaster of Waldzell, Otto Zbinden, was an original character who was apt to inspire a certain amount of fear in his pupils. He was at that time about sixty years old. Many of the entries concerning Joseph Knecht which we have examined are written in this tutor's beautiful and sensitive handwriting.

Knecht was less interested in his teachers than in his fellow students, with two of whom he entered into a lively and many-sided relationship. The first of these, a youth of the same age as himself, with whom he became friendly during the first few months, was called Carlo Ferromonte (he later became the Music Master's deputy, an office of the second highest rank among the authorities). To him we owe among other things a history of style in the lute music of the sixteenth century. He was known in the school as "the rice eater," and was considered a pleasant comrade. His friendship with Knecht began with conversations on music, which led to a series of studies and exercises lasting many years, some of which we know from Knecht's rare but lengthy letters to the Music Master.

In the first of these letters he described Ferromonte as a "specialist and connoisseur of music rich in ornament, embellishments and trills." They used to play Couperin, Purcell and other masters of the seventeen hundreds together. In one of these letters Knecht speaks at length of these exercises and of this music, "where in many pieces a flourish stands over nearly every note. When one has played nothing but trills, turns and mordents for a few hours," he continued, "one's fingers become charged with electricity."

Knecht made great progress in music, and in his second or third year at Waldzell could read and play with ease scores, clefs, abbreviations and figured basses of every century and style, and had acquainted himself particularly—as far as we can judge—with that type of western music which was in the nature of a handicraft, and which did not scorn a painstaking attention to and care for the sensual and technical in order to penetrate into the realms of the spirit. His very zeal in capturing the sensual, his striving to catch the spirit of various musical styles from the sensual and the harmonic, and from the sensation produced upon the ear, prevented him for a long time from devoting himself to the preliminary school of the Bead Game. He himself maintained in one of his lectures at a later date: "He who knows music only in the extracts which the Bead Game has distilled from it, may be a good bead-player but is far from being a good musician, and is presumably no historian. Music does not consist only in those pure spiritual lilts and configurations which we have abstracted from it, but arose down the centuries primarily from the joy of the senses, the outpouring of the breath, the beating of time, the colours, friction and excitement which ensue from the blending of voices and the harmony of instruments. Admittedly the spirit is the main thing, and is naturally older than the discovery of new instruments and changes, and the introduction of new keys; new constructive and harmonic rules and prohibitions are never more than a gesture and an external manifestation, no less than costumes and fashions among races. But one must have grappled with and tasted extensively of these external and sensual marks of distinction in order to understand various periods and styles from them.

One makes music with the hands and fingers, with the mouth and lungs, and not with the brain alone, and the man who can only read the notes and is unable to play an instrument perfectly should never discuss music. Therefore the history of music, too, is by no means to be understood as an abstract history of style. For example, the periods of musical decline would remain quite incomprehensible to us were we not to recognise in them the preponderance of the sensual and quantitative over the spiritual."

For a time it seemed as though Knecht had resolved to be no more than a musician. He neglected all the non-compulsory subjects, including preliminary instruction in the Bead Game, in favour of music, which resulted in the headmaster's calling him to account at the end of the first semester. Knecht, the student, did not allow himself to be intimidated, but stood obstinately by his student's rights. He is reported to have said to the headmaster: "If I fail to give satisfaction in any official subject, then you are entitled to blame me, but so far I have not given you any cause to do this. I, on the contrary, have the right, if I wish, to devote three-quarters or even the whole of my free time to music. I plead the school statutes." The headmaster Zbinden was intelligent enough not to insist, but bore this student in mind and apparently treated him for a long time with cold disfavour and harshness.

This curious period in Knecht's school life lasted for more than a year—probably nearly a year-and-a-half. He received normal but not brilliant reports, and it seems that after the clash with the headmaster he retired into himself in a quiet, somewhat insolent manner, made no outstanding friendships, but contented himself with his extraordinary and passionate zeal for music, and abstained from participation in all private subjects including the Bead Game. Certain traits in this youthful portrait of Knecht seem to indicate the stirrings of adolescence. During this period he probably only encountered the opposite sex on rare occasions, and then with mistrust: perhaps, like many Eschholzers—unless they happened to have had sisters at home—he was entirely without experience of women. He had read a great deal, and had studied in particular the German philosophers Leibnitz, Kant and the Romantics, of whom Hegel attracted him most.

We must now give our detailed attention to that other

fellow student who played such a decisive rôle in Knecht's life
at Waldzell—the guest student, Plinio Designori. This
young man was an extra-mural student, *i.e.*, he was passing
through the élite school as a guest, without intending to
remain in the pedagogic province or to enter the Order. Such
guests appeared from time to time but very seldom, for the
pedagogy was naturally disinclined to educate scholars whose
intention it was to return to their homes and to the outside
world after their term in the élite school. There were, however, several old patrician families in the land which had
rendered great service to Castalia at the time of its foundation, and among which the custom still ruled that from time to
time one of the sons would be privileged, provided his talents
were sufficient, to receive his education in an élite school. This
right had become traditional in respect of one or two families.
These extra-mural students, although subject to the same
rules as all the other élite scholars, formed an exception
among their comrades inasmuch as they did not become more
estranged from their families as the years went by but spent
all their holidays at home, and remained no more than guests
and strangers in Castalia on account of the fact that they
retained the customs and ways of thinking of the outside
world.

Home, a worldly life, a career and marriage awaited them,
and it only very rarely happened that such a guest scholar
would be so captivated by the spirit of the province as to
remain in Castalia (provided of course his family gave their
consent) and enter the Order. On the other hand, many of the
well-known statesmen in the history of our land who had been
guest scholars in their youth, took up the cudgels strongly at
times in favour of Castalia when public opinion was opposed
on various grounds to the élite schools and the Order.

Such a guest scholar was Plinio Designori, who came into
contact with the somewhat younger Joseph Knecht in Waldzell. He was a highly talented youth, brilliant in conversation
and debate, a fiery and rather restless individual, who caused
the headmaster Zbinden a great deal of anxiety, for, although
he was an excellent and blameless scholar, he took no pains
to forget the fact that he was a guest student by adapting
himself in the most unobtrusive manner possible, but on the

contrary stressed his non-Castalian and worldly outlook brazenly and energetically.

It was inevitable that a singular relationship should have arisen between the two scholars: both were talented and had a vocation, which made them brothers, although they were complete opposites by nature. It would have required a teacher of unusually great perspicacity and skill to have extracted the quintessence from the problem which ensued, and to have arrived at a synthesis according to the rules of dialectic between and concerning these antitheses.

The headmaster Zbinden was not lacking in gifts and strength of purpose. He did not belong to that class of teacher for whom geniuses are disconcerting phenomena, but in this particular case he lacked the most important prerequisite—the confidence of the students themselves.

Plinio, who revelled in his rôle of outsider and revolutionary, was very much on his guard against the headmaster. In Knecht's case there had been that unfortunate contretemps with regard to his private studies, which prevented his approaching the teacher for advice. Fortunately there still remained the Music Master. Joseph went to him for counsel and support, and the wise old man not only took the affair seriously but assumed control and dealt with it in the most masterly fashion, as we shall now see. In the hands of the Magister Musicæ, the greatest danger and temptation in the life of the young Knecht was sublimated into a task of distinction, in which Joseph rose to the occasion.

The inner history of this conflicting friendship between Joseph and Plinio—this musical study in two themes, this dialectical contest between two spirits—developed somewhat in the following manner.

It was of course Designori who first attracted and caught the attention of his opponent. Not only was he the elder, but he was also a handsome, bold and eloquent youth. But above all he was "from outside," a non-Castalian, a visitor from the mysterious outside world, with father and mother, uncles, aunts and cousins and one for whom Castalia with its laws, traditions and ideals was only a stage, a stepping stone, a caravanserai. For this exotic bird Castalia was not the world. For him Waldzell was a school like any other, and a return to the "world" no disgrace and punishment; the Order did not

lie before him, but a career, marriage, politics—in short that
"real life" about which each Castalian felt a secret desire to
know more. For the "world" was to the Castalian what once
it had been to the penitent and the monk—the inferior and
forbidden, but no less the mysterious, seductive and fascinating. Plinio made no secret of his belonging to that world,
was not in the least ashamed of it, but on the contrary,
extremely proud of the fact.

With a half boyish and theatrical—but also half serious—
zeal, and almost in the nature of a campaign, he stressed the
other mode of life and seized upon every opportunity to
contrast his worldly conceptions and norms with those of
Castalia, portraying them as being better, more natural,
just and human.

His favourite argument was to oppose "the natural" and
"the healthy commonsense attitude" with the unworldly,
exotic and pedagogic spirit. He was not sparing in his use of
slogans and hyperbole, although he was intelligent and had
taste enough to avoid provocation and to observe the form of
discussion customary in Waldzell. He endeavoured to defend
the "world" and the "normal" life against the "arrogant
scholastic intellectualism" of Castalia, but at the same time to
show that he was in a position to do so with the weapons of
his opponents. He by no means wished to be thought a
barbarian who blindly tramples the flowers of the cultural and
spiritual garden underfoot.

From time to time Joseph Knecht had stood, a silent but
attentive listener, on the fringe of the little group of students,
the central figure of which was Designori. He had listened
with curiosity, amazement and terror to this speaker, whose
conversation tended always towards a destructive criticism of
everything that was held sacred in Castalia, and threw into
doubt everything in which he himself believed, making it
appear questionable or merely laughable. He noticed, however, that his audience for the most part had long since ceased
to take these speeches seriously, and that many of the students
listened only by way of diversion, as one may listen to a
quack at a fair. He also heard frequent contradictions, in
which Plinio's attacks were repulsed either with irony or in
real earnest. However, certain of his comrades continued to
gather around Plinio, who was always the centre of interest:

whether he found an occasional opponent or not, he inevitably exercised a power of attraction over them bordering upon seduction.

And Joseph was affected no less than these others, who formed a group around our lively orator, listening to his tirades with astonishment and often with laughter: despite the feeling of fear, nay, almost of terror, which he experienced at such speeches, he felt himself attracted in some sinister way, not only because they were amusing but because they seemed to affect him seriously. Not that he had inwardly agreed with the speaker, but the latter tended to raise doubts in his mind, the possible authenticity of which one had only to recognise in order to suffer. At first it was not a grave suffering, but only a certain restlessness and feeling of contamination, a mixture of powerful impulse and bad conscience.

The time was bound to come, and it naturally did come, when Designori would notice that among his audience there was one to whom his words meant more than mere exciting or provocative diversion and satisfaction derived from the love of argument—a silent, fair-haired boy, engaging and delicate, but who looked somewhat chaste and who would blush and snap out embarrassed replies to his friendly questions. Obviously this boy had been attracted to him for a long time, Plinio thought, and he resolved to reward him with a friendly gesture and so win him over completely. He invited Joseph to his study for an afternoon visit, but discovered at once that the shy and demure boy was not so easy to tame. Plinio learned to his amazement that Joseph avoided any personal contact with him, and would not be drawn into conversation. Moreover he refused the invitation, and this so irritated and intrigued the elder boy that from that day onward he began to court the silent Joseph—at first out of conceit and later in all earnestness—for he sensed that here was an opponent, or possibly a future friend or enemy. He noticed Joseph constantly in his proximity, felt his keen attention, only to see him withdraw into his shyness once more when he tried to approach him.

This behaviour was not without cause. For a long time Joseph had sensed that something important awaited him in the shape of this fellow student; something beautiful perhaps, an enlargement of his horizon, some knowledge or revelation, or perhaps again a temptation and danger; in any event, something which had to be experienced. He had told his friend Ferromonte of the first stirrings of doubt and the desire to criticise which Plinio's arguments had awakened in him, but the musician had paid little heed, had dismissed Plinio as a conceited and consequential fellow to whom one had no need to listen, and had immediately retired to his musical practices. Joseph felt that he ought actually to have confided this sensation of doubt and discomfiture to the headmaster, but since their little passage of arms he had had no affectionate or frank relationship with him. He was also afraid of being misunderstood by the headmaster, and even more, that an exposure of the rebel Plinio would be construed as a denunciation. In this state of embarrassment, which increased daily as a result of Plinio's attempts at friendship, he returned to his patron and good genius, the Magister Musicæ, and wrote him a very long letter, which we have in our possession.

"It is also not clear to me," wrote Knecht among other things, "whether Plinio hopes to win me over as an accomplice or merely as a comrade. I hope the latter to be the case, for to convert me to his outlook would mean to incite me to disloyalty and to destroy my life, which is now deeply rooted in Castalia. I have no parents or friends in the world outside to whom I could return, even should I wish to do so. But even if Plinio's disrespectful speeches fail to influence or convert me, he none the less succeeds in embarrassing me; for, to be quite frank, revered Master, with regard to him there is something in his way of thinking to which I cannot reply with a simple negation. He appeals to a voice within me, which at times inclines me to agree with him. Presumably it is the voice of nature, and it stands in harsh contradistinction to my education and to our customary outlook. When Plinio describes our teachers and masters as a priestly caste, and ourselves as a castrated hoard of children tied to their mothers' apron strings, these are naturally coarse and exaggerated words, but they must contain a grain of truth or else they would not disturb so much. Plinio can give vent to the most astonishing and discouraging ideas—like the following, for example: 'The Bead Game is a reversion to the Age of the Digest, a purely irresponsible game of letters, into which we have resolved the languages of the different arts and sciences;

it is comprised of simple associations and plays with simple
analogies.' Or: 'The proof of the worthlessness of our whole
spiritual culture and behaviour lies in its resigned sterility.'
For example, he maintains that we analyse the laws and
technicalities of every style and period of music, and never
produce any new music ourselves: we read and interpret
Pindar or Goethe, and are ashamed to write verses. These are
reproaches which I cannot dismiss with a smile. And these
are still not the worst, or those which wound me most. It is
terrible when he says to all intents and purposes that we
Castalians lead the lives of artificially reared singing birds,
incapable of earning our own keep, ignorant of the misery and
struggle of life, not knowing or wishing to know anything of
that section of mankind whose work and poverty are the
foundations of our existence of luxury." The letter ends with
the words: "I have perhaps abused your friendship and kind-
ness, *Reverendissime*, and am therefore resigned to your
rebukes. By all means rebuke me, and impose penances upon
me. I shall be grateful, I assure you, but I am urgently in need
of advice. I cannot endure the present situation much longer,
for I am unable to bring it to a true and fruitful development
unaided: I am too weak and inexperienced. And perhaps,
which is worse, I cannot confide in the headmaster—unless
you expressly command me to do so. That is why I have
importuned you with this affair, which has begun to cause me
endless wretchedness."

It would have been instructive had we been able to see the
Master's answer to this call for help in black and white, but
the answer was only given by word of mouth. Shortly after
receiving Knecht's letter, the Magister Musicæ had appeared
in person at Waldzell to give a musical audition, and during
his stay there had received his young friend with the greatest
cordiality. We learn of this from Knecht's later writings. But
he did not make things easy for the boy: he began by telling
him that, having examined them carefully, he found his school
reports far too one-sided, by taking the part of the headmaster
and insisting upon Knecht's obedience. As far as his relationship with Designori was concerned he laid down an exact line
of conduct, and did not leave Waldzell before having discussed the matter fully with Zbinden. The results were not
only that remarkable and—for those who took part in it—

unforgettable contest between Designori and Knecht, but
also a new stage in the latter's relationship with the headmaster, which resumed its previous course, not on an
affectionate and mysterious plane such as with the Music
Master, but on one which had been clarified and from which
the tension had been removed.

The rôle which had now been allotted to Knecht determined
his life for a long time. He was allowed to accept Designori's
friendship and to place himself within the circle of his
influence and attacks without any interference or observation
on the part of the teachers. The actual task which had been
entrusted to him by his mentor, however, was that of defending Castalia against its critic, of raising the conflict between
the two opposing outlooks to the highest possible plane.
This entailed Knecht's becoming thoroughly versed in the
fundamentals of the discipline that ruled in Castalia and the
Order, and his continually bearing it in mind.

The disputes between the two antagonists—who were now
on friendly terms—soon became famous, and the other pupils
would flock to hear them. Designori's aggressive and ironic
tones became more refined, his postulations stronger and
more responsible and his criticism more professional. Until
then Plinio had had the advantage in the conflict: he came
from the outside world and had had experience of it, knew its
methods, its means of attack, and also something of its
unscrupulousness, and he knew, too, from conversations with
the adults at home, exactly what the world had to complain of
with regard to Castalia. But now Knecht's replies compelled
him to see that even if he did know the outside world better
than any Castalian, he by no means knew the inner spirit of
Castalia as well as those who were at home there and for
whom it was both country and destiny. He came to realise and
also to admit that he was simply a guest here and not a
resident, and that here in the pedagogic province were also to
be found a secular experience and things taken for granted,
that here too existed a tradition—even a "Nature"—which
he only partially knew, and whose claims were now postulated
by their defender Joseph Knecht.

Knecht, on the contrary, in order to succeed in his rôle of
apologist, was obliged with the help of study, meditation and
self-discipline, to acquaint himself even more deeply with that

which he was there to defend. Designori remained his
superior in rhetoric, for in addition to his natural fire and
ambition he had the advantage of a certain worldly schooling
and shrewdness. He understood in particular how to give the
audience food for reflection even in defeat, and to ensure for
himself a dignified or witty exit, whereas Knecht, when his
adversary had driven him into a corner, could only say:
"I must have time to consider that, Plinio. Wait a few days,
and I will remind you of it."

Even if this relationship had been raised to a more dignified
level—for the participants and audience of the disputes it had
become an indispensable element in the Waldzellian school
life of the period—it had hardly brought relief to Knecht's
personal distress and inner conflict.

Thanks to the high degree of trust and responsibility
which had been laid upon him, he accomplished the task, and
it is a proof of his strength and of his sound constitution that
he carried it out without visible harm to himself. In secret,
however, he suffered a great deal.

If he felt a sense of friendship for Plinio it was not for the
engaging and witty comrade alone, for the worldly and
elegant Plinio, but as much for that alien world which his
friend represented and which he was learning or imagined he
was learning from his figure, words and gestures—that
so-called "real" world, in which were to be found tender
mothers and children, starving men and almshouses, newspapers and elections, that world at once primitive and refined
to which Plinio returned every vacation, where he would visit
parents and relations, pay court to the girls, attend work-
men's meetings or be a guest in fashionable clubs, while he,
Knecht, remained behind in Castalia, walking with comrades,
fishing, practising Froberger *ricercari* or reading Hegel.

There was no question in Knecht's mind as to whether he
belonged to Castalia or not, and that it was right for him to
lead their life—a life without family, without all manner of
fabulous distractions, a life without newspapers but also
without misery and hunger. In parenthesis, Plinio, however
much he might have emphasised the drone existence of the
élite scholars, had never up to that time either gone hungry
or earned his own bread. No, the Plinio world was neither
better nor more seemly, but it was there and it had, as he

knew from world history, always existed, and had always been similar to what it was in his day. Moreover, many nations had known no other world, known nothing of élite schools and pedagogic provinces, of Orders, Masters and Bead Games. The greater majority of men in the outside world lived quite differently from the way in which one lived in Castalia—a simpler, more primitive, dangerous, unprotected and irrational existence. And every man had been born in that primitive world and still felt something of it in his own heart, a certain curiosity about it, a home-sickness and a compassion for it. The criterion was to be just towards it, to preserve a certain patriotic loyalty towards it in one's own heart, but still not to slide back into it. For there was also an adjacent and superior second world—the Castalian, the spiritual and artificial, ordered and protected, but a world that demanded constant attention and practice—in short, the hierarchy.

To serve that other world without being unjust or despising it, and also without casting secret glances or possessing some obscure longing and homesickness for it, must be the correct attitude, for the small Castalian world served the greater one, gave it teachers, books and systems, cared for the purification of its spiritual functions and morality, and stood as a school and a sanctuary for that small number of men whose destiny, it seemed, was to devote their lives to truth and the spirit. But why did the two worlds live presumably apart from each other in hostility and discord? Why could they not both unite and cherish each other?

One of the rare visits of the Music Master occurred at a time when Joseph, tired and harassed by his task, had had the greatest difficulty in maintaining his equipoise. The Master could divine this from certain of the youth's remarks, but read it far more clearly in his pinched and strained features, in his restless gaze and somewhat unsettled manner. The old man put a few pointed questions, only to encounter discontent and all manner of inhibitions, and wisely gave up his quest. Seriously worried, he led Joseph into one of the practice rooms under the pretext of imparting a little musical discovery to him. He ordered a clavichord to be brought in, and without more ado embarked upon a long and complicated dissertation on the origins of sonata form, capturing the student's attention and bringing him to forget his troubles to a certain extent. The latter surrendered himself, relaxed and listened gratefully to his words and playing. The Music Master was patient, and took time to allow this receptive and ready mood, which had previously been entirely lacking in his pupil, to take root. When he saw that he had succeeded, having finished his lecture and having played, by way of conclusion, one of the Gabrieli sonatas, he stood up and, walking slowly up and down the little room, related the following story:—

"Many, many years ago I was very preoccupied with this particular sonata. It was during the years of my post-graduate studies, before I became a teacher and eventually Magister Musicæ. At that time I had an ambition to work out a new history of sonata form from an entirely new viewpoint, but the time came when I not only made no progress but began to wonder more and more whether these historical researches into music had any value at all, or whether they were merely an empty game for leisured people and a tawdry artistic-intellectual substitute for a true and integrated life. In short, I was going through one of those crises in which all studies, all intellectual effort and all things spiritual become devalued and constitute a matter for grave doubt within us, when we are inclined to envy every peasant at his plough, every pair of nocturnal lovers, every bird that sings in the treetops and every cricket that chirps in the summer meadows, for they seem to us so natural, so full of life and so happy, although we know nothing of the distress, hardships, dangers and suffering of their lives. To be brief, I had apparently so lost my balance that I was in a truly lamentable condition. It was, in fact, quite intolerable. I thought out the most incredible schemes for a flight into freedom, planned to go out into the world as a travelling musician to play at wedding breakfasts and, had some foreign recruiting officer, as in the old romances, appeared and invited me to put on a uniform and follow him to some convenient war, I should have accepted. And, as so often happens in such circumstances, I became so desperate that I could not rid myself of my distress and was urgently in need of help."

He came to a standstill, and gave a little chuckle to himself.

"Of course," he continued, "I had a tutor, as is customary,

and naturally it would have been wise and in keeping with my duty to have asked for his advice. But, as is often the case, Joseph, when one falls into difficulties and has strayed so far from the path that one is earnestly in need of a corrective, it is precisely then that one is most reluctant to return to the normal path and to seek out the normal cure.

"My tutor had not been satisfied with my last quarterly report, and had raised serious protests, but I was convinced that I was on the road to new discoveries and viewpoints, and took his objections amiss. To put it in a nutshell, I did not wish to go to him. I did not wish to crawl to the cross and admit that he had been right. Nor did I wish to confide in my comrades. There was, however, an eccentric in the neighbourhood whom I knew only by sight and from hearsay, a Sanscrit scholar who bore the nickname of 'the Yogi,' and one day, when my condition had become almost unbearable, I went to visit this man, whose somewhat lonely and unusual figure I had as often ridiculed as admired. Wishing to talk with him, I sought him out in his cell, but found him sunk deep in contemplation. Furthermore, he had adopted the Indian inner attitude, and was unapproachable. With a smile on his face he was drifting in other spheres in perfect aloofness, and I could do nothing except stand near the door and wait for him to come out of his trance. This lasted for a considerable time— perhaps an hour or two—and finally I grew so tired that I slipped to the floor. I sat there leaning against the wall and continued to wait. At last I saw that the man was gradually regaining consciousness: he shook his head slightly, stretched his shoulders, slowly uncrossed his legs and just as he was about to stand up caught sight of me. 'What do you want?' he asked. I stood up and, without having reflected and without really knowing what I was saying, replied: 'It is the Andrea Gabrieli sonatas.' He got to his feet, sat me down in his own chair, and took up his position beside the table. 'Gabrieli,' he said. 'What had he done to you with his sonatas?' I began to tell him what had happened to me, and to confess my condition. He questioned me closely—a thing which seemed to me rather pedantic—about my history and my studies of Gabrieli and the sonatas, wishing to know at what hour I rose, how long I read, how often I practised music and at what times I ate and went to bed. As I had entrusted myself to him, I was compelled to suffer all these questions and to reply to them, although they put me to shame, for they penetrated ruthlessly into the details of my private, spiritual and moral life, all of which were analysed over the past weeks and months. Then 'the Yogi' fell suddenly silent, and as I could make no sense of this he shrugged his shoulders and asked: 'Can't you see for yourself wherein your fault lies?' No, I could not see. And then he recapitulated with astonishing accuracy everything that he had extracted from me as far back as the first signs of weariness, disinclination and spiritual constipation. He showed me that this could only have taken place in the case of a post-graduate, and that it was high time that I regained my self-control and strength and found catharsis through outside help. He suggested that, no sooner had I embarked upon my days of freedom, than I had renounced my regular practice of meditation, that I should have remembered this, and repaired the lapse immediately at the first evil consequences. And he was perfectly right: I had not only neglected my meditation for a considerable time, either through lack of leisure or through having always been too ill-disposed, distracted or preoccupied and excited with my work, but had in time even lost consciousness completely of my protracted neglect. And at last, when I had almost failed and become desperate, I had had to be reminded of it by an outsider. In actual fact I experienced the greatest difficulty in tearing myself out of my negligence, for I was obliged to return to school and take the beginner's exercises in meditation in order gradually to adapt myself once more to a capacity for self-discipline and contemplation.''

The Master came to a stop once more, and added with a little sigh: "That is exactly how it was with me at that time, and I still feel a little ashamed of myself to-day when I speak of it. But it is like that, Joseph: the more we demand of ourselves, or rather, the more our immediate task demands of us, the more we are thrown back upon that source of strength which is meditation, upon the ever-renewed reconciliation between mind and soul. And—I know many examples of this—the more intensive the task which makes demands upon us, alternately exciting and elevating, tiring and depressing, the easier it can become for us to neglect this fountain head, just as by absorption in an intellectual work it is quite easy to neglect the care of the body. All the really great men in world history have either understood the art of meditation or have unconsciously known the path that leads to it and its final goal. The other, even the most talented and the strongest, have always failed and been defeated in the end, because their task or their ambitious dream has possessed them and become an obsession, and they have lost the capacity to release themselves from the actual and to see things in their true perspective. Now you yourself know this, for you have already learned it in your preliminary exercises. It is irrefutably true, and one only observes this when one has strayed from the path and lost one's way."

This story had such a profound effect upon Joseph that he was able to weather the danger in which he had stood, and thenceforth devoted himself with increased zeal to his exercises. He had also been deeply impressed by the fact that the Master had, for the first time, given him a glimpse into his personal life from his youth and student days: for the first time it became clear to him that even a demi-god and a Magister could once have been young and pursued false paths. He felt grateful for the confidence which the great man had shown in him by his confession. One could apparently err and tire, make mistakes, contravene the precepts and yet recover—and even in the end become a Magister. The crisis passed.

During the two or three years at Waldzell, while the friendship between Joseph and Plinio lasted, the school experienced the unfolding of this friendly rivalry as a drama in which every one participated, from the headmaster to the youngest student. The two worlds and the two principles had become embodied in Joseph and Designori respectively. Each stimulated the other, and each debate became a ceremonious and representative contest which affected everybody. And just as Plinio on his return from vacation would bring back new vigour from his mother soil, so Joseph, from his reflections, from each lecture, each exercise in meditation and each new meeting with the Magister Musicæ, would gain new strength and equip himself to be the representative and defender of Castalia. Once, while still a child, he had experienced his first call: now he experienced the second, and these years welded and formed him into the perfect figure of a Castalian.

He had long since completed his preliminary instruction in the Bead Game, and during his holidays had begun to develop his own Games under the control of a Game Leader. In this he now discovered the most generous source of joy and inner relaxation: nothing had done him so much good, refreshed, strengthened, confirmed and entranced him so much since his insatiable cembalo and clavichord exercises with Carlo Ferromonte as these first encounters with the starry world of the Bead Game.

It was during these years that the youthful Joseph Knecht composed the poems which have been preserved for us in Ferromonte's handwriting. It is quite possible that there were more of them than have come down to us, that these poems were written before Knecht's initiation into the Bead Game and that they helped him to accomplish his rôle and to overcome those critical years.

Every reader will be able to detect here and there in these in part polished, in part hastily composed verses the traces of the deep upheaval and crisis that Knecht underwent at that time under Plinio's influence. In many of the lines a deep anxiety, a fundamental doubt in himself and in the meaning of his destiny rings out, until in the poem "The Bead Game" a pious state of devotion seems to have been reached. Furthermore, there lies in them a certain concession to Plinio's world, a trace of rebellion against the school rules of Castalia, in the actual fact of his having written these poems and of having shown them on occasions to several fellow students. For even if Castalia had rejected in principle the production of all works of art—even musical production was only known and tolerated in the form of rigidly stylised practice compositions—the composing of verses ranked as the most impossible, laughable and prohibited of all activities.

Nor are these poems merely a game, a leisurely rococo fretwork: some powerful pressure was necessary to bring about this productive urge, and it also required a certain sullen courage to have written these verses and to have admitted to their authorship.

It must be mentioned that Plinio Designori also underwent considerable transformation and development under the influence of his antagonist, and not in the refinement of his methods of attack alone. During this jovial yet belligerent polemic, in the course of their school years, he saw his opponent steadily mature into an exemplary Castalian, saw the spirit of the Province ever more clearly and vividly revealed; and to the same extent that he infected Joseph with the atmosphere of his own world, he breathed the Castalian air and succumbed to its charm and influence.

During his last year at Waldzell, after a two-hour debate upon the ideal of the monastic life and its dangers, which had been fought out in the presence of the highest Bead Game students, Plinio took Joseph for a walk and made the following admission to him, which we are quoting from one of Ferromonte's letters.

"I have known for a long time, Joseph, that you are not the hundred per cent bead-player and saint of the province such as you have portrayed so admirably in your rôle. Each of us has taken a firm stand in the struggle, and we both know perfectly well that the thing we severally dispute exists legitimately and has its uncontested value. You are the protagonist of intensive cultivation of the spirit, and I of the natural life. During our struggles, you have gained some inkling of the dangers of the natural life and have made capital out of it: your task is therefore to show how the natural, ingenuous life without spiritual discipline would degenerate into a morass and eventually lead back to the jungle. I, on the contrary, must ever and again recall how audacious, dangerous and ultimately sterile is a life based solely on the spirit. Good. Each of us defends that in which he primarily believes—you in the spirit and I in nature. But do not take it amiss if I tell you that it sometimes appears to me that, in actuality, you naïvely take me for something of an enemy to your Castalian way of life, for a man to whom your studies, exercises and games are at base a lot of fiddle-faddle even if he has for some reason or another participated in them for a time.

"Ah! my friend, what a mistake you would be making if you really believed that. I will admit to you that I have such an insensate love for your hierarchy that it often enchants and lures me like happiness itself. I will also confess to you that when I was at home recently with my parents I had a discussion with my father and succeeded in obtaining his consent to remain in Castalia and to enter the Order at the end of my school days, should that really be my desire and my resolve. Moreover, I was happy when he finally gave his permission. I shall however not make use of it, as I have come to know just recently. Oh! not that I no longer wish to do so, but I see more and more that to remain with you would constitute a flight, an honourable and noble flight perhaps, but a flight all the same. I shall return to the outside world and become a man of that world, but one who will always remain grateful to your Castalia and who will continue to practice many of your exercises and return each year to celebrate in the great public Games."

Knecht recounted this admission of Plinio's with deep emotion to his friend Ferromonte, who wrote in one of his letters the following words: "For me, as a musician, this confession on the part of Plinio, to whom I have never been entirely just, came like a musical experience. The antithesis: world and spirit—or rather, the antithesis: Plinio, Joseph—had sublimated itself before my eyes into an harmony out of the struggle between two irreconcilable principles."

When Plinio's four years school course came to an end and he was about to return home, he brought a letter from his father to the headmaster, inviting Joseph home for the holidays. This was an unusual request. Permission to travel and sojourns outside the pedagogic province were occasionally granted, but primarily for purposes of study. It was only given in exceptional cases, and only to the older and trusted scholars during their post-graduate studies, never to students.

However, the headmaster Zbinden considered the invitation important enough, as it had come from such a highly esteemed man and house, not to dismiss it on his own account but to leave the decision to the pedagogy, who replied immediately with a laconic NO. The two friends were obliged to say farewell to each other.

"We will try again later with the invitation," said Plinio. "One day it will be bound to succeed. You must see my house and get to know my people: you will see that we are men, too, and not just a bunch of worldly and business barbarians. I shall miss you very much. And now, see to it that you soon rise to the top of this complicated Castalia: you richly deserve some sort of niche in the hierarchy, and belong definitely more to the bonzes than to the underlings—with all due

respect to your name. I prophesy a great future for you, and
that one day you will be a Magister and be numbered among
the illustrious."

Joseph looked at him sadly.

"You can mock me," he said, struggling with the emotion
of this parting. "I am not so ambitious as you, and if I ever
attain to some office, you will long since have been president
or burgomaster, university professor or councillor. Think
kindly of Castalia, Plinio, and don't estrange yourself entirely
from us. There must be one or two people out there who
know more of Castalia than the jests which they make about
us suggest."

They shook hands, and Plinio departed.

Joseph's last year at Waldzell was very peaceful now that
his exposed and onerous function of having been to a certain
extent a public personage had suddenly come to an end.
Castalia no longer needed a defender. He devoted his free
time during the course of this year principally to the Bead
Game, which began to attract him more and more. A small
notebook of his, which dates from that period, on the meaning
and theory of the Game, opens with the following phrase:
"The whole of life, physical as well as spiritual, is a dynamic
phenomenon, of which the Bead Game embraces basically
only the æsthetic side, and that predominantly within the
image of rhythmic events."

Chapter Three

APPRENTICESHIP

JOSEPH KNECHT WAS now about twenty-four years old.
His school days had come to an end with his graduation from
Waldzell, and now began his years of free study. With the
exception of his innocent boyhood years at Eschholz, they
were the serenest and happiest of his life. There is always
something wonderful and moving about the fervent love of
discovery and conquest of a youth who, freed for the first
time from the fetters of school, encounters the boundless

horizon of the spirit, for whom no illusions have yet been shattered and for whom no doubt exists as to his own capacity for endless devotion or as to the limitations of the spiritual world.

For the gifted, such as Joseph Knecht, who had not as the result of a particular aptitude concentrated too early upon a special faculty but upon totality, synthesis and universality, this springtime of free study is often a period of intense happiness, not to say intoxication. Without the precursory discipline of the élite school, the spiritual hygiene of exercises and meditation and the mildly practised control of the pedagogy, this freedom would entail grave dangers for such talents and would be fatal for many, as it had been for countless highly gifted youths in times before our present Order in the pre-Castalian century. The colleges in those early days had teemed with young Faustian natures, who launched out with full sail upon the high seas of knowledge and academical freedom, and had naturally suffered every form of shipwreck upon the rocks of unbridled fanaticism. Faust himself is the prototype of genial dilettantism and of his own tragedy.

In Castalia to-day the students enjoy a greater intellectual freedom than they did in the universities of earlier periods, for the possibilities of study at their disposal are far more extensive. In addition to this, in Castalia there exists no constricting influence of material considerations such as ambition, anxiety, parental poverty, prospects of earning a living and a career, etc., etc. In the academies, seminaries, libraries, archives and laboratories of the pedagogic province all the students, irrespective of descent or prospects, are on a completely equal footing: the hierarchy is graded entirely according to the aptitudes and qualities of the students, in respect of intellect and character. From the material and spiritual point of view, on the contrary, the freedom, lures and dangers to which many of the talented youths from the colleges of the outside world succumb, for the most part do not exist in Castalia: of course, there are, here as well, dangers, demonism and blindness enough—where should the human destiny be free of them?—but many possibilities of back-sliding, disappointment and decline are removed from the path of the Castalian student. He cannot fall victim to drunkenness, or waste his youthful years in braggadocio or

secret society activities, which frequently ruined generations
of students in the old days, nor can he wake up one day to
discover that his student's degree has been a mistake and that
only during the course of his post-graduate studies does he
first stumble against *lacunæ* in his education. From these
inconveniences he is protected by the Castalian Order.

Furthermore, the danger of his wasting his substance upon
women or excessive sport is considerably diminished. As
regards women, the Castalian student knows neither
marriage, with its enticements and dangers, nor the prudery
of many former epochs which constrained the student either
to sexual abstinence or drove him into the arms of more or
less venal woman and prostitutes.

As there exists no marriage for the Castalian there also
exists for him nothing of the attendant morality of love, and
as there is no such thing as money, and to all intents and
purposes no personal property, the venality of love does not
exist either. It is the custom in the province for the daughters
of the townsfolk not to marry too early, and in the years
before marriage the students and teachers seem to them
particularly desirable as lovers: the latter demand nothing of
birth or fortune, are accustomed to placing intellectual and
vital capabilities on the same plane, and as they have no
money must pay for their favours to a greater extent with
their personality. The student's sweetheart in Castalia has no
knowledge of the question: will he marry me? No, he will not
marry her. It has actually happened on occasions that an élite
student has returned to the world through the door of
bourgeois marriage, renouncing Castalia and participation in
the Order, but these few cases of apostasy in the history of the
school and of the Order can only be regarded as curiosities.

The degree of freedom and self-determination in which the
élite scholar, after his graduation from these preparatory
schools, finds himself in relation to all fields of knowledge
and research is in fact a very high one. This freedom is
unrestricted in so far as the student's talents and interests are
not from the outset specialised, and only by undertaking a
free post-graduate plan of study for perhaps six months will
its execution be mildly supervised by the authorities. For the
students with many-sided talents and interests—and to this
group Knecht belonged—the first few years of free studies

have something wonderfully alluring and enchanting on account of this far-reaching freedom. To these particular students, unless they rush straight away into excesses, the authorities allow an almost paradisial freedom: they may dally at will with any and every science, mixing the most varying subjects together, be enamoured of six or seven of them at the same time or confine themselves to a narrower choice. Beyond the observance of the general rules of morality which hold good for the province and the Order, nothing is asked of them except a report upon the lectures they have attended, the books they have read and their work in the institutes.

A stricter control and examination of their achievements begins when they first attend specialist science courses and seminaries, which include the Bead Game and the College of Music. Here, naturally, every graduate has to submit to official examinations, and carry out the tasks demanded of him by the head of the seminary, which is quite understandable. But nobody compels him to attend these courses and he can, if he so wishes, sit for months and years on end in the libraries and listen to the lectures. These students who hesitate before devoting themselves to a single subject, and therefore delay their acceptance into the Order, will be allowed and are even encouraged to complete their excursions into all possible sciences and studies: nothing in the way of achievement is asked of them beyond their moral integrity and the composition each year of an "incarnation." We have to thank this old and oft-maligned custom for the three "incarnations" which Knecht wrote during his post-graduate years.

These three stories cannot be compared with the poems he wrote at Waldzell, which were in the nature of a voluntary and unofficial—even secret and more or less forbidden— literary activity, for these were a normal and official task. Already in the earliest years of the pedagogic province the custom had arisen for the younger graduates, i.e., those who had not yet been accepted into the Order, to produce from time to time a particular type of thesis or exercise in style—a so-called "incarnation" or fictitious autobiography, laid in a favourite period of the past. The student would be faced with the task of transporting himself into the surroundings, culture and spiritual climate of some earlier epoch, and of building around himself a corresponding existence. According to period and fashion, Imperial Rome, France of the seventeenth or Italy of the fifteenth century, the Athens of Pericles or the Austria of Mozart would be preferred, and in the case of the philologists it was the custom to write these life romances in the speech and style of the country and period in which they were played. At times there were highly ingenious "incarnations" written in the style of the Curia of Papal Rome around the year 1200, in monkish Latin, Italian of the "Cento Novelle," in the French of Montaigne or in the baroque German of the Swan of Boberfeld. A remnant of the old Asiatic belief in incarnation and the transmigration of souls was perpetuated in this free and imaginative form. All the teachers and students were familiar with the idea that their present existence could have taken place in other bodies at other times and under other conditions. This was of course not a belief in its strongest sense, nor was it by any means a doctrine: it was an exercise, a game of the imaginative powers to portray oneself in different localities and surroundings. One embarked, as was so often done in the seminaries of style-criticism and also in the Bead Game, upon a voyage of discovery into past cultures, ages and countries, learned to consider one's person as a mask, as the transitory raiment of an entelechy.

The custom of writing such incarnations had both charm and many advantages, or else it would not have endured for so long. Furthermore, there were very few students who not only believed more or less in reincarnation but believed in particular in the truth of their own self-discovered reincarnations, for naturally the majority of these imaginary pre-existences were not essays in style and historical studies alone but also wish-dreams and enhanced self-portraits: most of the authors portrayed themselves in the particular costume and character which seemed to fulfil their wishes and ideals. In addition to this, these studies were from the pedagogic point of view a far from unintelligent conception and a legitimate canal for the poetic needs of youth.

Even if for generations actual and serious poetry had been forbidden and partly replaced by the Bead Game, the artistic and creative urge of youth had by no means died out, and it

found a permissible outlet in these incarnations, which often
reached the length of short novels. Moreover, this practice
enabled authors to take their first steps into the land of
self-knowledge. It very often occurred—and was looked upon
by the teachers in general with benevolent complacence—that
students would utilise their incarnations to utter critical and
revolutionary tirades against Castalia and the contemporary
world. In addition to this, during a time when the students
were enjoying the greatest freedom and no strict control,
these theses were very illuminating as far as the teachers
were concerned, and gave them an often surprising knowledge
of the spiritual and moral life and thoughts of the authors.

We possess three such incarnations written by Joseph
Knecht, which we have reproduced word for word at the end
of this book, and which we consider perhaps to be the most
valuable part of our study. It is a matter of speculation as to
whether he only wrote three of these incarnations or whether
one or more have been lost. We only know for certain that
after Knecht had delivered his third—the Indian incarnation
—he was informed by the pedagogy that he might set his next
effort in an historical period nearer to modern times and
richer in documentation, and that he should apply himself
more to the historical details. We know from stories and
letters that he did in fact make some preliminary studies for
an incarnation set in the eighteenth century. He wished to
take the stage as a Swabian theologian who had later abandoned his ecclesiastical duties in favour of music, had been a
pupil of Johann Albrecht Bengel, a friend of Oettinger and for
some time a guest of the Zinzendorf congregation. We know
that at that time he had read and made notes on a mass of old
and for the most part out of the way literature upon the
constitution of the Church, Pietism and Zinzendorf, and also
upon liturgy and Church music of the period. We also know
that he was greatly enamoured of that legendary figure, the
Prelate Oettinger, that he had a true love and deep reverence
for the Magister Bengel—he had photographed a portrait of
the latter, which had stood for some time on his writing desk
—and had conscientiously bestirred himself to write an
appreciation of Count Zinzendorf, who had interested but at
the same time repelled him.

He finally abandoned this work, content with what he had

learned, but declared that he was incapable of making a
reconstruction of it, for he had undertaken too many individual studies and amassed too many details. This remark
corroborates our view completely when we see in the three
incarnations more the creative ideas of a poetic individual and
noble character than the work of a scholar. But we do not wish
by this to be unjust to him.

For Knecht, to the freedom of the self-chosen studies of the
post-graduate, was now added another freedom and relaxation. He had not been merely a pupil as all the others had
been, had not only received the strict schooling, the precise
partition of the day, the careful control and supervision of the
teachers and undergone all the efforts of an élite scholar, but
had besides all this, and far more than this, through his
relationship with Plinio been forced to play a part and assume
a responsibility which had alternately spurred him on
intellectually and spiritually to the very boundaries of the
possible, and which had at times almost overburdened him.
It had been an active and representative rôle, and a responsibility which was actually far in advance of his years and
strength, which had often constituted no small danger and
which, without a superabundance of will power and talent and
without the powerful support from afar of the Music Master,
he could never have carried out and brought to a successful
conclusion.

At the end of his unusual school years in Waldzell we find
him then a youth of about twenty-four years old, slightly
over-mature for his age, a little over-strained but oddly
enough not visibly impaired. As to how much this burdensome rôle had taxed him—at times apparently bringing him
nearly to the point of exhaustion—we are lacking in accurate
information, but we can recognise it as soon as we observe the
manner in which he made use of the freedom he had earned,
and which he must often have longed for. This graduate who,
during his last school years, had stood in such a prominent
position and had been to a certain extent a public figure, had
immediately withdrawn completely; and if we look for traces
of his life at that time we gain the impression that he would
have preferred to make himself invisible, that for him no
surroundings or company could have been simple enough and
no form of existence private enough. We can therefore

understand why he had at first only replied briefly, and without pleasure, to several long and stormy letters from Plinio, and had then ceased to reply at all.

The renowned scholar, Knecht, had disappeared and was not to be found, but in Waldzell his fame endured and became in time almost legendary.

At the beginning of his post-graduate years he avoided Waldzell altogether, and also temporarily renounced the upper and most advanced courses of the Bead Game. Nevertheless, although a casual observer might presume an obvious neglect of the Bead Game on the part of the scholar Knecht, we on the contrary know that during the whole of the apparently paradoxical, moody and quite unusual course of his free studies, he was influenced by the Bead Game and eventually led back into its service. We propose to deal with this at length, because this feature is characteristic of him. Joseph had used his free time in the most remarkable and original manner—in a disconcerting and at the same time genial manner.

During his years at Waldzell he had, as was customary, attended the official initiation into the Bead Game and taken the refresher course. Both then and in the course of his final year he had already gained the reputation among a circle of friends of being a good player, and had been so captivated by this Game of games that after finishing a further course he had, while still an élite scholar, been accepted into the second stage of the Game, which represented a very rare distinction.

Some years later at an official refresher course he told a comrade, his friend and later assistant, Fritz Tegularius, of the experience which not only determined his destiny as a player but also had the greatest influence upon the course of his studies. This letter had been preserved, and the paragraph runs as follows: "Let me remind you of the time when we both belonged to the same group, when we were working so fervently at our first dispositions in the Bead Game, and also of a certain day and of a particular game. Our instructor had given us different stimuli and all manner of schemes to choose from. We had just reached the tricky stage of transition from astronomy, mathematics and physics to philology and history, and the instructor was a virtuoso in the art of setting traps for us eager beginners, of luring us on to the thin ice of unprofitable abstractions and analogies. He would smuggle alluring etymological and comparative philological trifles into our hands, and enjoy himself immensely when one of us fell into his trap. We would count Greek spondees until we grew tired, only to find the ground suddenly cut from beneath our feet as we were confronted with the possibility—I should say the necessity—of finding an accented instead of a metrical scansion, or similar inconvenience. The instructor always carried out his duties formally, brilliantly and with great correctness, even if he did so in a spirit which did not particularly please me. He would lead us up false paths and entice us on with false speculations, quite obviously with the good intention of acquainting us with the dangers, but also a little in order to laugh at us foolish youngsters and to pour cold water as far as possible on the enthusiasm of the most eager among us.

"And then one day it happened that under his guidance and in the course of one of his vexing experiments, while we were feeling our way and timorously trying to develop a semi-possible problem, I was suddenly captivated by the meaning and greatness of our Game and was overwhelmed to my innermost vitals. We were dissecting a philological problem and were seeing to a certain extent at close quarters the zenith and golden age of a language; we had travelled for several minutes with it along the road which had taken several centuries to build, and the pageant of this transient passage made a powerful impression upon me. There, before my eyes, I saw how a complicated, ancient and venerable organism, which had been built up slowly throughout many generations, comes to flower, the very flowers of which already contain the seeds of its decline, and how then the whole meaningful limbed edifice begins to sink, degenerate and totter towards decline; and at the same time a shudder of joy and terror ran through me when I thought that even decay and death had not borne that language into the void, but that its youth, flowering and decline had been preserved in our memory, in our knowledge of it and in its history, and moreover that it could be built up again at any time and live on in the symbols and formulas of science as well as in the mysterious formularies of the Bead Game.

"I understood in a flash that in the language, or, at least,

in the spirit of the Bead Game, everything was in actual fact
all-significant, that each symbol and each combination of
symbols led, not hither and thither, not to single examples,
experiments and proofs but towards the centre, into the
mystery and vitals of the world, into primæval conscience.
I recognised in that split second that every change from sharp
to flat in a sonata, every transformation of a myth or cult,
every classical, artistic formulary, by the standards of true
meditative observation, was no more than a direct path to the
centre of world mysteries where, in the interval between
In and Out breathing, between Heaven and Earth and
between Yin and Yang, the sacred perfects itself. Although
previously I had assisted at many well-constructed and well-
conducted Games as a listener, and had at times received
great exaltation and much gratifying and profitable insight,
I had always until then been inclined to doubt the actual
worth and status of the Game.

"Ultimately, every well-solved mathematical problem
could bring intellectual enjoyment, every piece of good music,
when heard—or even more, when played—could elevate the
soul and make it expand into infinity, and each devotional
meditation could tranquilise the heart and bring it into
harmony with the cosmos; but, by very reason of this, the
Bead Game—so whispered my doubts—was perhaps no more
than a formal art, an ingenious *legerdemain* and witty
combination, and it would be better therefore not to play this
Game but busy oneself with pure mathematics and good
music. But now, for the first time, I had heard the inner voice
of the Game and seen its meaning: it had been brought home
to me conclusively, and since that moment I have believed
that our royal Game is in effect a *lingua sacra*—a sacred and
divine language.

"You will remember, for you remarked upon it yourself,
that a change had taken place within me and that I had
received a Call. I can only compare it with that unforgettable
call which had once stimulated and changed my whole life
when as a boy I was examined by the Magister Musicæ and
summoned to Castalia. You noticed that I really *had* felt it,
even though you did not mention the fact, and we will not
discuss the point any further to-day. But now I have a request
to make of you, and in order that I may the better explain it I

must tell you something that no one else knows or must ever know, namely, that my present vagaries of study are not the result of a mood but are based far more upon a definite plan.

"Can you recall, at least broadly, the outlines of that Bead Game exercise which we as students during the third course built up with the aid of an instructor, during the course of which I heard that voice and realised my vocation as a Lusor?

"That particular exercise began with a rhythmical analysis of a fugue theme, in the midst of which stood a phrase probably from Kung Fu Tze. I am now in the process of studying that whole Game from beginning to end, which means that I am working through each of its phrases and translating them from the speech of the Game into their original language—into mathematics, musical ornamentation, Chinese, Greek, etc.

"I intend at least once in my life to study and reconstruct professionally the entire content of a Bead Game. I have already completed the first part, and it has taken me two years, but as we are both now enjoying our famous free studies, I intend to employ mine in this manner. I already know the objections to this. Most of our teachers would say: 'We have invented the Bead Game and built it up over several centuries into an universal system and language, in order to express and bring every spiritual and artistic value and concept beneath a common denominator. Now you come along and want to check everything to satisfy yourself that it is correct! It will take you your whole lifetime to complete, and you will undoubtedly regret it.' No, it will not take my whole lifetime, and I sincerely hope that I shall not regret it. And now for my request: as you are for the moment working in the Games Archives, and as I wish, for particular reasons, to avoid Waldzell for a long time, I should like you now and again to answer a host of questions for me, *i.e.*, acquaint me with the unabbreviated forms of the official keys and symbols of all manner of themes, which you will be able to find in the Archives. I count upon you, and also hope that you will call upon me should you require any services which I can possibly render you in return."

We feel that this is perhaps the place to insert an extract from another of Knecht's letters in which he refers to the Bead Game, although it was written one or two years later and addressed to the Music Master.

"I think," wrote Knecht to his patron, "that one can be a very good—even a virtuoso—bead-player, and perhaps even an able Magister Ludi, without realising the actual secret of the Game and its ultimate meaning. Yes, it is possible that a man who knew and realised these, and who became a specialist or leader of the Game, could be more dangerous to it than any one else, for the inner meaning, the esoteric of the Game, aims as all esotericism does deep down into the One and All, into the depths where only the eternal In and Out breathing reigns in self-sufficiency. Whoever were to experience inwardly the meaning of the Game to its conclusion would no longer be an actual player, inasmuch as for him there would be no more variety and he would no longer be capable of the joy of discovery, construction and combination, because he would know quite another form of pleasure and enjoyment. Because I feel that I am very close to the meaning of the Bead Game, it will be better for me and for others if I do not make the Game my career but confine myself rather to music."

The Music Master, who was usually very sparing in his correspondence, was very disturbed by this letter and replied to it with a friendly warning. "It is an excellent thing that you yourself do not demand that a master of the Game should be 'esoteric' in your sense of the word—for I hope that you wrote this without irony. A master of the Game who worried primarily as to whether he stood sufficiently close to the 'innermost meaning' of the Game would be a very bad teacher. I, for example, to be frank with you, have never during my whole life mentioned a word about the 'meaning' of music. If such a thing exists, the pupil does not need my interpretation. But on the other hand I have always placed great value on the fact that my pupils should count their quavers and semiquavers well and accurately. Whether you now become teacher, scholar or musician, you should respect the 'meaning,' but not consider that it can be taught. With this academic desire for meaning the historian-philosophers once ruined half world history, brought about the Age of the Digest and made themselves co-responsible for the shedding of a great deal of blood. Were I also to initiate my pupils into Homer or the Greek tragedians I should not attempt to present the poetry to them as a phenomenon of the divine, but should take great pains to make the poetry available to them by an accurate knowledge of its linguistic and metrical mediums.

"The duty of the teacher and scholar lies in the examination of the medium and care for tradition, the preservation of systems in their purity, not in arousing excitement and in expediting incommunicable experiences, which are the prerogative of the chosen—who are also often defeated and fall victims in the struggle."

Apart from these references, Knecht's correspondence during those years, which does not seem to have been very extensive and which appears in part to have been lost, makes no further mention of the Bead Game and its esoteric conception. The largest and also best preserved part of this correspondence—with Ferromonte—deals almost exclusively with musical problems and the analysis of musical styles.

Thus, we can see in this remarkable zig-zag course which Knecht's studies took—they amounted to no less than the exact copying and year-long working out of a single Game scheme—the accomplishment of a very determined ambition and desire.

In order to master the content of this single Game, which had been composed for exercise purposes in the course of a few days during his student days and which, in the language of the Bead Game, could be read through in a quarter-of-an-hour, he now spent year after year sitting in lecture rooms and libraries, studying Froberger and Alessandro Scarlatti, fugues and sonata form, studying mathematics, learning Chinese, working at a system of acoustic figures and learning the Feustelian theory of the correspondence between the spectrum and the musical scales.

One asks oneself why he had chosen this laborious, capricious and above all lonely path, for his ultimate goal—outside Castalia one would say his choice of vocation—was without a doubt the Bead Game.

Had he, as a guest graduate and without any obligation, joined one of the institutes of the Vicus Lusorum in Waldzell, all the special studies in connection with the Game would have been made easier for him. He would have had access at all times to information and advice upon every detail, and furthermore he could have conducted his studies in company with scholars and fellow pilgrims, instead of torturing himself

in solitude and certainly very often in voluntary exile. But he
went his own way. He avoided Waldzell, we presume not
only in order to erase as far as possible the memory of his
erstwhile student rôle from the minds of others as well as
from his own, but quite as much in order to circumvent his
entry into the community of the bead-players in a new but in
many ways similar rôle, for since that time he must have felt
something fatal, some premonition of his future leadership
and representation, and he did all that was possible to outwit
the destiny that seemed to threaten him. He anticipated the
burden of his responsibility, as he already felt it now towards
his fellow students at Waldzell, who were enthusiastic about
him and from whom he had now withdrawn; and he felt it in
particular towards Tegularius, whom he knew instinctively
would go through fire and water for him.

He therefore sought seclusion and contemplative solitude,
whereas destiny sought to drag him forward into the public
eye. This is how we see his state of mind in those days. But
there was a still more important reason for his becoming a
lone wolf and being frightened away from the higher Game
Schools, namely, an urge to research, inspired by his early
doubts about the Bead Game, which would not be stilled.

Admittedly he had tasted of an experience which proved to
him that the Game could be played in the highest and most
sacred sense, but he had also seen that the majority of players
and students, and also a proportion of the leaders and instructors, were by no means players of this category, for they did
not see the language of the Game as a *lingua sacra* but as a
kind of intellectual shorthand, as an interesting or amusing
speciality, an intellectual sport or a contest of ambition. Yes,
he had already had a suspicion, as his letter to the Music
Master proves, that the quality of the player did not always
denote the quest for the ultimate meaning, that the Game
also needed an exoteric and that it was also a technique,
science and social institution. In short, doubts and discords
existed. The Game was a lifelong question, and had become
the major problem of *his* life. He was not in the least inclined
to lighten his struggles through the offices of benevolent
spiritual pastors, to allow them to be dismissed as trifles or
be put off by the friendly smile of an instructor.

Naturally he could have utilised, had he so wished, any one

of the ten thousand Games that had been played, or the millions of potential Games, as a basis for his studies. He was well aware of this, but concentrated nevertheless upon that casual Game which he and his comrades had constructed during his student course. It was the Game, we may remember, in which he had realised for the first time the meaning of all Bead Games, and which had decided him in his vocation as a player. A pattern of this Game in the customary shorthand accompanied him constantly throughout these years. In the designations, keys, signatures and abbreviations of the Game language, it was a formula of astronomical mathematics, the form principle of an old sonata, and an axiom from Kung Fu Tze, etc., etc.

A reader who knew nothing of the Bead Game might imagine such a Game pattern as the pattern of a game of chess, only that here the significance of the figures and the possibilities of their correlation and mutual influence were multiplied, and to each figure, each constellation, each chess move, through this very move, configuration, etc., could be attributed a definite symbolical content.

Knecht's post-graduate studies for the future consisted in the task of learning to the full the content, principles, workings and system of the Game plan and in tracing a way back through the different cultures, sciences, languages and arts of centuries; he had taken upon himself no less a task— inconceivable to any of his instructors—than the most detailed verification of the systems and possibilities of expression in the art of the Bead Game.

We can safely say that as a result of his studies he might have found here and there a lacuna or an insufficiency, but on the whole must have approved the Bead Game after his thorough assessment of it, or else he would not finally have returned to it.

Were we to be writing a study in cultural history it would be a profitable task to describe many of the places and scenes in which Knecht passed his post-graduate years. He preferred as far as possible those places in which he could work alone or with only a few collaborators, and incidentally retained a grateful loyalty to several of these places in after life. He often stayed in Monteport as the guest of the Music Master, and occasionally took a course in one of the music historical

seminaries. Twice we find him in Hirsland, the residence of
the Order, assisting in the "great exercise", the twelve days
of fasting and meditation. At a later date he used to tell his
students with particular pleasure and almost with tenderness
of "Bamboo Grove," the lovely hermitage and scene of his
studies in the I Ching. He had not only learned and experienced much that was decisive, but had also found—led there
by a wondrous premonition or guidance—a unique setting
and a most unusual man in the person of the so-called "Elder
Brother", the creator and owner of the Chinese hermitage,
"Bamboo Grove". It seems incumbent upon us to describe
this remarkable episode of his post-graduate days in greater
detail.

Knecht had begun his study of the Chinese language and
Classics in the famous college of Sinology which for generations had been affiliated to St. Urban, the seat of ancient
philology. He had made great individual progress in reading
and writing, had made friends with several of the Chinese
working there and had learned by heart many of the odes
from the Shih Ching, before in his second year he began to
take an ever more intensive interest in the I Ching—the
Book of Changes.

The Chinese gave him all manner of information but no
instruction, for no teacher was available, and when Knecht
renewed his request that they should find him an instructor
for an exhaustive study of the I Ching, they told him of
"Elder Brother" and of his retreat. Knecht had perceived for
some time that, with his interest in the Book of Changes, he
was aiming at territory which few in the College wished to
know anything about. He therefore adopted a more cautious
attitude in his enquiries, and on taking pains to acquire more
precise information about the legendary Elder Brother
became aware that this hermit enjoyed a certain respect and
even fame, but admittedly more as a droll eccentric than as a
scholar.

Joseph felt that in this case he must be self-reliant. He
brought his course in the seminary to a close as soon as was
possible, and announced his departure. He made his way to the
district in which the mysterious Elder Brother—who was
perhaps a sage and a master, but perhaps after all only a fool
—had built his Bamboo Grove. He had gleaned the following

information about him: some twenty-five years before the
man had been the most promising student of the Chinese
section, and seemed to have been born with a true vocation
for these studies. He had surpassed the best teachers, both the
Chinese by birth and the Occidentals, in the technique of
brush writing and the deciphering of old texts, and had
become at the same time somewhat notorious by virtue of his
having tried to make himself as Chinese as possible in
outward appearance. Thus he would obstinately address his
superiors, from the head of the seminary to the masters, by
their titles, invariably using the prescribed polite form as the
other students did, but with the additional form of address:
"My Elder Brother". This distinction remained with him for
ever in the form of an ironical nickname.

He had devoted particular care to the oracle game of the
I Ching, whose manipulation he practised in a masterly
fashion with the aid of the traditional yarrow stalks. Next to
the old commentaries on the Book of Oracles his favourite
reading was the work of Chuang Tzu. Obviously, as Knecht
had also discovered, the rationalist or rather the anti-
mystical and strongly Confucian spirit which reigned in the
Chinese section had been in existence in his time, too, for the
Elder Brother had one day left the institution—which would
have been delighted to retain him as a specialist teacher—and
taken to the road with brush, a box of Chinese ink and two or
three books. He had travelled towards the south, staying here
and there with the brothers of the Order, had sought and
found the requisite spot for his intended retreat and, after
obstinate petitions and oral representations, obtained permission from the Order to develop this place as a colonist.
Ever since that day he had lived a rigid, idyllic ancient
Chinese existence there, alternatively laughed at as a crank
and revered as a kind of saint, at peace with himself and with
the world, passing his days in meditation and in copying old
Chinese scrolls, when the work in his Bamboo Grove, in
which he had meticulously laid out a Chinese dwarf garden
protected from the north wind by a hedge, did not claim his
attention.

Thither Joseph Knecht also wandered, taking the journey
in leisurely stages, enchanted by the landscape which confronted him once he had crossed the mountain passes—blue

and perfumed, with sunny terraced vineyards, brown walls
covered with lizards, dignified chestnut groves, a spicy
mixture of mountain country and the south. It was late in the
afternoon when he reached Bamboo Grove. He entered, and
saw to his amazement a little Chinese house set in the centre
of a beautiful garden; a spring gurgled from wooden pipes,
and the water flowed along a bed of pebbles into a basin made
of bricks, in the cracks of which all manner of greenery grew
and where, in the crystal clear water, a pair of golden carp
were swimming. The feathery bamboos swayed with peaceful
grace on their firm, slender shafts: the lawn was broken
up by stone tablets upon which could be read inscriptions
in the classical style. A delicate little man dressed in greyish
yellow linen, a pair of glasses shading his blue expectant
eyes, rose up from one of the flower beds over which he had
been bending and came slowly towards the visitor. He was
not unfriendly, but had that somewhat awkward shyness
which is often to be found among those who lead a retiring
and solitary life. He looked quizzically at Knecht and waited
to hear what he had to say.

Not without embarrassment Knecht uttered the Chinese
phrases which he had thought out: "The young scholar makes
so bold as to attend upon the Elder Brother."

"The well-born guest is welcome. A bowl of tea and a little
agreeable conversation with a younger colleague is always
welcome, and he will find shelter for the night should he
so desire."

Knecht kowtowed, thanked his host, and was thereupon led
into the house. He was given tea, and next conducted round
the garden and shown the stones with their inscriptions, the
pond and the goldfish, whose age he was also told. They
sat down under the swaying bamboos until supper time,
exchanging courtesies, poems and maxims from the classics
and looking at the flowers and enjoying the rosy gleam of
twilight on the mountain peaks. Then they turned once more
into the house where Elder Brother brought out rolls and
fruit, baked a savoury pancake on the little stove for his guest
and himself, and after they had eaten asked Knecht in German
the object of his visit. Joseph told him of his journey and of his
desires, namely, that he would like to remain and be the
Elder Brother's pupil should he be acceptable.

"We will speak of that to-morrow," said the hermit, and showed the guest to his bedroom. On the following morning Knecht went out into the garden, sat down by the water's edge and looked down at the goldfish. He gazed into the small cool world of shadow and light where, in the dark blue-green water, the golden bodies were suspended. The whole world seemed enchanted and petrified in eternal slumber and in the spell of dreams when, with a gently elastic but terrifying movement, they would set off in lightning flashes of crystal and gold in the sleepy half light. More and more absorbed, perhaps more in reverie than in contemplation, he was unaware that Elder Brother had come out of the house with velvety footsteps and stood for a long time watching this guest who was so deeply engrossed in his observations. When Knecht at last stood up and shook his preoccupation from him Elder Brother was no longer there, but he heard his voice from indoors inviting him to tea. They exchanged a short greeting and sat listening to the trickle of the tiny spring in the morning quiet—the melody of eternity. Then the hermit rose, busied himself in the asymmetrically built room, blinked across at Knecht from time to time and suddenly asked: "Is the young scholar prepared to don his shoes and set out again immediately?"

Joseph hesitated, and replied: "If it must be so, I am prepared."

"And should it transpire that he were to remain here for a while, is he prepared to be obedient and keep as still as a goldfish?"

Knecht once more agreed.

"It is well," replied the Elder Brother. "Now I will read the sticks and consult the Oracle."

While Knecht sat watching, still as a goldfish, with a mixture of curiosity and awe, Elder Brother drew from a wooden beaker, or rather a kind of pot, a handful of little sticks. They were yarrow stalks. He counted them carefully, and replaced part of the bundle in the vessel; then he laid a stick to one side and separated the rest into two equal bundles, holding one in the left hand and from the other making minute bundles with the sensitive tips of his fingers. These he counted and laid side by side, until only a few remained which he stuck between two fingers of the left hand. After

he had reduced a bundle with ritual counting to a few
sticks, he repeated the procedure with the second bundle.
He removed the counted ones, took both bundles one after
the other, counted again and stuck the residue between
two fingers. All this he did with a sparing, tranquil dexterity,
so that it appeared as an occult game of skill, ordered by
strict rules which had been practised a thousand times and
brought to a pitch of virtuosity. After he had repeated
the game several times, three small heaps remained over,
and from the number of sticks in these he read a symbol
which he painted with a pointed brush on a small sheet of
paper. Now the whole complicated game began anew: the
stalks separated into two bundles, were counted, removed,
others stuck between the fingers until finally once more only
three small heaps remained, the result of which was the
second symbol. Like the movement of a dance, and with a soft
dry click, the sticks struck each other, changed places, were
formed into heaps, separated and counted afresh; the
sticks moved rhythmically and with almost spectral certainty.
At the end of each performance Elder Brother wrote down a
symbol, and at last six positive and six negative signs stood
opposed to each other. The stalks were collected and carefully
placed in the container, and the Mage crouched on the floor on
his reed mat with the answer to his consultation of the Oracle
on the piece of paper in front of him. He regarded this for
a long time.

"This is the sign Mong," he said at last. "This sign is
known as 'Youthful Folly.' Above stands the mountain Shan,
below the water Shui. Below the mountain springs the source,
symbol of youth. The judgment of the Oracle reads:

'Youthful folly has success.
I seek not the young fool,
The young fool seeks me.
At the first Oracle I give information.
Should he ask me again, it were importunate.
If he importunes me I give no information.
Perseverance is encouraging!' "

Knecht had been holding his breath in rapt attention. In the
silence that ensued he could not help giving vent to a deep sigh
of relief. He did not dare to ask any questions, but he thought
he had understood that the young fool had been accepted and

might remain. Even while he had been captivated and spell-bound by this sublime game of marionettes, of fingers and spelicans, which he had watched for such a long time and which had appeared so convincing and significant, although he had hardly understood its meaning, the experience had taken complete hold over him. The Oracle had spoken and decided in his favour.

We should not have described this episode in such detail had not Knecht himself often related it with a certain complacency to his friends and pupils. We shall now return to our serious study.

Knecht remained in Bamboo Grove for many months, and eventually learned to manipulate the yarrow sticks with a perfection approaching that of his teacher. He practised counting them for an hour each day with Elder Brother, and was initiated into the grammar and symbolism of the Oracle language. The latter allowed him to practice writing, and to learn by heart the sixty-four symbols, read to him from the old commentaries and on particularly good days would relate a story to him from Chuang Tzu. In addition to this Knecht learned to tend the garden, wash the brushes, prepare the Chinese ink, to make soup and tea, collect brushwood, observe the weather and use the Chinese calendar. His endeavours to bring the subject of the Bead Game and music into their rare conversations were completely fruitless: they might have been directed at someone who was hard of hearing, or else they would simply be brushed aside with an indulgent smile or answered with an axiom such as : "thick clouds, no rain" or "the noble is immaculate." But when Knecht had a small piano sent from Monteport, and played for an hour each day, there was no complaint. Once Knecht told his teacher that he wished one day to be able to incorporate the system of the I Ching into the Bead Game.

Elder Brother smiled.

"You can try," he said. "You will see. One can build a pretty little bamboo garden in the world, but whether the gardener could succeed in incorporating the world into his bamboo garden seems to me to be questionable."

But enough of this. We will only mention that some years later, when Knecht was already a respected figure in Waldzell, and had invited his former teacher to give a lecture there, Elder Brother did not reply to the invitation.

In later days, Joseph Knecht looked upon his months in Bamboo Grove not only as an especially fortunate period, but also described them as "the beginning of his awakening." From that time onwards, this image of "awakening" appears more frequently in his utterances, having a similar though not quite analogous meaning to his previously pictured Call. We must presume that "awakening" means a realisation at that time of his own self, and of the position in which he stood within the Castalian and the human scheme, and yet the accent seems to us to be laid more and more upon self-realisation in the sense that Knecht, from "the beginning of his awakening," was approaching nearer and nearer to a feeling of his own particular position and vocation, whereas the concepts and the categories of a general and special position attainable within the Castalian hierarchy became for him ever more relative.

Knecht's Chinese studies did not by any means come to an end with his stay in Bamboo Grove. He continued with them, and was particularly preoccupied in gaining a knowledge of old Chinese music. In all the older Chinese writings he had encountered a praise of music, where it was described as one of the primæval sources of all law, order, morality, beauty and health, and moreover he had already seen this wide and moral concept of music in the person of the old Music Master, who could be regarded as its complete apotheosis.

Without abandoning his basic plan of studies, which we know from that letter to Fritz Tegularius, he pressed open-mindedly and energetically forward in whichever direction he sensed something important to himself, *i.e.*, wherever the prescribed path of awakening appeared to him to lead. One of the most positive results of his apprenticeship with Elder Brother was the fact that he had overcome his shyness of returning to Waldzell: he thenceforward took part each year in one of the higher courses, and had already become—without rightly knowing how it had happened—one of the personalities who were being watched with interest and recognition in the Vicus Lusorum. He now belonged to that innermost and most sensitive organ in the whole existence of the Game, that anonymous group of trusted players in whose hands the momentary destiny or at least direction and fashion of the Game actually lay. This group of players, in which officials of the Game Institutes were not lacking but were by no means in the majority, was to be encountered chiefly in certain remote and quiet rooms of the Games Archives, occupied with critical studies of the Game, striving for the introduction or acceptance of new fields and material, debating for or against the continually changing directions of taste in form, outward practice and gymnastic possibilities. Each player in this circle was a virtuoso, and each knew his own talents and singularities so well that it was like being in the precincts of a ministry or an aristocratic club, where rulers and responsible persons met each other each day and got to know each other.

A subdued and polished atmosphere ruled there. One was ambitious without showing it, and observant and critical to a point of exaggeration. For many in Castalia, and also for certain people outside the province, this élite of the younger generation from the Vicus Lusorum represented the prize blossom of Castalian tradition and the cream of an exclusive aristocratic intellectuality. Many youths had dreamed ambitious dreams of one day belonging to it. For others again, this eclectic circle of pretenders to the higher posts in the hierarchy of the Bead Game was something detested and degenerate, a clique of arrogant wasters, of jaded and æsthetic geniuses with no sense for life and truth, a pretentious and basically parasitical society of dandies and pushers whose life and calling were simple tomfoolery and a sterile, selfish intellectual enjoyment.

Knecht was indifferent to both opinions. It meant nothing at all to him if he were prized by student chatter as a fabulous animal or scorned as a *parvenu* and climber. Perhaps the most important thing for him was still that one question: as to whether the Game really were the highest achievement of Castalia and one to which it was worth devoting his life. For, even as a result of his own probing into the innermost arcana of the Game's laws and possibilities, of his growing familiarity with the gay labyrinths of the Archives and the complex inner world of symbolism, his doubts had not been completely silenced, and he soon realised that belief and doubt belong together and rule each other like In and Out breathing; that, with his progress in all the fields of the Game microcosm, his own powers of perception and his susceptibility to all the problematical factors of the Game had also increased. His idyll in Bamboo Grove had perhaps tranquillised and deceived him for a short while. The example of Elder Brother had shown him that there were always ways of escape from these problems. One could, for example, become Chinese as he had done, shut oneself away behind a garden hedge and live in a satisfying and beautiful world of perfection. One could perhaps also become a Pythagorean, a monk or a scholastic; but these were only expedients, only slightly more possible and permissible renunciations of universality, renunciations of to-day and to-morrow in favour of perfection—but a past perfection. Knecht had at times felt that this was not his path. But which, then, was his path? Apart from his great talent for music and the Bead Game, he knew that he possessed other latent powers—a certain inner independence, a high degree of obstinacy, which by no means excluded or made service difficult but which demanded that he should only serve the highest. And these powers, this independence and obstinacy, were not only traits in his character directed and effective inwardly but also operative externally.

Already during his school years, and particularly during that period of rivalry between himself and Plinio Designori, Joseph Knecht had often found that comrades of his own age, and even more so those younger than himself, had not only liked him and courted his friendship but had been inclined to submit to him, to ask his advice and to accept his influence. Moreover, this experience had often been repeated. There was a highly pleasing and flattering aspect to this discovery, which encouraged ambition and strengthened self-consciousness; but it had, too, another side, a dark and terrible side, for one already felt the temptation at each counsel, at every direction or example offered to greedy comrades in their weakness, to look down upon their lack of dignity and backbone; one felt the occasional lurking desire at least so he thought—to make pliant slaves of them, and this had something hateful and forbidden about it. Furthermore, he had received a foretaste during his contest with Plinio of the toll in responsibility, exertion and inner strain that had to be paid for each illustrious and representative position. He knew no less how severely the Music Master was sometimes taxed. It was magnificent and alluring to have power over men and to shine before them, but this power also contained its demonism and danger. World history was composed of a continuous line of rulers, leaders, politicians and soldiers who, with very few exceptions, had all started admirably and all finished disastrously, who had all striven for power, presumably with good will, only later to be obsessed and intoxicated by it and to love it for its own sake. It was his task to consecrate and make salutary the nature-given power which he was to place at the service of the hierarchy. For him, this had always been an understood thing. But where was the position in which his powers could best serve and bring forth fruit? The capacity to attract others, particularly the young, and to influence them more or less might have been of value to an officer or to a politician, but there was no place for these gifts in Castalia. Moreover, these particular faculties were of use only to the teachers and educators, which professions did not appeal in the least to Knecht. If he could have followed his own inclinations he would have chosen the life of an independent scholar or that of a bead-player. And here again arose that old torturing question: was the Game really the criterion, and queen in the realm of the spirit? Was it not, despite everything, only a game in the last analysis? Was it really worthy of complete devotion and lifelong service? Generations ago this famous Game had begun as a kind of substitute for art, and had gradually become in concept, at least for many, a kind of religion, a collective stimulus and devotional potential for highly developed intelligences. One can easily see that the old conflict between the æsthetic and the ethical was taking place in Knecht. The never completely outspoken, but also never quite silent, question was the same which had loomed so menacingly and sombrely in his Waldzellian poems, and applied not only to the Bead Game but to Castalia itself.

One day, at the very time when he was particularly over-wrought by these problems, and in his dreams was reliving the disputes with Designori, he was walking across the spacious courtyard of the Vicus Lusorum when he heard a voice, which he did not immediately recognise although it sounded familiar, calling his name. On turning round he beheld a well-built young man with a small beard, who rushed forward enthusiastically to greet him. It was Plinio, and in an impulse of memory and tenderness he returned his greeting affectionately. They arranged to meet the same evening. Plinio, who had left his student days far behind and was already an official, had arrived as a guest on a short holiday to take a course in the Bead Game, as he had done several years previously.

Their meeting that evening brought nothing but embarrassment for the two friends. Plinio was in Waldzell only as a guest scholar, a tolerated dilettante from the outside world, who was admittedly following the course with great zeal, but certainly not the one for outstanding players and amateurs for this would have been too advanced for him. He was sitting opposite an expert, one of the initiated, who, even in his forbearance and courteous reception of his friend's interest in the Game, could not help making him feel that he was no colleague but only a child who was taking his pleasure on the periphery of a science which the other knew inside out. Knecht tried to divert the conversation away from the subject of the Game, and asked Plinio to tell him of his office, work and life in the outside world. Now it was Joseph who became the inexperienced one, the child asking inconsequential questions and having to be taught. Plinio had become a jurist, was striving for political influence and was about to become engaged to the daughter of the party leader. He spoke a language which Joseph only half understood, and for whom the expressions rang emptily or at least seemed to have no content. It was obvious that Plinio had attained a certain position in his own world, was well informed and had ambitious aims, but the two worlds which once, ten years previously, had aroused mutual sympathy and interest in two inquisitive youths, now seemed far apart, irreconcilable and alien. Joseph could see that this politician and man of the world had retained a certain attachment for Castalia, inasmuch as this was the second occasion on which he had devoted his holidays to the Bead Game; but in the long run, Joseph thought, it was not a very different situation from the one in which he, Knecht, might have found himself had he been in Plinio's district and office, and allowed himself to be shown a few court sessions, factories or charity organisations in the rôle of an interested guest.

Both of them were disappointed. Knecht found his former friend changed and coarsened. Designori, on the other hand, found his comrade particularly arrogant in his exclusive intellectualism and esotericism, one who seemed to him to have become completely "incorporeal" and who was enchanted with himself and his sport. However, they both made a great effort, and Designori told him all manner of things about his studies and examinations, of a journey to England and the south, and of political meetings and parliament. On one occasion, too, he uttered a phrase which rang like a threat and a warning: "You will see that there will soon be a time of great unrest, perhaps a war—and it is not impossible that your Castalian existence will be seriously menaced." Joseph did not take this too seriously, but simply asked: "And you, Plinio? Will you be for or against Castalia?"

"Ah!" sighed Plinio with a forced smile. "It will hardly rest with me. In any case, I am naturally in favour of non-interference with Castalia—or else why should I be here? Nevertheless, however modest your material claims may be, Castalia costs the country a pretty penny each year."

"Yes, of course!" laughed Knecht. "The sum represents, as I have been told, approximately a tenth of that which the country spent yearly during the warring centuries on armaments and munitions."

They met on several more occasions, and the nearer they approached to the close of Plinio's visit the more polished became their exchange of courtesies. They both felt very relieved when the two or three weeks came to an end and Plinio departed.

The Ludi Magister at that time was Thomas of Trave, a famous and much travelled cosmopolitan, conciliatory and accommodating with everyone he met, but of great vigilance and asceticism as regards the Game and a great worker, a fact which anyone who only knew him from the representative side would not have imagined had they seen him in ceremonial dress conducting the great Games or receiving delegates from abroad. He was reputed to be a cool, even cold, intellectual, who only paid lip service to the arts, and on occasions one heard deprecatory criticisms of him among young enthusiastic amateurs of the Bead Game. This was indeed, false criticism, for even if he were not over-enthusiastic and in the great public Games avoided contact with huge and exciting themes, his exquisitely constructed formal Games were unsurpassed, and even for connoisseurs showed a close intimacy with the underlying problems of the Game world.

One day the Magister Ludi summoned Joseph Knecht, received him in his own residence in informal dress, and asked him whether he would care to come each day for the next few days and spend half-an-hour with him. Knecht had never before been alone with the Magister, and accepted the command with great surprise.

The Magister handed him a voluminous script, a proposal which he had received from one of the organists. This was one of the many proposals, the examination of which was part of the work of the higher officials of the Game: they were chiefly suggestions for the acceptance of new material into the Archives. One man, for example, had worked out with special accuracy the history of the madrigal and had discovered a curve in the development of style, which he had drawn in the form of a musical and mathematical graph so that it could be incorporated into the vocabulary of the Game; another had examined the Latin of Julius Cæsar for its rhythmical characteristics and had found the most outstanding similarities with examples from his researches into the intervals in Byzantine chants. Again, an enthusiast had once discovered a new cabbala in a musical manuscript of the fifteenth century, and there were also stormy letters from abstruse experimentalists who were adept at drawing the most astonishing conclusions from some such subject as a comparison between the horoscopes of Goethe and Spinoza, which would often be accompanied by pretty and illuminating geometrical figures in many colours. Knecht tackled the daily courier eagerly, for he had often had similar propositions in his own head, even though he had never forwarded any. Every active bead-player dreamed of a perpetual expansion of the fields of the Game, until it should embrace the whole world; more than this even, he brought these expansions to perfection in his own performances and in his private exercises, continually cherishing the hope that those which seemed to prove satisfactory might be included in the official archives. The ultimate finesse in the private game of a highly developed bead-player consists in having perfect mastery of the explicit, enumerative and imaginative powers of the Game laws, in order that he may incorporate quite individual ideas into any game having objective and historical values. An eminent botanist once made the following comical statement: "Everything should be possible in the Bead Game, even that single plants should be able to converse in Latin with Linnæus."

Thus Knecht helped the Magister with the analysis of the proposals which had to be dealt with. The half-hour passed very rapidly, and he appeared from then on every day for two weeks to work for half-an-hour alone with the Magister Ludi. He had already noticed during the first few days, that this task, the uselessness of which had been obvious at first glance, was quite beneath him, but that it had to be carried out carefully and critically to the end. He wondered to himself how the Magister Ludi could possibly find time for such work, but gradually became aware that it was not simply a question of his rendering a service to the Master and taking a little work off his hands, but that this work, although necessary in itself, was above all being used as an opportunity for examining him, the young adept, more closely and in the most courteous manner possible.

And now, once again, there was a repetition of his boyhood days when the Music Master had appeared, and he had suddenly noticed that the behaviour of his comrades had become shyer, more distant and sometimes even ironically subservient. Something was being prepared, only it was less agreeable than before.

At their last session, the Magister Ludi said in a somewhat high-pitched voice, in his very exact, accentuated speech, without a trace of pomposity: "Good! You need not come to-morrow: our work is over for the moment, and in any case I must find something else for you to do. My best thanks for your help—it has been most useful to me. By the way, I think you should now propose yourself for admission into the Order: you will encounter no difficulties, for I have already notified the high officials. I hope you are in agreement Just one more word," he added as he stood up. "Presumably you are inclined, as nearly all good bead-players are when young, to use our Game as a kind of instrument for philosophising. Although my words alone will not prevent you from doing so, I must warn you that philosophising should be accomplished through its legitimate medium, *i.e.*, philosophy. Our Game is neither philosophy nor religion, but has its own discipline and in character is most related to art. It is in fact an art *sui generis*. One advances further if one bears this in mind as an objective than when one realises it after a hundred failures. The philosopher Kant—he is no longer well-known to-day, but was a great brain in his time—once said of theological philosophising that it was 'a magic lantern of chimæras.' We should not turn our Bead Game into this."

Joseph had been taken by surprise. In fact, he had hardly heard this last warning in his suppressed excitement. He had realised with lightning rapidity that the words meant an end to his freedom, the termination of his post-graduate studies, his acceptance into the Order and imminent enrolment into the hierarchy. He thanked the Magister with a low bow, and went immediately to the chancery of the Waldzell Order, where he found his name already on the list of new candidates for acceptance. He was moderately well acquainted, as were all the students of his grade, with the regulations of the Order, and remembered the concession which permitted any member of the Order holding an official position of higher rank to sanction an acceptance. Knecht therefore asked permission that the Music Master should perform the ceremony of initiation, duly received a pass and a short term of leave and set out on the following day to visit his friend and patron in Monteport. He found the venerable old man ailing, but received an affectionate welcome.

"You have come at the right moment," said the Magister. "In a short time I should have been unable to perform the ceremony of receiving you as a younger Brother into the Order. I am resigning from office, and my resignation has already been accepted."

The ceremony was very simple. On the following day, in accordance with the statutes, he invited two Brothers of the Order as witnesses, having previously given Knecht an

extract from the rules of the Order as his task for a meditation
exercise. The extract read as follows:

"Should the higher Authorities summon thee to office,
know that each promotion on the ladder of office is not a step
into freedom but into bondage. The higher the office, the
heavier the bondage. The greater the official power, the
stricter the service. The stronger the personality, the more
expressly forbidden is wilfulness".

They assembled in the Master's music cell, the same one
in which Knecht had received his first lesson in meditation.
In celebration of the occasion the Master had invited the
neophyte to play a Bach choral prelude. After this, one of the
witnesses read out a short summary of the Order rules, and
the Music Master himself posed the ritual questions and took
his young friend's oath. When the ceremony was over he
granted him another hour of his time and they sat together in
the garden, where the Master gave him a little friendly
advice as to the meaning of the rules and how they should
be observed.

"It is wonderful to think," he said, "that at the moment
when I am retiring you are filling the gap. It is as though you
were a son taking my place."

He noticed the sadness on Joseph's face, and added: "Now
there is no need for you to be unhappy, for I am not in the
least unhappy. I am only very tired, and am looking forward
to the leisure which I shall now enjoy, in which I hope you will
often share. The next time we meet, you may use the familiar
form of address to me—I could not suggest it while I was
in office."

He took leave of Joseph with that winning smile that his
pupil had known now for twenty years.

Knecht returned at all speed to Waldzell, for he had been
accorded only three days grace. He had no sooner arrived
than he was summoned to the Magister, who received him
genially as a colleague and congratulated him upon his
acceptance into the Order.

"And now, to make you the perfect colleague and collaborator," he went on, "only a prescribed place in our organisation
is lacking."

Joseph drew back a little. So he really was to lose his
freedom after all!

"Oh, well! I hope you will be able to make use of me in some humble post," he said modestly. "And yet I had hoped to win your permission to continue with my studies for a while."

The Magister looked him in the eyes with a light ironical smile. "For a while, you say? But how long is that?"

Knecht gave an embarrassed laugh. "Oh, I don't really know."

"I thought as much," said the Magister. "You are still speaking the language of the students, and thinking in terms of their concepts, Joseph Knecht. That is all right, but it will soon be all wrong—for we have need of you. You know quite well that you, too, can have leave at a later date for purposes of study even in the highest offices of the pedagogy, provided you can convince them of the value of those studies. My predecessor and teacher, for example, while he was still Magister Ludi, and an old man at that, requested a full year's leave for his London Archive studies and was granted it, although he was not given leave 'for a while' but for a prescribed number of weeks and days. This is how you will have to reckon in the future. And now I have a proposal to make to you: we need a responsible man who is not yet known outside our circle for a special mission. . . ."

It was a question of the following task. The Benedictine monastery, Mariafels, one of the oldest cultural centres of the land, which was on friendly terms with Castalia and for many years had been devoted to the Bead Game, had requested that a young instructor be sent to them for some time to teach the Game and also to stimulate the few advanced players who were to be found in the monastery. The choice of the Magister had fallen upon Joseph Knecht. This was the reason why he had been so carefully scrutinised, and why his entrance into the Order had been precipitated.

Chapter   Four

TWO   ORDERS

IN MANY RESPECTS a similar set of circumstances had
arisen around Knecht to those which had once arisen in his
grammar school days after the visit of the Music Master.
He had hardly looked upon his mission to Mariafels as a
particular distinction or as an energetic first step upon the
ladder of the hierarchy. He could, however, now read the
portents in the behaviour and attitude of his fellow graduates
with a more practised eye: for some time he had belonged to
the inner circle of bead-players who, as a result of this
unusual commission, now recognised in him one upon whom
the superiors had their eyes and thought to take advantage
of. His comrades and competitors of yesterday did not
immediately withdraw or become unfriendly, for these highly
aristocratic circles were far too well mannered, but they
allowed a certain distance to be felt. The comrade of yesterday
could become the superior of to-morrow, and this circle
registered such grades and differences in their mutual
relationships by giving expression to the most sensitive
shades of behaviour.

Fritz Tegularius was the exception. Next to Ferromonte
we can count him as the truest friend in Joseph's life. This
man, whose talents should have destined him to a place
among the highest, was heavily handicapped by ill health,
lack of balance and self-confidence. He was the same age as
Knecht, and had been about thirty-four years old at the time
of his acceptance into the Order. The friends had first met
during a Bead Game course, and Knecht had noticed at the
time how greatly this quiet and somewhat melancholy youth
had been attracted to him. With his perspicacity for judging
men which, even if unconscious, was well developed at that
time, he sensed the nature of this love as an unconditional
devotion and submission, a readiness for friendship and
veneration and a glowing enthusiasm of an almost religious

character, but which, by reason of its inner seemliness and because it was clouded over by a suspicion of its inner tragedy, was held severely in check.

At that time Knecht, shattered and sensitive after the Designori episode, had kept Tegularius at a distance with purposeful strength, although he, too, felt attracted to this interesting and unusual comrade.

For purposes of characterization, we shall reproduce a leaf from one of Knecht's secret reports, which some years later he placed at the disposal of the higher authorities. It read as follows:—

"Tegularius. A personal friend of the writer's. A scholar from Keuperheim with many distinctions. A good ancient philologist with a pronounced interest in philosophy, having worked on Leibnitz, Bolzano and later on Plato. The most talented and brilliant Bead Game player that I know. He would be an obvious choice for Magister Ludi were not his character completely unsuited to this post on account of his delicate health. Tegularius should never be allowed to attain a leading representative or administrative position, because it would be a misfortune both for himself and for his office. His shortcomings manifest themselves outwardly in states of depression, periods of insomnia and nervous pains; and spiritually, at times, in melancholy, an urgent need for solitude, a fear of responsibility and possibly thoughts of suicide. This heavily handicapped man has, with the aid of meditation and great self-discipline, held himself so courageously upright that most of his fellows have no conception of his sufferings and know only his great modesty and reserve. Although Tegularius is unfortunately unsuited to leadership in the high offices of the Vicus Lusorum, he is a jewel and a quite irreplaceable treasure. He has mastered our Game as a great musician does his instrument. He strikes the most delicate nuances of the Game instinctively, and is not to be despised as an instructor: in the advanced and highest refresher courses—he is too good for the lower classes—I could not have done without his help. The way in which he analyses the trial Games of the young students without discouraging them, sees through their artifices, recognising and exposing them as imitation or embellishment; how, in a well founded but still uncertain and badly composed Game, he discovers the source of the errors and demonstrates them as faultless anatomical compounds, is nothing short of miraculous. His incorruptible and eagle eye for analysis and correction ensures him, above all, the respect of his pupils and colleagues, which would otherwise be questionable owing to his uncertain, vacillating, shy and modest behaviour. To illustrate the geniality on the part of Tegularius as a bead-player such as I have described, I should like to give an example: in the early days of my friendship with him, when there was not very much more for either of us to learn in the course in the way of technique, he once gave me, in a moment of great confidence, an insight into certain Games that he had composed at that time. At first glance I found them to be brilliant, but somehow new and original in style. I borrowed these schemes for purposes of study, and found in their composition real poems—so astonishing and unique that I do not feel justified in remaining silent about them. These Games were little dramas of almost purely monological structure and reflected the individual—both the handicapped and genial spiritual life of their creator—like a perfect self-portrait. It was not only that a dialectical harmony and conflict existed between the different themes and groups of themes upon which the Game was based, the sequences and contrasts of which were highly ingenious, but also that the syntheses and harmonising of the opposing voices were not developed to the utmost in the usual classical manner; rather, this harmonising underwent a whole series of interruptions, stopping on each occasion as though tired or desperate, halting before the solution and ringing out in tones of question and doubt. As a result of this, such Games not only achieved exciting, and to my knowledge hitherto undared, chromatics, but the whole Game became the expression of tragic doubt and renunciation, and an imaginative affirmation of the doubtfulness of all spiritual effort. At the same time, ni their spirituality, as well as in their technical perfection and calligraphy, they were so extraordinarily beautiful that one could almost have wept over them. Each individual Game strove so soulfully and earnestly for solution, only in the end to reject the solution with such noble resignation that it was like a perfect elegy on the inherent transience of all beauty and the ultimate innate dubiety of all high spiritual aims.

"Item: Tegularius—in the event of his outliving my period of office—should be regarded as an unusually delicate, priceless but dangerous asset. He should be given great freedom, and his advice would be listened to on all questions pertaining to the Game. Individual pupils, however, should never be entrusted to him for instruction."

This remarkable man had in the course of time become one of Knecht's real friends. His relationship with the latter, whom he admired as much as a leader as for his intellect, was one of touching devotion, and we owe much of our knowledge of Knecht to his writings. Tegularius was perhaps the only one of the inner circle of the younger bead-players who did not envy his friend the new mission, and for whom his departure for an indefinite period was a deep, almost unbearable loss and cause for suffering.

Joseph himself, once he had overcome a certain terror at having suddenly lost his beloved freedom, was pleased with the new circumstances. He took pleasure in the thought of travel and activity and felt a curiosity about the new world to which he was being sent. We must mention that this young Brother, so new to the Order, was not sent immediately to Mariafels. He was placed for three weeks in the "Police," as this small department in the apparatus of the pedagogy was known to the students. One might almost say that it was the Castalian political department or Ministry for Foreign Affairs, but perhaps these are very high-sounding names for so small a department. Here Joseph learned the code of behaviour for members of the Order visiting the outside world.

The head of this office, M. Dubois, devoted an hour each day to him in person. That such an inexperienced and untried youth should be sent to so important an outpost had given this intelligent man much food for thought. He did not disguise the fact that he disapproved of the Magister Ludi's decision, and took double pains to instil into Joseph with friendly solicitude some knowledge of the dangers of the world and the means of countering them.

Knecht showed such great willingness to learn from this paternal, eloquent and anxious teacher that, during these hours of initiation into the rules of conduct to be employed towards the world, he became a great favourite of Dubois', who in the end released him on his mission with the utmost confidence. He even tried—more out of benevolence than for political ends—to entrust him with an auxiliary commission on his own account. M. Dubois was one of the few "politicians" of Castalia, and belonged to that small group of officials whose thoughts and studies for the most part centred around the legal and economic survival of Castalia, its independence and its relationship with the outside world.

Most of the Castalians—officials no less than tutors and graduates—lived in their pedagogic province and in their Order as though in a stable and eternal world which they took for granted. Admittedly they knew that it had not always existed, that it had once been created: that, in the times of bitter conflict at the end of the warring centuries, it had arisen as much as a result of the æsthetic-heroic self-realization and efforts on the part of the intellectuals as from a deep need on the part of the exhausted, decimated and desperate people for order, norm, intelligence, law and just measure. They also knew that the function of all the Orders and Provinces of the world was to eschew power and competition and to guarantee in exchange a permanence and stability of the intellectual basis of all measures and laws. But what they did not know was that this order of things could by no means be taken for granted, that it presupposed a certain harmony between the world and the spirit, the disruption of which could occur again; that world history, taken all in all, by no means strove for and favoured the estimable, the intelligent and the beautiful, but barely tolerated them—and then only in exceptional cases. The majority of the Castalians did not in the least realize the hidden problems of their existence, but were content to leave it in the hands of the few political brains, the leader of whom was Dubois.

Once Knecht had won his confidence, he received a summary initiation into the fundamental political position of Castalia. This had appeared to him at first—as it would have done to most of his colleagues in the Order—as a rather repugnant and uninteresting subject. It recalled to his mind that remark of Designori's, which he had apparently forgotten, about the possibility of Castalia's being endangered, and it also brought back the bitter memory of his youthful contest with Plinio, which now suddenly assumed great importance as a step on the way to his awakening.

"I think I can now release you," Dubois said to him when their last conference had come to an end. "You are to observe the orders that the venerable Magister Ludi has given you very strictly, and no less the rules of conduct which you have learned here from me. It was a great pleasure for me to have been of assistance to you, and you will discover that these three weeks we have spent together have not been wasted. Should you ever feel inclined to show your appreciation of my training and to renew our acquaintanceship, I will tell you how you can do so. You are going to a Benedictine monastery, and in the event of your staying there for some time and winning the confidence of the Fathers you will probably hear political conversations among those reverend gentlemen and their guests, and also become aware of their political opinions. Should you incidentally pass this information on to me, I should be very grateful. But please don't misunderstand me: I do not wish you to feel yourself in any way a 'spy,' or to abuse the confidence which the Fathers may place in you. You must only give me the information that your conscience allows you to divulge. I can guarantee that we should only take into account and make use of any such information in the interests of our Order and of Castalia. We are not really politicians in the true sense of the word and have no power, but we, too, are dependent upon the world, which perhaps needs but seldom does more than tolerate us. Under certain circumstances it might be of interest to us should a statesman visit the monastery, a Pope fall ill or new candidates be added to the list of future Cardinals. We are not dependent upon your information for we have many sources, but one insignificant one more or less cannot possibly do any harm You may go now, and you need not make a decision regarding my suggestions to-day. Take no heed of anything except first and foremost to carry out your official mission and to do us honour with the reverend Fathers. I wish you a pleasant journey."

Before setting out Knecht consulted the oracle from the Book of Changes by means of the yarrow stick ceremony, and met with the symbol Yu which signifies "The Wanderer," along with the judgment: "Success through humility.

Salvation comes to the wanderer through perseverance."
He found a six in the sub-dominant, and looked up the
meaning in the book, which read:
  "The wanderer comes to sanctuary.
  He carries his possessions with him.
  He gains the assiduity of a young servant."
His leave-taking passed serenely, but the last conversation
with Tegularius was a hard test of stoicism on both sides.
Fritz forced himself to keep cool, and maintained a rigid,
almost frozen, self-control, for this was the departure of the
best friend he possessed. Knecht's personality had no such
passionate and exclusive need for a friend, and he could if
necessary live without one and turn his sympathies freely
towards new objects and new people. For him this farewell
was by no means a trenchant loss, but he knew his friend well
enough to realize what a devastation and test it must be on
his side, and this made him all the more solicitous. He had
often reflected upon this relationship, had at times spoken of
it to the Music Master, and had learned to a certain extent to
analyse his own experiences and feelings objectively and
critically; and as a result he knew that he was not as though
held in passionate bondage by Fritz's great talents alone, but
by a combination of these, his heavy shortcomings and his
extreme fragility; that the one-sidedness and exclusiveness
of the love which Tegularius bore him was not only beautiful
but possessed a certain ingenuous quality and dangerous
charm, which tempted him on occasions to exercise his power
over one who was weaker in strength but stronger in love.
He had therefore seen fit to maintain to the last a great
reticence and self-discipline in this friendship. However fond
he may have been of Fritz, the latter had achieved no real,
deep meaning for him, unless it were by virtue of the fact that
his friendship with this tender creature, fascinated as he was
by his stronger and more self-assured companion, had made
him aware of the power of attraction and influence which he
possessed over so many men. He came to realize that some
of this power, which enabled him to attract and influence
others, was bound up to a large extent with his teaching and
educatory gifts, and that it entailed dangers and brought
with it a certain responsibility.
Tegularius was only one of the many admirers whose

appraising glances he so frequently observed around him.
At the same time, during the past year he had experienced
ever more clearly and consciously the tense atmosphere in
which he had been living in the Game town. He belonged to a
very sharply defined and unofficial circle, composed of a
narrow choice of candidates and coaches of the Bead Game,
the majority of whom were called upon to assist the Magister,
the Archivist or in the Game courses, but who were never
made use of in the lower or medium official teaching staffs and
were reserved for the filling of leading posts. In this circle
everyone knew everyone else very accurately—with painful
accuracy in fact—and there was no possible room for decep-
tion as to talents, character or achievements; and inasmuch as
here, among these coaches of the Game studies and aspirants
to the higher dignities, each one of them was well above the
average in his subject and possessed first class testimonials
for achievement and knowledge, every trait and shade of
character which predestined an aspirant to leadership and
success played a particularly great and carefully watched rôle.
A very small surplus or deficiency in ambition, good
demeanour, stature or appearance, in charm, amiability or
influence upon the younger members or upon the authorities
was of great weight and could prove decisive in competition.
Thus, while Fritz Tegularius belonged to this circle only as
an outsider, as a tolerated guest more or less on the periphery
because he obviously had no talent for leadership, Knecht
belonged to the innermost circle. The thing about him that
appealed to the young and brought him so many admirers
was his freshness and extreme youthful grace, seemingly
impervious to passion, incorruptible and almost childishly
irresponsible—a certain innocence, in fact. And what made
him agreeable to his superiors was actually the reverse side
of this innocence—his almost complete lack of ambition
and aspiration.

The effect of his personality, first upon his juniors and
gradually rising to his superiors, had only recently come to
his knowledge, and when he looked back, as one who had
been awakened, he found that both these effects led back in a
line even to his boyhood days, running through his life and
forming it: he had always enjoyed the friendship of his
juniors and the benevolent consideration of many of his

superiors. There had of course, been exceptions, such as the headmaster Zbinden, for example, but to offset this there had been the patronage of the Music Master and more recently that of the Magister Ludi himself and Monsieur Dubois.

All this pointed in one direction, which Knecht had never entirely recognised and which he would not have entertained in any case. He was obviously predestined to be numbered among the élite, to find admiring friends and high ranking patrons quite naturally and without any effort on his own part. His path would not allow of his remaining in the shadow, on the lower rungs of the hierarchy, but forced him to mount continually towards the peaks and into the bright light in which they were bathed. His fate was not to be a subordinate or private tutor, but a leader. The fact that he had noticed this later than his comrades who were in a similar position gave him just that extra magic and note of innocence. And why had he noticed this so late—so unwillingly? Because, in actual fact, he had not striven for it and had not really desired it, because he had felt no need to rule and found no pleasure in command, but would have preferred a contemplative rather than an active life, and would have been content to remain for many years—perhaps his whole life through—an insignificant post-graduate, an eager and respectful pilgrim, wandering through the temples of the past, the cathedrals of music, and the gardens and forests of mythology, language and ideas. Now that he saw himself being thrust irrevocably into the life of action he felt, more strongly than ever before, the tensions of striving, competition and ambition which surrounded him, felt his innocence menaced and no longer tenable, perceived that he must now agree to and accept that which had been indicated and ordained in order that he might overcome the feeling of being a prisoner and his homesickness for the lost freedom of the past ten years. And because inwardly he was still not quite disposed to take this course he saw the temporary absence from Waldzell and the Province, and his journey out into the world, in the nature of a redemption.

The monastery Mariafels and its seminary had for many centuries since its foundation participated and been a fellow sufferer in the history of the West. It had experienced its

times of renaissance and decline, many ups and downs, and
had been famous and illustrious in a variety of fields. Once
the high seat of scholastic learning and dispute, and still
possessing to-day a mighty library of mediæval theology, it
had risen after the era of negligence and indolence to a new
brilliance, but this time through its music, universally
appraised choir and the masses and oratorios which had been
composed and conducted by the Fathers. It still retained
from that epoch a magnificent musical tradition, half-a-dozen
walnut chests crammed with priceless music manuscripts, and
the most beautiful organ in the country. Then the political age
of the monastery had come, and left in its wake a certain
tradition and ritual. In the evil times of devastating wars
Mariafels had several times become a tiny island of intelligence and reason, where the more enlightened brains of the
two hostile parties had cautiously sought each other out in
order to arrive at some compromise, and once—this was the
high peak of its history—it had been the birthplace of a
Peace Treaty which had satisfied for a while the longings of
an exhausted people. When at last a new era had dawned
and Castalia had been founded, the monastery had stood
aside, but in all preparedness, having presumably asked
Rome for direction. An attempt on the part of the Pedagogy
to obtain hospitality for a scholar who wished to work in the
scholastic library was politely refused, as was the invitation
for Mariafels to send a representative to a musical history
conference.

Only since the Abbot Pius, who at an advanced age had
begun to take a lively interest in the Bead Game, had there
been a certain traffic and exchange of courtesies, which had
developed into a friendly though not particularly active
relationship. There had been an exchange of books and
mutual hospitalities—Knecht's patron, the old Music Master,
had once spent a few weeks in the monastery as a young man,
copying music manuscripts, and had played on the famous
organ. Knecht knew this and was pleased at the thought of
having been sent to the spot about which his adored master
had told him stories from time to time.

He was received with an unexpected courtesy and deference, which he found almost embarrassing. This was the first
time that Castalia had placed a Bead Game instructor from

the élite at the disposal of the monastery for an undetermined period. He had been advised by Dubois to regard himself at the beginning less as a person than as a representative of Castalia, to accept and to return courtesies and to retain a certain ambassadorial distance. This counsel helped him over his initial nervousness. He also overcame the feeling of strangeness, fear and slight excitement of the first few nights, during which he slept little; but, since the Abbot Gervasius treated him with good-natured and cordial benevolence, he soon felt at home in his new surroundings.

He found pleasure in the freshness and majesty of the landscape—a raw mountainous neighbourhood of crags, lush meadows and valleys, in which fine cattle grazed. He loved the expanse and spaciousness of the old buildings, in which the history of many centuries could be read, and the beauty and simple comforts of his apartments—he had been given two rooms in the upper storey of the rambling guest wing—captivated him. He was reassured by his explorations of the stately little town, with its two churches, cloisters, archives, libraries, Abbot's lodging, numerous courtyards, rambling stables full of well-fed cattle, playing fountains, huge vaulted wine and fruit cellars, two refectories, famous chapter house and well-tended gardens, not to forget the workshops of the lay brothers, coopers, cobbler, tailor, blacksmith, etc. which formed a little village in itself around the largest courtyard.

He already had access to the library, and the organist had shown him the organ and given him permission to play upon it. The manuscript chests lured him greatly, for he was certain that a large number of unpublished and still unknown musical scores of earlier ages awaited him there.

At first there did not seem to be any great hurry for him to start his official functions: it was not a question of days but of weeks before they began to consider the actual reason for his presence in the monastery. From the very first day some of the Fathers, the Abbot himself included, had been pleased to discuss the Bead Game with him, but no mention was made of instruction or any systematic activity. Apart from this, Knecht noticed in the demeanour, style of life and conversation of the Reverend Fathers a tempo which had hitherto been unknown to him—a certain venerable slowness, a deep breathing and good-natured patience which seemed common to them all, even to those who appeared to be by no means lacking in temperament. This was the spirit of their Order: it was the thousand-year-old breath of an ancient, privileged Order and community which had been safeguarded a hundred times in happiness and in sorrow, and in which they participated just as the bees participate in the destinies and fortunes of the hive, sleeping its sleep, sharing its sorrows and trembling when it trembled. At first glance, this Benedictine mode of life, when compared with the Castalian seemed less spiritual, less flexible and to have less acuity and activity, but on the other hand to be more unruffled and immune from influence, to be older and better preserved. A spirit and meaning that had long since become natural seemed to reign here, and Knecht, with curiosity, great interest and also great admiration, allowed this monastic life to take effect upon him—this life, already fifteen hundred years old, and almost the same as it had been before Castalia existed, and which appealed so much to the contemplative side of his nature.

He was a respected guest who received in fact far more respect than was obligatory, but he felt convinced that this was only an outward form and custom and had no bearing whatever upon himself, the spirit of Castalia or the Bead Game, but was simply the majestic politeness of an ancient and greater power towards a younger. He had only been partially prepared for such treatment, and after a while, despite all the comfort of his life at Mariafels, he felt so unsure of himself that he wrote to his authorities for more precise instructions. The Magister Ludi replied in person in a few lines.

"Do not be concerned," read the reply. "if you have to sacrifice an unlimited amount of time to your study of the life at Mariafels. Keep yourself occupied, learn, try to make yourself useful and beloved as far as the Fathers will allow you, but do not force the issue. Never appear to be impatient, and always look as though you had as much leisure as your hosts. Even if you are obliged to act in this manner for a whole year as though it were your first day there as a guest in their house, go forward calmly and behave as though for you, too, another two or even ten more years would make no difference. Look upon it as a contest in the art of patience.

Meditate carefully! Should your leisure time appear to you too protracted, you may devote a few hours daily—not more than four—to some regular work such as the study or copying of manuscripts; but do not on any account give the impression that you are working, and be sure that you find time for everyone who wishes to gossip with you."

Knecht observed these instructions and soon felt much easier in mind. He had until then given far too much thought to his commission for teaching the amateurs of the Bead Game, which was ostensibly the purpose of his present mission, whereas the monastery Fathers had treated him much more as the ambassador of a friendly power whose amicable disposition they wished to retain. When at last the Abbot Gervasius remembered this teaching mission, and sent him as a start a few of the Fathers who had already received their initiation into the Bead Game, and to whom he was now to give extra instruction, to his astonishment and in the beginning to his great disappointment it became apparent that the culture of the noble Game in this hospitable place was of a superficial and dilettantish order, and that they were apparently content with a very moderate standard of playing. On the heels of this discovery another thought slowly dawned upon his mind—that he had not been sent here on account of the Bead Game and to promote its culture in the monastery alone. The task of encouraging the few Fathers who were interested in the Game, and of bringing them to a moderate degree of efficiency in order to increase their contentment, was very easy—all too easy—and could have been accomplished by any other candidate who had not even belonged to the élite. This instruction therefore could not have been the purpose of his mission. He began to realize that he had been sent here less to teach than to learn. At all events, shortly after he imagined that he had seen through this stratagem, his standing in the monastery underwent a sudden change for the better, thereby strengthening his self-confidence; for, despite all the charms and guest privileges, he had begun to look upon his sojourn almost as a punishment. One day, during a conversation with the Abbot, Joseph made a chance reference to the I Ching. The Abbot looked up, asked a few questions, and could not conceal his joy at discovering that his guest was so unexpectedly versed in Chinese and in the

Book of Changes: Gervasius had a predilection for the
I Ching, and even though he understood no Chinese and his
knowledge of the Oracle Book and other Chinese mysteries
was of that harmless superficiality which seemed to suffice for
the present inmates of this monastery in all their scientific
interests, it was easy to see that this intelligent man who, in
comparison with his guest, was so experienced and worldly,
really had an affinity with the spirit of ancient China and
its life.

An unusually animated conversation took place, which for
the first time broke down the barriers of courteous behaviour
between the Abbot and his guest, and which resulted in
Knecht's being requested to give the Reverend Father an
exposition in the I Ching twice a week.

While his relationship with his host, the Abbot, had
blossomed into something more lively and effectual, his
friendship with the organist had also increased. Gradually
this little religious community in which he was living took
him into its confidence, and in addition to this the promises of
the Oracle which he had consulted before leaving Castalia
now began to show signs of fulfilment. Not only had "the
wanderer who carries his possessions with him" reached the
promised sanctuary, but he had also "gained the assiduity of
a young servant." The "wanderer" took it as a good sign
that the promises were now unfolding according to prophecy,
that he really carried his possessions with him, and that he,
too, far from the schools, teachers, comrades, patrons,
benefactors and helpers, far from the native, nourishing and
helpful atmosphere of Castalia, had been able to summon the
spirit and strength within himself to embark upon a useful
and valuable life.

The heralded young servant had approached him in the
figure of a seminarist called Anton; and even if this young
man was later to play no part in Knecht's life, he was at that
time, in that strange transitional period of his first days in the
monastery, a hint, a harbinger of new and greater things, a
prophet of future events. Anton, a silent but spirited and
apparently talented youth, almost mature enough to be
accepted into the noviciate, quite often met the bead-player
whose origin and art he found so mysterious, whereas the
remainder of the little band of seminarists, in their segregated

wing to which no guest had access, remained quite unknown to him and were kept strictly out of sight. These pupils were not allowed to participate in the Game course. Anton, however, was on duty as a helper in the library several times a week and Knecht, who had entered into conversation with him, noticed more and more that this young man with the dark brown eyes beneath bold black eyebrows was attracted to him with that enthusiasm and readiness for service peculiar to admiring adolescence and boyish love. He had often met with this and on each occasion had felt the desire to escape from it, although he realised it to be a living and important element in the life of the Order. He decided to be doubly cautious in the monastery, for it would be in the nature of an insult to its hospitality should he attempt to influence this youth who was undergoing a religious education. He was also fully aware of the strong vows of chastity that prevailed, and he saw that a boyish passion could become doubly dangerous on this account. The realization that he had at all events to avoid any conflict finally determined his attitude.

In the library, the only place where he came face to face with young Anton, he also made the acquaintance of another, a certain Father Jacobus, whom he had almost overlooked during his first tentative appearances there, but whom in time he learned to know better and grew to love with a grateful veneration such as he had only felt once for his old Music Master. This figure, who was the foremost historian of the Benedictine Order, was at that time a lean and elderly man of about sixty, with a hawklike head and a long sinewy neck. His face, when seen from the front, had something lifeless and extinguished about it, but his profile with the bold chiselled lines of the forehead, the deep furrows above the bridge of the razor-sharp aquiline nose, and the somewhat short but attractively clean cut chin, denoted a decisive and individual personality.

This silent old man who, incidentally, on closer acquaintance could be very temperamental, had his own private table, which was covered with maps and manuscripts, in a small inner room of the library. He seemed to be the only scholar who was really working seriously in this monastery, which possessed such a treasure of priceless books.

We might mention that it was the seminarist Anton who had inadvertently drawn Knecht's attention to Father

Jacobus. He had already noticed that this inner room was treated almost as a private study and was only used when absolutely necessary—and then quietly and respectfully, on tiptoe—although the Father who was working there did not give the impression that he was easily disturbed. One day, the Father having ordered some books from Anton, Joseph saw the latter returning from the inner sanctum: he stood for a moment in the open doorway looking over at the table where the Father was working, with an enthusiastic expression of admiration and awe mixed with that almost tender consideration and readiness to help which good-hearted youths at times display towards bald-pated and fragile old age. Knecht's heart was immediately gladdened at the thought that Anton's enthusiasm for admirable and praiseworthy older men contained no physical element, but at the next moment a second ironical thought crossed his mind: how meagrely scholarship must be represented in this institution when the only actively employed scholar was gaped at like some fabulous animal or some figure out of a saga! However, this tender look of respectful admiration which Anton had cast towards the old man opened Knecht's eyes to the presence of the Father, and from time to time he began to cast glances in his direction as well. He discovered his Roman profile, and gradually many other things about this Father Jacobus, which seemed to indicate that he was a man of unusual spirit and character. He had already known that he was an historian and ranked as one of the greatest authorities on the history of the Benedictine Order.

And then one day the Father spoke to him. He did not use the broad, benevolent, genial and somewhat avuncular tone which seemed to be the style of the house, but invited Joseph simply to pay him a visit in his cell after vespers.

"You will see that I am no expert in the history of Castalia," he said in a soft, almost timid but well modulated voice, "and you will see that I am still less a bead-player, but since—or so it seems to me—our two very different Orders are becoming more and more friendly, I do not wish to be entirely excluded and for my own part should like occasionally to profit by your presence here among us."

He said this in all earnestness, but the soft voice and the old shrewd face gave to his words that strange mixture of seriousness and irony, devotion and gentle scorn, pathos and suggestion of ambiguity such as one may find in the patient courtesies and endless bowings when two holy men or two princes of the Church meet.

This well-known Chinese blend of superiority and scorn, of wisdom and rigid ceremonial, acted as an immediate restorative upon Knecht. He suddenly realised that he had not used this tone—the Magister Ludi Thomas had mastered it to perfection—for a very long time. He accepted the invitation gratefully and with pleasure.

That same evening, when he was searching for the Father's remote lodging at the far end of a quiet side wing and was wondering upon which door to knock, he heard to his amazement the sound of piano music. He stopped and listened. It was a Purcell sonata played modestly and without virtuosity but with accuracy and in perfect tempo. The clear serene music with its sweet triads rang out with friendly intimacy, reminding him of the days at Waldzell when he had practised music of this kind with his friend Ferromonte. He listened with sensuous enjoyment, and waited for the sonata to end. It rang out in the still dim corridor, lonely and unworldly, brave and innocent, childlike and perfect, as all good music does in the unregenerate muteness of the world.

He knocked on the door and heard Father Jacobus call out: "Come in!" The Father received him with modest dignity. Two candles were still burning on the piano. "Yes," he replied to Knecht's question, "I play every evening for half-an-hour or an hour. I finish my daily task at nightfall, and do not read or write during the hours before I go to sleep."

They spoke of music, of Purcell and of Handel, of the age-old musical culture of the Benedictines—that truly musical Order—the history of which Knecht was eager to learn.

The conversation grew animated and touched upon a hundred topics. The old man's historical knowledge seemed truly remarkable, but he did not deny that he had hardly studied the history of Castalia and Castalian thought at all, for he had actually very little interest in the subject. He did not disguise his critical views about this Castalia, whose "Order" he looked upon as an imitation of the Christian Congregations, and a blasphemous imitation at that inasmuch as it had no religion, no God and no Church as its foundation. Knecht listened respectfully to these criticisms, and voiced the opinion that as regards religion, God and Church, other conceptions were possible and had existed apart from the Benedictines and the Roman Catholic Church. No one could deny, he pointed out, that the purity of will and effort of these had had a deep influence on spiritual life.

"I agree with you," said Jacobus. "You are thinking, among others, of the Protestants. They were not able to preserve their religion and Church, but at times they showed great courage and produced some outstanding men. I devoted a few years of my life to studying the different attempts at reconciliation between the hostile creeds and churches, and this actually became one of my favourite studies, in particular the period round about 1700 where we find men like the philosopher and mathematician Leibnitz, or again that remarkable Count Zinzendorf, trying to bring about a reconciliation and to re-unite the enemy brothers. But above all it is the eighteenth century that I found remarkably interesting and equivocal, although its spirit may often seem superficial and dilettantish—and I have studied the Protestants of that period even more closely.

"I once discovered a philologist, teacher and educator of great merit, a Swabian Pietist and a man whose moral influence clearly lasted for at least two hundred years—but we are getting on to different ground there. Let us return to the question of the legitimacy and the spiritual mission of the individual Orders."

"Oh, no!" cried Joseph. "Please continue about this teacher you mentioned. I think I can almost guess his name."

"Well?"

"At first I thought of Francke of Halle, but as you said that he was a Swabian I can think of no one else but Johann Albrecht Bengel."

The old scholar laughed, and a gleam of joy lit up his face. "You surprise me, my friend," he exclaimed excitedly. "It was in fact Bengel whom I had in mind. But where did you learn about him—or is it a foregone conclusion that in your amazing Province one is familiar with such abstruse and forgotten names and things? You can rest assured that were you to ask all the Fathers, teachers and pupils of our monastery, including those of the past few generations, not one of them would ever have heard of that name."

"There are few people in Castalia who have heard of him—perhaps no one with the exception of myself and a couple of my friends. I was once studying the eighteenth century and Pietism, but for my private ends alone, and in the course of those studies I came across one or two Swabian theologians who aroused my admiration and respect, and in particular Bengel, for he seemed to me to be the ideal teacher and leader of youth. I was so intrigued by this man that I even had his portrait photographed from an old print and kept it for a long time on my work table."

The Father's laugh rang out once more. "We have really met under the most unusual auspices," he said. "It is extraordinary that both you and I should have stumbled across this forgotten man in the course of our studies, but what is even stranger is the fact that this Swabian Protestant could have succeeded in influencing almost simultaneously a Benedictine Father and a Castalian bead-player! Besides, I imagine your Bead Game to be an art which requires a great deal of fantasy, and I am surprised that so sober a man as Bengel could have attracted you so much."

It was now Knecht's turn to laugh.

"Well," he said. "If you consider for a moment Bengel's studies on the Revelation of St. John the Divine, and recall his interpretation of the prophecies in that book, you must admit that our friend was not altogether lacking in the antithesis of sobriety."

"I agree," replied the Father serenely. "And how do you account for such contradictions?"

"If you will forgive me if I sound frivolous, I should say that what Bengel lacked and what he was unconsciously striving and yearning for was the Bead Game. I count him among the unrecognised forerunners and ancestors of our Game."

"It seems a little audacious," Jacobus replied with cautious gravity, "to annex Bengel of all people for your Honour Roll of ancestors. How exactly do you justify this claim?"

"It was a joke, of course, but one that can be defended. While he was still young and was busy on his great biblical work, Bengel once informed a friend that he hoped to compile

a work of encyclopædic dimensions incorporating and classifying all the knowledge of his age symmetrically and syn-
optically within one central system. That is nothing other
than the function of the Bead Game."

"It is the encyclopædic thought with which the whole
eighteenth century flirted," exclaimed the Father.

"It certainly is," agreed Joseph. "But Bengel did not
merely strive for a parallelism of science and fields of research
but a unification, an organic arrangement, and he was on the
way to a quest for a common denominator. Now that is one
of the elementary thoughts of the Bead Game, and I must
point out further that had Bengel been in possession of a
similar system to that of our Game he would have been
spared the great errors which he made in his conversion of
the prophetic numbers, his prediction of the anti-Christ and
the Thousand-year Kingdom. Bengel did not quite find the
longed-for direction towards a common goal for the varied
talents which he possessed, and so he devoted his mathematical genius along with his philological acuity to that fabulous
"calendar," a mixture of ἀκρίβεια and fantasy, which
occupied him for so many years."

"It is a good thing you are not an historian," insisted
Jacobus, "for you are too inclined to whimsical speculation—
but I understand what you mean. I am only a pedant in my
own subject."

It was a productive conversation, which led to better
understanding and to the beginnings of a friendship. To the
learned Father it seemed more than a coincidence, or at least
a very strange one, that both of them—he in his Benedictine
and the young man in his Castalian studies—had discovered
the poor Würtemburger monastery preceptor, that man who
was tender-hearted but steadfast as a rock, extravagant and
at the same time sober: there must have been something
behind it all which had created this bond and had exerted so
obscure a magnetic influence upon them both. From that
evening onwards, which had begun with the Purcell sonata,
that something and that bond was there.

Jacobus enjoyed the exchange of ideas which ensued with
so schooled yet so malleable a young spirit, for this was
indeed a rare pleasure for him. For Knecht, on the other hand,

this relationship with the historian and the schooling he now began to receive was a new stage on the path of awakening, in which light he now considered his life.

To sum up: from Father Jacobus he learned history, the laws and anomalies governing the study of history and its writing. In the years following he learned, too, to see the present and his own life as historical reality.

Their conversations often led to real disputes, attacks and justifications, but in the beginning it was Father Jacobus who showed the greatest bellicosity. The more he grew to know the spirit of his young friend, the more it pained him to realise that this promising young man had grown up without the discipline of a religious education and in the pseudo-discipline of an intellectual-æsthetic spirituality alone. Everything which he found reprehensible in Knecht's mode of thinking he attributed to the "modern" Castalian spirit, with its remoteness from reality and its tendency towards frivolous abstractions; and when Knecht surprised him with unspoiled concepts and utterances which approached his own way of thinking, he would rejoice in the fact that his young friend's sound nature had achieved so powerful a resistance to his Castalian upbringing. Joseph accepted his criticism of Castalia very calmly, and when the old man in his enthusiasm and passion seemed to go a little too far he countered his attacks dispassionately. Moreover, among the Father's unfavourable utterances against Castalia there were some which Joseph was obliged to recognise, and on one point he learned to change his opinion completely during his stay at Mariafels. It was the question of the relationship between the Castalian spirit and world history, which the Father described as "completely lacking in historical sense."

"You mathematicians and bead-players," he insisted, "have distilled for yourselves a world history which is made up of the several histories of the spirit and art, while your own is bloodless and lacking in reality. You have an intimate knowledge of the degeneration of Latin syntax in the second or third centuries and have no conception of Alexander, Cæsar or Jesus Christ. You deal with world history as a mathematician deals with mathematics, where nothing exists except laws and formulas—where there is no reality, good or

evil, no time, no yesterday or to-morrow but only an eternal
flat mathematical present."

"But how is one to deal with history without bringing
some order into it?" asked Knecht.

"Naturally one must bring order into it," growled Jacobus.
"Every science is among other things an ordering, a simpli-
fication, a making digestible of that which the spirit cannot
digest. We believe that we have recognised in history
certain laws, and we try, once we recognise them, to take
heed of historical truth, just as for example, when an
anatomist dissects a body, he does not find himself faced with
fresh and surprising discoveries but with an empirical organ,
muscle, ligament and bone-world beneath the epidermis and
finds a fixed scheme on the pattern which resides in his own
body. If, however, the anatomist only recognises his scheme
and overlooks the single individual reality of his objects, then
he is a Castalian and a bead-player who is using mathematics
on a most unsuitable object. Whoever elects to study history,
as far as I am concerned, may bring to bear the most pathetic
and childish belief in the classifying power of our spirit and
methods, but apart from this and in spite of it he should have
respect for the incomprehensible truth, reality and singularity
of events. To deal with history, my friend, is no jest and no
irresponsible game. History presumes in advance that one is
striving with something impossible and yet necessary and of
the greatest importance. To deal with history means to
abandon oneself to chaos and yet to retain a belief in the
ordination and the meaning. It is a very serious task, young
man, and perhaps also a tragic one."

Among the pronouncements of the Father which Knecht
communicated in letters to his friends at that time is another
phrase which can be taken as characteristic.

"Great men are for the young like currants in the cake of
world history. They have their own particular substance,
admittedly, and it is not so easy and so simple as one might
imagine to differentiate the really great from the pseudo-
great. In the case of the latter, it is the historical moment and
their conjecture and grasping of it that gives the appearance
of greatness. There is no lack of historians and biographers,
not to mention journalists, for whom this conjecture and
seizing of opportunity will mean that the momentary success

already indicates greatness. The corporal who from one day to the next becomes a dictator, or the courtesan who for a short while manages to dominate over the good or evil caprices of a sovereign, are favourite figures for such historians. Idealistically inclined youths, on the contrary, prefer tragic failures, martyrs who have arrived too early or too late on the historical scene. For myself, being admittedly first and foremost an historian of our Benedictine Order, the most attractive, astonishing and most worthy of study in world history are neither individuals nor their coups, successes and failures: my love and insatiable curiosity is reserved for such a phenomenon as our Congregation, which is one of those very long-lived organisations in which an attempt has been made to garner the spirit and soul of man and to educate and transform it, to ennoble it through education as opposed to eugenics, through the spirit and not through the blood, in order to make it capable of service as well as rule. In the history of the Greeks, it is not the starry firmament of the heroes and the importunate turmoil of the Agora, but attempts like those of the Pythagorean and the Platonic academies, in the history of the Chinese no other phenomenon so much as the longevity of the Confucian system, and in our Western history, above all, the Christian Church and in particular the serving Orders within its framework which seem to me to be historical values of the first degree. That an adventurer may once have had the luck to conquer or found a kingdom lasting some fifty or a hundred years, that a well-meaning idealist, king or emperor has striven for a more honourable type of politics or to realise some cultural wish-dream, that under conditions of high pressure a people or a community has been capable of unheard of achievements or feats of endurance has for me long since been of less interest than the fact that ever and again attempts have been made to found such edifices as our Order, and that certain of these attempts have been able to endure for a thousand or two thousand years. I will not speak of the Holy Church itself, for it stands outside discussion for us believers; but that congregations such as the Benedictine, Dominican and later the Society of Jesus, etc., etc., have lasted for many centuries, and after this length of time, despite all developments, degenerations, adaptations and constraints have retained their countenance, voice, gesture

and individual soul is for me the most remarkable and
venerable phenomenon of history."

Knecht admired the Father equally in his angry injustice.
At that time he had no conception at all as to whom Father
Jacobus really was, and had seen in him only a profound and
genial scholar. He knew nothing of the fact that he was also
in himself a world historical figure who had played a great
part in its creation, that he was the leading politician of his
Order and was approached from many sides for information,
details and advice as a specialist in political history and
contemporary politics. For about two years—until his first
vacation—Knecht associated with Father Jacobus entirely as
a scholar, and knew absolutely nothing of the reverse side of
his life, activities, vocation and influence. This learned monk
had understood how to keep silent even in friendship, and his
brothers in the Order also practised this art to a more subtle
degree than Joseph would have given them credit for.

After two years Knecht had adjusted himself to the life of
the monastery as fully as any guest or outsider could possibly
have done. He had been of assistance to the organist from
time to time by modestly helping him to bring the thin
threads of age-old tradition into his tiny motet choir. He had
made various finds in the monastic musical archives, and had
despatched a few copies of musical works to Waldzell and
especially to the Music Master; he had inaugurated a small
beginners' class of bead-players, in which the young Anton
was one of the most eager pupils; and had taught the Abbot
Gervasius, if not Chinese, at least the manipulation of the
yarrow sticks and a superior method of meditation upon the
maxims of the Oracle Book. The Abbot had grown quite used
to him, and had long since given up his attempts to make his
guest drink wine. His half-yearly reports in reply to official
enquiries from the Magister Ludi as to whether he were
satisfied with Knecht were panegyrical. The attendance lists
of Knecht's Game Course were examined more closely than
the Abbot's reports: the standard was found to be modest, but
satisfaction was expressed with the way in which the teacher
had adapted himself to the spirit and customs of the monastery. But the thing that pleased and really surprised the
Castalian authorities most—without, of course, their informing their emissary of this—was the constant, confidential and

positively friendly relationship that existed between Knecht
and the famous Father Jacobus. This intercourse had borne
all manner of fruit, about which we have allowed ourselves to
deal at some length, or rather about the particular fruit that
Knecht appreciated most. It ripened slowly, very slowly, and
matured, hesitant and distrustful as the seeds of mountain
trees which have been transplanted on to fertile plainland.
These seeds, entrusted to a luxuriant soil and mild climate,
bear within them as a legacy the tardiness and mistrust in
which their forbears have grown and the slow tempo of
which has become an inherited characteristic. Thus the
shrewd old Father, accustomed as he was to controlling any
possibility of being influenced, very slowly and grudgingly
allowed all that which his young friend and colleague had
brought him from the opposite pole of the Castalian spirit to
take root; and it gradually bore seed. Of all that he had
experienced in his years at Mariafels, what Knecht appreciated most, and what seemed to him above price, was a
gradual increase of confidence and an expansion on the part
of the experienced old man from an apparently hopeless
beginning, and his slow-growing understanding not only for
the person of his young admirer but also for that in him
which was of specific Castalian imprint. Step by step the
young man, seemingly only a pupil, had led the attentive and
learning Father, who in the beginning had been wont to use
the words "Castalian" or "bead-player" with ironical inflec-
tions or even as outspoken insults, to recognise—at first to
tolerate and finally to admit his respect for—this other
conception and Order, this new attempt to build a spiritual
aristocracy. The Father ceased to carp at the extreme youth
of this Order, which had admittedly only been in existence
for about two hundred years and was therefore fifteen
hundred years younger than the Benedictine Order, ceased to
see in the Bead Game nothing more than an æsthetic dandy-
ism and to brush aside the idea that any fraternisation and
alliance between the two disparate Orders was out of the
question.

Joseph did not realise for a long time that the authorities
saw in this partial winning over of Father Jacobus, which he
himself looked upon as a completely personal and private
piece of good fortune, the peak of his Mariafels mission and

achievement. Now and then he would reflect somewhat inconclusively as to how things stood with regard to his task in the monastery, as to whether he was actually of use and was achieving results in this place, which had seemed at first a promotion and distinction much envied by his competitors, or whether it would not in the long run prove to be an inglorious sinecure and a relegation to a dead end. But there was something to be learned everywhere, so why not here? In the Castalian sense, however, this monastery—apart from the scholarly Father Jacobus—was no flower garden or shining example of learning, and he could not be certain that in his isolation among these mediocre dilettantes he was not growing rusty in the Bead Game. His lack of aspiration as well as his highly developed *amor fati* helped him at that time in his uncertainty. He felt, by and large, that his life as a guest and small specialist teacher in this cosy old monastic world was to a certain extent more pleasant than it had been among the ambitious members of his most recent Waldzell circle, and that, should destiny wish to detain him for ever in this little colonial outpost, he would even try to alter his life a little by manœuvring things so that some of his friends might come and join him, or at least would request a long yearly vacation in Castalia, but beyond this he would try to be content with his lot.

The reader of this biographical sketch may perhaps have been waiting for a description of the other side of Knecht's life in the monastery—the religious side. We can only offer him a few very cautious hints on this subject.

It is not only probable but quite clear from many of his later utterances and from much of what we know of his later behaviour that he came in close contact with religion and a daily practised Christianity in Mariafels. The question as to whether, or to what extent, he became a Christian there we must leave unanswered, as this does not come within the scope of our research. From the respect for religion which was fostered in Castalia he had obtained a certain inner reverence which we might call piety, and during his school days he had been well instructed in the Christian doctrine in its classical form, especially in the study of music. Above all he was familiar with the sacrament of the Mass and the rite of High Office.

Among these Benedictines he had now become acquainted, not without amazement and respect, with a living religion which he had previously only known theoretically and historically. He had attended many of their services and, since the day when Father Jacobus had first entrusted some of his writings to him and whose conversations he had allowed to influence him, the phenomenon of this Christianity had become a visible reality—this Christianity which throughout the centuries had become so out-dated, antiquated and petrified, and had yet refreshed and renewed itself once more at its source, leaving behind the modern and victorious of yesterday. He did not defend himself earnestly against the idea that was born of his conversations with Jacobus and the Father's more closely revealed thoughts—that possibly the Castalian culture, likewise, might be no more than a worldly and transitory late by-product of the western Christian culture and might one day be absorbed and incorporated in it once more.

Be that as it may, he once told the Father that his own particular place and service was once and for all within Castalia and not within the Benedictine Order, that he had to work in Mariafels and to keep an open mind as to whether the Order of which he was a member laid claim to an eternal or only to a temporal existence. He would have considered his conversion only as a very worthy form of escape. In a like manner he had revered Johann Albrecht Bengel who, in his age, had served in a small and transitory church without lacking thereby any service to the Eternal. Piety, which may be described as orthodox service and loyalty to the point of life devotion, is possible in every creed and in every stage of development, and for the rectitude and value of each personal piety this service and loyalty is the only valid test.

Knecht's stay with the Fathers had lasted for more than a year when one day a mysterious guest arrived in the monastery, who was kept away from him with the utmost caution and to whom he was not even allowed a fleeting introduction. This made him curious, and he began to watch this stranger who, as a matter of fact, only stayed a few days but who had succeeded in arousing all manner of speculations in his mind. The religious habit that he wore Knecht believed to be a disguise. He had long sessions with the Abbot and with Father Jacobus behind closed doors, and frequently received and sent dispatches, and Knecht, who knew, by reputation at least, the political connections and traditions of the monastery, guessed that he must be some high statesman on a secret misision or a prince travelling incognito. While he was thus occupied with his musings he recalled also the several other guests who had appeared during the past month and who, on second thoughts, seemed mysterious and somehow significant to him. At this moment his thoughts turned to the "Chief of Police," the friendly Dubois, and of his request that he should occasionally have an eye for such occurrences; and, although he still felt no particular desire to send any such reports, his conscience smote him because he had not written to him all this time and felt that he was probably a great disappointment to this well-intentioned man.

He immediately wrote a long letter to Dubois trying to justify his silence, and in order to give some substance to his letter related to him a little of his relationship with Father Jacobus. He had no idea how carefully and by whom this particular letter was read.

Chapter Five

THE MISSION

THIS FIRST STAY OF Knecht's in the monastery had lasted nearly two years, and he was then in his thirty-seventh year. One morning, towards the end of this period as guest at Mariafels, and some two months after he had written his long letter to Dubois, he was summoned to the Abbot's study. He had thought that the affable old man might have felt an inclination to have a little talk about the Chinese, and announced himself without delay.

Gervasius came forward to meet him with a letter in his hand.

"I have been honoured with a commission for you, my worthy friend," he cried cheerfully in his comfortable and patronising manner, lapsing immediately into the ironical, teasing tone which he had adopted as the form of expression he thought most suited to the unclarified friendship that existed between the religious and the Castalian Order, and which, incidentally, had been instigated by Father Jacobus. "Oh! and by the way—all my respects to your Magister Ludi. He certainly knows how to write a letter! He has written to me in Latin—the good Lord alone knows why. One never knows when you Castalians do something whether it is meant to be polite, mocking, respectful or merely an object lesson. So your venerable Dominus writes to me in Latin—but in a Latin such as no one has ever been capable of using in our old Order with the possible exception of Father Jacobus. It is a Latin that definitely originates from the Ciceronian school but is flavoured with a well-balanced pinch of Church Latin, which naturally leaves one in doubt as to whether it is meant ironically, naïvely as bait for we 'black birds,' or arises simply from an irresistible desire to frolic, stylise and embellish. In any case the most worthy man has written to say that they are desirous of seeing you once more and of embracing you, and they also wish to ascertain how far your stay among us semi-barbarians has corrupted and influenced your style and morals. In short, if I have read this lengthy literary masterpiece aright, you have been granted a vacation, and I have therefore been asked to dispatch my guest to Waldzell for an unspecified time but not for ever, since the authorities apparently have the intention of your returning, if we are agreeable. In any case I should never have been capable of interpreting all the subtleties of this letter, and Magister Thomas could certainly not have expected it of me, so you must excuse me. You may now go and consider whether and when you will leave. We shall miss you, my dear friend, and should you remain away from us for too long we shall not fail to reclaim you from your authorities."

In the letter he had been handed Knecht was informed that a holiday had been granted him, in order that he might relax and also that he might discuss matters with his superiors; that he was expected forthwith in Waldzell. Unless the Abbot expressly wished it, ran the letter, he need not wait for the completion of the current Game Course for beginners. The old Music Master also sent his greetings, and as he read these lines, Joseph gave a start and began to reflect: how came it that the writer of this letter, the Magister Ludi, had been entrusted with the forwarding of this greeting, which was hardly appropriate in an official letter? There must have been a conference of the entire Pedagogy, including the ex-Magister Musicæ. Well! the sessions and decisions of the Pedagogy were no concern of his; but this greeting moved him strangely, and had a remarkably familiar ring. At all events, whatever questions may have been discussed at the meeting, this message certainly showed that they had discussed him, Joseph Knecht. Was something new afoot? Was he to be recalled, and would this be an advancement or a setback? But the letter spoke of a vacation! Yes, indeed, he was delighted with the idea of this holiday and would have liked to set out on the following day, but would have at least to say good-bye to his pupils and leave instructions for them. Anton would be very sad at his departure—and he would also have to say farewell to several of the Fathers. He thought of Father Jacobus, and to his astonishment felt a slight pang of regret which told him that his heart inclined more to Mariafels than he had realised.

Much of that to which he had been accustomed and which had been dear to him was missing in the monastery, and moreover, two years of absence and privation from Castalia had made it appear even more beautiful; but at this moment he recognised quite clearly that he possessed something in Father Jacobus that was irreplaceable and would be missing in Castalia. At the same time he realised more clearly than ever all that he had experienced and learned here, and although he felt a certain joyful confidence at the thought of his journey, of seeing Waldzell again, of the Bead Game and his holiday, he would have been far less jubilant had he not had the certainty of returning to Mariafels.

He came to a sudden decision. Seeking out Father Jacobus he told him the news of his forthcoming holiday in Waldzell, and admitted that to his own surprise beneath the joy of returning home there was another joy—that of returning to Mariafels. As this was largely due to the presence of Father Jacobus, he plucked up the courage to ask him, as a great favour, whether on his return he would give him a little instruction, even if it were only an hour or two each week.

Father Jacobus laughed protestingly, and once more paid him a polished ironical compliment—that a simple monk like himself could only stand in mute admiration and could only shake his head in wonder before the unsurpassed comprehensiveness of Castalian culture. Joseph, however, noticed that the implied refusal was not to be taken too seriously for, as the Father gave him his hand on taking leave of him, he said in a friendly manner that he was not to worry his head about the request he had made and that he would be pleased to do anything in his power to grant it. He said good-bye to Joseph affectionately.

Knecht set out for his holidays gay at heart and with the knowledge that his sojourn in the monastery had not been in vain. He felt like a boy again, but very soon realised that he was no longer a boy or even a youth. He was made acutely aware of it by the feeling of shame and inner contradiction that checked him immediately he wished to give way to a gesture, a cry of joy or some childish outburst in his present mood of freedom and school holiday happiness. No, what had once been spontaneous and a release of his feelings—such as a joyous whistle to the birds in the trees, a loud and lively marching song or a gay frolicking dance—he found no longer natural, for the result would have been stiff and artificial, would have been stupid and childish. He realised that he was now a man—young in heart and in body maybe but no longer free to devote himself to the moment and to the transitory mood—aware, fettered and constrained to duty. But why? Because of an office—because of his task of representing his Province and Order among the monastery folk? No, it was on account of the Order itself, the hierarchy into which, as a result of this sudden self-analysis, he found himself incorporated and welded. It was the responsibility, the embrace of the General and the Higher, which made many young men appear old and many old men young, which held one fast and at the same time supported one, curtailing one's freedom like the stake to which a young tree is bound and taking away one's innocence while demanding an ever more immaculate purity.

In Monteport he visited the old Music Master, who in his youth, as we have already mentioned, had once been a guest at Mariafels where he studied Benedictine music. The old man asked him many questions about the monastery. He was somewhat lighter in heart and more absent-minded, but looked stronger and more serene than he had done at their last meeting. The weariness had partially disappeared from his face, and although he looked no younger he seemed even more handsome and sedate now that he had laid down his office. Joseph was surprised when he asked after the organ, the music chests and the choral music at Mariafels, when he enquired as to whether a tree in the cloisters was still standing but seemed to evince no interest in his own activities there, in the Bead Game course or in the object of his holiday. The old man did, however, say something about his forthcoming journey, which proved useful.

"I have learned," he said in jesting tones, "that you have become something of a diplomat—not a very seemly vocation I feel, but it appears that they are contented with you. You can take that whichever way you like. Should it not be your ambition to remain for ever in that profession, then be on your guard, Joseph! I think they intend to embroil you! You must protect yourself—and don't forget, you are quite entitled to do so! No . . . you must not ask me any questions, for I cannot tell you any more. You will soon see for yourself."

Despite this warning, which he felt as a thorn in his side, he found, on his arrival in Waldzell, a pleasure at homecoming such as he had never experienced before. He felt that this Waldzell was not only his country and the most beautiful spot in the world but that during his absence it had become even more lovely and interesting—or perhaps he was now seeing it in a new perspective, having returned with heightened powers of perception. And this applied not only to the gates, towers, trees, the river, courtyard and halls, the figures and well-known faces, for during this vacation he felt an ever-increasing appreciation for the Order and for the Bead Game as though with the grateful understanding of a prodigal, of a traveller who has grown more mature and more intelligent.

"It seems to me," he confided to his friend Tegularius, at the end of a lively panegyric in favour of Waldzell and Castalia, "that I have spent all my years here asleep—that I was happy, but only unconsciously so. It is now as though

I have awakened, and can see everything sharply and clearly, bearing the stamp of reality."

His vacation was in the nature of a festivity for him, particularly the Games and the discussions with comrades in the élite circle of the Vicus Lusorum, the fact of seeing his friends again and the *genius loci* of Waldzell. But, to be sure, this high peak of gaiety and happiness was first reached after his reception by the Magister Ludi, for until then it had been mingled with a sense of fear.

The Magister Ludi had put fewer questions to him than Knecht had anticipated. He had hardly mentioned the beginner's course or Joseph's studies in the musical archives, but could not hear enough about Father Jacobus and continually brought the conversation round to him, and no detail that Joseph could relate seemed to be too insignificant.

That they were pleased with him—very pleased indeed— and with his mission to the Benedictines was obvious not only from the Magister's great cordiality but far more from the behaviour of M. Dubois, to whom the Magister Ludi had immediately sent him.

"You have accomplished your task admirably," the Police Chief said with a little smile. "My instinct really must have been at fault when I discouraged your mission to the monastery. That you have won over Father Jacobus in addition to the Abbot and made him better disposed towards Castalia is a great deal—far more than anyone would have dared to hope."

Two days later the Magister Ludi invited him to dinner with Dubois and the headmaster of the élite school— Zbinden's successor—and after dinner the new Music Master and the Archivist to the Order also put in an appearance, along with two other members of the Pedagogy, one of whom accompanied him later to the guest house for a long conversation. This invitation now drew Knecht publicly into the innermost circle of candidates for high posts, and raised an immediately perceptible barrier between himself and the average members of the Game élite. The more sophisticated Knecht felt this immediately. In addition he was given four weeks of leisure and a customary official's pass, valid for the guest houses of the Province. Although no duties of any kind were imposed upon him—not even the obligation to report as to his whereabouts—it soon became apparent that he was being watched by his superiors, for when he paid a few visits and made a few excursions to Keuperheim, Hirsland and the College of Sinology he instantly received invitations from the high functionaries of those places. In actual fact, he was introduced to the entire Pedagogy and most of the Magisters and instructors.

Had it not been for these official invitations and introductions, his holiday would have been more in the nature of a return to the world and the freedom of his post-graduate days. He curtailed his visits, partly out of consideration for Tegularius, who found any interruption of their reunion difficult to bear, and partly on account of the Bead Game, for he was very anxious to learn and take part in the newest exercises and problems: in this Tegularius was of invaluable service to him. His other close friend, Ferromonte, was now on the new Music Master's staff, and Knecht only saw him on two occasions. He found him hard at work and happy in his work. He had just undertaken an onerous task in musical history— the study of Greek music and its survival in the folk songs and dances of the Balkan countries. Ferromonte told his friend excitedly of his latest work and discoveries; it dealt with the period of the gradual decline of Baroque music, approximately from the end of the eighteenth century onwards, and the absorption of new musical matter into it from the side of Slav folk music.

Knecht spent the best part of this happy holiday in Waldzell occupied with the Bead Game and, with Tegularius, practising the extracts from a private session which the Magister had given for advanced players during the last two semesters. After a two years' abstinence he lived once more to the full in the noble Game world, the magic of which seemed so bound up with and as indispensable to his life as music.

He was not sent for by the Magister Ludi until the last few days of his vacation to discuss his Mariafels mission and his immediate future and tasks. Opening the interview in a conversational tone and then becoming more earnest and compelling, the Magister told Joseph of a plan in which the Pedagogy, with the support of nearly all the Magisters as well as Dubois, was very interested, namely, the creation in the future of a permanent Castalian embassy in the Holy See in Rome. The historic moment had arrived, Master Thomas elaborated in his winning and exquisite tones, or was at least at hand, when the century-old gulf between Rome and the Order should be bridged, for in the event of any future dangers they would undoubtedly have common enemies, would be partners in destiny and natural allies. In the long run the present position with the two powers of the world whose historical task was the preservation and culture of the spirit of peace living side by side and almost in alienation, was highly undignified. Despite grave losses, the Roman Church had survived the last great war period, had been regenerated and had purified itself, while the worldly cultural centres of science and the humanities had succumbed in the general decline of culture. Out of their ruins the Order and Castalian thought had arisen, but on account of its illustrious age, precedence had to be conceded to the Church. It was the older and more distinguished, and also a power that had weathered many storms. It was primarily a question of awakening and cultivating in the Roman Church a realization of the affinity between the two powers, and of making them see that it would be mutually advantageous to hang together in all future crises.

Knecht thought: "Oh! so they want to send me to Rome— and possibly for ever!" And then, recalling the old Music Master's warning, made up his mind to put forward a defence.

An important step forward in this development, the Magister Thomas continued, and one which had long been desired on the part of Castalia, had resulted from Joseph's mission to Mariafels. This mission, in itself only an attempt, a courteous and noncommital gesture, had been undertaken at the invitation of the Catholic partner without ulterior motives, or else the Pedagogy would obviously not have sent a politically ignorant bead-player but some younger official from M. Dubois' office. But this attempt, this innocent little mission, had had surprisingly good results, for a leading spirit of present day Catholicism, Father Jacobus, had become closer acquainted with and had gained a more favourable conception of the Castalian spirit, which he had previously categorically rejected. For this they had to thank Joseph for the part that he had played. Herein, therefore, lay the meaning and success of his mission, and from this point onwards, not only had the whole attempt at an approach, but particularly Knecht's mission and work, to be further examined and continued. He had been granted a vacation which could, if necessary, be prolonged. He had now been made familiar with the matter, the Magister pointed out, and furthermore, he had been introduced to most of the members of the Pedagogy, who had pronounced their confidence in him and had instructed the Magister Ludi to send him back to Mariafels, with a special task and wider powers, where he would be sure of a friendly reception.

He paused for a moment, as though to give his listener time to voice an opinion, but the latter made it clear by a courteous gesture of devotion that he had understood and was ready for the commission.

"The commission which I now have to give you," went on the Magister, "is as follows: we are planning sooner or later to inaugurate a permanent representation of our Order in the Vatican, and if possible a reciprocal one. We, as the younger organisation, are prepared to observe a very respectful but by no means servile attitude towards Rome, and we shall willingly accord them precedence and take second place. It is possible—I know no more about this than M. Dubois—that the Pope might even agree to our request to-day, but what we must expressly avoid is a rebuff. However, there is a certain well-known man, to whom we have access, whose opinion has the greatest possible weight in Rome—Father Jacobus. Now your commission is to return to the Benedictine Monastery, take up residence there again, continue your studies and hold a harmless Bead Game course, but in particular you are to devote all your attention and solicitude towards winning Father Jacobus over to our side so that he may one day inform you that he has recommended us in Rome. This time, therefore the ultimate goal of your mission is accurately defined. As to how long you will need before you achieve this is quite immaterial. We think that it will take at least a year, but it might easily be two or even more. You know the Benedictine tempo and have learned to adapt yourself to it. Under no circumstances must we give the impression of impatience or eagerness, and the whole undertaking must be allowed to ripen quite naturally. Don't you agree? I hope that you are content with this commission? If not, I must ask you to raise any objections that you may have. You may have a few days to think the matter over, if you wish."

Knecht who, as a result of many recent conversations was no longer surprised, replied that time for reflection was superfluous, accepted the commission obediently, but added: "You are aware that tasks of this kind succeed best when the one to whom they are entrusted, has no inner resistances or inhibitions to contend with. I have no personal objection to this one for I understand its importance and hope to be able to fulfil it, but as I feel a certain fear and anxiety as to my future, will you be kind enough, Magister, to give an ear to my own private, selfish requests and views. I am, as you know, a bead-player, and as a result of my having been sent to stay with the Fathers I have already missed two full years of study, have learnt nothing new and have neglected my art, and now this will mean another year's delay and probably more. I therefore request that frequent short vacations in Waldzell be granted to me and that I also be put in radio communication with the lectures and special exercises of your seminary for advanced players."

"I grant that gladly," said the Magister with a certain note of dismissal in his voice. But Knecht added that he was also afraid that if the Mariafels plan succeeded he might be sent to Rome or would perhaps be used again for some diplomatic service.

"And this prospect," he concluded, "would have a depressing and constraining influence on my work in the monastery, for to be relegated permanently to the diplomatic service would be in complete opposition to my own wishes."

The Magister frowned and raised a reprimanding finger.

"You mentioned relegation, and I find that word singularly ill-chosen for no one has had the slightest intention of relegating but rather of conferring distinction and advancement. I am not empowered to give you any information or to make any promises as to the way in which you will be made use of later, but I can, everything considered, appreciate your hesitation, and shall presumably be capable of assistance to you should your fears prove right. And now listen to me: you have a certain gift of making yourself agreeable and beloved —an ill-wisher might even call you a charmer—and this gift may possibly have influenced the Pedagogy in their decision

to send you to Mariafels for a second time; but do not make
too much use of your gift, Joseph, and do not try to put a
premium on the price of your achievement. Should you
succeed with Father Jacobus, that will be the right moment
for you to address a personal request to the authorities.
To-day it seems to me to be premature. Let me know when
you are ready to set out."

Joseph received these words in silence, and took more note
of the hidden benevolence behind them than of the admonition. He left shortly afterwards for Mariafels.

He soon found the security which a specified commission
can give to be very salutary. Furthermore, the task he had
been entrusted with was important and admirable inasmuch
as it accorded with his innermost wishes, namely, to associate
with Father Jacobus as much as possible and to gain his full
friendship. That his new mission was taken very seriously,
and that he was now considered promoted in rank, was
noticeable by the changed behaviour of the monastery's chief
dignitary, the Abbot. His behaviour was no less cordial, but a
shade more respectful, than before. Joseph was no longer
the young guest of no standing towards whom one was
pleasant on account of his personality and out of kindly
regard for his origin. He was now received and treated like
a high Castalian official almost like an ambassadorial pleni-
potentiary. No longer blind to these things, Knecht drew his
own conclusions.

At all events, he could discover no change in his relationship with Father Jacobus; the friendliness and joy with which
he had been greeted, and the way the Father had immediately
referred to their projected work together without his having
to be reminded, touched him deeply.

His working plan and daily routine now took on quite a
new countenance and colour. In his curriculum the Bead
Game course was no longer of primary importance, and it
was no longer a question of his studying in the musical
archives or of collaborating with the organist; first and
foremost now was his instruction with Father Jacobus. They
covered several branches of the science of history simultaneously, for the Father initiated his prize scholar not only
into the pre- and early history of the Benedictine Order but
also into the sources of the early Middle Ages, and at certain

specified hours would read one of the old chroniclers with him in the original text. It pleased the Father when one day Knecht importuned him with a request that Anton should be allowed to participate in these lessons, but did not find it difficult to convince him that even the best intentioned third party could not help but merely seriously hinder this type of private tuition; and it turned out that Anton, who had known nothing of Knecht's intercession, was only invited to attend the readings from the chroniclers and was highly delighted with this privilege. Without a doubt these hours were a distinction, a joy and a spur of th? highest type for this young novice, upon whose life we are lacking any further documentation: as a listener he was able to participate in some small measure in the work and exchange of ideas of the two purest spirits and most original brains of his time. Knecht's return service to the Father consisted in giving him a cursive introduction, with occasional epigraphic readings from original sources, into the history and structure of Castalia and the underlying ideas of the Bead Game. In these, the pupil became the teacher and the worthy teacher an attentive listener, but often a critic and an interrogator who was difficult enough to convince. His distrust of the whole Castalian mentality had not been quieted: because he found in it a lack of religious principle he doubted its value and its capacity to produce a really serious and acceptable type of man, even though he found himself in the presence of such a noble example of this education in the person of Knecht.

Although, as far as this were possible, he had long since undergone a kind of conversion through Knecht's instruction and example, and had for some time been resolved to support the advances of Castalia to Rome, this mistrust would not be completely stilled. The notes which Knecht jotted down at the time are full of glaring examples of this mistrust, such as the following dialogue.

FATHER JACOBUS: "You are great scholars and æsthetes, you Castalians. You measure the weight of the vowels in an old poem and correlate its formula with a planetary orbit. That is enchanting, but it is a game. Your highest secret and symbol is also a game—the Bead Game. I will admit that you have attempted to raise this pretty game almost to the height of a sacrament, or at least to a means of building it up into one; but sacraments do not ensue from such efforts, and a game always remains a game."

JOSEPH: "You mean, Father, that we lack the foundation of a theology?"

FATHER JACOBUS: "Oh, we won't talk about theology, for you are too far removed from it. You could for example have used a simpler foundation, such as anthropology—a true doctrine and a true knowledge of mankind. You know nothing of mankind, neither his bestiality nor the fact that he was created in the image of God: you only know the Castalian man, a speciality, a caste, an exclusive attempt at breeding."

This task of winning over the Father for Castalia and of convincing him of the value of an alliance between the two Orders was an extraordinary piece of good fortune for Knecht, and during these hours the most favourable and widest fields were covered.

He had been offered a situation which represented so perfectly any desires that he might conceivably have entertained that he soon began to feel certain twinges of conscience: it seemed shameful and unworthy to him to see the esteemed Father sitting trustingly and devotedly opposite to him or walking with him up and down the cloisters, while at the same time being the object and goal of secret political designs and intentions. Knecht could not have endured this situation for long in silence, and was thinking out some way in which he could unmask himself when to his surprise the old man forestalled him.

"My dear friend," he said one day quite inconsequentially, "we have discovered a highly agreeable, and I hope a fruitful, mode of exchange. The two activities which all my life have been most dear to me—learning and teaching—have now found a magnificent combination in our joint work, and for me this has come at the right moment for I am getting old and could not have devised a better cure and rejuvenator than our studies. So, as regards myself, I am in any case the gainer in our exchanges; but on the other hand, my friend, I am not so sure whether you, or rather the people whom you represent, stand to win so much in the affair as they perhaps hope. I should like to guard you against any disappointment in the future and also to allow no misunderstanding to come between us, and so I am sure you will permit a practical old

man to ask you a question: I have naturally often thought
about your stay in our tiny monastery, although it is a great
pleasure to me, and until recently—that is to say, until your
vacation—I thought that I could be safe in surmising that the
meaning and object of your presence here was not altogether
clear to you. Am I correct?" As Knecht agreed, he went on:
"Good! But since your return from Waldzell things have
altered. You no longer think about the reason for your being
here, for you are now well aware of it. Am I right? Excellent!—then I have not judged badly. Presumably I am also
correct in surmising that I know the reason for your presence
here: you have been entrusted with a diplomatic commission
which concerns neither the monastery nor the Reverend
Father Abbot, but no one other than myself. You see—very
little remains of your secret. In order to clarify the position
completely, I suggest that you tell me the rest. What is the
actual wording of your commission?"

Knecht had sprung to his feet and now stood opposite him,
surprised, embarrassed and also quite crestfallen. "You are
right," he exclaimed, "but although you have relieved me,
I am also very ashamed that you have forestalled me. For a
long time I have been considering how I could possibly
clarify our relationship, which you have now brought to light
in one stroke. It is a lucky thing for me that my request for
instruction and your agreement to initiate me in your subject
were made before I went away on vacation, or it really would
have seemed like diplomacy on my part and our studies only
a pretext."

The old man reassured him in the most friendly manner.
"I only wanted to help us both one step forward. I need no
assurance as to the integrity of your intentions. If I have
anticipated you and have done no more than fulfil your
apparent desire, everything is in order."

Regarding the content of Knecht's mission, which he was
now told, he said: "Your authorities in Castalia are not
particularly genial, but they are quite acceptable diplomats
and are also fortunate. I will think over your commission in
peace, and my decision will depend upon how far you can
enlighten me as to your Castalian organisation and ideology,
and upon how far you can make them appear plausible to me.
We will give ourselves plenty of time."

As Knécht still looked a little crestfallen, he laughed
heartily and said: "You can look upon my behaviour as a
kind of lesson, if you like. We two are diplomats whose
association is an unending conflict, although it is conducted
on a friendly basis. In our tussle I was momentarily at a disadvantage, for the facts of the affair had eluded me: you knew
more than I did. But now we are quits. The chess move was
successful, and it was also just."

If it appeared of value and importance to Knecht to win
over the Father for the intentions of the Castalian authorities,
it seemed still more important to learn as much as possible
from him and on his own side to be a trustworthy exponent of
the tenets of the Castalian world for the benefit of the
scholarly and influential man.

Knecht had been envied many things by a great number of
his friends and pupils, just as outstanding men are always
envied, not because of their inner greatness and energy alone
but also on account of their apparent luck, their apparent
preferment through Destiny. The smaller man sees in the
greater only what he wishes to see, and Joseph Knecht's rise
and career had in fact something unusually brilliant, rapid
and seemingly effortless about it from everyone's point of
view: one is tempted to say of that period of his life that
"He was lucky!" We have no wish to attempt to describe
this "luck" in a rationalist or moralist sense, be it as a casual
result of external circumstances or as a kind of reward for
his special virtues. Luck has nothing to do either with ratios
or morals: it is in essence something magical, belonging to an
early, youthful stage of human life. The ingenious lucky man,
endowed with gifts by good fairies, the darling of the gods,
is no subject for rational observations on the part of his
biographers, and stands outside the personal and the historical. And yet there are outstanding men from whose lives
the phenomenon of luck cannot be dismissed, even if only
because of the fact that they have been born neither too early
nor too late, that their respective tasks appear actually to
suit their characters historically and biographically. Knecht
seems to have belonged in this category. Thus his life—at
least for a period—gives the impression that everything
desirable simply fell into his lap. We will not deny this
aspect of his life, nor will we dismiss it out of hand, but we

could only reasonably account for it along biographical lines
that we ourselves do not savour and which would actually be
forbidden in Castalia—by an exhaustive research into the
most personal and private details of his life and feelings, in
health, sickness, and in every possible curve and aberration.
We are convinced that such a biography, which in any case
is out of the question here, in an attempt to strike a perfect
balance between his luck and sufferings, would still both
falsify his figure and distort the picture of his life.

Enough of digressions. We were saying that Knecht was
envied by many who knew him, and by many who had only
heard of him; but for the smaller fry nothing seemed more
enviable than his relationship with the old Benedictine monk,
which was at once apprenticeship and exposition, a receiving
and a giving, submission and conquest, and also a friendship
and collaboration. None of Knecht's conquests since that of
Elder Brother in Bamboo Grove had been so entirely
felicitous, and in none of them had he felt at once so favoured
and so abashed, so graced and stimulated as in this one.
Hardly a single one of his later prize pupils did not confirm
that he often and willingly spoke of Father Jacobus, and
always with pleasure. From this Benedictine he learned
something that he could hardly have learned in Castalia: he
acquired a comprehensive view of the methods of historical
perception and research and a practical knowledge of their
rise, but far more than this came to experience history not
merely as a field of knowledge but as reality, as life and as
the conformity of the changes and rises of the individual
personal life to history. This he could not have learned from
a pure scholar. Father Jacobus was far more than a scholar, an
onlooker and a sage: he was one who lived and created. He
had not used the position which fate had given him to live the
secure and cosy life of an observer, but had allowed the
currents of the world to flow through his study and the
miseries and forebodings of his epoch to flow through his
heart. In the events of his time he had been co-active, co-
guilty and co-responsible, but not merely as a reviewer, an
examiner and classifier of events of long past eras, for he had
had to deal with ideas no less than with the recalcitrance of
matter and man. Together with his collaborator and counter-
part, a Jesuit Father who had been long dead, he was

regarded as the virtual founder of the diplomatic and moral power, and the high political influence, which the Roman Church had regained after a time of resignation and great indigence.

Even if the conversations between teacher and pupil hardly touched upon the political present—not because of the Father's habit of silence and reserve, but because of the pupil's fear of being dragged into diplomacy and politics—the political position and activity of the Benedictine so permeated his views upon world history that in each of his observations and in each of his glances into the intricacies of world affairs, the practical politician also spoke—no ambitious or intriguing politician at all events, no regent or leader, and no climber, but a counsellor and an intermediary, a man whose efforts and activities, as the result of a deep insight into the shortcomings and difficulties of the human being, had been mellowed by wisdom, and to whom fame, experience, knowledge of men and conditions, and not least his selflessness and integrity as a person, had given a significant power.

Of all this Knecht had known nothing before he came to Mariafels. He had never once heard the name of Father Jacobus mentioned, for the majority of the inhabitants of Castalia lived in the blissful and unsuspecting ignorance that had once been a feature of the scholar class of earlier periods: one possessed no political rights or duties and one never saw a newspaper; and if this summed up the outlook of the average Castalian, the terror of reality, politics and newspapers was far more acute among the bead-players, who considered themselves the élite and cream of the Province and were very careful not to allow the rarified atmosphere of their scholarly artistic existence to be disturbed by a trace of anything morbid.

Knecht had not originally appeared in the monastery as the bearer of a diplomatic brief but actually as a teacher of the Bead Game, and had no knowledge of politics other than that which he had assimilated during his short three weeks with M. Dubois. Although, compared with that time, he had become far more versed in this respect, he had by no means renounced all the unwillingness of the Waldzellian to busy himself with actual politics. If now, as a result of his association with Father Jacobus, he had become far more alive to political issues, it was not because he felt a need for such knowledge as he had done in his eagerness to learn history, but because it was unavoidable and purely incidental.

To expand his armoury, and to carry out his worthy task of being an efficient exponent *de rebus Castaliensibus* to his pupil, the Father, Joseph had brought with him from Waldzell certain works dealing with the organisation and history of the Province, the system of the élite schools and the development of the Bead Game. Some of these books had served him twenty years before in his conflict with Plinio—he had not set eyes upon them since—others, which had been kept from him at that time because they were reserved for the use of Castalian officials, he now read for the first time. So it transpired that, simultaneously with the expansion of his present fields of study, he was compelled to observe, understand and strengthen anew his own spiritual and historical foundations. In his attempt to simplify as far as possible, and to demonstrate for the Father's benefit, the essence of the Order and the Castalian system, he immediately encountered —a thing which could not be avoided—the weakest point of his own as well as of the whole Castalian culture: it showed that he was only capable of depicting the world historical condition which had caused, encouraged and made possible the rise of the Order and all its consequences, in the form of a schematised and anæmic picture which was lacking in clarity and order. This led to a lively exchange of views and to a collaboration on a high level, inasmuch as the Father was anything but a passive pupil: while he attempted to expound the history of the Castalian Order, Jacobus helped him in many respects to see and experience this history correctly himself and to find its roots in a universal world—and state-history. We shall see that these intensive conflicts which, owing to the temperament of the Father, often rose to the most heated arguments, bore their fruit many years later and eventually had an active influence upon Knecht's end. On the other hand, as to how attentively the Father listened to Knecht's expositions, and to what extent he learned and grew to recognise Castalian background, is demonstrated by his later behaviour. The concordat between Rome and Castalia which is still in force to-day, and which began with a genial neutrality and an accidental exchange of ideas between two scholars, growing in time to be a real collaboration and an active alliance, owes its existence to these two men. The Father even expressed the desire to be initiated into the theory of the Bead Game, which in the beginning he had laughingly rejected, for he sensed that therein lay the secret of the Order, and to a certain extent its faith or religion. Because he was now prepared to explore this world which he had previously only known of by hearsay, and for which he had had little sympathy, he set out in his energetic and cunningly resolute manner straight for the centre. If he did not actually become a bead-player—he was far too old in any case—the spirit of the Game and of the Order had rarely found so earnest and valuable a friend outside Castalia as in this great Benedictine.

Very often, when Knecht took leave of him after their studies, the Father would give him to understand that he was at home during the evening leisure hours. These were happy moments that they spent together, after the strain of the lectures and the heat of the discussions. Joseph would bring his clavichord or his violin and the old man would sit down at his piano by the soft light of the candles, and the room would be filled with the sweet smell of wax and the music of Corelli, Scarlatti, Telemann or Bach which they would play alternately or as duets. The old man was accustomed to retiring early, but Knecht, fortified by these little musical vespers, would prolong his studies far into the night and sometimes to the limit of his endurance.

In addition to his studies with the Father, his perfunctory Game course in the monastery and an occasional Chinese colloquy with the Abbot Gervasius, we find Knecht busily engaged in a very strenuous task, for he now took part—a thing which he had omitted to do on the two previous occasions—in the annual competition of the Waldzellian élite. In these competitions the entrants were required to develop three or four specified major themes into Bead Games. Great value was laid upon new, bold and original associations of highly formal purity and calligraphy, and on these occasions the candidates were allowed to overstep all the canons, which meant that they had the right to employ new figures which had not yet been accepted into the official Codex and Dictionary of Hieroglyphics. Next to the great public festival Games this competition was the most exciting event in the Vicus Lusorum, and also a trial of skill for the most ingenious prospective inventors of new Game symbols. The highest conceivable distinction for the victor—which, incidentally, was very seldom given—was not only that the winning Game was ceremoniously performed but also that all the new suggestions in the grammar and vocabulary of the Game were recognised and accepted into the Game Archives and language. The present Magister Ludi, Thomas of Trave, had won this rare distinction twenty-five years before with his new abbreviations for the alchemical significance of the Zodiacal signs, just as he had later added a great deal towards the knowledge and classification of alchemy as an elaborate code.

For this occasion Knecht renounced the use of the new Game words, although like every other candidate he had many such a word in readiness, nor did he make use of his knowledge of psychological Game methods—to which he would have been more inclined. He constructed a Game perfectly modern and personal in structure and theme, but which was above all rigidly symmetrical and of a crystal-clear classical composition, although highly decorative, old master-like and graceful in execution. Perhaps this choice was due to his remoteness from Waldzell and from the Game Archives, or perhaps to the strong claims that his historical studies made upon his time and strength, or again it may have been the result of an unconscious wish to stylise his Game so that it might conform in the highest possible degree to the taste of his friend and teacher, Father Jacobus. We do not know.

We have just used the term "psychological game methods," which may perhaps be a little puzzling to some of our readers. In Knecht's time it was a very much used slogan. In each age there were currents, modes, conflicts and opposing schools of thought, and also changing outlooks and interpretations among the initiated, and at that time there were two primary conceptions of the Game, around which many controversies and discussions raged. One differentiated between two distinct types of Game—the formal and the psychological—and we know that both Knecht and Tegularius, although they refrained from taking any open part in the discussions, were supporters and protagonists of the latter, only Knecht preferred to speak of the psychological Game as the "pedagogic." The formal Game sought to portray to the greatest extent possible a concise, uninterrupted and perfect formal unity and harmony from the positive contents of each Game—mathematical philological, musical, etc., etc. The psychological Game, on the contrary, strove after unity and harmony, cosmic sphericity and perfection, not so much in the choice, arrangement, limitation, association and opposition of contents, as in the meditation that followed each stage of the Game, upon which it laid all the emphasis. The "pedagogic Game" did not ask for a glimpse of perfection from without but led the player as the result of his exact prescribed meditation to an experience of perfection and the divine. "The Game, as I interpret it," Knecht once wrote to the old Music Master, "encompasses the player at the conclusion of his meditation in the same way as the surface of a sphere encloses its centre, and leaves him with the feeling of having resolved the fortuitous and chaotic world into one that is symmetrical and harmonious."

The particular Game which Knecht used as his entry in the great competition was therefore a formal and not a psychologically constructed one. It is possible that he also wished to bring to the notice of the Pedagogy the fact that, in spite of his beginners' course in Mariafels and his diplomatic mission, his play had lost nothing in practice, elasticity, elegance and virtuosity. He certainly succeeded in this demonstration. As the final execution and fair copy of his Game plan could only be completed in the Waldzell Game Archives, he had entrusted this task to his friend Tegularius who, incidentally, was a rival competitor. He was able to hand the rough drafts to his friend personally, to discuss and go through them with him, for Fritz had come to stay in the monastery with him for three days. Magister Thomas had at last granted this request after two previous refusals.

Although Tegularius was delighted with the idea of this visit and, as an insular Castalian, was full of curiosity, he felt extremely uncomfortable in the monastery. This sensitive individual nearly fell ill as a result of all the strange impressions he received among these friendly but simple, healthy and somewhat coarse men for whom none of his thoughts, anxieties and problems had the least significance.

"I cannot understand it at all, and I admire you for having endured three years of it. Your Fathers are being very nice to me, of course, but I feel rebuffed and thrust aside by everybody. Nothing is obvious: nothing can be assimilated without resistance and suffering. To live here for two weeks would be like being in hell for me."

Knecht took great pains with him, but with the eyes of a spectator, and with extreme discomfort, saw and felt for the first time the alienation that existed between the two Orders and worlds, and realised that his oversensitive friend would not make a good impression here with his timorous helplessness. They would read over their plans for the competition together thoroughly and critically, and when, after these sessions, Knecht went off to visit Father Jacobus in the other wing or to a meal, he would also have the feeling that he had suddenly come out of a country with quite another soil and atmosphere, another climate ruled over by other stars.

After Fritz had gone Joseph provoked Father Jacobus into giving an opinion as to his impressions of Tegularius.

"I hope that the majority of Castalians are more like you than your friend," was the worthy man's retort. "I am afraid that you have brought an unreliable, overbred weakling and at the same time an arrogant type of man to see us. I will not say any more for fear of being unjust to your kind, but I cannot help feeling that this poor, sensitive, over-intelligent, floundering creature could sicken one against your whole Province again."

"Now wait a minute! Among you Benedictine gentlemen, in the course of the centuries, you must also have had a few ailing, bodily weak but intellectually well-integrated men such as my friend Tegularius. It was probably a mistake my having invited him here, where everyone has a sharp eye for his weaknesses but is blind to his great talents. He has rendered me a very friendly service by coming here!"

He proceeded to tell the Father of his entry in the competition. The latter was pleased that he had stuck up for his friend.

"Good for you!" he said with a friendly laugh; "but it seems to me that you have many friends whom one finds it difficult to deal with." He enjoyed Knecht's bewilderment and

pained expression, and then added quickly: "No this time
I mean another one—have you any news of your friend
Plinio Designori?"

Joseph's surprise was even greater than before. He asked
Father Jacobus for an explanation. Designori, he was told,
had given vent in a political pamphlet to certain ardent anti-
clerical views, and had attacked Father Jacobus with great
energy. This information was passed on to him by friends in
the Catholic press, who had also mentioned Plinio's accredited
student relationship with Knecht in Waldzell. Joseph asked
whether he might read Plinio's article, and this gave rise to
his first actual political discussion with the Father, a precedent which was, however, not often repeated.

"It was strange—almost terrifying," he wrote to Ferromonte, "to see the figure of our Plinio, and myself as an
accessory, suddenly on the world political stage. It was an
aspect which I could never possibly have foreseen."

Furthermore, the Father had gone on to speak of Plinio's
pamphlet with some recognition, and certainly without a
trace of rancour. He had praised Designori's style and form,
maintaining that one could recognise the élite school stamp,
for in everyday politics one had to be content with a far lower
level of intellect.

It was about this time that Knecht received from Ferromonte a copy of the first part of his great work, which was
later to become famous. It bore the title: "The Acceptance
and Incorporation of Slav Folk Music into German Musical
Art from Joseph Haydn Onwards." We have seen Knecht's
acknowledgment of this gift in which he writes, among
other things: "You have certainly composed a most con-
clusive treatise out of your studies—studies in which I was
allowed for a while to participate. I number the two chapters
on Schubert, particularly the one dealing with the quartets,
among the most sterling criticisms of musical history that
have been written in modern times. Consider my position,
for example: I am far removed from any such a harvest as
that which you have been successful in reaping. Although I
ought to be content with my present existence, for my mission
here in Mariafels does not seem to have been entirely fruitless, I still find my remoteness from our Province and the
Waldzell circle to which I belong, oppressive at times. I am

learning a great deal here, an incredible amount actually, but what I am gaining does not seem to be an increase in security and professional ability but an increase in problems—although admittedly also a broadening of horizon. As regards the uncertainty, strangeness and lack of assurance, serenity, self-confidence and all the other evils that I often felt during my first two years here, I am, I admit, now much more tranquil. Tegularius was here recently—only for three days—but despite his pleasure at seeing me and his curiosity about Mariafels he could hardly endure it. On his second day a feeling of oppression and of alienation had already begun to assail him. However, considering that a monastery is more in the nature of a protected, peaceful and hospitable world and by no means a gaol, a barracks or a factory, I cannot but conclude that we people from our beloved Province are far more spoiled and susceptible than we realise."

Shortly after receiving Carlo's letter Father Jacobus was moved to write a short note to the Head of the Order in Castalia giving his blessing to the diplomatic question at issue, and the Father also added the request that they might "allow the bead-player, Joseph Knecht, who is generally beloved in the monastery, and who is at present giving me a private course *de rebus Castaliensibus*, to remain here for a while." The Pedagogy naturally considered it an honour to grant his wish. Knecht, however, who had still thought himself to be far removed from his goal, received a special joint letter of recognition from the Head of the Order and M. Dubois upon the execution of his mission. The feature in this high official letter that at the moment seemed to him of the greatest importance and delighted him most (he announced it triumphantly in a letter to Fritz) was a short phrase telling that the Order had, through the good offices of the Magister Ludi, heard of his desire to return to the Vicus Lusorum, and that upon the completion of his present mission they were favourably inclined to grant this request. He read this extract out to Father Jacobus with great pleasure, and confessed how afraid he had been lest he should be banned from Castalia for ever and be sent to Rome. The Father replied with a smile: "Yes, indeed! Orders have something about them, my friend. One would certainly rather live in their lap than on the outskirts or in exile. You can safely forget your little political interlude, for you are no politician but you must never be untrue to history, even though it remain an amateur subject in your curriculum, for you have all the makings of a good historian. And now we will make the most of each other while I still have you here with us."

Joseph Knecht seems to have made little use of his permission to spend frequent short spells in Waldzell, but he listened to a seminary course and to many lectures and Games on the radio. And so, from a distance, in his well-appointed guest room he also listened to that "Solemnity," wherein the results of the competition were announced from the Feast Hall of the Vicus Lusorum. He had, as we know, sent in a rather impersonal and not in the least revolutionary work, but one that was concise and highly elegant, and, being fully aware of its value, had expected to gain perhaps a second or a third prize. To his surprise he heard that he had been awarded the first prize, and before he could recover heard the deep voice coming through the loudspeaker from the Game Hall announcing that the second prize had been awarded to Tegularius. It was a moving and enchanting experience indeed that the two friends should both have been crowned victors in this competition! He sprang up and, without waiting to listen any further, ran down the steps through the echoing dormitories into the open air.

In a letter to the old Music Master which was written during those days, we read: "I am very happy, my revered friend, as you can quite imagine. First of all, the success of my mission and its honourable recognition by the Pedagogy; next, the prospect of my returning home to my friends and to the Bead Game, instead of being used further in the diplomatic service; and now this award of the first prize for a Game in which I was painstaking enough as regards construction but did not exhaust everything I knew—on very good grounds—and in addition to this my friend's success as well! This was, you must admit, a great deal, to happen all at once. I am happy, Yes! but I cannot say that I am gay. After a difficult time—or one that has appeared so to me—for all these fulfilments to come at once seems somehow too sudden and too abundant, and my gratitude is mixed with a certain trepidation, as though one more drop would be required to make everything questionable. But please forget that I have said all this, for another word would be superfluous at this time."

We shall soon see that the vessel, which had been filled to the brim, was soon to have more than a single drop added. During the short period before this happened, Knecht lived his happiness in an admixture of fear, devotion and intensity, as though he already sensed great changes that were approaching. These months were also happy and radiant ones for Father Jacobus. He regretted the fact that he would soon be losing his pupil and colleague, and tried during their working hours, and even more during their leisure conversations, to impart and bequeath to him to the utmost possible degree all the knowledge that he had gained of the heights and depths of the lives of men and races from his work and from a richly contemplative life. He also spoke at times of the significance and of the consequences of Joseph's mission, of the possibility and value of an alliance and political unity between Rome and Castalia, and advised him to study that period, the fruits of which were the founding of the Castalian Order and the gradual regeneration of Rome after a humiliating time of trial. He also recommended two works on the Reformation and the Church schisms of the sixteenth century, and most strongly of all counselled him always to prefer fundamentally the direct sources of study and the occasional limitations of visible fields to the reading of world historical tomes, and made no bones about voicing his deep distrust of all philosophies of history.

Chapter Six

MAGISTER LUDI

KNECHT HAD DECIDED to postpone his final return to Waldzell until the spring which was the season of the great Public Game—the *Ludus anniversarius aut sollemnis.*

Even though the zenith in the memorable history of the Game, the period of week-long Games which dignitaries and representatives from all countries used to attend had been

passed and belonged for ever to the realms of history, these
spring days of solemn festival, lasting from ten to fourteen
days, were a great annual occasion for the whole of Castalia,
a feast which was not lacking in high religious and moral
significance for it united all the representatives of the Province, who were not always of the same mind and leanings, in
the semblance of a harmonious whole: it made peace between
the egoisms of the individual Faculties and awakened a
memory of unity transcending their infinite variety.

For the believers it possessed the sacramental strength of a
true consecration and for the faithless at least a substitute for
religion: for both of them it was a bath in the pure source of
beauty. In a similar way, the Passions of J. S. Bach were once,
not so much at the time of their creation but after their
rediscovery in the following centuries, a true religious
ceremony and consecration for some of their listeners and
performers, for others a devotion and a religious substitute,
and for all of them a ceremonious manifestation of art and of
the *Creator spiritus.*

Knecht had no difficulty in persuading the monastery folk
and his own authorities to agree to his decision. He could not
quite envisage his position once he was incorporated in the
little republic of the Vicus Lusorum, but he imagined that he
would not be left idle for long and would soon be burdened
and honoured with some office or mission. For the moment he
was looking forward to his homecoming, to seeing his friends
and to the approaching festival, and enjoyed those last days
with Father Jacobus intensely. He noticed with satisfaction
that the Abbot and the other members of the monastery
showed many marks of their benevolence towards him on
his departure. He set out, not without a certain sadness at
having to say farewell to this place which he had grown to
love, and at leaving behind him an important section of his
life, but he had already keyed himself up for the coming
festivity through the preparatory contemplative exercises, in
which admittedly he had been without guidance and companions but which he had undertaken most precisely according
to the programme that had been issued.

This mood was by no means marred by the fact that he had
not succeeded in persuading Father Jacobus—who had been
sent a formal invitation by the Magister Ludi for the annual

Game—to accompany him, for he understood the reserved behaviour of the old anti-Castalian well enough, and felt for the moment absolved from all duties and restraints and was ready to devote himself wholeheartedly to the immediate future.

Now there is a peculiar thing about festivals. A true feast can never wholly and entirely fail unless it be through some unfortunate interference on the part of the higher powers: for the pious even a procession in the rain retains its sanctity and a feast spoiled in the cooking cannot sober a zealot. Thus, for bead-players, each annual festival is to a certain extent hallowed. And yet, as we all know, there are feasts and games in which everything and everybody is in harmony, where each stimulates, inspires and exalts the other, just as there are theatrical and musical performances which, for no recognisable cause as and though by a miracle, are high peaks and great occasions, while others, no less carefully prepared, simply remain gallant achievements. Insofar as the success of that great experience is founded upon the morale of the participants, Joseph Knecht ought to have been prepared for it in the best possible manner, as he was totally carefree, had just returned from his mission with honour, and was looking forward to the forthcoming events with joyful anticipation.

This particular *ludus sollemnis* was not destined to be touched by any miraculous breath or to reach the height of a consecration and a radiance. It was in fact a joyless Game and was frankly luckless—almost a failure. Even though many of the participants felt edified and elated as is usually the case, the actual players, organisers and responsible parties felt more and more inexorably that atmosphere of apathy, gracelessness and failure, of frustration and ill luck with which the heavens had menaced this feast.

Although Knecht naturally also experienced this, along with a certain damping of his high pitched mood of expectancy, he was by no means one of those who suffered this adversity most directly: although he was not an active performer and bore no responsibility for this particular Game, and despite the fact that its performance failed to blossom and find favour, he was able to follow its course with appreciation as a pious participant, to let himself be inspired by the meditations quite undisturbed, and in grateful devotion perfect within himself that well-known experience common to all the guests of the Game—a celebration and a sacrifice, a mystic unification of the community at the feet of the divine—which was not possible for the narrow circle of the wholly initiated in this "uninspired" performance. Nevertheless, he did not remain unaffected by the evil star which ruled over the ceremony. The Game itself, of course, in plan and construction was exemplary, as Magister Thomas' Games invariably were—it was in fact one of his most impressive, simple and direct but its execution stood under a particularly adverse conjunction and has not been forgotten in the annals of Waldzell.

When Knecht arrived a week before the great Game and announced himself in the Game Town, he was received not by the Magister Ludi but by his deputy, Bertram, who welcomed him politely but informed him rather absentmindedly that the worthy Magister had been ill for some days and that he himself was not sufficiently informed as to Knecht's mission to receive his report. He was therefore to report to the Head of the Order in Hirsland, notify him of his arrival and await further instructions.

As Knecht, on leaving, unwittingly betrayed a certain astonishment, either by his tone of voice or by some gesture, at the coolness and brevity of his reception, Bertram apologised quite profusely. His colleague had to forgive him, he said, if he had disappointed him, but he had also to understand the delicacy of the situation: the Magister was ill and the great Annual Game was imminent. It was by no means certain that the Magister himself would be able to lead them, or whether he might not have to deputise for him. The illness of the Magister could not have taken place at a less convenient moment. He was, of course, as always, ready to superintend all the official duties in place of the Magister Ludi, but he was afraid that to take over the leadership of the great Game at such short notice would be a task beyond his powers.

Knecht pitied this sorely disconcerted man who had been thrown off his balance, and regretted the fact that perhaps the responsibility for the festival would now rest in such hands. He had been absent from Waldzell too long to know how well-founded were Bertram's fears, for the latter—always the worst thing that can happen to a deputy—had for some time past lost the confidence of the élite, the so-called "tutorship," and was in fact in an extremely uncomfortable predicament.

Knecht thought with sorrow of the Magister Ludi—that hero of classical form and irony, that ideal Magister and cavalier. He had been looking forward to a reception and an audience, and had hoped perhaps to be given some post of confidence in the little community of the players. He had so earnestly desired to witness a Festival Game conducted by Magister Thomas, to continue to work under his supervision and to win his recognition. It was a bitter disappointment to find him ill and to be addressed to other courts. He was however compensated for this disappointment by the respectful goodwill with which the Secretary to the Order and M. Dubois received him, and also by the fact that they both treated him as a colleague. After the very first conversation he grasped that, for the moment, the Pedagogy had no intention of using him any further for the Rome plan, and that his request to return permanently to the Game had been respected. He was at once invited in the most friendly manner to stay in the guest house of the Vicus Lusorum, to have a good look round in order to get his bearings once more, and to attend the annual Game. In company with his friend Tegularius he devoted his mornings to the fasting and meditation exercises, and piously and thankfully prepared for that strange Game which has remained an unpleasant memory for so many people.

The post of a deputy Magister, or "shadow" as he is popularly called, particularly to the Music Master or to the Magister Ludi, is a highly exceptional one. Each of the Magisters has a deputy, who is not chosen for him by the authorities but whom he himself elects from the narrow circle of élite candidates and for whose actions and writings he bears full responsibility. It is therefore a great distinction for the candidate who is chosen, and a mark of the highest confidence on the part of his Master: he will in future be recognised as an intimate collaborator and the proverbial right hand of the all-powerful Magister, and will carry out his duties when the latter is prevented from doing so—but by no means all of them. For example, in the voting conclaves of the Pedagogy, he may only reply with "yes" or "no" in the name of the Magister and can never be a spokesman, a mover of resolutions or decide upon any major precautionary measures. Although his appointment to deputy raises him to a very high and exposed position it constitutes in actual fact something in the nature of a dead end. It tends to separate him from the other members of the hierarchy, and although he is frequently entrusted with the most important functions, involving high honours, it deprives him of certain rights and possibilities which all the other aspirants enjoy. There are two points by which this exceptional position can be clearly recognised: the deputy bears none of the responsibility for his official actions and he cannot rise any higher within the hierarchy. Although it is an unwritten law, it can be clearly read in the history of Castalia, and never on the death or retirement of a Magister does his "shadow" step into his shoes, into the part which he has so often understudied and into the position to which he would seem predestined as a natural successor. It is as though the custom arose from a desire to demarcate an apparently fluid and movable barrier and to make it intentionally insuperable—the barrier between Magister and deputy, representing the metaphorical barrier between office and individual. Therefore, once a Castalian accepts the highly trusted post of deputy, he renounces any chance of becoming a Magister himself or of assuming the official costume and insignia, which he has so often worn as a representative in his own rights, but at the same time he receives that remarkable right which can be a two-edged sword of having no personal responsibility in office and of leaving it for the Magister, who has to answer for him, to bear on his own shoulders. It has often happened that a Magister has become the victim of some great error that his deputy has committed, for which he has been obliged to accept the guilt and has sometimes even been obliged to retire from office. The nickname used in Waldzell when referring to the deputy of the Magister Ludi is very appropriate to this curious position of interdependence: he might almost be described as one who is identical with the Magister, but one whose official existence is illusory and unsubstantial. On this account he is known as the "shadow."

Magister Thomas of Trave had been served for many years by his "shadow," Bertram. This man seems to have been lacking more in luck than in talent and goodwill. He was naturally an outstanding bead-player, and was also a moderately efficient teacher, a conscientious official and was devoted to his master. In the course of the last few years, however, he had become more or less disliked by the officials and had antagonised the younger members of the élite, and since he did not possess the frank cavalier nature of his Master this disturbed his serenity and self-assurance. Magister Thomas had not once deserted him, and had for many years protected him as far as possible from friction with the élite, had given him less public duties to perform and had used him more and more in the chancellery and in the archives.

This man, who had never actually been reprimanded but who was at the same time unpopular and obviously not favoured by fortune, now suddenly saw himself, through the sickness of his Master, at the head of the Vicus Lusorum and, should he be obliged to conduct the Annual Game, in the most prominent position in the whole Province. Had he been fitted to this task, and had he been supported by the confidence of the majority of the bead-players and the tutorship, everything would have been in order, but unfortunately this was not the case. And so it came about that this *ludus sollemnis* proved to be a hard test and almost a catastrophe for Waldzell.

Only a few days before the Game was due to start was information given out that the Magister was seriously ill and that it would be out of the question for him to preside. We do not know whether this witholding of information had been dictated by the wish of the sick Magister, who had hoped up to the last moment to recover and still be able to carry out his task. It is probable that he was too ill to nourish such thoughts, and that his "shadow" had made the mistake of keeping Castalia in the dark too long as to the actual position in Waldzell. It is naturally still a debatable question as to whether this procrastination on his part was really a mistake or not. It was doubtless done with the good intention of not discouraging the admirers of Magister Thomas from paying their annual visit. Had everything passed successfully, and had there been a sufficient reciprocal confidence between the Waldzell community and Bertram, it is quite conceivable that the "shadow" would have acted as a genuine deputy and that the absence of the Magister would have been overlooked. But it is a waste of time to discuss these possibilities any

urther: our personal opinion is that Bertram was not such a
failure and despicable person as public opinion in Waldzell
would have had him appear. He seems to have been more a
victim than a culprit.

The stream of yearly visitors began to arrive for the great
Game. Many came in ignorance of the true situation and
others with sorrow in their hearts for the Magister Ludi in his
illness, along with unpleasant forebodings of how the festival
would transpire. Waldzell and the adjacent settlements were
soon filled to overflowing. The Order and the Pedagogy were
in full strength, and all the guest houses were packed out with
festive travellers from many remote parts of the country.

As usual, on the evening prior to the Game the festival was
opened with an hour of meditation, while the great peal of
bells plunged the entire community into an awed silence. The
following morning the first of the musical performances took
place, and the first Game phrase, was announced. Bertram,
robed in the Magister Ludi's costume, displayed a seemly and
controlled behaviour, but was very pale and as the days went
by appeared to become more and more exhausted, ailing and
resigned, until on the last day he looked really no more than
a shadow.

Already on the second day, the rumour having spread that
Magister Thomas' condition had taken a turn for the worse
and that he was dangerously ill, here and there and above all
among the initiated the first seeds of that gradually developing legend concerning the Magister and his "shadow" was
born. This legend, which started among the tutorship in the
innermost circle of the Vicus Lusorum, had it that the Master
had been prepared to officiate as leader of the Game and
would also have been able to do so, but had sacrificed himself
to the ambition of his "shadow" by leaving the festive task in
his hands; that, now Bertram had proved himself not quite
capable of his high rôle, and the Game threatened to be a
disappointment, the sick man, knowing that he was responsible both for the Game and for his "shadow," had
accepted the responsibility and was prepared to expiate the
latter's faults: and that this and nothing else had been the
cause of the rapid deterioration of his health and the increase
of his fever. This was naturally not the only version of the
legend, but it was the one favoured by the élite and which

showed clearly that they—the ambitious aspirants—had viewed the situation as a tragic one and were determined to tolerate no compromise, clarification or anything in the nature of an excuse. Reverence for the Magister tipped the scales in his favour and to the detriment of his "shadow," whose failure and discomfiture was desired by this clique, which also insisted that he should pay the full penalty along with his Master.

The following day one could hear reports that the Magister, from his sick bed, had implored his deputy as well as the seniors of the élite to make their peace so as not to endanger the Game, and on the next day it was maintained that he had dictated his last wishes and given the authorities the name of the man whom he wished to be his successor. Names were actually mentioned.

Together with the news of the deteriorating condition of the Magister, these and other rumours were bruited about the feast hall as well as all the guest houses. The general mood grew worse from day to day, although no one actually failed to attend the performance and returned home. A dark and heavy oppression lay over the whole institution. To all outward appearances the Game ran its course in the correct form, but there was no trace of the joy and exhilaration that one usually expects from this festival; and when, on the day before the closing phase, its creator, Magister Thomas, closed his eyes for the last time, the news spread despite all the efforts on the part of the Pedagogy to suppress it, and curiously enough many of the participants looked upon his death as the cutting of a Gordian knot. Moved by an unanimous impulse, the Game students, and in particular the élite, although they were not allowed to put on mourning until the end of the *ludus sollemnis,* and although they did not dare to interrupt in the least detail the rigidly prescribed course with alternate hours of performance and meditation exercises, behaved throughout the last act of the Game as though it were a mourning feast for the beloved dead man, leaving the over-tired, pale and sleepless Bertram, who continued to officiate with half-closed eyes, in an icy atmosphere of isolation.

Joseph Knecht, although still in active touch with the élite and the other players through Tegularius, and sensitive to all these currents and moods, had not allowed them to infect him personally, and from the fourth or fifth day onwards had actually forbidden Fritz to enlighten him as to the state of the Magister's health. He had fully realised and appreciated the tragic cloud which had descended upon the feast, and had thought with deep grief and mourning of the Magister and, with increasing discomfort and compassion, of the "shadow" Bertram who was condemned to die with him. He had resolutely refused to be influenced either by true or legendary rumours, had practised the severest concentration, giving himself over wholeheartedly to the exercises of this well-constructed Game, and despite all the disharmony and obfuscation had experienced it with grave exaltation.

Bertram, as vice Magister, was spared the final congratulations and the customary reception by the Pedagogy. The ensuing holiday for the Bead Game students was also abandoned. Directly after the musical finale the authorities announced the death of the Magister, and a period of mourning began in the Vicus Lusorum, which Joseph Knecht also observed at a distance in his guest house. The burial of this deserving man, who is still remembered to-day with high esteem, was carried out with the usual Castalian simplicity. Bertram, his "shadow," who had come to the end of his resources as a result of the exigencies of the feast, understood his position. He asked for a vacation and wandered into the mountains.

In the Game Town, and in fact everywhere in Waldzell, it was a time of mourning. Perhaps no one had known the dead Magister intimately or had had a friendly relationship with him, but the superiority and sincerity of his illustrious personality, his shrewdness and delicacy and cultured sense of form, had raised him to the height of regent and representative of Castalia—a position that was rare indeed in its basically democratic constitution. They had been proud of him. Even though his person seemed to have been far removed from the realms of passion, love or friendship, this very factor had been a great stimulus to the hero-worshipping needs of the younger generation, among whom his dignity and princely grace had inspired the half affectionate nick-name of "Excellence," and had given him, despite stiff resistance during the course of the years, a somewhat special position in

the high councils, sessions and communal work of the
Pedagogy.

The question as to the filling of his high office was of course
eagerly discussed, and nowhere so much as among the élite
bead-players. The functions of the Magistracy after his death
and the downfall and departure of the "shadow," which this
circle had desired and accomplished, were divided between
three provisional deputies chosen by the votes of the élite
themselves, but this naturally only applied to the internal
functions of the Vicus Lusorum and not to the official ones in
the Council of Education. This regency, pending the appointment of a new Magister, was not to last for more than three
weeks. In cases where a dying or retiring Magister had
stipulated a decisive and uncontested successor, the office was
immediately filled after a full session of the Pedagogy. On
this particular occasion it would naturally take somewhat
longer.

During the period of mourning Joseph Knecht frequently
discussed the Game which had just come to a close under such
remarkably gloomy circumstances with his friend.

"This deputy, Bertram," he maintained, "not only played
his rôle tolerably well to the end—I mean, his rôle of trying
to play the real Magister—but in my opinion did far more.
He actually sacrificed himself in this *ludus sollemnis* as his last
ceremonious act of office. You were harsh to him—gruesome
in fact! You had the power to rescue him, and did not do so.
I will not pass a judgment, for perhaps you had your reasons
for such behaviour, but now that this poor Bertram has
retired and you have had your way, you should be magnani-
mous. When he returns you must be kindly disposed towards
him and show him that you have understood his sacrifice!"

Tegularius shook his head. "We have understood, and we
have accepted it. You were fortunate in having been able to
participate in this Game as a guest without having to take
sides, and therefore you have not followed events so closely.
No, Joseph, we shall have no more opportunity of reversing
our feelings in any way as regards Bertram, whatever they
may be. He knows that it was necessary for him to be sacrificed and will not try to repeal the decision."

For the first time Knecht understood, and was quite
dumbfounded. He realised that he had in fact participated in

this festival not as a true Waldzellian and comrade but more in the manner of a guest, and at last saw Bertram's sacrifice in its true perspective. Previously the latter had appeared to him as an ambitious man who had succumbed to a task that was beyond his capacity, who ought to renounce any further ambitious goals and try to forget that he had once been the "shadow" of a Magister and the leader of the Annual Game. Now at last, as a result of his friend's words, he realised to his amazement that Bertram had definitely been condemned by his judges and would not return. He had been allowed to bring the Game to an end, and had been helped only to the extent of avoiding a scandal: it had not been done in order to aid him, but to spare Waldzell.

The position of a "shadow" apparently demanded not only the full trust of the Magister—in this Bertram had not been wanting—but to no less a degree the confidence of the élite, and this the unfortunate man had not been able to inspire. Were he to commit a blunder, there stood behind him—as also behind his Master and model—the hierarchy for his protection; but unless he were fully recognised by his former comrades there was virtually no authority to support him, and these comrades from the tutorship would become his judges. If they were unrelenting, the "shadow" was ruined. In actual fact Bertram never returned from his excursion to the mountains, and after a while it was given out that he had fallen from a steep cliff. He was never referred to again.

In the meantime, day after day high officials of the Order and of the Pedagogy began to appear in the Game Town, and every minute individuals from among the élite and the Waldzellian bureaucrats were summoned for interrogation, the purport of which was only discussed among the élite themselves. Joseph himself was sent for and questioned several times, once by the Magister of Philology, once by M. Dubois and several times by two other high members of the Order.

Tegularius, who had also been interviewed, was pleasantly excited and made mordant witticisms about the "conclave complex," as he called it. Joseph had already noticed during the course of the Game how little remained of his former close relationship with the élite, and came to realise it even more acutely during this period of conclaves. It was not only that he was living as a stranger in the guest house and that the superiors appeared to treat him as an equal, but the members of the élite itself, of the tutorship, no longer accepted him intimately and in a comradely manner but addressed him with mocking politeness or, at the least, with a cool reserve. They had already withdrawn from him when he had been sent on his Mariafels mission, which had been quite natural and in order: whoever took the step from freedom, from the student grade of the tutorship, into the service and into the hierarchy was no longer a comrade but was well on the way to becoming a superior and a bonze: he no longer belonged among the élite, and had to realise that they would be critical of him from that moment onwards. This is exactly what took place in his case. He felt the remoteness and coolness particularly acutely during these days, firstly because the élite had been orphaned and had to choose a new Magister, entrenching themselves behind an even closer barrier of defence than usual, and secondly because in their inexorable resolution they had shown themselves so harsh in their dealings with the "shadow" Bertram.

One evening Tegularius arrived at the guest house in great excitement. He drew Knecht aside into an empty room, shut the door and burst out: "Joseph, Joseph! my God, I should have realised it! I ought to have known it—it was not so improbable as all that . . . Oh, I am quite beside myself! I don't really know whether to laugh or to cry!"

Being well in touch with all the sources of information in the Game Town, he told him eagerly that it was more than probable, in fact almost a certainty, that he, Joseph Knecht, would be chosen as Magister Ludi. The Head of the Archives, whom many had considered to be the obvious successor to Magister Thomas, had announced his retirement from the narrow choice on the previous day, and of the three remaining élite candidates whose names headed the list neither of the other two had apparently been given any special recommendations by a Master or by the heads of the Order. On the other hand, M. Dubois, along with two members of the Order, had spoken in favour of Knecht, and in addition there was the very important voice of the old Music Master, whom everyone knew had been visited several times during the past few days by a number of the Masters in person.

"Joseph, they will make you Magister Ludi!" he repeated excitedly. Knecht silenced his friend. At first he had been hardly less surprised and disturbed than Fritz at the suggestion, for it had seemed so improbable; but while his friend was imparting all the rumours as to the state and course of the conclave he began to see that this presumption might actually be true. Moreover he had felt something in the nature of a "yes" in his soul—that he had known and expected it, and that it was just and natural—and this is why he had quelled his friend's excitement. He had looked at him with the eyes of a stranger and had repelled him as though a distance had suddenly sprung up between them.

"Do not talk so much, *amice!*" he said. "I do not wish to hear anything of this gossip! Go back to your comrades!"

Tegularius, whatever else he might have wished to add, was dumbfounded by this look. It was as though a complete stranger now stood before him. He paled and left the room immediately.

Some time later he related that Knecht's remarkably calm behaviour and coldness at that moment had at first impact been like a blow and an insult, almost like a slap in the face, a betrayal of their old friendship and intimacy, and a hardly conceivable overemphasis and foretaste of his approaching position of Principal Superior. Only as he was on his way—and he really had left the guest house like someone who had been thrashed—did he begin to realise the significance of this unforgettable look, this distant, kingly but for all that sorrowful look, and understood that his friend had accepted what had occurred not with pride but with humility. He had, he said, unwittingly recalled Joseph Knecht's reflective look, and the tone of deep compassion in his voice, when a short time before he had voiced his opinion about Bertram and his sacrifice. His friend's face, as he looked at him, had been so decorous and devoted, so lonely and resigned to fate that it might have been he himself who, like that "shadow," had resolved to sacrifice and extinguish himself. He seemed to epitomize, in that moment, all the Magisters who had ever been in Castalia. "Go back to your comrades!" he had said to him. Hardly a second had elapsed, therefore, than this incomprehensible man had already adapted himself to his new dignity and had seen the world from a new focal point wherein he was no longer a comrade and would never be one again.

Knecht could quite easily have forecast his nomination to this latest and highest call, or could at least have recognised it as probable, and yet, on this occasion, he had once again been horrified and surprised. He might have known it, he said to himself afterwards, smiling at the thought of the eager Tegularius who had not expected it from the first but had only calculated and anticipated it several days before the actual decision and announcement.

There had been nothing in fact against the choice of Joseph for Magister except possibly his youth: most of his predecessors had assumed high offices at the age of at least forty-five or fifty, whereas Joseph was hardly forty. There was however no law that stood in the way of such a youthful nomination.

When Fritz had so surprised his friend with the results of his observations and surmises—observations of a mature élite player who knew the complicated apparatus of the little Waldzell community in its minutest details—Knecht had immediately seen that he was right, had realised and accepted the fact of his nomination and destiny immediately, but his first reaction had been to repel him with the words "I do not wish to hear anything of this gossip!" No sooner had Tegularius, hurt and deeply offended, departed, than Joseph sought to achieve a state of composure through meditation. His reveries began with a memory picture which had returned to his mind with great vividness.

He saw a bare room with a piano. A cool serene morning light streamed in through the window, and in the doorway stood a handsome friendly man, an elderly man with greying hair and an untroubled face, the very personification of goodness and dignity. Joseph himself, however, was only a small secondary schoolboy waiting in the room, half fearful, half happy, for the Music Master, whom he was seeing for the first time—the honoured Magister from the fabulous province of the élite schools, who had come to show him what music really was, who had later guided and accepted him, step by step into his province, his realm, into the élite and the Order, and whose brother and colleague he had now become —while the old man, having laid aside his magic staff or sceptre, had changed into a friendly, silent but still benevolent, venerable and mysterious ancient, whose gaze and example lay over Joseph and who, as a patron and model, in dignity, modesty, excellence and mystery, vastly his superior, was gently to lead him through a generation and several stages of life, in the same way that a rising and setting planet attracts its satellite.

As long as Knecht abandoned himself freely to the stream of his inner images, which manifested themselves in the form of dreams in this first stage of relaxation, two major scenes came to the fore—two images or fantasies, two allegories. In the first, the boy Knecht was following the Music Master along many winding paths. The latter strode before him as a leader, and each time he turned round his face seemed to grow older, calmer and more venerable, each time approaching more and more the ideal picture of timeless wisdom and dignity, while he, Joseph Knecht, devoted and obedient, strode behind the paragon, always remaining the same age, alternately ashamed and jubilant over this fact, and feeling— yes, an almost arrogant satisfaction! The second picture was as follows: the scene in the music room, the entrance of the old man and his reception of Knecht repeating itself time after time, endlessly. The Magister and the boy followed each other again and again as though drawn by mechanical wires, so that it soon became impossible to recognise who came and who went, who led and who followed—the old or the young. Now it seemed to be the youth who was paying homage and obeying the old man, authority and dignity: now it seemed as though it were the latter who was obliged to serve and adore, as he followed this slim figure of youth hurrying by—his serene successor. And while he followed this irrational though significant dream-sequence across the screen of his own mind the dreamer felt himself alternately identified with the old man and with the boy. Now he was the reverer and now the revered, now the leader and now the led, and in the course of this fluctuating interchange of personalities there came a moment when he was both of them together, simultaneously master and small pupil, or rather, he stood above both of them, the originator, conceiver, leader and spectator of the circle, of this fruitless, frolicsome competition in the round of age and youth which, to the tune of his changing sensations, he slowed down or accelerated to a great speed. From this stage a new aspect of the scene developed—already more a symbol than a dream, more a cognition than an image—namely that this ambivalent whirl of master and pupil, this courtship of youth and wisdom and the search of youth after wisdom, this endless balanced Game, was the symbol of Castalia, the very scheme of life which flowed in endless duality, in old and young, in day and night, in Yang and Yin without end. From then on the meditator found his way from the picture world into tranquillity, and after a long period of contemplation returned to consciousness strengthened and serene.

When, a few days later, he was summoned by the Head of the Order administration, he went consoled, and received the fraternal handshake of the leader and the suggestion of an embrace which he gave him with serene gravity. He was informed of his nomination to the post of Magister Ludi, and was told that the investiture and the swearing-in would take place in two days time in the Festival Hall—the same hall in which a short time before the dead Master's deputy had discharged that oppressive feast like some gold-adorned beast of sacrifice.

The day of grace before the investiture was reserved for a precise and ritual meditation, accompanied by a perusal of the form of the oath and the preliminaries under the direction and observation· of two superiors, who in this case were the Chancellor of the Order and the Magister Mathematices, and during the mid-day recess of this extremely tiring day Joseph vividly recalled his erstwhile acceptance into the Order and the preliminary preparation with the Music Master.

On this occasion, however, he was not led by the prize scholar, as an exceptional distinction, at the head of hundreds through a wide door into the great community, but everything took place as though in camera among the highest and narrowest circle of the Magisters. He confessed to the old Music Master later that during his intensive self-searchings on that day he had thought continually of one quite ridiculous little possibility: he had actually been afraid that the moment would come when one of the Magisters would hint how unusually young he was to be receiving this high dignity. He had had to struggle with his fear, with this vain and childish thought, and in the event of any such insinuations about his age being made, with his desire to retort: "Then let me grow old in peace, for I have never striven for this promotion!" Further self-searching had shown him that the thought of his nomination and the desire for it could not have been so far removed from his mind. He had admitted this to himself, had recognised and rid himself of the vanity of his thought; and in actual fact neither on that day nor on any later occasion did any of his colleagues refer to his age.

At all events the choice of the new Magister was discussed and criticised all the more eagerly by those who had hitherto been his fellow aspirants. There had been no outspoken opposition, but he had certainly many competitors, and among these some were older than himself. They did not intend to sanction the choice without a struggle and without reservations, or at least until after a period of close and critical observation. In nearly every case the assumption of an office and the early days of a new Magister are very much in the nature of a purgatory.

The investiture of a Magister is not a public festival, and apart from the higher members of the Pedagogy and the administration of the Order, only a certain number of the elder pupils take part—the candidates and the officials of the particular Faculty which is being appointed with a new Magister. The Magister Ludi has first to take his oath of office and to receive his insignia—certain keys and seals—from the hands of his superiors in the Feast Hall, and is then robed in the ceremonial dress, the festal overmantle which the Magister wears on high occasions and above all at the Annual Game, by the Speaker of the Order. This ceremony lacks the *brio* and slight intoxication of the public festivals, and is more ceremonious and sober, but it is given unusual tone by the full presence of both sections of the high officials.

The little republic of the bead-players thus receives a new lord at its head, who has henceforward to represent them before the collective officials of the Province. It is a significant and rare event. Even should the scholars and younger students not realise its full importance and perhaps see in it only a ceremony and a spectacle, all the other participants are fully aware of its importance and are sufficiently wrapped up in and identified with their community to experience the event personally and intimately. On this occasion the festive gaiety was not only clouded over by the death of the late Magister and the period of mourning, but also by the subdued mood that still reigned as a result of the Annual Game and the tragedy of the deputy Bertram.

The ceremony of the investiture was accomplished by the Speaker of the Order and the Chief Game Archivist. Jointly they raised the official robe on high and laid it over the new Magister Ludi's shoulders. Short speeches were then made by the Magister Grammaticæ, the Magister of Classical Philology from Keuperheim, and finally one of the members of the élite representing Waldzell handed over the keys and the seal.

Near the organ the age-old Music Master could be seen in person. He had arrived for the investiture of his favourite pupil in order to give him a pleasant surprise, and perhaps also to offer him a little advice. The old man would have liked nothing better than to play the music with his own hands, but he did not dare attempt such an exertion and left the task to the organist of the Game Town. Instead he stood behind him and turned over the pages of the music. He looked over at Joseph with a smile of admiration, saw him receive the robes and the keys, heard him take the oath and listened to the impromptu speeches made in honour of his pupil and future colleague. Never had this boy Joseph appeared to him so attractive and so beloved as to-day, when he had nearly ceased to be Joseph, and had now become not only the bearer of a distinction and an office but a jewel in the crown and a pillar in the edifice of the hierarchy. He could only speak to his Joseph for a few minutes. Smiling serenely, he hurriedly whispered some encouragement in his ear.

"Take care that you come well through the next three or four weeks, for much will be asked of you! Think continually of the whole, and remember constantly that a neglect of detail at this stage does not matter a great deal. You must devote yourself entirely to the élite, and pay no attention to anything else. You will be sent two people to be of assistance to you, one of whom will be the yoga expert, Alexander: I have personally given him instructions, and you must pay great heed to him for he knows his vocation. What you need now, Joseph, is an unshakable conviction that the superiors were right in nominating you. Have confidence in them, and trust those whom they send to your aid—and furthermore, have blind trust in your own strength! The élite, however, observe with a cheerful but ever-watchful distrust, for they expect nothing else. You will succeed, Joseph, I am absolutely convinced of it!"

The majority of his magisterial duties were already well-known to the new Magister, or were familiar activities that he had previously carried out on his own or as an assistant. The most important of these were the Bead Game courses, starting with those for pupils and beginners, the festive and guest courses and rising to the exercises, lectures and seminaries for the élite. These duties, with the exception of the last named, were fully within the capacity of any newly appointed Magister, whereas the new functions which he would not have had occasion to practice would naturally give him more anxiety and care, and this was also the case with Joseph. He would have preferred to devote himself to these new duties with undivided zeal, particularly the actual magistral ones such as the collaboration in the highest educational council, the co-operation between the Council of Magisters and the Order Administration and the representation of the Bead Game in the Vicus Lusorum before the collective authorities. He was burning to make himself acquainted with these tasks and to encounter the menacing aspect of the unknown. He would have liked to have retired for a few weeks in order to study more closely the constitution, the formalities, the protocol of the sessions, etc. For information and instruction on this subject he knew that, apart from M. Dubois, the most experienced connoisseur and master of the magistral forms and tradition stood at his disposal in the person of the Speaker of the Order Administration who, although not a Magister himself, and therefore beneath them in rank, conducted the sittings of the Pedagogy and assisted in preserving a traditional behaviour like some chief master of ceremonies at a princely court. How greatly would he have liked to beg a private course of instruction from this shrewd, experienced man, who was so inscrutable in his brilliant courtesy and at whose hands he had been invested with his robes, had the latter but resided in Waldzell instead of half a day's journey away in Hirsland! How glad would he have been to have hurried to Monteport for a while, and have been taught these things by the old Music Master! Alas, they were both out of the question, and a Magister could not entertain any such private and student-like wishes. He had far more to devote his entire care and devotion for the first few days to those functions that he had thought would cause him but little effort. What he had experienced during Bertram's Game, where he had seen a Magister abandoned by his own comrades, the élite, to struggle in empty space and be ruined, what he had guessed at at that time, and what the words of the old man from Monteport had confirmed on the day of his investiture, now showed him at each moment of his official day and at each waking moment what his own predicament was—he had above all things to devote himself to the élite and the tutorship, to the highest grades of study, the seminary exercises and to enter into an entirely personal relationship with the tutors. He could safely leave the Archives to the Archivist, the beginners' course to their present teachers, the correspondence to the secretaries, and nothing much could go wrong: but he could not afford for one instant to leave the élite to their own devices, had to constrain them and make himself indispensable to them, had to conquer, court and win them over and measure swords with any candidate who seemed disposed to argument, and of these there was no lack.

In this struggle much came to his aid which he had formerly overlooked, particularly his long absence from Waldzell and the élite, in whose eyes he was now almost a *homo novus*. His friendship with Tegularius now proved of great service to him, for that witty, sickly outsider obviously did not come in the running as a competitor and had so little ambition that a few favours from the new Magister would not necessarily mean any disadvantage to the other aspirants. But the greatest and best part of his work of storming this highest, most active, restless and sensitive stratum of the Game world Knecht had to do for himself. He had to tame these men much as a rider does a thoroughbred horse, for in each Castalian institution and not only in the Bead Game circles, the élite comprised an already matured cultural element—still studying no doubt and not yet in the service of the Order or actually accepted into the Order, and still called coaches—but men who were the most precious assets and actually the reserve and blossoms of the future. Everywhere, not only in the Game Town, this arrogant *cream*, this newest brood of future teachers and superiors, not only showed criticism and reserve and accorded only the minimum requisite courtesy and submission to the new leader, but had to be won over by the personal achievements of the newcomer and be convinced and conquered before they recognised him and submitted readily to his leadership.

Knecht approached the task fearlessly, but was amazed at its difficulty; and while he was in the process of resolving it, which assumed the nature of a highly tiring and exciting game, those other duties and tasks which he had been inclined to think of with anxiety slipped into the background and seemed to demand less and less of his attention. He confessed to a colleague later that he had attended the first full session of the Pedagogy—to which he had gone and returned in a fast conveyance—almost as in a dream, and had been able to devote no further thought to it afterwards because he had been so completely absorbed by the work in hand. Even during the council itself, although the subject under discussion had interested him and although he had thought of this first appearance before the Pedagogy with a certain trepidation, he had caught himself several times with his thoughts not among his colleagues and in the debate but far away in the blue distempered room of the Archives where every third day he held a dialectical class for only five participants, each hour of which demanded a greater degree of attention and was more telling on his strength than the whole of the rest of the day, which was by no means light and from which he could not withdraw, for the Pedagogy had sent him, as the old Music Master had told him they would, a taskmaster and controller to observe his routine hour by hour, advise him upon his timetable and to preserve him from onesidedness and overwork during this, the first period of office. Knecht was grateful to this man, and even more so to the representative of the Order Administration, the highly reputed master of the art of meditation, whose name was Alexander. The latter took good care that, even on the most tiring days, he observed thrice daily the "little" or "short" exercises, and also that he paid accurate heed to the length of time, down to the number of minutes laid down for such exercises. Before both these helpers—the crammer and the contemplative Order Brother—he was obliged each day, just before the evening meal, to recapitulate his day of office, to reveal his progress and defeat, to "feel his own pulse" as the meditation teacher called it, *i.e.*, to recognise and take his own measure, his momentary position, his health and the distribution of his powers, his hopes and anxieties, to see his daily work objectively and to take to sleep with him nothing unsolved or of the morrow.

While the coaches looked upon the colossal work of their Master in part with sympathetic and in part with belligerent interest, and missed no opportunity of setting him little trials of strength, patience and ingenuity, of increasing his work or frustrating it, a fatal emptiness had taken hold of his friend Tegularius. He fully understood that Knecht could now have no time, attention, thought or compassion to spare for him, but somehow failed to make himself hard and indifferent enough to withstand the perfect oblivion into which he had so suddenly been thrust. To make things even harder for him it not only appeared that his friend of yesterday was lost to him to-day, but that he was now also to be treated with a certain amount of distrust by his comrades and he was in fact almost ignored. This of course was not remarkable, for even if Tegularius could not really stand in the way of the ambitious he was still in the running as a coach and still had an arrow in his quiver in the person of the new Master. None of this was of course beyond Knecht's comprehension, and it was in keeping with his task of the moment to eliminate this friendship along with all other personal and private affairs for the time being. He did not actually do this wittingly and intentionally, however, as his friend admitted later, but simply forgot all about him. He had turned himself so entirely into a tool that private things such as friendship had completely disappeared from his consideration; and when Fritz's face and figure appeared anywhere before him—as in that seminary of five members—it was not Tegularius a friend and an acquaintance, a person, but Tegularius a student, a candidate, a coach and one of the élite, a portion of his work and task, a soldier in the troop, one whom it was his objective to school and conquer. Fritz had realised with a shudder that this alienation and objectivity was not assumed but genuine and uncanny, and that the man before him, who treated him with this professional politeness and great intellectual awareness, was no longer his friend Joseph but only a teacher and examiner, only the Magister Ludi, entirely dedicated to and absorbed by the strenuousness of a task, resembling nothing so much as a brilliant glazed object which had been moulded and petrified beneath the flames.

As a matter of fact, during the course of these restless weeks Tegularius happened to figure in a small disturbance. Suffering from insomnia, and inwardly exhausted by his recent experience, he committed a misdemeanour in the little seminary: he was guilty of a small outburst, not against the Magister, but against one of his colleagues who had irritated his nerves with his mocking remarks. Knecht noticed it and at the same time realised the nervous condition of the delinquent. He raised an admonitory finger, but after the class sent the culprit his meditation master so that the latter might practise a little spiritual healing upon him. Tegularius saw in these attentions, after a week-long privation, the first signs of a re-awakening friendship, for he took it as a personal recognition and submitted readily to the cure. In actual fact, Knecht had hardly taken this possibility into account when he had prescribed this cure but had acted entirely as a Magister: he had noticed signs of irritation and a lapse of good behaviour on the part of one of his coaches and had reacted to it professionally, without for one moment looking upon this coach as a person and bringing him into relationship with himself. When, some months later, Fritz reminded him of this scene and assured him how overjoyed and consoled he had been by this sign of goodwill Knecht remained silent, because he had completely forgotten the incident and did not bother to contradict him.

At last his goal had been reached, and the conflict won. It had been a great struggle to bring the élite to heel, to exercise them to the point of weariness, to tame the unruly, to win over the undecided ones and to impress the arrogant; but at last the task was completed. The aspirants of the Game Town had recognised their Master and surrendered to him.

Suddenly everything went smoothly as though only a few drops of oil had been lacking. The taskmaster laid down a final programme of work for Knecht, assured him of his recognition by the authorities and disappeared. The meditation adept, Alexander, did the same. In place of the morning massage he would now go for a walk, and although for the moment it was not possible to think of anything in the nature of study or private reading, on many an evening he was able to enjoy a little music before retiring.

At his next appearance before the Pedagogy Knecht felt quite clearly, without a word having been spoken, that he was now looked upon by his colleagues as one of their permanent peers. After the fire and devotion of his struggle for majority there now came an awakening, a cooling and a sobering. He saw himself in the innermost circle of Castalia and on the upper rung of the hierarchy, and realised with strange sobriety and almost with disappointment that it was also possible to breathe in this rarified atmosphere, but that he, who was now breathing it as though he had never known any before, had been completely transformed. This was the fruit of that hard testing period which had kindled him as no other exertion had previously done.

The recognition of the regent by the élite this time was marked by a curious gesture. Now that Knecht sensed the absence of any resistance and a definite confidence and comprehension on the part of the tutorship, and realised that the greatest difficulty was over, he decided that the moment had come for him to choose a "shadow" for himself. In fact he had never been more in need of such an unburdening than in this moment after victory, when the almost superhuman trial of strength had left him with a relative freedom. Many a man would have succumbed at this point of the way. Knecht now renounced his right to choose from among the candidates and asked the tutorship to place a "shadow" of their own choosing at his disposal. Still under the spell of Bertram's destiny, the élite took this accommodation doubly seriously, made their choice after several sessions and secret discussions and presented the Magister with one of their best men as deputy—in fact the man who had been the obvious choice for Magister Ludi before his own nomination.

Now that the hardest period had been passed there was music and walking again: he could think of reading; friendship with Tegularius was possible, and at times an exchange

of letters with Ferromonte. From time to time there was a
free half-day, and sometimes a small holiday excursion. All
these pleasant things alone would have been a boon to
another, but not to the former Joseph who had considered
himself to be an industrious bead-player and a moderately
good Castalian, and yet had been so ignorant of the innermost circle of the Castalian organisation, who had lived such
a naïvely self-seeking, childishly frivolous, indescribably
private and irresponsible life. He often recalled Magister
Thomas' ironical words of admonition on the occasion when
he had expressed the wish that he might be allowed to
continue his free studies for a while. "For a while?" the
Magister had asked. "How long is that? You are still speaking the language of the students, Joseph." That had been only
a few years before. He had listened to him with deep admiration and awe, but also with a slight feeling of horror at the
impersonal perfection and discipline of the man; he had felt
how Castalia also wished to clutch *him* and draw him to
itself, and perhaps one day make of him such a man as this
Thomas—a master, a regent and servant, a perfect tool.
And now he was in this very position himself, and when he
spoke with one of his coaches—one of these shrewd sophisticated players and private scholars, one of these industrious and
arrogant princes—he looked at him as though he were living
in another beautiful but alien world of the past, exactly as
Magister Thomas had once looked at him while he was in his
strange student world.

Chapter Seven

IN OFFICE

IF AT THE OUTSET Knecht's appointment to the office of
Magister seemed to have brought with it more loss than gain,
if it almost consumed his strength and personal life putting an
end to all habits and hobbies and leaving a cold tranquillity in
the heart and a feeling of giddiness in the head from over-
exertion, the later days brought acclimatisation, recuperation,

a clearer outlook along with many new observations and experiences. The greatest of these was his confidential and friendly collaboration with the élite after the victorious conflict. He now lived, in the conferences with his "shadow," in the work with Fritz Tegularius, whom he used on probation as assistant in his correspondence, in the gradual studying, checking and amplifying of the testimonials and other reports on pupils and collaborators which his predecessor had left behind, with a rapidly growing love for this élite whom he had thought he had known so well but whose character, together with the peculiarity of the Game Town and its rôle in Castalian life, was now revealed to him for the first time in all its reality. He may for many years have belonged to this élite and tutorship, to this musical and ambitious Game Town in Waldzell, and have looked upon himself as a part of it, but now he was no longer only a part, living within it in spirit alone, for he could now consider himself the brain, the consciousness and also the conscience of this community, whose disturbances and destinies he not only led and was responsible for, but shaped.

In an exalted moment at the end of a course for perfecting Game teachers for beginners he once uttered these words: "Castalia is a small state on its own, and our Vicus Lusorum a tiny state within a state—a small but old and proud republic, ranking with and possessing the same rights as its sisters, but strengthened in its self-consciousness and raised above them through the special, musical and we might almost say sacral nature of its functions, for we are distinguished by our task of guarding the actual Castalian holy of holies, its unique mystery and symbol, the Bead Game. Castalia raises outstanding musicians and art historians, philologists, mathematicians and other scholars. Each Castalian institution and each Castalian should know only two ideals: to achieve the utmost possible perfection in his subject, and to keep both his Faculty and himself, living and elastic, so that he may know himself to be permanently bound to all other subjects and inwardly on good terms with all of them. This second ideal, the idea of the inner unity of all intellectual human effort, the thought of universality, has its perfect expression in our illustrious Game. The physician, the musical historian or whatever teacher you like may at times display a stern and ascetic perseverance in his own subject and renounce the thought of a universal culture in favour of the special high achievement of the moment; but we—we bead-players— whatever we do, must never approve and practise this limitation and self-sufficiency, for it is our definite task to preserve the idea of a *Universitas Litterarum* and its highest expression, the noble Game, and ever and again to rescue it from the inclination of the individual Faculties towards self-sufficiency. But how then can we rescue something that has no wish to be rescued, and how can we force the archæologists, pedagogues, astronomers, etc., to renounce their self-sufficient specialisations and continually to open their doors to all the other Faculties? We could not do it by compulsory methods, such as making the Bead Game an official subject in the schools, nor could we do it simply by recalling what our precursors intended with this Game. We can only prove our Game and ourselves indispensable by maintaining our whole intellectual life perpetually at the peak, by watchfully adapting ourselves to every new achievement, every new aspect and question of knowledge, and by presenting and performing our universality, our noble and also dangerous Game, with the ever-renewed thought of unity, and by so doing make it so beautiful and convincing, alluring and attractive that even the most serious research worker and industrious specialist will be forced to recognise its message, its seduction and its spell. Let us imagine that for a time we players were to work with less zeal, that the Game courses for beginners were to grow tedious and superficial, that the specialists were to become the living, pulsating life in the Games for advanced players, the spiritual actuality and interest were to be lacking, that our great Annual Game was three or four times in succession to be no more than an empty ceremony—a dead, outdated and fossilised relic of the past—how quickly would both the Game and ourselves be shelved. We are already no longer at the brilliant high peak at which the Bead Game stood a generation ago, when the Annual Game did not last for a week or two but three or four and was the great event of the year, not only for Castalians but for the whole country. To-day a representative of the Government attends the Annual Game more often than not as a bored guest, and only a few towns and classes send emissaries. Towards the end

of the Game many of these representatives make it apparent
in the most courteous manner that the length of the feast
keeps many a town from sending its representatives and that
perhaps for considerations of time it would be better either to
shorten it very considerably or in future to hold it only every
second or third year. Now we cannot stop this development
or this decline. It is quite possible that our Game will very
soon find no understanding in the outside world, and that the
festival will only be celebrated once every five or even ten
years or perhaps not at all. We must prevent this at all costs,
and what we can do is to see that the discrediting and
devaluation of the Game does not take place in our own
country—in our Province. Here our struggle is hopeful and
continually leads to victory: every day we may see young
élite scholars, who have joined the Games courses without
any great enthusiasm, who have shown good conduct on the
whole and carried out their studies rather perfunctorily
suddenly being seized by the spirit of the Game, by its
intellectual possibilities, venerable tradition and emotional
powers, and becoming our most passionate followers and
partisans; every year at the *ludus sollemnis* we can see scholars
of rank and renown, who have made no secret of their
contempt for us bead-players during their whole busy working
year and have not always wished our institution well,
becoming more and more redeemed and being won over by
the magic of our art, alleviated and exalted, rejuvenated and
uplifted and ultimately, completely conquered and strengthened in heart, taking their leave with words of almost
shamefaced gratitude. Let us examine for a moment the
means at our disposal for the fulfilment of our task: we see a
precious, beautiful and well-ordered apparatus, the heart and
centrum of which is the Game Archives, which we all make
use of gratefully and which each one of us serves, from the
Magister and Archivist down to the lowest assistant. The
best and most vivid characteristic of our institution is the
ancient Castalian principle of the choice of the best—the
élite. The schools of Castalia collect the best scholars from
the whole land and educate them. In the same way we in the
Game Town try to select the best of these, who have a
special love and talent for the Game, to retain, develop and
perfect them. Our courses and seminaries receive hundreds

and let them go again, but we cultivate the best of them as true players, as artists and adepts of the Game, and each one of you know that in our art as in every art there is no end point of development, that each one of us, once we belong to the élite, will for the rest of our lives work for the further development, refinement and adaptation of ourselves and of our art, irrespective of whether we have a bureaucratic post or not. Accusations have often been made against us that the existence of our élite is actually a luxury and that there is no further need to educate élite players in order to fill our official posts; but officialdom is not a sufficient institution in itself, and again, everyone is not suited to be an official any more than every good philologist is suited to be a teacher. In any case, we officials know and feel very acutely that the tutorship is not merely a reservoir of talented and experienced players from which to fill our gaps and to furnish us with successors. I might also say that this is only an auxiliary function of the Game élite—as I invariably do when stressing their importance to the heedless every time the question crops up as to the meaning and justification of our institution. No, the coaches are not in the first degree future Magisters, course leaders or Archive officials: they are a means in themselves. Their little band is the actual substance and future of the Bead Game. Here, in a few dozen hearts and brains, the development, adaptation, rises and conflicts of our Game are played out, with the time spirit, and the individual sciences. Only here is our Game played accurately and justly, to its full value and with maximum stakes; only here in our élite is it a self-goal and sacred service, devoid of amateurish or pseudo-cultural vanity, devoid of pomposity or superstition. The future of the Game lies in the hands of you Waldzell coaches. It is the heart and vitality of Castalia, and you are the innermost and most vital members of our settlement—you are, in fact, the salt of the Province, its spirit and its restlessness. There is no danger that your number will grow too large, your zeal too ardent, your passion for the wonderful Game too heated, for if you rise, it rises too. There is, however, as for all Castalians, one particular danger against which we must every one of us guard day by day. The spirit of our Order and our Province is based on two principles—upon objectivity and love of truth in our studies, and upon the culture of contemplative wisdom and harmony. For us, to maintain a balance between these two principles is synonymous with being wise and worthy of our Order. We love all branches of knowledge, each man his own, and yet we know that devotion to a subject cannot save a man from selfishness, vice and absurdity. The history of the sciences is full of such examples, and the figure of Dr. Faustus is the popular literary symbol of this danger. Other centuries sought flight in the unification of spirit and religion, in research and ascesis, and theology reigned in their *Universitas Litterarum*. In our case it is with meditation, the many-graded yoga praxis, that we endeavour to exorcise the beast within us and the diabolus in each branch of knowledge. Now you know as well as I do that the Bead Game houses its own private diabolus, which can lead to empty virtuosity, artistic vanity as a form of self-indulgence, competition, the striving for power over others and thus to the abuse of power. We were in need, therefore, of another education in addition to the intellectual, and we have submitted ourselves to the morality of the Order, not so that our active spiritual life should conform to a soulful, vegetative dream-existence, but on the contrary in order to be capable of the highest spiritual achievements. We must not flee from the *vita activa* into the *vita contemplativa* or the reverse, but we should continually try to strike a mean between the two and be at home in each and participate in each."

We have quoted these words of Knecht's because they throw such a clear light upon his conception of office, at least during the first years of his magistracy. Many similar examples have been recorded by his pupils. That he was an outstanding teacher—to his own amazement at the outset— we can see by the surprising number of lectures that have been preserved to us in his own writings: that teaching should afford so much pleasure and should have come so easily to him was one of the discoveries and surprises which his office brought him from the very beginning. He would never have dreamed that such should be the case, for he had never previously yearned for a teaching position. He had, as every member of the élite has done, occasionally held teaching posts of short duration, had taught as a deputy in the various grades of the Bead Game courses and frequently served as

co-examine r of the participants; but at that time the freedom
of his studies and his lonely concentration upon his favourite
subjects had been so important and so dear to him that he had
looked upon these teaching tasks—although he had been
capable and beloved—as irksome disturbances. Finally, he
had also taken courses in the Benedictine monastery, but
intrinsically they had been of little importance and had been
of even less account to himself; he had allowed all other work
there to be subordinated to his course of instruction with
Father Jacobus and to his relationship with him. His major
efforts during those days had been directed towards becoming
a good scholar, to learning, absorbing and cultivating his
mind; but now out of the pupil a teacher had developed, and
it was as a teacher above all that he had mastered his great
task during his first period of office—the struggle for
authority and for an exact identification between person and
office. He made two discoveries at this period, firstly the joy
that ensues from the transplanting of knowledge already
gained into other minds and of seeing it take on completely
new appearances and radiations—in other words the joy of
teaching—and secondly, the struggle with the personalities
of the students and scholars and the gaining and practising of
authority and leadership—otherwise the joy of educating.
He had never really separated the two, and during his
magistracy had not only trained a great number of very good
and first-class bead-players but had also, through his personal
example, through his resolute type of patience and through
the strength of his personality and character, developed the
greater proportion of his pupils to the utmost of their
capabilities,

If we may be allowed a digression here, he had made
another characteristic discovery. At the beginning of his
official duties he had had to do exclusively with the élite,
with the highest branch of his subordinates, with students
and coaches, many of whom were the same age as himself and
many of whom were already expert players. Gradually, as he
became more sure of them, he began slowly and cautiously,
year by year, to relax his power and to devote less time to
them until eventually he could leave them almost entirely to
the care of his trusted assistants and collaborators. This
procedure lasted for several years, during which Knecht

extended his lectures, courses and exercises so as to embrace ever lower grades until, on several occasions, he found himself—a thing that a Magister Ludi has seldom done—taking beginner courses for pupils who were not yet even qualified students. He found that the younger and more ignorant scholars were, the more pleasure he derived from teaching them, and it was sometimes almost a burden, and would cost him a perceptible effort, to return from these younger and youngest pupils to the élite. At times he felt a desire to go even further back still and make an attempt with pupils for whom there was not yet a Bead Game course—to Eschholz for example, or to one of the other preparatory schools, where he would have liked for a while to instruct the little boys in Latin, singing or algebra. There the atmosphere would be far less intellectual even than in the preliminary courses of the Bead Game, the practice of teaching and the idea of education more closely related, and he would at least be dealing with frank and malleable pupils. In the last two years of his Magistracy he had twice signed himself "Schoolmaster," thereby recalling the fact that the title "Magister Ludi," which for Generations in Castalia had only signified "The Master of the Game," had originally been synonymous with "Schoolmaster."

In any case the fulfilment of any such schoolmasterish wishes was out of the question: they were dreams, such as one may dream on cold grey winter days, of a blue summer sky. No new road lay open to Knecht now, for his freedom to choose was curtailed by the demands of his office; but as this office was one that gave him far-reaching personal liberty to fulfil his duties as he desired, he had from the beginning quite unconsciously turned towards his major interest—the guidance and instruction of the youngest grades accessible to him. The older he grew the more youth attracted him. This is how we of to-day see it, but a critic at that period would certainly have found it difficult to discover any trace of private enjoyment or self-interest in his conduct of office. This high post compelled him ever and again to return to the élite, and at such times when, for example, he had to leave the seminaries and Archives almost entirely to his helpers and his "shadow" during the lengthy work entailed by the yearly Game competition or the preparations for the Annual Game, he was brought into daily and vivid contact with them.

He once said jestingly to his friend Fritz: "There have been princes who, throughout their whole lives, were tormented by an unhappy love for their underlings. While their hearts were drawn towards the peasants, shepherds, artisans, schoolteachers and schoolchildren they seldom managed to see anything of them for they were continually surrounded by their ministers and officers, who stood like a wall between them and their people. This is exactly what happens to a Magister: he would like to go to the common man and sees only colleagues, would like to go to youth and children and sees only advanced scholars and the élite."

However, we have been anticipating somewhat, and we must now return to Knecht's first official year. Once he had achieved a desirable relationship with the élite, his next important task was to become a friendly but watchful master over all the officials of the Archives. He had to learn the routine of his office, and to attend to the many letters that arrived summoning him to sessions or, in the form of circular letters from the collective officials, demanding duties and tasks of him which as a relative newcomer he did not find easy to understand and organise correctly. They were often to do with questions in which the Faculties of the Provinces were interested and in which they were inclined to be jealous of one another and sometimes questions of jurisdiction, and only gradually but with growing admiration did he learn to appreciate the secret and powerful function of the Order, of this living soul of the Castalian state and the constitution of its watchful protector.

Thus the strenuous and over-filled months went by without there being any place in Joseph's thoughts for Tegularius, except—and this was done half instinctively—that he allotted a great deal of work to him in order to protect him from too much idleness. Fritz had lost his comrade, who overnight had become his master and his highest superior: he no longer had private access to him but had to obey him and address him formally as "Reverence." Yet he accepted all that the Magister required of him as a personal sign of care and solicitude, and this somewhat moody lone wolf found himself, through the promotion of his friend and the highly excitable mood of the whole élite, participating in this excitement and being of service to him by the work which he had been given. In any case, since that moment when he had announced the news to Knecht that he was destined to be Magister Ludi and had been so brusquely dismissed, he had endured the completely changed position better than he would have thought possible. He was also intelligent and compassionate enough to understand, or at least to have some idea of, the colossal exertions and trials of strength that his friend had to undergo at that time: he witnessed the ordeal by fire, and as he was the more sensitive he suffered inwardly more than the man on trial himself. Although he took the utmost pains with the commissions that the Master entrusted to him, and although he seriously regretted his disinclination for office work and responsibility, recognising it to be a great failing, he would have liked most of all to have been a helper and an official, and to have stood at the side of this friend whom he so admired as his "shadow."

Autumnal gold had already begun to tinge the beech woods above Waldzell when one day Knecht, taking a little book with him, entered the Magister's garden near his residence —that pretty little garden that the dead Magister Thomas had loved so much and which Knecht, like all scholars and students, had once imagined as a holy of holies, a hallowed spot for the relaxation and recuperation of the Master, like some magic island of the Muses or Tusculum, and which he himself had visited so seldom since he had become Magister Ludi and its owner. Even now he had only come to spend a few carefree moments after dinner, and was walking up and down between the high bushes and shrubs beneath which his predecessor had planted so many evergreens from the south. He drew a light cane chair into a sunny spot—for it was very cool in the shade—sat down and opened the little book. It was the "Pocket Calendar of a Magister Ludi" which Ludwig Wassermaler, the Magister Ludi of that time, had composed seventy or eighty years before and which since then had been augmented with many corrections, deletions and additions by each of his followers. This calendar was a *vade-mecum* for Magisters, particularly for those who were inexperienced, during their first years of office: it embraced the whole work of the official year week by week, showing the most important duties, many of them in an abbreviated form but many in detail and supplemented with personal advice. Knecht looked up the current week and read it through attentively. He found nothing surprising or particularly urgent, but at the foot of the extract he read the following lines: "Begin to turn your thoughts gradually to the next year's Game. It seems premature—in fact, it may seem to you unduly early. Nevertheless, my advice is: should you not have a plan for the Game in your head, let no week or at least no month pass by from now onwards without giving a thought to the future Game. Jot down your ideas; study the scheme of some classical Game for half-an-hour or so, and take it with you on a few official journeys; prepare yourself, not by forcing good ideas to come but by thinking as often as you can of the fact that in the coming months a beautiful and festive task awaits you, for which you should perpetually be preparing your mood, bracing and collecting your thoughts."

These words had been written two or three generations before by a wise old man and a master of his art at a time when the formal Bead Game had perhaps reached its highest cultural level: in the Game at that time there had been a delicacy and rich ornamentation in its exposition comparable with the late gothic or rococo in the art of architecture and decoration, and for two decades the Game really had been with beads and was apparently glassy and somewhat shallow, but a coquettish arrogant Game full of tender embellishments like a dance—sometimes almost a tightrope dance—swaying in the most differentiated rhythm. There were players who spoke of a lost magical key to that style, while others found it superficial, over-decorated, decadent and effeminate. The composer of these friendly and well-considered counsels and admonitions in the Magister's Calendar, which Knecht now read through critically for a second and third time, had been one of the masters and joint creators of that style. He felt a serene delicious stirring at his heart, a sensation which he had once experienced, and which had never been repeated, during the meditation before his investiture which had inspired that wondrous roundelay, that whirling dance between the Music Master and Joseph, between master and beginner, between old age and youth. Magister Ludwig, he thought, had already been an old man when he had written down these thoughts: "let no week pass by . . ." and "not by forcing good ideas to come . . ." He had perhaps already filled this high office for some twenty years or more, and in that age of joyous rococo had doubtless often had to deal with a highly spoiled and self-assured élite. Having invented and conducted no fewer than a score of brilliant Annual Games, which at that time had lasted for four weeks on end, the recurrent task of composing a great *sollemnis* each year must have been far less an honour and a joy to the old man than a burden and a great exertion—a task for which he had to inspire the mood, use self-persuasion and resort to certain stimuli. Knecht felt nothing but a grateful veneration for this wise, experienced old counsellor and for his Calendar, which had often proved to be a valuable guide; but at the same time he could not help giving way to an ebullient, gay and arrogant feeling of superiority—the superiority of youth—for of all the cares of a Magister Ludi of which he had already learned, this particular one did not come into the picture: one could not think early enough of the Annual Game, could not possibly be lacking in a joyous anticipation for this task or in ideas. No, the Knecht who during the past month or so had often appeared out-wardly old, at this moment felt young and strong. Unfortunately he could not savour or devote himself to this beautiful gay feeling any longer for his leisure hour was all too short and already nearly past, but he retained it and bore it away with him. Thus, his short rest in the Magister's garden had not been in vain, for it had given rise to something new. Not only had he experienced a profound sense of relaxation and a gaily exalted feeling of life, but two ideas had been born, both of which had taken on the quality of resolutions: firstly, when he became too old and tired and when for the first time he found the composition of an Annual Game to be a burdensome duty and the discovery of new ideas to be an embarrassing proposition, he would lay down his office; and secondly, he would soon start work upon his first Annual Game, with his comrade Tegularius as collaborator. This would be a satisfaction and a joy for his friend and would be a first attempt on his part to give their friendship, which had lain fallow for some time, a new lease of life—for Fritz could not possibly make the opening move, and it had to come from the Magister himself.

This project would entail a great deal of work for Tegularius. Since his Mariafels days Knecht had carried in his head an idea for a Bead Game which he now decided to use for his first ceremonial Game as Magister. It was based upon the pretty concept of taking for its structure and dimensions the building of a Chinese house according to the old Confucian ritual scheme—the orientation in accordance with the cardinal points, replete with the gateways, walls to keep out the spirits, and observing the relations and requirements of the buildings and courtyards, their arrangement to the planets, the calendar, family life and also to the symbolism and rules of style obtaining in the garden. Once, when he had been studying a commentary on the I Ching, the mythical order and significance of these rules had appeared to him to be a particularly apposite and genial simile of the cosmos and the position of man in the world. He also found the age-old mythical folk spirit in this tradition of house construction remarkably compatible with the spirit of the speculative scholarly mandarin and with the spirit of the Magister. He had often enough worked lovingly upon the plan for this Game, admittedly without making notes, in order to have the whole of it ready in his mind, but since his appointment to office he had no longer had time to do so. Now, in this moment of resolution, he decided that he would build up his ceremonial Game upon this Chinese idea and Fritz, should he be capable of appreciating the spirit of it, would now have to begin his studies for its development and its translation into the Game language. There was only one difficulty in the way: Tegularius knew no Chinese, and it was far too late in the day for him to start learning it, but as in this case it was not so much a question of philology, with the help of the literature upon the subject and from the hints that could be given him, partly by Knecht himself and partly by the College of Sinology, he could be initiated quite adequately into the magical symbols of the Chinese house. In any event it would require a lot of time, particularly for a spoiled creature like his friend who did not feel inclined to work every day, and it was therefore a good thing to tackle the affair immediately. He realised with a smile of pleasant surprise that the cautious old man had been perfectly right in his observations in the pocket calendar.

The very next day, as his audiences were over quite early, he sent for Tegularius. The latter arrived, bowed with the somewhat exaggerated devotion and humility which he had now adopted towards the Magister, and was greatly astonished when, instead of being spoken to in the usual brief terms, Knecht nodded to him and asked with a certain roguery: "Do you remember how once in our student days we had a great argument, in which I failed utterly in converting you to my way of thinking? It was about the value and importance of eastern studies, particularly Chinese, and I wanted to make you spend a certain time in the College of Sinology learning the language—do you remember? Now, to-day for the second time I am regretting that I could not persuade you to agree with me. How excellent it would have been now if you could understand Chinese: we could have undertaken the most wonderful work together."

He teased his friend a little, arousing his anticipation before finally coming into the open with his proposition. He told him that he wished to begin working out the details of the Great Game immediately, and if it would give him any pleasure he would like Fritz to carry out a large proportion of the work, just as he had done in Knecht's competition Game for the *sollemnis* while he had been staying in the Benedictine Monastery.

Fritz looked at him incredulously, greatly surprised and already thrilled by the friendly tone and smiling face of his friend, whom for so long he had only seen as a lord and master. Deeply touched, he realised not only the honour which this proposal afforded and the confidence which was being placed in him, but also saw and appreciated the full significance of Knecht's fine gesture. It was an attempt at reparation, a re-opening of the closed door between his friend and himself. He took the former's reflections about his knowledge of Chinese lightly, and without more ado declared himself ready to place his talents wholeheartedly at the disposal of his Reverence in the compilation of the Game.

"Good!" replied Knecht. "I shall hold you to your promise. At certain hours then, we shall be working companions once more, as we used to be in those days which now seem so far away when we used to prepare and think out so many Games together. It will be a great pleasure, Tegularius.

And now you must give your whole attention to the idea upon which I propose to build this Game. First of all you must be able to understand exactly what a Chinese house is and what the rules in its construction signify. I will give you a letter of recommendation to the College of Sinology where they will help you. No, I have a far better idea than that: we can try Elder Brother, the man who lives in the Bamboo Grove about which I have already told you so much. It may possibly be beneath his dignity, or he may consider it too much bother to have anything to do with someone who knows no Chinese, but we will make the attempt none the less. If this man feels so inclined he is quite capable of making a Chinaman out of you."

A message was sent at once to Elder Brother cordially inviting him to come to Waldzell as a guest of the Magister Ludi, explaining that his office allowed him no time to pay any visits and informing him of the service that was required of him. The "Chinaman," however, did not leave his Bamboo Grove, and the messenger returned with a little scroll upon which had been written in Chinese characters: "It would be an honour indeed to see the Great Man, but travel leads to hindrances. Two little bowls are customary for sacrifice. The younger greets the Eminent One."

At this, Knecht, not without great difficulty, succeeded in persuading his friend to go to Bamboo Grove to ask Elder Brother to receive and instruct him. But this little journey also remained without results: the hermit, in his grove, received Tegularius with an almost servile politeness, but refrained from answering a single one of his questions except in friendly axioms couched in the Chinese language; nor did he invite him to remain, despite the magnificent letter of recommendation painted with a brush on exquisite paper in the Magister Ludi's calligraphy.

With his mission unaccomplished and in a rather subdued mood, Fritz returned to Waldzell bringing a second scroll upon which was painted a poem to a goldfish. He was now obliged to try his luck in the College of Sinology, where Knecht's recommendations proved more productive. The petitioner and ambassador from the Magister was helped to the utmost and he was soon as perfectly versed in this theme as was possible without a knowledge of Chinese and,

incidentally, found so much joy in Knecht's idea of founding
his Game plan on this house symbolism that he soon forgot
his failure in Bamboo Grove.

When Knecht had heard by report that his messenger had
been repulsed by Elder Brother on his visit to Bamboo Grove,
and as he read the goldfish poem at his leisure he was moved
by the atmosphere surrounding the writer and by a nostalgic
memory of his earlier stay in his hut, with the swaying
bamboos and the yarrow sticks—memories of freedom,
leisure, student days and the bright-coloured paradise of
youthful dreams. How well this courageous and crotchety
hermit had known how to withdraw and preserve his freedom; how hidden from the world he was in his silent Bamboo
Grove, living inwardly and strongly in his pure, pedantic,
wise Chinese fashion, which had become second nature to
him; how circumscribed, concentrated and firm had the magic
of his life-dream kept him year after year, decade after decade,
turning his garden into China, his hut into a temple, his goldfish into divinities and himself into a sage! With a sigh,
Knecht tore himself away from this picture. He had taken
other paths, had been far more constrained and was beholden
to go this appointed way loyally and not to compare it with
the ways of others.

Devoting whatever time to it that he could spare, he outlined and composed his Game with Tegularius, to whom he
left its entire development in the Archives, as well as the first
and second draft. With this new project their friendship took
on life and form once more. It had changed entirely in
character, and the Game upon which they were working also
underwent many changes bearing unmistakable marks of the
originality and sensitive fantasy of the strange collaborator.

Fritz belonged among those never contented and yet self-
sufficient people who busy themselves hour after hour with a
completed bouquet or a laden table which for anyone else
would be ready and perfect with restless pleasure and loving
handling, knowing how to turn the smallest task into an indefatigable and trustworthy day's work. This was to be seen
no less in the forthcoming Game. This year the great
sollemnis was a partnership achievement and a double gratification for Tegularius, in that he had been of such assistance
to his friend and Magister—even to the point of indispensa-

bility—in such an important affair, and had been able to experience the public performance of the Game as an unnamed co-author but fully recognised by the members of the élite.

In the late autumn of that first year of office, while his friend was still busy with his preliminary Chinese studies, the Magister came across a note on his office pad: "The student, Petrus, has arrived with a recommendation from Monteport, bringing special greetings from the Magister Musicæ and asking for hospitality and access to the Archives."

Well, he could safely leave the student's request to the officials of the Archives as this was a matter of daily occurrence, but special greetings from the old Music Master could concern only himself. He sent for the student.

He was a pensive, silent though ardent looking youth, who obviously belonged to the élite of Monteport for he seemed to be quite used to having audience with a Magister. Knecht asked him what the old Music Master had commissioned him to say.

"Greetings," replied the student—"Most affectionate and respectful greetings to you, Reverence, and also an invitation to go and see him."

Knecht asked the youth to sit down.

"The revered ex-Magister," Petrus went on, choosing his words with great care, "enjoined me to convey his greetings to you, as I have just said. At the same time he hinted at a wish to see you in the near future—as soon as possible, that is. He invites you or, rather, suggests that you should go and see him shortly—always provided, of course, that the visit can be an official one and does not take up too much of your time. That is my message."

Knecht looked at the young man and summed him up. He was certainly one of the old man's protegés.

"How long do you intend to remain in the Archives, *Studiose?*" he asked cautiously.

"Until the time, Reverend Magister . . . until I see you are ready to leave for Monteport."

Knecht reflected for a moment. "Good!" he said. "But why have you not repeated to me the exact wording of the old Master's message, as is customary?"

The student returned his gaze obstinately and answered slowly, even more cautiously than before, choosing his words as though he were speaking in a foreign language: "There was no message, Reverence—and no actual text. You know my worthy Master, and you know that he was always an extraordinarily modest man. In Monteport they say that in his youth, while still a coach but already recognised by all the élite as the future Music Master, he was given the nickname 'the great Would-be-Little.' Now this modesty, and to no less a degree his piety, obligingness, thoughtfulness and patience have increased since he laid down office and has grown old, and doubtless you know this better than I. It would therefore have prevented him from asking you to come and visit him even though he wished to do so inordinately—and this is why, *Domine*, as I was not entrusted with a commission of any kind, I took one upon myself. If it was a mistake, then it is for you to consider this fictitious commission as actually non-existent."

Knecht smiled a little. "And your work in the Game Archives, my friend: was that also an excuse?"

"Oh, no! I have a number of abbreviations to look up, and should have been obliged to ask for your hospitality in any case in the near future. But it seemed to me a good thing to make my journey slightly in advance."

"Very well," nodded the Magister, looking quite serious again. "And may one ask the reason for this speed?"

The youth closed his eyes for a moment and wrinkled his forehead, as though the question disturbed him. Then he turned the enquiring and critical look of youth upon the Magister. "The question cannot be answered unless you should decide to elaborate it."

"Very well, then," replied Knecht. "Is the old man's health bad and giving rise to anxiety?"

Although the Magister had spoken with great calm the student could sense his loving care for the old man, and for the first time since the beginning of this interview a ray of good will appeared in his dark eyes and his voice became a little more direct and friendly as though he had at last determined to unburden himself of his suffering.

"Reverence," he said, "you may reassure yourself. The health of the worthy Music Master is not at all bad. He has always been a man of excellent health and is still so to-day, although his great age has weakened him very much. It is not that his appearance has altered a great deal or that his strength has suddenly taken a turn for the worse. On the contrary, he goes for little walks, plays the piano every day and recently gave two pupils instruction on the organ— beginners, for he has always had a preference for the youngest pupils. The fact that for the past fortnight he has given up these two pupils is a symptom that has caught my attention, and ever since I have been watching the worthy Master even more carefully and have been thinking a great deal about him. This is the reason for my presence here to-day. If there is anything that can justify such thoughts and steps, I suppose it is because I myself was once one of his scholars—I might almost say one of his prize scholars—and because about a year ago his successor appointed me as a kind of famulus or companion to the old musician and commissioned me to look after his well being. It was a very pleasant task for me, for there is no man living for whom I have the same respect and sympathy as for my old teacher and patron. Furthermore, it was he who revealed the mystery of music to me and fitted me for its service; and everything that I possess in the way of thoughts, in appreciation of the Order, in maturity and inner serenity is all due to him and to his efforts. And so, for the past year, I have been at his side— although also busy with my studies and one or two courses —but always at his disposal, his companion at table, accompanying him on his walks and at his music, and sleeping in the room next to his own. As a result of this close proximity I can observe quite clearly the stages of his growing old—his physical ageing—and some of my comrades make scornful and pitying jokes about me and about this wonderful office which makes so young a man as myself a life companion to an age-old man. But you do not know—and no one knows as well as I do—what an unexacting master the old man is, how he grows gradually weaker and more feeble, takes less and less nourishment and returns more and more tired from his short walks—without actually being ill, mind you—and how at the same time, in the tranquillity of his dotage, he grows more spiritual, devout, worthy and simple. If there are any difficulties in the way of my office as famulus or attendant they are due to the fact that the worthy man will not be served and cared for but insists upon giving and never taking."

"Thank you," said Knecht. "It is a great joy to me to know that my old friend has so devoted and grateful a pupil. But now tell me, as you are no longer speaking on behalf of your master: why do you actually set so much store by my visit to Monteport?"

"You asked after the old Music Master's health with solicitude," replied the youth. "Therefore my request must have raised the thought in your mind that he might be ill, and possibly that it was high time to pay him a visit again. But although his end does not seem to me to be near, his manner of saying farewell to the world is very strange. During the past few months he has gradually lost the use of speech, and even though he always preferred to be brief rather than loquacious he has now lapsed into a silence that I find rather disturbing. When I speak to him or ask him a question he does not reply, and at first I thought that his hearing must have failed, but he hears as well as ever for I have tested him on several occasions. Then I began to think that he was becoming absent-minded and could not concentrate his attention any more, but that was not the solution either. It is far more probable that he has already been on his way for a long time past, and that he no longer lives entirely among us but more and more in his own world. This is why he has refrained from seeking people out or allowing them to visit him, and apart from myself he sees no one for days on end. Therefore, this aloofness has begun to set in, and since he is now no longer in the world, I have been trying to bring the few friends whom I knew he most loved to his side. If you would pay him a visit, *Domine*, you would doubtless be giving your old friend some pleasure—I am quite convinced of this, in fact—and you would also still be able to see the same man more or less whom you have always honoured and loved, for in a few months' time— perhaps even in a few weeks—his pleasure in seeing you and his compassion for you may have diminished and he may no longer know you or pay any attention to you."

Knecht stood up. He went over to the window and stood there for a moment in silence, looking out and breathing the fresh air. When he turned to the student once more the latter was standing up, as though he had considered the audience to be at an end. The Magister stretched out his hand.

"I must thank you once more, Petrus," he said. "You know, of course, that a Magister has all manner of duties and that he cannot just take his hat and set forth—that everything must be arranged and prepared. I hope to be ready the day after to-morrow. Will that be time enough, and could you have finished your work in the Archives by then? Yes? . . . Very well, I will send for you when I am ready."

A few days later Knecht left with Petrus for Monteport. As they approached the pavilion of the old man's garden, a graceful and peaceful retreat, they heard music coming from the back room—a tender thin, serene music, played in perfect tempo. The old man was sitting there playing a melody for two voices with two fingers; Knecht recognised it as the Bach Bicinium, which had been written towards the end of the sixteenth century. They both stood still until he had come to the end and then Petrus called out to his master, announcing his return and the fact that he had brought a visitor with him. The old man appeared in the doorway and looked at them with a smile of welcome.

This greeting smile of the Magister Musicæ, which was absolutely enchanting, had always been full of childish, frank radiant friendliness and affection. Joseph Knecht had seen it for the first time nearly thirty years before, and his heart had opened at once to the genial man on that oppressive but happy morning in the music room at Eschholz. Since then he had seen it many times and on each occasion had been deeply moved; and as the Master's hair had turned gradually to grey and then to white, as his voice had grown softer, his handshake weaker and his gait more stiff, his smile had lost none of its clarity, grace, purity and sincerity. This time, upon seeing his friend and pupil, it was unmistakable: the radiant living message on the laughing old face, whose blue eyes and delicate, pink cheeks had grown lighter with the years, was not only the same old familiar one but had become now even more spiritual, mysterious and intense. For the first time, at this greeting, Knecht really understood the full significance of Petrus' request, and realised that he was the gainer although he had intended to grant the other a favour by sacrificing some of his time.

Several hours later he visited his friend, Carlo Ferromonte, who was then librarian of the famous Monteport
library—he was actually the first person to whom he spoke
of this transformation—and Carlo has recorded their
conversation in a letter.

"Our old Music Master," said Knecht, "was also your
teacher, and you were very devoted to him. Do you often see
him now?"

"No," replied Carlo, "that is to say I see him frequently
when he goes for his walks, and sometimes when I am
returning from the library, but I have not spoken to him for
months. He retires more and more and does not seem to
enjoy society now. Formerly, he used to keep an evening for
people like myself—early pupils of his who are still officials in
Monteport—but that ceased about a year ago, and we were
all amazed that he went to your investiture in Waldzell."

"Yes," said Knecht; "but when you see him now, do you
notice any particular change in him?"

"Indeed I do. You mean how well he looks—his serenity
and his remarkable radiance? Naturally, we have all noticed it.
While his strength fails, this serenity increases continually.
We have become used to it, but it must be very apparent
to you."

"His famulus, Petrus, sees more of him than you do,"
replied Knecht, "and he has not become used to it as you
imply. He came to Waldzell on his own—naturally with a
plausible excuse—to propose this visit to me. What is your
opinion of him?"

"Of Petrus? Oh, he is quite a good connoisseur of music,
more pedantic than gifted, but rather a ponderous and dark-
blooded creature. He is absolutely devoted to the old Music
Master, and would give his life for him. In my opinion he is so
completely absorbed by his service to his adored Master and
idol that he is obsessed by him. Don't you get that
impression?"

"Obsessed? Yes, but I am inclined to think that this young
man is hardly obsessed by a predilection or a passion alone.
He has not simply become enamoured of his old teacher and
made an idol of him, but is obsessed and enchanted by an
actual and genuine phenomenon which he sees or senses more
acutely than anyone else. I will try to tell you what I mean.

I came here to-day, to visit the old man who, as you know, I have not seen for six months. From the hints that his famulus made, I expected very little or nothing at all from this visit: I had simply been afraid that he might suddenly be leaving us, and so hurried here in order to see him at least once more. When he recognised and greeted me his face seemed to light up, but he said nothing except my name and gave me his hand, and even this movement and his hand seemed to glisten: the whole man, his eyes, white hair and pale rosy skin seemed to give out a gentle cool radiation. I sat down opposite him, and after he had sent the student away there began the most remarkable conversation that I have ever had. At the outset it was very alienating and oppressive, even embarrassing, for I went on talking and asking questions, to which the old man made no other answer but a look. I could not tell whether my questions or remarks reached him in any form other than a burdensome jumble, with the result that I felt confused, disappointed, tired out—as though I were somehow in the way or being importunate. No matter what I said to him I received a smile and a brief glance in reply, and had these looks not been so benevolent and affectionate I should have been forced to think that the old man was making fun of me, of my tale and my questions—of the whole unnecessary rigmarole of my journey here and of my visit to him. Well, something in this nature *was* intended by this silence and smile: it was actually a defence and perhaps a warning, only it was a warning on a different plane and with another grade of meaning than anything in the nature of mocking words. I began to wilt, and it seemed as though I had to suffer complete shipwreck in my patient and courteous attempts at opening a conversation before I began to realise that the old man was capable of a patience, endurance and courtesy a hundred times greater than mine. This state of affairs lasted for perhaps a quarter- or half-an-hour, but it appeared to me to last for half-a-day. I began to grow sad, tired and ill-disposed and to regret my journey, and my throat became quite dry. There sat the worthy man, who had been my patron and friend ever since I could first think for myself, who had possessed my heart and my trust and who had never refused to answer any of my questions; there he sat, having retired and completely fortified himself behind a radiant smile, unattainable behind a golden mask, already belonging to another world and governed by other laws. Everything that one wished to communicate to him from our world ran off him like rain off a stone. At last—I had already given up hope—he broke through his magic world and came to my aid. At last he uttered a word. It was the only remark that I heard him make to-day. 'You are tiring yourself, Joseph,' he said gently in that voice of infinite friendliness and solicitude which you know so well, as though he had been watching me for a long time at too strenuous a task and wished to rebuke me. The words came with some effort, as though he had not used his lips in speech for a very long time. At the same time he laid a hand as light as a butterfly upon my arm, looked me directly in the eyes and smiled. I was completely conquered. Something of his calm, patience and serenity came over to me, together with a sudden comprehension of the course which the old man's life had taken— away from humans into a realm of silence, away from speech and thoughts into music and unity. I realised then what I had been vouchsafed, and understood for the first time the significance of this smile and radiance. I had been sitting there before a saint and a perfect one, who had allowed me to participate for an hour in his aura and I, clumsy oaf that I am, had talked, questioned and tried to engage him in conversation. I thank God that I had seen the light in time! He might have dismissed me and witheld himself from me for ever, and I should thus have missed the most remarkable and wonderful experience that I have ever known."

"Really?" said Ferromonte thoughtfully. "So you regard the old Magister Musicæ almost in the nature of a saint? It is a good thing that it is actually you who have brought all this to my notice. I admit that I should have accepted such a report from anyone else with the greatest mistrust. Taking everything into consideration I am not a great lover of mysticism, particularly as I am a musician and historian, a pedant and friend of pure categories. As we in Castalia are neither a Christian congregation nor an Indian or Taoist brotherhood, it seems to me that this elevation into the company of the saints, and therefore into a purely religious category, is not actually admissible to us. If it had come from anyone but yourself—you will pardon me *Domine*—I should

have considered the presumption of such an apotheosis as a
lapse from grace. But then, I imagine that you hardly intend
proposing a canonisation of the venerable old Music Master,
for it would not correspond in the least with the existing ideas
of our Order and the Pedagogy. No, please do not interrupt
me—I am speaking in all earnestness, and my remarks are
not meant in the least as a joke. You have related an experience to me, and I must admit that I feel a little ashamed
that neither I nor my Monteport colleagues have fully
appreciated the phenomenon you portray; we have only
noticed it vaguely and have paid little attention to it. I am
fully aware of my lack of sensitivity in this respect, and its
cause. The fact that the transformation of the old Music
Master struck you so forcibly and was something of a
revelation while I hardly noticed it can naturally be explained.
It took you unawares, you see, and as a *fait accompli*, while I
have been witness to a slow process of development: for you
the old Music Master of some months ago and the one you
saw to-day are two completely different persons, while we,
his neighbours, meeting him from time to time, have hardly
remarked any perceptible changes. I admit, however, that
this explanation does not altogether satisfy me. If a miracle
has happened before our eyes, whether gently and gradually
or not, we ought, even if we are quite impartial, to be much
more strongly moved than it has fallen to my lot to be—and
here I stumble against the cause of my obtuseness. I was by
no means impartial. The fact that I did not notice the
phenomenon was because I did not wish to notice it: like
everyone else I observed the increasing withdrawal and
silence of our honoured friend and the corresponding increase
of friendliness, the ever brighter and unearthly radiance of his
face when he replied mutely to a word of greeting. Yes, this I
noticed like everyone else, but I defended myself against
seeing anything more in it. I defended myself not out of lack
of reverence for the old Master but partly on account of my
aversion to personal cults and fanaticism in general, and
partly from my dislike for the particular type of enthusiasm
that the *studiosus* Petrus displays towards his Master and idol.
All this has become perfectly clear to me from your story."

"Well!" laughed Knecht, "that was one way of discovering
your aversion for the poor Petrus . . . but what is the position

now? Am I also a mystic and a fanatic? Am I also practising a
forbidden cult for persons and saints, or do you grant me
what you refuse to grant to the student: that we have seen
and experienced something, not dreams or fantasies, but
something very real and material?"

"Naturally I grant it to you," said Carlo slowly and
thoughtfully. "No one will cast a doubt upon your experience,
or upon the beauty and serenity of the old Music Master who
smiles at one so enchantingly, but the question is: what are
we to do with this phenomenon, how are we to describe and
explain it? What I am about to say may smack somewhat of
the schoolmaster, but we Castalians are really only school-
masters, are we not? In trying to understand and describe
your experience I do not wish to destroy its reality and
beauty through abstractions and generalities, but to affirm it
to the utmost possible degree and to explain it lucidly. If, on
one of my journeys, I hear a peasant or a child humming a
melody which I do not know, I look upon even that as an
experience, and if I try to write down the notes of the melody
as accurately as possible it is no callous disregard or denial of
the experience but an honouring and perpetuation of it."

Knecht nodded his head in the most friendly manner.

"Carlo, it is a shame that we do not see more of each other.
It is not all the friends of one's youth who retain their charm
at each subsequent meeting. I came to you with my story of
the old Magister because you are the only one in this place to
whom I could impart it and whose sympathy I could count
upon. I must of course leave it to your discretion as to what
use you intend to put my story, and how you choose to
classify the transfigured state of our former master. I should
be pleased if you would visit him once and stay for a short
while in his aura. This state of grace, perfection, sanctity, the
wisdom of his old age, or whatever we may like to call it may
possibly belong to the religious life, and although we
Castalians do not know confession and have no church we are
not ignorant of piety: our old Music Master has always been
a pious man, and as there are stories of those who have been
graced and become perfected, radiant and transfigured in
many religions, why should our Castalian piety not produce
such a flower? But it is late, my friend, and I must go to bed
for I am starting early in the morning. I hope to return soon.

But let me tell you the end of my story. After he had said to me: 'You are tiring yourself, Joseph,' I at last not only succeeded in controlling my efforts to involve him in conversation and in remaining silent, but also in repressing my desire to fathom and profit by the secret of this silent man through the medium of words and conversation. From that moment onwards, having renounced this desire and having left everything to him, it all transpired quite smoothly. I give you full leave to alter some of the expressions I may use if you wish to repeat this story—but now listen to me, even if I should appear obtuse or appear to confuse my categories. I remained with the old man for an hour or perhaps for an hour-and-a-half, and I cannot impart to you what transpired or what passed between us, for words would be inadequate to describe it. Once my resistance was broken down I felt only that he had accepted me into his peace and illumination, and that it enclosed the two of us completely in security and a miraculous calm. Without my having meditated voluntarily and consciously, it was comparable with the experience of a particularly successful and gratifying meditation, the theme of which was the life of the aged Magister. I saw, or rather sensed, both him and the entire path of his life from the moment when I first met him as a boy up to that very instant. It had been a life of devotion and toil, but freed from all constraint and all ambition, and simply saturated with music; it had developed as though, as a musician and Music Master he had chosen music as the way to the highest goal of man, to inner freedom, to purity and perfection; as though he had done nothing else since then but let himself become more and more impregnated with music, be transformed, exalted from the relative, from the clever hands of the cembalist and his rare, gigantic musical memory to all the parts and organs of his body and soul, into the pulse and breathing, into spell and dream, until he was now only a symbol, an apparition, a personification of music. At last I experienced all that radiated from him, or all the rhythmic In and Out breathing between him and myself, as nothing but music—completely immaterial, esoteric music, which accepted each new entrant into the magic circle just as a choral work introduces a new voice.

"Perhaps a non-musician would have described this grace in terms of other pictures: an astronomer might perhaps have

seen it as a moon circling a planet, or a philologist might
have spoken of it as an all-significant, magic, primæval form
of speech. Enough! I shall now take my leave. It was a great
pleasure having this talk with you, Carlo."

We have related this episode in detail, because the Music
Master had played so great a part in Knecht's life and had
occupied so important a place in his heart. Another factor
that prompted us to a lengthier treatment was that this
conversation had been preserved in one of Ferromonte's
letters, and his account of the old Music Master's "transfiguration" is undoubtedly the earliest and the most reliable.
At a later date there was no lack of legends and explanations
on this theme.

Chapter Eight

THE TWO POLES

THE ANNUAL GAME, which is still known to-day and is
often referred to as "The Chinese House Game," brought
Knecht and his friends an ample reward for their work and
proved to Castalia and the Pedagogy that Knecht's appointment to the highest office had been a wise measure. Once
more Waldzell, the Vicus Lusorum and the élite experienced
the gratification of a brilliant and highly exalted festival:
the Annual Game had not for many a year been comparable
with this one, in which the youngest and most discussed
Magister had appeared in public for the first time and proved
to Waldzell that the loss and failure of the previous year
could be rectified. This year no one lay ill and there was no
terrified deputy to view the great ceremony with growing
nervousness and distrust, to be regarded with icy coldness by
the élite and to be supported resolutely by officials who were
loyal but nervous.

Noiseless, unapproachable, the complete high priest, the
central figure robed in white and gold upon the ceremonious
chessboard of symbols, the Magister celebrated his and his

friend's joint work. Radiating calm, power and dignity, impervious to any profane summons as he appeared in the Feast Hall among his innumerable ministrants, he opened act upon act of his Game with the ritual gestures, wrote delicately with a gleaming golden stylus symbol after symbol upon the little board before him, which were immediately repeated in the Game calligraphy a hundred times enlarged on the giant tablet on the rear wall of the hall, to be copied down amidst the murmur of a thousand whispering voices, broadcast by the loudspeaker and relayed by the long distance announcers into the land and the world. At the end of the first act, as he gave a *resumé* of the formulas and announced the phrases for meditation with a graceful and impressive demeanour, laid down his stylus and sat down with exemplary poise to take up the meditation position, not only in the hall, in the Game Town and in Castalia but also outside in many countries of the world the believers of the Bead Game also sat down in devotion to the same meditation, to concentrate upon the phrases the Magister had given until the moment when he should arise once more in the hall.

Of course it was always the same and had taken place many times before, and yet it all seemed to be very moving and new. The abstract and apparently timeless world of the Game was elastic enough to react in a thousand shades upon the spirit, voice, temperament and handwriting of a personality—the personality great and cultivated enough not to consider its own conceits as more important than the inviolable innate principles of the Game. The helpers, fellow players and the élite alike obeyed like well-drilled soldiers, and yet each one of them—even when he did no more than bow or help to raise the curtains around the meditating Magister—seemed to be celebrating his own living Game inspired by his own imagination. But from the multitude, from the crowd in the great hall and over-filled community of Waldzell, from the thousand souls who followed the Master down the fantastic hieratic path through the unending many-dimensioned realms of the Game's pageantry, came the basic feeling of the celebration like a fundamental chord, like the deep quavering note of a base bell, which for the less sophisticated members of the community is the best and nearly the sole experience of the festival but which is also felt

with a shudder of awe by the inspired Game virtuoso and
critic of the élite, from the lowest ministrant and official up to
the leader and Magister.

It was a magnificent occasion. The ambassadors from the
outside world realised this at once and sent home glowing
reports, and many a novice was won over for ever to the
Bead Game.

However, the words with which Joseph Knecht described
his own experience to his friend Tegularius at the end of the
ten-day celebration were very remarkable. "We can rest
content," he had said. "Yes, Castalia and the Bead Game are
wonderful things—almost perfect in fact—only perhaps too
much so, and too beautiful. They are so beautiful that one can
hardly observe them without feeling some alarm as to their
future. One should hate to think that they must one day
disappear in the same way that everything else disappears,
and yet one must give thought to this eventuality."

This utterance constrains the biographer at this juncture to
approach the most delicate and mysterious part of his task,
which he would have preferred to postpone for a while in
order to portray in peace and comfort those things which are
clear and of single meaning—to have unfolded his tale of
Knecht's successes, his superlative conduct of office, and the
brilliant high peak of his life—but it appears to us that it
would be a mistake and hardly in accordance with our subject
if we were to refrain from mentioning and recognising the
duality or polarity that existed in the worthy Magister's life
and being, which had not been visible to anyone with the
possible exception of Tegularius. It is perhaps our task from
now onwards to accept or to affirm this gulf, or rather this
perpetual vibrant polarity in the worthy master's soul, as an
original trait in his personality. It would not actually be
difficult for an author, in writing a biography of a Castalian
Magister completely in the sense of a saintly life *ad majorem
gloriam Castaliæ*, to consider it permissible to depict Joseph
Knecht's years of magistracy, with the exception of the final
dénouement, as a complete and glorifying account of merit,
fulfilment of duties, and successes, for no life and office of any
individual Magister Ludi—including that Magister Ludwig
Wassermaler, who was in office in Waldzell during the most
happy epoch of the Game—can appear to the eye of the

historian in possession of all the documents and facts as more
exemplary and praiseworthy than that of Magister Joseph
Knecht.

Nevertheless, this office had a most unusual, spectacular,
and in the opinion of many judges, scandalous end, and
because this end was not a coincidence or an accident but
transpired quite logically, it is a part of our task to show that
it does not in the least contradict the brilliant and renowned
achievements and successes. Knecht was a great and magnificent administrator and representative of his high office, and a
blameless Magister Ludi; but he saw and felt the brilliance
of this Castalia which he was serving as a menaced and
vanishing greatness. He did not live within it heedlessly and
unthinkingly as the majority of his fellow Castalians did, but
knew its origin and history intimately, and looked upon it as
an historical entity subordinated to time, laved and shaken
by its pitiless violence.

This awakening to a vivid sense of historical continuity and
this sensation of his own person and activities being in the
nature of a co-propelled and co-active cell in the stream of
becoming and metamorphosis, had ripened within him and
been brought fully home to him through his historical studies
and under the influence of the great Father Jacobus, but the
germs and the seeds had already been there long before; and
whoever wishes to reconstruct and vivify Joseph Knecht's
personality and is really on the track of the originality and
meaning of this life will easily discover these germs and
seeds. That this man who, at the close of the most brilliant
day of his life, at the end of his first public Game and after
an unusually successful and impressive tribute to the Castalian
spirit, could say: "One should hate to think that Castalia and
the Bead Game must one day disappear again and yet one
must give thought to this eventuality," shows that he had
from an early age, long before becoming an initiated
historian, possessed a certain world-feeling and had been
conscious of the transience of all events and the problematical
nature of all that had been created by the human spirit.

When we look back to his boyhood and schooldays we
shall recall that each time a fellow pupil disappeared from the
élite school of Eschholz, having disappointed a teacher, and
had been returned to a normal school, he had found this a

source of deep oppression and unrest. We have no record that any one of these expelled boys had been a personal friend of Knecht's; but it was not the loss or the expulsion and disappearance of the individual which had excited and grieved him, but far more the gentle disruption of his childish belief in the duration of the Castalian organisation and Castalian perfection. That there could be boys and youths who had had the good fortune and grace to be accepted into the élite schools of the Province and who had frivolled or simply thrown away this grace, appeared to one who took his vocation so seriously as something devastating, as a testimony to the power of the non-Castalian world. Perhaps too—although we have no proof of this—such events sowed the first doubts in the boy's mind as to the hitherto accepted infallibility of the Pedagogy, inasmuch as they brought pupils to Castalia from time to time who after a short while had to be sent away again. Incidentally, as to whether this thought also played a part in the earliest arousing of his criticism of authority or not, the misdemeanours and expulsion of an élite pupil were always regarded by the boy, not only as a misfortune but as an impropriety, a hateful and glaring stain, the very possibility of which was a reproach against Castalia, and made it co-responsible. We believe this factor to have been the cause of the bewilderment and distress which the pupil Knecht was so prone to experience after such occurrences. Beyond the borders of the Province lay a world and a human existence which stood in direct contradiction to Castalia and its laws, which did not apply to its ruling order and calculations and could be neither tamed nor sublimated by them. Moreover, he naturally knew of the existence of this world in his own heart: he also had urges, fantasies and desires which were contradictory to the laws under which he stood—impulses which he gradually learned to tame, but only at the expense of great hardship. These urges could apparently be so strong in many pupils that they transcended all admonitions and punishments and led those who fell a prey to them out of the Castalian élite world into the other, which was ruled neither by discipline nor culture but by the urges of nature and which would inevitably appear to one trying to attain the Castalian virtues as an evil under-world or a theatre and arena of seduction. For generations many young consciences have experienced their conception of sin in this Castalian form.

Many years later, as an adult and amateur of history, he was to recognise that history cannot evolve without the material and dynamism of this sinful world of egoism and urge, and also that such sublime edifices as the Order can be born from this desolate flood and once again be swallowed up by it. Thus it was the problem of Castalia that lay at the foundation of all the powerful movements, strivings and upheavals in Knecht's life, and it had never been a matter for speculation alone but one which concerned him intimately and one for which he knew himself to be co-responsible. He belonged to those natures who fall ill, waste away and die when they see a cherished article of faith, a cherished fatherland or community ailing in distress.

When we pursue these threads further we come to Knecht's early Waldzell days, his last student years and the significant meeting with the extramural student, Designori, which we have described in an earlier chapter. This meeting between the fanatical protagonist of the Castalian ideal and the child of the world Plinio was not only violent and had many repercussions but was also a deeply important and symbolical experience for the student Knecht, for he was at that time, as we remember, forced into a significant and exacting rôle which had been allotted to him as though by accident, but which corresponded so closely to his whole being that one could almost say his later life was no more than a resumption of this rôle and an even more perfect adaptation of it, *viz.*, the rôle of defending and representing Castalia, which he was obliged to play anew some ten years later against Father Jacobus and which he played to the end as Magister Ludi—a defender and representative of the Order and of its spirit, but one who was inwardly ever ready to learn from his opponents and who, far from demanding that Castalia should be sealed off in petrified isolation from the outside world desired above all that it should co-operate actively with and adapt itself to the life of the latter.

What had still been very much a game in the intellectual and rhetorical dispute with Designori later became grave and earnest in his friendship and tussle with the important Father Jacobus; he had defended himself against each of these opponents and had adapted himself to each, learning much and actually receiving as much as he gave in the conflict and exchange of ideas, had in neither case conquered the opponent —which had never been the aim of the struggle—but had succeeded in forcing from him an honourable recognition both of his person and of the principle and ideal that he represented. His dispute with the scholarly Benedictine had resulted in the creation of a semi-official representation in the Holy See in Rome, but even had it not achieved this practical success it would nevertheless have been of greater value to him than the majority of Castalians would have imagined.

It was through this very competitive friendship with Plinio Designori and later with the wise old Father that Knecht, who had otherwise not come into closer contact with the outside world, had gained a knowledge or conception of that world such as few Castalians possessed. With the exception of his stay in Mariafels, which could not have brought him any real acquaintance with actual life as it is led in the world at large, he had never lived or seen this phenomenon except in his very early childhood, but he had at least gained an acute idea of its reality through Designori, Father Jacobus and his study of history—an idea that was nine-tenths theory and one-tenth experience, but which resulted in his being more knowledgeable and open-minded than the majority of his fellow Castalians, the Pedagogy hardly excluded. He was and remained a genuine and loyal Castalian, but he never forgot that Castalia is only a part—a very small part—of the world, even though it was the most precious and cherished part of all.

And now we will examine his friendship with Fritz Tegularius, that difficult and enigmatical character, that sublime artist of the Bead Game, that spoiled and timorous super-Castalian who had found his short stay in Mariafels among the coarse Benedictines so sinister and wretched that, as he had admitted, he could not have endured it for a week, and admired his friend for having stayed there for two whole years. We have given much thought to this friendship which lasted for so many years and have discarded many of our conclusions, but certain of them seem to hold good: they apply mainly to everything that had a bearing upon its course and significance. Above all, we must not forget that in all Knecht's friendships—with the exception of the one with the Benedictine—he had never been the seeking, courting and needy party: he had attracted, had been admired, envied and loved simply on account of his noble personality, and—from a certain stage of his awakening onwards—he was conscious of this gift. In exactly the same way he had also been admired and courted by Tegularius in his early student years, but had always kept him at a certain distance. There are many signs, however, which show us that he was really attached to his friend. We believe that it was not Tegularius' extraordinary talents and restless and obvious genius for all the problems of the Bead Game alone that had in them something attractive for Knecht, but that the latter's strong and enduring interest was aroused no less by his faults and weaknesses—in fact by everything that the other Castalians found disturbing and at times intolerable. This strange man was so Castalian that his whole existence would have been inconceivable outside the Province; he had become so acclimatised to the atmosphere and high niveau of culture that, had he not been so strange and difficult of approach, he could have been described as the arch-Castalian; and yet this very arch-Castalian did not get on at all well with his comrades and was no more liked by his superiors and the officials, was a constant source of nuisance, was perpetually offended, and would probably have been ruined very early on in life had it not been for the protection and leadership of his shrewd, courageous friend. His malady was primarily a failing of character, what one might have called a depraved capacity for insubordination: in the deepest sense he was totally unhierarchical and individualistic in outlook and mode of life, and only complied with the existing code to the extent that was necessary in order to be tolerated by the Order. He was a good and even brilliant Castalian insofar as he had a many-sided, tireless and insatiable spirit for scholarship and for the Bead Game, but was rather an indifferent one in character and in his attitude towards the hierarchy and the morality of the Order. His greatest vice was an incorrigible casualness and a neglectful attitude towards his meditation, the intention of which is the subjugation of the individual and a greater attention to which

might possibly have healed him of his neurasthenia, for it
so often proved efficacious after a crisis of excitation or
melancholia and after a period of bad behaviour, when he
was constrained to rigid exercises under observation as a
punishment. These methods the well-wisher and tolerant
Knecht had often been forced to employ.

No, Tegularius was an obstinate and moody character,
quite unsuited to a practice of serious self-control: he was
admittedly often enchanting in his vivid spirituality and in
certain hectic hours when his pessimistic wit sparkled, and no
one could escape from the audacity and often sinister
splendour of his conceits, but fundamentally he was incurable
for he did not wish to be cured. He cared nothing for harmony and submission, loved nothing so much as his freedom,
his eternal studenthood, and preferred all his life to be a
sufferer, an unreliable and disrupted lone-wolf, a genial fool
and nihilist instead of following the path of submission to
the Order and achieving the resulting peace of mind. He
cared nothing for peace, cared not in the least for the
hierarchy and was indifferent to blame and ostracism—a most
disquieting and indigestible element, therefore, in a community whose ideal is harmony and order—and because of
this difficulty and indigestibility was a permanently living
disturbance, a reproach, admonition and warning to this little
well-ordered world, an instigator of new bold forbidden and
insolent thoughts, a black and fractious sheep in the fold;
and this we think was above all what won over his friend. It is
certain that in Knecht's relationship with him there existed
also a large measure of compassion—the appeal, shall we
say, of the endangered and most unfortunate to all his
knightly feelings—but this element would not have been
sufficient to have allowed this friendship to continue after
Knecht's promotion to the rank of Magister and in the midst
of an over-burdened official life with its toil, duty and responsibility. We are of the opinion that this Tegularius
was no less necessary in Knecht's life than Designori and
the Benedictine Father had been and that, like these two, he
was an awakening influence, a casement opening on to new
horizons.

Knecht had sensed in his remarkable friend the representative of a type, and in time had come to recognise him

as something in the nature of a precursory figure—or should we say a forerunner—of the type that all Castalians could become unless they were rejuvenated and strengthened by new encounters and life impulses. Tegularius was of course, like the majority of lonely geniuses, a forerunner. He lived virtually in a Castalia that did not yet exist, but which could come about to-morrow in a still more enclosed atmosphere, and with age and the lure of the contemplative order morality would represent, in the light of the world, a merely degenerate Castalia, in which the loftiest cultural flights and the deepest devotion to the high values were still possible but wherein a highly developed and plastic spirituality had in its over-refined capacity, no other goal save self-enjoyment. Tegularius was, in Knecht's eyes, simultaneously the embodiment of the highest Castalian capacities and the admonitory sign of its demoralisation and decline. It was wonderful and beyond price that there was such a person as Tegularius, but the disintegration of Castalia into a dream-world peopled with Tegulariuses had to be avoided at all costs. The danger that this could occur was still far distant, but it was evident: the Castalia that he knew had only to build its walls of elegant isolation a little higher, the order discipline had only to be relaxed and the hierarchic morality to suffer a decline, and Tegularius would no longer be a fabulous unicorn but a typical representative of a degenerating and collapsing Castalia. This most important recognition on the part of Magister Knecht, and the anxiety he felt at the hypothesis that the tendency towards and commencement of such a decline was impending, would presumably have come far later, or perhaps never have come at all, had not this Castalian of the future been there before him, a living specimen for his study. To Knecht's awareness he was a symptom and a warning cry, just as the first attacks are a symptom of an undiagnosed malady to the doctor; but as Fritz was no average man—he was an aristocrat and a talent of the first degree—were the still unknown disease which had appeared in this forerunner to spread and change the face of Castalian man, then the Province and the Order, once it had degenerated, would take on the figure of the sick man and these Castalians of the future would not just be Tegulariuses, would not possess his rare talent, his melancholy genius, his glowing artistic temperament, but the majority of them would have only his unreliability, inclination to frivolity and lack of discipline and community sense.

Knecht may have been a prey to such gloomy visions and premonitions in his hours of anxiety, and it is certain that their sublimation, through meditation or increased activity, must have taxed his strength.

The case of Tegularius gives us a particularly fine and instructive example of the way in which Knecht perserveringly strove to help and master the problematical, the difficult and the ailing whom he encountered. Without his watchful care and instructive leadership not only would his imperilled friend have succumbed but would most certainly have brought endless disruption and inconvenience to the Game colony, of which there had been no lack since his entry into the ranks of the Game élite. The art with which the Magister eventually both kept his friend on the rails and adapted his gifts to the service of the Bead Game, raising them to noble achievements, the protectiveness and patience with which he suffered his moods and idiosyncrasies, appealing tirelessly to what was best in his nature, we must look upon as a masterpiece of dealing with men.

It would be an attractive task, and one which would perhaps lead to surprising conclusions—and we should like to recommend this most earnestly to our future historian of the Bead Game—to study the Annual Game of Knecht's first year of office and to analyse those estimable and precious conceits and sparkling formularies, those brilliant, rhythmic, original and delectable themes that were yet so far removed from virtuosity, the basic plan and construction of which, as well as the leading up to the meditation sequences, was entirely Knecht's own spiritual work, whereas the chiselling and technical details were to a great extent the result of the efforts of his collaborator Tegularius. These Games could be lost and forgotten without Knecht's life and capabilities losing too much of the power of their attraction and example for future generations. Fortunately for us they have not been lost, for they were recorded and preserved, but not neglected, in the Archives. They still live on to-day in tradition, are studied by the young students and used as favourite examples for many Game Courses and in many seminaries, and in them too is perpetrated the life of that collaborator who would otherwise have been forgotten or would have been relegated to the position of a strange ghostly figure gliding through many anecdotes of the past. Inasmuch, therefore, as Knecht was able to designate a place and a field of activities for his friend Fritz, who was so difficult to manage, so he was able to assure as a memorial for his friend a certain permanence in the spiritual inheritance and history of Waldzell. We should also like to point out that this great educator was not unaware of the most effective means at his disposal as an educatory influence in dealing with his friend, and found the latter's love and admiration to be the clue in this case. These sentiments and this enthusiasm for Knecht's powerful and harmonious personality, for his nobility, were not peculiar to Fritz alone: he had recognised them in many of his colleagues and pupils and had built far more upon them than upon his authority and power of high office which, despite his good-natured and conciliatory personality, he had enforced upon so many of them. He seemed to sense exactly what a friendly word or a recognition, a withdrawal or a lack of notice could achieve. One of his most eager pupils related many years later that, for a whole week of a seminary, Knecht had not spoken a word to him, had appeared to look right through him and had treated him as though he did not even exist. This, he averred, had been the bitterest and most effective punishment that he had experienced throughout the whole of his student years.

We have considered these observations and glimpses back into the past necessary in order, at this juncture, to make the reader aware of the two fundamental and paradoxical tendencies in Knecht's personality and, having brought him so far—in fact, to the Magister's high peak—in order to prepare him for the last phase of this rich career. The two basic tendencies or poles of his life, his Yin and Yang, were on the one hand the tendency to preserve, to be loyal and to devote selfless service to the hierarchy, and on the other to press forward, to grasp and conceive the reality. For Joseph Knecht, the believer and devotee, the Order, Castalia and the Bead Game were something holy and definitely estimable: for Knecht the awakened, the seer and pioneer, they were,

irrespective of their value, creations which had been fought
for, which were changeable in form, were subject to the danger of growing old, of becoming sterile and of declining
into out-dated institutions. The idea behind Castalia remained
for him always untouchable and sacred, but the reigning
conditions he had recognised to be transient and in need of
constant criticism.

He served an intellectual community, the power and
meaning of which he admired, but which he saw in danger as a
result of the tendency on the part of its members to regard it
purely as an end in itself, to forget its task of co-operation
with the whole of the land and the world, and which he saw
finally condemned to succumb in a brilliant but more and
more sterile segregation from the whole of life. He had had an
intuition of this danger in his youth, in the face of which he
had always hesitated and been afraid to devote himself
entirely to the Bead Game. It had been in the forefront of his
consciousness during his discussion with the monks, and in
particular with Father Jacobus, however courageously he may
have defended Castalia against the latter's criticisms, and
since he had come to live in Waldzell and been appointed
Magister Ludi it had become even more noticeable, with
visible symptoms in the loyal but unworldly and purely
formal manner of work in many official posts and among his
own officials, in the belletristic but arrogant specialisation of
his Waldzellian tutorship, and last, but not least, in the
touching and terrifying figure of his friend Tegularius.

After completing his first difficult years of office, during
which he had had no spare time or private life, he now turned
once more to the study of history and delved for the first time
with wide open eyes into the history of Castalia. He came to
the incontestable conclusion that the facts were not at all as
current opinion within the Province would have held, but
that in actual fact its relationship with the outside world, the
effective exchange between it and the life, politics, and culture
of the land had for many years shown an adverse balance.
Admittedly the Pedagogy had their say in educational and
cultural affairs, and the Province still supplied the land with
good teachers and exercised their authority in all questions of
scholarship, but even this had taken on an aspect of custom
and had become automatic. Less and less frequently did eager

young men from among the Castalian élite apply for the post of schoolteacher *extra muros;* less frequently did the authorities and individuals in the land turn for advice towards Castalia, whose opinion had formerly been courted and listened to eagerly in weighty affairs of state. When one compared the *niveau* of culture obtaining in Castalia with that of the world outside one saw immediately that, far from approaching each other, they were striving in a fatal manner to separate: the more cultured, differentiated and over-refined the Castalian intellectuality became, the more inclined was the world to leave the Province to its own devices and the more inclined were its inhabitants to look upon it not as a necessity and a source of daily sustenance but as a foreign body of which they were slightly proud by reason of its antique preciousness, which for the moment they should not give away and dispense with, but from which they preferred to keep at a certain distance and which they felt, without knowing why, possessed a mentality, morality and self-consciousness no longer suited to real and active life. The interest of the inhabitants as regards the life of the pedagogic Province, their participation in its institutions and in the Bead Game, was as much behind the times as was that of the Castalians in the life and destiny of the country. That the fault lay here he had long since realised, and that, as Magister Ludi in his Game Town, he had exclusively to do with Castalians and specialists, was a constant source of grief to him: hence his striving to devote himself more and more to the beginners' courses and his wish for the youngest possible pupils—the younger they were the less trained and specialised they were, and the greater remained their bonds with the whole of life and the world. He often felt a hungry longing for the world, for men, and for an ingenuous life—if such should exist in the unknown world outside. Something of this yearning and this feeling of emptiness of a life lived in too rarified an atmosphere has been felt by most of us, and this difficulty has always been known to the Pedagogy; it has sought to counter it from time to time with increased care for physical exercise and games and, in an attempt to compensate for it, with all manner of handiworks and gardening activities. If we are correct in our surmises there has in recent times been a tendency on the part of the Order Administration to do away with many of the specialities in scientific subjects that have been found to be over-cultivated in favour of an intensification of the practice of meditation: one need therefore be no sceptical pessimist or unsatisfactory brother of the Order to agree that Knecht was right when he had recognised a long time in advance of us that the complicated and sensitive apparatus of our republic was an out-of-date organism much in need of repairs.

We find him therefore, as we have already mentioned, turning once more to his historical studies and, in addition to his reading of Castalian history, occupied with the major and minor works that Father Jacobus had written on the Benedictine Order. In certain conversations with M. Dubois and one of the philologists from Keuperheim who was acting as secretary in the sessions of the Pedagogy, he found the opportunity of bringing these historical topics to the fore, and of arousing their interest in them. This was always a welcome recreation and pleasure, for in his daily surroundings the opportunity to discuss such things was lacking. The general dislike of history in Waldzell was epitomised in the person of his friend Fritz: we have discovered a notebook giving details of one of their conversations in which Tegularius stated passionately that for a Castalian history was a subject hardly worth studying. Admittedly he had said, one could amuse oneself by reading the philosophy of history as a witty, entertaining, and perhaps highly pathetic type of historical interpretation. That would at least be a pastime, like any other philosophy, and he had nothing against it if it brought one any pleasure; but the thing itself, the subject of this pastime—this history in fact—was something so ugly, so banal and devilish and at the same time so loathsome and boring, that he failed to understand how anyone could entertain such a thing. Its content was made up entirely of human egoism, and always of the same brand; always the same over-estimation of the self and the same struggle for self-glory and power—for material, brutal and bestial power —for a thing therefore that could not be envisaged by a Castalian and had not the slightest value. World history was an endless account, devoid of spirit and interest, of the enslavement of the weaker by the stronger; and to try to bring it into line with, and through it to explain, the real and true history, the timeless history of the spirit—*i.e.*, through these age-old ridiculous scuffles between the ambitious for power and a place in the sun—had already been a betrayal of the spirit, and reminded him of a populous sect of the nineteenth or twentieth century of which he had learned, who had fostered the earnest belief that the gods and the offerings brought to them by the ancient peoples, their temples and myths like everything else had been the result of a calculable lack or surplus of food and work, of a tension caused by the fluctuation of wages and the price of consumer goods, and that the arts and religions had been stucco façades—so-called ideologies—of a humanity occupied entirely with hunger or guzzling.

Knecht, who had been amused by this conversation, had immediately asked whether the history of the spirit, culture and art had not always stood in close relationship with that other history. His friend had replied violently that he would not even admit to that. World history, he had maintained, was a competition in time, a race for profit, power and riches, and it was all a question of who had strength, luck or roguery enough not to miss his opportunity. The deeds of the spirit, culture and art, on the contrary, were the exact antithesis of this: they always constituted a breaking away from the thraldom of time, a slipping away on the part of man from the filth of his urges and his slothfulness, and his projection on to another plane—into the timeless, the freedom-from-time, the divine, the totally un- and anti-historical.

Knecht listened to him with pleasure, encouraged him to further outbursts which were by no means lacking in wit, and finally brought the conversation to a close with the following observations: "I congratulate you on your love for the spirit and its accomplishments but spiritual creation is something in which one cannot indulge as easily as many people would imagine. A dialogue of Plato's or a choral phrase from Heinrich Isaac—in fact, everything which we call a work of art or an objectification of the spirit—is an end process or final result of a struggle for purification and deliverance. These works are as far as I am concerned, as you say, a breaking away from time into the timeless, and in the majority of cases the most perfect are those which leave no hint of the struggle and conflict which preceded them. It is a great piece of good fortune that we possess these works and that we Castalians live almost entirely in and through them, for we are no longer creative except in reproduction. We live continually in that remote sphere where there is neither time nor conflict, but which is comprised of those works and which we should not know without them. We become more and more intellectualised or, if you wish, more and more occupied with abstractions: we dismember these works of the sages and artists in our Bead Game, draw up rules of style, schemes of form and sublimated conclusions from them, and use these abstractions as though they were bricks. Now that is all very fine and no one will disagree, but one cannot breathe, eat and drink nothing but abstractions one's whole life through. History has an advantage over that which the Waldzellian tutor finds of value: it has to do with reality. Abstractions may be enchanting things in themselves, but I am of the opinion that one also needs fresh air to breathe and bread to eat.''

From time to time Knecht was able to pay short visits to the old Music Master, who was now in his dotage. This wonderful old man, whose strength was rapidly failing and who had long since given up the use of speech, remained serene and disciplined to the very last. He was not ill, and his death was not an actual dying but a rapid disintegration, a disappearance of the living functions and substance whilst his life seemed to concentrate more and more in the look in his eyes and in the radiance of his gradually sinking, ancient face. To most of the inmates of Monteport he was a well-known and highly respected phenomenon, but only very few people, among them Knecht, Ferromonte and the young Petrus, participated in and were graced by this afterglow and illumination of a pure and selfless life. These few, when they foregathered in the little room where the old Magister sat in his armchair, entered into this soft gleam of dissolution, this fellow-feeling of perfection which had outstripped all words and they lingered as though in the realm of invisible rays, participating for a happy moment in the crystalline sphere of this soul, to the accompaniment of un-earthly music, and returned to their daily tasks as though from a high mountain peak. One day Knecht learned that the old man had died, and he hurried to Monteport, where he found him lying on his couch as though quietly sleeping. His tiny face had disappeared into a calm rune or arabesque, a magic symbol no longer legible and yet still telling of a smile and of perfect happiness. Both Knecht and Ferromonte made speeches at the graveside. Knecht spoke not of the illuminating sage of music or of the great teacher, or of the benevolent, shrewd and oldest member of the Pedagogy, but of the grace of his old age and death, of the immortal beauty of the spirit which had revealed itself from within to his comrades during his last days on earth.

We know from several sources that Joseph had nourished a desire to write a life of the old Magister Musicæ, but his duties left him no time for such a task and he had learned by now to accord little place to his own personal wishes. He is reported to have said once to a student: "It is a pity that you students are not really conscious of the abundance and luxury of your lives—but of course the same could have held true for myself when I was young. You study and work and have no apparent leisure, and may actually believe that you are considered industrious, but you hardly realise everything that you could do and achieve with all this freedom. And then one day comes the summons from the Pedagogy: the time has come for you to be employed. You receive a teaching commission, a mission or an office; you are promoted on to a higher plane and unsuspectingly find yourself caught in a net of tasks and duties that becomes narrower and tighter, until you can no longer stir. There are great and small tasks, but each one will be attended to in due course and you will find that the official day has many more duties than hours. That of course is excellent and should not be otherwise; but when, between classrooms, archives, chancellery, audience room, sessions, and official journeys you remember for a moment that freedom which you once possessed and have lost—the freedom to pursue independent studies, unrestricted far-reaching studies—then you long for them and imagine that if you possessed them once more you would enjoy their pleasures and possibilities to the full."

He had a particularly fine sense as to the qualifications of his pupils and officials for service in the hierarchy: he carefully chose people for each commission and position and the testimonials and reports that he wrote concerning them show a great certainty of judgment in all that referred to the human side of the characters. In cases of judging and handling difficult characters, he was frequently approached for advice. There was, for example, the case of the student Petrus, the last prize-pupil of the old Music Master. This young man, who was a type of quiet fanatic, had remained to the last in his strange rôle of companion-nurse and devoted disciple to the venerable old man. As these duties naturally came to an end with the Magister's death he lapsed into a state of melancholy and mourning, which was fully understood and tolerated for a while but the symptoms of which soon became a source of anxiety to the head of Monteport, the present Music Master Ludwig. Petrus insisted upon living and remaining in that pavilion which had belonged to the dead man and in keeping watch over the little house. He kept it neat and clean, and regarded the room where he had died, with its armchair couch and cembalo, as an untouchable hallowed spot, and in addition to the preservation of these relics recognised only one care and duty—that of tending the grave in which his beloved master rested. He saw his life vocation as a prolonged cult for the dead man in this place of memory and a preservation of the hallowed spot in the guise of a temple servant; he also perhaps nursed the hope of seeing it become a place of pilgrimage. For the first few days after the funeral he had eaten nothing at all, and had then limited himself to small and rare meals such as had sufficed the Master during his last weeks: it looked as though he had every intention in this manner of following his Master to the grave.

He did not, however, endure this for long, and began to behave as though he ought to have been appointed as steward of the house and grave—an eternal custodian of this memorial spot. It was quite apparent that this stubborn young man who had enjoyed for a long time what for him had been a charming position, intended to retain this particular post and under no circumstances return to everyday life, which in secret he no longer felt capable of facing. "That Petrus, who was allotted to the old Magister Musicæ, is cracked anyhow," was the curt judgment in a letter from Ferromonte.

Now the Monteport music student was no affair of the Waldzell Magister; he was not in any way responsible for him, and doubtless felt no necessity to interfere in a question that concerned only Monteport, and thereby increasing his own work, but the miserable Petrus, whom they had been obliged to remove forcibly from the pavilion, refused to be consoled, and had in his mourning and distress fallen into a state of isolation and remoteness from reality to which the normal rules in cases of disciplinary infringement could not be applied. Since Knecht's benevolent relationship with him was a well-known fact, a letter was despatched from the Music Master's chancellery asking for advice and action, while the recalcitrant was for the moment looked upon as ill and retained under observation in a cell of the infirmary. Knecht at first felt disinclined to interfere in this matter, but after he had given it some thought decided to be of assistance and took things into his own hands with his usual energy.

He offered to take Petrus on trial, on condition that he was to be treated as a healthy individual and allowed to travel alone. He enclosed a short friendly invitation to the youth asking him to come to Waldzell for a short time if he felt so inclined, and telling him that he hoped to hear many revelations concerning the last days of the old Music Master. After some hesitation the Monteport doctor agreed, and the invitation was handed to the student. As Knecht had foreseen, nothing could have pleased him more than to be speedily removed from the scene of his distress. Petrus announced himself to be in agreement with the journey, and without having to be pressed, ate a hearty meal, was given a travel pass and set out for Waldzell.

He arrived in a pitiful condition, but his unsettled and nervous condition was ignored on Knecht's instructions and he was taken in as a guest of the Archives. He found himself treated neither as a delinquent nor as a sick man—nor, in fact, as being in any way out of the ordinary. He had not actually been ill enough not to appreciate the present atmosphere and to seize this opportunity of returning to a normal life, although for the first few weeks of his stay he was burdensome enough to the Magister, who kept him busy with plausible but well-supervised duties revising the last musical exercises and studies of his late Master, and gradually gave him small duties to perform in the Archives. He was asked whether he would care to be of assistance, as they were busy and short-handed: in short, the youth was helped back on to the road from which he had strayed. Once he was calm again and obviously of a willing disposition, Knecht began to apply his educatory influence upon him during the course of a few conversations, cured him completely of his folly and made him realise that his idolatrous cult for the dead man was not a hallowed and seemly thing in Castalia. As Petrus could not overcome his terror of being sent back to Monteport, and as to all intents and purposes he was now quite cured, he was given a post as assistant to one of the music teachers in a junior élite school, where henceforth he behaved admirably.

There is no lack of such examples of Knecht's educatory and soul-healing capacities, or of young students who were won over in a similar manner by the gentle persuasion of his personality to a life of true Castalian spirit—as he himself had once been won over by the Magister Musicæ.

All these examples show us that the Magister Ludi was by no means an enigmatical character, and they are all testimonies to his sanity and balance; only the loving care which this great man displayed towards unstable and imperilled characters like Petrus or Tegularius, and a peculiar sensitiveness and awareness for such maladies or tergiversations among Castalians, show his untiring and unequalled devotion to the problems and dangers which lay within the Castalian life itself. To ignore these dangers casually and complacently as the majority of his fellow citizens did was quite alien to his clear and courageous character, and presumably the tactics of most of his colleagues in the Pedagogy, who knew of the existence of these dangers but treated them fundamentally as non-existent, had never been his way of behaving. He saw and recognised them—or at least many of them—and his familiarity with the early history of Castalia made life in their midst appear very much in the nature of a conflict, made him affirm and love this danger-fraught existence, whereas so many Castalians looked upon their community life as nothing more than an idyll. He was, as we know, familiar with Father Jacobus's works on the Benedictine Order, and his presentation of it as being a militant community and of piety as being a bellicose form of behaviour. "No noble and exalted life can exist," he had once said, "without a knowledge of the devil and of the demons, and without a perpetual conflict against them."

Outspoken friendships between the highest officials are very rare among us, and therefore we are not surprised that during his first years Knecht did not encourage any such relationship with his colleagues. He felt a great sympathy for the Ancient Philologist of Keuperheim and a deep respect for the Head of the Order, but in this sphere the private and personal is almost completely subordinated and objectivised and, apart from official collaboration, hardly any serious intimacies and fraternisations are possible. And yet, we feel, that he must have experienced something in this nature.

The secret Archives of the Pedagogy are not available to us, and we only know of Knecht's capabilities and behaviour at the sessions and voting conclaves from reports of his actual utterances that have been recorded by his friends. He does not seem to have maintained the silence of his early magisterial days, but appears never to have been a spokesman even when he himself was the instigator or mover of a resolution. The speed with which he mastered the prevailing code which rules at the peak of our hierarchy, and the gracefulness, creativeness and adaptability with which he practised these forms, must be particularly emphasised.

It is well known that the higher members of our hierarchy, the Magisters and members of the Order Administration, are accustomed to using not only a carefully prescribed ceremonious style towards each other but also—and we do not quite know when this originated—a form of obeisance or secret precedent, the protocol of which demands a more meticulous observance of this carefully polished courtesy the greater the differences of opinion reigning between them and the more important the questions under discussion. Presumably this traditional courtesy, in addition to whatever other functions it may have served, was first and foremost in the nature of a defence measure: the exaggerated tone of politeness in debate not only protected the speakers against yielding to passion and helped to preserve a high standard of behaviour, but also protected and preserved the dignity of the Order and Pedagogy itself, swathing it, so to speak, in ceremonial robes and bright-coloured veils. This art of the compliment, therefore, so often ridiculed by the students, was not without its good reasons. Before Knecht's time his predecessor, Magister Thomas of Trave, had been greatly admired for his artistry in this respect, and one cannot really say that Knecht was his true successor or imitator: he was far more a pupil of the Chinese school and his mode of courtesy was less pointed and tinged with irony, but for sheer courtesy he was the equal of his former colleague.

Chapter Nine

A CONVERSATION

WE HAVE NOW REACHED a point in our study where our attention will be centred upon the development which took place during the last years of the Magister's life, which led to his resignation from office and departure from the Province, to his crossing over into another circle of life and ultimately to his end. Although, up to the very moment of his farewell, he had administered his office with exemplary loyalty and had continued to enjoy the love and confidence of his students and colleagues, we have refrained from any further description of his official leadership because we consider that he had grown weary of office and had already turned his face towards other goals.

He had exhausted the full circle of possibilities and whatever scope for development this office had held out to him and had reached the point where great natures abandon the way of tradition and obedient compliance and with confidence in higher, unnamed powers feel themselves obliged to attempt and make themselves responsible for the new, the uncharted and the unknown.

As soon as he had become fully aware of this, he had summed up his position carefully and soberly and had pondered long over the possibilities of changing it.

He had, at an unusually early age, reached the highest

position that a talented and ambitious Castalian could possibly conceive as being desirable and worthy of attainment, and had, moreover, achieved it not through ambition and effort or by attempting to adapt himself consciously, but almost against his will. An inconspicuous, independent scholarly life without official duties would have been more in keeping with his own personal desires.

He had by no means laid equal store by all the special perquisites and privileges which his position had brought him, and several of these distinctions and power privileges had after a short term of office already seemed to have become worthless. For example, he had always looked upon the political and administrative co-operation with the higher Pedagogy as particularly onerous, but naturally without devoting himself any the less conscientiously to it. Furthermore, the most unique, singular and characteristic task demanded by his position—the selection of an eclectic group of perfect bead-players, which at times gave him so much pleasure—was in the long run perhaps more of a burden than a delight, however proud this group might in turn have been of their Magister.

What actually brought him the greatest joy and contentment was teaching and education. In this, he had discovered that his joy and success were in direct proportion to the youth of his pupils, so that he found his office a privation and a sacrifice insofar as it did not bring him children and boys but youths and adults.

There were also other considerations, experiences and opinions during the course of his magistracy which had led him to become critical of his own activities and to disagree with many of the conditions ruling in Waldzell, or again to find his office a great hindrance to the utilization of his best and most fruitful capabilities. Much of this we know and much we must assume.

The question as to whether Magister Knecht, in his striving to be free from the burdens of his office, his desire for less obvious but more intensive work, his criticism of the conditions ruling in Castalia, was actually in the right or whether he is to be regarded as a progressive and courageous warrior or as a kind of rebel or renegade we will also leave in peace, for it has been discussed often enough. This question has for a long time past split both Waldzell and the Province into two camps, and has still not been silenced. Although we admit to our grateful admiration for the great Magister, we do not wish to take part in this controversy, for the synthesis of the many conflicting judgments and opinions upon Joseph Knecht's personality and life has already been dealt with at length in this portrayal.

We neither wish to pass a judgment nor to convert our readers, but to relate as truthfully as possible the history of our revered Master's end, which is actually less in the nature of a history than what we might almost call a legend—an account, a mixture of true fact and pure hearsay like the blending of calm and troubled waters—current among us younger members of the Province.

Just at the time when Joseph Knecht's thoughts were already turning to his quest for a way to freedom, that once trusted and half-forgotten figure of his youthful days—Plinio Designori—unexpectedly crossed his path once more.

This scion of an old family and erstwhile guest-scholar, who had rendered valuable service to the Province and who had now become an influential man as a statesman and political writer, had appeared one day, on official business with the highest authorities of the Province. There had been a newly elected State Commission to control the expenses of Castalia which sat every few years, and Designori was one of the members of this Commission: he first appeared in this capacity at a session in the Residence of the Order at Hirsland, at which the Magister Ludi had been present. The meeting had made a deep impression upon Knecht, and was not without consequences. We know a great deal about this from Tegularius and also from Designori himself who, during this somewhat obscure period of Knecht's life, soon became his friend and even his confidant once more. The members of the newly elected State Commission were presented to the Magisters as usual, and when Joseph heard the name Designori, which he had not heard for so many years, he was surprised and not a little ashamed for he had not immediately recognised this companion of his boyhood days.

As he held out his hand to him in a cordial and friendly manner—dispensing with the official bow and the formal greeting—he had looked at him intently, trying to discover the changes which had made his old friend so unrecognizable, and during the session his gaze frequently wandered across to that once well-trusted face. Designori, however, had addressed him formally and with his full magisterial title, and Joseph had been obliged to ask him twice before he would make up his mind to use the old familiar form of address.

Knecht had known Plinio as a stormy, hilarious, brilliant and communicative youth, a good scholar and at the same time a young man of the world who had felt somewhat superior to the unworldly young Castalian, whom it had so often amused him to challenge. He had perhaps not been entirely devoid of vanity, but had for all that been a frank and open creature without a trace of pettiness, and was in the eyes of most of his contemporaries an interesting, attractive and agreeable personality—for many of them even scintillating, on account of his handsome appearance, sureness of manner and that trace of mystery which had surrounded him as a stranger and child of the outside world.

Years later, towards the end of his student days, Knecht had seen him again, when he had given him the impression of having dulled, coarsened and entirely lost his charm. This had disappointed Knecht very much, and there had been a sense of embarrassment and coolness on either side; but now he seemed once more to have changed his personality. The most outstanding thing about him was that he had lost or laid aside his youth and gaiety, his joy in conversation, disputes and polemics, and to all appearances was a different person from his active, engaging extraverted self.

Far from drawing attention to himself at this reunion by coming forward to greet his former friend, he had waited for the Magister to greet him first, and after the introduction had only rather unwillingly accepted the latter's affectionate invitation to address him familiarly. So, too, in his behaviour, in his look, his mode of speech, his gestures and movements, in place of the former pugnacity, frankness and verve, there was now a certain restraint or subdued air, as though he were withholding himself, a kind of cramp or rigidity . . . or perhaps simply weariness.

The charm of youth had vanished and been extinguished, as had also the signs of superficiality and over-coarse worldliness. The entire man, but in particular his face, seemed to have been partly destroyed and partly ennobled, and bore the unmistakable imprint of suffering.

Throughout the proceedings the Magister Ludi's attention kept returning again and again to this phenomenon, and he found himself reflecting as to what kind of suffering it could have been that had impressed itself so deeply upon this lively, handsome and joyous man.

It seemed to Knecht to be a type of suffering that was beyond his own experience, and the more he pursued his reflections the more he felt drawn towards the sufferer in sympathy and compassion. There even entered into this sentiment a feeling that he was in some way responsible for his sad looking friend and that he owed him some reparation. After many conjectures—only to be as quickly abandoned—as to the cause of Plinio's sorrow, the following thought came to him: "The suffering in this face is of no ordinary origin, but is founded rather upon some noble or perhaps tragic experience, and in its expression it is quite unknown and alien to Castalia. I can remember having seen similar expressions on the faces of non-Castalians and men of the world, but never to so marked and striking a degree. I have also seen such manifestations in the portraits of men of past ages, in the portraits of many scholars or artists, in which I could detect a moving, half ailing, half fatal mourning, loneliness and helplessness."

For the Magister, who possessed such a keen artistic sensibility for the secrets of expression and, as a teacher, such an aware sense for character, there had for a long time been certain physiognomical signs which, without turning them to any systematic use, he had trusted to instinctively. Thus, for example, there was a special Castalian and a special worldly type of smile, laugh and serenity, and also a special type of suffering and sorrow.

He imagined that he now saw this worldly sorrow written upon Designori's face: it was so strong and purely impressed that it might have been the express purpose of this face to deputize for many scores of others and to portray the sufferings and ills of many.

Knecht was at once disturbed and intrigued. It seemed to him not only significant that the world had now sent his long

lost friend back to Castalia, and that Plinio and Joseph—as
had once been the case in their student debates—now really
and truly represented the world and the Order respectively,
but even more important and more symbolic still that in this
lonely and mournfully-shadowed countenance the world had
for once sent the very opposite of its laugh, smile, love of
life, joy of power and coarseness as an emissary to Castalia—
to wit, its misery and suffering.

It also gave him great cause for thought, and by no means
displeased him, that Designori seemed to avoid rather than to
court him and only surrendered himself slowly and with great
reluctance. Furthermore—and this was a great relief to
Knecht—his former school comrade was no heavy, surly and
actively hostile member of this Commission so vital to
Castalia but, as he had already ascertained, was one of the
admirers of the Order and patrons of the Province, both of
which had already received great service at his hands despite
the fact that he had given up the Bead Game for a number of
years past.

We are unable to give more intimate details as to how the
Magister gradually regained the confidence of his friend. We
must leave it to the appreciative reader who has managed to
grasp from our exposition the tranquil serenity and affectionate courtesy of the man to imagine it after his own
fashion. Knecht did not hasten his courtship of Plinio—but
who could have resisted it once he was really in earnest?

Some months after the first meeting, Designori finally
accepted Knecht's oft-repeated invitation to pay an informal
visit to Waldzell. One cloud-swept windy afternoon in
autumn the two of them drove through the twilight towards
the town of their school days and early friendship. Knecht was
unruffled and serene and his companion and guest was outwardly calm but inwardly restless like the empty fields
between sun and shadow, trembling between the joy of
reunion and sorrow at their estrangement.

As they approached the settlement they alighted, and
climbed the old paths, which they had often taken together as
students, on foot. They recalled many comrades and teachers
and many of their former conversations.

Designori was Knecht's guest for one day, during which he
had been promised that he should attend all the Magister's

official duties and functions as a spectator. In the evening—
the guest wished to leave early on the following morning
—they sat together almost in their old intimacy in Knecht's
living-room.

That day, when he had been able to watch the Magister at
his work hour by hour, had made a great impression upon
Designori, and on his return home he committed to paper the
conversation which arose between them. If to a certain extent
the content is found to be unimportant and irrelevant by
many readers we are none the less determined to include it in
full just as Designori wrote it down.

"I had intended to show you so much," the Magister
began, "and yet I have been unable to do so for sheer lack of
time. For example, my charming garden . . . do you remember the Magister's garden and Magister Thomas' wonderful
plants? Yes, and so many other things as well—but that will
be for another occasion, I hope. In any case, many memories
will have been revived for you since yesterday, and you have
also had a glimpse into my official duties and daily round."

"I am very grateful," replied Plinio. "I only began to-day
to realize some of the actual facts about your Province and the
great and remarkable secrets it possesses, although during
my years of absence I have thought about you all far more
than you might imagine. You have given me a good insight
into your office and life, and I hope, Joseph, that it will not be
the last time. I hope that we shall often be able to talk about
what I have seen here to-day, which I do not yet feel capable
of discussing. On the other hand, I feel that your confidence
has laid me under an obligation and I am sure that my previous reserve must have estranged you. You must visit me
some day too and see where I live. To-day I can only tell you
a little of my life—only as much as will enable you to know
something about me, and even if the relation of it is shameful
and in the nature of a punishment for me it will bring me
some small relief.

"You know that I come from an old patrician family, a
conservative family of land owners and high officials, which
has always been well-disposed towards your Province—but
you can see for yourself that this information in itself already
raises the gulf which separates us! I say 'family' and think of
it as something simple, self-evident and unequivocal, but is it

really that? You of the Province have your Order and your hierarchy, but you have no family. You do not know the meaning of family, blood and descent and you have no conception of the mysterious and powerful magic which that single word 'family' holds for us. Well, that applies to most of the words and ideas which can express the content of our lives. Most of those which are important to us are not so to you: some of them are totally incomprehensible, and others mean something quite different to you from what they do to us—so how can we speak to each other? Look! When you speak to me it is as though a foreigner were speaking—a foreigner, of course, whose language I had learned in my youth and which I had spoken and could partially understand —but the converse does not apply. When I speak to you, you are listening to a language half the nuances, idioms and expressions of which are quite unknown to you: you hear stories of a human life, a form of existence which is not your own, and most of it, even if you were to find it interesting, must remain foreign and at best half-intelligible.

"Do you remember the many debates and conversations of our school days? On my side they were nothing but one of my many attempts to bring the world and speech of your Province into harmony with mine. You were the frankest, most loquacious and eager of all those upon whom I practised these attempts, and you stood up courageously for the rights of Castalia without being indifferent or contemptuous of the other world and its rights. At that time we came moderately close together—but we will return to that later . . ."

He fell silent for a moment, and Knecht broke in cautiously.

"This not being able to understand each other is not really so bad as you think. Naturally two peoples speaking two different languages will never find each other so comprehensible, nor will they be able to speak to each other so intimately, as two individuals who belong to the same nation and speak the same language; but that is no reason to renounce all understanding and communication. Even between people of the same country and speech there are limitations which prevent perfect communication and complete mutual understanding, such as the barriers of culture, education, talent and individuality.

"One might argue that every man on earth can communi-

cate fundamentally with others, but one might equally assume
that no two men in the world exist between whom a complete,
unbroken, intimate communication and understanding is
possible. Both assumptions are equally valid. It is the Yin and
the Yang, the day and the night: both are right and we must
perforce be reminded of both at their appointed times. I give
you right insofar as you may think—although I do not
believe it myself—that we could strive perpetually and not be
able to understand each other wholly and completely. You
may be an Occidental and I a Chinaman and we may both
speak different languages, but even so if we are of goodwill
we shall still be able to impart much to each other and from
this be able to judge and imagine a great deal more. At all
events, let us try."

Designori nodded his head and then went on: "I will begin
by telling you the little that you need know in order to have
some inkling of my situation. I must therefore refer first of all
to the family—the supreme power in the life of a young man,
whether he recognizes the fact or not. I was on excellent
terms with mine during the time that I was an extra mural
student in your élite school. Throughout the year I was being
well educated there and during the holidays was being fêted
and spoiled at home. I was the only son. I was devoted to my
mother with a tender and almost passionate love, and parting
from her was the only pain I felt each time I left home. I
stood in a cooler yet friendly relationship to my father—at
least during my boyhood and youth, which I spent among
you. He was an old admirer of Castalia, and proud of the fact
that I was being educated in the élite school and initiated into
such sublimities as the Bead Game.

"These holidays spent at home were often of a really
amicable and festive nature, and the family and I still knew
each other to a certain extent only in holiday garb. Very
often, as I left for my holidays I felt sorry for you others who
had to remain behind, and who knew nothing of such happiness. I need not tell you very much about those days, for you
knew me better than any one else at Waldzell. I was almost a
Castalian—a little gayer, coarser and more superficial
perhaps, but full of happy exuberance, verve and enthusiasm.
They were the happiest days of my life, which of course I did
not realize then, for throughout those years at Waldzell I had

expected that the time of good fortune and the zenith of my life would come when I returned home, released from school and studies, and free to conquer the world with the aid of the superiority I had gained among you.

"Instead of this, from the moment of my departure there began that inner conflict which has lasted until this day, and a struggle in which I have certainly not been the victor.

"For the world to which I returned no longer consisted of my parent's house alone, and had by no means been waiting to embrace me and to recognize my Waldzellian superiority. Even at home there were disappointments, difficulties and discords. This state of affairs lasted for quite a while until I realised that I was protected by my ingenuous trust, my boyish belief in myself, and protected, too, by the morality of the Order which I had learned among you and by the practice of meditation.

"But what disappointment and disenchantment I experienced in the college to which I was sent in order to study politics! The manners of the students, the *niveau* of their general culture and social life, the personalities of many of the teachers—what a come down from all that I had grown accustomed to at Waldzell!

"Do you remember how I once defended our world against yours, and how I loudly extolled the naïve and traditional life that was led there? If I deserved punishment for that, my friend, then I have been well and truly punished, for this naïve, innocent life of impulse, this childish and artless geniality of the ingenuous may possibly exist somewhere— perhaps among the peasants and craftsmen—but I failed to catch a glimpse of it or share in it. You remember, too, I'm sure, how in my speeches I criticized the overweening affectation of the Castalians, that conceited and effeminate caste with their caste spirit and élite arrogance. Well, the people of the outside world were no less proud of their bad manners, of their lack of culture and coarse vulgar humour, their peasant-sly confinement to practical, selfish aims, so that they appeared no less precious, sanctimonious and eclectic in their narrow-minded naturalness than the most affected Waldzellian prize scholar. They laughed at me or slapped me on the back, but many of them reacted to the unusual and the Castalian in me with the open, blank hatred

which the vulgar have for everything well bred, and which I
had firmly decided to adopt as a mark of distinction."

Designori paused for a moment and looked at Knecht,
uncertain as to whether he were tiring him or not. His eyes
caught those of his friend and found in them an expression of
deep attention and friendliness, which reassured him. He saw
that Knecht was completely absorbed by his confession and
was listening to it not as one listens to idle chatter or to an
interesting story but at once with the intensity and devotion
of the meditator and with a pure, affectionate benevolence
which moved him deeply, for it seemed so loving and almost
childlike. He was amazed to see such an expression in the
face of the man whose many-sided day's work and authority
he had so recently admired. He continued lightened in spirit.

"I still do not know whether my life was useless and a pure
misapprehension, or whether there really was some sense in
it. If indeed this last was the case then its logic could have
been described somewhat as follows: a single ordinary man of
our age had recognised and experienced most clearly and
painfully how widely removed Castalia was from his mother-
land. Or conversely, if you like: how vastly untrue had our
land become to its noblest province and spirit; how wide in
our land was the rift between body and soul, between ideal
and reality, and how little did they know or wish to know of
each other.

"Were I to have had a task and an ideal in life it would
have been to incorporate in my person a synthesis of the two
principles, to become an intermediary, interpreter and
mediator between the two. I have tried it and failed lament-
ably, and because I cannot possibly relate my whole life to
you—which, incidentally, you would be unable to understand
—I will only tell you some of the situations which are illus-
trative of my failure.

"The difficulties which I experienced at the outset of my
studies in the college did not arise so much from the fact that
I had to put up with the ridicule and hostility which was my
portion as a Castalian, and almost a model pupil at that. In
actual fact the few of my new comrades for whom my arrival
from the élite school signified a distinction and a sensation
gave me far more trouble and embarrassment. No, the most
difficult and perhaps impossible thing for me was to continue

to lead a life in the midst of worldliness in the Castalian sense of the word.

"At the beginning I hardly noticed this and continued to observe the rules which I had learned among you. For a long time they seemed to be valid here also, seemed to strengthen and protect me, to preserve my vigour and my spiritual health, and above all they appeared to strengthen me in my purpose, alone and independently to pursue my student years as far as possible in the Castalian manner, to follow my thirst for knowledge and not to allow myself to be forced into a branch of study which required nothing of its students except that, in the shortest possible time and with the greatest possible thoroughness, they should specialize for some 'bread and butter' occupation and destroy every notion of freedom and universality that they possessed. But the protection which Castalia had afforded me soon proved to be dubious and also rather dangerous, for I found that I did not wish to preserve my peace of mind and meditative spiritual calm with resignation and asceticism, but to conquer the world and to understand it, to force my will upon it and also to make it understand me. I wished to affirm and whenever possible to rebuild and better it: I even wished to unite Castalia and the world and to reconcile them in my own person.

"When, after some disappointment, conflict or disturbance, I withdrew into meditation, I found at first that it brought me relief, relaxation, a deep breathing and a return to the good benevolent powers. But in time I observed that it was this very contemplation, care and exercise of the spirit which isolated me and made me appear so uncomfortably strange to the others, and also made it impossible for me really to understand them. I saw that in order to understand the others, the men of the world, I could only do so if I were to become like them once more, and then I should have no advantages over them—this escape into meditation included.

"Naturally it is possible that I am glossing over the facts when trying to describe them briefly like this. Perhaps, or presumably, it was simply due to the fact that I had been cut off from comrades of the same schooling and ideals, with no control from above by a teacher and without the proven and healing atmosphere of Waldzell that I had lost all sense of discipline, had become indolent and heedless and had fallen into a humdrum routine. Perhaps also in a moment of guilty conscience I had made the excuse that the humdrum was only one of the attributes of this world, and one to which I must concede in order to arrive at a closer understanding of my new surroundings.

"I am not trying to embellish things for you, but neither do I wish to deny or disguise the fact that I made the effort, strove and struggled even when and where I was at fault. It was a serious matter for me. But whether or not my attempt to understand and discipline myself was only conceit on my part, in any event the natural thing resulted—the world was stronger than myself and slowly overpowered and swallowed me up. It was as though I had been taken at my word and become exactly like the world, the fairness, ingenuousness, strength and ontological superiority of which I had so inordinately praised in our discussions at Waldzell, and which I had defended against your logic. Do you remember?"

"And now I must remind you of something else—something which you have probably long since forgotten because it can have had no significance for you. For me, however, it had a very great significance: for me it was important— important and terrible. My college years were over and I had adapted myself, had been conquered—but by no means entirely. On the contrary, I considered myself spiritually as one of you, and believed these shifts and compromises to be voluntary and a matter of intelligence rather than as a proof that I had actually suffered a defeat. Therefore I had held fast to many customs and needs of youthful years, including the Bead Game, which presumably had little sense, for without constant practice and contact with equal or superior players one can learn nothing, and solitary playing can at best only be a substitute in the same way that a monologue is only a substitute for true and genuine intercourse.

"Without rightly knowing how things stood with myself, with my art of playing, my culture and my élite scholarship, I took the trouble to rescue at least a part of these assets. Whenever one of my friends attempted to discuss the Bead Game without having the slightest knowledge of its spirit, and I outlined a Game subject or analysed a phrase, it would seem to this man, who was completely ignorant, to be in the nature of magic.

"During the third or fourth years of my college studies I took a refresher course in the Game in Waldzell. Seeing the neighbourhood again, the little town and our old school afforded me a somewhat melancholy pleasure; but you were away either in Monteport or in Keuperheim, and had the reputation for being a zealous and, if I may say so, an eccentric character.

"My course was only the 'holiday refresher' for us poor dilettantes and men of the outside world, but it entailed some effort and I was proud to receive at the end of the proceedings the usual 'third'—that 'adequate,' which allows its possessor to attend a further holiday course.

"Then, a few years later, I pulled myself together and put my name down for a course under your predecessor, and did my level best to get myself into presentable shape for Waldzell. I had read through my old exercise books and had tried to re-accustom myself to meditation and concentration exercises, and had in short with the modest means at my disposal practised, collected myself and prepared my mood in the same way as every bead-player does for the great Annual Games.

"So I arrived in Waldzell where, after an absence of some years I found myself even more of a stranger, but at the same time still as enchanted as ever and as though returning once more to a lost homeland, but in whose speech I was now not very fluent. And on this occasion my most ardent wish was also fulfilled—to see you again. Can you remember the incident, Joseph?"

Knecht was looking at him earnestly. He nodded his head and smiled faintly, without saying a word.

"Good," Designori went on, "so you do remember. But what exactly do you remember? A transient meeting with an old school comrade, a little encounter and a disappointment; one goes on one's way and gives no more heed to it than that one had been rather impolitely reminded of a few decades before by another. That is so, is it not? Was there anything more in it than that—anything more for you?"

He was exceedingly moved, although quite obviously struggling to control himself, and seemed to be trying to unburden himself of something which had piled up and been smouldering within him for many years.

"You are anticipating me," said Knecht cautiously. "We will talk about that when my turn comes, and then I will try to give you an account of what it was like on my side. You have the word now, Plinio. I can see that that meeting was no more pleasant for you than it was for me. But go on with your story as to what happened, and speak quite unreservedly."

"I will do my best, then," answered Plinio, "and I will not attempt to reproach you. I must admit that you behaved extremely correctly towards me—no, you did even more than that. When I accepted this present invitation to Waldzell, which I had not seen since that second holiday course—yes, even when I was chosen to sit as a member of the Castalia Commission—it was my intention to confront you and discuss that experience, however pleasant or unpleasant it might have proved for both of us. And now I will continue with my story. I arrived for the holiday course and was given a room in the guest house. The other members of the course were nearly all of my own age, although some of them were considerably older. There were not more than twenty of us— Castalians for the most part—but either bad, indifferent or negligent bead-players, or beginners who had felt a tardy desire to learn some rudiments of the Game. It was a great relief to me that I knew none of them. Although our course leader—one of the assistants from the Archives—put himself to the greatest trouble and was extremely friendly towards us, the whole thing from the very beginning savoured of the second-class and futile school, of a detention class in which neither the hastily assembled members nor the teacher had any belief.

"One might have asked with astonishment why this handful of people had gathered together of their own free will in order to perform something which they were incapable of performing, and for which they had neither the strength, endurance nor capacity for sacrifice, and why a scholarly expert should have lent himself to the undertaking in order to give them instruction and to busy himself with the exercises, from which he himself could hardly expect any success.

"I did not know at the time, and only learned later from

people of experience, that I had been frankly unlucky in this course, and that a slightly different composition of the participants could have made it enthralling and challenging, not to say inspiring. It would have been possible, so I was told, for two members present, who were capable of kindling each other or who had previously been on intimate terms, to have given an elevating swing to such a course, and to have carried with them all the other members including the teacher. After all, you are the Magister Ludi and must know all about this. So I was unlucky in our casual community inasmuch as that little vivifying cell was absent, no warmth or elevation transpired, and it remained a dull repetition class for grown-up schoolboys.

"The days went by, and with them my disappointment increased. However, besides the Bead Game there was still Waldzell—a sacred place of cherished memories. And even if the Game course had been a failure, there was still that festive feeling of homecoming, the contact with former comrades and perhaps also the chance of seeing again the one comrade of whom I had the most vivid memories and who in my eyes represented our Castalia more than any other figure— yourself, Joseph.

"Perhaps, I thought, if I could just see a few of the companions of my youth and schooldays once more; if, on my walks through the beautiful and beloved place, I could meet once again the good spirits of my youthful years; if only *you* were to approach me, and we could enter into a conversation again such as we used to have in our disputes—less between you and I personally than between my own Castalian problem and myself—then the holiday would not have been wasted and the course and everything else could go its own way.

"The first two old comrades who crossed my path were harmless enough; they slapped me cheerfully on the back and asked me childish questions about my fabulous life in the outside world. A few of the others, who belonged to the Vicus Lusorum and to the younger élite, were not so harmless. They asked me no ingenuous questions, but greeted me as they would a person whom they could not avoid in the realms of their sanctuary with a pointed, somewhat exaggerated politeness or rather condescension, and they could not show clearly enough their preoccupation with other important things which were beyond my reach, their lack of time, curiosity and sympathy, and that they had no wish to renew an old acquaintanceship. Well, I did not importune them, and left them in peace—to their Olympian, serene, ironical Castalian peace. I looked across at them and their busy tranquil life like some prisoner through the bars, or as some poor hungry serf might look at a group of serene, handsome, refined and well-rested aristocrats with their well-tended faces and hands.

"And then you appeared, Joseph. As I caught sight of you, joy and new hope were born within me. You were walking across the courtyard, and I recognised you at once by your walk and called out to you quite spontaneously. A man at last! I thought. At last a friend . . . an opponent, perhaps, but one at least with whom I could speak; a veritable Castalian admittedly, but one in whom the Castalian had not become petrified into a mask and an armour, a man, an understanding man!

"You must have noticed how glad I was and how much I expected of you, and indeed you received me with the greatest courtesy. You remembered me—I still meant something to you, and you seemed pleased to see my face again.

"Nor did it remain a short friendly greeting in the courtyard, but you invited me in to your study and devoted—nay, sacrificed—an evening to me.

"But, my dear Knecht, what an evening that was! How we both tortured ourselves to appear jovial, polite and to try and be comradely towards each other. How hard it became to lead the halting conversation from one subject to another. If the others had been indifferent towards me this was far worse: this tiring and useless effort to revive a former friendship was far more hurtful. That evening destroyed my illusions once and for all. It had been made bitterly apparent to me that I was no comrade and co-striver, no Castalian or man of rank but an importuner, a hobnobbing loon, an uneducated foreigner. That all this took place in so correct and mannered a form, and that the disappointment and impatience you felt remained so impeccably masked seemed to me the worst blow of all. Had you but railed at me and reproached me, or had you upbraided me and said 'What has happened to you, my friend? How could you have so degenerated?' I should have been happy, and the ice would have been broken. But nothing of the sort occurred. I saw that I no longer belonged to Castalia, that my love for the Province, my studies in the Bead Game and our companionship had come to naught. The private tutor, Knecht, had graciously accepted my tiresome visit to Waldzell, had allowed himself to be irked and bored with me for a whole evening and had then shown me the door in the most impersonal and courteous manner."

Designori, struggling with his emotion, broke off and looked with tortured eyes at the Magister. Knecht sat there not in the least disturbed, a most attentive and devoted listener, smiling in a friendly and compassionate manner at his old friend. As Designori did not continue with his narrative, Knecht allowed his gaze to rest upon him, a gaze full of benevolence, satisfaction and pleasure, which his friend bore for a moment or two with darkened countenance.

"You are laughing!" cried Plinio violently, but without any anger in his voice. "Do you find everything in order, then?"

"I must admit," said Knecht, still smiling, "that you have described the incident admirably, most admirably. It was exactly as you have painted it, and possibly the residue of injury and accusation in your voice was necessary in order to reconstruct the scene for me so perfectly. You have also, although unfortunately you cannot quite see it with the eyes of yesterday and have not completely recovered from it, told your story with true objectivity—the story of two young men in a somewhat painful predicament who were both obliged to dissemble, and one of whom committed the fault of hiding his real and earnest suffering in the situation beneath a dashing demeanour instead of breaking through the game of masks. It seems to me even a little as though you still to-day blame the futility of that meeting upon me rather than upon yourself, although it definitely lay in your hands to alter the situation. Have you not yet understood that? But I must say once more that you have told the story uncommonly well. In actual fact I have been re-experiencing all the oppressiveness and embarrassment of that strange evening, and for a few moments I thought that I should be obliged to struggle all over again to preserve my good behaviour and to feel a little ashamed of both of us. It was a pleasure to hear such a tale."

"Well," began Plinio, and there was still a ring of mortification and distrust in his voice, "it is gratifying if my story has at least been diverting. But it has not been particularly diverting for me, I can tell you!"

"Don't you see, though," said Knecht, "how complacently we can now view this affair, which showed neither of us up in a very good light? We can actually laugh over it!"

"Laugh—but why?"

"Because this story of our ex-Castalian Plinio who bothered so much about the Bead Game and about the recognition of a former comrade is obsolete and fundamentally at an end, just as much as the story of our courteous private tutor Knecht who, in spite of all Castalian usage, knew so little how to disguise his embarrassment before the gravely disconcerted Plinio that it can still, after so many years, be held up before him as an indictment. Yes, Plinio, you have an excellent memory. It is fortunate for us that the story is so completely dead and buried that we can both laugh at it."

Designori was bewildered. He could feel the warmth of the Magister's mood as something pleasant and affectionate, far removed from any irony, and he realised too that behind this geniality there lay a profound seriousness; yet he had sensed as he told the story, all too painfully and with all the bitterness of that experience, that it was far too near to being a confession for him to have dared to change the tone of his voice.

"You are forgetting perhaps," he said undecidedly and still half in disagreement, "that what passed that evening did not have the same effect on both of us. For you it was at most an unpleasant episode, but for me it was a collapse and a defeat, and furthermore marked the beginning of important changes in my life. When I left Waldzell at the end of the course I resolved never to return again, and came near to hating Castalia and the lot of you. I had lost my illusions and realized that I no longer belonged among you—perhaps never had really belonged as much as I had imagined—and that it did not require much for me to become a renegade and your outspoken enemy."

Knecht looked at him serenely but at the same time penetratingly.

"Naturally I hope that you are going to tell me all about

this," he said slowly. "But to-day the position as I see it is as follows: we were friends in early youth, were parted and travelled in very different directions. We met again at the time of your unfortunate holiday course, when you had become half or entirely a man of the outside world and I a somewhat obscure, thoughtful Waldzellian of the Castalian mould. We have to-day recalled that disappointing and ignominious meeting. We have seen ourselves and our former embarrassment once more and we have been able not only to endure the sight of it but to laugh at it, for to-day the position is quite different. I will also not disguise the fact that the impression you made upon me at that time caused me extreme embarrassment. It was a thoroughly unpleasant and negative impression, and I did not even know how to begin for you seemed in some unexpected, disturbing and irritating manner, to be immature, coarse and worldly. I was a young Castalian, ignorant of the world and not wishing to find out anything about it, whereas you were a young stranger whose visit I could in no way account for. Nor could I understand why you were taking a course in the Game, for you seemed to have nothing at all left of the élite scholar. You aggravated my nerves as I did yours. Naturally I must have appeared to you as an arrogant Waldzellian devoid of any special merit trying carefully to maintain a distance between himself and a non-Castalian, a mere dilettante of the Game. And on my side, I saw you as a kind of barbarian or half-educated person who, in an importunate and unwarranted manner, seemed to be laying claims to my interest and friendship. We defended ourselves mutually and came very near to hating each other. We could do nothing but pursue our several ways, for neither had anything to give nor was either in the position to be fair to the other.

"But to-day, Plinio, it was necessary that we should renew the shameful buried memory and that we should both laugh at that scene, because to-day we are different and have come together with quite other intentions and possibilities, without sentimentality and without suppressed feelings of jealousy and hatred, for we have long since become men."

Designori smiled with relief. "But are you so sure?" he could not refrain from asking. "Have we not always in the long run been of good will towards each other?"

"Oh, I agree with you," laughed Knecht. "We have even tried our goodwill to the point of torture and overstrain. In those early days we were instinctively opposed to each other: we were each of us suspect, disturbing, alien and repugnant in the eyes of the other and only an illusory sense of duty, an equality of breeding had compelled us to play that tedious comedy that evening. That much became clear to me soon after your visit. Neither of us had entirely overcome our former friendship or our former antagonism. Instead of allowing it to perish, we thought we could dig it up again and in some manner revive it: we both felt under an obligation, and we did not know how we could pay off our debt to each other. Is that not so?"

"I think," Plinio replied thoughtfully, "that even to-day you are still a little too polite. You say 'both,' but it was not both of us who sought and were unable to find. The seeking and the love were entirely on my side, and also the disappointment and the suffering. What, I ask you, has been altered in your life as a result of our meeting? Nothing! For me, on the other hand, it has meant a deep and painful change, and therefore I cannot join in the laughter with which you dismiss it."

"Forgive me," answered Knecht amicably, "perhaps I have been a little hasty, but I hope eventually to be able to bring you round to my way of thinking. You were right. You were wounded, though not through me—as you thought and as you still seem to think—but through the gulf and the alienation that existed between yourself and Castalia, which both of us seemed to have bridged during our school friendship, only for it suddenly to yawn wide and deep again that evening. As far as your personal accusation against me goes I beg you to give vent to it freely and courageously."

"Oh, it was never an accusation: it was merely a plaint. You did not hear it then, and it seems that you do not even hear it to-day. You answered it then with a laugh and with courteous behaviour, and you are doing exactly the same thing to-day."

Although Designori was aware of the benevolence and deep friendship in the Magister's bearing he could not refrain

from harping on this point. It was as though this long
endured pain had now to be assuaged once and for all.

Knecht's expression did not change. He sat immersed in
thought for a moment or two. "I am beginning to understand
you now for the first time, my friend," he began cautiously.
"Perhaps you are right, and the matter must be thrashed out
here and now. I should like to remind you first of all that you
would only have had the right to expect an answer to your
"plaint" as you term it, had you really given utterance to that
plaint. But in actual fact, on that very evening in the guest
house you by no means complained, but behaved exactly as I
myself did—in as hale and hearty and courageous a manner as
possible. You played your part impeccably and so did I—
I, who had nothing at all to complain of. But in secret, as I
now gather, you expected that I should hear your hidden
plaint and recognise the true face behind the mask. Now I
could easily have noticed something at that time, but
certainly not everything; and how was I, without wounding
your pride, to make you understand that I was worried about
you and that I actually pitied you? What use would it have
been for me to stretch out a hand to you, inasmuch as my hand
was empty and had nothing to give—no advice, no consolation and no friendship—because our ways lay so far apart?
Yes, at that time the concealed discomfiture and misfortune
which was quite evident behind your lusty behaviour was,
I admit, burdensome, disturbing and repulsive, for it presumed
a compassion and sympathy on my part which by no means
corresponded with your behaviour. It appeared to me as
something cloyish and childish, and helped my feelings to
grow colder towards you. You had raised claims upon my
friendship, you wished to be a Castalian and a bead-player
and yet seemed so uncontrolled, so strange and so entirely
given over to selfish feelings.

"This was more or less my judgment at the time, for I
saw full well that practically nothing of the Castalian had
remained in you and that you had even forgotten the basic
rules of behaviour. Good. That was not my affair. But why
had you come to Waldzell and wished us to greet you as a
comrade? That was, as I have already said, annoying and
repellent, and you were perfectly right in judging my
polished courtesy at the time as a rejection. Yes, I rejected

you instinctively, not because you were a child of the outside world, but because you were making demands upon me and trying to rank as a Castalian.

"When, however, you reappeared once more after so many years, there was nothing at all of Castalia to be observed in you. You looked worldly and spoke like one from the world outside, and I found your expression of mourning, grief and unhappiness particularly that of a stranger; but everything, your behaviour, your dignity and even your sadness, pleased me; they were beautiful, they suited you and were worthy of you. Nothing offended me and I could accept and approve of you without any inner contradiction. This time no exaggerated politeness and behaviour was necessary on my part: I approached you immediately as a friend, and have made every endeavour to show you my sympathy and love. But on this occasion it was quite the reverse of our previous meeting, for it was I who bestirred myself on your account and courted you, while you witheld yourself to the utmost. Naturally I accepted your presence in our midst and your interest in our destiny as a kind of recognition of affection and loyalty. Well, at least you responded to my advances, and here we are opening our hearts to each other and able—I hope—to renew our old friendship.

"You said just now that our youthful meeting was something painful for you and meaningless to me. We will not quarrel over that. You may be right. But our present meeting, *amice*, is by no means purposeless: it means far more to me than I am able to tell you now, and more than you can possibly imagine. To give you some brief idea, it not only means the return of a lost friend and at the same time a resurrection of the past to new strengths and transformations, but above all constitutes a call, a compromise, an opening up of a new avenue to your world, and it also poses once more the old problem of finding a synthesis between you and myself, between your world and mine. It could not have happened at a more appropriate time, I assure you. The call finds me this time not deaf but more aware than I have ever been, for actually it has come as no surprise and, mark you, does not seem to have arrived from a strange outside source, to which one could open or shut one's ears at will, but from within myself and to be the answer to a longing which has

grown strong and urgent—to a distress and an inner yearning. But we will speak of that another time, for it is already
late and we both need rest.

"You spoke anon of my serenity and of your sadness, and
you suggested—or so it appeared to me—that I was unjust to
what you term your 'plaint,' and no less so to-day since I have
answered you with a smile. This is something which I cannot
properly understand. Why should a lament not be listened to
with serenity, and why must it not be answered with a smile
but with sadness?

"The mere fact that you have returned to Castalia once
more with your sorrow and your burdens leads me to think
that it has something to do with our serenity. If even now I
do not participate in your sadness and heaviness of heart and
do not allow myself to be infected by it, it does not necessarily
mean that I refuse to countenance it or take it seriously. Your
entire mien and all that which your life and destiny in the
world has left imprinted upon your face I have fully recognised and accept. It suits you and is a part of you, and I love
and respect it—although I hope to see it changed. Its origin
I can only presume—perhaps later you will tell me as much
or as little about it as you consider seemly—but I can only say
with certainty that you seem to have had a pretty difficult life.
Will you tell me what makes you think that I could not be
and should not wish to be just to your sorrows?"

Designori's face had clouded over once more.

"Sometimes," he said resignedly, "it seems to me as
though we not only possess two completely different
codes and languages, which can only be translated into
terms approximating each other, but as though we are two
fundamentally different beings with no possibility of ever
understanding each other; and it always seems to be a
question of doubt for me which of us is the true and complete
man, or whether either of us actually fits this description.
There were times when I looked up to you bead-players and
members of the Order with veneration, and with a feeling of
inferiority and envy for the way in which you gods and
supermen, whom no suffering could touch, enjoyed your
existence eternally serene and ever at play; but at other
times you appeared to me alternately pitiable and con-
temptible, as eunuchs, petrified artificially in an eternal

childhood, childlike and childish in your passionless, neatly circumscribed, well-furnished world of games, your kindergarten where every nose was scrupulously clean and where every unseemly sensation and thought was pacified and suppressed, where one played pretty, safe, and bloodless games one's whole life long, and where every disturbing life impulse, powerful sensation, true passion or heart throb was controlled immediately by meditative therapy, canalized and neutralized. Is it not, I thought, an artificial, sterilized, pedagogic emasculated world, a pure half-world, a world of appearances, in which you cowards vegetate; a world without crimes, passions or hunger, without salt or sap, a world without family, mother or children—almost without women? The life urge is contemplatively fettered; dangerous and audacious activities or matters entailing heavy responsibility such as administration, law and politics have for generations been left to the care of others; you lead a cowardly and well-protected drone's existence without food problems and with but few onerous duties, and lest it grow tedious you devote yourselves with fervour to those scholarly specialities, toy with syllables and letters, play music and indulge in the Bead Game, while outside in the filth of the world poor harrassed men live the real life and do the real work."

Knecht had been listening to this tirade with friendly and unflagging attention.

"My dear friend," he said thoughtfully, "how much your words remind me of our schooldays and your criticisms and love of your argument. But to-day I do not have to play the same part as I did then; to-day my task does not lie in defending the Order and the Province against your attacks, and I am very thankful, considering the difficulty and the strain, that it does no longer exist. It is certainly very hard to parry such magnificent attacks as the one you have just launched. You spoke, for example, of the people outside in your world as those who 'live the real life and who do the real work.'

"Now that has such a clear, beautiful and candid ring, almost like an axiom, and should one wish to contest it, one must definitely be unfair and remind the speaker that part of this world's 'true work' consists in running a commission for the maintenance of Castalia. But jesting aside for the moment, it is clear from your words and from your tone of voice that your heart is still filled with either hate, envy or yearning for us. In your estimation we are cowards and drones or irresponsible children in a kindergarten, and yet there have also been times when you have looked upon us as eternally serene gods. One thing I think I may assume from your words: that Castalia is not to blame for your sorrow or misfortune, as you are pleased to call it, and that we must look elsewhere for the causes. Were we Castalians really to blame, your reproaches and objections would not be the same to-day as they were in your boyhood days.

"In later conversations you shall tell me more, and I have no doubt that we shall find a way to making you serener and happier, or at least to making your relationship with Castalia a freer and more agreeable one. As far as I can see you have built up a false, constricted and sentimental attitude towards myself and towards Castalia, and at the same time towards your own youth and schooldays. You have split your own soul between Castalia and the world, and tortured yourself unduly over things for which you were not responsible. On the other hand, it is possible that you take many other things, for which the responsibility lies entirely within yourself, far too lightly. I imagine that you have not practised your meditation for a long time . . . is that not so?"

Designori laughed bitterly. "How perspicacious you are, *Domine!* For a long time, you say? It is many, many years now since I renounced the charms of meditation. But how anxious you have become about me all of a sudden! At that time when I was in Waldzell on my holiday course, when you showed me so much courtesy and contempt and so politely rejected my comradeship, I returned home with the firm resolution of making an end of everything Castalian within me for ever. I renounced the Bead Game from that day onwards, have never meditated since, and for a long time even music was unbearable to me. In place of these I found new comrades, who instructed me in pleasure. We drank and whored, and tried all manner of narcotics, and we spat upon everything decent, worthy and ideal. Naturally that filth did not last for long, but long enough to eat away completely the last traces of Castalian varnish. And then, some years later, when on a certain occasion I realised that I had abused even these intoxicants and had urgent need of meditation, I was too proud to start again."

"Too proud?" asked Knecht softly.

"Yes, too proud. I had in the meantime become submerged in the world, and had become a man of the world. I wished for nothing better than to be as one of them and to have no other life than theirs—that passionate, childish, gruesome, uncontrolled life that vacillates between happiness and fear. I scorned the idea of resorting to your expedients in order to provide a modicum of relief or to create certain advantages for myself."

The Magister looked at him sharply.

"And for how many years did you endure that? Have you made use of no other expedients in order to be rid of it all?"

"Oh, yes!" admitted Plinio, "I have indeed, and still do so to-day. There are times when I drink really heavily and use all manner of drugs in order to sleep."

Knecht closed his eyes for a moment as though suddenly weary, then looked up at his friend again, long and questioningly and in silence. Gradually his look assumed an even more tender and friendly serenity.

Designori confessed afterwards that he had never in his whole life seen a look in a man's eyes at once so inquiring and affectionate, so innocent and appraising, so radiantly friendly and so omniscient. He admitted that it had at first confused and irritated him, but had gradually calmed him with its gentle compelling insistence. And yet he had tried to defend himself against it.

"You said just now," he went on, "that you know of an anodyne to make me serener and happier, but you do not dream of asking me whether that is actually what I desire."

"Well," laughed Joseph Knecht, "if we can make a man serener and happier, we do so irrespective of whether he asks us to do so or not. And why pray should you not seek and desire it? That is why you are here—why we are now sitting opposite each other, and why you have returned to us. You hate and despise Castalia; you are too proud of your worldliness and sorrow to lighten it with a certain amount of intelligence and meditation, and yet a secret and irresistible longing for us and for our serenity has guided and nourished you all these years, prompting you to come and try your

luck with us once more. And I tell you, you have come at
the right moment—at a time when I, too, yearn for a call
from your world and for one of its doors to open. But we
will talk about that next time. You have confided a great
deal to me, my friend, and I thank you for your confidence:
you will see that I, too, have something to confess to you.
It is late, however, and you are leaving early to-morrow
morning; I have also a hard official day before me, and we
must soon go to sleep—but be good enough to grant me
another quarter of an hour before you retire."

He stood up, went over to the window and looked up into
the sky, where drifting clouds could be seen in dark patches
in the starry night heaven. As he remained standing there
his guest also rose and went over to join him. The Magister
was breathing rhythmically, inhaling the thin cool air of the
autumn night. He raised his hand and pointed. "Look," he
said, "at that cloud landscape dappling the heavens. At the
first glimpse one might think that the depth was there
where it is darkest, but one sees at once that those soft dark
patches are only clouds, that space with all its profundity
first begins beyond the borders and fjords of that cloud-
mountain and sinks into infinity where the stars reign
supreme—those grand and highest symbols of clarity and
order for us humans. It is not there in the clouds and in the
darkness that the depths of the world and its secrets reside,
but in the open and the serene. I implore you, before you
go to bed stay and look for a while at these bights and narrows
with their host of stars, and do not thrust aside the thoughts
and dreams that they may inspire in you."

A curious trembling sensation welled up in Plinio's heart,
and he was uncertain as to whether it were due to grief or
joy. He remembered that an unconscionably long time
before, in the lovely serene spring of his Waldzell schooldays he had been initiated into his first exercises in meditation
with these very words.

"And allow me one more word," the Magister began in a
soft voice: "I should like to talk to you about serenity—
that of the stars and the spirit, and also about our own
particular Castalian serenity. You have an aversion to it,
probably because you have been obliged to follow the path
of sadness and because now all sunniness and geniality, our

Castalian brand especially, seem to you shallow and childish—cowardly too—and seem to constitute a flight from the terrors and the abysmal truths of reality into a clear well-ordered world of pure pattern and formulas, of pure abstractions and refinements. But, my dear mournful one, even though this flight exists, and even though there may be Castalians who are cowardly and timorous and who play with formulas, even though this should apply to the majority of us, it does not contradict the serenity of the heavens and the spirit, and does not detract from their value and splendour. The easily content and pseudo-serene among us can be opposed by others—men and generations of men for whom serenity was not merely a superficial game but a serious and deep preoccupation. I have known one of them. He was our former music master, whom you saw from time to time at Waldzell, a man who in the latter years of his life possessed this virtue to such a degree that it radiated from him like light from the sun, that it flooded everything and was reflected in everyone—as benevolence, love of life, good temper, confidence and reliability—who accepted and absorbed its glow seriously.

"I, too, was illuminated by this light, and partook to some small measure of his sunniness and the warmth from his glowing heart, just as Ferromonte and many others did. To achieve this serenity is my highest and noblest aim, and also that of many others: you will find it very often among the Fathers of our Order. This serenity is neither a pose nor self-complacency but the highest knowledge and love, the acceptance of all truth, the awareness at the edge of all depths and abysses, the virtue of the Saint and the Knight. It is imperturbable and increases with age and the approach of death; it is the secret of all beauty, and the quintessence of all art. The poet who, in the dancing metre of his verses, praises the glorious and the terrible in life, the musician who lets it ring as pure Present, are both bringers of light, spreading joy and brightness upon earth, even though at first they may lead us through tears and painful tension. The poet whose verses enchant us may be a sad recluse, and the musician a melancholy dreamer, but their work also has a part in the serenity of God and the stars. What they give us is no more than their sombreness, sorrow or fear, but it is a drop of the pure light of Eternal Serenity. When, too, whole peoples and languages seek to plumb the depths of the world by means of myths, cosmogonies and religions, their highest achievement is this serenity. Think for one moment of the ancient Indians of whom our teacher at Wald-zell often told us: they were a people of suffering, reflection, penance and ascesis, but the ultimate fund of their spirit was light and serenity—serene the smile of the world conqueror and the Buddha, serene the figures of their eschato-logical mythologies. The world, as their myths portray it, was in the beginning divine, radiant and happy, beautiful as spring—a golden age. But suddenly it grows sick and begins to degenerate, becomes more and more coarsened and wretched, until finally, at the end of four ever declining aeons, it is ripe to be stamped underfoot and destroyed by the dancing feet of Shiva. That is not the end of the world, however. It begins anew with the smile of the dreaming Vishnu who, with his playing hand, creates a new, young, beautiful and radiant world. It is truly marvellous: these people, discerning and capable of suffering as hardly any other, looked upon the gruesome game of world history with horror and shame—the ever-turning wheel of lust and suffer-ing. They saw and understood the decay of creation, the lust and devilry of man and simultaneously his deep longing for purity and harmony, and discovered this glorious allegory for the whole beauty and tragedy of creation—the aeons and the decline of creation, the powerful Shiva who tramples the putrefying world to pulp and the laughing Vishnu who lies in slumber and allows a new world to be born of his divine golden dreams.

"Now as regards our Castalian serenity, it may be only a small and late variety of this great one, but it is entirely legitimate. Scholarship has not always and everywhere been serene—as of course it should have been. With us it is the cult of truth closely bound up with the cult of the beautiful and, in addition to this, with the contemplative care of the spirit, and thus can never entirely lose its serenity; but our Bead Game unites within itself all three of these principles—science, reverence of the beautiful and meditation. Thus, a true bead-player should be permeated with serenity like a ripe fruit with sweet juices, and above all should possess the serenity of music, which is naught else but courage—a serene, smiling, striding and dancing amidst the terrors and flames of the world, the festive offering of a sacrifice.

"I have been preoccupied with this serenity ever since, as a scholar and student first I began to understand something about it, and I would never forego it again—even in unhappiness and sorrow.

"Now let us go to sleep, my friend. To-morrow you will be leaving us, but you must return soon, and tell me more about yourself. You shall learn that here, too, in Waldzell and in the life of a Magister, doubts, disappointments, despair and evil spirits are not unknown. But you must not retire to sleep without first hearing a little music. A glance at the stars and a little sweet music are better than all your sleeping draughts."

Knecht sat down and played softly and gently. He played a phrase from that Purcell sonata which had once been a favourite of Father Jacobus'. The notes fell like golden drops of light in the silence of the room, so gently that the murmur of the fountain in the courtyard could still be heard. The voices of the beautiful music met and merged—gentle and powerful, chaste and sweet. Courageously and serenely, they strode in their innermost ranks through the void of time and the transitory, making space and the night hour, while they lasted, enduring and cosmic. As Joseph Knecht bade farewell to his guest the latter's face had changed and grown lighter, and there were tears in his eyes.

Chapter Ten

PREPARATIONS

KNECHT HAD SUCCEEDED in breaking the ice, and a vivid and mutually refreshing relationship and exchange of ideas now began between Designori and himself. This man, who for many years had lived in a resigned state of melancholy, had been forced to acknowledge that Knecht was right: it had in actual fact been a yearning for revival, for sunniness and Castalian serenity that had drawn him back towards the Pedagogic Province. He was a frequent visitor now quite apart from his missions and official duties, and was regarded by Tegularius with a somewhat jealous distrust.

Knecht soon learned all that he needed to know about him and about his life, which had not been so unusual and complicated as the Magister had imagined by his first revelations. Plinio had in his youth suffered the disappointments and humiliations of his enthusiastic and action-thirsty existence, as we have already learned. Instead of becoming a go-between and a conciliator between the world and Castalia he had become a lonely and embittered outsider incapable of forming a synthesis between the worldly and the Castalian sides of his origin and character, and yet he had not simply been a failure, but had carved out for himself in defeat and renunciation an individuality and an especial destiny. His education in Castalia seemed to have proved a disaster and to have brought him nothing but conflicts and disappointments and an isolation and loneliness difficult for one of his nature to bear, and it seemed as though, now that he had been forced on to the thorny path of the lonely and the unadaptable, everything that he undertook or did only tended to separate him more and more and to increase his difficulties.

Already as a student he had brought himself into irreconcilable opposition to his family and above all to his father. The latter, although he was not actually to be numbered among the political leaders, was like all his forebears a supporter of everything conservative, true to the government in his politics, an opponent of any claims of the lower orders to rights and privileges, distrustful of men without name or rank, loyal to the old order and prepared to make sacrifices for everything that appeared to him legitimate and sacred. Thus, without having any religious needs, he was a friend of the Church, and although he was not lacking in a sense of justice, benevolence and readiness to charity and good deeds, he obstinately and basically set his face against every effort on the part of the peasants to better their lot. He justified this pseudo-logical harshness with the slogans and programmes of his party. In reality he was actuated not by conviction and discernment but by a blind loyalty to his peers and to the tradition of his house, which could be summed up as a certain chivalry and knightly honour and a downright contempt for everything that in his eyes was modern, progressive and up to date. In view of this attitude it is not surprising therefore that he was disappointed, irritated and embittered when his son Plinio, while still a student, approached and joined an outspoken opposition and modernistic party. At that time a leftish, youthful branch of an old bourgeois liberal party had been formed, led by Veraguth, a publicist civil servant and orator of great and outstanding influence. This slightly ecstatic and emotional friend of the people and lover of freedom, whose courtship of academical youth through the medium of public speeches in the college towns had not been without success, had among other enthusiastic listeners and followers captured the interest of the young Designori. The youth, disappointed with the college and in search of an anchorage—some substitute for the Castalian morality, which had ceased to exist for him— was attracted by Veraguth's speeches. He had admired the latter's pathos and fire, his wit and accusing demeanour, his handsome appearance and speech, and had joined a group of students from among the many followers who were in favour of his party and aims.

When Plinio's father learned of this he fell into a terrible rage and for the first time in his life thundered at the boy, hurling epithets at him such as "conspirator," "traitor to father, family and tradition" and gave him strict commands to repair his errors forthwith by severing connections with Veraguth and his party. This was by no means the most fruitful way of influencing Plinio, who from that moment onwards began to look upon his own behaviour as a kind of martyrdom. He faced the paternal thunder and announced that he had not spent ten years in the élite school and a few more in the university simply to renounce his own convictions, judgments and views upon state administration and justice and to be dictated to by a bunch of selfish, feudal barons. He stressed the fact that he appreciated the school of Veraguth which, taking the great tribunes as an example, knew nothing of selfish or class interests and struggled for nothing else in the world except justice and humanity.

The elder Designori broke into a bitter laugh and pointed out to his son that he might at least finish his studies before he began mixing himself up in men's affairs and imagining that he, a degenerate and reprehensible scion, knew more about human life and justice than generations of more revered and noble races, whom he was now stabbing in the back with his treachery. The two of them quarrelled bitterly and used insulting words to each other which increased in violence until the elder man, as though seeing his anger-distorted face in a mirror, suddenly fell into a shamefaced silence and left the room without another word.

From that day onwards, the old harmless and intimate home life came to an end for ever for Plinio. Not only did he remain true to his group and their neo-liberalism but upon the completion of his studies actually became Veraguth's constant pupil, helper and collaborator and a few years later, his son-in-law.

Although the balance in Designori's soul had been disturbed and his life faced with a burning problem as the result of his education in the élite school—or rather, through the difficulties in adapting himself to the outside world and to his country—these new relations brought him altogether into an exposed, difficult and tricky situation. There was no doubt that he had acquired something valuable—a kind of belief, a political conviction and a sense of unity with the party—which had satisfied his youthful need for justice and progress; and in the person of Veraguth had found a teacher, leader and elder friend, whom in the beginning he had loved and admired blindly and who seemed moreover to need and to value him, but above all he had gained a sense of direction, an aim and a life task. These were no mean acquisitions, and they had to be paid for dearly. Even though the young man had been able to bear the loss of his natural inherited position in his father's house and the ostracism and animosity on the part of the privileged members of his class with a certain fanatical pleasure and sense of martyrdom, there yet remained much to which he could not become reconciled—least of all to the gnawing feeling of having caused sorrow to his beloved mother, who was placed in an unenviable and equivocal position between his father and himself, a circumstance which probably shortened her life.

She died shortly after his marriage, and after her death Plinio was hardly seen again in the old family residence, which he sold upon his father's decease.

There are natures which are capable of so loving and making their own position in life that has been paid for by a sacrifice—an office, a marriage or a vocation—such that it constitutes, simply because of this sacrifice, a perpetual source of happiness and satisfaction. Plinio Designori was not one of these.

Although he remained true to his party and leader, his political standpoint, his marriage and his idealism, he found that in time they became just as problematical as his whole existence. His outlook upon politics and the world began to lose its youthful enthusiasm. He found the struggle for justice in the long run as little cause for happiness as the consolation of suffering and sacrifice, and to these cares were added the daily experiences and disenchantments of his profession. Finally, he began to wonder whether it had been a sense of truth and justice alone which had prompted him to become a follower of Veraguth's or whether the latter's eloquence and platform skill, charm and aptitude for public speaking, the sonorous ring of his voice, his masculine winning smile and the intelligence and beauty of his daughter had not partly influenced him. The question as to whether his father, with his conservative loyalty and his severity towards the peasants, had really possessed the less noble standpoint became more and more debatable in his mind, no less than the question as to whether there really existed such things as good and evil, right or wrong, and whether in the last analysis the voice of one's own conscience was not the only valid judge: if all this were true then he, Plinio, was in the wrong for he now lived neither in happiness, peace and harmony, nor in confidence and security, but on the contrary in insecurity, doubt and with a bad conscience. His marriage, in the coarsest sense, had not been unhappy or a failure, but was full of tensions, complications and contradictions; it was perhaps the best thing that he had achieved so far, although it did not bring him that peace, happiness, innocence and clear conscience that he so lacked but demanded great circumspection and cost a great deal of effort. His attractive and gifted little son, Tito, had at an early age become a source of conflict and diplomacy, courtship and jealousy, and the spoiled boy, upon whom too much love had been lavished, began to side more and more with his mother and finally became her supporter against him. This was the latest and apparently the bitterest blow that Designori had had to suffer during his life. It had not broken him, however: he had overcome it and had been able to maintain a dignified mode of conduct in face of the world, but it left him nevertheless serious, grave and melancholy.

While all this slowly came to light during the course of many meetings and visits, Knecht told his friend in exchange about his own experiences and problems. He did not by any means leave Plinio in the invidious position of one who comes and confesses and then, with the change of hour and mood, regrets what he has said and would withdraw it, but strengthened and retained the latter's confidence through his own frankness and devotion. His life was gradually revealed to his friend as an apparently simple, direct, exemplary and well-ordained existence within a clearly constructed hier-archical system, a career of success and recognition, and yet in actuality a hard and lonely one full of sacrifices. Yet, if much of it was hardly comprehensible to this man from the outside world, he was able to grasp the main streams and basic trends, and nothing was easier for him to understand and sympathize with than Knecht's longing for youth, for young and unspoiled pupils, for a modest task devoid of glamour, as for example the post of grammar or music teacher in one of the lower schools. It was quite in the style of Knecht's curative and instructive methods that he not only succeeded in winning over this patient by his great frankness but also managed to put the suggestion into his head that he could be of service to him, and at the same time imbued him with the desire to put it into effect. In actual fact, it was possible for Designori to be of great assistance to the Magister, not of course upon the major issues of his office but to the extent of satisfying his curiosity upon the hundred and one details of life in the outside world.

Why Knecht took it upon himself to teach this melancholy friend of his youth to smile and laugh again, which was not an easy task by any manner of means, and whether the con-sideration of Plinio's usefulness was partly the solution, we

cannot tell. Designori, the one who was in the best position
to be a judge of this, did not seem to think so.

"When I try to clarify my mind on this point," he declared
later, "how it was that friend Knecht began to influence so
resigned and reticent a man as myself—I see ever more
clearly that it was due to a great extent to magic and, I must
also add, roguery on his part. He was a far greater rogue than
his people realized, full of fun, wit and impulses, love of
magic, dissimulation and the surprise of sudden disappear-
ances and re-appearances. I believe that at the very moment of
my arrival before the Castalian authorities he had made up
his mind to capture me and to influence me after his own
fashion, *i.e.*, to awaken and improve me. I think that men of
his type do it to a great extent unconsciously, as a sort of
reflex action: hearing themselves summoned by a call of
despair, they feel that a task has been placed before them and
obey the call without more ado. He found me, his friend who
had formerly been so open and communicative, disillusioned
and reticent, distrustful and shy and not in the least ready to
fall into his arms or to ask him for help, and this barrier, this
considerable difficulty, seemed to be exactly what intrigued
him most. He did not abandon his efforts however refractory
I proved to be, and in the end he achieved what he wanted.
To accomplish this he made use among other things of the
device of allowing our relationship to appear a mutual one, as
though my strength and worth corresponded with his, and as
though his need for help was but a reflection of my own. In
our very first long discussion he hinted to me that he had in
some way expected my arrival and had even longed for it.

"Gradually he involved me in his plan for laying down his
office and abandoning the Province, continually insisting upon
how much he needed my advice, my support, and also my
silence, for apart from myself he had no friends in the outside
world nor any experience of it. I must confess that I listened
to all this with pleasure, and knew that it would require very
little more for me to give him my full confidence and to
surrender myself to him completely. I believed in him
implicitly, but later, as time passed, it seemed to me once
more questionable and even improbable that he could really
have expected anything substantial of me, and I could not
have said whether his manner of captivating me was innocent

or diplomatic, ingenuous or with some ulterior motive, upright or merely artificial and frivolous. In any case he was far too much my superior in every way, and had displayed far too much goodness towards me, for me to have dared entertain any such considerations. To-day I consider the fiction that his predicament resembled my own, that he was just as dependent upon my sympathy and devotion as I upon his, to be a winning and pleasant fantasy which he wove around me; but I should not care to hazard how far his game was consciously thought out and intentional, and to what extent, everything considered, it was ingenuous and natural, for Magister Joseph was a great artist. On the one hand he could so little resist the urge to educate, influence, save, help and develop that the means was almost a matter of indifference to him, and on the other hand it was virtually impossible for him not to lavish his complete devotion upon even the most insignificant task. The way in which he handled me, for instance, as a friend, a great doctor and leader, and the fact that he did not slacken and ultimately succeeded in awakening and healing me as far as it was humanly possible, was certainly a mark of great devotion. It was an apt and truly remarkable characteristic of his for, while he behaved as though he were accepting my help in his claim to secede from office, while he listened to and even applauded my often coarse and naïve criticisms, doubts and insults against Castalia, all the while struggling to free himself from its toils, he had really and truly lured me and led me back, reaccustomed me to meditation, taught and changed me through Castalian music and contemplation, and made me one of you again, transforming my unhappy love for you into a fortunate one once more—I who, despite my yearning for you, was so un- and anti-Castalian."

Thus Designori expressed himself. He had indeed good grounds for his admiring gratitude, for although it may not be a difficult matter, with the aid of our old and trusted methods, to educate boys and youths to the style of life prevailing in the Order, it must inevitably have been a difficult task in the case of a man nearly fifty years old, even though he brought great goodwill to bear in the task himself. Not that Designori ever became a perfect or exemplary Castalian, but it is quite clear that Knecht achieved what he had set out to do—to dissipate the sorrow and bitter weight of sadness, to restore harmony and serenity in a distressed and over-sensitive soul which had become reticent, and to exchange a number of his bad habits for good ones.

Naturally the Magister Ludi could not have carried out the whole mass of insignificant details which this work entailed in person: he made use of the apparatus and might of Waldzell and the Order in attending to the welfare of his guest of honour, and for a certain length of time sent a master of meditation from Hirsland, the seat of the Order, to Designori's home so as to ensure that the latter's exercises were under constant surveillance. Their general plan, however, remained in his own hands.

During the eighth year of his office as Magister, he at last accepted his friend's invitation to visit him at his home in the capital. Having gained the permission of the Pedagogy, whose leader, Alexander, stood very close to his heart, he made use of a holiday in order to pay this visit, which he had postponed year after year partly because he wanted first to be quite sure of his friend and partly because of a very natural fear, for this was his first step over into that world from which his comrade Plinio had returned a prey to such a mute sadness and which yet contained so many important secrets for him.

He found the modern house, which Plinio had exchanged for the old town residence, presided over by a stately, extremely intelligent and reserved lady, who in turn was ruled by her pretty, rather naughty and precocious son, around whose small person everything seemed to revolve and who seemed to have inherited from his mother a certain dogmatic behaviour and a somewhat humiliating attitude towards his father. In addition he encountered an atmosphere of coolness and distrust for everything Castalian, but neither mother nor son were able to resist for very long the personality of the Magister, whose office to them seemed shrouded in mystery, sanctity and legend. On this first visit, however, everything remained extremely formal and constrained. Knecht was on his guard, expectant and silent. The lady of the house received him with an aloof, formal politeness and an inward rejection, and behaved towards him as she might have done towards some high officer who had been billetted on her. Tito, the son, was the least impressed of all; he must have been the

spectator and perhaps amused witness of many similar situations. His father seemed to be no longer the true master of the
house. Between himself and his wife there existed a gentle,
solicitous and somewhat anxious note, a sort of tip-toe politeness, practised in a far easier and more natural manner by the
woman than by the man. Plinio made every effort to display a
comradeship towards his son, of which the boy at times took
advantage and at others rebuffed with impudence. In short, it
was a painstaking, guilty and rather sultry association, full of
tension and the fear of an interruption or perhaps an outburst.
The style of speech and behaviour was, like the style of the
whole house, a little too mannered and acquired, as though the
protective wall against onslaught and attack could not be
built thickly and securely enough. Knecht also observed that a
greater part of Plinio's recaptured serenity had disappeared
from his features. In Waldzell and in Hirsland, the residence
of the Order, he had appeared almost to have lost his melancholy and sadness, and now in his own home he seemed once
more to stand completely under its shadow, and to warrant
both criticism and compassion.

The house was beautiful and savoured of wealth and luxury.
Each room was of seemly dimensions and was decorated in a
harmonious scheme of two or three colours. Knecht allowed
his eyes to wander here and there over the valuable art
treasures and yet all these perspectives seemed to lead
ultimately to an exaggerated degree of beauty, too perfect
and well thought out and too much in the nature of a stage
setting. He felt that this beauty had the sense of an attempted
conjuration, a protective gesture, and that these rooms,
pictures, vases and flowers accompanied and circumscribed a
life which yearned after harmony and beauty but was unable
to achieve anything beyond a preoccupation with harmonious
surroundings.

It was shortly after this visit, which had in part proved so
unproductive, that Knecht sent an instructor of meditation to
the Designori home. Having spent a day in this house, in
which the atmosphere was so heavily loaded, Joseph had
learned much that he had not desired to know but at the same
time much about which he was ignorant and was most eager
to learn, and on account of which he had accepted his friend's
invitation. Nor was this his only visit. He received many more

invitations, which inevitably led to discussions on the subject
of the young Tito's education, in which his mother took a
prominent part. The Magister gradually won the confidence
and sympathy of this shrewd and suspicious woman. On one
occasion, when he put forward the suggestion that it was a
pity that her little son should not be sent at an early date to be
educated in Castalia, she took his observation as a personal
reproach and defended herself. It was highly doubtful, she
said, as to whether Tito would be acceptable. Admittedly he
was talented enough, but very difficult to handle, and she
would never allow of any interference in his life, even though
a similar attempt had been made by his father without
success. Moreover, neither her husband nor herself had
realised that they still held a right to claim the old privilege
of the Designori family for their son, inasmuch as they had
completely broken with the tradition of the old house, and
finally, she added with a wry smile, she would under no
circumstances be parted from her child, as apart from him she
had nothing in life worth living for. This involuntary and
unconsidered remark gave Knecht much food for thought. So
her beautiful house, in which everything was outwardly so
decorous, magnificent and harmonious, her husband, her
politics and the inheritance of her once adored father were
insufficient to give meaning and value to her life: this only her
child could do, and she would prefer to allow this child to
grow up under the same unfavourable and harmful conditions
that ruled here in her house and in her marriage than be
separated from him for his own salvation! This he felt was an
astonishing outlook on the part of so shrewd and intellectual
a woman. Knecht could not of course help her in as direct a
manner as he could her husband, and never dreamed of
trying to do so, but thanks to his rare visits and to the fact
that Plinio was now more under his influence, a certain sense
of measure and caution came into the distorted and perverse
family circumstances.

The Magister, however, while gaining influence and
authority each time he visited the Designori house, saw the
life of these world folks grow richer in problems the better he
began to know them; and yet we know very little, and must
content ourselves with the suggestions that we have already
given as to what he saw and experienced in the capital.

The Head of the Order in Hirsland had not previously approached Knecht more closely than official duties demanded. He saw him at every full session of the Pedagogy which took place in Hirsland, and on such occasions confined himself for the most part to the more formal and ornamental offices, such as the reception and leave-taking of his colleagues, while the main work of the session fell upon the speaker. The former Head had already been an old man at the time when Knecht had assumed office, a man whom he had very much revered but who had never invited him to lessen the distance between them, and who already appeared to him less as an individual than a figure who hovered like some high priest—a symbol of dignity and poise, the silent peak and crown—over the edifice of the Pedagogy and the whole hierarchy. This worthy man was now dead and his place had been taken by Alexander, who was in actual fact the Meditation Master whom the Order had given to Joseph Knecht to assist him at the beginning of his official leadership. He was an exemplary Order brother, to whom the Magister Ludi had been grateful and whom he had admired, for he had been in daily contact with the trials of the new Magister and had to a certain extent become his confessor; he had been near enough to him to have gained an insight into his private character and behaviour and to have grown to love him. This friendship which had hitherto remained latent and which now both were conscious of had taken shape from the moment when Alexander had become his colleague as President of the Pedagogy. They now saw more of each other and had more work to do in common. Admittedly this friendship lacked daily intimacy, as also a common background of youthful experiences, but there existed a certain professional sympathy between them; their exchanges were confined to a little extra warmth at meeting and departure, an unbroken and quicker mutual understanding and a few minutes gossip in the recesses between sessions.

Although constitutionally the Head of the Order, or Master of the Order as he was called, did not rank higher than his colleagues the Magisters, his authority had grown proportionately within the Province and the hierarchy—though of course not outside it—as a result of the tradition according to which the Master of the Order presided over the sessions of the Pedagogy, and to the extent to which the Order had during the last decades become more contemplative and more monastic. In the Pedagogy, the Master of the Order and the Ludi Magister had both become the virtual exponents and representatives of the Castalian spirit: as opposed to the secular faculties such as grammar, astronomy, mathematics or music, which had derived from pre-Castalian eras, meditative spiritual discipline and the Bead Game were characteristic Castalian properties.

It was therefore not without significance that the two representative leaders should stand in a friendly relationship towards each other: it was a ratification and an exaltation of their dignity, and added a warmth and contentment to life and a spur to the fulfilment of their tasks, which were to portray and live out in their innermost persons the sacral assets and powers of the Castalian world.

But for Knecht it also meant an additional bond, one more counterweight to offset his growing tendency to total renunciation and to his break-through into another and new sphere of life. And yet this tendency developed unceasingly. Since he had grown aware of it, which may have been in the sixth or seventh year of his magistracy, it had become stronger and had been freely accepted into his conscious beliefs and thoughts, accustomed as he was to his "awakenings." Since approximately that time, we believe we are right in saying, the thought of his approaching departure from office and from the Province was familiar to him—in much the same way as a prisoner believes in his eventual release or as a grievously sick man realizes his approaching death.

In that first conversation with the friend of his youth, Plinio, he had put it into words for the first time, possibly only in order to encourage his friend who had become so silent and reserved, but also perhaps in order to impart his new "awakening" to another, to communicate his new orientation to an audience, a preliminary turning to the outside and to give it a first thrust towards realization. In the ensuing conversation with Designori, Knecht's wish in some way to lay aside his present form of life and to dare a leap into the unknown had already assumed the aspect of a decision. In the meanwhile, he carefully consolidated his friendship with Plinio, who was now not only bound to him in admiration but as much through the gratitude of a convalescing and partially cured invalid, and possessed in him a bridge to the outside world and its problem-laden existence.

The fact that the Magister only granted a glimpse into his secret and plans to his friend Tegularius does not surprise us. The more well-disposed and challenging he had made each of his friendships, the more independently and diplomatically he was able to keep them under observation and to direct them. With the advent of Plinio into his life once more, a competitor had appeared upon the scene for Tegularius, a regained friend with claims upon Knecht's heart and interest, and the latter could hardly have been surprised if Tegularius had immediately reacted with profound jealousy. For a while he may have found Tegularius' smouldering retirement rather welcome, until he had completely won over and set Designori upon his feet once more, but taking a longer view there was another far more important consideration; how could his desire to withdraw gently from Waldzell and from his magistracy be explained and made palatable to Fritz? Once Knecht really left Waldzell, his friend was lost to him for ever: to take Fritz with him on the narrow and dangerous path which lay before him was unthinkable, even if—contrary to all expectations—the latter should pluck up the courage and wish to do so.

Knecht waited, ruminated and hesitated a long time before making Fritz a party to his intentions. However, when his determination to break away had become irrevocable he finally did so, for it would have been altogether against his nature to have left his friend in ignorance right up to the last moment and to have made his plans and prepared his dispositions behind the back of one who would certainly have to bear some of the consequences. He wanted, as far as possible, not only to make him as much privy to his plans as Plinio, but to procure him as a true or imagined helper and participator because activity always eases tension.

Tegularius had naturally known Knecht's thoughts upon the subject of the threatened decline of the Castalian existence for a long time—as far, that is, as the latter was willing to impart them and the former to receive them. The Magister seized upon this as an opening once he had decided to disclose his intentions to his friend. Contrary to his expectations, and

to his great relief, Fritz did not take the information too
tragically; in fact, the idea that a Magister should fling his
high dignity back in the teeth of the authorities and shake the
dust of Castalia from his feet to lead a life more in accordance
with his own tastes seemed to please and even to amuse him.
As an individualist and enemy of all conformity, Tegularius
had always been on the side of the individual against the
Pedagogy, and he could always be relied upon whenever it
was a case of fighting, riling or outwitting the official powers
in some subtle manner. This gave Knecht an idea. Breathing
more freely and with a hidden smile, he went on to try out his
friend's reactions. He stated his case as though the whole
thing were merely a form of a practical joke upon the
Pedagogy and its red tape, and allotted him the rôle of
colleague and fellow conspirator. A "petition," he told him,
or a statement had to be compiled and sent to the Pedagogy
containing an elucidation of all the grounds which warranted
Knecht's retirement from office. The preparation and compilation of this was to be mainly Tegularius' task. He would
have to acquaint himself above all with the Magister's
historical conceptions of the birth, rise to greatness and
present position of Castalia, and collect historical data to
strengthen his wishes and proposals. The fact that he would
be obliged to delve into a subject which he had hitherto
despised and neglected, namely History, did not seem to
deter him, and Knecht proceeded to give him the necessary
documentation. Without any further ado, Tegularius engrossed himself in his task with all the zeal and tenacity that
he was capable of bringing to abstruse and solitary under-
takings.

This recalcitrant individualist derived a remarkably grim
pleasure from these studies which enabled him to point out to
the bonzes and the hierarchy their shortcomings and weaknesses, and frankly to irritate them.

Knecht took as little part in this pleasure as he had belief in
the success of his friend's efforts. He was resolved to shake
off the fetters of his present position and of the tasks which
he felt awaited him, but he saw quite clearly that he would
neither be able to defeat the Pedagogy on the grounds of
reason nor achieve even a part of what had to be done
through Tegularius. That the latter was occupied and

sidetracked for the time being while he was still living in his proximity, was a welcome realization. He disclosed this to Plinio Designori at their next meeting, and added: "Friend Tegularius is kept busy and is being recompensed for what he imagined he had lost by reason of your return. His jealousy is nearly cured; the work which he is doing for me on the affidavit against the Pedagogy suits him admirably, and he is almost happy. But don't imagine, Plinio, that I expect very much from this affidavit apart from the good that it will do him personally. That our highest authorities will grant any success to the petition which we have planned is very, very improbable—I might say impossible—and the most they will do is to reply with a gently reproachful rebuke. The thing that stands between my intentions and their fulfilment is the fundamental law of the hierarchy itself, and I must say a Pedagogy that released its Magister so easily and gave him leave to take up a profession outside Castalia would not please *me* very much! Furthermore, the Master of the Order, Alexander, is a completely intransigent character. No! I must fight out this struggle alone. But we will allow Tegularius to sharpen his wits: we are only losing a little time and I need just that to put everything in such impeccable order that my departure can cause no damage whatsoever to Waldzell. In the meantime you must obtain a lodging for me out there and a possibility of work, however modest it may be; at the worst I shall be content with a post as a music teacher, which need only be a beginning and a jumping off place."

Designori maintained that they would easily find something and assured him that when the moment arrived his house remained open to his friend for as long as he wished. But Knecht would not agree to this.

"No," he said, "I will not simply be a guest: I must have work. Furthermore, a stay in your house, however charming it might be, should it last for more than a few days, would only increase the tension and difficulties. I have great confidence in you, and your wife has grown more friendly and accustomed to my visits, but it would immediately take on a different aspect if I were no longer a visitor and a Magister Ludi but a fugitive and permanent guest."

"You are seeing everything in too much detail," Plinio

replied. "You can be certain that, once you are free and have
your residence in the capital, you will be offered a post in
keeping with your dignity, at the least a professorship in a
university. But these things take time, as you know, and I can
naturally only begin making provisions for you once your
release has been completed."

"Quite so," replied Knecht: "until then my resolution must
remain a secret. I cannot place myself at the service of your
authorities until my own have been notified and have come to
a decision, that is obvious. But I do not wish for a public post
right away. My needs are very modest—more modest
perhaps than you can understand—for I need only a tiny room
and my daily bread, but above all work, a task as a teacher
and educator. I shall need one or more pupils and apprentices,
with whom I can live and whom I can influence. I am not
greatly impressed by the idea of a university, and would just
as soon be a private tutor to a boy, or something in that
nature. What I am looking for now is a simple natural task—
a human being who has need of me. . . . The post in a college
would from the outset bring me once more into a traditional,
hallowed and mechanised official organisation, and what I
covet is the absolute antithesis of this."

Designori now hesitatingly made a request which had lain
near his heart for a very long time.

"I should like to make you a proposal," he said, "and I
earnestly hope that you will give it your serious consideration. Perhaps you will find it acceptable, in which case you
will also be rendering me a great service. You have done a
great deal to help me since that first day when I was your
guest, and you have also come to know my life and my family
and how things stand there. They are far from satisfactory,
but certainly better than they have been for many years. The
greatest difficulty lies in the relationship between myself and
my son: he is impertinent to me, and I am afraid he has been
very much spoiled. He has created for himself a privileged
position in our home, which was made possible during those
early years when his mother and I both vied for his affections.
He eventually sided with his mother, and gradually all the
means of education were taken out of my hands. I adapted
myself to this in the same way that I have adapted myself to
my unsuccessful life. I became resigned to it. But now, since

I am more or less cured thanks to your aid, I have regained hope. Perhaps you see what I am driving at? In a word, I should be more than content if Tito, who has great difficulties with his schooling in any case, could have an expert private tutor to take him in hand. It is a selfish request, I know, and I cannot presume that the task would appeal to you, but you have at least given me the courage to come into the open with my proposal."

Knecht smiled at his friend and stretched out his hand.

"I thank you, Plinio. No proposal could possibly have been more welcome. The only thing we lack now is your wife's consent. There is one condition that I make, however: you must both resolve to entrust your son completely to me; in order that I may control him, the daily influence of his home must be removed. You must discuss this matter with your wife and make her agree to this condition, but set about it cautiously, Plinio, and take your time."

"And do you think that you can really achieve anything with Tito?"

"Indeed I do, and why not? He comes of good stock and has inherited good qualities from both his parents, only the harmony between these qualities is missing. My task will be to awaken in him a desire for this harmony, and finally to strengthen and make it a permanent part of his character. I shall undertake the task with pleasure."

In this manner Joseph Knecht was able to busy both his friends in quite different ways with his own affairs. While Designori at home in the capital was putting the new plans before his wife and trying to make them acceptable to her, Tegularius sat in his working cell in Waldzell collecting material for the proposed circular letter from Knecht's documentation. The Magister had baited him well with the reading matter he had chosen. Fritz Tegularius, the great detractor of history, now succumbed to the charm and became enamoured of the history of the "warring centuries." Always a prodigious worker at his hobbies, he amassed with insatiable appetite so much anecdotal material symptomatic of that gloomy pre-Order period that Knecht, on receiving the work some months later, could hardly utilise a tenth part of it.

During these months Knecht paid several visits to the capital, and because a sane and harmonious man can so often find easy access to heavily burdened people Madame Designori began to gain more and more confidence in him and was soon won over to her husband's plans. We know that Tito during one of the Magister's visits behaved somewhat saucily, demanding to be addressed in the polite form, which everyone in his school including the teachers were wont to use. Knecht thanked him for the information with the greatest courtesy, apologised and told him that in his Province the teachers used the familiar form to all pupils and students, and also to people who had long since grown up. After a meal he asked the boy to go for a walk with him and show him something of the city, and Tito led him along a stately street in the old part of the town where stood an unbroken row of secular houses belonging to the leading landed and patrician families. The boy came to a halt before one of these trim houses and pointed to a shield over the doorway.

"Do you know what that is?" he asked, and as Knecht admitted his ignorance, went on: "Those are the arms of the Designori family, and this was our old residence. It was in the family for three hundred years, but now we live in an indifferent everyday modern dwelling just because father had the caprice after grandfather's death to sell this noble mansion and build himself a fashionable barrack which, incidentally, is no longer particularly modern. Can you credit such a thing?"

"Do you regret losing the old house very much?" Knecht asked in a friendly tone.

Tito admitted to this with passion and repeated his question: "Can you credit it?"

"One can understand anything when one throws a little light upon it," replied Knecht. "An old house is a beautiful thing, and if the new one had stood next to it and one had had the choice, one might well have retained the old one. Yes, old houses are beautiful and dignified, and this one is no exception. But to build a house oneself is also something fine, and if an energetic and ambitious young man had the choice as to whether he would remain comfortable and devoted in a ready-made nest or wish to build a new one, one can well understand that the latter may be his choice. Now as regards your father, whom I new as a passionate go-getter when he was your age, the sale and loss of the house hurt no one so much as himself. He had a hard conflict with his father and family, and it seems

that his upbringing with us in Castalia was not the right one
for him— or at least it could not protect him from certain rash
and hot-headed acts. One of these was undoubtedly the sale of
this house. By selling it he wished to declare war on and to
administer a slap in the face to the family traditions, his
father and his whole past dependence. At least, that seems
quite a conceivable explanation to me. But man is a strange
animal, and therefore another explanation arises which does
not appear so very improbable: that the vendor of this old
house did not wish to hurt the family alone but also himself.
They had disappointed him. They had sent him to an élite
school and allowed him to be educated there after a fashion,
and then on his return had received him with tasks, demands
and claims of which he was incapable. I do not wish to enlarge
upon the psychological aspect, but the story of this sale shows
how powerful the conflict between father and son—this hatred
which is so intimately bound up with love—can be. This conflict seldom spares lively and talented natures, and world
history is filled with examples of it. One can, however, easily
imagine a later young Designori making it his life task to
retrieve the house at any cost and to bring it into the
possession of the family once more."

"Well!" exclaimed Tito, "and would you not approve if
he were to do that?"

"I would not like to be a judge of that, my young sir. If a
later Designori were to consider the greatness of his race as
synonymous with his life duty, and if, by serving the state,
city, people, laws and charity with all his strength he incidentally accomplished the repurchase of this house, then he
would be a worthy man and one to whom we should be proud
to raise our hat: but, should he have no other goal in life save
the acquisition of the house, then he would be no more than
one obsessed, a fanatic, a man of passion and very probably
one who had never recognised any such youthful conflict with
his father and had carried it around with him all his life, even
when he had become a man. We should even pity him, for he
would certainly not increase the renown of his house. It is a
wonderful thing when an old family is attached to its house,
but rejuvenation and new greatness come to it only when its
sons serve higher goals than that which the family serve."

Although on these walks Tito listened with attention and

apparent willingness to his father's guest, on other occasions he displayed renewed outbursts of rejection and defiance. He sensed in this man, whom both his parents—who were usually so much in disagreement—seemed to esteem, a power that could be dangerous to his spoiled independence, and as a result showed himself on occasions to be frankly unbearable: each time of course there followed regrets and a desire to atone, for it hurt his pride to feel so exposed before the serene courtesy with which the Magister surrounded himself like a coat of mail. Secretly, he also felt in his inexperienced and somewhat unruly heart that here was a man whom perhaps one could revere and love very much.

He had felt this particularly during a certain half-hour when he had found Knecht waiting alone for his father, who had been detained by pressing affairs.

As Tito entered the room he saw the guest sitting motionless, in a statuesque pose, with half-closed eyes radiating peace and calm in his contemplation. He involuntarily slowed down his steps, and was about to retire on tiptoe when the seated figure opened its eyes, greeted him in a friendly manner, stood up and pointing to the piano in the room asked him if he enjoyed music.

Tito admitted that he had not taken any music lessons for a long time and had not practised either, for he did not stand well in school and was plagued enough by the "crammers" but told him that he always found pleasure in listening to music.

Knecht opened the piano, sat down, tried it carefully to see whether it were in tune and played an andante theme from Scarlatti which he had recently used as a basic example for a Bead Game exercise. When he stopped playing, and finding the boy appreciative and attentive, he began in a few words to explain how such a Bead Game exercise transpired. He split the music into its component parts, showed him several ways of analysing it, pointing out how these parts or voices could be used, and also demonstrated how the music could be translated into the Game hieroglyphics.

For the first time Tito saw the Magister not as a guest, not as a famous scholar whom he repulsed because he felt a loss of self-esteem, but as a man at his work, a man who had mastered a very subtle art and practised it as an adept—an art the meaning of which he could only guess at but which seemed to dominate the entire artist and his devotion. Furthermore, the fact that he had been taken for a grown person and intelligent enough to take an interest in such complicated things was flattering to his sense of dignity. He grew thoughtful and began, during that half-hour, to suspect the source of this remarkable man's serenity and unruffled calm.

Knecht's official activities during the last days of his magistracy were nearly as intensive as they had once been in the difficult period of assuming office, for he laid great store by leaving every thread of his duties in an exemplary condition. He achieved this goal even if he had failed in his intended object—to appear dispensable or easily replaceable. As is nearly always the case in the highest offices, the Magister Ludi glides over everything like an ornament, like a glittering ensign over the complicated maze of his official kingdom. He comes and goes quickly, amiable as a friendly guest, says a word or two, nods in acquiescence, suggests a task by means of a gesture and has gone—he is already talking to the next man. He plays on his official apparatus as a musician upon his instrument, seems to use no strength and to need no reflection, and everything runs as it should; but every official in this apparatus knows what it means when the Magister is absent or falls ill, when they are obliged to replace him, if only for a day or for an hour or two.

While Knecht was carefully reviewing the whole little settlement of the Vicus Lusorum, and in particular giving all his attention to handing over his duties unobtrusively to his "shadow" so that the latter could represent him shortly in all earnestness, he was at last able to maintain how inwardly free and aloof he had become from it all, how the costliness of this well-devised little world no longer captivated or held any joys for him. He already saw Waldzell and his magistracy as something that lay behind him, something which had both given and taught him a great deal but which could no longer entice him to new strengths and deeds. It became more and more clear to him during this time of gradual secession and leavetaking that the actual cause of his alienation and desire to depart had not arisen from his knowledge of the dangers which lay in store for Castalia and his care for its future, but lay simply in the fact that an empty and idle residue of himself, of his heart and his soul, now desired its rights and wished to fulfil them.

He made a thorough study of the Statutes of the Order once more, and saw that his departure from the Province would not, theoretically, be so difficult as he had once imagined it. He was free to lay down his office and even to leave the Order on grounds of conscience, for the oath was not a lifelong one, even though in practice members had very seldom—and never before a member of the Pedagogy— availed themselves of this privilege. No, what had made this step appear so difficult was not the harshness of the laws but the hierarchic spirit itself and the loyalty and allegiance in his own heart. Certainly he did not wish to depart furtively, for he was preparing a circumstantial petition demanding his freedom, and the egregious Fritz was working with ink-stained fingers to accomplish this. However, he personally did not believe in the success of this petition: he would be pacified, warned, perhaps offered a vacation in Mariafels where shortly before Father Jacobus had died, or even be sent to Rome, but released—never. This, he thought he knew for certain. To release him would be in contradiction to all the traditions of the Order. Moreover were the Pedagogy to acquiesce they would be acknowledging the justification of his request, and this would be tantamount to admitting that life in Castalia, and even in the highest posts, could under certain circumstances be gravely inadequate and signify only renunciation and imprisonment.

Chapter Eleven

THE CIRCULAR LETTER

WE ARE NEARING THE end of our story. As we have already stated, our knowledge of Knecht's end is fragmentary and more in the nature of a legend than an historical record. We must be content with this. It is, therefore, all the more pleasurable for us to amplify this penultimate chapter of Knecht's career with an authentic document, namely, with that extensive letter in which the Magister Ludi gave his own reasons for the decisions which he had taken and wherein he requested to be released from his office.

We must admit quite honestly that Joseph Knecht, as we have seen for a long time, not only had little faith in the success of this "petition" which he had prepared in such detail but, now that it had gone so far, would actually have preferred not to have written or dispatched it.

The same law applied to him as to all those who practise a natural and primarily unconscious power over other men: this power cannot be used by the wielder without consequence. Although the Magister had been glad enough to win over Tegularius to his point of view, once having allowed him to become his agent and confederate, events proved stronger than his own thoughts and desires. He had inspired Fritz or rather seduced him into undertaking a work, in the value of which he, the author, no longer believed, but he could not cancel this work, which was at last presented to him, nor could he dismiss it or leave it unused without wounding and disappointing his collaborator, for whom he had merely wished to make the inevitable separation bearable.

We ourselves think that Knecht's intentions would have been better represented had he simply announced his secession from the Order and retired from office without more ado, instead of choosing this devious route entailing a laborious "petition," which had almost assumed the proportions of a comedy in his own eyes. Consideration for Tegularius, however, induced him to control his impatience for a while.

It would be extremely interesting to peruse the manuscript of the industrious Tegularius. It was mainly composed of historical data which he had collected as a testimony and for purposes of illustration, and we should be making a great mistake if we thought that it contained a plethora of apposite and witty criticisms of the hierarchy, of the world or of world history. Even if this manuscript, which had been compiled after months of unusually hard toil, were still in existence and still at our disposal, we should have to renounce the use of its contents inasmuch as this study would not be the correct place for its publication.

The only thing that is of interest to us is the use to which the Magister Ludi put his friend's work. When Tegularius ceremoniously handed it to him he accepted it with hearty words of thanks and gratitude and, knowing that it would give his friend pleasure, bade him read it out to him. For several days Tegularius sat with the Magister for half an hour or so in his garden—for it was summer—reading the many pages of his manuscript to him with relish, and the reading would often be interrupted by loud bursts of laughter from both of them.

These were happy days for Tegularius. After this Joseph withdrew and, making use of a great part of his friend's manuscript, composed his letter to the authorities, which we reproduce here *verbatim* and upon which no comment is necessary.

THE LETTER OF THE MAGISTER LUDI TO THE PEDAGOGY

Various considerations have led me, your Magister Ludi, to lay this especial petition before the authorities in the form of a separate and more or less private letter rather than incorporate it in my solemn account of stewardship. Although I am appending it to the proper official reports and await an official reply, I consider it to be more in the nature of a circular letter from a colleague to my fellow Magisters.

It is the duty of a Magister to inform the authorities when obstacles or dangers arise which threaten the stability of his rigidly prescribed office. The administration of my office, although I am determined to serve it assiduously to the best of my powers, is in my opinion threatened by a danger which resides in my own person, but which has not its origin there; for I consider the moral danger of a weakening of personal ability as Magister Ludi to be both objective and outside my own control. To express it briefly: I have begun to doubt my own capacity to carry out my duties to the full because I am forced to consider the object of my office—the Bead Game itself—to be in danger. The intention of this letter is to inform the Pedagogy that this suggested danger exists, and by very reason of this discovery that I now feel called imperatively to other spheres than those which I now occupy.

Perhaps I may explain the situation better by means of an analogy. A man is sitting in an attic room intent upon a subtle work of scholarship, and suddenly realizes that a fire has broken out somewhere in the house below. He will not even bother to reflect whether it were his duty or not to rescue his calculations and take them to a place of safety, but will hurry downstairs and endeavour to save the house. In much the same way I find myself sitting here in the top storey of our Castalian edifice, engrossed in the Bead Game and handling many delicate instruments. I realise instinctively and can smell that somewhere below me there is a fire, that our entire building is threatened and endangered and that it is now my duty to refrain from analysing the anatomy of music or differentiating between the many Game rules and hasten to where it is smouldering.

The greater part of us Order brothers take our Castalian institution, our Order, our scientific and academic activities, not to forget the Bead Game, as a matter of course just as the ordinary man takes the air he breathes and the soil upon which he treads. Hardly one of us gives a thought to the possibility that this air and soil might not perhaps be so secure and that one day the atmosphere might fail and the soil disappear from beneath our feet. We have the good fortune to live a well-protected life in a small, compact and serene world and, strange though it may seem, the majority of us live under the illusion that this world has always existed and that we have been born into it. In my earlier years I myself lived under this highly agreeable illusion, although the facts were well known to me that I was not born a Castalian but was summoned through the official channels and simply educated here, and that Castalia, the Order, the Pedagogy, the schools, archives, and Bead Game had by no means always existed and been a work of nature but a late, noble and transitory creation, like all constitutions founded by human endeavour. I knew all this but it had no reality for me: I merely overlooked it and am quite certain that more than three-quarters of us live and will presumably die in this most curious and delectable error.

However, just as in the past there have been centuries and aeons in which no Orders and no Castalias have existed, so these times will recur again in the future. When to-day I remind my colleagues and the worthy authorities of this fact, of this truism, and challenge them to cast their eyes for a moment upon the danger which threatens us; when I take it upon myself for an instant to assume the rather distasteful rôle of prophet, warner and preacher of penitence, which almost invariably arouses scorn, I am none the less ready to accept this scorn, but always in the hope that the majority of you will read my letter to the end and that some of you will even agree with me on a few points. This, I realise only too well, is a great deal to expect.

An edifice like our Castalia—a little spiritual colony—is exposed to both internal and external dangers. We are fully aware of the inner dangers, or at least many of them, and we watch for and combat them. We frequently send individual pupils back home from the élite schools because we have discovered in them ineradicable traits and impulses which would make them dangerous or unsuited to our community. Most of them are men of no less merit on account of these un-Castalian traits and will—we hope—be able to find conditions more favourable to them on their return to the outside world where they will become strong and qualified men. This practice has proved effective, and we can say of our Community, by and large, that it has retained its dignity and self-discipline, and that its aims have sufficed to maintain an ever renewed upper crust, an aristocracy of the intellect. We have presumably allowed no more of the unworthy and indolent to dwell among us than was normal and tolerable.

Much less incontestable among us, however, is that conceit of the Order, that arrogance of rank to which every nobility and every privileged class is tempted, and of which they are invariably accused either with or without foundation.

In social history there have always been attempts to form a nobility representing the peak and crown of society, and some type of aristocracy or rule of the best seems to be the actual if not always the admitted goal and ideal of any attempt at building a society. The ruling powers have always, whether they have been monarchic or anonymous, been ready to encourage a rising nobility by giving it protection and privilege —whether a political or any other form of nobility, either of birth, selection or education. This favoured clique has always been strengthened by this protection, and from a certain stage of development onwards its privileged place in the sun has always been a temptation which has finally led to its corruption.

If for a moment we regard our Order as a nobility and try

to examine ourselves in this light—as to how far our behaviour towards the people in the world as a whole justifies
our special position and as to how far the characteristic
maladies of nobility (*hubris*, conceit, arrogance, priggishness
and ungrateful usufruct) have already attacked and dominated
us—we may well find great cause for reflection. The present-
day Castalian may not be lacking in obedience to the rules of
the Order, in application and in cultivated intellectuality, but
does he not often fall short in his attitude towards his place in
the structure of humanity, the world and world history? Is he
conscious of the fundamentals of his existence? Does he see
himself as a leaf, blossom, branch, or root of a living organisation? Has he any idea of the sacrifices which the people bring
to him insofar as they nourish and clothe him and make his
schooling and many sided studies possible? Moreover, does he
trouble his head very much about the meaning of our
existence and special position; does he possess a real picture
of the aims of our Order and life? With exceptions—many and
praiseworthy exceptions—I think that we could reply to this
question with a definite No. The average Castalian may perhaps look upon the man of the outside world and the unscholarly individual without contempt, envy or hatred, but he
certainly does not consider him as a brother or even see in
him a provider, nor does he feel in the least responsible for
what is happening out there. To him the aim of his life appears
to be the culture of knowledge for its own sake, or perhaps
only a pleasant stroll through the garden of culture which he
likes to hold up as universal without its actually being
anything of the kind.

In brief, this Castalian culture, which is certainly a high and
noble one and one to which I am profoundly grateful, is
hardly in the hands of most of its possessors and representatives, an organ and instrument directed actively towards any
fixed goal, for it is not consciously of service to anything,
neither higher nor lower, but tends, if only slightly, towards
self-enjoyment and self-appraise, towards the development
and intensive cultivation of intellectual specialities. I know
that there are many Castalians who are valuable and of
integrity, who really demand no more than to serve; but
there are among us also many educated teachers—I mean
those in the schools of the outside world—who carry out a

self-sacrificing, inestimable service there, far from our pleasant climate and the intellectual luxury of our Province. These brave outside teachers, to put it bluntly, are the only ones among us through whose work we are able to reimburse the world for what it gives us. The fact that our highest and most sacred task lies in maintaining the spiritual foundations of the world, namely, in preserving the meaning of truth, which is also the basis of justice has been proved a moral element of the highest efficacy. Each of us Order brothers knows this quite well, but if some of us were to look into our hearts for a moment we should find that the well-being of the world, the spiritual probity and purity outside our clean and immaculately preserved Province, is certainly not the most important thing—nay, actually of very little importance to us—and that we are well content to leave this task to those courageous teachers to bear on their own shoulders through their work of devotion, besides paying off our debt to the world and to a certain extent justifying the privileges of us bead-players, astronomers, musicians and mathematicians. This goes hand in hand with the arrogance and caste spirit that I mentioned earlier—that we do not care very strongly one way or the other whether we earn our privileges through achievement or not, and that not a few of us look upon our ordained abstemiousness in our material conditions of life as a virtue, practising it purely for its own sake, whereas it is actually the minimum of return due to the country which renders our Castalian existence possible.

I will content myself with this hint as to the inner damages and dangers, which are not inconsiderable, although in times of peace they would not endanger our existence for a long time to come.

We Castalians, however, are not only dependent upon our own morality and intelligence, but have also to rely to a great extent upon the conditions ruling in the country and the will of the people. We eat our daily bread, make use of our libraries, go on building schools and amplifying our archives, but should the people cease to wish to make this possible, or if the country became incapable of doing so through poverty, war, etc., then our lives and studies would very quickly come to an end. Our land will one day no longer be able to maintain its Castalia and our culture; the people will one day look upon

Castalia as a luxury that it can ill afford and, instead of being proud of us as hitherto, in a kindly spirit, will look upon us as parasites and vermin—nay, as corrupters and enemies. These are the dangers that menace us from without.

Were I to attempt to portray these dangers to an average Castalian I should first of all have to take historical examples, and I know that I should meet with a certain passive resistance, an almost childish ignorance and a complete lack of sympathy. As my worthy colleagues know, the interest in world history is very weak among us Castalians, and I might say that for most of us here there is not only indifference but also little sense of justice felt towards history and certainly no respect for it. This aversion for the study of world history, which contains an admixture of indifference and presumption, has often impelled me to enquire into its possible sources and foundations. I have discovered that it is based upon two facts. Firstly, the content of history appears to us of very little value; I am speaking now of course not of spiritual and cultural history, which we cultivate intensively, but of world history which consists, insofar as we have any conception of it, of brutal struggles for power, property, lands, raw materials and gold—in fact, for the material and the quantitative, the very things which we look upon as unspiritual and more or less despicable. In our eyes, for example, the seventeenth century is the age of Descartes, Pascal, Froberger and Schutz; not of Cromwell or of Louis XIV. The second reason for our dislike of world history consists in our inherited and, in my opinion, partly justifiable distrust for a certain manner of historical observation and writing which was very popular in the age of decline just prior to the foundation of our Order, and in which *a priori* we have not the least confidence—the so-called "philosophy of history," the most spiritual flowers and at the same time the most dangerous effects of which we find in Hegel but which, in the centuries that followed him, led to a repulsive perversion of history and to an utter demoralization of the meaning of truth. To our way of thinking, preference for this "philosophy of history" belongs to the major signs of that epoch of spiritual beggary and far reaching political struggles for power which we know as the "warring centuries," but generally refer to as the Age of the Digest. Out of the wreckage of that period, out of the conflict and victory over its spirit—or rather out of its spiritual malpractice—arose our present culture, the Order and Castalia.

Now as regards our present-day spiritual arrogance, we stand towards world history, particularly modern history, in almost the same position as the ascetics and eremites of early Christianity stood towards the world stage. History seems to us a battleground of urge and fashion, covetousness, avarice and greed for power, blood lust and despotism, ravages and wars, of ambitious ministers, venal generals and of towns bombarded into ruins, and we forget all too easily that this is only one of its many aspects. We forget, above all, that we ourselves are a fragment of history, something that has become and something that is doomed to die out should it lose the capacity for further progress and transformation. We ourselves are history, and are co-responsible to world history and our position within it. The realization of this responsibility is very much lacking among us.

Let us cast a glimpse at our own history, at the time of the rise in our land as in so many others of our modern pedagogic Provinces, at the rise of the different Orders and hierarchies, of which our Order is merely one, and we shall see at once that hierarchy and homeland—our dear Castalia—was by no means founded by people who were so resigned to world history or who were so arrogant in behaviour as we are. Our predecessors and founders began their work at the end of the warring centuries in a decimated world. We are accustomed rather one-sidedly to account for the world conditions of that period, which began with the first so-called World War, by maintaining that the spirit had no validity and had only been utilized incidentally by the violent usurpers of power as a secondary weapon, which we see as a direct result of the corruption of the "Age of the Digest." Now it is easy to maintain the unspirituality and brutality with which those struggles for power were waged, although when I call them unspiritual I do so not because I am overlooking the potent achievements in intelligence and methodology, but because we are used to, and make a point of looking upon the spirit primarily as the will to truth, and what was abused in the way of spirit in those struggles had nothing whatever in common with truth. The misfortune of that age was that no one had any moderately resolute moral code to oppose the unrest and dynamism of the monstrously rapid increase in populations, and whatever critical faculties he still had were forced into line by the prevailing slogans. Many strange and appalling facts come to light in reviewing those struggles. Exactly as, during the Church schisms in the time of Luther four hundred years earlier, the world was suddenly filled with indescribable unrest. Everywhere suddenly arose deadly enmity between young and old, between patriotism and humanity, between red and white and we of to-day can no longer reconstruct the power and inner dynamism of that "red" and "white," the actual meaning and content of all those devices and war cries, not to mention being able to understand or sympathize with them, just as in Luther's time we see the whole of Europe— we might say half the world—believers and heretics, young and old, reactionaries and progressives, springing at each other's throats in enthusiasm or despair. The frontiers often ran right through countries, splitting whole peoples and families asunder, and we should not doubt that for the majority of the combatants themselves or at least for their leaders this was all of great significance, nor should we deny a certain robust good faith, a certain idealism as it was called in those days, to many of the ringleaders and spokesmen: everywhere they fought, killed and destroyed and everywhere, on both sides, in the belief that they were fighting for God against the devil.

For us this savage age of great enthusiasm, wild hatred and indescribable suffering has fallen into a kind of oblivion, which we hardly realize because it is bound up so closely with the rise of all our organisations and of which it was the premise and the cause. A satirist could compare this oblivion with the obliviousness which ennobled and successful adventurers have for their birth and parents. Let us dwell for a moment upon those centuries. I have ready many of their documents and have interested myself less in the subjugated races and the destroyed towns than in the behaviour of the intellectuals of that period. They had untold difficulties, and the majority of them did not stand firm. There were martyrs both among the scholars and the clergy, and their martyrdom and example did not remain without effect even in those horror-sated ages. Most of the representatives of the spirit did not endure the pressure of that period of violence. Some of them surrendered and placed their talents, knowledge and methods at the disposal of the rulers—there is the well-known reply of a university professor in the Republic of the Massagetes: "The sum total of twice two is not for the Faculty to determine but for his Highness the General!" Others put up a resistance for as long as they were able in their half-protected sphere, and lodged protests. A world-famous author of that period—we read of this in Ziegenhals —signed over two hundred such protests, warnings and appeals to reason in one year, many more than he probably ever read. Most of them, however, learned to remain silent, to hunger and freeze, to beg and keep out of the clutches of the police. They died prematurely and those who died were envied by the survivors. Countless numbers of them took their lives. It was really no longer a joy and an honour to be a scholar or man of letters: he who entered the service of the rulers and produced slogans for them held an office and earned his daily bread, but at the same time the contempt of the best among his colleagues and in most cases a really bad conscience; whoever rejected this service was forced to starve, to live as an outlaw and die in exile or in misery. A gruesome, harsh and unheard of selection was inaugurated. Research, insofar as it was useless to power and to military ends, declined rapidly, as did also the school curricula; but above all, world history, seized upon by the nation that happened to be in power at the time, was unceasingly simplified and re-written entirely for that nation's own ends. Philosophies of history and the "feuilleton" reigned even in the schools.

Enough of details. Suffice it to say that they were wild and stormy times, chaotic and Babylonian times, in which nations and parties, young and old, red and white had no under-standing for each other whatsoever. Ultimately, after a satiety of bloodshed and misery, a growing longing was felt by everyone for reason, for the re-discovery of a common idiom, for order, morality and valid measures, for an alphabet and a multiplication table no longer dictated by power interests and liable to be changed from one moment to the next. A colossal need arose for truth and justice, for reason and for some form of order out of the chaos. We have to thank this vacuum at the end of a violent and totally extraverted period for our Castalia and our very existence—this indescribably urgent and universal hankering after a new beginning and a new order. The infinitesimal, courageous, half-starved cohort of true intellectuals began to realize their opportunity, began with ascetic-heroic self-discipline to create an order and a constitution, began everywhere in small and insignificant groups to resume work, to sweep away the slogans and to build up from the very bottom a new spirituality, curriculum, research and culture. Their efforts were successful and out of the poor heroic beginnings the building has grown into a superb edifice. Through many centuries the Order, the Pedagogy, the élite schools, the archives and museums, specialist schools, seminaries and the Bead Game have been created, until to-day we live as heirs and beneficiaries in this almost too magnificent edifice—and, I should like to repeat, we live in it as seemingly inconsequential guests, unwilling to know more about the gigantic human sacrifice upon which the foundation stones were laid, anything about the piteous experiences of which we are the heirs or about world history, which in the first place brought about or at least tolerated our edifice, which still supports and tolerates us and will certainly continue to do so for many Magisters and Castalians to come, but which will one day overthrow and swallow us up as it always eventually swallows what it has allowed to grow.

To return from history, we find that its result and import as far as we are concerned to-day is as follows: our system and Order has surpassed the peak of its golden age, the time of good fortune which the enigmatical game of world events allows the beautiful and estimable to achieve from time to time. We are already on the decline. It is possible that we shall endure for a long time yet, but in any case nothing higher, more beautiful or more estimable can come our way than that which we already possess. The path leads downward. Historically, I believe, we are ripe for destruction, and this will undoubtedly ensue—perhaps not to-day or to-morrow, but eventually. I have arrived at this conclusion less from an all too moral criticism of our achievements and capabilities than from the movements which I see being prepared in the outside world. Critical times lie ahead, and everywhere one can see signs of the world's once more losing its centre of gravity. New dispositions of power are being prepared and a menace not only to peace but also to life and freedom lowers from the Far East. Even if our country and its Province remain neutral, even if our whole people were of one accord (which is not the case) in their present-day determination to remain true to the Castalian ideal, it will be in vain. Already many of our parliamentarians speak openly on occasions about Castalia's being somewhat of an expensive luxury to our country. It need only come to serious rearmament for war—even armament for defence—and that might soon occur, for us to be hit very hard in the time of great economy that will inevitably ensue in spite of the goodwill on the part of the Government towards us. We are very proud of the fact that our Order and the permanence of the spiritual culture that it has attained calls for a reasonably modest sacrifice on the part of the country. In comparison with other ages, such as the earlier "feuilleton" period with its conceited and well-endowed high schools, its innumerable privy councillors and luxurious institutions, this sacrifice is by no means a great one, and insignificant when compared with the sums that armaments swallowed up during the warring centuries. But this armament may shortly take priority again; generals may predominate in Parliament, and if the people were faced with the choice of sacrificing Castalia on the one hand or of averting the threat of war and destruction on the other we have a shrewd idea as to which way they would vote. A belligerent ideology will immediately be set in motion which will seize upon youth in particular—a slogan outlook in which scholars and scholarship, Latin, mathematics, culture and the care of the spirit will only have the right to exist to the extent that they can be put to warlike ends. The breakers are ahead, and one day they will capsize us. Perhaps it is a good thing—perhaps it will be necessary—but before this, my most worthy and esteemed colleagues, we have an option, each according to the degree of his insight into events, and each according to his awareness and courage—that limited freedom of resolution and behaviour which is accorded to man and which makes world history the history of men—we can, if we wish, shut our eyes to the danger, for it is still quite far distant. Presumably, we who are Magisters here to-day will terminate our office in time of peace before it matures and becomes apparent to all. For myself, however, and certainly not for me alone, this peace would not be one of clear conscience. I could not continue my office and peacefully go on playing the Bead Game content in the knowledge that I should not be affected during my lifetime. No—but it seems important to remind myself that we unpolitical figures also have a place in world history, and ought therefore to help in it. That is why I said in the beginning of my letter that my capacity for office was endangered: I cannot prevent a greater part of my cares and sorrows from being directed towards the future danger. I refuse to indulge in the game of hypothesis as to what form the misfortune could take as far as we are concerned, but I cannot help raising the question: "What have we and what have I to do in order to combat the danger?" and on this subject I hope that I may be allowed a few words.

I should hardly care to postulate the axiom of Plato's—that the scholar, and above all the sage, should rule the State—for the world was considerably younger then and Plato, although the founder of a kind of Castalia, was by no means a Castalian: he was a born aristocrat and of royal descent. We too are aristocrats and form a nobility, but it is an aristocracy of the intellect and not of the blood. I do not consider that mankind will ever succeed in building a nobility which is at once hereditary and of the intellect—it would be the ideal of course, but it remains a dream. We Castalians, although highly intelligent and moral people, are not suited to be rulers: were we to rule, we should do so without the strength and ingenuousness which are the prerequisites of a true regent, and our own particular field—the cultivation of an exemplary spiritual life—would very soon fall into neglect. In order to rule it is not by any means necessary to be brutal, as conceited intellectuals have sometimes maintained, but what one does need is an untrammelled joy in extraverted activity and the faculty of identifying oneself with goals and aims, besides a certain speed and lack of reflection in the choice of the means to achieve success—characteristics which we scholars (we will not call ourselves sages) should not and do not possess, for whom observation is more important than action, and in whose choice of means and methods in order to reach our goal we have learned to be as scrupulous and sceptical as is humanly possible. Thus it is not for us to rule or to mingle in politics. We are the specialists in research, dissection and measurement; the preservers and perpetual verifiers of all alphabets, multiplication tables and methods, and above all the gaugers of the spiritual weights and measures. But our potentialities do not end there, for we may under certain circumstances also be innovators, discoverers, adventurers, pioneers and interpreters, although our primary and most important function, on account of which the people need and support us, always remains the same—that of the sanitation of all sources of knowledge. In trade, politics and in fact anywhere where an accidental achievement or act of genius is possible an X may be turned into a Y and vice versa, but never with us.

In earlier epochs, in turbulent, so-called "great ages," in war and upheaval, it was demanded of the intellectuals that they should take part in politics. This was particularly the case during the "Age of the Digest," but to these demands were also added the politicizing and militarizing of the spirit: just as the church bells were melted down to make cannons and the still immature schoolboys were used to replace the decimated troops, so was the spirit to be dragooned and abused.

Naturally we cannot entertain this demand. That the scholar, in cases of dire necessity, may be dragged from his catheder or desk and be turned into a soldier, that under certain circumstances he may even enlist his services voluntarily, and further, in a country that has been bled by war, that he should be prepared to forego material things to the utmost and sometimes to the point of starvation, is a foregone conclusion and we need waste no further words-upon it. The higher a man's culture and the greater the privileges he enjoys, the greater should be his sacrifice in times of distress, and this will, I hope, be accepted as a matter of course by every Castalian. However, even if we are ready to sacrifice our well-being, our comfort and even our lives to the people if the country is endangered, it does not hold good that we should be prepared to sacrifice the spirit itself, along with the tradition and morality of our spirituality, to the interests of the day, the people or the generals. The coward is the man who attempts to avoid the trials, sacrifices and dangers that his people have to undergo, but no less a coward is he who betrays the principles of the spiritual life for material interests —who for example, is prepared to leave the decision as to the product of twice two to the rulers! To sacrifice the sense for truth, intellectual probity and loyalty to the laws and methods of the spirit to any other interest is treachery. If, in the struggle of interests and slogans, truth is imperilled, devalued, mutilated and violated, like the individual, speech, the arts and like everything organic and artificially cultivated, then it is our duty to resist and to rescue the truth, *i.e.*, to persist in striving after truth—the highest canon of our faith. The scholar who, as an orator, author or teacher, wittingly utters falsehoods and supports lies and perjuries, not only acts against organic and basic laws but is, contrary to all appearances, of no use to his people whatever. He causes them nothing but harm, for he poisons the air and the earth, their food and their drink, not to mention thought and justice, and aids everything evil and inimical that threatens to destroy them.

The Castalian should therefore be no politician. He should, if need be, sacrifice his person but never his loyalty to the spirit. The spirit is beneficent and noble only in its obedience to truth: once it betrays the latter, as soon as it lays aside reverence and becomes venal and complacently pliable, it has all the potentialities of the devil and is far worse than the animal urge towards bestiality, which still retains something of the innocence of nature.

I leave it to each of you, my esteemed colleagues, to give a thought to this matter, to determine wherein the duty of the Order would lie in the event of law and order being menaced. There will, in face of such an eventuality, naturally be many different interpretations. I, too, have my own, and after much reflection upon the above questions have arrived at a very clear picture as to what constitutes my duty and as to what is worth while achieving. This now brings me to the point where I must put forward my personal petition to the Authorities, with which I shall close this memorandum.

Of all the Magisters who compose our Pedagogy, I, as Magister Ludi, am by very reason of my office the farthest removed from the outside world. The mathematicians, philologists, biologists, pedagogues and the rest all work in fields which have a common link with the profane world: in the ordinary non-Castalian schools of our own and every land mathematics and philology forms the basis of the curriculum, and in the high schools of the world astronomy, physics and also music is practised by the completely unscholarly. All these subjects are age-old; they were in existence long before our Order, and they will certainly outlive it. The Bead Game alone is our own discovery—our speciality, our darling, our toy—the ultimate, most differentiated expression of our Castalian type of spirituality. At the same time it is the most costly, most useless, most beloved and the most fragile jewel in our treasury. It will be the first thing to go if the survival of Castalia is ever in doubt, not only because it is the most breakable of our possessions but because, in the eyes of the layman, it is the very part of Castalia most easily dispensed with. If and when it becomes a question of saving the country every unnecessary expenditure, we shall find that the élite schools will be curtailed in number, the funds for the upkeep and expansion of our libraries and archives reduced and finally discontinued, that our food will be cut down, our clothes no longer renewed and, although several of the major Faculties will be allowed to continue, it will not be so with the Bead Game. They will always need mathematicians out there to discover new weapons of artillery, but no one, least of all the military, will believe that the closing down of the Vicus Lusorum and the disappearance of the Game might be harmful to the country and the people. The Bead Game is at once the pinnacle and the most vulnerable part of our edifice. Perhaps it is for this reason that the Magister Ludi, the head of our most unworldly faculty, should be the first to feel this danger, and that he should bring his suspicions to the notice of the authorities.

I consider the Bead Game to be doomed, therefore, with the advent of any new political upheavals of a warlike nature. It will disintegrate very rapidly, despite the devoted individuals who continue to practise it, and it will never be revived. In the atmosphere following upon a new period of war no such thing will be allowed. We know that certain highly cultivated fashions in the history of music have disappeared, such as were found in the choirs of professional singers about 1600 or in the dominical figural music in the churches around 1700. At that time the human ear could appreciate tones that no science and no magic can conjure up to-day in all their angelic and radiant purity. The Bead Game will also disappear, and like these fashions will not be forgotten but will be impossible to revive; and those who in later ages come to study its history, rise and golden age will sigh and envy us because we were fortunate enough to live in such a peaceable, cultured and harmonious spiritual world.

Although I am now Magister Ludi, I do not by any means consider it my (or our) task to interfere with or postpone the end of our Game. Even beauty and the most beautiful is transitory once it has become history and taken on an earthly form. We are aware of this and it may make us sad, but we cannot seriously try to change it, for it is immutable. When the Bead Game dies, both Castalia and the world will suffer, but they will be so occupied with their great crisis and with rescuing everything that can still be rescued that they will hardly notice their loss. A Castalia without the Bead Game is perfectly conceivable, but not a Castalia without respect for truth, and loyalty to the spirit. A pedagogy can survive without a Magister Ludi; but we seem almost to have forgotten the original meaning of the title "Magister Ludi," for it does not signify the high speciality to which we have fitted the word. In its original sense Magister Ludi simply meant schoolmaster—and the schoolmaster, the good and courageous schoolmaster whom our land will need increasingly the more Castalia is threatened and the more its treasures crumble away or grow stale. Above all else we need teachers, men who will bring to our youth the capacity for moderation and judgment and who, by their example, will instil a reverence for truth, obedience to the spirit and service to to the word. And this holds good not primarily and solely for our élite schools, which will one day cease to exist, but also for the schools outside in the world where the burghers and peasants, the artisans and soldiers, the politicians, officers and rulers are educated and moulded while they are still children and still malleable. Therein lies the basis of the spiritual life of the land, and not in the seminaries or in the Bead Game. We have always provided the land with teachers and pedagogues and, as I have already said, they are the best of us; but we must do far more than has yet been done. We must no longer rely upon the fact that the cream of the talented from out there flock to us and help us to maintain Castalia: we must recognise our humble and heavy responsibility to the schools of the world as the most important and the most honourable part of our task, and we must elaborate it more and more.

Finally, I come to my own personal request. I hereby formally request that the authorities release me from the office of Magister Ludi, and that they entrust me with a large or small school outside in the world, that they allow me to gradually attract to that school a staff of young Order brothers as teachers in whom I may have confidence, and who will loyally help me to make our basic principle, flesh and blood in the young boys out there.

I beg the worthy authorities to give their favourable consideration to my petition and its grounds, and to make known to me their commands.

The Magister Ludi.

Postscript:

May I be allowed to add a pronouncement that I once heard the Reverend Father Jacobus make during the time of my unforgettable private instruction with him.

"Times of terror and the deepest misery may arrive, but if there is to be any happiness in this misery it can only be a spiritual happiness, related to the past in the rescue of the culture of early ages and to the future in a serene and indefatigable championship of the spirit in a time which would otherwise completely swallow up the material."

Tegularius did not know how little of his work remained in this missive, for he was not shown the final draft. Knecht had given him two of the earlier and more complete versions to read. He had forwarded the letter and had awaited the reply with far less impatience than his friend. He had resolved not to make Tegularius an accessory to his next step, and had therefore forbidden him to allude to the subject again, hinting that it would be a long time before he received an answer; and when, shortly afterwards, the reply arrived—far more promptly than he had expected—Tegularius learned nothing of it. The letter from Hirsland read as follows:

His Worthiness the Magister Ludi in Waldzell.

Most esteemed colleague,

Both the Leaders of the Order and the Conclave of Magisters have taken note of your circular letter, which was warmhearted and brilliant. Your historical references have captured our attention no less than the anxious glimpses you have given into the future, and it is certain that we shall bear many of these disturbing and highly plausible hypotheses in mind in order that we may put them to the best use. We have all recognised the sentiments which inspired you with joy and appreciation—the sentiments of a true and selfless Castalian with a deep inner devotion, and at times an anxious, somewhat timorous love for our Province, the life and morals of which have become as second nature to him.

We appreciate the mood of this love, its personal and momentary distress, its readiness for sacrifice, urge to action, its gravity, zeal and heroic nature. In all these traits we recognise only too well the character of our Magister Ludi, his energy, fire and audacity. How typical that this pupil of the famous Benedictine should not have studied history to purely scholarly ends or merely as an æsthetic pastime as an unimpassioned observer might have studied it, but that he should feel impelled to utilize his knowledge of history to the needs of our time in terms of active and positive assistance! How perfectly also, most esteemed colleague, does the goal of your personal wishes fit your character: the fact that it is so extremely modest, that you do not feel drawn towards political tasks and missions or to influential and honourable posts, but desire no more than to be a Ludi Magister—a schoolmaster!

These are a few of the impressions and thoughts that arose upon first reading your circular letter. They were the same or very similar in the case of all your colleagues. In their further judgments of your communication—your warnings and your requests—the members of the Pedagogy could, on the contrary, not arrive at such a unanimous opinion. In the session which was held expressly for this purpose, the questions, as to how far your views regarding our threatened existence were acceptable and as to the type, dimensions and approximate date of the foreshadowed dangers, were brought up and gave rise to an animated discussion. The greater part

of the members, obviously took these questions very
seriously and evinced a lively interest in them; and yet, as I
must inform you, upon none of these questions was a majority
of voices raised in favour of your hypotheses. The imagination and farsightedness of your historical and political
observations were duly recognised but as regards the
individual assumptions, or should we say prophecies, no single
one of them was wholly approved or accepted as convincing.
Furthermore, the question as to how far the Order and the
Castalian organisation has been co-responsible for the
preservation of an unusually long period of peace, and as to
how far it can be considered as a basic factor in political
history and world conditions, was agreed by only very few,
and then with reservations. The interpretation of the majority
was that the enduring peace on our continent after the
warring centuries had run their course could be attributed
partly to the general exhaustion and loss of blood as a result
of the appalling wars, but far more to the fact that the West
had ceased at that time to be the focal point of world history
and the cockpit of claims to hegemony. Without casting any
aspersions on the services of the Order, one could not
possibly recognise Castalian thought—the thought of a high
cultural development under the sign of contemplative
spiritual discipline—as an actual history-making power, as a
living influence on world political conditions, for an impulse
or ambition of this kind was entirely alien to its nature. It
could neither be the intention nor the desire of Castalia—and
this point was stressed in several very earnest speeches—to
have a political influence or an influence on peace or war:
there could be no question of any such intention because
everything Castalian was based upon reason and operated
within the sphere of intelligence, which could not be said of
world history, and this course would merely be a reversion to
the poetic-theological enthusiasms of the romantic historical
philosophies and a recognition of the whole murder and
annihilation apparatus of the powers which made history as
the method of universal intelligence. It was illuminating,
even from the most casual glance into the history of the
spirit, to discover that the golden ages of the spirit could
never be explained basically in terms of political conditions,
but that the culture of the spirit or the soul had its own

separate history—a second, secret, bloodless and consecrated history—running parallel to the so-called world history, to the never-ending struggles for material power. Our Order, at one with this secret and consecrated history, had nothing to do with the "real" brutal world history, and it could never be our task to watch over political history or help in its making.

Whether the world political situation really was or was not as serious as your circular letter suggested, it was in neither case for the Order to do anything except take up a patient position of waiting towards them; and thus your interpretation, with the exception of a few votes in favour of our accepting this situation as a call to taking an active stand, was rejected by the majority. As regards your portrayal of the present-day situation of the world and your hints as to the immediate future, most of your colleagues were visibly impressed and your remarks were in the nature of a sensation for one or two of the gentlemen. Yet a quorum in your favour was not forthcoming despite the fact that most of the speakers announced their respect for your knowledge and perspicacity. There was a far greater inclination to regard your utterances as remarkable and of great interest but to dismiss them as exaggerated pessimism. Several voices were raised asking whether it were not dangerous and blasphemous—frivolous at the very least—for a Magister to terrify his Authorities with such a forlorn fantasy of forthcoming dangers and tribulations. Naturally an occasional reminder of the transience of all things is permissible and every man, even in the high and responsible posts, must from time to time cry out a *memento mori*, but to announce an ostensible approaching end to the whole Order and the whole hierarchy in such general and nihilistic terms was not only an unworthy attack upon the peace of mind and imagination of his colleagues but also a threat to the Pedagogy itself and to its competence. The efficiency of a Magister could gain nothing by the thought as he went to work each morning that his office, his work, his pupils, his responsibility to the Order and in fact the whole life in Castalia would come to an end and be destroyed to-morrow or the day after. Even if these speeches were not supported by the majority, they received a certain amount of applause.

We are making this reply a brief one, but we are fully

prepared, if you wish, to discuss the matter verbally. You will already have perceived that your circular letter did not achieve the result that you perhaps expected. To a great extent its failure was due to professional factors—to the actual difference between your ideas and those of the majority—but there were also formal grounds, the least of which in our opinion is the fact that a direct verbal discussion between yourself and your colleagues would have been decidedly more harmonious and would have had more positive results. It is not only your adoption of this circular letter form which has been an obstacle to your proposals, but much more the fact that it is unusual to add a personal petition to an official communication. Most of the members who were present saw in this unhappy combination an unfortunate attempt at innovation and others pronounced it as frankly unprofessional!

And now we come to the most delicate part of your affair— your request to be released from office and to be used in the school service outside in the world. That the authorities could not accept such an abruptly worded and curiously founded petition, that they could neither approve of it nor even entertain it, must have been known to the petitioner in advance. The Pedagogy naturally answers you with a categorical "No." What would happen to our hierarchy if each man was no longer given his position by the Order under the direction of the Pedagogy? What would happen to Castalia if each man took himself at his own estimate, assessed his own gifts and suitabilities and tried to seek out a post for himself? We recommend that the Magister Ludi reflect a little on these matters, and we bid him continue to administer the worthy task which we have entrusted to him. This is the reply to your letter. We could not give you the answer which you may have hoped for, and yet we cannot remain silent as to our recognition of the disturbing and warning value of your document. We intend to discuss its content with you in person in the near future, for even if we of the Order still believe that we can rely upon you, the point at which you speak of a threat to or a lessening of your capacity for further official duties gives us grounds for anxiety.

Knecht read the letter without undue expectation but with

the greatest attention. He could well understand that the Pedagogy had "grounds for anxiety," and thought that he could also conclude as much from a certain telltale incident. A guest, a quiet, attentive and handsome elderly man, had recently arrived in the Game Town from Hirsland with a regular pass and a recommendation from the Head of the Order begging right of hospitality to work (ostensibly) in the archives and in the library. He had asked to be allowed to attend certain of Knecht's lectures, and had also put in an appearance in nearly all the departments and halls of the settlement, had asked questions about Tegularius and had several times visited the headmaster of the Waldzell élite school who lived in the neighbourhood. There could be little doubt that the man had been sent to see how things stood in the Vicus Lusorum, to see whether there were any signs of negligence, whether the Magister Ludi was in good health and in his right mind, and that the pupils were not disturbed in any way. He had remained for a whole week, had not missed a single one of Knecht's lectures, and his ubiquitous omnipresence had been remarked upon by two of the officials. The Head of the Order had undoubtedly waited upon the report of this spy before despatching his answer to the Magister Ludi.

What was there to be gathered from the reply, and who could have been the composer? The style betrayed nothing, for the letter was couched in cursive, impersonal pedagogic style such as the occasion demanded; but on closer examination it betrayed more originality and character than one might have imagined at first reading. The whole document was based on the hierarchic spirit of the Order, upon justice, and the love of order. Knecht could plainly see the unwelcome, uncomfortable and importunate effect that his petition must have had, and its rejection had most certainly been made by the composer of this reply as soon as he had read it, quite uninfluenced by the judgments of others. On the other hand, as opposed to the reticence and air of defence there was another tendency, another mood—a perceptible sympathy in the stressing of all the mitigating and comradely judgments and utterances that had been made at the session. Knecht did not doubt that Alexander, the Head of the Order, had composed this reply.

We have reached the end of our journey, and hope that we have imparted everything of importance concerning the career of Joseph Knecht. About the latter part of this career a future biographer will no doubt be able to ascertain and impart many additional details.

We have renounced the pleasure of giving our own portrayal of the Magister's last days, for we know no more about them than every Waldzellian student knows, and we could not improve upon the "Legend of the Magister Ludi," which was probably the work of a few privileged students and of which many copies have been circulated. We should like to bring our book to a close with this legend.

Chapter Twelve

THE LEGEND

WHEN WE LISTEN to the conversations of our comrades on the subject of our Master's disappearance, its causes, the right or wrong of his decisions and steps, the meaning or paradox of his destiny, we find them as charming as the arguments of Diodorus Siculus upon the probable causes of the flooding of the Nile, and it seems to us not only useless but unfair to elaborate these arguments. We prefer to pre-serve intact in our hearts the memory of our Master who, so shortly after his mysterious foray into the world, passed over into a stranger and more mysterious beyond. In order to do justice to his memory, which is so dear to us, we wish to relate these events exactly as they have come to our ears.

After the Magister had read the letter in which the Pedagogy had rebuffed his petition, he felt a slight shudder— an early morning feeling of coolness and sobriety—which told him that his time was at hand and that hesitation and delay were now no longer possible. This strange feeling, which he used to call his "awakening," had been known to him at decisive moments all through his life. It was a senti-ment at once vivid and painful, having in it a mixture of

farewell and departure, like the rustling of spring storms
deep in the unconscious. He looked at the clock and saw that
in an hour's time he was due to give a lecture. He decided to
devote this hour to self-communion, and repaired to his
private garden. As he entered through the wicket gate the
lines of a poem suddenly occurred to him: "For each beginning has its special magic . . ." He repeated it to himself, not
knowing where he had read it, but the line impressed him and
seemed appropriate to the present hour. He sat down on a
seat in the garden, which was already strewn with the first
faded leaves of autumn, controlled his breathing and
struggled for inner calm until, with a lightened heart, he
sank into contemplation arranging the constellations of this
hour in his life in general and supra-personal images. On the
way to the lecture room the verse came once more into his
head and he was obliged to reflect upon it; he felt certain that
it must run slightly differently. Suddenly his memory cleared
and came to his aid. He declaimed the words softly:

"A magic dwells in each beginning and
protecting us, it tells us how to live . . ."

but not until the evening, after he had finished his course and
completed all manner of work did he discover the origin of
those lines. They were not from some old poet but from one
of his own poems which he had written as a student, and
which ended with the line:

"Courage, my heart, take leave and fare thee well."

On the same evening he sent for his deputy and announced
to him that he would be leaving on the following day for an
indefinite time. He informed him of all the current affairs,
gave him a few brief hints and took leave of him amicably and
formally as though he were going away on short official
business.

It had been clear to him for quite some time that he would
have to leave his friend Tegularius without letting him into
the secret, or burdening him with a leavetaking. He had to
take this course not only in order to spare his sensitive friend
but also to avoid endangering his whole plan. Fritz would
presumably be able to accustom himself to an accomplished
action and fact, whereas a surprise discussion and a parting
scene might bring about an unseemly lack of self-control.
Knecht had even thought of leaving without seeing him at all,

but on second thoughts he had found that this would be too much in the nature of a flight from the unpleasant. However shrewd and correct it might seem to spare his friend a scene, excitement and an opportunity to do anything foolhardy, so much the less ought he to spare himself by avoiding the issue. There was still about half-an-hour before bedtime and he could seek him out without disturbing anyone. It was already dark as he crossed the broad inner courtyard. He knocked on the door of his friend's cell with a curious sensation that it was for the last time. He found Tegularius alone. Surprised in his reading, Fritz greeted him with joy, laid aside his book and offered his visitor a chair.

Knecht started to gossip amicably.

"I recalled an old poem to-day—or rather several lines from it. Perhaps you know where it comes from: 'A magic dwells in each beginning . . .'"

This gave Tegularius little trouble. He recognised the poem after a few moment's reflection, stood up and fetched from a desk drawer the original manuscript of Knecht's poems, which his friend had once given him as a present. He searched for a second or two, drew out two leaves which bore the first version of the poem, and handed them to the Magister.

"Here you are," he said, smiling, "you can see for yourself. It is the first time for many a long year that you have remembered these poems!"

Knecht looked at the leaves attentively not without a certain emotion. As a student, during his stay in the College of Sinology, he had filled the two sheets of paper with these verses. A far distant past looked out at him now from the faintly yellowing paper, the youthful handwriting, the deletions and corrections in the text. They spoke of an almost forgotten, an admonitory and painfully revived "once upon a time." He seemed to remember not only the year and the season when these verses had been written but the very day and hour, even the mood and the strong sensation of pride which had inspired them and filled and overjoyed his heart. They had been composed on the very day upon which he had experienced that sensation which he always referred to as his "awakening."

Obviously the title had been thought of before the poem

itself. It was written in a flamboyant hand, and read:
"TRANSCENDENCE!" but later, at some other time during a
different phase of life and in another mood this title and the
exclamation had been scored through and, in a smaller,
neater and more modest handwriting, changed to "STEPS."

Knecht realised how, fired by the conception of this poem,
he had written the word "Transcendence!" as a summons and
a command, a warning to himself, as a newly formulated and
strengthened resolution to place his life and actions beneath
this sign and to make of it a "transcendence," a serenely
resolved passage, a fulfilment and a leaving behind him of
every realm and stage. He read out a few of the strophes:

> "High purposed we must traverse realm on realm,
> cleaving to none as to a home. The world
> of spirit wishes not to fetter us
> but raise us higher, further, step by step."

"For many years I had completely forgotten those verses,"
he said, "and when one of them recurred to me to-day I no
longer knew its origin and that I had written it myself. What
do you think of the poem to-day? Does it mean anything
to you?"

Tegularius reflected. "Actually, this particular one has
always had an unpleasant effect upon me," he said slowly.
"It was one of the few of your poems that I did not like, and
which always disturbed or repelled me. I did not know at the
time what there was about it that rankled, but to-day I think
I realise. This fragment, my friend, to which you gave the
title 'Transcendence' almost as a marching order, and for
which praise God you substituted a far better one, never
pleased me very much because it had something authoritarian,
moralizing or schoolmasterish about it. Could this element, or
rather this coat of paint, have been removed, it would have
been the finest of all your poems, as I have often maintained.
The actual content is represented quite well by the title
'Steps,' but you could just as well or perhaps even better have
called it 'Music' or, 'The Essence of Music' for, after the
moralizing or predicatory opening, it is really a discussion
upon the nature of music or, if you like, a song in praise of
music, of its eternal presence, its serenity and resolution, its
flexibility and unceasing determination and its readiness to
hurry forward and abandon the first realm or section of space

that it has occupied. Had this discussion or this pæan remained on this level, on the spirit of music, and had you not—obviously already dominated by an ambition to educate —made it a warning and a sermon, it might have been a perfect jewel. As it stands it seems to me not only too instructive and too pedagogic, but also to suffer from faulty reasoning. For moral effect it puts music and life on the same level, which is at once questionable and contestable: it makes out of an amoral and natural driving power, of which music is the mainspring, a 'life' which, through a summons, through commands and good doctrines, is designed to educate and develop us. In short, in this poem, a vision, something unique, beautiful and magnificent has been utilized and falsified for educational purposes, and that is what has always put me against it."

The Magister listened to his friend with pleasure, and noticed a certain angry heat in his speech which he always liked.

"You may be right," he said, half in jest. "You are right anyway as far as its connection with music is concerned. The 'traverse realm on realm' and the basic thought of my rhymes came inadvertently and quite unconsciously from music. As to whether I have spoiled the thought and falsified the vision I do not know—perhaps you are right. When I composed those verses I was preoccupied less with music than with an experience—an experience in which that beautiful musical allegory had shown its moral side, had become an awakening and a summons to a life vocation. The imperative form of the poem which specially displeases you is not the expression of a command and a will to teach but a command and warning directed towards myself. Even if you were not fully aware of this, my friend, you could have read it in the closing lines. I experienced an insight, you see, a realization and an inner vision, and wished to impress and hammer the moral of this vision into myself. That is the reason why this poem has remained in my memory. Whether the verses are good or bad they have achieved their aim, for the warning has lived on within me and has not been forgotten. It rings anew for me again to-day, and that is a wonderful little experience which your scorn cannot take away from me. But it is time we broke up this meeting! How pleasant were those days when as students, we used to break the house rules and remain talking together far into the night! As a Magister Ludi one cannot do such things any more. It is a pity!"

"Oh!" replied Tegularius. "It could still be done, you know—if only one had the courage to do it . . ."

Knecht laid his hand on his friend's shoulder with a laugh. "As regards courage, my dear Fritz, I should be capable of far greater pranks! Good-night, old grouser!"

Knecht left the cell in a happy mood, and only as he crossed the dark deserted corridors and courtyards of the settlement did his gravity return—the gravity of parting. Leavetaking always arouses images and memories, and he now remembered his first exciting and hopeful walk through the town and the Vicus Lusorum as a boy, as a newly arrived Waldzellian. He now realized, with a deep and painful feeling as he walked among the silent trees and buildings, that he was seeing all this for the last time, was seeing for the last time the quiet and slumber of the settlement after the day's activity, the little light over the porter's lodge reflected in the fountain basin and the night clouds above the trees of the Magister's garden. He walked slowly along the paths and visited every corner of the Game Town. As he neared his garden he felt an impulse to open the gate once more and enter, but he had not the key with him and this quickly brought him back to sobriety and consciousness. He returned to his house and wrote a few letters, including one to Designori announcing his imminent arrival in the capital. He then released himself from the disturbing tumult of his soul in a painstaking meditation, in order that he might be strong on the following day for his last act in Castalia—his speech with the Head of the Order.

On the following morning the Magister rose at his usual hour, ordered his conveyance and drove away. Few people noticed his departure, and no one gave the matter a thought. He drove through the early morning countryside, already shrouded in autumn mists, and arriving at mid-day in Hirsland, where he had himself announced to Magister Alexander. He was carrying, wrapped up in a cloth, a fine metal casket which he had taken from a secret drawer in his chancellery containing the insignia of his office—the seals and key.

He was received with some surprise in the great official hall of the Presidency, for it rarely happened that a Magister appeared there unannounced and uninvited.

He was given hospitality in the name of the Order and conducted to a rest cell in the old cloister. Shortly afterwards a messenger arrived and informed him that the Head of the Order hoped to be free to see him in two or three hours time. Knecht asked for a copy of the Order rules, and sat down and read through the whole brochure to assure himself once more of the simplicity and legality of his intended step, the meaning and inner justification of which even now still seemed to him impossible to put into words.

He recalled a phrase in the rules upon which he had been made to meditate during his last post-graduate days of youthful freedom on the occasion of his acceptance into the Order. He read the phrase again and pondered over it carefully, just as he had done once before as a somewhat timorous private coach. It read: "Should the Higher Authorities summon thee to office, know that each promotion on the ladder of office is not a step into freedom but into bondage. The higher the office the heavier the bondage. The greater the official power, the stricter the service. The stronger the personality the more expressly forbidden is wilfulness."

How final and incontestable it had sounded at that time, and how greatly had many of the words, such as "bondage," "personality" and "wilfulness" changed their meaning for him since then—had, in fact, become their absolute antitheses in meaning—and yet how superb, clear, well defined and admirably suggestive were these phrases; how absolute, timeless and incontrovertibly true could they appear to a young spirit! Yes, and this they would have been, had Castalia been the world, the universe, the many-sided and yet indivisible, instead of only a little world within the world, or a bold and powerful portion of it. Had the earth been an élite school, the Order the community of all men and the Head of the Order God, how perfect would these phrases and all these values have been! Ah, had it only been thus, how beautiful, flowering and innocent would life have been! Once upon a time he really had seen it like this—had seen the Order and the Castalian as mankind and the non-Castalian part of the universe as a type of childish world or jumping-off stage for the Province, a fallow primæval soil still awaiting redemption and the ultimate culture, looking up to Castalia with awe and from time to time sending such amiable ambassadors as the young Plinio.

To what a remarkable pass then had Joseph Knecht and his own spirit come! Had he not considered his own particular type of vision and realization—that experience of reality which he had in former times, and even yesterday, termed his "awakening"—as a gradual progress towards the heart of the world, into the centre of truth, as something to a certain extent absolute, as an advance along a path which could only be traversed step by step, but which in idea was continuous and direct? Had there not once, in his youth, been an awakening, a progress, and had it not seemed essential and just to recognize the outside world in the figure of Plinio, but consciously and meticulously to keep one's distance from it as a Castalian? And again, had it not been an act of progress and a sincere step when he had chosen the Bead Game and the Waldzellian life after year-long doubts, when he had allowed himself to be received into service by Magister Thomas, to be accepted into the Order by the Music Master and later to be appointed to the post of Magister Ludi? They had been only major and minor steps on an apparently direct path, and yet he now found himself, at the end of this path, by no means at the heart of the world and in the centre of truth, and saw also that his present awakening was only an eye opening, a reorientation and an adaptation to new conjunctions. The same stern, clear, single and direct path which had led him to Waldzell, Mariafels, into the Order and to the office of Magister Ludi, was now leading him out of it again. That which had been a sequence of acts of awakening had at the same time been a series of leavetakings: Castalia, the Bead Game, the dignity of magistracy had each been a theme to be transformed and fulfilled, a realm to be traversed and transcended. Already they lay behind him, and obviously in the past, when he had thought and done the antithesis of what he was thinking and doing to-day, he had already known or divined this questionable state of affairs. Had he not placed as title above that poem which he had written as a student and which dealt with stages and departures, the summons: "Transcendence!"?

His way had therefore come full circle, or rather had taken the form of an ellipse or a spiral, following as ever no straight unbroken line, for the rectilinear belongs only to Geometry and not to Nature and Life. After his first awakening he had loyally followed the self-exhortation and self-encouragement of his poem, which he had long since forgotten; not to perfection perhaps, not without hesitation, doubts, deviations and struggles, but courageously, consciously and with tolerable serenity, pushing forward step by step and stage by stage; not by any means so radiantly as the old Music Master, but tirelessly and without lapsing into melancholy, apostasy or disloyalty; and if, according to Castalian lights, he was now about to enter upon a stage of apostasy and disloyalty, if he was about to act in a manner contrary to all the moral laws of the Order and to outward appearances egotistically, that is to say wilfully, then this phase would also be lived out serenely and harmoniously, in a spirit of courage and music, however things might transpire for him in the future. Would he be able to convince others and prove to them what seemed so clear to himself—that the "wilfulness" of his present behaviour was in truth service and obedience, that in reality he was not going towards freedom but towards new, unknown and strange ties, not a fugitive but one who had been called, not obstinate but obedient, not a master but a victim?

What then was the state of his courage, his inner serenity and harmony? He would henceforth be humble, but these virtues would remain in force. If there were no such thing as a departure but only a form of guidance, if there were no arbitrary transcendence but only a rotation of space around the central figure, then the virtues must remain in all their pristine value and magic: they would consist in accepting instead of refusing, in obeying instead of shirking, and would perhaps be valid by virtue of the fact that one behaved and thought as though one were master over one's fate, because one accepted this life and self-deception unquestioningly—this mirage—with the appearance of self-determination and responsibility, and because for some unknown reason one had been created fundamentally more to act than to understand and driven more by impulsive urges than by the spirit. Oh! if only one could have had a discussion with Father Jacobus on this subject! These were approximately the thoughts and reveries of his meditation. An "awakening," it appeared to him, was not so much a question of realizing truth but of experiencing reality and of sustaining it.

Upon "awakening," one was drawn nearer to the core of things, to truth; but one grasped, achieved or suffered it only to the extent that one's ego was attuned to the momentary position of things. In this one discovered no laws but only resolutions, one did not attain the centrum of the world but only the centre point of one's own ego, and in consequence all that one experienced was so difficult of communication, so remarkably inimical to linguistic formulation that any intelligence from this realm of life seemed beyond the scope of human speech. Were one in exceptional cases to convey a little more through this medium, then it was only because the listener was a man in similar circumstances, a fellow-sufferer and a fellow seer. Fritz Tegularius had on occasions gained this extra insight, and Plinio's understanding had been even more far reaching. Whom else could he name? No one.

Night had already fallen and he had sunk deep in reverie, completely enmeshed in the web of his thoughts. There was a knock at the door, but he was still far away and did not answer. The messenger waited a little and then knocked a second time. Knecht now replied, stood up and followed him to the chancellery buildings. He was led straightway into the Head of the Order's study. Magister Alexander came forward to greet him.

"It is a pity," said the latter, "that you arrived so unceremoniously and that I was obliged to keep you waiting. I am very curious to know what has brought you here so suddenly. Nothing serious I hope?"

"Oh, no!" smiled Knecht, "nothing serious. But is my appearance really so unexpected—have you no idea as to what may have brought me here?"

Alexander looked at him gravely, and there was a suggestion of anxiety in his eyes. "Well, yes," he replied, "I can imagine all manner of things. Only to-day, for example,

I thought that the question of your circular letter to the Pedagogy would be far from finished as far as you were concerned. The Authorities were obliged to reply somewhat curtly, and for you, *Domine*, perhaps in a somewhat disappointing manner and tone."

"That is not quite so. Fundamentally I could hardly have expected anything beyond what was contained in their reply. As regards the tone, it did me good. I noticed that the writer had taken the trouble—he seemed almost solicitous in fact— to instil a few drops of honey into a letter which might otherwise have proved both unpleasant and shaming. He succeeded admirably, and I am grateful to him."

"And so, my esteemed colleague, you have accepted the content of the letter?"

"Well, I have taken note of it and more or less understand and approve it. Their reply can obviously have been nothing but a rejection of my petition, combined with a mild reproach. My circular letter was a somewhat unusual one for the Pedagogy to receive, and I have no doubt that it proved extremely disturbing. It was also, insofar as it contained a personal request, presumably not very appositely constructed and I could hardly have expected any other answer."

"That is very gratifying," said the Head of the Order with a trace of asperity. "It is a good thing that you see it in that light, and that our reply did not come as an unpleasant surprise. But there is one thing I do not understand: if, when you were composing your letter—that is, if I have interpreted you rightly—you believed neither in its chances of success nor that you would receive an affirmatory reply, that it was doomed in advance to failure, why did you complete and despatch this circular letter, which must have entailed a considerable amount of work?"

Knecht looked at him with a friendly smile as he replied: "My esteemed Master, my letter had a double content and also a double purpose, and I do not believe that both of these have proved quite fruitless. It contained a personal request that I should be relieved of office and made use of in another place, but this request should have been regarded to an extent as an incidental matter, considering that every Magister ought always to put his personal affairs in the background. The plea was rejected, and I have nothing to say against that.

However, my circular letter contained very much more than this mere request, for I had introduced into it a mass of data and thoughts which I considered it my duty to bring to the attention of the Pedagogy. All of the Magisters, or at any rate the majority of them, read what I had to say and understood my warning, even if most of them did not relish this diet and reacted unfavourably to it. That they did not greet my words with applause constitutes no failure to my mind, for I sought neither applause nor agreement: it was my intention that they should produce a disquieting and rousing effect. I should regret it very much had I refrained from sending the letter on the grounds you have just mentioned for, whether it has had an insignificant or a vital effect, it has at all events been a call to arms and a notification."

"Yes, there I must agree," said the Head of the Order hesitantly; "and yet you have still not solved my problem. If you had hoped, with your warning, your call to arms and your exhortations to the authorities to achieve any measure of success, why did you weaken or endanger the effect of your golden words by appending a personal petition, in the possible fulfilment of which you yourself did not believe? I do not grasp that at all for the moment, but it will no doubt be cleared up when we have discussed the matter fully. At all events therein lies the weak point of your circular letter—in your having amalgamated a call to arms with a request, a warning with a plea. It seems to me that you were ill-advised, to use a petition as a vehicle for a warning missive. You could easily have reached your colleagues by word of mouth if you had thought it necessary to give them a jolt and the petition would have followed through the normal official channels."

Knecht continued to regard him in the friendliest possible manner.

"Yes," he said calmly, "it may be that you are right. But look at the rather distorted affair once more. Neither the warning speech nor the petition dealt with everyday, ordinary and normal matters, and both of them very definitely belonged together inasmuch as they arose from unusual circumstances involving distress: consequently, both were outside the conventions. It is neither customary nor normal for a man without urgent reasons suddenly to conjure his

colleagues to remember their mortality and the dubiety of
their whole existence, nor is it a matter of everyday occurrence for a Castalian Magister Ludi to hanker after a humble
schoolmaster's post outside the Province. Thus far both
purports of my letter are in perfect accord. A reader who
really took the whole letter seriously would, in my opinion,
have considered that this was not simply the case of a
somewhat whimsical man giving vent to his intuitions and
taking his colleagues to task, but that the petitioner really
had taken his thoughts and his distress so seriously and
earnestly that he was prepared to abandon his office, his
dignity and past and to begin afresh in the most modest
position; that he had become satiated with dignities, peace,
honour and authority and desired nothing better than to be
rid of them and to cast them aside. From this hypothesis—I
am still attempting to place myself in the position of my
reader—I should conclude either that the writer of this
tiresome homily was a little mad, and in consequence no
longer to be thought of as a Magister, or that on the contrary
he was quite sane and healthy but that more must lie behind
his preaching and pessimism than a mere mood or whimsy—
in fact, a reality and a truth. This is to a certain extent how
I imagined the reader would argue, but apparently I mis-
calculated: instead of my 'sermon' and my call to arms being
supported and strengthened, neither have been taken
seriously and both have been shelved. I am actually not very
dismayed at this rejection because, fundamentally, I must
repeat, I had expected it in spite of everything, and I must
also admit that my petition deserved such treatment, for I did
not really believe in its success and looked upon it more as a
kind of feint, a gesture and a formula."

Master Alexander's face had grown more serious and had
almost darkened, but he did not interrupt the Magister.

"But sending in this petition," Knecht continued, "and
hoping for a favourable reply, which I should have been
overjoyed to receive, did not necessarily mean that I was
prepared to accept a refusal obediently as a final decision."

"Not prepared to accept the reply of your authorities as a
final decision—did I hear rightly?" the Magister interrupted,
stressing each syllable. He had presumably at last recognized
the gravity of the situation.

Knecht bowed slightly. "Certainly you heard rightly. It
was a fact that I could hardly have expected to have any
success with my petition, but I had to carry it out in order to
comply with form and order. Thus, to a certain extent, I gave
the authorities the opportunity of dealing with the matter
indulgently. Even if they had not inclined towards this
solution I had already decided not to restrain myself or allow
myself to be pacified, but to act."

"And how, may I ask?"

"According to the dictates of my heart and reason. I was
determined to lay down my office and assume a position
outside Castalia with or without the permission of the
Pedagogy."

The Head of the Order had closed his eyes and no longer
seemed to be listening. Knecht saw at once that he had
resorted to that well-known remedy practised by members of
the Order whereby they were able to attain inner calm in
moments of distress or sudden danger by emptying the lungs
and suspending the breath for a double length of time. He
saw the face of this man, for whose grave discomfiture he had
been responsible, grow pale and then gradually regain colour
with the commencement of the inbreathing from the
diaphragm, saw the eyes of the Master whom he esteemed so
highly—nay, loved—look petrified and lost for an instant,
only to awaken and recover their strength again immediately.
With a slight shudder he beheld the clear controlled and
constantly disciplined gaze of this man, who was equally
great in obedience as in command, now turn upon him with
cool composure, observe, sum him up and judge him. For a
long time he was obliged to endure this look in silence.

"I think that I have now understood you," Alexander said
at last in a calm voice. "You have long been tired of office or
of Castalia, and been tormented by a desire to lead a worldly
life. You have decided to obey this mood in preference to the
laws of your Order. You have also, apparently, felt no need to
confide in us or to ask for our counsel and support. In order to
satisfy convention and to unburden your conscience you have
addressed a petition to us which you knew would be unacceptable but which, when the affair came to a decision, you
could fall back upon. Let us suppose that you had good
grounds for your most unusual behaviour and that your

intentions were honest and estimable, which incidentally I cannot conceive to have been otherwise. How then was it possible that, harbouring such thoughts, desires and resolutions, already a deserter in your heart, you could remain so long in office and apparently continue to conduct it in a faultless manner?"

"I am here," the Magister Ludi replied with undaunted friendliness, "in order to talk things over with you now—to answer all your questions—and now that I have embarked upon my way of independence I am resolved not to leave Hirsland or your office until I have made you understand as far as possible my actions and my position."

Master Alexander appeared to reflect. "Does that mean that you expect me to approve of your conduct and your plans?" he asked at length rather hesitantly.

"Oh, I can hardly expect you to approve of them, but what I hope and expect is to be understood by you, and I also hope to retain a little of your respect when I leave here. It is the only leavetaking from the Province that I intend to make. I have to-day left Waldzell and the Vicus Lusorum for ever."

Alexander closed his eyes again for a few seconds. This astounding information was quite overwhelming.

"For ever?" he asked. "So you never intend returning to your post! I must say that you are a master in surprise tactics, but one question if I may be allowed it: do you actually still consider yourself to be Magister Ludi or not?"

Joseph Knecht reached for the casket which he had brought with him.

"I was until yesterday, and I think that I can now consider myself entirely free of this post, inasmuch as I am handing back to the authorities the seals and the keys. They are intact, and you will find everything in order in the Game Town if you care to verify it."

Alexander rose slowly from his chair. He looked suddenly tired and seemed to have aged.

"We will leave your casket for to-day," he said drily. "If the acceptance of your seals means the completion of your release from office, then I am not competent to grant it for at least a third of the entire Pedagogy must be present. Formerly you had so much respect for the old customs and forms that I cannot adapt myself so rapidly to this change.

Perhaps you will be good enough to give me until to-morrow before we talk of this again?"

"I am entirely at your Reverence's disposal. You know me very well indeed, and you must be aware of the regard in which I have held you for so many years. I can assure you that nothing has changed in this respect. You are the only person from whom I am taking leave before I depart from the Province, and this has nothing to do with your office as Head of the Order! Once I have handed over the seals and keys into your hands, and once we have discussed the matter to its full, I hope, *Domine*, to be released from my oath to the Order by you personally."

Alexander looked at him earnestly and sadly. He gave a sigh. "Leave me alone now, my esteemed friend, you have brought me enough sorrow and matter for thought for one day. We must call a halt for this evening and resume our talk again to-morrow. Come here about an hour before mid-day."

He dismissed the Magister Ludi with a courteous gesture, but there was about it an air of such resignation that it seemed no longer to be that of a colleague. This totally alien politeness hurt Joseph Knecht far more than all his words could have done.

The famulus, who called later to escort him to supper, led him to one of the guest tables and informed him that Magister Alexander had retired for a long exercise in meditation, having concluded that the worthy Magister Ludi would not be desirous of company that evening, and that one of the guest rooms was at his disposal.

Alexander had been taken completely by surprise by the Magister Ludi's visit, although he had foreseen his appearance at an early date. It had been he who had composed the letter from the Pedagogy in reply to his petition, and he had thought of the inevitable conversation with a certain amount of anxiety; but that the Magister Knecht, with his exemplary obedience and exquisite manners, his modesty and sensitive tact, should demand an interview unannounced, lay down his office without previous notification to the authorities and in this overwhelming fashion flout every custom and precedent, he had considered absolutely out of the question. Admittedly Knecht's outward demeanour, his tone, manner of speech and impeccable courtesy had been the same as ever, but how surprising and appalling, how insulting even and how completely un-Castalian had been the content and spirit of his announcements! No one who had seen and heard the Magister Ludi could have suspected that he were ill, overworked, irritated or not perfectly master of himself, and the recent careful investigations instituted by the Pedagogy in Waldzell had brought to light nothing that gave the slightest indication of any disturbance, disorder or monotony in the life and work of the Magister Ludi. And yet this amazing man, who until to-day had been the dearest of all his colleagues, had stood there before him, had discarded his casket and insignia of office as though they were so much junk and had declared that he had ceased to be a Magister, ceased to be a member of the Pedagogy, and Order brother, and had simply come to bid him a hasty farewell. It was the most alarming, difficult and most hateful position into which his office had yet brought him. He had had the greatest difficulty in maintaining his self-control.

And now what? Ought he to use force? Ought he to place the Magister Ludi under some form of house arrest and immediately, this very evening, send a fast messenger to all the members of the Pedagogy summoning them to a meeting? What was there against this procedure? Was it not the easiest and the most correct thing to do? And yet, what could be achieved by such methods? Nothing but humiliation for the Magister Ludi, nothing gained for Castalia, and for himself, the Head of the Order, at best only a certain unburdening and lightening of conscience, relieving him of the sole responsibility in this distasteful and difficult affair. If anything were still to be made good, and if something in the nature of an appeal to Knecht's sense of honour, with a resultant change of mind, were conceivable, then this could only be achieved between the two of them. Knecht and Alexander had to fight this conflict out alone, with no one else present. As he thought this over he was forced to admit that Knecht, fundamentally, had been right and that he had behaved nobly by ignoring the authorities, whom he no longer recognized, coming instead to challenge and finally take leave of him, the Head of the Order. This Joseph Knecht then, even when he did something forbidden and hateful, was still to be relied upon for his tact and behaviour!

Master Alexander decided to have faith in his intuitions and to leave the whole official apparatus out of the issue, and once he had decided upon this course he began to consider the affair in all its details and to ask himself above all, whether the Magister, who had given every indication that he was entirely convinced of his own integrity and the justice of his projects, was right or wrong in his actions. Now that he began to analyse the Magister Ludi's audacious deed and to verify it by the Order rules which, incidentally, he knew better than anyone else, he came to the surprising conclusion that Knecht had neither broken nor had had any intention of breaking the rules, inasmuch as any member was entitled to secede from the Order at any time, even though he had belonged to it for decades, thereby simultaneously renouncing all rights in the community life of Castalia. By returning his seals, announcing his secession from the Order and going out into the world he might be doing something which had been unheard of in the memory of the institution, something unwonted, terrifying and perhaps very unseemly, but he would not be acting in contravention to the written rules of the Order. The fact that he had not taken this incomprehensible but in no way illegal step behind the Magister's back, and the fact that he had stopped to discuss it face to face with him was more than he was in duty bound to do; but how had this worthy man, one of the pillars of the hierarchy, come to such a pass? How could he have taken into account the written laws to justify his behaviour, which amounted after all to desertion, when a hundred unwritten but no less sacred and obvious laws must forbid such a step?

He heard the clock strike one. Tearing himself away from these fruitless thoughts, he took a bath and practised his deep breathing exercises for ten minutes before retiring to sleep, so as to garner a little strength and peace within himself and to avoid thinking any further about the matter until the following morning.

The next day a young famulus from the guest house conducted Magister Knecht to the Head of the Order and was able to witness their greeting. It struck the youth, who was accustomed to seeing the Masters of meditation and self-discipline at close quarters, that there was in the outward appearance, behaviour and greeting of these two notable

Magisters something novel and altogether peculiar, an unusual and very pronounced degree of poise and suavity. It was, so he told us later, not quite the customary greeting between two of the highest dignitaries, which took the form either of a serene and slightly exaggerated ceremonial or of a pompous festive act entailing on occasions a certain competition in courtesy, submission and exaggerated humility. In this case it might have been a foreigner or a great Yoga adept from a far-off land who had come to pay his respects to the Head of the Order and to measure swords with him. Words and gestures had been modest and very sparing, the looks and faces of both men had been calm, and serene, but behind their equanimity there had been a secret tension as though both had been somehow illumined or laden with an electric charge. Our witness did not of course see any more of the interview for the Magisters vanished into an inner room, probably Alexander's private study, where they would be undisturbed. All that we know of this conversation has reached us through the numerous anecdotes recorded by the delegate Plinio, to whom Knecht must have confided certain details.

"You surprised me yesterday," Alexander began, "and nearly made me lose countenance. Since then I have had a little time to think things over. My standpoint has naturally not altered, for after all I am a member of the Pedagogy and Head of the Order. You are perfectly within your rights according to the letter of the Order rules to announce your secession and to lay down your office. You have pleaded that your vocation has become burdensome and that you now find it necessary to attempt a life outside the Order; but if I were to propose to you that you should consider this essay not in the light of your violent decisions but somewhat as a prolonged or indeterminate vacation, would that fit in at all with your petition?"

"Not quite," replied Knecht. "Had my petition been granted, I should have remained in the Order but not in office. What you now so generously propose would be no more than an expedient, and furthermore, Waldzell would be indifferently served by a Magister Ludi who was absent on vacation for an unspecified period and of whose eventual return no one could be sure. Even if he did return after a year or two, as regards his office, his efficiency and the Bead

Game, he would only have forgotten all that he had known and would have learned nothing new."

"On the other hand he might have learned a great deal," put in Alexander. "He might, for instance, have discovered that the outside world is quite different from what he had imagined it to be, that he liked it as little as his own and that he would be only too glad to return to the old and trusted one and remain there."

"Your generosity is very far-reaching, and I am truly grateful to you, but unfortunately I cannot take advantage of it. What I am in search of is not so much the gratification of a curiosity or a passion for worldly life, but something far less conditional. I do not wish to go out into the world with an insurance policy in my pocket guaranteeing my return in the event of a disappointment, like some cautious traveller who would be content with a brief glimpse of the world. On the contrary, I desire that there should be hazards, difficulties and dangers to face; I am hungry for reality, for tasks and deeds, and also for privation and suffering. I beg of you not to persist in your kind proposals or attempt to make me vacillate or lure me back. It will lead nowhere, I assure you. My petition would lose its value and consecration if it were to bring me the belated permission that I no longer need. I have not remained idle since I sent in that petition; the path which I have chosen is now all I have—my law, my country and my service."

Alexander ceded the point with a sigh. "Let us accept," he said patiently, "that you cannot be swayed and that you cannot be made to change your mind, that, contrary to all appearances, you are simply a drunkard who has run amok, a berserker who no longer recognises any authority, reason or good counsel and with whom one must not interfere. I will therefore give up all attempts for the time being at influencing you in your decision; but will you kindly tell me what you have come here to tell me. Will you, for our enlightenment, lay bare the whole story of your downfall and enlarge upon the actions and resolutions with which you are terrifying us! Whether it be in the nature of a confession, a justification or a complaint, I will hear it out!"

Knecht nodded. "The berserker thanks you and will be only too pleased to grant your request. I have hardly any complaints to make, but what I have to say—if only it were not so incredibly difficult to put into words—is for me more like a justification than anything else, although it may sound like a confession to you."

He leaned back in his chair and looked up at the domed ceiling where the pale remains of earlier paintings from Hirsland monastery times were to be seen—dreamy faint patterns of hues and colours, flowers and decorative motifs.

"The idea that one can become satiated with and have to relinquish a magistracy first came to me a few months after my appointment as Magister Ludi. I was sitting in my garden one day perusing a little diary written by my famous predecessor, Ludwig Wassermaler, in which he reviewed his office from month to month and gave advice and directions to his successors. I read his warning that one ought to begin to think of the Public Games for the following year well in advance and, in the event of one's not feeling inclined to do so or if one lacked ideas, to stimulate oneself through concentration. As I was then, so to speak, revelling in the prime of my new office I could not help smiling a little, in my youthful cleverness, at the old man's anxieties, but his words nevertheless had a serious and somewhat disturbing ring, as though warning me of some danger. Were the day to come when the thought of the next Annual Game should inspire me with care instead of joy, fear instead of pride, I resolved there and then that I would hand back my insignia of office to the Pedagogy and leave instead of tormenting myself with worries about the future festivals. This was the first time that I had occupied myself with such thoughts, and in any case I could hardly believe in all seriousness at that time—don't forget I had just weathered the first difficult period of my office and was in full sail—that I could grow old and tired of my work and life, that I could one day approach the task of conjuring new Bead Games out of my hat with embarrassment and with sullenness. But be that as it may, the resolution came to me then—and you knew me very well then, Domine, better perhaps than I knew myself, for you were my father confessor and adviser and you had only just left me and returned to Hirsland."

Alexander looked at him quizzically. "And I have hardly ever had a finer task,.' he said. "I was content with both you and myself to a degree that very seldom happens with me. If it is just that one should have to pay for all the pleasures one has had in life, then I suppose that I am now atoning for my exaltation of that period. I was really proud of you then, but I cannot say the same to-day. If the Order experiences a disappointment through your actions, or if Castalia receives a shock I know that I am partially to blame. It may well have been advisable, when I was your companion and counsellor, had I remained a few weeks longer in your Game settlement, or had I treated you more harshly and controlled you more rigidly."

Knecht returned his gaze serenely. "You need have no qualms, Domine, on that score, or else I shall have to remind you of the many warnings that you gave me when, having only just assumed Magistracy, I was wont to take my duties and responsibilities too seriously. I recollect quite well that you said to me on one such occasion that even if as Magister Ludi I were to become an evil genius or an incompetent, even if I did everything that a Magister ought not to do and, with the great powers at my disposal, made a point of causing as much damage as possible, it would affect or disturb our beloved Castalia no more than if I had thrown a stone into a lake—a few wavelets, a few ripples, and it would be gone—so steadfast and sure was our Castalian foundation and so untouchable its spirit. Do you remember? No, it is certain that as regards my attempts to be a bad Castalian and to cause the Order as much damage as possible you are entirely innocent— and you know full well that I could never succeed in seriously disturbing your peace. However, I will continue with my story. The fact that I could already make that decision and not forget it at the outset of my Magistracy is bound up with a kind of spiritual experience which I have undergone from time to time and which I call an 'awakening'—but you already know of that because I used to tell you of it when you were my mentor and Guru, and I even complained to you, if you remember, that I had been spared this particular experience upon taking up my new post and that it seemed to be fading more and more into the past."

"I remember quite well," said Alexander. "I was very impressed by your propensity for this type of experience, which is rarely found among us and which manifests itself in such a variety of forms in the active world—in geniuses, statesmen and army commanders, but also in weak, semi-pathological and men of lesser talent, men such as clairvoyants, telepathists and mediums. You seemed to me to have nothing in common with these two types of men—the warrior heroes or the clairvoyants and water diviners. Until yesterday you appeared to be far more the perfect Order brother—lucid, clear thinking and obedient—the visitation or domination by secret voices, either divine or demonic, did not seem to suit you at all. Therefore I looked upon this condition of awakening, as you described it to me, as a coincidental realization of personal development. It was therefore, to my way of thinking, quite natural that these spiritual experiences had not recurred. You had assumed an office and a task which fitted you like a cloak and you had simply grown into it. But tell me—have you ever looked upon these awakenings as something in the nature of a revelation from the higher powers, an intelligence or a summons from the realms of an objective, eternal or divine truth?"

"On that point," replied Knecht, "we stumble against a momentary difficulty in my present task—I mean, as to how one may express in words things that are beyond the bounds of speech, to present rationally what is supra-rational. No, I have never thought of these awakenings as manifestations of a God or a demon or even of an absolute truth. What gives them weight and credibility is not their contact with truth, their high origin, their divinity or anything in that nature, but their reality. They are monstrously real in their presence and inescapability, like some violent bodily pain or surprising natural phenomenon, such as a storm or an earthquake which seem loaded with quite another element of reality than those prevailing in normal times and under normal conditions. The rush of wind that precedes the oncoming thunderstorm, which drives us at all speed into the house and tries to wrench the door from our hands, or a violent toothache, which seems to concentrate all the tension, pain and conflict of the world in our jaw—these are things, the reality and significance of which we may begin to analyse later, if we feel inclined for such levity, but at the actual moment of the event they allow of no doubt and are pregnant with reality. My 'awakenings' had a similar form of intensified reality, and from this very fact they received their name. It would

actually seem as though I had been dormant for a long time
or in some sort of trance, and that suddenly I was wide awake
and more clear headed and sensitive than at any other time.
In world history moments of great anguish or upheaval also
have their convincing necessity. They kindle a feeling of
oppressive actuality and tension, and as a result of the
upheaval beauty and illumination may ensue, or on the
contrary something insane and altogether sinister. In any
case whatever happens will bear the semblance of greatness
necessity and importance, and will differ and stand out from
daily occurrences.

"But let me approach the question from another angle," he
went on, after a pause to recover his breath. "Do you remember the legend of St. Christopher? As you know, he was a man
of great strength and courage, but one who did not wish
either to be a master or a ruler: he wished only to serve.
Service was his *forte* and his art, and in this rôle he realised
himself. Yet it was by no means a matter of indifference to
him whom he served: his master had to be the greatest and
most powerful ruler, and whenever he heard of one who was
mightier than his own he would offer his services to him. This
great servant has always appealed to me, and I think that I
must resemble him a little. At least, during the only time of
my life when I was a free agent—in my post graduate years—
I also searched and vacillated as to which ruler I would serve,
and I held myself in check with scepticism and mistrust for
many years against the Bead Game, which I had long since
recognised as the costliest and most singular product of our
Province. I had nibbled at the bait and knew that nothing on
earth was more intriguing or more different, but I had noticed
quite early on that this enchanting and by no means ingenuous
parlour game demanded not merely an amateurish interest
but total and complete service. And so, before devoting all my
strength and interest permanently to this magic, I defended
myself. An instinct, a naïve sentiment for the simple, the
whole and the healthy, warned me against the spirit of the
Waldzell Vicus Lusorum as being a specialist and virtuoso
spirit, highly cultivated and richly elaborated admittedly, but
one which was severed from the whole of life and humanity
and which had become an arrogant solipsism. For years I
hesitated, throwing out feelers, checking and double-

checking everything until the time was ripe for my decisions, and in spite of all this I decided in favour of the Bead Game. I did it because that urge within me told me to seek out the acme of fulfilment and only to serve the greatest master."

"I understand," said the Magister Alexander. "But as I see it, and however you may explain it, I still run up against the same basic reason for all your idiosyncrasies. You have had too much feeling for your own person, or have been too dependent upon it, which is not the same thing as being a great personality. One can be a star of the first magnitude in talent, will-power and endurance, and be so well-poised that one revolves in the system to which one belongs with the minimum of friction and waste of energy, while another whose axis is out of alignment with the centre, wastes half his energy in eccentric movements which leave him so much the weaker and his surroundings all distorted. You must belong to the latter type, but I must say that you have been able to conceal the fact surprisingly well. So much the graver, however, does the evil appear now that it comes to light. You call to mind the analogy of Saint Christopher and I must admit that, although this figure has something magnificent and moving about it, it is hardly representative of the true servant of our Hierarchy. Whoever wishes to serve should devote himself only to the master to whom he has sworn fealty, in good times or bad, and not with the secret proviso that he can change masters as soon as he finds a more illustrious one. In the latter case he becomes a judge of his master, and this is exactly what you are doing. You wish only to serve the highest master, whom you yourself decide to choose, and you are really only loyal to his rank."

Knecht had been listening attentively and a shadow of despondency had crossed his face. "To be honest," he said, "I could have expected no other judgment. But have patience with me for a while. I became a bead-player there-fore, and for a long time was convinced that I was serving the highest master. My friend Designori, our patron in the League Commission, once painted a very true portrait of me as an arrogant, superior, blasé virtuoso and élite unicorn, as indeed I used to be. But I have yet to tell you what the word 'transcendence' has meant to me since my student days and my first awakening. I imagine that it came to me after reading one of the philosophers of the Age of Reason at a time when I was very much under the influence of Master Thomas of Trave, and it has ever since signified something truly magical, like the word 'awakening'—something encouraging and compelling, consoling and full of promise. My life, as I saw it, was to be a transcendence, a progress from step to step, a series of realms to be traversed and left behind one after another, just as a piece of music perfects, completes and leaves behind theme after theme, tempo after tempo, never tired, never sleeping, always aware and always perfect in the present. I had noticed that, coincidental with the experience of awakening, there actually were such steps and realms, and that each time a life stage was coming to an end it was fraught with decay and a desire for death before leading to a new realm, and awakening and to a new beginning. I am giving you this picture of 'transcendence' as another means whereby my life may become easier to understand. My decision in favour of the Bead Game was an important step, and was my first conscious submission to the hierarchy. I have also been aware of such stages during my term as Magister Ludi. The best that this office brought me was the discovery that teaching and education, besides music and the Bead Game, were joy-inspiring activities, and gradually I discovered further that education could be increasingly pleasurable the younger and more unformed the pupils were. This and other factors led me to crave for younger and younger pupils, until finally I should have liked most of all to be a teacher in an elementary school. In short, my imagination began at times to focus itself upon things that lay outside my office."

There was a short silence, after which the Head of the Order remarked: "You surprise me more and more, Magister. You talk to me about your life, and you hardly reveal anything except private, subjective experiences, personal desires, personal developments and decisions! I really did not know that a Castalian of your rank could regard himself and his life in such a manner!"

Knecht was wounded by the note of reproach and regret in his voice, but he controlled himself and replied gaily: "But, your Reverence, we are not at the moment discussing Castalia, the Pedagogy and the hierarchy but myself alone, the psychology of a man who has unfortunately been obliged to cause you great inconvenience. It is not for me to speak of my official administration, the fulfilment of my duties, my value or shortcomings as a Castalian or as a Magister. My administration of office, together with the whole external side of my life stands open to your later investigation and I do not think that you will find much room for complaint. The question under review is quite a different one. It is to make quite clear to you the path which I have taken as an individual, which has already led me out of Waldzell and will to-morrow lead me out of Castalia. Be so indulgent as to hear me a little further.

"The fact that I know a little about the world outside our Province I have not my studies—in which it only appeared as a far distant peak—to thank, but first and foremost my fellow scholar Designori, who was a guest from out there, and later my stay with the Benedictine monks and Father Jacobus. I had indeed seen very little of the world with my own eyes, but through Father Jacobus I began to gain some insight into what one calls history, and this may well account for the feeling of isolation I experienced on my return to Castalia. It seemed as though I were entering a land almost without a history, a province of scholars and bead-players, a highly cultured and highly agreeable society but one in which my curiosity about the world, and my compassion for it seemed to be unique. There was however enough there to make up for this: a few men whom I revered, and with whom it would be a pleasure and an honour to collaborate, a host of well-educated and extremely cultured people and also work enough and many truly talented and amiable students. The trouble was that I had discovered during the course of my instruction with Father Jacobus that I was not only a Castalian but also a man and that the whole world affected me and made demands upon me as a fellow human being. Out of this discovery were born needs, desires, demands, which I knew I ought by no means entertain. The life of the world as the Castalian saw it was something antiquated and inferior, a life of disorder and coarseness, of passions and vagaries in which there was nothing beautiful or desirable, but in actuality it was far greater and richer than any description that I could possibly give as a Castalian. It was pregnant with future, history, efforts and eternal new beginnings; it was perhaps chaotic, but it was the homeland and the mother soil of all destinies, all revolts, all arts, all humanity; it had languages, peoples, states, cultures and had also engendered us Castalians, would see us all die and still go on. My teacher Jacobus had awakened in me a love for this world, which waxed continually and sought for nourishment but there was nothing in Castalia that it could feed upon for here one was outside the world and was oneself a little perfect, static, sterile world."

He took a deep breath and fell silent for a while. As Alexander did not reply but only looked expectantly at him, he nodded and continued: "I now had two burdens which I knew I should have to bear for many years. I had an important office to administrate, with all its attendant responsibilities, and I had to make an end of my love for the world. My office had not to suffer as a result of this love, and this was clear to me from the start, but were I—a thing which I hoped would not occur—to carry out my work less perfectly and efficiently than was to be expected of a Magister, I still knew that I was more aware and alive in heart than many of my impeccable colleagues, and that I still had a great deal to impart to my pupils and fellow workers. I saw that my task lay in slowly and gently broadening and vivifying Castalian life and thought without causing any break with tradition, to bring new blood into it from the world and from history. It was a gratifying coincidence that a man from the outside world had simultaneously thought and felt as I did, had dreamed of a friendship and an amalgamation of Castalia and the world. This man was Plinio Designori."

Master Alexander's lips curled slightly as he replied: "I never expected anything very pleasant to accrue from that man's influence upon you, any more than I did from your mischievous protégé Tegularius. So it is Designori who has brought you to break completely with our organisation?"

"No, Domine, but he has unwittingly helped me in this to a certain extent. He brought a little fresh air into my tranquillity, and through him I came into contact once more with the outside world. Thus it was possible for me to realise and become quite convinced that I was at the end of my present career, that all pleasure in my work had vanished and that it was time to put an end to the torment. Another step had been left behind me; I had traversed a sphere, and this time the sphere was Castalia."

"The way you express yourself!" Alexander remarked with a shake of the head. "As though the sphere of Castalia were not large enough to occupy you worthily your whole life through! Do you really seriously believe that you have exhausted and outgrown this sphere?"

"By no means," replied Knecht excitedly. "I have never once believed any such thing. When I say that I have arrived at the frontier of this sphere I only mean that what I, as an individual, can achieve in my post here has already been accomplished. I have been for some time past on this frontier where my work as Magister Ludi has only been an endless repetition, an empty exercise and a meaningless formula which I have carried out without pleasure and without enthusiasm, at times even without faith. It was high time to make an end of it."

Alexander sighed. "That is your conception, but it is not the interpretation of the Order and its rules. The fact that a brother can have moods and that he can grow weary of his work is neither new nor remarkable. The rules show him the way in which he can orientate himself and regain his harmony under such circumstances. Had you forgotten that?"

"I do not think so, Reverence. You are free to examine the details of my administration, and I am aware that recently, after you had received my circular letter, you sent someone to investigate the Game Town and to watch my activities. You were then able to maintain that the work was being carried out efficiently, that the chancellery and the archives were in order and that the Magister Ludi was neither ill nor obviously moody. I have even those very rules, into which you once initiated me in so masterly a fashion, to thank for the fact that I have been able to hold out without losing either my strength or my composure; but it has cost me a great effort, and now unfortunately costs me hardly less effort to convince you that I am allowing myself to be driven neither by moods, passions nor by caprices. Whether I succeed in this or not, I at least insist that you should recognise that up to this moment my person and my capacities, which you have controlled for the last time, have been of integrity and of use. Would this be too much to expect?"

Master Alexander's eyes twinkled a little ironically.

"My worthy colleague," he said, "you are talking to me as though we were two private people indulging in an unofficial conversation, but this holds good only on your side. You are now virtually a private person, while I am still the Head of the Order: all that I think and say is done on behalf of the Pedagogy, to whom I am responsible for every word. Whatever you say here to-day will be without consequences, and however seriously you may take your words they still remain those of a private individual speaking in his own interests; but in my case my office and responsibility continue, and certain consequences can ensue according to what I say or do. I am representing you and your affairs before the Pedagogy, and therefore as to whether they accept your explanation of events or even recognise it is not a matter of indifference to me. You have portrayed yourself to me as an exemplary Castalian and Magister, although you have been harbouring all manner of thoughts which seem to give it the lie, and have admitted to temptations and attacks of weariness which, apparently, you have fought and subdued in the approved manner. Even if I grant you this much, how am I to interpret the monstrous occurrence of a sudden desertion on the part of a blameless, integrated Magister who, until yesterday, had complied with all the rules. It seems more reasonable to suppose that your disposition had suddenly taken a change for the worse, that you had been ailing for a long time and had been taking yourself for a good Castalian, which you were not. I must also ask myself why you lay so much store by your having been a loyal Magister up to the last moment. Once you had so much as taken the first step, been disobedient and started on the way of desertion, this description could no longer apply to you."

Knecht defended himself. "Pardon me, Excellence, and why should not this description apply? My vocation, my good name and the memory that I leave behind me are at stake, and there is also the question of my being of some use to Castalia outside in the world. I am not here to salvage anything for myself or to win the approval of the Pedagogy as regards my project. I had reckoned with the fact that I would henceforth be regarded by my colleagues with despair as an enigmatical phenomenon, and was resigned to this fact, but I will *not* be regarded as a traitor or as a madman. That is a judgment that I find quite unacceptable. I have done something of which you cannot but disapprove, but I have taken this course because I felt called to do so, because I am fulfilling a mission in which I believe and which I accept with good grace. If you cannot grant me this, then I have suffered a defeat and have spoken to you in vain."

"It always reverts to the same question," replied Alexander: "I am supposed to grant that under certain circumstances the individuals may break certain laws in which I believe and which I am here to represent; but I cannot at once believe in our Order and in your right to contravene its laws—no please do not interrupt me. I can concede that, according to appearances, you are convinced of the rectitude and intelligence of your fatal step and that you believe in a call that justifies your behaviour, but that I should approve of the step itself you could not possibly have expected. On the other hand you have succeeded in one thing— in making me abandon my original intention of trying to win you back and making you change your mind. I accept your secession from the Order and will notify the authorities of your voluntary abdication. Further than that I cannot accommodate you, Joseph Knecht."

The Magister Ludi bowed, to show his submission.

"I thank you, Sir," he said quietly. "I have already handed you the casket. I now also submit to you a few memoranda upon the condition of things in Waldzell, and mainly upon the state of the Tutorship and those few candidates who, in my opinion, may be considered as possible choices for succession to my office."

He took a few sheets of folded paper out of his pocket and laid them on the table. Then he stood up, and the Master followed suit. Knecht approached him, looked him long and sorrowfully in the eyes and bowed. "I should have liked you to shake my hand before leaving, but I suppose I must now forego this too. You have always been very dear to me, and the events to to-day have made not the least difference to my feelings. Live well, my dear and much admired friend!"

Alexander stood still. He was very pale and for a moment it seemed as though he would give way and stretch his hand out to Knecht. He felt that his eyes were moist, but he lowered his head, returned the bow and allowed him to depart.

After Knecht had closed the door, Alexander stood motionless listening to his receding footsteps. When he could no longer hear them and the last echo had died away he began to pace up and down the room, until footsteps were once again to be heard outside and there was a faint knock at the door. The young servant entered and announced that a visitor wished to speak to him.

"Tell him that I can receive him in an hour's time, and that I must beg him to be brief, as I have many urgent affairs to attend to. No—wait a minute! Go to the chancellery and inform the First Secretary that he must convene the entire Pedagogy for the day after to-morrow. He must notify every single member that only serious illness will be accepted as an excuse for non-attendance. Then go to the Master of the household and tell him that I have to go to Waldzell to-morrow and that he must have the conveyance ready for seven o'clock. . . ."

"Excuse me," put in the youth, "but the vehicle of His Excellence the Magister Ludi is available.

"How is that?"

"Magister Knecht arrived in it yesterday, but he has just left informing us that he will be continuing on foot and that he has no more need of it—that it is now at the disposal of the authorities."

"Good. I will take his conveyance to Waldzell to-morrow, then. Repeat my instructions, please!"

The servant did as he was bid: "The visitor will be received in one hour's time and should be as brief as possible. The First Secretary is to convene a meeting of the entire Pedagogy for the day after to-morrow. Full attendance is imperative, and only serious illness will be acceptable as an excuse. To-morrow morning at seven o'clock Your Excellency will take the Magister Ludi's vehicle to Waldzell."

Master Alexander relaxed once the famulus had left the room. He went over to the table where he had sat with Knecht, and for some reason the footsteps still rang in his ears, the footsteps of a man whom he had loved above all others and who had just caused him so much sorrow. He had cherished this man ever since he had first assisted him many years before and among his many singularities he had liked most his walk, an assured and rhythmic, light almost swaying step, half sedate and half childish, like a priest's or a dancer's, a peculiar, amiable and aristocratic step which had so suited his appearance and especially his voice. It had matched equally well his own particular brand of Castaliahood and magistracy, of lordship and serenity, which at times had reminded him of Magister Thomas and at times too of the winning and simple old Music Master. Now he had departed, in haste and on foot, no one knew where. Presumably he would never see him again during his lifetime, nor hear his laugh again nor see his beautiful tapering fingers writing down the hieroglyphics of a Bead Game phrase. He snatched up the pages that were lying on the table and began to read them. It was a brief testament, very concise and professional containing often only catchwords instead of sentences, but he saw at once that it would be of great service to the Pedagogy in their forthcoming revision of the Vicus Lusorum and in their choice of a new Magister Ludi. The shrewd comments, written in small elegant letters, stared up at him from the white paper—words and handwriting that were just as representative of the once steadfast character of this Joseph Knecht as his face, voice and gait. The authorities would be hard put to discover a man of his merit as a successor, for true masters and personalities were just as rare, and each such figure was just as much a jewel here in Castalia and the élite Province as in the world outside.

Knecht enjoyed his walk, for he had not travelled on foot for many years. The last journey that he had made on foot, he reflected, was on the occasion of his return to Waldzell for the Annual Game that year when everyone had been so gravely handicapped by the death of his predecessor, the worthy Magister Thomas of Trave. Previously, whenever he had recalled those days, his student years and his idyll at Bamboo Grove, it had always been as though he were looking out from an austere, cool room into a wide joyous and sunny neighbourhood, into the never-to-be-revived, into a Paradise of the memory. These thoughts had always, even when unaccompanied by melancholy, been a view of the far distant past, of a yesterday which had been mysteriously festive and unlike to-day or every other day. But now, on this fine clear September afternoon with its brilliant colours in the foreground and its gentle, delicate and dreamy tones blending from blue into violet towards the horizon, wandering at ease and indulging in idle observation, that pilgrimage which had been made so long ago appeared not like a distant paradise viewed from a resigned to-day but seemed actually to be the present day journey undertaken by the former Joseph Knecht, because to-day he resembled so much his brother of that time. It was all perfectly new again, mysterious and of great promise; everything that had once been could be revived, and much that was new besides. It seemed ages since the day and the world had looked so beautiful, innocent and undismayed. The joy of freedom and independence flowed through his veins like a strong potion, and he recalled how long it was since he had felt this precious sensation, this lovely and enchanting illusion! He remembered also the occasion on which it had been crushed and led into chains during a conversation with the Magister Thomas, and relived the forebodings of that hour, under the latter's ironical but friendly gaze, in which he had lost his freedom: it had not been exactly a pain or a sharp sorrow but more a fear, a slight shivering in the spine, a warning feeling in the pit of the stomach, a change in temperature and in particular in the tempo of the life stream. The sensation of that fatal hour, so fearful, contracting and warning, almost like that of a drowning man, was compensated for and cured by to-day.

The previous day, on his journey to Hirsland, Knecht had decided that whatever might happen there he would not regret it. For to-day he forbade himself to think of the details of his talk with Alexander and of his duel with him, of the struggle he had undergone on his account. He gave himself up completely to the feeling of relaxation and freedom which flowed through him like the holiday feeling that assails the peasant after a hard day's work. He knew himself to be secure and answerable to none, knew for a perfect moment that he was dispensable and excluded, in duty bound to no work, no thought and no responsibilities. The bright coloured day

embraced him with its gentle radiance, a complete picture and
completely in the present without demands, without yesterday and without to-morrow. At times he broke into a
marching song out of sheer exuberance—a song which, long
ago as a small élite scholar in Eschholz, he had sung with
three or four other accompanying voices, and the memories
and notes flew back to him like the twitter of birds from the
serene early morning of his life.

He came to a halt under a cherry tree, whose foliage was
already turning an autumnal purple, and sat down on the
grass to rest. From the breast pocket of his tunic he brought
out an object which Magister Alexander would hardly have
expected to find in his possession—a small wooden flute—
which he examined with a certain tenderness. He had not long
been in possession of this ingenuous and childlike instrument,
a bare six months perhaps, and remembered with pleasure the
day he had acquired it. He had gone to Monteport to discuss
certain musical questions with Carlo Ferromonte, and during
the conversation the topic of certain woodwind instruments of
bygone ages had cropped up: he had asked his friend to show
him the Monteport collection of instruments. After an
enjoyable stroll through several halls filled with ancient
organ manuals, harps, lutes and clavichords, they had come
to a storeroom where the school instruments were kept, and
Knecht had noticed a whole shelf full of little flutes, had tried
one and asked his friend whether he could take it away with
him. Carlo had told him to choose one for himself, had
laughingly given him a receipt to sign and had then proceeded
to explain to him thoroughly the construction of the instrument, its fingering and the playing technique. Knecht had
taken this pretty toy away with him. Since the reed flutes of
his Eschholz days he had not played a wind instrument and
had often intended to learn one again. He now began to practise in his spare time. Once he had mastered the scales he made
use of a book of old melodies for beginners which Ferromonte
had given him, and the soft notes of the little flute could
frequently be heard coming from his garden or through the
windows of his bedroom. He was still far from being an
expert but he had learned to play a number of chorals and
songs, many of which he knew by heart. One of these songs
seemed especially to fit the present occasion, and came almost

automatically into his mind. He recited a few of the verses aloud to himself:

"My head and limbs lay deep
Beneath the sod,
But gay and carefree
Now I stand
And look t'ward heaven and God!"

Then he placed the instrument to his lips and played the melody, looked into the gentle gleaming distance, towards the far distant mountain peaks, heard the serene and pious song echo in the sweet notes of his flute and felt at one and contented with heaven, mountains, song and day. He felt the smooth round wood between his fingers and thought how, apart from the clothes that he was wearing, this little flute was the only object of property he had allowed himself to take away from Waldzell with him. During the course of the years he had collected much that was more or less his own personal property, particularly sketches, books of excerpts, etc. Now he had left all these behind. They could be used by members of the Game Town if necessary, but the one thing that belonged to him was the little flute and he was glad that he had it with him. It was a modest and consoling travelling companion.

On the second day the wanderer entered the capital and arrived at Plinio's house. His friend ran down the steps and embraced him affectionately.

"We have been waiting impatiently for you!" he cried, "and we were beginning to grow a little anxious. You have taken a serious step, my friend. May it turn out to be a fortunate one. But to think they allowed you to go! I would never have believed it!"

Knecht laughed.

"Well, here I am as you see—but I will tell you all about that in good time. Now I should like most of all to greet my new pupil—and of course your wife—and then I should like to discuss everything about my new duties with you. I am anxious to start as soon as possible."

Plinio called one of the maidservants and told her to fetch his son immediately.

"The young gentleman?" she asked, somewhat surprised, but went off right away while Plinio showed his friend to the guest room and began telling him eagerly everything that he had thought out and prepared for his arrival and his life with Tito. Everything had happened according to Knecht's wishes; his wife had also been agreeable and given her consent after a certain amount of resistance. They owned a summer house in the mountains called Belpunt with a fine position on the lake, and at first Knecht was to live there with his pupil. An old peasant maid would look after them. This was of course only a temporary dwelling, at most until the winter, but during these first days a certain remoteness of this nature was inevitable. He was also glad to say that Tito loved the mountains and Belpunt, so that he would be going there with pleasure and not with reluctance.

Designori suddenly remembered that he had an album of photographs of the house and the surrounding country. He led Knecht into his study, found the album and began to show him the pictures, describing in great detail the pleasant dining-room, the stove, the arbours, the bathing-place on the lake and the waterfall.

"Do you like it?" he asked eagerly. "Will you be able to feel at home there?"

"And why ever not?" asked Knecht calmly. "But where is Tito? It is some time now since you sent for him."

They went on talking for a while, and then footsteps were heard outside. The door opened and someone entered the room. It was neither Tito nor the maid who had been sent to find him, but Madame Designori herself. As Knecht rose to greet her she stretched out her hand and smiled with a somewhat constrained friendliness; he noticed that there was an expression of anxiety and irritation behind her smile. She had hardly uttered a few words of welcome before she turned to her husband and unburdened herself of the thought which was disturbing her.

"It is really lamentable," she said: "the boy has disappeared and is nowhere to be found."

"Oh, he has probably gone off somewhere," said Plinio, reassuring her. "He will soon return."

"I am afraid that is not very likely," she replied. "He has been missing all day—I noticed his absence quite early this morning."

"And why have I only just been told?"

"Because I naturally thought each hour that he would be returning and I did not want to disturb you unnecessarily. At first I did not think that there was anything amiss for I assumed that he had merely gone for a walk, but when he failed to turn up at mid-day I began to get a little worried. You were not at home for the mid-day meal, or I would have told you then. I also wanted to persuade myself that it was only thoughtlessness on his part in keeping me waiting so long, but this was apparently not the case."

"May I ask a question?" interrupted Knecht. "Had the young man been informed that I was coming, and was he aware of your plans concerning him and myself?"

"Of course, Magister, and he seemed to be almost pleased with the idea—or, should we say, he made it quite clear that he preferred to have you as a teacher than to be sent to some other school."

"Well, then," answered Knecht, "everything is in order. Your son, madam, has been accustomed to a great deal of freedom, particularly just recently, and therefore it is quite conceivable that the idea of a teacher and disciplinarian might be distasteful to him. He has apparently run away at the very moment when he was due to be handed over to his new tutor, perhaps less in the hope of really escaping his destiny than in the belief that he could be losing nothing by a short postponement, and presumably also he wanted to cock a snook at his parents and this schoolmaster whom they had ordered for him—in fact, to show his defiance of the whole world of grown-ups and teachers!"

Designori was pleased that Knecht had taken this event so lightly, although he could not prevent himself from feeling anxious and restless and from imagining all sorts of dangers that might have overtaken his son. Perhaps he has fled for good, he thought, or maybe he has done himself some injury. Everything that had appeared false and neglected in the education of this boy now seemed to be wreaking its vengeance upon the household, and just at the moment when one had hoped to make good all past mistakes.

He insisted, in spite of Knecht's advice, that all was not well and that steps ought to be taken at once. He felt incapable of restraining his impatience and waiting passively for the boy to return, and gave way to a nervous irritability which his friend found displeasing. It was therefore decided that word should be sent to several houses where Tito sometimes visited comrades of his own age and Knecht was pleased when Madame Designori left to see to this, for he then had his friend to himself once more.

"Plinio," he said at once, "you are making a face as though they had brought your son home dead on a stretcher. He is no longer an infant and he will not have fallen under a car or eaten deadly nightshade, so pull yourself together, my dear friend! As your son is not here I must put you in his place for a moment, and take you to task. I have been watching you and I find that you are not at all in good trim.

"When an athlete suffers an unexpected shock to his system, his muscles automatically react in the necessary way, expanding or contracting, and help him to become master of the situation. So. Plinio, when you receive a shock like this, or what you exaggeratedly regard as a shock, you ought to use the first defence measure against a spiritual attack and think immediately of controlling it by carefully regulated breathing. Instead of this you begin to breathe like an actor who is trying to portray dismay. You are not well enough armed, you people of the world: you seem to be vulnerable to suffering and cares in a special way. There is something helpless and pitiful, and also something magnificent, about it when it is a case of true suffering or martyrdom, but for everyday events this renunciation of defence is no weapon at all. I will see to it that your son is far better armed for such occasions. And now, my friend, be so kind as to do a few exercises with me, so that I may see whether you really have forgotten them all."

With the breathing exercises, which he directed with strong rhythmic commands, he was able to lead his friend away from his self-torment, found him willing to listen to reason and to build up a certain resistance to his fears and cares. Later they climbed up to Tito's room, and Knecht noticed with pleasure the disorder of all the boyish paraphernalia. He took a book from the little bedside table from which he noticed a sheet of paper protruding, and saw at once that it was a message from the truant. He handed the sheet of paper to Designori with a laugh. The latter's face now became quite reassured again.

In the note Tito informed his parents that he had left early in the morning and was going up to the mountains alone. He would wait for his new tutor at Belpunt. He could at least be granted this little pleasure in view of the fact that his freedom was to be curtailed once more so tediously. He had had an overwhelming distaste for undertaking that little journey in company with the tutor, of making it, so to speak, as a prisoner and already under observation.

"Very understandable," said Knecht. "I shall follow him there to-morrow, and I am sure that I shall easily be able to find your country house—but now go and tell your wife of our discovery!"

For the rest of the day the mood in the house was serene and agreeable. That evening Knecht, at Plinio's insistence, told him briefly of the events of the last few days and of his two conversations with Master Alexander, and that evening, also, he scribbled on a slip of paper that curious verse which Designori still possesses to-day. It bears some relationship with the following incident.

The master of the house had left Knecht alone for an hour before the evening meal and the latter had seen a case full of old books which had aroused his curiosity, for this was a pleasure that he had forgotten during his many years of continence and it now reminded him of his student years. Oh, simply to stand before a row of unknown books, to take out a volume here and there at will, the title or the author of which attracted one, and to size up the gilt lettering, the format or the colour of the leather binding! He cast his eye with delight along the titles on the shelves, and found that they contained the best literature of the nineteenth and twentieth centuries. At last he took out a faded linen-bound volume bearing a title which intrigued him, "The Wisdom of the Brahmans." At first, while standing there, he dipped into it and then, becoming more and more engrossed, he drew up a chair and sat down. This remarkable and moving book, with its many hundred pages of didactic poetry—a curious jumble of scholarly verbiage and real wisdom, of narrow-mindedness and true poetic genius—seemed to him to be by no means lacking in esotericism, but he found that it was hidden in coarse homely wrappings and that the poems which strove after doctrine and wisdom were far less beautiful than those in which the poet's mood, his robust yeoman character and his inheritance of love, probity and humanity found expression.

As he delved more deeply into the mind of this poet with a mixture of respect and amusement, he came across a verse which he absorbed with satisfaction and agreement and he could not help nodding his head with a smile for it seemed so particularly appropriate to the day. It read as follows:

"Our good days fade, and yet we do not grieve
If something dearer in their place they leave:
Within our garden some rare blossom white,
A child we teach, a booklet that we write."

He opened a drawer of the writing table, found a sheet of notepaper and copied down the verse. Later in the evening he showed it to Plinio.

"I like these verses," he said. "There is something original about them—so dry and at the same time so poignant —and they suit my present position and mood admirably. Even though I am no gardener whose life is devoted to tending rare blooms, I am nevertheless a teacher on the way to my task, to the child whom I will educate. How I am looking forward to that! As regards the author of these verses, the poet Ruckert, he presumably possessed all three of these noble passions—that of the gardener, the educator and the author. The last of these must have taken precedence over the other two as he shows in the first and most significant stanza, for he is so enamoured of his subject that in his delicacy he does not call it a 'book' but a 'booklet.' How enchanting that is!"

Plinio smiled. "Who knows," he said, "whether the diminutive was not only a necessity on the part of the rhymster because he needed a two-syllable word instead of a monosyllable."

"We must not underestimate him," said Knecht in defence of the poet. "A man who had written ten thousand couplets in his lifetime would not have allowed himself to be hampered by a wretched metrical exigency. No, listen to him for a while—how tenderly and slightly embarrassed he reads. Perhaps it is not out of love alone that he makes a booklet out of the book: perhaps it is also intended as an extenuating and conciliatory gesture. I cannot help feeling that this poet was so scrupulous an author that he may have looked upon his leaning towards writing as a kind of passion and blasphemy. In that case the word booklet was not meant in an amatory sense and tone but in an extenuating, diverting and apologetic sense, such as a player may use when invited not to a 'game' but to 'a little game,' or a drinker when asking not for a 'glass' but for 'a little glass' or 'a thimble full.' But these are only speculations. In any case I fully endorse the singer's attitude towards the booklet that he will write and the child he wishes to educate, for not only am I familiar with the passion for education but the desire to write a small book has for a long time also not been far from my thoughts, and now that I am free of my office this desire has assumed the proportions of a precious and alluring promise—to write a book in all good-humour and at my leisure, a pamphlet, an insignificant booklet for my friends and fellow thinkers."

"And upon what subject, may I ask?" put in Designori with curiosity.

"Oh, the subject would not matter so much. It would merely be an opportunity for me to weave my thoughts around some theme and to enjoy the good fortune of having a great deal of free time. The chief thing in my case would be the tone—a tone not of scholarship but a decorous mean between respect and intimacy, between gravity and playfulness, a friendly communication and utterance of sundry things that I believe I have experienced and learned. The manner in which this Friedrich Ruckert mixes the didactic with reflection and the communication of true knowledge with gossip in his verses would not be my style, and yet there is a certain amiability about his art, for without conscious intention it is personal, playful and yet based upon hard and fast rules of form, which pleases me. In the immediate future I cannot anticipate the joys and problems of writing my little book, for I have to prepare myself for other tasks, but I think that later I might allow myself the luxury of blossoming into authorship, as I see it, with a comfortable but careful presentation of things, not for my solitary pleasure but always bearing in mind a few good friends and readers."

On the following morning Knecht set out for Belpunt. Designori had told him the previous evening that he should have liked to accompany him but Knecht had refused point blank, and when the other had tried to put in a convincing word he had come near to reprimanding him.

"The boy," he said shortly, "will have enough to do in meeting and accommodating himself to a new teacher and we should not give him the additional burden of having his father present, which would hardly be a pleasure to him at a time like this."

During his journey through the fresh September morning in the car that Plinio had hired for him, the same joyous mood of travel he had felt on the previous day returned. He talked freely with the chauffeur, made him stop or drive slowly from time to time when he found the landscape attractive, and even played a tune or two on his little flute. It was a lovely and exciting journey from the capital across the foothills to the high mountains. They drove out of the fast vanishing summer deeper and deeper into the autumn, and about mid-day began the last great climb in broad sweeping curves through the sparse pine forests, skirting the foaming, leaping mountain torrents between the gorges, crossing bridges and leaving behind lonely, sturdily built farmhouses with tiny windows, into the stony, starker and ever more barren mountain world, where little flowery paradises seemed to bloom with redoubled charm in the severe, bleak atmosphere.

The small country house, which they reached at last, lay hidden among the grey rocks from which it was hardly distinguishable. At first sight the traveller was struck by its sternness and the sinister appearance of this type of architecture that fitted so well into the rugged surroundings, but a happy smile soon crossed his face when he caught sight of a figure standing in the doorway—a boy with a bright jacket and shorts, who could be none other than his pupil, Tito. Although he had not been unduly worried about him he breathed a sigh of relief and thankfulness: as long as Tito was here and greeting his teacher from the threshold of the house, everything was in order and many complications, the possibilities of which he had thought of more than once during his journey, would be avoided.

The boy came forward to greet him with a friendly smile and with a slight show of embarrassment. As he helped him from the car he said: "You must not take it amiss that I allowed you to make the journey alone," and before Knecht could reply, added confidentially: "I imagine you understand how it was intended otherwise you would have brought my father along, too. I have already let him know of my safe arrival."

Knecht took his hand with an answering smile and allowed himself to be led into the house, where he found the maid already busily preparing their evening meal. Now, for the first time he noticed how astonishingly tired he was after his beautiful drive and, giving way to a most unusual need, lay down on a sofa before the meal. He was quite exhausted in fact, and while he chatted with his pupil and was being shown the latter's collection of alpine plants and butterflies, this weariness increased and he felt a hitherto unknown emptiness and giddiness in his head, an oppressive weakness and an irregularity in his heart beats.

The boy wondered why the Magister mentioned no word about the start of lessons, curricula, previous reports and such-like things, and when he tried tentatively to exploit this good mood by proposing a long walk for the following morning, so as to show the tutor his new surroundings, his proposal was gladly accepted.

"I shall indeed look forward to it," Knecht answered, "and I should like to ask a favour of you at the same time. While I was looking at your plant collection it was quite obvious to me that you know far more about the subject than I do. One of the objects of our being together is that we should exchange our respective interests and make them similar. Let us begin, then, by your checking my botanical knowledge and helping me on in this subject."

By the time they came to say good-night Tito was very happy and had made one or two good resolutions. Once more this Magister Knecht had pleased him immensely. He was delighted at the thought that he had not used long words, had not spoken of knowledge, virtue, the aristocracy of the spirit and all the other things that his school professors had always drummed into him, and that this serene and friendly man had in his personality and speech alone something dutiful, which denoted nobility, goodness and a knightly striving after higher things. It could be fun and even profitable to outwit or deceive any schoolmaster, but who could dream of such a thing as regards this man. He was . . . what was he, in actual fact? Tito reflected long upon this—why he should be so pleased and impressed by this stranger—and found that it was his nobility, breeding and lordliness above all that attracted him. His new tutor was courteous, was a lord and a nobleman, although no one knew anything of his family and his father might quite conceivably have been a cobbler; he was far superior to and nobler than most of the men whom Tito knew, including his own father. This proud and fiery youth, who held the patrician instincts and traditions of his house in high esteem and who had not forgiven his father for renouncing them, had met here for the first time one of the intellectual, cultivated nobility, a protagonist of that power which under fortunate circumstances can work miracles and which, by leaping a long sequence of ancestors and generations, can convert a proletarian child into an aristocrat in the course of a single lifetime. He felt an exciting intuition that to belong to this type of nobility and to serve it could perhaps become a duty and an honour, that perhaps here, embodied in the figure of this teacher who in his gentleness and friendliness was a perfect aristocrat, was something that approximated to the essential meaning of his life and was destined to be his goal.

Knecht did not go to bed immediately upon being shown to his room, although he felt a great longing to do so. The evening had been extremely tiring for him, for he had felt the tiresome necessity to control his expression, his behaviour and the tone of his voice in front of this young man, who had without doubt taken a good view of him, in order to prevent him from seeing any signs of his growing weariness and indisposition.

At all events he seemed to have succeeded, but now he had to deal with and master this disquieting emptiness, this feeling of oppression, disagreeable giddiness and deathly weariness. As soon as he had come to recognise its origin he accomplished this without undue difficulty, although it took a considerable time: he found this ailment to have no other cause than the journey, which had brought him so suddenly from the plains to a height of some six thousand feet. Since early childhood he had been unused to staying at such heights, and apparently he had not been able to endure the swift change of pressure. He would probably have to suffer this for a day or two, and if he really could not hold out would have to return home with Tito and the housekeeper, and in that case Plinio's plans for his stay in beautiful Belpunt would have proved a failure. This would be a pity, but not an irreparable misfortune.

After these reflections he went to bed but slept little, alternately musing upon his journey since his departure from Waldzell and trying to calm his heartbeats and over-excited nerves. He also could not prevent his thoughts from turning ever and again, and not without a certain contentment to his pupil, but he did not make any plans. It seemed to him that he would be far better able to tame this noble and obstreperous colt with wise handling and goodwill than by trying to hurry or compel him in any way. He had to bring the youth by gradual stages to a realization of his gifts and powers, and at the same time nourish that excellent curiosity, that well-born discontent within him which gives a spur to the love of knowledge, the spirit and the beautiful. It was a fine task and, moreover, his pupil was not any casual young talent that had to be brought out and formed: he was the only son of an influential landed patrician and was a future master, destined to be a social and political figure for country and people, an example and a leader. Castalia still remained indebted to the old Designori family to a certain extent in that it had not educated the father of this Tito sufficiently well, had not stressed his difficult position between the world and the spirit strongly enough, and as a result not only had the amiable and talented young Plinio lived an unbalanced and badly orientated life but his son was still in danger, having been drawn into the paternal problems. This had to be remedied and made good. It was a debt which had to be paid, and it pleased him that this very task had fallen to his lot—to him, the disobedient Castalian and ostensible renegade.

On the following morning, as he heard sounds of life awakening in the house, he arose and, finding a bathing wrap ready at the bedside, put it on over his light sleeping attire and went out through the back door, as Tito had shown him the previous evening. He set out along the semi-enclosed pathway that led from the house to the bathing stage.

Before him lay the little grey-green tranquil lake, beyond which towered a steep high cliff, still completely in shadow.

Its sharp jagged crest cut sheer and cold into the misty, greenish early morning sky. The sun was coming up behind this crest and its light already winked here and there on a razor edge in tiny golden spangles. In a few minutes it would be in full view, and the lake and valley would be flooded with light. Knecht watched the scene attentively and gravely, for he found that this silence, gravity and beauty, to which he was so unaccustomed, possessed a strange admonitory import. He felt, even more acutely than yesterday, the height, the cold and undignified aloofness of this mountain world which made no compromise with man, which refused to invite him and in fact hardly tolerated him. It seemed indeed significant that his first step into the new-found freedom of the life of the world should have led him up to this austere and icy terrain.

Tito appeared in bathing trunks, took the Magister's hand and said as he looked up at the cliffs: "You have arrived at just the right moment: the sun will be rising at any minute now. Oh—isn't it absolutely marvellous up here?"

Knecht smiled at him and nodded. He had long been aware of the fact that Tito was an early riser, a runner, wrestler and walker and that, on these grounds and also as a protest against the slovenly and undisciplined behaviour of his father, he had despised all intoxicating drinks. These habits and leanings naturally led him to pose as an "open-air fiend" and to effect a contempt for the intellect. An inclination to exaggerate seemed to be a family failing, but in him Knecht found it welcome and was determined to make use of his sport, as a means of taming this ebullient youth and winning his comradeship. It was only one means, however, and not the most important for music would obviously have more far-reaching results; nor did he for one moment think that he would become the boy's equal in physical feats or wish to surpass him. A harmless participation would be sufficient to show him that his teacher was neither a coward nor a stay-at-home.

Tito looked eagerly across at the dark ridge, behind which the sky was bathed in morning light. Very soon a particle and then a whole section of the rugged backbone became ablaze like glowing molten metal, the ridge gradually lost its contours and suddenly seemed to lose height as, through a saddle, the flaming planet that rules the day swam into view. In next to no time the soil, house, bathing hut and the near side of the lake were illuminated and the two figures standing in the strong rays felt the agreeable warmth of this light. The boy, filled with the majestic beauty of the moment and exulting in his youthful strength, stretched his limbs with rhythmic motions, first his arms and then quickly followed by his whole body, building up into an enthusiastic dance to celebrate the dawn and to express his inner comprehension of the seething and radiant elements around him.

His steps flew for a full minute in joyous homage to the all-conquering sun and then, recoiling in awe before it and drawing mountains, water and sky to his heart with outstretched arms, he knelt down and seemed to pay homage to the earth-mother and the wisp of mountain lake, offering as a ceremonious sacrifice to the powers his youth, freedom and the life instinct that burned within him. The sunlight played on his brown shoulders, his eyes were half closed against the bright light and his young face stared like a mask in an expression of fervent, almost fanatical earnestness.

The Magister was also seized by the impressive, ceremonious spectacle of daybreak in this rocky mountain solitude, but what moved him more than all else was the human spectacle that was taking place before his eyes—the festive morning dance of his immature pupil to greet the sun. This impetuous youth, in a transport of almost religious awe, had revealed to the onlooker his deepest and most noble inclinations, talents and vocations in just as sudden, radiant and lucid a manner as had the sun lit up the cold, dark mountain lake.

The young man now appeared even stranger and more significant than he had previously imagined him to be, but also tougher, less approachable, spiritually more remote and more pagan. This ritual and sacrificial dance on the part of the uncontrolled enthusiast was far more vital than any of the speeches or poems of the young Plinio had been: it raised him many stages higher than his father, but seemed also to leave him harsher, less sensitive and open to the summons.

The boy himself was completely possessed by his enthusiasm without quite knowing what had happened to him. It was not a familiar dance that he practised daily, no

ritual sun or dawn dance that he had learned and, as he
discovered later, had no trace of magical obsession: it had
simply been inspired by the raw mountain air, the dawn, the
sun and an ecstatic feeling of freedom, but to no less a degree
by the approaching change in his life, by the new stage or
departure that had appeared to him through the friendly and
awe-inspiring figure of the Magister. So much that was
concentrated met in the destiny and soul of the young Tito
during this early morning hour that it was distinguished from
a thousand others as an exalted, festive and consecrated
occasion. Oblivious of what he was doing, quite spontaneously and without suspicion he carried out what the
hallowed moment demanded of him—danced his devotion,
prayed to the sun, made known through his gestures his joy,
his belief in life, his faith and reverence, proudly offering his
pious soul to the sun and the gods and no less to the admired
but feared sage and musician, the Magister of the magic
Game who had come from such mysterious realms, his future
teacher and friend.

All this, like the brilliant pageant of the sunrise, had lasted
only a few minutes, and Knecht had watched the wondrous
scene with amazement. His pupil had become transformed,
had revealed himself before his eyes and now appeared to him
new and alien and completely his peer. They were both still
on the footpath between the house and the hut, bathed in the
splendour from the east and deeply excited by the whirlwind
of events, but Tito, having only just completed the last steps
of his dance and having hardly awakened from his happy
bewilderment, stood like a wild beast surprised at its solitary
gambols, on the alert and realising that he was not alone,
realising that he had not only experienced and done something unusual but that he had also had an audience. Swift as
lightning he took the only way of escape open to him from
this position, which he suddenly saw as something dangerous
and shameful, and the only way he could possibly break
through the powerful magic spell of this ecstatic moment
which had so completely enthralled and overwhelmed him.

His ageless mask-like face took on a somewhat crazed
expression like that of a child too suddenly awakened from a
deep sleep. His knees were trembling slightly as he looked
his teacher with mute astonishment in the face as though he

had just remembered something very important that he had nearly forgotten. Stretching out his right arm and pointing to the further side of the lake, half the breadth of which still lay in deep shadow but which was gradually growing narrower beneath the sunlight as it stormed the cliffs, he cried with boyish eagerness: "If we swim quickly we can reach the other side before the sun!"

He had hardly uttered this challenge to the encroaching sun than with a mighty spring he dived head first into the lake and disappeared, as though out of arrogance or embarrassment he could not make off quickly enough and draw a veil over the ceremonious act in heightened activity. There was a splash and the water had closed over him, and some seconds later his head, shoulders and arms re-appeared and began receding into the distance, across the blue-green mirror of the water.

Knecht had had no intention of bathing when he came out, for he had decided that the water would be far too cold for him after his half sleepless night; but now, in this beautiful sunlight, excited by the recent spectacle and called upon by his pupil's comradely invitation, he found the hazard less terrifying. The one thing he feared above all was that the promise this morning hour had set in motion might be lost again for ever if he left the boy alone now and disappointed him by renouncing the test of strength with the cool reasoning power of the adult. His feeling of uncertainty and weakness nevertheless warned him that he had already overtaxed his strength with the too rapid mountain journey but he made up his mind that perhaps this ailment would be the more speedily cured by force and by making a bold attack. The summons was stronger than the warning, the willpower stronger than the instinct: he quickly slipped off his bathing wrap, took a deep breath and flung himself into the water in the same spot where Tito had disappeared.

The lake, fed from glacier waters and even in the hottest summer only suitable for hardened swimmers, received him with icy coldness and a cutting hostility. A mighty shudder ran through him, which was not altogether on account of the gruesome cold that hemmed him round with louring flames and after a moment began to penetrate to his very marrow with a sense of intolerable burning. He had come to the

surface quickly after his dive and had seen the great lead that
Tito had won over him: bitterly beset by his chilly savage
enemy, he had been thinking more of narrowing the distance,
of the goal of the swimming contest, of the mutual respect and
comradeship and of struggling for the soul of the boy than of
the fact that he was already wrestling with Death, which had
him in its embrace. He held out with all his strength as long
as his heart still beat.

The young swimmer had often cast backward glances over
his shoulder, had noticed with satisfaction that the Magister
had followed him into the water, but now when he looked
back he could see him no longer. He began to grow anxious
and called out, then turned back and swam at full speed to
give him support. There was no trace of him to be found.
He swam backwards and forward and dived time and again
until his strength began to fail and the bitter cold overcame
him. He scrambled out at last completely out of breath, saw
the bathing wrap lying at the water's edge, put it on and
began to rub his body and limbs mechanically until the
warmth returned to his frozen skin.

He sat down in the sun as though in a trance and stared
into the water. The cold blue-green now seemed strangely
evil and empty. With the disappearance of his bodily weakness the realization of what had happened was gradually
brought home to him and he was overcome with perplexity,
terror and deep sorrow.

"Alas! What have I done?" he cried in horror. "Now I am
guilty of his death!" And now for the first time, when pride
was of no avail and there was no more need for resistance, he
felt with a pang in his terrified heart how much he had
already grown to love this man. Inasmuch as he felt partially
responsible, despite any excuses that could be made, for the
Magister's death, a feeling of sacred awe took hold of him
which foretold that this guilt would change him completely
and would make more demands upon him than he had
hitherto ever demanded of himself.

THE END

JOSEPH KNECHT'S
POSTHUMOUS WRITINGS

*The Poetic Fragments from
Knecht's Student Days*

LAMENT

IN US LIFE never is fulfilled. A stream
That shapes itself to every mould are we:
Traversing day and night, the pit, the dream
Vault of the heavens, thirsting but to be.
Shape upon shape we thus assume, nor rest
Where fortune smiles or pipes a dirge forlorn,
Urged ever onward, always but the guest
Whom no home calls, nor plough, nor ripening corn.
We do not know what God with us intends,
We are his playthings, clay beneath his hands,
Dumb, inarticulate, stuff which he bends
And kneads, yet never in the furnace brands.
Could we be turned to stone but once, endure!
For this we crave all our uneasy days,
Yet dread alone retains its sinecure,
And nothing on our pilgrimage allays.

COMPROMISE

'TIS TRUE the simpletons who nothing dare
The harvest of our doubts will never reap:
The world is flat they solemnly declare,
An old wives' tale the legend of the deep.
For were dimensions to exist as well
As those in which our childish trust we place,
How should a single soul in safety dwell,
How should men live untroubled and at peace?
To safeguard, then, the freedom of our minds
Let us cast one dimension to the winds!
If honest is the ingenuous man's intention,
And is so perilous the mind's declension,
We will make do without a third dimension.

YET SECRETLY WE THIRST . . .

Airy, delightful as an arabesque,
Our lives appear to dance like those of elves
Lightfoot about the void, encompassing
Our present being and our future selves.
O loveliness of dreams, sweet dalliance,
So gossamer and poised so gracefully,
Deep down below your sun-bright surface lurks
The urge t'ward night, blood-lust, barbarity.
Spin through the void by no necessity
Impelled our lives, as light as breath,
Yet secretly we thirst for violence,
For love's embrace, birth, suffering and death.

CALLIGRAPHY

FROM TIME to time we take up pen or pencil
and make set signs upon the page appear
which this or that convey, for we are playing
a game with rules to which we all adhere.
But were a moon-man or a tribal savage
to come across this pen-ploughed runic zone,
intent to solve the secret of our writing,
he'd be confronted with a world unknown,
a gallery of strange and magic pictures.
As man and beast he would interpret A
and B, as eyes and tongues and limbs in motion,
here circumspect, to passions there a prey,
like crowsfeet in the snow imprints be tracing,
he'd run and pause, try like a bird to fly;
he'd see potential sources of creation
beyond the stiff black strokes in his mind's eye
and spooks among those ornamental symbols,
he'd see love glow, and feel the stab of pain.
Yea, he would marvel, laugh and weep and tremble,
for all the world of Yahweh and of Cain
would there appear in miniature before him
with features dwarfed, like creatures in a dream;

and so confined within their latticed prison
each would resemble each, till none could tell
life-force from death, nor lusting from affliction—
so like unto twin brothers would these seem—
And in the end dream-haunted would this wild man
recoil in abject terror, rave and yell,
but soon stoke up his fire and with chantings
consign the hieroglyphics to the blaze.
And then perhaps he'd sense as he grew drowsy
how this black-magic-world and all its ways,
this vision unendurable was drawn
into the void before life's primal dawn,
and he would sigh, and smile and, stretching, yawn.

UPON READING AN OLD PHILOSOPHER

WISDOMS which brimmed with charm and nobleness,
Thought-worlds but yesterday upheld and praised,
Turn empty on the instant, meaningless
As music score from which has been erased

Both key and accidentals: disappears
The magic mortar of our hall of dreams,
It totters, falls apart, disintegrates,
And where was harmony all discord seems.

Thus can a wise old face which we of old
Have reverenced, when set for dying, be
Distorted, lose itself in fold on fold
Of lamentable, blank futility.

So do exalted moods while still the dew
Of morning's on them fail to satisfy,
As though long since within our hearts we knew
All things on earth must rot and fade and die.

Above this corpse-strewn valley of dismay
Soul incorruptible in agony
Of longing torches forth to light the way
Death challenging to immortality.

THE   LAST   OF   THE   BEAD-PLAYERS

HIS PLAYTHINGS, bright-hued beads, clutched in his hand,
He sits with bended back; all round the land
Ravaged by war and pestilence now lies,
Whilst in the ivied ruins hum the flies.
Peace with a sad and lute-like threnody
Drones in the age of ancients, wearily.
The old man counts his coloured beads, selects
A white one first, then sets by it a blue,
Picks out a large and then a small, effects
At last the magic pattern in a circle true.
One time in symbol-play was he well skilled,
Master of many tongues, versed in the arts,
Man of the world whose travels would have filled
A book and brought him fame, a man of parts
Whom old and young once lent a ready ear.
Now he is all used up, age-worn, alone,
Disciples for his blessing draw not near
Nor dons to pick an academic bone;
They are no more, the temples, libraries
And schools of fair Castalia are gone . . .
Amid the shards the ancient rests, and sees
The pearls within his palm which lately shone
With all the radiance of inspired creeds
Are nothing more than brightly-coloured beads.
Slowly they trickle from his palsied hands
Without a sound, and vanish in the sands . . .

A   BACH   TOCCATA

PRIMEVAL silence reigns . . . Darkness abounds . . .
A sudden ray pierces a jagged cloud
and wrests from blind-eyed chaos cosmic deeps,
constructs space-realms, and floods the night with light;
great bluffs reveals, peak precipice, abyss,
the air with blue suffuses, knits the earth.

Then with creative lust it splits in twain
her womb to germinate the world,
which burgeons forth in fearful pregnancy;
where falls the seed of light all is transformed,
takes purpose on, while Beauty hymns the quick
in honour of the great creator, Light.

And striking farther yet, still God-impelled,
infects all living creatures with the urge
toward the holy spirit whence they came.
Delight and sorrow spawn, speech, art and song,
while worlds rise up in one triumphal arch
of flesh and spirit, fortune, war and love.

A DREAM

GUEST AT a monastery in the hills,
I stole, when all had gone to evening prayers,
into a library. Around the walls
the wondrous titles of a thousand books
in vellum bound gave back the sun's last rays.
By thirst for knowledge drawn delightedly
I reached toward a shelf, took down a tome,
and read: "Squaring the Circle—Final Stage."
This book I'll take, I there and then resolved!
Another work, a quarto volume tooled
in gold, bore this strange legend on its spine:
"How from the Other Tree too Adam ate."
The other tree? Which one: the Tree of Life!
Is Adam then immortal? Now I knew
there was a purpose in my presence here,
and I espied a folio whose boards
and edges shone with all the rainbow's hues.
Its hand-illumined title bore these words:
"Colour and Music, their Relationship:
Primary and Refracted Colours Shown
to Correspond with Notes of Varying Pitch."
O, how the colour-choirs danced and gleamed
before my eyes! And then I realised—
each book was proof of this—that I had strayed

into the Library of Paradise;
life's every problem that had bowed me down
was here resolved, and here too could be slaked
all thirst for knowledge parching mind and soul.
For, did I let my roving eye rest but
a moment on a book, a title full
of promise would flash forth; here every need
was catered for, at hand was every fruit
that schoolboy ever longed for in his dreams,
that mind of master dared investigate.
Here was the inmost meaning crystal clear
of all wise men had spoken, poets sung,
for every door to knowledge and delight
the open sesame, quintessence of
men's noblest thoughts, within these books contained.
The key to every problem lay at hand,
no secret but could be unlocked by him
whom fortune favoured at the magic hour.

Upon a reading desk with trembling hands
I laid one of these volumes and began
deciphering the magic scripture there,
which seemed like some enigma in a dream
that is resolved with unexpected ease.
Whereat, as if on pinions borne, I sped
through star-hung spirit-realms which circumscribed
the zodiac, and all about me spread,
fell into place all that had been vouchsafed
to men in vision since the world began,
forever changing and forever merged
in new relationships in time and space;
old wisdoms, symbols and discoveries
flowed into newer moulds without surcease,
till I, in that brief moment while I read,
re-lived the whole long pilgrimage of man,
and so absorbed within my flesh and bone
the inmost spirit of the human race.
I read, and saw the figures on the page
each with the other pair, then separate,
as in a minuet close up and part,
in endless new configurations flow,

kaleidoscope of allegoric forms
which took on ever fresh significance.
But when, bedazzled by this spectacle,
I lifted up my head to rest my eyes,
I saw that someone else was in the room.
Facing the rows of books an old man stood—
the Keeper of the Archives it might be—
who earnestly intent upon his task
was busying himself with book on book;
and all at once I felt I had to know
the nature and the purport of the work
he plied so zealously. I watched, and saw
how with a delicate white hand the old
man chose a book, read what was written on
the back and breathed, his pale lips pursed, upon
the lettering—a title promise-filled
with hours of bliss for all who chose to read—
with wetted finger wiped it clean away
and, with a smile upon his face, wrote down
a wholly different title in its place,
then sought out other books, one here, one there,
erased their titles, and wrote others in.

For long, perplexed, I watched him, then I turned,
since this beyond my comprehension lay,
back to my volume, into which I had
no more than dipped; but now I could not find
those picture-sequences which had incurred
my high delight; it seemed the symbol-world
in which I had so briefly wandered and
which had laid bare life's true significance,
was fast dissolving, vanishing away;
it danced before my eyes, grew blurred and dim,
and dissipating left behind no more
than grey-white lustre of the empty sheet.
I felt a touch upon my shoulder, turned,
saw that the ancient stood by me, and rose.
Now, with an enigmatic smile, he took
my book, and as his anger moist expunged
the lettering, a shiver froze my spine;
upon the unmarked leather now he wrote

fresh titles, postulations, promises,
of age-old problems new analyses,
spelling with slow, painstaking pen. Then took
away without a word both pen and book.

DEDICATION

IN THE beginning reigned the sovereign princes
who consecrated meadow, corn and plough
demanding sacrifice and seemliness
from this poor race of mortals thirsting for
the righteous rule of the invisible powers;
holding the sun and moon within their courses,
these ever-shining presences know nothing
of sorrow and the shadowed world of death.

The sacred line of godlike sons of men
is long extinct, and humankind is left
alone in grief's and pleasure's turbulence,
forever inchoate, no longer blessed.

Yet has our intimation of true being
never died, and it behoves us in the days
of our decline, through symbol-play and parable
and song, this holy admonition to sustain.

Some day perhaps the darkness will disperse,
maybe the times will one day change again;
reign over us the sun in likeness to a god,
and welcome votive offerings at our hands.

SOAP BUBBLES

FROM HOMESPUN learning and much earnest thought
An old man weaves the cloth of life years after,
Threaded with gentle wisdom which is caught
Within the warp of pain, the weft of laughter.

Aflame with zeal an ardent student plies
His pen, with debt to better minds' devising,
And writes a young man's book which testifies
To months of genial philosophising.

A boy sits blowing bubbles through a straw,
And soon with living light each one is glowing;
They seem the brightest worlds he ever saw,
His soul takes wing in ecstasy of blowing.

Out of the Maya-foam of worlds, all three—
Old man, young boy and undergraduate
Their unsubstantial magic dreams create
Wherein, all wreathed in smiles, they seem to see
The light eternal beckon joyously.

After Reading the SUMMA CONTRA GENTILES

ONCE, SO IT seems, life was more genuine,
the world was better ordered, thought more lucid,
wisdom and science were not yet divorced.
They lived more fully, did those men of old
of whom we read such wondrous tales in Plato,
the Chinese and the other ancient writers—
and, ah! whenever we set foot within
Aquinas' perfectly proportioned fane
a world of truth, mature and honey-sweet,
appeared to beckon to us from afar:
there all seemed light, enspirited all nature,
men dwelt with God behind them and before,
rules were obeyed and kept were law and order,
existence formed a round unbroken whole.
But we, the living, seem to be condemned
to journey on through barren wildernesses,
beset by doubts and bitter ironies,
oppressed by conflict and a ceaseless yearning.
Yet later generations will maybe
see us as we our forbears see, transfigured,
as wise and happy men, for they will hear
only the tuneful echoes of the wild
and disconcerted chorus of our lives,
their tumult will have mellowed into legend.
And he of us who trusts himself the least,
doubts most and questions most, will be the one
perhaps whose impress carries down the ages,

a yardstick for the youth of times to come.
And he who harbours doubts about himself
may well be envied for his happiness,
as one who knew no sorrows and no fears,
who lived in days when life on earth was good,
whose blissful state was like to that of children.

For in our souls the Spirit Everlasting
lives on, and makes soul-brothers of all men:
IT shall survive the Now, not you or I.

STEPS

AS EVERY blossom fades and all youth sinks
into old age, so every life's design,
each flower of wisdom, every good, attains
its prime and cannot last for ever.
At life's each call the heart must be prepared
to take its leave and to commence afresh,
courageously and with no hint of grief
submit itself to other, newer ties.
A magic dwells in each beginning and
protecting us it tells us how to live.

High-purposed we must traverse realm on realm,
cleaving to none as to a home. The world
of spirit wishes not to fetter us
but raise us higher, further, step by step.
Scarce in some safe, accustomed sphere of life
have we established house, than we grow lax;
he only who is ready to inspan
and journey forth can throw old habits off.

Maybe death's hour too will send us out
new-born toward undreamed-of lands, maybe
life's call to us will never find an end . . .
Courage, my heart, take leave and fare thee well!

THE BEAD GAME

MUSIC OF THE spheres, music of the masters
We venerate and gladly hearken to,
To glorify with taintless celebration
The spirits of the great of long ago.

We let the secret kindle and uplift us,
The magic formula which is our pass,
Under whose spell life's shoreless, roaring ocean
Pours into images as clear as glass.

Like constellations crystalline they echo,
Life dedicate to them takes purpose on,
And none of us can fall from out their courses
If not toward the holy colophon.

THE THREE INCARNATIONS

THE RAINMAKER

MANY THOUSANDS of years ago the women were supreme in tribe and family. It was the mother and grandmother to whom respect and obedience were due, and the birth of a maiden was more important than that of a boy.

In the village there was an ancient woman—more than a hundred years old—who was so venerated and feared by everyone that she might have been a queen, although she had seldom raised a finger or spoken a word within the memory of man. Day after day she sat before the entrance of her hut, surrounded by a train of obsequious relatives, where the village women would come to pay their respects, tell her of their affairs, show her their children for appraisal and her blessing. Pregnant women would come and beg her to touch their bellies and give them a name for their expected child. Sometimes the old woman would raise her hand, sometimes merely nod, shake her head or remain quite motionless. She hardly ever spoke: she was just there. She simply sat and ruled. Thin strands of yellowish white hair framed her leathery face with its sharp eagle eyes. She received homage, presents, pleas, news, reports and complaints, and was known to all as the mother of seven daughters, the grandmother and great-grandmother of many nieces and great-nieces. Behind her wrinkled features and her brown forehead lay the wisdom, tradition, laws, customs and honour of the village.

It was a spring evening. The sky was cloudy and night had fallen early. The great-grandmother was not in evidence before the mud hut, but her place had been taken by her daughter, who was hardly less white and worthy, and also not much younger, than the old woman herself. She was seated quietly at the threshold upon a flat stone, over which, in cold weather, a skin used to be spread. Some distance away, in a half circle around her, a few children, women and boys squatted in the grass or in the sand. They would assemble there every evening, except when it rained or froze, for they wanted to hear the tribal mother's daughter tell stories or chant incantations.

Previously, of course, the tribal mother herself had done this, but now she had grown too old and was no longer communicative, and her daughter crouched in her place telling the same stories and singing the same incantations. As she had learned all these from her old mother, and had also inherited her voice, figure, calm dignity of behaviour, gestures and speech, the younger ones among the audience knew her better than her parent, and no longer realised that it was not the other who sat there passing on the stories and wisdom of the tribe. Of an evening the fountain of all know-ledge would flow from her lips, for there beneath her white hair, behind that gentle, wrinkled old forehead, was preserved the treasure of the race, there dwelt the memory and spirit of the tribe. Whoever was wise and knew incantations and stories had learned them from her. However, apart from herself and her mother, there was still one wise man in the race, but one who remained distant and aloof, a mysterious and very silent man—the weather prophet or Rainmaker.

Among the listeners crouched the boy Knecht, and beside him a little girl called Ada. He was very fond of this girl and often accompanied and protected her, not exactly out of love —for of this he knew nothing, being himself still only a child—but because she was the daughter of the Rainmaker. Knecht revered and admired this wise man almost as much as he did the tribal mother and her daughter. But of course they were women: one could revere and fear them, but one could not possibly entertain the thought and the wish to become like one of them. The Rainmaker, however, was a somewhat unapproachable man, and it was not easy for a boy to gain access to him. It was necessary to use oblique tactics, and his preoccupation with the child was simply one of these. He would fetch her as often as possible from the Rainmaker's somewhat isolated hut, and they would go and sit together in the evening before the old woman's hut, after which he would accompany her home. He had called for her again this evening, and they were now squatting in the midst of the dark company, listening.

The grandmother was telling them of the witches' thorp or village, and this is what she told:—

"Sometimes in a village there is a bad woman who has evil designs upon everyone. These women hardly ever have any children, and sometimes one of them is so evil that the villagers will no longer allow her to stay. When this is the case she is fetched in the night, and her husband is made fast with chains. She is beaten with rods and then driven far out into the woods and marshes; a curse is put upon her, and she is left all alone in the wilderness. After this the man is released from his chains, and if he is not too old is allowed to choose another wife for himself. The outcast, however, if she does not die, wanders in the woods and the marshes, learns the speech of the animals, and after wandering and struggling for a long time may one day find a little village which is known as the Witches' Thorp. There dwell all the evil women who have been driven from their villages, and have therefore built this one for themselves. There they live, plot evil and practise magic; and, as they have none of their own, like nothing better than to entice children away from honest villages to their own. If a little one wanders off into the forest and does not return, it does not mean to say that she has been drowned in a marsh or eaten by a wolf, for she may have been lured away by a witch and taken off to the Witches' Thorp.

"In the days when I was still young, and my grandmother was the tribal mother here, a little girl once went out with her companions to gather bilberries, and it happened that after some time she grew tired and fell asleep. As she was quite small the ferns towered high above her head, and the other children went on, not noticing, until they had reached the village and it was already nightfall, that the little girl was no longer with them. The boys were sent out to look for her, and they called to her in the forest until it was too dark, but returned without her.

"The little one, however, had woken up and had plunged deeper into the forest. The more frightened she became the quicker she had run, but she no longer knew where she was, and was running ever further and further away from her village into country where no one had ever been before. She was wearing around her neck a boar's tooth on the end of a strip of twine, which her father had given her one day after hunting. He had bored a hole in the tooth with a flint, through which the cord could be drawn, having first boiled it three times in boar's blood and sung powerful incantations over it, so that whoever wore such a tooth would be protected from magic.

"At this moment a woman came out from among the trees. She was a witch.

" 'Good evening, my pretty child,' she said, smiling sweetly. 'Have you lost your way? Come along with me: I will take you home.'

"The little girl followed her. But she remembered what her father and mother had told her—that one should never show the boar's tooth to a stranger—and so, as she walked, she stealthily removed the tooth from the cord and hid it in her girdle. The strange woman walked with the child for several hours, and it was already night when they came to a village— which was not our village but the witches'. The little girl was locked in a dark shed, and the witch went off to sleep in her own hut.

"On the following morning, the witch said to her: 'Do you not wear a boar's tooth?' The child denied this, and said that she had once had one but that she had lost it in the forest. She pointed to her necklet of twine, from which the boar's tooth had been removed. At this the witch brought a stone pot filled with earth, in which three plants were growing. The child looked at the plants and asked what they were. Pointing to the first one the witch said: 'That is the life of your mother,' and to the second: 'That is the life of your father.' And finally, as she came to the third plant, she said: 'And that is your own life. As long as these plants are green and flourishing, both your life and theirs will be healthy: should one of them fade, then whoever's life it stands for will begin to ail: should one of them be torn from the earth, as I am now going to tear one out, then that particular life will die!' Seizing the plant which stood for the father, she began to draw it out slowly with her fingers, and when a portion of the white root was to be seen, the plant gave off a deep sigh . . ."

At these words the little girl who was sitting next to Knecht sprang up as though she had been bitten by a snake, let forth a scream and ran off as fast as her legs would carry her. For a long time she had been struggling against the fear which the story had aroused in her, but now she could bear it no longer. An old woman laughed. Several of the other listeners had been almost as frightened as the little one, but they controlled themselves and remained seated. Knecht, however, was no sooner awakened from his dream of fearful listening, then he too sprang up and ran after the child. The old woman went on telling her story.

The Rainmaker's hut stood near the village green, and thither went Knecht to look for the fugitive. He tried to entice her out of hiding and attract her to him with high-pitched croonings and cluckings, long drawn out notes, sweet and full of enchantment, such as women make when they call to chickens.

"Ada!" he chanted. "Ada, little Ada, come here! Don't be frightened, Ada. It is only I, Knecht." He sang this again and again, and suddenly, before he had heard a sound or caught a glimpse of her, he felt a soft little hand grasp his own. She had been standing at the wayside with her back to one of the hut walls waiting for him ever since she had heard his first call. Breathing a sigh of relief she snuggled up against him, for he appeared to her as tall and strong as a man.

"So you were frightened, then?" ne said. "You need not be, you know. Nobody will do you any harm. Everyone likes Ada. Come, we will go home!"

She was still trembling and sobbing a little, but was already calmer, and followed him gratefully and with great confidence in him.

A faint red light gleamed from the hut door, and within crouched the Rainmaker over his oven. The red glow lit up his long hair: he was cooking something over the fire in two

little pots. Before Knecht entered with Ada, he looked inside
with curiosity once or twice. He saw immediately that it was
not food that was being cooked, for that was done in a different kind of pot, and in any case it was already far too late.
The Rainmaker had heard him.

"Who is standing there outside the door?" he called.
"Ah! is it you, Ada? Come in, my dear!" He replaced the lids
on his pots, banked up the embers and ashes and turned round.

Knecht continued to cast sidelong glances at the mysterious
pots, for he was inquisitive, awed and uncomfortable, as was
always the case when he visited this hut. He came as often as
he possibly could, and invented many excuses and pretexts
for doing so, but always experienced, besides his curiosity
and joy, that tickling, warning sensation of slight embarrassment mingled with fear. The old man must have noticed that
Knecht had been pursuing him for a long time, for he would
appear before him whenever he could anticipate his whereabouts, like a hunter on the chase mutely offering his services
and company.

Turu, the weather prophet or Rainmaker, looked at him
with his clear, falcon's eyes. "What do you want here?" he
asked coldly. "This is no time for a visit to strange huts,
my young friend."

"I have brought Ada home, Master Turu. She was listening to the tribal mother telling stories of the witches, and
suddenly became frightened and started to scream. So I
brought her home."

The father turned to his daughter. "You are a frightened
little mouse, Ada. Sensible little girls have no need to be
afraid of witches, and you are a sensible girl, aren't you?"

"Of course, but the witches can practise many evil arts,
and if one hasn't a boar's tooth . . ."

"Oh! So you would like a boar's tooth, would you? Well,
we shall see. But I know something much better than that:
I know of a root, which I will bring for you one of these days.
We must go and find one in the autumn. It protects sensible
little girls from all manners of sorceries, and at the same
time makes them much prettier."

Ada smiled and was pleased. She was already quite calm
again now that the protecting smell of the hut and the little
glimmer of fire were around her.

"Couldn't I go and look for the root?" asked Knecht diffidently. "You could describe it to me . . ."

Turu screwed up his eyes. "Ah! A great many young men would like to know that!" There was no anger in his voice, but only a trace of mockery. "There is plenty of time, plenty of time. We will see when the autumn comes."

Knecht withdrew. He made off in the direction of the dormitory where he slept, for he was an orphan—and for this reason found magic in Ada and in her hut.

The Rainmaker, Turu, had little use for words, nor did he particularly like to hear other people talk. Many people regarded him as eccentric, others as sullen, but he was neither. He knew much more about what went on around him than people would have given him credit for in view of his learned and hermit-like absentmindedness. He knew well enough, among other things, that this tiresome but attractive and obviously intelligent boy was running after him and watching him. He had noticed it from the very beginning, and it had been going on now for a whole year. He also knew exactly what this meant. It meant a great deal to the boy and also a great deal to himself. It showed that this lad was enamoured of weathermaking, and desired nothing more earnestly than to learn it. There were always such boys to be found in the village, and Knecht had had many precursors. Many of them were easily frightened away and discouraged, but others not so, and Turu had already had two who had stayed with him for many years as pupils and apprentices. They had eventually gone away to other villages, where they had married and become rainmakers or herb gatherers, and since that time Turu had remained alone. But were he once again to take a pupil, he would do so in order to have a successor. It had ever been thus, and it was right and could not be otherwise. Ever and again a talented boy must appear, approach and pursue the man whom he saw to be a master of his craft. Knecht was talented and had certain signs to recommend him: above all, an enquiring and at the same time sharp and dreamy look, something reserved and noiseless about him, and in the expression of his face and head something questing, divining and aware—a sense for noises and smells—something birdlike and hunterlike. It was certain that a weather prophet could be made out of this boy—

perhaps also a magician. He was good material. But there was no hurry, for he was still too young, and there was no need to show him any recognition: it was not wise to make things too easy for him, and he should be spared no test. If it turned out that he could be disconcerted, frightened or discouraged, then it would do him no harm. He should be made to wait and serve, creep after him and win him over.

Knecht hurried back to the village through the approaching night, satisfied and happily excited. The sky was cloudy and only two or three stars were to be seen. Of the enjoyment, beauty and refinement which we to-day find quite natural and indispensable, and which are the property of even the poorest, the villagers knew nothing. They knew neither culture nor art, nor houses other than mud huts, and they knew nothing of iron and steel tools. Things such as wheat or wine were also quite unknown, and discoveries such as candles or lamps would have been regarded by these men as glittering marvels. The life of Knecht and his world of imagination were no poorer on account of this, since the world around him was an endless secret picture book, of which he captured a new little fragment every day, from the lives of animals and the growth of plants to the firmament. And between mute, mysterious nature and the heart that beat in isolation in his timorous boy's breast resided every relationship and every tension, fear, curiosity and pleasure of assimilation of which the human soul is capable. Even if there was no written knowledge, no history book or alphabet in his world, and everything that lay three or four hours away from his home was entirely unknown and unattainable, he lived in complete harmony with the life of his own village.

The village, the country and the community of his tribe, under the leadership of the mothers, gave him everything that state and society can give to a man—a soil full of a thousand roots, in whose woof he himself was a single thread participating in everything.

So, in this contented mood, he hurried home. The night wind whispered in the trees and made the branches creak. There was a smell of damp earth, of reeds and slime, of smoke from half-green wood, a fatty and somewhat sweet odour which above all others spelt for him his home country, and, as he approached the dormitory, there was the smell of boys, of young human bodies. He crept noiselessly under the reed mat into the warm breathing darkness, laid himself down on his bed of straw and thought of the witch tale, the boar's tooth, of Ada and of the Rainmaker with his little pots on the fire, until he fell asleep.

Little by little Turu softened towards the boy, but did not make it easy for him. The youngster was always at his heels, and was attracted to the elder man often without knowing the reason why. Sometimes, when Turu was somewhere in the most hidden part of the wood, marsh or heath, setting a trap, examining a wild beast's spoor, digging up a root or gathering seed, he would suddenly feel the eyes of the boy who had been following him silently and invisibly for hours, watching him. Then he would act as though he had noticed nothing, but would sometimes growl and chase his persecutor away quite rudely. But sometimes he would beckon to him, keep him at his side for a whole day and allow him to serve him. He would show him this and that, give him advice, test him, tell him the names of herbs, teach him to divine water or make fire, and at each performance instruct him in useful tricks, secrets and formulas which the youth was told to keep strictly to himself.

When Knecht was a little older, Turu accepted him permanently as his apprentice and transferred him from the boys' dormitory to his own hut; and in this way the boy became recognised by the whole tribe. He was no longer a boy: he was the Rainmaker's apprentice, which meant that, should he endure the tests and prove of value, he would become Turu's successor.

From the time when Knecht had been received by the elder man into his hut, the barrier between them had fallen—not the barrier of awe and obedience, but that of mistrust and reticence. Turu had surrendered and allowed himself to be conquered by Knecht's spirited assault. In this apprenticeship there were no concepts, manuals, methods, scripts or numbers, and only very few words, and it was far more Knecht's senses than his understanding that were being developed by his master. It was not simply a question of administering and practising a large legacy of tradition and experience—the entire knowledge of the men of that period about nature—but of passing it on. A great and compact system of experiences,

observations, instincts and experiments was revealed slowly
and obscurely to the youth. Practically nothing was put into
words, for everything had to be felt through the senses,
absorbed and verified. The basis and focal point of this
knowledge, however, was the study of the moon, its phases
and influences; how, peopled by the souls of the dead, it
constantly waxed and waned, sending them out once more
to be born again and to make room for those who had
just died.

Just as the hour that evening when he had left the story
teller and seen the pots on the old man's oven had been
impressed upon Knecht's memory, so yet another hour,
between night and morning, when the master awakened him
two hours after midnight and they went out together into the
pitch-black night to look at the last phase of the waning
moon crescent, remained a poignant memory. The master
stood silent and motionless with the youth, who was somewhat fearful and shivering from lack of sleep, in the midst of
the wooded hills on a rugged cliff plateau, until, in the spot
he had designated and in the shape and direction exactly that
he had described, the moon arose like a slender arched bow.
Knecht stared fearfully, as though bewitched, at the slowly
rising planet, which sailed gently into a clear island in the
heavens between the dark clouds.

"Soon she will change her form and wax again, and then it
will be time to sow the buckwheat," said the Rainmaker,
counting the days upon his fingers. Then he lapsed once
more into silence, and as Knecht cowered on the dewy stone,
trembling with cold, the long drawn-out hoot of an owl came
from the depths of the forest. For a long time the old man
meditated, and then stood up, laid his hand on Knecht's head
and said softly, as though speaking in a dream: "When I am
dead, my spirit will fly to the moon. You will then be a man
and have a wife, who will be my daughter, Ada. When she
begets you a son, my spirit will return and dwell in him, and
you shall call him Turu, as I am called."

The apprentice heard this with astonishment, and did not
dare to utter a word. The fragile silver sickle had descended,
and was soon half-swallowed up by the clouds. The young
man was strangely moved by an intuitive sense of the many
relationships and associations, repetitions and cross-currents

between things and events. Wondrous indeed, as a spectator and participant, had he found this strange nocturnal heaven where, over the boundless forests and hills, the slender crescent had appeared at the time and place forecast by the master. Marvellous indeed, and shrouded in a thousand secrets, appeared to him the master himself, who had thought of his own death and whose spirit would linger in the moon and thence return into a man, who should be Knecht's son and who should bear the name of his former master. Wonderfully open and transparent in parts like the cloudy heaven seemed his future, seemed destiny to lie before him: that one could know of these, name them and speak of them seemed to him like a glimpse into infinite space, full of marvels and yet full of order. For a moment everything appeared to him comprehensible to the spirit, everything knowable, everything audible—the smooth sure path of the stars above, the life of man and beast, their communities and entities, friendships and conflicts, everything great and small together in that life enclosed by death. All this he saw or felt as a whole in a first shudder of foreboding, with himself incorporated within it and placed as something ordered, ruled over by laws, with access to the spirit. This was a first presentiment of the great secrets and of their value and depth, as much as a comprehension of them which touched the young man like a spiritual hand in this cool semi-nocturnal forest on the cliffs above the thousand whispering tree-tops. He could not speak of this, either at that moment or throughout his whole life, but he was forced to think about it, and during his later instruction and experience this hour was always present within him.

"Think," it warned, "think of it—that all this exists between the moon and you and Turu and Ada, that rays and currents pass, that there is death, a land of souls and a return; that there is an answer in your heart to all the images and phenomena of the world, that all this concerns you and that you shall know as much of everything as it is possible for any one man to know."

In this way the voice spoke to him. For Knecht it was the first time that he had heard the call of the spirit, with its enticement, claims and magic aspirations. He had often seen the moon climbing the heavens and had often heard the

nocturnal hooting of the owl; and from the mouth of his
master also, however sparing in words he may have been, he
had heard many a word of ancient wisdom or single observations; but in the present hour it was new and different. It was
a prescience of the whole which had struck him, a feeling of
the associations, relationships and order which drew him into
the picture and made him co-responsible. Whoever should
hold the key had not simply to be able to recognise a beast by
its track, a plant by its root or seed, but the whole universe—
stars, spirits, men, beasts, healing balsams and poisons. He
had to embrace everything in its totality and be able to read
each portion and sign from the other portion. There were
good hunters who could recognise more than others from a
spoor, from droppings, a hair or some other remnant; from a
few insignificant hairs they could determine not only the type
of beast to which they belonged, but also whether it were old
or young, male or female. Others could foresee in a cloud
form, in some odour in the air, in the particular behaviour of a
beast or plant the weather for days in advance. His master
was unequalled and almost infallible in this respect. There
were yet others who possessed a kind of innate dexterity: for
instance, there were boys who could hit a bird at thirty paces
with a stone, and they had never been taught this but could do
it quite naturally. It did not happen through effort but
through magic or grace—the stone simply flew from their
hands of itself, desiring to hit, and the bird would be hit.
Others, apparently, knew how to read the future, knew
whether a sick man would die or not, or whether a pregnant
woman would give birth to a boy or a girl. The daughter of
the tribal mother was very renowned for this, and it was
reputed that the weather maker also had some knowledge of
the art. There must, it appeared to Knecht at that moment,
be a central point in that gigantic net of associations from
which everything known, everything past and future could be
seen and read. Whoever should stand at this focal point must
run towards wisdom, like water to the valley or the hare to
the cabbage. His word must hit sharply and unerringly, like
the stone from the hand of the slinger. He had with the
strength of the spirit to allow all these single wonderful gifts
and capabilities to unite and have play within himself. Such
a man would be perfect, wise and incomparable! To become

like him, to approximate to him, to be on the way to him—
that was the path of paths, that was the goal, that gave a
purpose and an inspiration to life.

This is in some measure what the boy felt, and what we
have tried to express in our articulate speech—which was of
course unknown to him and which cannot possibly reproduce
the awe and ardour of his experience. The rising in the night,
the adventure of being led through the dark silent wood full
of danger and mystery, the sojourn on the rock plateau high
up in the morning cold, the appearance of the thin, ghostly
moon, the sparse words of the wise man and the solitude
with his master at that extraordinary hour—all this was
experienced and preserved by Knecht as a feast and a
mystery, as the mystery of initiation and as his acceptance
into a union and cult, into a menial but honourable relationship with the unnameable, the cosmic mystery. This experience and many similar ones can never be expressed in
thoughts or in words, and even more remote and more
impossible were those which we may sum up as follows:
"Is this experience peculiar to myself, or is it objective
reality? Does the master feel the same as I do, or is he
laughing at me? Are my thoughts on this experience new
and original, or have the master and many before him
experienced and thought exactly the same things?" No,
there were no such shades and differentiations. Everything
was reality, was saturated and permeated with it like
dough leavened with yeast—the clouds, the moon and the
whole changing theatre of heaven; the damp, cold chalky soil
beneath naked feet; the wet, trickling, dewy cold in the wan
night air; the comforting odour of the homeland, of oven
smoke and the litter of leaves which impregnated the fur that
the master had wrapped around himself; the ring of dignity
and the gentle timbre of old age and readiness for death in
his harsh voice. All this was super-real and had penetrated
into the senses of the youth in the nature of a violation, for
impressions upon the senses are a deeper soil for memories
than the best systems and modes of thought.

Although the Rainmaker belonged to the few who practised a vocation and had developed his own special art and
capacity, his daily life was not so very different from that of
his contemporaries. He was a high official, enjoying esteem

and also receiving gifts and rewards from the tribe whenever he had any public duties to perform, but this was only on special occasions. By far his most important and pontifical, almost sacred, function was to decide upon the day in spring when each type of fruit, herb and cereal was to be sown. He would do this after careful consideration of the moon's phases, partly in accordance with ancient rules and partly from his own experience. The festive occasion of the sowing itself, the strewing of the first handful of corn and seed on the community land, no longer belonged to his office, for no man stood high enough in the hierarchy: it was performed every year by the tribal mother herself, or by her oldest relative. But the master, in his rôle of weather prophet, was undoubtedly one of the most important figures in the village. This immediately became apparent when cold weather, an extensive drought or a flood laid seige to the fields and menaced the tribe with famine. On these occasions, Turu had in his possession various known means of counteracting drought and bad harvests—to wit, sacrifices, incantations and intercessions. According to legend, when in times of persistent drought or interminable rain all other methods had proved useless, and the spirits were not to be appeased by any amount of persuasion, pleas or menaces, a last infallible remedy remained, namely, the sacrifice of the weathermaker himself to the community. In the time of the primæval mother and the great grandmother it had often been put into practice, and the present tribal mother, it was said, had seen this happen.

In addition to his cares about the weather, the master also had a kind of private practice as exorciser of spirits: he would prepare amulets and magic potions, and frequently act as doctor—excepting in the case of the tribal mother. In every other respect, Master Turu lived the same life as everyone else. He owned a little plant garden near his hut, and in the season also helped to sow the community land. He collected fruits, mushrooms and firewood, and stored them against the winter, occasionally fished and hunted, and kept one or two goats. As a peasant he was like any other man, but as a huntsman, fisherman and herb gatherer he was unique and a genius, and was reported to know many natural and magical tricks, crafts and antidotes far beyond the reach of the common tribesman. No captured beast could escape from the willow noose that had been prepared by his hands; he knew how to make bait for fish in a special manner so that it was sweet smelling and tasty, understood how to attract crayfish, and many people believed that he could also understand the speech of the wild beasts. However, his own personal province was magic, the observation of the moon and the stars, the knowledge of the weather signs, the forecasting of thunder and the growth of the crops, a preoccupation with everything possessing magical properties which would serve as an expedient. He was therefore a great expert and collector of those types of plants and animals that could be used as medicinal remedies or poisons, and as amulets for protection against the powers of darkness. He knew and could find even the rarest herb, knew exactly where and when it bloomed and bore seed, and when the time was ripe to dig out its root. He knew and could find all manner of snakes and toads, knew the uses of horns, hooves, claws and hair, and was also well acquainted with deformities and all stunted, ghostly and grotesque formations such as the knots, excrescences and warts in wood, leaf, corn, nut, horn and hoof.

Knecht had to learn much more with his senses—with his feet and hands, eyes, skin, ears and smell—than with his intelligence, and Turu taught him much more by example and demonstration than with words and lessons. It was very seldom that the master ever spoke coherently, and if he did so his words were only an attempt to clarify his curious emphatic gestures. Knecht's lessons differed very little from those that a young hunter or fisherman receives from a good teacher, and they brought him great pleasure, for he was really only developing that which was latent within him. He learned to observe, to listen, to stalk and to spy, to be alert and aware, to scent and sense. The quarry that he and his master hunted, however, was not only fox and badger, viper and toad, bird and fish, but the spirit, the whole, the meaning and the association. They were occupied in determining the elusive and moody weather, in knowing, advising and forecasting, in recognising the lurking death in berries and snake bite, in surprising the secret by which the clouds and the storms correspond to the phases of the moon, their consequen influence upon sowing and growth and upon the rise and

decline of life in man and beast. In this way they strove
actually after the same goal as did the science and technics
of later centuries—to dominate nature and play with her laws.
But they did this in a completely different way. They did not
isolate themselves from nature and try to penetrate with
violence into her secrets: they were never opposed and
hostile to nature, but always a part of her and devoted to her
in awe, and it is quite possible that they knew her better and
dealt more intelligently with her. One thing, however, was
quite impossible for them, even in their most foolhardy
moments: they could never regard nature and the spirit
world without fear or feel themselves superior. This *hubris*
was unthinkable in their case, and to have any relationship
with the powers of nature, with death and with the demons,
other than that of fear would have appeared impossible to
them. Fear dominated the life of man, and to overcome it
seemed out of the question; but the various forms of sacrifice
served as a means of appeasing, banishing, outwitting, mask-
ing and absorbing it into the whole of life. It was the pressure
under which the life of these men stood, and without the high
pressure of this terror the intensity would have been lacking
in their lives. Whoever succeeded in ennobling a part of his
fear into awe had accomplished much, and men of this type,
men whose fear had turned to piety, were the good and
enlightened members of that age. There was much and
varied sacrifice, and a certain part of this sacrifice and its
rites belonged within the province of the weathermaker.

In the hut at Knecht's side little Ada grew up, a pretty
child and the favourite of her father, who in due course gave
her to his apprentice as a wife. From this time onwards
Knecht was regarded as the Rainmaker's assistant. Turu
introduced him to the village mother as his son-in-law and
successor, and allowed him to deputise for him in many
functions and affairs of office. Gradually, as the seasons went
by, the old Rainmaker sank into the solitary contemplation
of old age and left his entire office in Knecht's hands. When
he died—he was found dead crouching by his fire over a
cauldron of magic brew, his white hair singed by the flames—
the pupil Knecht had long since been considered by the village
as the Rainmaker. He demanded an honourable burial for his
teacher from the village council, and burned a whole bundle of

noble and costly healing herbs and roots as a sacrifice over his grave. This, too, is long in the past, and among Knecht's many children who filled Ada's hut to overflowing, there was a boy named Turu: in his person the old man had returned from his death journey to the moon.

From now on Knecht's life took a similar course to that of his teacher. A part of his fear was turned to piety and spirit: a part of his youthful striving and deep yearning remained alive, and the other died within him and was lost with age and in his work, in love and care for Ada and the children. His greatest love and most urgent concern was for the moon and its influence on the seasons and the weather. In this he soon equalled his master, Turu, and finally surpassed him. Because the waxing and the waning of the moon is so closely concerned with the birth and death of man, and because of all the fears in which men live the deepest is the knowledge of death, the moon lover and worshipper, Knecht, through his near and living relationship with the moon, also attained a consecrated and deep relationship with death. In his riper years he was less susceptible to the fear of death than other men. He could speak reverently, imploringly or tenderly to the moon, for he knew himself to be bound in tender spiritual bonds to her. He knew the moon's life very accurately, and identified himself with her adventures and destinies. He lived her waning and her resurrection like a mystery within himself, and with her he suffered and was terrified when the monster arrived, when she appeared sick and in danger and seemed to have suffered some change or damage, when she lost her brightness, her colour altered, or she was darkened almost to extinction.

Naturally at such times everyone took a vital interest in the moon and trembled with fear for her, recognising the menace and the approach of evil in her eclipse, and stared up anxiously into her old sick visage. One thing, however, showed that the Rainmaker, Knecht, had inner bonds with her and knew more about her than anyone else. However much he may have suffered her fate with her, and his heart have constricted with fear, his recollection of similar occurrences was sharper and more cultivated, his confidence more fundamental, his belief in eternity and reincarnation and in the corrective and transcendence over death greater; and greater, too, at such times was the degree of his devotion, for he felt himself ready to participate in the fate of the great star, in its destruction and its rebirth. At such times he would feel a sentiment almost of impertinence, of something in the nature of foolhardy courage and resolution—a readiness to defy death through the spirit and to strengthen his ego through devotion to superhuman agencies. Something of this feeling was transmitted to others, and he was considered a wise and pious man, serene and fearless in the face of death, one upon whom the powers looked favourably. He had had to substantiate these gifts and virtues through many hard tests. Once he had had to pass through a period of bad harvests and hostile weather which had lasted for two whole years, and this was the greatest trial of his life. Adversity had set in and ill omens had begun to appear immediately upon the postponement of the sowing, and from then on every conceivable misfortune and disaster had befallen the crops, until finally almost everything had been destroyed. The community had suffered grievously, and Knecht had been no exception. That he was able to survive this year, that he, the Rainmaker, did not lose his faith and influence, and was able to help the tribe to bear their misfortune with humility and self-control, was already a great triumph. But when in the following year, after a hard winter of many deaths, all the distress and misery of the previous year returned; when the community land dried up and lay scorching in the summer heat under an obstinate drought, and the mice multiplied inordinately; when even the invocations and sacrifices of the Rainmaker remained unanswered, as did the public ceremonies, the chorus of drums and the supplicating processions of the entire community; when conditions grew appalling and the Rainmaker still could make no rain, then indeed it was no trifle, and required more than an ordinary man to bear the responsibility and hold himself erect before the terrified and maddened villagers. For two or three weeks Knecht had stood quite alone with the whole community opposed to him. In hunger and desperation the old superstition, that only the sacrifice of the weather-maker could once more propitiate the powers, was revived. He had offered no resistance to this thought of sacrifice, and had proposed himself as an oblation. Furthermore, he had co-operated with unheard of courage and devotion towards lightening the burden. Time and time again, he had found water. The discovery of a trickling stream at the height of the distress had prevented the entire herd of cattle from being slaughtered. He had even prevented the tribal mother, who had been seized with a fatal desperation and spiritual weakness in this time of constraint, from collapsing and allowing everything to take an unreasonable course by his support, counsel, warning, magic and prayer and by his example and resolution. It clearly showed that in times of unrest and general trouble a man is more useful to the degree that he has based his life and thought upon the spiritual and the suprapersonal, the more he has learned to revere, watch, pray, serve and sacrifice. These two terrible years, which had almost destroyed him and brought him to sacrifice, had left him eventually more highly esteemed and more trusted—not of course by the irresponsible majority, but by the few who felt the responsibility and who knew how to judge a man of his nature.

Passing through these and many other trials, he reached maturity and the zenith of his life. He had helped to bury two tribal mothers, and had lost a pretty six-year-old son who had been carried off by a wolf. He had survived a grievous malady without outside aid, having always been his own doctor, and had suffered hunger and cold; and all this was pictured on his face, no less than in his soul. He had also made the discovery that a spiritual man in some curious way arouses resentment and opposition in others, who esteem him from afar and make claims on him in times of distress, but by no means love or look upon him as one of themselves and are more inclined to avoid him.

He had learned from experience that old-fashioned or home-made magic formulas and spells were more willingly acceptable to sick people or victims of misfortune than intelligent advice. He had learned that man prefers misfortune and external penance rather than attempt to change himself inwardly, and had found that he believes more easily in magic than in intelligence, and in formulas more readily than in experience—many things in fact which in the few thousand years that have elapsed have presumably not altered so much as many history books would have us believe. He had also learned that a man in quest of the spiritual should never

abandon love, that he should encounter human desires and
follies without arrogance, but should, however, never allow
them to dominate him; for, from the sage to the charlatan,
the priest to the mountebank, from the helping brother to
the parasitical sponger, is only a short step, and people
fundamentally prefer to pay a rogue or allow themselves to
be exploited by a quack than to accept selflessly offered
assistance for which no recompense is asked. They would not
readily pay with confidence and love, but preferably with
gold or wares. They cheated each other and expected to be
cheated in return. One had to learn to regard man as a weak,
selfish and cowardly being, but one had also to see how
greatly one participated in all these characteristics and urges
oneself. And therefore one ought to believe, and nourish
one's soul upon the fact that man, too, is spirit and love, and
that within him something dwells which off-sets his urges and
longs for ennoblement. But these thoughts are already far too
abstract and over-formulated for Knecht to have been capable
of them. Let us say that he was on the way to them, that his
way would one day lead him to them and help him to
transcend them.

Following this path, yearning after these thoughts and yet
living far more in the senses, in a state of bewitchment
through the moon, the perfume of a herb, the salts of a root,
the taste of a bark, the culture of healing plants, the preparation of salves and the devotion to weather and the atmosphere,
he developed many capacities which we of later ages no
longer possess and only half understand. The most important
of these was naturally the making of rain. Even though on
many occasions the heavens remained obdurate and seemed
ruthlessly to mock his efforts, Knecht had made rain a
hundred times, and on each occasion in a slightly different
manner. He had of course not dared to alter or to interfere in
the least with the sacrifices, rites, supplicatory processions,
invocations and the music of the drums. But these were only
the official and public aspects of his activities—their official
and priestlike manifestation. It was certainly a magnificent
triumph and brought with it great exultation when, on the
evening of a day upon which sacrifices and processions had
taken place, the heavens surrendered themselves, the horizon
clouded over, the wind began to smell damp and the first

drops began to fall. For this the weathermaker had recourse to his art only to the extent of choosing a good day, and not striving blindly against the unforeseen. One had, of course, to implore the powers and assail them, but with intelligence and moderation and by bowing to their will. But far more cherished than these fine successes and the pleasure of being listened to, were certain other achievements of which no one knew, and which he himself only knew with humility, and more with the senses than with the intellect. There were conditions of weather, tensions of air and heat, certain types of cloud and wind, different varieties of water, earth and dust scents, warnings and promises, moods and caprices of the weather demons, which Knecht felt beforehand in his skin, hair and in every sense, so that he could never be surprised or disappointed by anything, so that he compelled the weather to concentrate within himself, and absorbed it in such a manner that it enabled him to order the clouds and the winds. This was naturally not achieved arbitrarily or at will, but resulted from the unity and bond which the difference between himself and the world, between Within and Without, had perfected. He could stand and listen, or huddle enraptured, with all his pores open and not only feel the life of the air and the clouds in his innermost being but conjure them up and direct them, in exactly the same way as we are able to awaken and reproduce a phrase of music within ourselves. Then he had only to hold his breath and the wind or thunder would fall silent, only to nod or shake his head for the hail to break loose or cease, only to give expression through a smile to the corresponding struggle within himself, and the cloud masses above would concentrate and veil the thin blue light. On certain occasions, when his mood was particularly pure and his condition of soul favourable, he could reflect the weather for the coming day accurately, as though the whole score about to be played by nature was written in his blood. These were his good and best days, his rewards and his joys.

Whenever these inner connections with the outside were interrupted, when weather and the world were untrustworthy, incomprehensible and incalculable, his inner conditions would also be disturbed and the stream broken. He would feel himself to be no true Rainmaker, and find his office and his responsibility for weather and harvest onerous and unjust.

At such times he would stay at home and be obedient and helpful to Ada, assist her industriously with the household duties, make toys and tools for the children, concoct medicines, thirst for love and feel the urge to differ as little as possible from other men, to enter so completely into their usages and customs that he could even listen to the otherwise burdensome stories of his wife and the neighbours about the life, health and fortunes of other people. In good times, however, one saw little of him at home, for he would be roving about outside, angling, hunting, looking for roots, lying in the grass, perching in trees, sniffing the air, listening, imitating the voices of wild beasts, burning little fires and comparing the smoke clouds with those in the heavens, drenching his skin and hair with mist, rain, wind, sun or moonlight. In addition to this he would collect, as his master and predecessor, Turu, had done throughout his whole long life, articles in which Being and forms of appearance seemed to belong to different provinces, in which the wisdom or mood of nature seemed to betray a particle of her playing rules and creative secrets. He would collect, for example, objects that incorporated in their forms widely disassociated comparisons, such as knotted branches with faces of men or beasts, water-polished pebbles with a pattern of wood, fossilised animals of previous ages, deformed or twin fruit kernels and stones in the form of a kidney or a heart. He would read the veinings of a leaf, the network lineaments on the head of a morel, and vaguely suspect in them the secret, the spiritual, the future and the possible—the magic of symbols, a forecasting of numbers and writing, the transformation of the infinite and multiform into the simple, into the system and concept. For in him lay all the possibilities of world concepts through the spirit, nameless and unnamed admittedly, but not impossible and not unsuspected, still seed and bud, but growing singly and organically within himself to no small degree. And if we could go back a few thousand years before this Rainmaker and his primitive and graceful age, we believe that we should already meet everywhere with men of the spirit—of the spirit that has no origin and which has ever contained that which later ages have brought forth.

The Rainmaker Knecht could not perpetuate or codify his intuitions and bring them nearer to proof, but in any case this was hardly necessary. Admittedly he was not one of the discoverers of writing, geometry, medicine or astronomy: he remained an unknown link in the chain, but he was as indispensable a link as any other. He passed on everything that he had received, besides adding to it the hard-won results of his own experiences—for he, too, had pupils. During the course of his term of office he educated two pupils as rainmakers, one of whom became his successor.

For many years he had carried out his experiments unwatched and alone, and now for the first time—it was not long after that great season of bad harvests and famine—a youth, one of those whose urge was to be a rainmaker, began to visit, watch, spy upon, revere and persecute him. He felt, with a wondrous melancholic throb of his heart, the return and reversal of that great experience of his youth, and also for the first time that strong and at once strangling and awakening presentiment that youth was over, that the meridian had been passed and that the blossom had become fruit; that he was doing that which he had never dreamed of doing—witholding himself from the boy and behaving exactly as once old Turu had behaved towards himself. And this reserved withdrawal, this expectant and hesitant behaviour, came quite naturally and instinctively to him: it was neither an emulation of his dead master, nor did it arise from deliberations of moral and educational principles, such as the initial testing of a young man for a long period in order to see whether he were serious enough, the witholding of secrets and the placing of difficulties in his way, or similar considerations. No, Knecht behaved towards his pupil quite simply as any somewhat elderly, solitary and scholarly original may towards his admirers and pupils—in an embarrassed, shy, retiring and evasive manner, full of fear for his cherished loneliness and freedom to stray into the wilderness, for his free and lonely hunting and plant gathering, dreaming and listening; full of jealous love for all his habits and preferences, secrets and contemplations. He by no means opened his arms to the persistent young man who approached him with respectful curiosity, nor did he encourage him in his persistence. He did not for one moment consider it as a joy and a reward, as recognition and pleasant success that the world of the others had at last sent him an ambassador with a declaration of love,

that someone was courting him, that someone felt attracted
and related to him, and like him was called to the service and
its secrets. On the contrary, he felt it primarily as a wearisome importunity and an attack upon his rights and customs,
a theft of his independence which, for the first time, he realised
how much he loved. He struggled against it, and became
an expert in stratagem and self-concealment, in erasing the
traces of his journeys, in circumvention and disappearance.
But at length the same thing happened to him as had once
happened to Turu—the long mute courtship of the youth
slowly softened his heart, slowly wore down his resistance,
slowly tired and melted him so that, the more the young man
won ground the more he turned towards him and relented,
confirmed his longings and accepted his courtship. He
accepted the often burdensome duty of taking an apprentice
and pupil, which was inevitable, was ordained by destiny and
was the wish of the spirit. Ever more was he obliged to say
goodbye to dreams, to the sensation and enjoyment of
boundless possibilities that the future held in store. Instead of
his dream of endless progress towards the sum total of all
wisdom, a pupil now stood there, a small, ever present,
nagging reality, an interloper and a disturber of his privacy,
but not one to be repelled or discouraged—the only entry
into the true future, the only really important duty, the only
narrow path through which the Rainmaker's life and deeds,
theories, thoughts and surmises could be saved from death
and live further in a new tiny bud. Alternately sighing,
gnashing his teeth and smiling, he accepted his duty. And
in this important, perhaps the most important branch of his
office—the imparting of tradition and the education of his
successor—the Rainmaker was not spared a very deep and
bitter experience and disillusionment.

The first boy who made demands upon his favour, and
whom he had accepted after much delay and resistance as his
pupil, was named Maro. This youth brought him nothing
but endless disappointment. He was subservient and engaging, and for a long time observed a rigid obedience, but he
had many failings: above all he was lacking in courage, and
was afraid of darkness and the night, a weakness which he
endeavoured to conceal and which Knecht, as soon as he had
noticed it, had for a long time considered to be a legacy from

childhood, which would eventually disappear. But Maro never lost this fear. Moreover, he was completely lacking in the gift of selfless and dispassionate observation, and of devoting himself in thoughts and conjectures to the execution and demands of his calling. He was clever, had a clear quick understanding and learned everything that can be learned without devotion, easily and surely. But as time went on he displayed more and more selfish aims and intentions, and to these ends he had wished to learn the art of rainmaking.

His desire was above all to be esteemed, to play a leading part and to make an impression. He had the vanity of the talented but was without vocation, and in his eagerness for praise boasted of the first things he had learned before comrades of his own age. Even that, thought Knecht, might be pure childishness, and might perhaps be outgrown. Maro did not, however, seek only applause, but soon began striving for power over others and for profit. As soon as the master began to notice this he became terrified, and gradually withdrew his heart from the youth. This led to three or four serious misdemeanours of a nature which were only made possible by virtue of his having studied for several years with Knecht. The boy allowed himself to be led astray without either the permission or knowledge of his master, and in return for presents took the liberty of treating a sick child with medicaments and of chanting spells against a plague of rats in one of the huts. Eventually, when he was once more caught in the act of performing such practices despite all threats and promises, the master released him from his service, informed the tribal mother and endeavoured to dismiss the ungrateful and useless young man from his memory.

He was recompensed for this unfortunate experience by both his later apprentices, and in particular by the second of them, who was his own son, Turu. He loved this youngest and last of his pupils and disciples with a great love, and believed that more could be made of him than even he had made of himself, for without a doubt his grandfather's spirit had returned to earth in his person. Knecht experienced the profound spiritual satisfaction of passing on the sum of his knowledge and belief to the future through the instrument of a man who was twice his own son, and to whom he would be able to relinquish his office when it became too onerous. But

his misguided first pupil was not to be banned so easily from
Knecht's life and thoughts. Even if not highly esteemed, he
was a very well liked and not uninfluential man in the village.
He had married, was popular as a kind of mountebank and
jester, was leader of the drums and remained a secret and
envious enemy of the Rainmaker's, at whose hands the latter
was obliged to suffer many great and small injuries. Knecht
had never been a sociable and friendly man: he needed solitude
and freedom, and had courted neither respect nor love except
once as a boy from his master, Turu. But now he began to
experience what it means to have an enemy and someone who
hates, and it spoilt many a day of his life for him. Maro
belonged in that category of pupils who possess high talents
and who, despite this, are at all times disagreeable and
burdensome to their teachers, because in their case talent has
not grown from below and within, founded on organic
strength—the tender ennobling sign of a good nature, valiant
blood and valiant character—but is rather something
coincidental, accidental, usurped or stolen. A pupil of little
character, but one who possesses great intelligence or
outstanding imagination, inevitably causes the teacher
embarrassment. He has to impart to this pupil his legacy of
knowledge and method, and make him capable of co-operating
with him in the spiritual life, and yet he must feel that it is his
personal higher duty to protect science and art from the
sacrilegious hands of the merely talented; for the teacher has
not to serve the pupil alone, but both of them are there to
serve the spirit. This is the reason why a teacher has a dread
and horror of certain dazzling talents, for that particular type
of pupil falsifies the entire meaning and service of the
teaching profession. Each promotion of the pupil who seems
to shine but is not fundamentally capable of service is
detrimental to the profession. and constitutes in some
measure a betrayal of the spirit. We know of many periods of
culture in history in which, as a result of deep-reaching disturbance of spiritual laws, a host of the merely talented were
to be found in the leadership of the community schools and
academies, when highly talented officials, who wanted to rule
without wishing to serve, occupied all the high offices. To
recognise this type of talent sufficiently early, before it has
absorbed the fundamentals of a spiritual profession, and to

divert it with necessary harshness into the channels of unspiritual occupations, is often a very difficult task. Knecht had made mistakes as well, and had been far too lenient with his pupil Maro. He had entrusted much adept wisdom to an ambitious and superficial individual, which was a great pity. The consequences to himself were to be heavier than he could have imagined.

A year arrived—Knecht's beard had already turned grey—when the relation between heaven and earth seemed to have been driven mad and destroyed by demons of unusual strength and cunning. These disturbances began in the autumn with terrifying majesty, appalling every soul to its foundations and filling all the villagers with a cloying fear. They began with a heavenly spectacle which had never been seen before. The winter solstice was approaching, an event which normally was always watched and marked by the Rainmaker with a certain ceremonious and awed reverence and with heightened attention. And then came an evening—a cool evening with a slight breeze blowing. The sky was glassy, and a few restless clouds, which retained the rosy light of the setting sun for an unusually long time, swept by at a great height—fleeting, alluring light bundles of foam in pale icy space. For several days Knecht had felt something stronger and more remarkable than it was usual for him to feel each year at the time of the shortening days—some influence of the powers in space, a trepidation over the earth and among the plants and beasts, an unrest in the air, something intangible, expectant, fearful and full of foreboding in the whole of nature. The slow, tremulous oriflamme of clouds also seemed to belong to this evening hour with its billowing motion, which did not correspond to the gentle winds of earth, and which suddenly became invisible once the imploring and mournful red light, which seemed loath to be extinguished, had grown cold and died. Everything was quiet in the village. The open space before the tribal mother's hut was deserted, and the visitors and children had long since departed; only a couple of boys chasing and wrestling with each other were to be seen. Everyone else had long since returned to their huts, and many of them were already asleep. Possibly no one except the Rainmaker was watching the scarlet clouds at this sunset hour.

Knecht went into his tiny plant garden behind the hut and

began walking up and down, tense and restless, with his eye
on the weather. At times he sat down on a tree bole which
stood among the stinging nettles, and which served as a block
for chopping wood. With the extinction of the last cloud
beacon the stars suddenly seemed to have become more
visible, and to have increased in power and number in the
greenish after-glow that flooded the sky: where before only
two or three had been visible, there now stood ten or twenty.
The Rainmaker knew many of their groups and families, for
he had seen them a hundred times before. There was something reassuring in their unchanging reappearance. Stars were
comforting, although they stood cold and far distant; and
although they gave out no warmth they were reliable, well-
appointed and denoted a heavenly order that told of permanence. Seeming so alien and remote, so opposed to the life
of earth and man, so untouched—to the point of mockery—in
their superior, cold majesty and infinity by his warmth, fears,
sorrows, and ecstacies, the stars stood nevertheless in relation
to humans, perhaps led and ruled over them; and if some
human knowledge, some spiritual property or security and
superiority of the spirit had been achieved and maintained
over the transitory, then they too were like the stars, shone
like them in cool tranquility, consoled with their cool wonder,
and looked down eternally and somewhat ironically. Thus had
it often seemed to the Rainmaker, and although he by no
means had that close, exciting, constantly changing and
proven relationship with the stars that he had with the moon
—that giant, near, damp, fat, magic fish in the ocean of
heaven—he was bound to them deeply in many a belief. To
gaze at them intently for a long time and to accept their
influence, to surrender his puniness, warmth and anxiety to
their ice-cold stare, had often been to him like a bath and a
healing potion. And to-night they looked no different except
that they were very bright and sharply defined in the thin
taut air, but he found no rest in giving himself to them. A
power from· unknown space attracted him, made his pores
tingle and his eyes smart, working upon him insidiously
without cease like a current or a warning shock. Near-by in
the hut the weak light from the oven embers glowed a forlorn
red. A little warm life flowed from it and rang like a summons,
a smile, or a yawn, redolent of the odour of men, the warmth

of skin, maternity, the sleep of children, and through its
harmless proximity seemed to make the oncoming night
darker and to drive the stars even further back into their
immeasurable distance and remoteness.

And then just as Knecht heard the voice of Ada inside the
hut calming a child with a low crooning melody, there began
in the heavens that catastrophe which the village was to
remember for many a year. A mighty shimmering and
flickering started up in the tranquil naked net of stars above,
as though the otherwise invisible strands of this net were
vibrating and single stars began to fall like burning hot
stones which had been hurled through space, only to be
rapidly extinguished. At first it was only one or two, perhaps
a pair, and the eye had not lost sight of the first disappearing,
falling star, and the heart had not recovered from the first
surprise and begun to beat again, than they began to fall sheer
through the heavens in gentle curving lines in their dozens
and hundreds—lights falling or flung in countless showers as
though driven by a hurricane through the silent night, falling
as though a cosmic autumn of the world was tearing all the
stars like faded leaves from the tree of heaven and was
chasing them noiselessly into the void. Like faded leaves, like
gently cradled snowflakes, they flew in their thousands,
hither and thither in the terrifying stillness, to disappear
somewhere in the abyss behind the wooded mountains to the
south-east where, in the memory of man, no star had ever
fallen. With frozen heart and burning lids Knecht stood, his
head thrust deep into his neck in terror, looking with insatiable curiosity into this bewitched and transformed
heaven, mistrusting his eyes and yet only too well aware of
the appalling event. Like all the others who observed this
nocturnal phenomenon, he believed that the well-known stars
themselves were rocking, stumbling, and apparently falling:
he expected that the arch of heaven, unless it were first
swallowed up by the earth, would soon be blank and empty.
After a while he realised that which the others were not
capable of doing—that the familiar stars, here and there and
everywhere, were still in their accustomed places, and that
the star steeds were not playing their frantic games among
the old and trusted ones but in the intervening space between
heaven and earth; that these new lights which were falling

or being hurled by some invisible hand and which appeared
and disappeared so quickly, were glowing with a somewhat
different coloured fire to the true stars. This consoled Knecht
and helped him to compose himself. But even if they were
only other new and transitory stars, which were filling the
air with their disintegration, it was gruesome and evil, a
disorder and a catastrophe, and a deep sigh came from his
dry throat. He looked around him and listened, to ascertain
whether he had been the sole spectator of this ghostly
spectacle, or whether others had also seen it. Soon he heard a
moaning and screaming, and cries of terror coming from the
other huts: other villagers had seen it, had passed on the
news, and had aroused the unconscious sleepers. In a trice,
fear and panic had taken hold of the whole village. With a
deep sigh, Knecht assumed responsibility.

As Rainmaker this misfortune concerned him more than
all the others—he, who to a certain extent was responsible
for order in the heavens and in the air. He had always
recognised or felt in advance great catastrophes such as
floods, hail or great storms, had each time warned and prepared the tribal mother and the elders, had averted the worst
and had placed himself, by his knowledge, courage and confidence in the higher powers, between the village and despair.
Why, on this occasion, had he known nothing about it in
advance and taken his precautions? Why had he not said a
word to anyone of the dark warning presentiments which he
had most certainly felt?

Cautiously he raised the mat at the entrance to the huts and
softly called his wife's name. She came towards him with her
youngest at her breast, but he took the little one away from
her and laid him on the straw. Then he caught hold of Ada's
hand, laid a finger on his lips, demanding silence and led her
out. He noticed how her patient, quiet face had immediately
filled with fear and terror.

"The children must sleep and see nothing! Do you hear?"
he whispered vehemently. "You must let none of them go
outside—not even Turu. And you are to remain inside
yourself!"

He unconsciously hesitated as to how much he should say or
as to how much he should betray his own thoughts, and at last

added resolutely: "Nothing will happen to you and the children!"

She believed him implicitly, although her look betrayed that she had by no means recovered from the shock that she had suffered.

"What is it, then?" she asked, looking past him into the sky. "Is it very bad?"

"Very bad, indeed!" he said softly. "Yes, I think it is very bad—but it will not affect you and the little ones. Remain in the hut and keep the door well closed. I must join the villagers and talk with them. Go inside, Ada!"

He guided her through the hut entrance, arranged the mat carefully and stood there for a few moments with his face turned towards the unceasing rain of stars. At last he lowered his head, sighed once more with a heavy heart and went quickly through the night towards the village, to the hut of the tribal mother.

Half the villagers had already collected there. A subdued hubbub, half stricken and half suppressed, arose from them in their fear and despair. A few men and women, in their terror and with a foreboding of disaster, were giving way to a display of mad rage and voluptuousness; others stood stiff and trembling, or stumbled about with uncontrolled limbs; one man was foaming at the mouth and dancing a desperate and obscene solo dance, and tearing his long hair out by the handful. Knecht saw everything. It was already in progress: bewitched and maddened by the falling stars, they had already all but abandoned themselves to their intoxication, which would perhaps culminate in an insensate orgy of rage and suicidal lust. It was high time to gather the few courageous and enlightened members of the tribe and to fortify their courage. The ancient tribal mother was quite calm. She thought that the end of everything had come, but did not defend herself against it and presented a firm, hard, almost ironical face, with its network of autumnal wrinkles, to destiny.

Knecht forced her to listen to him. He tried to point out to her that the old stars, which had been there from time immemorial, were still in the sky; but she could not realise this, perhaps because her eyes no longer had the strength to see them, and perhaps because her conception of the stars and her relationship with them differed from that of the Rain-maker's, so that neither could understand the other. She shook her head and preserved her courageous grin, but when Knecht implored her not to abandon her people in their in-toxication of fear to themselves and to the demons, she was immediately in agreement. A small group of frightened but clear-headed men who were ready to be led formed itself around the Rainmaker and herself.

When Knecht had appeared on the scene he had hoped to be able to avoid panic by means of example, intelligence, speech, explanation and exhortations; but after his conversa-tion with the tribal mother, he discovered that it was too late. He had hoped to allow the others to participate in his own experience, to present and transmit it to them; he had hoped that they would, under his exhortations, realise that not all the stars had been dragged from the sky by the hurricane and fallen to earth, and that, as a result of this knowledge, he would be able to lead them from helpless fear and astonish-ment to active observation and thus endure the catastrophe. But, as he quickly perceived, there were only a very few in the whole village who were susceptible to his influence, and unless he soon won them over the others would succumb to complete madness. No, as is so often the case, nothing could be done here with reason and with wise words. Fortunately, another method was at hand. Even though it were impossible to exorcise the fear of death by an appeal to reason, it was still possible to control and organise this fear of death, to canalise it and give it form, to transform it from a hopeless turmoil and insanity into a unity, by building a choir out of the uncontrolled and savage single voices.

No sooner had Knecht attempted this method than it began to take effect. He appeared before the people and intoned the well-known opening words of the prayer that was used on occasions of public mourning and penance, also as the Death Lament for a tribal mother, at the sacrifices or penitential feasts and in times of danger such as pestilence and flood. He screamed out the words in their tempo and reinforced the rhythm with hand-beats. Screaming and clapping his hands, he bent forward almost to the soil, rose up, bent and rose again, repeating this ten or twenty times while the old village mother stood muttering rhythmically, and approving his ritual movements with little nods of her head. All the villagers from the other huts entered without further ado into the mood and spirit of the ceremony. The few who had been wholly possessed soon collapsed from exhaustion and lay unconscious on the ground or were captivated by the choral murmur and the nodding rhythm of the ceremony. He had succeeded. Instead of a despairing horde of madmen, there stood a people ready for sacrifice and penitential prayer, each one of them benefiting and being strengthened in heart, not burying his terror and his fear of death within himself or raving for himself alone, but co-operating and following the beats of the well-ordered choir of the community in a ceremony of conjuration. Such an exercise possesses many occult powers. The greatest consolation deriving from it lies in the uniformity and the doubled communal feeling, the most infallible catharsis being moderation and order, rhythm and music.

While the entire nocturnal heavens were covered with an army of falling stars like a silent cascade of diamonds, which for a further two hours dispensed its giant red drops of fire, the terror of the village changed into devotion and surrender, into a summons and a feeling of penance; as opposed to this heaven-ordained cataclysm the fear and weakness of man was transformed into an order and an harmonic cult. Before the rain of stars began to diminish and grow weary, the miracle had already taken place, radiating healing strength; and when at last the heavens were at peace once more and seemed to have recovered, all the exhausted penitents had the redeeming feeling of having appeased the powers with their exercise and of having restored the heavens to law and order.

The night of terror was not forgotten, and was spoken of throughout the whole autumn and winter—no longer in whispers and in secret, but in an everyday tone of voice and with the satisfaction that one may feel when looking back upon a well-weathered catastrophe or a danger averted. One recalled the details with relish, for everyone had been surprised at the unheard of phenomenon in his own fashion, and each wished to be considered the first to have discovered it. People permitted themselves to make fun of the most terrified and overwhelmed ones, and a certain excitement remained for a long time in the village. They had all experienced something, something gigantic had happened, something had definitely gone wrong.

To this mood and to the gradual loss of interest and forgetfulness of the great event, Knecht did not subscribe. For him this sinister experience remained as an unforgettable warning, a thorn that refused to be removed, for it represented for him something which had by no means been left behind, or been averted, exorcised, and appeased by the dancing procession, penance and ritual prayer. For him, in fact, the remoter it became the more meaningful it became; and it eventually assumed so great a significance that it made of him a thinker and cogitator. In his eyes this event, this magnificent performance of nature, was in itself an enormous and weighty problem with several perspectives. A man who had once seen this could very well reflect upon it for the rest of his life. Only one other person in the village now looked upon the rain of stars with similar premises and similar eyes, and this was his own son and pupil, Turu. Only his having witnessed it could have held any value as a corroboration of Knecht's own observations and correctives. But he had allowed his son to sleep, and the more he reflected upon the reason for his having done this, why he had renounced the single co-witness and observer who could be taken seriously on the subject of this unheard of event, the more he was strengthened in his belief that he had acted well and correctly and had obeyed a wise presentiment. He had wished to protect his own kin from seeing it, and also his pupil and colleague, but in particular the boy himself, for whom he cared more than anyone else. He had therefore concealed and witheld the fall of stars from him, for he believed in the good spirits of sleep and in the necessity of youthful sleep. And further, if his memory did not deceive him, he had at that moment, at the beginning of that heavenly portent, actually thought that it was less a sign of a forthcoming catastrophe than a present mortal danger for all, and especially for one who was as vulnerable as a rainmaker.

Something was being prepared up there, something in the nature of a danger and a threat from that sphere to which he was allied by reason of his office, and in whatever guise it appeared it would always first and foremost specifically concern him. To meet this danger in a resolute and alert

manner, to prepare himself spiritually to that end, to accept
it but not to be demeaned or belittled by it, was the attitude
and resolution which he had adopted as regards the great
phenomenon. It would require a mature and courageous man
to meet this approaching destiny, and therefore it would not
have been a good thing to have embroiled his son in it and to
have made him a co-sufferer and witness, for despite his high
opinion of the boy he was not convinced that a young and
unproven mortal would have been able to withstand it.

Turu was admittedly very displeased that he had slept
through and missed the great spectacle. Whatever conflicting
reports might say, it had undoubtedly been a great occasion,
and one perhaps that he would never see again during his
lifetime. He had missed an experience and a cosmic wonder,
and on account of this he was sulky with his father. This
resentment, however, was not of long duration, for the old
man compensated him for the loss with increased tenderness
and attention, and drew him closer than ever before into the
ramifications of his office. He gave him a visible foretaste of
coming events, and took the trouble to make of Turu the
most perfect and enlightened successor possible. Although he
spoke but seldom about the rain of stars, he took the boy ever
more ruthlessly into his secrets, practices, knowledge and
research, allowing him to accompany him on all his walks and
to watch experiments and nature observations which he had
previously confided to no one.

The winter came and went—a mild and damp winter. No
more stars fell from the heavens, no great and unusual things
happened in the village, and the people were reassured. The
hunters went eagerly about their business, and in the frosty
weather bundles of stiff frozen hides could be seen everywhere hanging from poles above the huts. Wood was
dragged from the forests over the snow on long, polished
sleighs. During the short period of frost an old woman died
in the village, and could not be buried immediately; they
were obliged to wait several days until the soil unfroze, and
in the meanwhile the corpse lay near her hut door.

The advent of spring partially confirmed the evil forebodings of the Rainmaker. It was a bleak and joyless spring,
abandoned by the moon, a spring without drive or sap. The
moon's phases were always in retard, and the signs necessary

for determining the day for sowing never favourable. The
wild flowers bloomed sparsely and unopened buds hung dead
upon the twigs. Knecht was very perturbed, but took pains to
hide his fears, and only Ada and Turu could see how tortured
he was. He did not order the usual invocations, but offered up
private and personal sacrifices, cooking sweet-smelling
stimulating brews and potions for the demons. On the night
of the new moon he cut his beard short, added resin and bark
to the hairs and burned them in a chafing dish, which gave off
a thick smoke. As long as possible he avoided public ceremonies such as communal sacrifice, penitential processions
or the choir of drums, and allowed this bewitched weather
and infernal spring to remain his own personal affair.
Nevertheless, as the accustomed time for sowing was long
passed, he was obliged to report to the tribal mother. Here
again he met with misfortune and frustration. The old mother,
who had been a good friend to him and who looked upon him
almost maternally, would not receive him. She felt ill, lay in
bed and had given over all her duties and cares to her sister,
who was far from well-disposed towards the Rainmaker. She
did not possess the strong upright character of the older
woman and had a leaning towards distractions and frivolities;
and, moreover, this addiction had been encouraged in her by
the mountebank Maro, who knew well how to divert and
flatter her . . . and Maro was Knecht's enemy. The Rainmaker
sensed her coolness and hostility at the first meeting,
although she did not once contradict him. His explanations
and proposals to postpone both the sowing, certain sacrifices
and the procession for a little longer were sanctioned, but the
old woman had received and treated him as an inferior, and
his request to be allowed to see the tribal mother and to treat
her with medicine was curtly refused. Knecht returned from
this interview despondent and in some way poorer. It had left
an evil taste in his mouth. For half a moon he worked in his
own fashion to produce weather conducive to sowing.

But the weather, which had so often obeyed his inner
radiations, remained obstinate and hostile and was impervious either to sacrifice or to magic. The Rainmaker was
left with no alternative but to visit the tribal mother's sister
once more. This time it was with a petition for patience and
postponement. He noticed immediately that she must have

discussed both himself and the situation with the clown Maro,
for in pointing out the need for deciding upon either a day for
the sowing or for public intercession the old woman over-
played the omniscient and made use of several expressions
which she could only have learned from Maro, his first
apprentice. Knecht asked for three days grace, forecast that
the whole constellations would be differently dispersed and
more favourable, and recommended the day for sowing as the
first of the moon's third quarter. The old woman agreed, and
uttered the ritual phrases. The village was informed, and
there was a general preparation for the feast of the sowing.
And now, when for the moment everything seemed to be in
order again, the demons showed their displeasure once more.
On the day prior to the longed-for and well-prepared day for
the sowing, the tribal mother died. The feast had to be postponed, and arrangements made for her burial instead. It was a
celebration of the first order. Behind the new village mother,
her sisters and daughters, the Rainmaker took his place in the
finery of the great funeral procession in his high, pointed
fox-fur head-dress, assisted by his son Turu, who beat the
double-toned hard wood clappers. Great honour was paid to
the dead woman and also to her sister, the new tribal mother.
Maro was well to the forefront with his drums, and was
applauded and admired. The villagers wept and feasted,
enjoyed the keening and the ritual, the music of the drums
and the sacrifices.

It was a wonderful day for everyone, but the sowing had
again been postponed. Knecht stood there sedate and calm,
but nevertheless deeply perturbed: it seemed to him as though
with the old woman he had buried all the good things of
his life.

Very soon, at the request of the new mother, the sowing
took place, and was carried out with great pomp. The
procession filed majestically across the fields, and with a
stately gesture the new mother flung the first handful of seed
on to the community land. On each side of her walked a sister
carrying a pouch of corn, into which the tribal mother dipped.
Knecht breathed a little more freely once this ceremony
was over.

But the sowing, which had passed with such festivity, was

destined to bring neither joy nor harvest. It was a graceless
year. There was a sharp return of winter and a late frost fell.
The weather during that spring and summer played all
manner of tricks and vagaries, and when at last in mid-
summer the fields were covered with a meagre and sparse
harvest the last and worst disaster occurred. An unheard of
drought set in, worse than any in human memory. Week after
week the sun beat down with a shimmering white heat; the
small brooks dried up, and the village pond became no more
than a dirty quagmire—a paradise for dragon-flies and a
monstrous brood of mosquitoes. Cracks appeared in the soil,
and one could watch the harvest sicken and wither before
one's eyes.

From time to time clouds would gather, but the weather
remained dry, and whenever a drop of rain fell it was
followed for days on end by a searing east wind. The lightning struck the tallest trees, and their dry tops were set
ablaze like fiery beacons.

"Turu," Knecht said one day to his son, "these things will
not turn out well, for we have all the demons against us. I
think that it will probably cost me my life. Take heed now:
when the moment comes for me to be sacrificed, assume my
office and as your first duty demand that my body be burned
and the ashes strewn over the fields. Then the evil spell will
be broken. You must take care that no one seizes the corn
stocks of the community—the penalty for this must be death.
Next year things will improve, and it will be said: 'It is good
that we have a new young Rainmaker'."

Despair reigned in the village. Maro incited the inhabitants, and on several occasions threats and curses were
flung at the Rainmaker. Ada fell ill, and lay racked with fever
and vomiting. The processions, offerings and the long
heartrending drum choirs were all in vain. Knecht was always
at their head, for this was his duty, but once the people had
broken up he stood alone, a man whom all avoided. He knew
what was required, and knew too that Maro had already
demanded his sacrifice of the tribal mother. For the sake of his
own honour and out of love for his son, he took the final step:
dressing Turu in the great ceremonial dress, he led him
before the old woman, recommended him as his successor,

and laid down his office. He then offered himself as a sacrifice. She watched him for a moment with curiosity, and then nodded her head in agreement.

The oblation took place on the same day. The whole village attended, except those who lay sick in their huts with dysentery. Ada, too, was grievously ill. Turu, in his ceremonial dress with the high fox head-dress nearly succumbed to sunstroke. All the notables and dignitaries who were not ill were present, together with the tribal mother and her two sisters, the elders and the drum leader, Maro. Behind them came the people. No one insulted the old Rainmaker. Everything took place in an uneasy and heavy silence. They entered the forest, and made for the round clearing which Knecht himself had appointed for the sacrifice. The majority of the men had brought their stone axes to cut wood for the stake. When they finally arrived at the clearing, they left the Rainmaker standing in the centre and formed a narrow ring around him, while beyond this the crowd formed an outer circle.

As an irresolute and embarrassed silence had fallen upon the whole assembly, the Rainmaker himself took the initiative. "I have been your Rainmaker," he said to them, "and I have plied my trade to the best of my ability for many years. Now the demons are against me and I shall have no more success: therefore I have offered myself as a sacrifice. That will appease the demons! My son, Turu, will be your new Rainmaker. Now slay me, and when I am dead follow the counsels of my son! Live well! And who will kill me? I suggest Maro as the most suitable man for the deed."

He fell silent and no one moved. Turu, flushed and hot beneath the heavy head-dress, looked round anxiously. A look of scorn had curled on his father's lips.

At last the tribal mother stamped her foot in rage and made a sign to Maro, crying: "Proceed, then! Take your axe and accomplish the deed!"

Maro, axe in hand, stood in front of his former teacher, hating him more than ever, for the look of scorn on that silent mouth wounded him. Raising his axe, he compelled himself to self-control and stood there aiming and swaying, staring his victim in the face and waiting for him to close his eyes. But Knecht kept his eyes open and looked unflinchingly at the man with the axe, almost without expression. Only, in those fine old eyes there could be discerned an admixture of compassion and scorn.

In a rage, Maro threw away his axe. "I will not do it!" he muttered, and pushed his way through the circle of the elders to disappear among the crowd.

A few laughed softly. The tribal mother was pale with rage, both at the conduct of the useless and cowardly Maro and at the arrogance of the Rainmaker. She beckoned to one of the elders—a worthy, tranquil man who stood leaning on his axe and who seemed to be ashamed of this uncomfortable scene.

He stepped forward, gave a curt and friendly nod to the victim—they had known each other since childhood. Knecht now willingly closed his eyes and lowered his head a little. The old man struck him with the axe, and he collapsed.

Turu, the new Rainmaker, could hardly utter a word, but gave the necessary orders with a gesture. A wooden clump was soon brought and the dead man laid upon it. The festive ritual of firemaking with the two consecrated sticks was Turu's first official act.

THE FATHER CONFESSOR

IN THE DAYS WHEN Saint Hilarion was still living, although he was well advanced in years, there dwelt in the town of Gaza one Joseph Famulus who, until his thirtieth year or more, had lived a worldly life, studied the pagan books and at last, through the instrument of a woman whom he had coveted, had become acquainted with the heavenly doctrines and the sweetness of Christian virtues.

He submitted to the sacrament of baptism, abjured his sins and sat for many years at the feet of a priest of his town listening with burning curiosity to tales from the lives of the pious hermits who dwelt in the desert, until one day, when he was nearly thirty-six years old, he took that way which Saint Paul and Saint Anthony had taken before him and which so many pious men have taken since. He presented the rest of his goods to the elders to be distributed among the poor of the community, took leave of his friends by the gate and wandered out of the town into the desert—out of the iniquitous world to assume the life of a penitent.

For many a year the sun scorched and withered him and he grazed his knees in prayer on the rocks and sand, waiting until sunset before chewing his few dates. The devil tortured him with temptations, scorn and tribulations, but he exorcised him with prayers, penances and self-sacrifice such as one can find written in all the lives of the holy Fathers. Many an evening he would look up at the stars, but these too brought him temptation and confusion: he still interpreted the constellations as histories of the Gods and images of humans —a science in which he had once been proficient, which was held in abomination by the priest and which still persecuted him with the fantasies and thoughts that remained with him from his pagan days.

In the neighbourhood at that time, wherever a spring, a handful of grass or a large oasis was to be found in the bare unfruitful soil, lived the hermits, many of them in solitude, many in brotherhoods such as can be seen in the frescoes in the Campo Santo in Pisa. They practised poverty and love for one's neighbour and were adepts in the melancholy *ars moriendi*—the art of dying—in the release from the world and from the ego through mortification and in the translation through death into light and the immortal, to the Redeemer. They were visited by angels and devils, composed hymns, exorcised demons, healed and blessed and seemed to have taken it upon themselves to atone for the world lust, barbarity and sensuality of many previous and many future ages. This was the result of a powerful wave of enthusiasm and devotion and of a superlative ecstasy in renunciation of the world.

Many of them still followed the old heathen practices of purification and the methods and exercises taken from the highly cultivated secular experience of asiatic spiritualisation. This, however, was no longer referred to and these methods and yoga practices were no longer taught, but stood under the ban which Christianity had imposed more and more upon everything pagan.

This ardent life developed remarkable gifts in many of these penitents—the gift of prayer, healing through the laying on of hands, prophecy, exorcism and gifts of dispensing judgments and punishments, consolations and blessings. In Joseph, too, slumbered a gift which came slowly to fruition as his hair began to turn white. It was the gift of listening. When a brother from one of the hermitages or some child of the world with a troubled and guilty conscience found himself in Joseph's presence and told him of his deeds, sorrows, temptations and failures, of his life, his struggle for good and defeat in the struggle, or of some loss, pain or mourning, Joseph understood how to listen, to lend him his ear and open his heart to him, and how to assimilate the other's sorrow and care, leaving him purged and comforted.

Slowly, after many years, this office claimed him completely and made of him a tool, an ear in which one confided. His virtues were a certain patience, a receptive passivity and a great gift for silence. More and more people came to him to open their hearts and to unburden themselves of their pent-up distress: many of them, even if they had travelled a long way to his hut, and once having arrived and greeted him, did not confess freely and courageously but were hesitant and ashamed, exaggerated their sins, sighed or remained silent for hours on end. He behaved in the same manner with each of them whether they spoke with pleasure or unwillingly, whether they were fluent or stammering, or whether they blurted out their secrets angrily and laid too much stress upon them. They were all alike to him, if they blamed God or themselves, if they exaggerated or minimised their sins and sufferings, if they had committed a murder or only confessed to an immorality, complained of an untrue lover or had imperilled their hopes of salvation.

It did not shock him if one of his visitors told him of his traffic with the devil, with whom he would seem to be on intimate terms; nor did it anger him if one of them talked at great length upon all manner of subjects obviously without revealing the major trouble; nor did he grow impatient if one of them confessed to hallucinations and sins of his own invention. Everything in the nature of laments, admissions, complaints and pangs of conscience appeared to be absorbed by his ear like water by the desert sand. He pronounced no judgment and seemed to feel neither pity nor contempt for the penitent, and in spite of this—or even perhaps because of it—nothing which was confessed to him seemed to have been uttered in vain, but to have been changed, understood, relieved and absolved.

He very seldom spoke a word of warning or admonition, and even less often did he give a word of advice or a command—this did not appear to be part of his vocation, and the visitor would also seem in some way to sense it. His vocation was to awaken and to receive confidences, to listen patiently and lovingly, and with these gifts to aid the half-formed confession to perfection, to release what was dammed up or encrusted in the soul and give it a free passage, to take it upon himself and to enshroud it in silence. Only at the end of each confession, whether it had been appalling or harmless, contrite or vain, would he kneel down beside the penitent, say a paternoster and, before dismissing him, kiss him on the forehead.

To prescribe penances and punishments he did not feel to be his duty, nor did he feel entitled to give priestly absolution; nor was he concerned with judgment or forgiveness of sin. By listening and understanding he seemed to accept part of the guilt and to be anxious to help. By his silence the confession seemed to have sunk into the past, and when he prayed with the sinner after confession it was as though he had accepted him as a brother and had recognised him as one of his own kind. With his kiss he seemed to have blessed him in a manner more brotherly than priestly, more tender than pontifical.

His fame spread throughout the whole region of Gaza. He was known from far and wide and was compared with the venerable and great Father Confessor and hermit Dion Pugil, whose calling dated from ten years earlier and whose capabilities and customs had quite other foundations. Father Dion was famous for his intuitive reading of the souls entrusted to him, which told him more than spoken words. Thus it would happen that a diffident penitent would often be surprised to be told of sins to which he had not yet confessed. This expert in souls, of whom Joseph had heard a hundred astonishing stories, and with whom he would never have dared to compare himself, was also an accomplished adviser of transgressors, a great judge, chastiser and supervisor: he prescribed penances, castigations and pilgrimages, consecrated marriages, compelled enemies to reconciliation, and his authority was almost as great as that of a bishop. He lived in the neighbourhood of Ascalon, but received petitioners from as far distant as Jerusalem and even further afield.

For many years, like most of the hermits and penitents, Joseph Famulus had waged a passionate and exhausting conflict. Although he had abandoned his worldly life, given away his goods and his house and fled from the town with its abundant temptations of worldliness and lusts of the flesh, he had been obliged to take himself in hand, and found that he possessed every urge in both body and soul that can lead a man to wretchedness and temptation. Above all he had struggled against his body, had been ruthless and harsh with it, accustomed it to heat and cold, hunger and thirst, scars and callouses, until it had slowly withered and almost dried up. And yet even in this haggard ascetic's shell he could still be ignominiously surprised and angered by the unreasonable lusts, desires, dreams and fantasies of the old Adam. We know only too well that the devil devotes special attention to penitents and to those who have fled from the world. Therefore when seekers of consolation and those who felt the need to unburden their souls had sought him out, he recognised in this a sign of grace and at the same time experienced an alleviation of his ascetic life. He had been granted a purpose and content outside his own self, and a duty had been entrusted to him through which he could serve others and simultaneously serve as an instrument of God to attract souls to Him. This had been a truly wonderful and elevating thought; but from experience he learned that the souls of the good are also earthbound and can be the object of temptations and traps. For example, when a wanderer, on foot or upon some beast, came to rest before his rocky grotto to drink a mouthful of water and to confess, Joseph would often be seized with a feeling of self-sufficiency and contentment, of vanity and self-love, the realization of which horrified him. Many a time he would implore God on bended knees to send him no more penitents, either from the huts of his neighbourhood or from the villages and towns of the world, for he was unworthy of receiving them. But then at other times, when his flock did not appear, he would feel no better, and once they resumed their visits he would find himself guilty of a new sin: as he listened to this or that admission he now

experienced sentiments of coldness and uncharitableness—
even of contempt—towards the penitents. With a sigh he
accepted this conflict as well, and there were times after such
confessions when he would inflict penances and mortifications
upon himself. In addition to this he made it a rule to treat all
the penitents not only as brothers but with a certain deference
and to a greater degree the less the individual happened to
appeal to him. He received them as messengers from God
who had been sent to test him. And so with the passing
years he found, late enough in life, a certain equipoise of
conduct, with the result that everyone who approached him
considered him a blameless man who had discovered the
peace of God.

Now peace is to a certain extent a living thing, must wax
and wane, adapt itself and undergo tests and transformations;
and the peace of Joseph Famulus was no exception to this
rule. It was unstable and liable to change, at times visible and
at times not, now like a candle held in the hand, now remote
like a star in the wintry heaven. And gradually a completely
new type of sin and temptation began to make his life a
burden. It was no strong, passionate emotion, no increase or
diminution of the life-urge, but seemed to be quite the
opposite: it was a feeling which in its early stages was fairly
easy to bear, and was in fact hardly noticeable—a condition
devoid of any suffering or privation, a faint, lukewarm and
wearisome condition of the soul which only showed itself in a
negative fashion as an ephemeral waning and ultimate
complete lack of joy. Just as there are days when there is
neither sunshine nor rain, when the sky sinks into itself and
withdraws, and the weather is not black but grey, sultry and
yet not entirely thundery, so did the days of the ageing Joseph
gradually become: less and less was he able to distinguish
morning from evening, feast days from working days, days of
elation from those of defeat. They passed in a numbing
exhaustion and boredom. He grew sad because he had
expected an alleviation from his urges and an increasing
enlightenment with old age, to have arrived a step nearer the
hoped for harmony and repose of the soul; and he was sad
because old age now seemed to have disappointed and
deceived him inasmuch as it had brought him nothing but this
tired, grey, joyless desert, this feeling of unconquerable

MAGISTER LUDI

satiety. He felt glutted with everything—with existence itself, with breathing, sleeping and his life in the grotto at the edge of the little oasis with its eternal sequence of evenings and mornings, the approach of travellers and pilgrims, riding on camels or asses, with the comings and goings that so closely concerned him of those mad, timorous and at the same time credulous men whose need it was to relate their lives, sins and fears, temptations and complaints. It seemed to him at times that, just as the little spring in the oasis collected in the stone basin, and then flowed away through the grass in a tiny stream to seep into the desert waste and there quickly to be conquered and die, so did these confessions, this catalogue of sins, these life stories and plagueings of conscience, large and small, serious and vain, flow unceasingly into his ear in their myriads, ever renewing themselves.

But this ear was not dead like the sand of the desert. It was alive and could not sip, drink and absorb for ever: it inevitably tired, felt misused and filled to overflowing, and longed for the spate of words, admissions, cares, laments and self-chastisements to cease for once, longed for peace, death and silence to take the place of this endless flux. Yes, he desired an end to it all: he was tired and had had enough and more than enough. His life had become shallow and worthless, and he had reached the point where he felt tempted to put an end to his existence, to punish and exterminate himself just as the traitor Judas had done when he had hanged himself.

Whereas previously he had sown desires, visions and dreams of sensual and worldly lust within his soul, the devil now taunted him with visions of self-destruction, forced him to test the branch of every tree to see whether it were capable of bearing his weight, every cliff in the neighbourhood to see whether it were high and steep enough for him to cast himself down to his death. He resisted the temptation, struggled and did not weaken, but his nights were passed in a welter of self-loathing and lust for death and his life had become insupportable and repugnant.

This was the sorry state into which Joseph's life had fallen.

One day, when he had climbed to the top of a pile of rocks and seen in the distance on the horizon three small figures approaching—travellers, pilgrims or perhaps people who wished to visit him and confess—he was suddenly seized

with an irresistible longing to run away from this place
and from this mode of life at the greatest possible speed.
The longing was so powerful and compelling that it swept
away all other thoughts, objections and considerations—
and naturally these were plentiful, for how could a pious
penitent have obeyed such an urge without experiencing
pricks of conscience? He ran and ran, and was soon in his
cliff grotto once more, the scene of so many years of struggle,
the vessel of so many exaltations and defeats. In frantic
haste he seized a few handfuls of dates and a gourd of water,
which he stuffed into an old knapsack and slung it across his
shoulders. Grasping his staff he then left—left the peaceful
green of his home, a fugitive and a wanderer, a fugitive
before God and men, and most of all before that which he had
once envisaged as his call and mission. He fled at first like
one pursued, as if in reality those far-off figures which he
had observed from the cliff were persecutors and enemies
But in the course of an hour his terror-stricken haste had
left him, for the movement had done him good, and during
the first halt, when he did not allow himself to break his fast—
it had become a sacred habit with him never to eat before
sunset—his reason, practised in solitary thought, had already
began to reassure him and to form judgments upon his
impulsive behaviour. Furthermore it did not disapprove of his
behaviour, however erratic it might have appeared, but
rather looked upon it with favour, and for the first time for
many a year found his action harmless and innocent. It was a
flight upon which he had embarked, a sudden and unconsidered
flight, but one which had nothing despicable about it. He had
abandoned a post to which he was no longer competent, and
had, by his running away, admitted his abdication both to
himself and to those whom it might concern. He had
renounced a daily repeated and useless struggle, had admitted
himself to be beaten and defeated. This action was not
particularly admirable—so reason told him—by no means
heroic and saint-like, but it was upright and seemed to have
been unavoidable. He was amazed that he had taken to flight
so late and that he had endured it all for so long: the struggle
and misery in which he had maintained himself in his deserted
post he now looked upon as an error, more in the nature of a
struggle and a revulsion against his selfishness, against his

old Adam, and thought that he now understood why this
misery had led to such evil, indeed devilish, consequences, to
such dismemberment and dejection, even to demonic obsession culminating in ideas of death and suicide. Although
Christ might be no enemy of death, and although a penitent
and holy man might look upon his life as a sacrifice, the
thought of taking one's own life was wholly inspired by the
devil and could only be born in a soul whose master and
protector was no longer God's angel but an evil demon.
For a while he sat there forlorn and downcast, and finally,
deeply shattered and contrite, as though these few miles of
wandering had given him a new perspective, his recent
existence became visible and he realized the desperate and
persecuted life of an ageing man who had failed in his goal
and had been perpetually tortured by the hideous temptation
of hanging himself from the nearest bough as the betrayer of
the Lord had done.

If the idea of this voluntary death horrified him so much
there obviously existed in it the spectral remains of that
primitive pagan knowledge of pre-Christian times—
knowledge of the age-old custom of human sacrifice, to
which king, saint and the elect of the race would be designated
but which they could not bring about with their own hands.
But this forbidden custom from pagan times was not so
appalling as the thought that the death which the Redeemer
had suffered on the Cross was nothing more than a voluntarily undertaken human sacrifice. And in reality, if he judged
himself correctly, there had been in that lust for suicide on his
part an intuition of this knowledge, something in the nature
of an evil savage urge to offer himself and in a forbidden
manner to imitate the Redeemer—or rather, in a forbidden
manner to suggest that His work of redemption had not been
completely successful. He was appalled by this thought, but
felt, too, that the danger was now passed.

For a long time he reflected upon the contrite man that he
had now become. Instead of following the example of Judas or
of the Crucified, he had taken to flight and had thereby placed
himself in God's hands. Shame and sorrow mounted within
him the more clearly he perceived the Hell from which he had
escaped, until at last his wretchedness seemed to become
lodged in his throat like a strangling morsel and he suddenly

found release in a storm of tears, which relieved him marvel-
lously. How long since he had been able to weep! The tears
flowed until his eyes could no longer see, but the deathly
feeling of strangulation had disappeared, and when he tasted
the salt tears upon his lips he realised that he was weeping,
and felt as though he had become a child once more and knew
nothing of evil. He smiled, a little ashamed of his tears, and at
last rose and went on his way. He was quite uncertain as to
whither his flight would lead him or what would become of
him, but went forward like a child. There was no more
struggle or desire within him and he felt lighter, as though
led forward at the behest of a far-off "good" voice luring
him onwards, as though his journey were not in the nature of
a flight but a return home. At last he grew weary and his
reason, too, began to flag, was stilled or at least became
tolerable.

At the drinking place where Joseph passed the night, a few
camels were resting, and as there were two women in the
little party of travellers he contented himself with a gesture of
greeting and avoided any speech with them. He ate a few
dates in the twilight, prayed and laid himself down to rest,
and after a while began to overhear a whispered conversation
between two of the men—a young man and an older one—for
they were lying quite close to him. He could only hear
snatches of their conversation, for it was for the most part
conducted in a low whisper; but a fragment of it caught his
attention and left him meditating half through the night.

"Yes, it is a good thing," he heard the voice of the elder
man say—"a very good thing indeed that you wish to go and
confess to a pious man. Those brothers understand everything, I can tell you: they are quite out of the ordinary, and
some of them can work miracles. If one of them simply cries a
word of command to a springing lion, the marauder stops
dead in its tracks and then slinks away with its tail between
its legs. I tell you they can even tame lions! A couple of these
beasts once dug the grave of a particularly holy man when he
died, arranged the earth tidily over his corpse and kept watch
over his grave for a long time. And it is not only lions that
these brothers know how to tame: one of them once brought
a Roman Centurion to prayer—a cruel beast of a soldier and
one of the biggest whoresons in the whole of Ascalon—and

softened his wicked heart, so that the fellow was made to feel humble and ran away and tried to hide himself in a hole like a timorous mouse. After this he became so peaceful and unassuming that he was almost unrecognisable. In any case it gives rise to thought, for he died shortly afterwards."

"Who—the holy man?"

"Oh! no, no—the centurion. His name was Varro. Soon after the holy man thus overwhelmed him and awakened his conscience, he fell to pieces, had two severe bouts of fever and was dead within three months. Well, I am not sorry for him . . . But in any case I have often thought that the confessor might have first driven the devil out of him and then uttered some incantation which put him under the sod."

"Such a pious man? I can hardly believe that!"

"Believe it or believe it not, my friend. From that day onwards the man was a changed being, almost as though bewitched, and three months later . . ."

There was a silence for a while, and then the younger voice went on: "There is a hermit who apparently lives near a little spring on the way to Gaza—it must be somewhere near here. His name is Joseph—Joseph Famulus. I have heard a great deal about him."

"Really! What have you heard?"

"He is incredibly pious, and never looks at a woman. If a few camels approach his isolated retreat and a woman is riding upon one of them he turns his back on her, however heavily veiled she may be, and disappears at all speed into the rocks. Many people go and confess to him."

"He can't be as famous as all that or I should have heard of him. But what can he do—your Famulus?"

"Oh, people go to him to confess, and if he were not so good and understanding the people wouldn't run to him. Another thing: they say he never speaks a word, never abuses and thunders . . . no punishments or suchlike. He seems to be a thoroughly gentle and sober man."

"Well, what does he do, then, if he doesn't rave and punish, and never opens his mouth?"

"He simply listens, sighs unobtrusively and makes the Sign of the Cross."

"Well, I never! A fine parlour saint you have there, I must

say! You are not going to be so foolish as to run after this silent uncle, are you?"

"Yes, indeed I am. I shall find him somehow: he cannot be far from here. There was a poor brother here this evening at the drinking place. I shall ask him to-morrow morning—he looks like a hermit himself."

The elder man became quite heated. "Leave your hermit to cower in his grotto! A man who only listens and signs and is afraid of women can do nothing and understands nothing! A long way from here, beyond Ascalon, lives the best penitent and Father Confessor of all. Dion is his name, and he is known as Dion Pugil—which means Dion the boxer, because he fights with all the devils—and if one confesses one's shameful deeds to him, then, my dear, Pugil doesn't sigh and keep his mouth shut, but lets loose and gives one a good rowsting, which is his way of going on. He has apparently given many of them a good thrashing, and he once made a sinner kneel all night on the stones on his bare knees, and then on top of that made him give forty *denarii* to the poor. That is a man, my friend! You will see him and be amazed. When he looks at you directly, your legs will tremble . . . he looks right through you. There won't be any sighing, I assure you, and if a man can't sleep any more or has bad dreams and visions, then he is the man to put you right again. And I am not telling you this because I have been listening to old women's chatter: I am telling you because I've been to see him myself. Yes, I myself, poor imbecile that I may be, went to see Father Dion, the boxer, the man of God! I tell you, as true as my name is David, that I went to him a sick man and full of shame with sins on my conscience, and came away as bright and pure as the morning star. Dion his name is, with the surname Pugil. Seek him out as soon as you can, and you will have your miracle. Prefects, elders and bishops have all gone to him for advice."

"All right," agreed the other, "I'll think it over if I am ever in those parts. But to-day is to-day, and as I am here at present and as Joseph, of whom I have heard so much good, must be in the neighbourhood . . ."

"Heard so much good! What has bitten you with this fool of a Famulus?"

"It pleases me to hear that he does not scold and rave. Yes, I must say that pleases me! I am no centurion, neither am I a bishop: I am only an insignificant man and rather shy at that, and I could not suffer much fire and brimstone. I have, God knows, nothing to find fault with if, on the contrary, one is a little gentle with me."

"A lot of people would like that. Treat you gently! When you have confessed and been punished, done penance and been purified, then it is perhaps time enough to be treated gently, but not when one is foul and stinking like a jackal and standing in front of one's Father Confessor and judge!"

"All right, all right! But we mustn't talk so loudly—the people want to sleep."

He suddenly gave a chuckle of pleasure in the darkness. "There is another thing I have heard about him, which is rather quaint."

"Of whom?"

"Of him—the hermit Joseph. He has a strange custom when you go and tell him your troubles and confess: he blesses you at leavetaking, and gives you a kiss on the forehead or on the cheek."

"Does he really, now? He's got some curious habits!"

"And he is so very shy in front of women. It appears that a whore once visited him disguised in man's clothing, and he did not notice it but listened to all her pack of lies; and when she had finished her confession he bent down to her to give her a ceremonious kiss——"

The elder man broke out into a hearty laugh, and his companion immediately warned him to be quiet. After this Joseph heard nothing further except a half-stifled laugh.

He looked up at the sky. The sickle moon hung slender and clearly outlined behind the tops of the palm trees. He shivered in the cold night air. The evening conversation of the camel drivers seemed to have thrown both his own person and the vocation to which he had been disloyal into sharp relief, although grotesquely, as in a distorting mirror. And so a whore had played that jest upon him! But that was not the worst of all, although it was bad enough. He thought for a long time about the conversation of these two strangers, and when at last he fell asleep it was only because his reflections had not been in vain. He had reached a conclusion and had made a decision, and with this new resolution in his heart fell asleep and did not wake until daybreak.

His resolution was identical with that which the younger of the two camel drivers could not decide to make—in other words, to follow the advice of the elder man and to seek out Dion, surnamed Pugil, of whom he had long since known but whose praises he had just heard sung so loudly. This famous Father Confessor, judge of souls and counsellor of men would also have some advice to give *him*, some verdict, some punishment, would know some way. He wished to place him in the position of a representative of God, and was willing to accept whatever he might prescribe.

On the following day he left the resting place while the two men were still asleep, and the same evening, after a strenuous journey, reached a spot which he knew to be inhabited by pious brothers and whence he hoped to reach the main route to Ascalon.

On his arrival a little green oasis landscape greeted him with a friendly smile. He saw palm trees and heard the bleating of goats. He thought that he could see the outlines of human dwellings and could sense the presence of people. As he approached somewhat hesitantly he had the impression that someone was watching him, and came to a standstill. Upon looking round, he saw a figure seated under the first group of trees with its back against a tree trunk. It was the upright figure of an old man with a pure white beard and a venerable but strong and frozen face, who was looking at him and might have been observing him for some time. The old man's gaze was firm and sharp but quite devoid of expression, like the gaze of a man who is used to watching but who is neither inquisitive nor personally concerned, who allows men and things to approach and tries to learn about them, but does not beckon to them or invite them to do so.

"Praise be to Our Lord!" said Joseph.

The old man returned his greeting.

"May I ask," Joseph went on, "whether you are a stranger like myself or an inhabitant of this beautiful settlement?"

"A stranger," replied the old man.

"Perhaps, then, Reverend Father, you can tell me whether I may reach Ascalon by this route?"

"It is possible," said the white-bearded one, rising slowly like some gaunt giant to his feet, for his limbs were stiff. He stood still and gazed into the distance.

Joseph felt that this tall man had very little inclination to talk, but he ventured to put a second question to him.

"Allow me to ask you one more question, Reverend Father," he said politely, and noticed that the eyes of the old man returned slowly as though from far away. They looked coolly and attentively at him.

"Do you by any chance know the place where Father Dion is to be found—the man whom they call Dion Pugil?"

The stranger frowned and his look became even colder.

"I know him," he replied shortly.

"You know him?" cried Joseph. "Oh! then please tell me of him, for my journey leads to Father Dion."

The tall man looked down at him with interest, and kept him waiting a long time before answering. Then he walked back to his tree trunk, sat slowly down and leaned against it in the same position as before. With a little gesture he beckoned to Joseph to do the same.

Joseph obeyed, feeling for a moment the acute weariness of his limbs, but forgot all about them again immediately in his interest in the old man. The latter had apparently lapsed into deep meditation, for a trace of forbidding strength seemed to appear on his worthy face like a transparent mask above that other expression—that other face—an expression of solitary suffering which pride and dignity would not allow of utterance.

It was a long time before the old man turned to him once more. He examined Joseph closely with his sharp look and suddenly questioned him in a peremptory voice: "Who are you, then?"

"I am a penitent," replied Joseph, "and for many years I have lived the life of a recluse."

"That is obvious. I asked you who you are!"

"My name is Joseph—Joseph Famulus."

At the mention of this name the old man, although he still remained motionless, drew his eyebrows so closely together that his eyes disappeared completely beneath them. He seemed overwhelmed, horrified or disappointed at Joseph's information. But perhaps his eyes were simply tired, or it was just an absentmindedness—one of those fits of weakness such as old men have. In any case, he retained a perfect immobility, keeping his eyes screwed up for a long time, and when at last he opened them again his look seemed to have changed or if possible to have grown older, more lonely, stonier and more aloof than ever. Slowly he unpursed his lips and said: "I have heard of you. Are you he to whom the people go and confess?"

Joseph admitted to this with embarrassment, finding in the recognition an unwelcome revelation and in the reference to his vocation an additional cause for shame.

The old man asked again in his terse manner: "And why do you wish to visit Dion Pugil? What do you want of him?"

"I want to confess to him."

"And what do you hope to gain?"

"I do not know. I have trust in him, and it seems to me as though a guiding voice from above has sent me to him."

"And when you have confessed, what then?"

"I shall do as he tells me."

"And if he commands and advises you falsely?"

"I shall not question whether it be false or true: I shall obey him."

The sun was low on the horizon, and a bird screamed in the tree-tops. As the old man had fallen silent, Joseph stood up and turned soberly towards him.

"You told me that you knew the place where I could find Father Dion. May I ask you to tell me that place and to point out the way?"

The old man drew his lips into a kind of wry smile. "Do you think," he asked softly, "that you will be welcome?"

Joseph was strangely perturbed by this question and did not reply. He stood there embarrassed.

"May I at least hope to see you again?" he asked at last.

The old man made a gesture of assent. "I shall sleep here and remain until sunrise. Go now, you are tired and hungry."

With a respectful bow Joseph retired, and made his way into the little settlement as night was falling. Here the so-called eremites, a group of Christians from different towns and villages, lived a monastic life. In their isolation they had built a dwelling place in order to devote themselves undisturbed to a pure and calm life of contemplation. He was given water, food and a bed, and no one bothered him with questions and conversation for they saw how weary he was. One of the congregation said a prayer and the others participated on their knees, all intoning the "Amen" together.

This community of pious men would at other times have been an experience and a joy to him, but he had now only one thing in mind, and at daybreak hurried to the place where he had left the old man on the previous evening. He found him lying rolled in a thin blanket on the ground, and sat down to wait until he should wake.

The sleeper soon grew restless, woke up and scrambled from his blanket. He stood up heavily and stretched his cramped limbs, and then knelt down again to say his morning prayer. When Joseph saw that he had finished, he approached and bowed to him in silence.

"Have you already eaten?" asked the stranger.

"No. I eat but once a day—after sunset. Are you hungry, Reverend Father?"

"We are on a journey," replied the other, "and we are neither of us young men any more. It is better that we should eat a little before we set out."

Joseph opened his knapsack and offered the old man a few dates. The friendly people with whom he had spent the night had also given him a millet loaf, which he shared with his companion.

"Now we can go," said the old man when they had finished their repast.

"Oh! are we going together?" cried Joseph with joy.

"Certainly—you asked me to lead you to Father Dion, didn't you? Come!"

Amazed and happy, Joseph looked at him. "How good you are!" he exclaimed, and tried to express his gratitude further, but the old man compelled him to silence with a sharp gesture of his hand.

"Only God is good," he said. "Let us go now—and please use the familiar form of address to me as I do to you. What need is there of formality and civilities between two old penitents?"

The tall man strode forwards and Joseph fell into step at his side. Day had broken. The former seemed to know the way and told Joseph that they would reach a shady spot by midday where they could rest during the hottest part of the day.

Not another word was spoken throughout the journey. Only during the burning hours which they spent in their resting place in the shade of the hollow cliffs did Joseph venture to address another question to his companion. He asked how many days they would have to travel before they could reach Dion Pugil.

"It all depends upon yourself," replied the old man.

"Upon me?" asked Joseph. "Ah! if it only depended on me I should be standing in front of him right now!"

The stranger still seemed indisposed to talk.

"We shall see," he said shortly, as he lay down on his side and closed his eyes. It was embarrassing for Joseph to watch him as he slept, so he moved somewhat further away, and it happened that he soon fell asleep himself for he had remained awake far into the night. His guide awakened him when he considered it time to continue on their journey.

Late in the afternoon they came to another resting place with water, trees and grass and, after they had washed and drunk the old man decided to remain. Joseph was not in agreement and raised shy remonstrances.

"You said yesterday," he insisted, "that it all depended upon me as to how quickly I should reach Father Dion. If I could possibly arrive to-day or even to-morrow morning, I am still ready to walk for several hours."

"No," replied his companion, "we have gone far enough for to-day."

"Forgive me," put in Joseph contritely, "but you do understand my haste, don't you?"

"Oh, I quite understand. But it will avail you nothing."

"Why did you say, then, that it lay in my power?"

"It is so, as I have said. As soon as you really desire to confess, and show yourself ready and prepared to begin, then you will be able to start."

"To-day?"

"To-day."

Joseph looked with astonishment into the old face.

"Is it possible," he cried in his bewilderment, "that you are Father Dion?"

The old man nodded.

"Rest here under the trees," he said with a smile, "but do not sleep. Collect your thoughts, and I too will rest and reflect. Then you may say what you wish to say to me."

At last Joseph realised that he had arrived at his goal, and could not understand why he had not been able to recognize the worthy man at whose side he had journeyed for a whole day. He retired, knelt down in prayer and concentrated all his thoughts upon what he would have to say in his confession. After an hour had elapsed he returned and asked Dion whether he were ready to receive him.

And now followed his confession. All that which he had endured for years, and which for a long time had seemed more and more to have lost its value and meaning, now poured from his lips in the form of tale, plaint, question, self-accusation— the whole story of his life as a Christian and a penitent, which he had undertaken as a purification and sanctification and which had at last turned to confusion, obscurity and despair. Nor did he remain silent about his recent experiences, his flight and the feeling of redemption and hope that this flight had brought him; about the origin of his resolution to seek out Father Dion, their meeting and how immediately he had been attracted to him in confidence and love even though the other had regarded him coldly and strangely and even ill-humouredly during the course of that day and on several occasions since.

The sun was setting as he came to the end of his confession. Old Dion had listened to him with tireless attention and had refrained from any interruption or question. And even now, when it was all over, no word fell from his lips. He stood up heavily, looked at Joseph with the greatest friendliness, bent down and kissed him on the forehead and made the Sign of the Cross over him. Only later did it occur to Joseph that this was the self-same uncensorious and brotherly gesture with which he himself had dismissed so many penitents.

Shortly afterwards they broke their fast, said their evening prayer together and lay down to sleep. Joseph reflected and pondered for a while. He had in actual fact expected to be condemned or given a severe sermon, and yet he was neither disappointed nor disturbed for the brotherly kiss of Dion had been enough, and he soon sank into a refreshing sleep.

On the following morning, without wasting any words, the old man led him forth. They walked for the whole of that day and for the next four or five days before they came at last to Dion's hermitage. There they now lived together, Joseph helping Dion with his small daily tasks He learned to share and soon became familiar with this life, which was very different from that which he had led for so many years, for now he was no longer alone—he lived in the shadow and under the protection of another.

Seekers of advice and those who were in need of confession came from the neighbouring settlements and from Ascalon and from even further afield. At first, on the occasion of each such visit Joseph would retire and only show his face when the visitor had departed; but Dion began to call him back more and more often, as one calls a servant, would tell him to bring water or to assist with a ministration, and after a while

Joseph accustomed himself to stay and listen to the confession
if the penitent had no particular objection. Many of them—
most of them in fact—were only too pleased not to be left
alone, standing, sitting or kneeling before the terrifying
Pugil, and were glad to have this calm, friendly servitor
at hand.

Thus he learned the manner in which Dion carried out his
office, the way in which he consoled, exhorted, attacked or
scolded, and the nature of the punishments he meted out and
the counsels he gave. He seldom allowed himself to ask any
questions, such as he had done on the occasion when a scholar
and man of culture happened to pass by on his journey.

This man had, according to the tales he told, friends
among the magicians and stargazers. Resting for a while at
Pugil's hut, he sat for an hour or two with the two old
penitents, a polite and loquacious guest. He spoke learnedly
and at length about the stars and about the orbit which men
and gods alike had to follow from the beginning to the end of
an age, passing through all the houses of the Zodiac. He
spoke of Adam, the first man, of how he was one and the
same as Jesus, the Crucified, and called the redemption
through Him "Adam's change from the Tree of Knowledge
to the Tree of Life"; the Serpent of Paradise, however, he
referred to as "the preserver of the Sacred Primal Fount
and the dark watery depths whence issued all creatures,
men and gods."

Dion listened attentively to the scholar, whose Syrian was
strongly intermingled with Greek, and Joseph found this
tolerance remarkable. He felt resentful that the Father
Confessor did not dismiss these pagan errors with anger and
scorn, that he did not refute and ban them, instead of to all
intents enjoying the clever monologue of this omniscient
pilgrim who seemed to have aroused his sympathy. But no, he
listened not only with devotion but often smiled and nodded
at some phrase of the speaker's as though it pleased him.

When he had departed Joseph asked Father Dion in a tone
of zeal and almost of reproach: "How comes it that you
listened so patiently to the false doctrines of that unbelieving
heathen? In fact, it seemed to me that you listened to him not

only with patience but also with sympathy and with a certain amount of pleasure. Why did you not take up the cudgels against him? Why did you not try to confute this man, punish him and try to convert him to a belief in Our Lord?"

Dion's head swayed gently to and fro on his thin neck, and he replied: "I did not confute him because it would have been useless, and even more because I was not in a position to do so. In speech and in the combinations of mythology and the stars this man is by far my superior, and I could have scored nothing against him. And furthermore, my son, it is neither your affair nor mine to contradict the belief of a man on the assumption that what he believes in are lies and errors. I did, I admit, listen to this clever man with a certain pleasure, because he spoke admirably and was very learned, but above all because he reminded me of my youth when I was occupied a great deal with similar studies and theories.

"The things about which our friend chattered so pleasantly are by no means errors. They are representations and allegories from mythology, and embody beliefs to which we no longer subscribe because we believe in Jesus the one Redeemer. But that man, who has not yet found our faith and perhaps never will find it, does possess a belief, which comes from ancient wisdom and is worthy of respect. Admittedly, my friend, our belief is quite, quite different, but because our faith does not need the doctrine of the planets and the æons, of the primal waters and world mothers and all the host of allegories, even so those doctrines are by no means errors and lies."

"But our faith is better!" cried Joseph. "Jesus died for all men, and therefore those who know it must fight against that outmoded teaching and put it in its right place."

"This you and I and many others have long since done," replied Dion wearily. "We are believers, because we have been granted a belief in the Redeemer and in His death. But those others, the mythologists and theologians of the Zodiac, have not been accorded this grace—not yet—and it is not in our power to compel them to accept it. Did you not notice, Joseph, how charmingly and ably this mythologist knew how to chatter and compose his game of pictures, how

suited it was to him and how peaceably and harmoniously
he lived in his lore of pictures and comparisons? Now this is a
sign that he has never suffered, that he is a happy man and
that things are well with him. Men for whom things go well
have nothing to say to such as us. In order that a man may
accept the Redeemer and a belief in redemption, in order that
he may lose the pleasure in the wisdom and harmony of this
thought and accept the great hazard of belief in the miracle
of redemption, things must first have gone badly with him—
very badly—he must first have endured suffering and disappointment, bitterness and despair, and the waters must
have reached up to his neck. No, Joseph, let us leave this
pagan to his contentment; let him remain fortunate in his
wisdom, his thoughts and in his oratory! Perhaps to-morrow,
perhaps within a year or in ten years he will experience some
suffering which will shatter his art and wisdom to pieces—
perhaps the woman whom he loves or his only son will die,
or he will succumb to wickedness or poverty. When we meet
him on the next occasion we will receive him and tell him of
the manner in which we have tried to master our sufferings,
and should he then ask: 'Why did you not tell me this
yesterday or ten years ago?' we will answer: 'Things had
not gone badly enough with you!' "

Dion had fallen into a very serious vein, and remained
silent for a while. Then he added as though from a dream
memory: "I myself once dallied and found enjoyment in the
wisdom of the ancients; and even when I was already on the
way to the Cross I often took pleasure in theologising, which
naturally brought sorrow enough. My thoughts hinged
chiefly around the idea of Genesis and that after the creation
of the world everything should have been good and perfect,
for it is written: 'And God saw everything that he had made,
and behold it was very good.' But in actuality it was only
good and perfect for an instant—the instant of Paradise—for
at the very next instant guilt and malediction descended upon
the perfection, Adam's having eaten of that tree which had
been forbidden him. There were teachers who maintained
that the God who created Adam and the Tree of Knowledge
was not the sole and highest God but only a part of him—an
underling, the Demiurge—and that the creation had not been
good but unsuccessful; that it had, moreover, been accursed

for an æon and given over to the evil one, until He himself, the One Spirit of God, had through His only Son decided to put an end to the accursed æon. From then onwards, so they taught—and this was also my belief—the decline of the Demiurge and his creation set in and the world slowly began to wither and die, and this process would continue until a new age should arise in which there should be no creation, no world, no substance, no envy and sin, no carnal procreation, birth and death: a perfect spiritual and redeemed world would arise, freed from Adam's curse, freed from the eternal compulsive urge of desire, procreation, birth and death. We blamed the Demiurge more than the first man for the current evils of the world, for we believed that it should have been an easy thing for the Demiurge, had he really been a god, to have created Adam differently and to have spared him from temptation. And thus, finally, as a result of our deductions, there were two Gods—the Creator-God and the Father-God —and we were not abashed to sit in judgment upon the former. There were some who went a step further and maintained that the creation did not come from a god at all but was the devil's handiwork. We thought, with all our cleverness, to be helpful to the Redeemer and to the coming æon, and so we made gods and worlds and world-plans, and disputed and theologised. But one day I fell ill with a fever and came very near to dying, and in my fevered dreams I had considerable dealings with the Demiurge, was obliged to make war and to shed blood. The visions and terrors grew ever more fearful, until one night when my fever was at its height I imagined that I had to kill my own mother in order to extinguish my own carnal birth. The devil tormented me in my fever with all the hounds of hell. I recovered, however, and to the disappointment of my former friends returned to life a lean, silent and listless man, whose bodily strength had returned but not his joy in philosophising; for, during those days and nights of convalescence, when the hideous fever dreams had faded and I had begun to sleep soundly again, I sensed at each waking moment the Redeemer at my side and felt his strength flowing into me; and when I had fully recovered I was sad because I could no longer feel his presence. From then on I felt a great longing for that presence, and I found that whenever I heard disputes again, this longing—it was then my best asset—was falling into danger, was disappearing and escaping in thoughts and words just as water is swallowed up by the sand. But enough, my friend! That was the end of cleverness and theology. I have ever since belonged among the simple minded. But, mark you, one must not hinder or despise the man who knows how to philosophise and to mythologise, and who understands how to play those games that I once tried. Just as I was once forced to conclude that Demiurge and God, creation and redemption were to remain an inconceivable, relative and comparative riddle, insoluble to me, so was I also forced to decide that I could not convert philosophers into believers. That is not part of my vocation."

Once, after a man had confessed to murder and adultery, Dion said to his companion: "Murder and adultery may sound mad and remarkable enough—and they are of course evil, in all conscience—but I tell you, Joseph, that these men of the world are not true sinners: however much I try to penetrate into their very depths, they always appear to me as children. They are not courageous, not good, not noble, and are admittedly selfish, lascivious, arrogant and wrathful, but actually and fundamentally they are innocent—innocent in the manner of children."

"And yet," replied Joseph, "you often rail at them and paint a picture of hell before their eyes."

"Precisely. They *are* children, and when they have pangs of conscience and come to confess, then they wish to be taken seriously and also wish to be rated in all earnestness. At least, that is how I see it. You were wont to act in a different manner: you neither railed nor punished nor exacted penances, but were friendly and dismissed the penitents with a brotherly kiss. I will not blame you for that, but I could not do the same."

"That is all well and good," said Joseph slowly. "But tell me then, why, when I came to confess, did you not treat me as you treat all your other children but kiss me in silence and speak no word of rebuke?"

Dion Pugil turned his penetrating gaze upon him. "Did I not do right?" he asked.

"I did not say that what you did was not right. It was obviously right, for otherwise the confession would not have done me so much good."

"Well, then, let us leave it at that. But I have also laid a long and strenuous penance upon you, even if not in words. I have taken you in and treated you as my servant, and compelled you to take up again the duty from which you wished to flee."

Dion turned away, for he did not favour long speeches. But this time Joseph was persistent.

"You knew in advance that I would obey you: I had told you as much before my confession, and had promised obedience before I came to recognise you. Tell me: was it really on these grounds alone that you treated me as you did?"

The old man walked up and down a few times, came to a standstill in front of Joseph and laid his hand upon his shoulder. "Mortals are children, my son," he said, and saints do not come and confess to us. But we—you and I and those of our kin, we penitents, seekers after truth and fugitives from the world—are not children and are not innocent, and cannot be brought to order by thundering sermons. It is we who are the actual sinners, we who think and know, who have eaten of the Tree of Knowledge, and we should not treat each other as children whom one strikes with the rod and then dismisses. After a confession and a penance we do not run away into the world of children, the world of business and festivity, where upon occasions they kill each other. We do not experience sin as a short evil dream which one can be rid of by means of confession and sacrifice: we dwell in it and are never guiltless, we dwell in sin perpetually, dwell in sin and in the fire of our conscience and we know that we can never expiate our great guilt; and it may be that after our death God will look upon us with favour and receive us in his mercy. This, Joseph, is the reason why I cannot prescribe sermons and penances in your case and mine. We have nothing to do with this or that fall from grace or misdemeanour, but must apply ourselves to original sin itself. Thus we can only assure each other of our mutual knowledge and brotherly love, but we cannot heal each other with punishment. But did you not know this?"

"It is so. I knew it," replied Joseph softly.

"Well, then, let us not talk any further, for it is useless," concluded the old man, turning towards the stone that lay in front of his hut and upon which he was wont to pray.

Several years went by and Father Dion was stricken with weakness. Joseph had to help him in the mornings as he could not rise unaided, and then the old man would sit the whole day through, staring into the distance. But on some days Dion would be able to rise alone. On the days that he could not hear confessions, and when one of his flock had confessed to Joseph, Dion would call to him and say: "The end is near, my child, the end is near. Make it known that Joseph is my successor." And if Joseph made a gesture of refusal or tried to remonstrate, the old man would give him a terrible look that would pierce him through like an icy ray.

One day, when Dion had risen unaided and seemed to be a little stronger, he called Joseph to him and led him to a spot at the end of their tiny garden.

"Here," he said, "is the place where you must bury me. We will dig the grave together, for we still have time enough for that. Bring me the spade."

Each morning early they would dig a little portion of the grave. When Dion had enough strength he too would lift a spadeful of earth with great difficulty but with a certain cheerfulness, as though the work brought him pleasure. Neither would this cheerfulness leave him during the rest of the day: ever since they had begun to dig he was always in a good mood.

"You will plant a palm tree over my grave," he said once, while they were at work. "Perhaps one day you will even eat of its fruit—or if not you, then someone else will. From time to time I have planted trees, but far too few of them—far too few. Many people say a man should not die without planting a tree and without leaving a son behind him. Now I am leaving behind a tree, and you are my son."

He was quite imperturbable and serener than Joseph had ever known him, and this serenity increased. One evening, as it was growing dark and they had already eaten and prayed, he called to Joseph from his bed and bade him sit with him for a little while.

"I have something to say to you," he said in a friendly voice—he seemed to be wide awake and not at all weary. "Think back for a moment, Joseph, to the time when you were in your cell in Gaza, when things were going so badly· with you that life seemed to have become intolerable—how you took to flight and were determined to visit old Dion and tell him your story, and how in the brothers' settlement you met the old man whom you questioned as to the whereabouts of Dion Pugil? Was it not a miracle that the old man turned out to be Dion himself? Now, then—I will tell you how it came about, because for me too it was remarkable and in the nature of a miracle.

"You know how it is when a penitent and Father Confessor grows old? He has heard the many sins of his children, who have always taken him for a holy man but who have never known that he is a greater sinner than they themselves. His whole life seems to him vain and useless, and that which once appeared sacred and important—that God had graced him, and allowed him the privilege of listening to the garbage of the human soul and of bringing relief—now seems to him a great burden, far too great a burden, I might almost say a curse; and finally he shudders before every poor creature who comes to him with his childish sins, and wishes him gone—wishes himself gone, even if at the end of a rope hanging from a tree. That is what happened to you, is it not? And now the time has come for me to confess, and I am confessing. It happened to me just as it has happened to you, and I thought that I was useless and worn out. I could no longer bear the idea that people should always come to me full of trust, bringing all the filth and stench of human life which they could not get rid of—and of which I too could not rid myself.

"Now I had often heard tell of a penitent named Joseph Famulus. Men came readily to confess to him too, so I gathered, and many preferred to visit him rather than me because he was more gentle and friendly, asked nothing of people and never railed at them, but treated them rather as brothers and dismissed them with a kiss. That was not my way, as you well know, and when I first heard the story of this man I thought that his method was insane and childish; but now that everything had become so questionable for me, I wondered whether indeed my own method was valid and if in fact I was justified in passing judgment and of knowing better than this Joseph? What kind of power might this man not have? I knew that he was younger than myself but that he was nevertheless also an old man, and that pleased me for I should not have trusted a younger man so easily. I felt drawn towards him. So I decided to undertake a pilgrimage to this Joseph Famulus in order to acquaint him of my distress, to ask his counsel; and even were he to give me no counsel I thought I might receive consolation and renewed strength from him. The decision itself did me good and made me feel easier in mind.

"I set off on my journey and made my pilgrimage towards the place where he was reputed to have his cell. But in the meantime Brother Joseph had experienced the same urge as myself and had acted in exactly the same way: each of us had taken to flight in order to ask advice of the other. Before I had even found his hut I came face to face with him, and recognised him at once by his speech; he even looked like the man I had expected to see. But he was a fugitive, and things had gone badly with him—as badly as they had gone with me if not worse—and he was in no mood to listen to confessions but himself desired to confess and to lay his sorrow in other hands. This was, in that first moment, a bitter disappointment, and I was very sad. This Joseph, who did not know me, had grown tired of his service and was in despair as to the meaning of his life—and did this not seem to mean that both of us had come to naught and that we had both foundered, that we had lived in vain?

"I am only relating what you already know, so let me make it brief. I remained outside the settlement that night when you found shelter with the brothers. I sank into deep contemplation and projected myself into the mind of this Joseph. What will he do, I thought to myself, when to-morrow he learns that his flight has been to no purpose and that he has put his trust in Dion Pugil in vain; when he learns that Pugil is also a fugitive and one who has given up the struggle? The more I thought about this, the more I pitied Joseph and the more it seemed to me that he had been sent to me by God, so that through him I might come to know myself and be healed. At last I was able to sleep; the night was already half spent.

The next day you started on your pilgrimage with me, and became my son.

"I have been wanting to tell you this story . . . Yes, weep, my son! Weep—for it will do you good. And now, as I have already become so unusually loquacious, do me the favour of hearing me out, and please take it to heart.

"Man is a strange creature, and can be little relied upon, so it is possible that the time will come when these sufferings and temptations will overwhelm you again, and will try to encompass your undoing. May Our Lord then send you just such a consoling, patient and friendly son and ward as He has sent me! As regards the bough of the tree and the death of Judas Iscariot of which the tempter once made you dream, I can tell you one thing: it is not only madness and a sin to prepare oneself for such a death—although it is a little thing in the eyes of our Redeemer and is a sin too which is to be forgiven—but it is also a wretched thing if a man dies in despair. God does not send us despair in order to kill us, but to awaken new life in us. But when he sends us death, Joseph, when he releases us from the earth and from life and calls us over there, that is a great joy. When one is tired and is allowed to let fall the burden that one has carried for so long, that is a precious and wonderful thing. Now, since we have begun to dig the grave—and please do not forget the palm tree which you are to plant—I have felt happier and more content than I have felt for many a year.

"But I have chattered long enough, my son, and you must be tired. Go and sleep—go to your hut, and God be with you!"

On the following day Dion did not come to morning prayers, and did not call for Joseph. Joseph became afraid and went to the old man's hut, where he found him in his last sleep with a radiant, childlike smile upon his face.

Joseph buried him and planted a palm tree on the grave, and lived to see the year in which the tree bore its first fruit.

THE INDIAN LIFE

VISHNU—OR RATHER VISHNU in the earthly guise of Rama, the slayer of the powers of darkness with the sickle moon arrows—had taken on human form once more in the circle of Karma, was known as Ravana and lived as a warrior prince on the banks of the great Ganges. This was Dasa's father. His mother had died while still young, and no sooner had her successor, a beautiful and ambitious woman, born a son to the prince than she found the little Dasa in her way, for she wished to establish her own son Nala as ruler in place of the first born. She contrived to estrange Dasa from his father and was determined to be rid of him at all costs.

One of Ravana's high Brahmans however, Vasudeva the sacrificer, was not blind to her intentions and was clever enough to thwart her. The boy, who seemed to have inherited a sense of justice and a leaning towards piety from his mother, aroused his pity. He therefore kept an eye on Dasa so that no harm should befall him and awaited an opportunity to remove him from his stepmother's clutches.

Now Ravana, the Rajah, owned a herd of sacred cows, whose butter and milk were frequently sacrificed to Brahma, and the best pasturage in the land was reserved for this herd. One day one of the herdsmen, who was delivering a cartload of butter to the palace, announced that there were signs of an approaching drought in the neighbourhood where the cows were grazing. All the herdsmen, he announced, were in agreement that they should drive the cattle towards the mountains where, even in the driest season, they would not lack for water and fresh fodder.

The Brahman took this man, who was loyal and well disposed into his confidence, and when on the following day the little Dasa was nowhere to be found Vasudeva and the herdsman were the only two who knew the secret of his disappearance. The boy had been taken away by the herdsman into the hills where they had joined the slow, wandering herd.

Dasa was delighted with his new companions and grew up as one of them. He helped to tend and drive the herd, learned how to milk, played with the calves, lay under the trees, thrived upon the sweet milk and butter and perpetually bore the stains of cow-dung upon his feet. He thoroughly enjoyed this existence. Before long he was completely familiar with the life of the forest, with its trees and fruits, and grew to love the mango, the wild fig and the varinga tree. He would gather the lotus roots from the green forest pond and wear a garland of red blossoms on feast days; he learned to be on the alert for wild beasts, to avoid the tiger, to make friends with the wise mongoose and the peaceful hedgehog and to weather the rainy season in a shady hut. He also played childish games, sang verses or plaited baskets and reed mats.

Dasa did not completely forget his former home and life, but they had already assumed the proportions of a dream.

One day, when the herd had moved on to other pastures, Dasa went into the forest to look for honey. He had loved the forests ever since he had first come to know them and this one seemed to him especially beautiful. The daylight trickled through branch and leaf like golden serpents and the cries of the birds, the fluttering in the treetops and the chatter of monkeys were like the sound of music. It was an intricately woven, soft gleaming tapestry, approaching, uniting and separating again, like the light in the foliage, the odours, the scents of blossoms, woods, leaves, waters, moss, beasts, fruit, earth and decay—bitter and sweet, wild and mysterious, waking and sleeping, gay and oppressive. Waters foamed from a hidden torrent; a velvety green moth with black and yellow spots dancing over the white blossoms; a branch creaked in the deep blue-shadowed mass of foliage; a wild beast roared in the darkness and an ill-tempered she-ape scolded her mate.

Dasa forgot his quest for honey and, while he was watching a bright lightning-swift humming bird, noticed a track leading through a thicket of high ferns which rose like a tiny wood within the forest. It was a narrow winding footpath. Noiselessly and cautiously he set out to explore it, and discovered beneath the copious branches of a banyan tree a little tent-shaped hut built of woven ferns. On the ground nearby a man was sitting motionless and erect. His hands lay idle between his crossed legs and beneath his white hair and broad forehead a pair of eyes, calm and unflinching, looked down at the ground. They were wide open but their gaze was turned inwards.

Dasa realised that this was a holy man, a Yogi. It was not his first encounter with one of his sect—he knew that they were venerable and the elect of the gods, and that it was good to bring them gifts and to pay them homage—but this particular Yogi, sitting here erect with arms relaxed in deep contemplation before his well-concealed hut of ferns, appealed to him more and seemed to be more venerable than any of the others he had seen.

An aura of sanctity, an enchanted circle of dignity and a flame-like intensity of yoga-strength, through which the boy dared not penetrate or even disturb with so much as a word of greeting, surrounded this man who sat so still, but as though swaying gently, and whose far-away gaze seemed to see and know everything. The dignity and greatness of his figure, the light from within which lit up his face, the concentration and iron intransigence of his features sent forth waves and rays, in the midst of which he sat enthroned like a moon. The accumulated spiritual strength and tranquil concentrated will power wove around him such a magic orbit that one began to feel that this man, by a simple wish or thought and without even raising his eyes, could kill and bring one back to life.

Betraying less movement than a tree as it breathes through its branches and foliage, motionless as a graven image, sat the Yogi in his retreat. The boy, from the moment he had seen him, stood as though rooted to the spot, staring at the Yogi, spellbound and attracted by this image.

Dasa noticed a fleck of sunlight on the master's shoulder, a patch of sunlight on his resting hands, saw the light spangles slowly move and reappear, and began to realise in awe and astonishment that these dappled patches meant no more to this man, than the bird song and monkey chatter from the surrounding forest, than the brown wood bees that settled on the face of the contemplator, smelling his skin, crawling over his cheek only to rise and fly away again, than the whole variegated life of the forest.

All this, all that the eye can see and the ear can hear—
everything beautiful or ugly, loveable or frightening—Dasa
felt, had no connection whatever with the holy man. Rain
could not chill or disturb him, fire could not burn him, the
whole world around had become superficial and meaningless.
As he watched, the herdsman prince felt intuitively that
perhaps the whole world was no more than a superficial
game, no more than a breath of wind or a ripple of the waves
above uncharted depths. It was less a thought than an
impression, accompanied by a light physical shudder and a
feeling of giddiness, a sensation of horror and danger and at
the same time a yearning and voluptuous attraction. He felt
that the Yogi had sunk deep below the surface of the world,
through the superficial world into the abyss of Being, into the
mystery of all things, that he had broken through and
sloughed the magic net of the senses, the playing of the light,
the scents, colours and sensations and dwelt firmly rooted in
the essential and the unchanging. The boy, although he had
once been taught by the Brahmans and had received many a
ray of spiritual light at their hands, hardly perceived this with
his reason and would not have known how to express it in
words, but rather sensed it as one senses the presence of the
divine in an hour of grace, felt it with a shiver of awe and
admiration for this man, with love for him and with a longing
for a life of contemplation such as he seemed to be living.

In this wondrous fashion, Dasa as he stood at the edge of
the fern thicket, was moved in spirit and through the old man,
saw his origin and recalled his princely birth: he left the
birds to fly and the trees to continue their sweet rustling
speech, left the forest and the herd to their own devices,
surrendered to the magic and looked at the meditating
ascetic, captured by the inconceivable calm and untouchability
of his figure, by the bright tranquillity of his countenance,
by the strength and equanimity of his bearing and by his
perfect devotion to service.

He could not have said afterwards whether he had remained
two or three hours or whether he had been days near the hut.
When at last the enchantment released him from its thrall
and he stole noiselessly through the ferns again on his return,
seeking his way out of the forest and finally reaching the

grazing grounds and the herd, he did so unconsciously for his
soul was still bewitched, and the spell was only completely
broken when one of the herdsmen called out to him.

The latter received him with violent abuse on account of
his long absence, but Dasa looked at him with such wide open
eyes and in such astonishment that he might not have understood a word he said. The herdsman fell silent when he
noticed the unusual far distant look in the boy's eyes and his
arrogant behaviour.

"Where have you been then, my dear?" he asked after a
while: "Have you seen a god or perhaps met a demon?"

"I was in the forest," replied Dasa. "I went there to look
for honey, but I forgot all about it when I saw a man—a
hermit—who was sitting deep in meditation or in prayer.
When I saw how his face shone I had to stay and look at him
for a long time. I must go back this evening and take him
a gift, for he is a holy man."

"Yes, do that by all means!" said the cowherd. "Take
him some milk and some sweet butter—one must always
respect holy men and bring them gifts."

"But how shall I address him?"

"There is no need to address him, Dasa. Simply bend down
before him and place the gifts at his feet. No more is
necessary."

This Dasa did. It was some time before he could find the
spot again, and when he did so the clearing before the hut was
empty. He did not dare to enter the hut, but placed his gifts
on the ground before the entrance and withdrew.

Every evening for as long as the herd remained in the
neighbourhood he brought offerings, and also went once
more during the day, to find the sage deeply immersed in
meditation as before Nor was the lure to receive a ray of the
holy man's strength and happiness as a favoured onlooker
any the less powerful on this occasion, and long after he had
left the neighbourhood and had helped to drive the herd in
search of new pastures he could not forget his experience in
the forest. As is the way with boys, he often yielded to day
dreams when he was alone, and at times saw himself as a

hermit and yoga adept. However, as the years went by the memory began to pale, especially as he was rapidly growing into a sturdy youth who took a vivid pleasure in wrestling and in games with the boys of his own age; yet there always remained in his soul a slight, shimmering presentiment to the effect that his lost princehood and kingship might one day be replaced by the dignity and power of Yoga.

One day, when the herd had arrived in the neighbourhood of a town, one of the herdsmen brought the news that a mighty feast was about to take place: the old Prince Ravana, who had lost his pristine strength and grown infirm, had appointed the day upon which his son Nala should succeed him.

Dasa wished to take part in this feast in order to see for the first time since his exile, the town of his childhood of which hardly a trace of memory remained in his soul, to hear the music and see the procession of nobles, to see once more the world of townsmen and the great whom he had so often heard described in legends and fairy tales, for he knew that once in a previous age, just as in a legend or a fairy tale, this world had also been his own world.

The herdsmen had received an order to deliver a consignment of butter to the court for the feast day sacrifice, and Dasa was one of the three who had been chosen by the chief herdsman for this task. In order to deliver their butter, they entered the court on the previous evening and were received by Vasudeva, for it was he who was in charge of the sacrifice. The old Brahman did not, however, recognise the boy.

The three herdsmen took part in the feast with the greatest gusto. At this early hour of the morning they already saw the beginnings of the sacrifice conducted by the Brahmans: the gleaming golden butter, licked by the fire, was transformed into high rising flames, and the fat-drenched smoke acceptable to the thrice ten gods rose high up into the infinite. In the procession they saw elephants bearing golden-roofed palanquins, upon which the riders sat, saw the flower bedecked royal car and the young raja Nala and heard the throbbing beat of drums.

Everything was magnificent and splendid and also a little ridiculous—or so it appeared to the young Dasa. He was

enchanted and intoxicated by the deafening noise, the cars
and the caparisoned horses, by all the splendour and
ostentatious extravagance, and was especially charmed by the
dancing girls who danced before the prince's car with limbs
slender and wiry as lotus stalks. He was astonished at the
size and beauty of the town, but in spite of it all and in the
midst of his joyous intoxication he nevertheless observed
everything with the sober eyes of the herdsman who in his
heart is wont to despise the town dweller. It did not occur
to him that he was actually the first-born, for no memory of
this remained, and that here before his eyes his step-brother,
Nala, was being anointed, consecrated and fêted while he
himself, Dasa, ought to have been riding in his place in the
flower-covered car. In any case this young Nala displeased
him intensely, for he seemed to Dasa to be stupid and ill-
tempered in his spoiled luxury, to be puffed up with unbearable
vanity and self-adoration. He would very much have liked to
play a trick on this youngster who was acting the princeling
and teach him a good lesson, but he quickly forgot this in all
that there was to see, hear, laugh at and enjoy. The women
of the town were comely and had saucy exciting looks and
movements. Their language was no less so and the three
herdsmen heard many a word that rang for a long time in
their ears, but these words were not said without a trace of
mockery for a similar sense of animosity applied in the case of
the townspeople towards the herdsmen. They both despised
each other and yet the strong, handsome youths, nourished
upon milk and cheese and living almost the entire year under
the open sky, pleased the townswomen exceedingly.

On his return from this feast Dasa had suddenly become a
man. He now courted the women and had many serious fights
and wrestling matches with the other youths. The herd came
in due course to another neighbourhood with flat meadows
and marshes where reeds and bamboo canes grew in profusion. Here he saw a maiden, named Pravati, and was seized
with an all-consuming love for her. She was the daughter of a
farmer, and Dasa's passion for her was so great that he forgot
all else in his preoccupation with possessing her. When after
some time the herd left the neighbourhood once more he
ignored his comrades' warnings and advice, took leave of
them and of his herdsman's life which he had loved so much

and took up a sedentary life among the farmers. He succeeded in winning Pravati for his wife, and thenceforward administered his father-in-law's millet and rice fields, helped in the mill and with the woodcutting, and built his wife a hut from mud and bamboo trunks to which he retired with her.

It must indeed have been a powerful urge that could influence a young man to renounce his former friends, companions and customs, to alter his life and to take over the unenviable position of a son-in-law among strangers, but so great was Pravati's beauty, so ensnaring the inner warmth and passion that radiated from her body and her countenance, that Dasa was blind to everything else; he surrendered himself completely to her and in fact found his greatest happiness in her arms. Many tales have been told of gods and holy men who have been enchanted by an alluring woman and have remained with her for days, moons and years on end in close embrace, joined together in molten lust and oblivious to all other activities. Thus Dasa might have desired his own fate to be, but other things were in store for him and his happiness was not of long duration. It lasted for perhaps a year, but even during this time he did not enjoy complete happiness for it was marred by many things such as the burdensome demands of his father-in-law, the envenomed shafts of his brother-in-law and the caprices of his young wife. But whenever he repaired to his couch all these irritations were forgotten and compensated for, because he found such incredible sweetness in caressing her slender limbs and young body, where the garden of passion bloomed with a thousand blossoms, scents and shadows.

His happiness was hardly a year old when a day of unrest and turmoil broke over the whole settlement. Messengers on horseback appeared announcing that the young Rajah was arriving on a visit with men, horses and a baggage train to hunt in the neighbourhood. Tents were hastily erected and there was a great sound of horses and of horn blowing. Dasa did not trouble himself in the least about all this but continued to tend the mill, to work in the fields and he avoided the huntsmen and the courtiers. One day, however, upon returning to the hut he found that his wife was not there, although he had strictly forbidden her to go out. He felt a contraction in his heart and a presentiment of impending misfortune. Hastening to his father-in-law's hut he learned that Pravati was not with him either and that no one seemed to have seen anything of her. The gnawing fear in his heart increased. He searched the cabbage gardens and the fields round about, and for two whole days wandered this way and that, searching his own and his father-in-law's hut a thousand times, exploring the meadows, going down into the well, praying, calling her name, enticing, cursing and looking for footprints. Eventually the youngest of his brothers-in-law, who was still a boy, divulged to him that Pravati was with the Rajah, that she was living in his tent and that she had also been seen riding his horse.

Dasa now haunted Nala's encampment day and night, carrying in his hand the sling he had once used as a herdsman, and whenever the prince's tent appeared to be unguarded he would stalk cautiously up to it, but each time a guard would show up and he would be obliged to flee. One evening, from the branches of a neighbouring tree, whence he could look down upon the tent, he saw the Rajah whose face he recognised from the feast in the town and which even then had been so repugnant to him, mount his horse and ride away. When he returned after a few hours and opened the tent door Dasa saw a young woman come forward from the shadows to greet him. He almost fell out of the tree, for he recognised in this young woman his wife Pravati. Now that he possessed the certainty the numbing pressure over his heart grew even stronger. Although his love for Pravati had been very great, his sorrow, anger and the feeling of his loss and affront were no less so—even greater perhaps. This is always the way when a man has lavished all his store of love upon one object: when he loses it everything collapses and he remains a pauper among the ruins.

For a night and a day Dasa wandered about aimlessly in the neighbouring thickets, and during each short respite the misery welled up afresh in his heart. He felt a compulsion to be on the move, as though he must wander to the end of the world, to the end of his life, which had lost its meaning and splendour; and yet his feet did not carry him·far afield, into the unknown and the beyond, but hovered continually around the scene of his misfortune, encircling his hut, the mill, the fields and the Rajah's camp. At last, overcome by a wave of angry bitterness, he hid himself once more in the branches overlooking the tent and, crouching like a hungry beast of prey in this leafy hiding place, waited until the moment came for which he had been conserving his last ounce of strength—until Nala appeared from the doorway. Then he slipped lightly from the branches, prepared his sling with a large stone and hurled it straight between the eyes of his enemy, who fell and lay lifeless on the ground. No one seemed to have seen. Through the storm of passion and the joy of revenge which swept through Dasa's senses, there entered a second or two of terrifying, strange deep calm.

Even before the noise of discovery and the whimpering cries of the servants had begun he had disappeared into the thicket and thence into the wilderness of bamboos that led to the valley.

In jumping down from the tree and in the intoxication of the act of whirling his death-dealing sling it had seemed to him as though, in these actions, he were extinguishing his own life as well, as though, having put every bit of energy he had behind the fatal stone, he himself were flying with it into the abyss of destruction and that he would be content with his downfall if only the hated enemy fell before him in that instant; but now that the deed was done and had been followed by that awful moment of silence, a love of life of which he had never previously dreamed drew him back from the yawning abyss, took possession of his senses and limbs with a violent primitive urge and cautioned him to seek out the forest and the bamboo jungle, bid him flee and remain invisible.

Only when the first danger had been averted and he had reached comparative safety did he realise what had happened. He sank to the ground completely exhausted and gasping for breath, and as his excitement died down he felt a sense of bitter disappointment and repugnance at the knowledge that he had escaped with his life: but hardly had he recovered his breath and the giddiness of exhaustion had passed than this cloying and repulsive feeling changed to one of consolation. The will to live and the wild joy of his deed returned once more with violence to his heart.

There was soon great activity in his proximity for the search for the murderer had begun. It lasted the entire day and he only escaped detection because he remained obstinately in his hiding place in the forest, which no one dared penetrate too deeply on account of tigers. Persistently on the alert, he slept but little and pressed forward in short stages until on the third day, having crossed the chain of foothills, he wandered without a halt into the high mountain districts.

This homeless existence led him hither and thither, made him tougher and more indifferent but also more intelligent and more resigned. He still dreamed of Pravati and his erst-while happiness as he liked to think of it and also many times of his flight—terrifying and disturbing dreams somewhat of the following nature: he would be fleeing through the forest and behind him would hear the drums and hunting horns of the pursuers. He would always be carrying through forest, bog and thicket and across rotting bridges a burden, a package, something wrapped up, shrouded and mysterious, of which he knew nothing except that it was precious and that under no circumstances had he to let it out of his hands— something valuable and in danger, a treasure, something stolen perhaps, enveloped in a cloth, a coloured material with a reddish brown and blue pattern such as the material of Pravati's dress. Laden with this bundle, this loot or treasure, he would be creeping amidst great dangers and tribulations, beneath overhanging branches and under frowning cliffs, avoiding snakes and crossing small vertiginous footbridges over crocodile infested rivers. At last, coming to a halt, tormented and exhausted, he would fumble with the knots of his package, untying them one by one and spread out the cloth, to find that the treasure he would then extract from it and hold up in his trembling hands was his own head!

He lived perpetually on the move and in hiding, no longer actually fleeing from men but simply avoiding them. One day his travels led him through a grassy and hilly district which reassured and encouraged him by its beauty and its serenity, which seemed in some strange way to welcome him as though he had been there before. He saw a meadow with gently swaying grass and a cluster of sallows which reminded him of the calm and innocent days before he had known aught of love and jealousy, hate and revenge: it was the self-same pasture land where he had once tended his flock with his comrades. Those had been the most tranquil days of his youth, and they now looked aross at him from the irrevocable past. Sweet sorrow found an answering chord in his heart to the voices that welcomed him here—the wind rustling the silver leaves of the willows, the gay swift marching song of the little brooks, the trill of the birds and the deep buzzing of the golden bumble bees. All the sounds and smells suggested a sanctuary and a homeland, and in spite of the fact that he was so used to the vagabond life of a cowherd, it seemed to him that he had never discovered a place at once so homely and so harmoniously attuned to his feelings and disposition.

To the accompaniment of these voices in his soul and with something of the feelings of a returning prodigal, he wandered slowly through the friendly land and for the first time for six desperate months felt no longer a stranger, a fugitive and an outlaw but light in heart, thinking of nothing, desiring nothing, enjoying to the full the enchanting present in these surroundings, grateful to and a little bewildered by this new unusual state of mind, by this imperturbable serenity and this gratifying pleasure of observation. It drew him across the meadows to the forest and into the twilight under the trees, dappled with patches of sunlight. Here the feeling of return and homecoming grew even stronger and led him on to a path which his feet seemed to find unaided until, making his way through a fern jungle he reached a giant banyan tree and a little hut before which sat the motionless Yogi to whom he had once before brought gifts of milk and butter.

Dasa stood as though he had just been awakened from a long sleep. He found everything just as it had once been. Time had not moved here: there had been no conflict or murder here. It seemed to him as though life and time had become crystallized in the eternal. He looked at the old man and all the admiration, love and longing that he had once felt for him returned to his heart once more. One glance at the hut was enough to tell him that it would be necessary to make some improvements before the next rainy season. Venturing a few steps forward, he then entered the hut and examined its contents: he found a bed of leaves, a gourd containing a little

water and an empty wicker basket. Taking the basket he went
away to look for food in the forest and returned with fruits
and sweet resin. Next he took the bowl and filled it with
fresh water. He had now accomplished all that could be done
—one needed so little here in order to live—so he squatted
down on the ground and fell into a deep reverie, content with
the silence, content to be resting and dreaming in this forest,
with himself and with the inner voice that had led him back to
the spot where, as a youth, he had once felt happiness and joy
and which he had felt to be his home.

He remained with the old man, renewed his bed of leaves,
provided food daily for both of them, repaired the hut and
began to build a second one close at hand for himself. The old
man seemed to tolerate him but Dasa could not be absolutely
certain as to whether he had realized his presence or not.
When the Yogi came out of his deep meditation it was only
to enter the hut and sleep, to eat a mouthful or to go for a
short walk in the forest. Thus Dasa lived with the silent one,
obliging and hardly noticed, as a servant in the presence of a
great man, or rather as a small house pet, a tame bird or a
mongoose might live among men. Because he had existed for
so long as a fugitive and in hiding, unsure of himself, with a
guilty conscience and perpetually aware of pursuit, this rest-
ful life, effortless work and the proximity of the Yogi, who
seemed to be completely unaware of him, suited him well
enough for a time: he slept dreamlessly and without fear,
forgetting for days on end what had happened. He gave no
thought to the future, and if he had any desires at all they
were to remain here, to be accepted and initiated by the Yogi
into the mysterious life of an ascetic, to participate in yoga
and eventually to attain all their proud freedom from care.

He had begun to imitate more and more often the behaviour of the venerable hermit, to sit motionless with his
legs crossed, to peer into an invisible world and to become
insensible to all that was happening around him. For the most
part it simply tired him out; his limbs suffered agonies from
stiffness and his back ached; he was importuned by mosquitoes
or attacked by a curious sensitivity of the skin, an itching and
an irritation which compelled him to fidget and scratch himself and finally to abandon his sitting posture. Sometimes
however, he experienced quite a different sensation, an

emptiness, a feeling of lightness and levitation such as some-times occurs in dreams: one seems to glide above the earth like a cloud, and when occasionally one comes down to touch it one is swiftly repelled again. In these moments he obtained a glimpse into what it must be like to soar perpetually, how his own body could shed its weight and enable his soul to swing in the rhythm of a greater, purer, sunnier life, elevated and impelled by the permanent, the timeless and the infinite. But these remained moments and presentiments and when, disappointed, he returned to everyday life he decided that he would try to persuade the master to be his teacher, instruct him in his exercises and secret arts and perhaps make of him a Yogi. Yet how could he achieve this? It did not seem as though the old man would ever recognise him with his eyes or as though words could ever be spoken between them for he appeared to be beyond days and hours, forest and hut and also beyond speech.

One day, however, Dasa plucked up enough courage to break the silence. He had once more fallen a prey to dreams which recurred night after night, alternately sweet and nightmarish, either of his wife Pravati or of the terror of the fugitive's life, and he made no progress by day: he could not sit and practise his exercises for any length of time but was constrained to think of women and love. It may of course have been on account of the thundery weather, for the days were sultry with burning gusts of wind. One particularly disturbing day, when the mosquitoes had swarmed, Dasa dreamed a heavy dream which left him fearful and tense, the content of which he could not remember in detail but which seemed on awakening to signify a piteous and shameful retrogression to an earlier stage and condition of life. He slunk about in the vicinity of the hut the whole day long, sombre and restless, playing at this task and that, settling down more than once to practise his meditation but on each occasion being over-come by a feverish unrest. His limbs trembled, the soles of his feet tickled as though besieged by a swarm of ants and his neck burned intolerably. He endured it for a while and then looked shyly and rather shamefacedly over at the old man, who was sitting there in a perfect attitude and whose face, with the inwardly turned eyes, swayed gently and with the calm serenity of a lotus flower.

When the Yogi arose and went over to the hut, Dasa, who had long waited a propitious moment to speak to the sage, confronted him at last.

"Oh most venerable one," he said, "forgive me for intruding upon your peace. I myself am in search of peace and should like to be like you and to live as you do. Look, I am still young and yet I have already suffered much and destiny has played many a hideous trick upon me. I was born a prince only to be banished among the cows and the herdsmen. I became a cowherd myself, and grew up joyful and strong as a young ox and innocent in heart. But then my eyes became aware of women, and as the most beautiful of them all came before my gaze, I placed my life in her service. I should have died had I been unable to possess her, so I abandoned my fellow travellers and courted Pravati. I became a son-in-law and a servant and worked hard, but Pravati was mine and loved me, or so I thought, and every evening I returned to her arms and lay upon her breast. And then one day the Rajah arrived in the neighbourhood—that same step-brother on whose account I had been driven out as a child—who came and took Pravati away from me. This was the greatest sorrow that I had yet suffered and it transformed my entire existence. I slew the Rajah and have since led the life of a criminal and a fugitive, for pursuers have been on my heels ever since and my life has not been safe for an hour until the moment I arrived here. I am a madman, Oh venerable one—I am a murderer—and perhaps they will catch me and tear me limb from limb. I cannot endure this terrible life a moment longer, and I would be free of it."

The Yogi had listened in silence to Dasa's outburst with downcast eyes. He now raised them slowly to the level of Dasa's face and gave him a piercing, almost unbearably direct and concentrated look. As he watched Dasa's face and pondered upon his hasty tale, his mouth suddenly changed to a smile until finally, shaking his head with a noiseless laugh he cried: "Maya! Maya!"

Confused and ashamed Dasa remained standing there while the old man calmly went off for his usual walk, before taking his meal, along the narrow path through the ferns. He walked up and down with well measured steps and when, after a few hundred paces, he returned and went into his hut his face, as usual, was turned once more away from the world of appearances. What manner of laugh had it been that had come from the Yogi's motionless face in reply to the wretched Dasa? He was forced to reflect upon it for a long time. Had this appalling laugh at the end of Dasa's confession and request been benevolent or scornful, consoling or condemning, godlike or infernal? Had it been only the cynical bleating of old age no longer to be taken seriously or the amusement of a sage over an alien madness? Was it a rejection, a gesture of farewell, a dismissal, or did he wish it to be a counsel, a challenge for Dasa to imitate him and to laugh with him? He could not solve the riddle. He thought far into the night of this laughter which his life, happiness and misery seemed to have inspired in the old man. His thoughts chewed upon this laughter as though it were a hard root, which did however have a certain odour and savour; and furthermore he reflected long upon the word that the old man had called out so clearly and serenely and the fact that he had appeared so incomprehensibly pleased with himself. "Maya! Maya!" What did it signify?

He had already known and half-sensed the significance of the word, and the manner in which the old man had uttered it had half betrayed its meaning. Maya—illusion. He thought of his life, his youth, his sweet happiness and his bitter sorrow. It had all been Maya. The lovely Pravati was Maya; love and its lusts, and the whole of life—Maya! Dasa's life and the lives of all men were, in the eyes of this old Yogi all illusion— something in the nature of a childish spectacle, a theatre, a figment of the imagination, a bright painted nullity, a soap bubble, at which one could laugh with a certain delight and at the same time despise, but which under no circumstances could one take seriously.

Even though Dasa's life had been brushed aside and dismissed by the old Yogi in that laughter and with the single word Maya, it was by no means the case with Dasa himself. However much he might himself have desired to be a laughing Yogi and to recognize in his own laughter nothing but Maya, and inasmuch as during these restless days and nights everything which he had seemed to have forgotten for a while in this sanctuary after the exhaustion of his fugitive days had become reawakened and vivid once more, the hope that he could really learn Yoga or resemble the old man seemed to have grown extremely small. To what purpose then had his sojourn in the wood been? The old man's hut had been a haven wherein he had been able to breathe a little more freely and to collect a little strength, wherein he had come a little more to his senses—all of which had been of use and of great value; and perhaps, in the meanwhile, outside the forest the hunt for the prince's assassin had been abandoned and he could now go on his way without undue danger. He decided to do this and determined to leave on the following day. The world was large and he could not remain in this hiding place for ever. This resolution brought him a little peace of mind.

He had wished to leave in the early morning, but upon awakening he found the sun already high in the heavens and the Yogi sitting in deep meditation. Dasa did not wish to depart without taking his leave of the old man, for whom he still felt a great affection, and waited therefore until the hour when the hermit arose, stretched his limbs and began to pace up and down. Then he placed himself in his path, bowed low and did not desist until the master turned a questioning gaze upon him.

"Master," he said humbly, "I would now go on my way. I do not wish to disturb your peace any longer. But, most venerable one, grant me one last favour: when I told you of my life you laughed and called out 'Maya'! I implore you—let me know a little more about this 'Maya'!"

The Yogi turned towards the hut and beckoned Dasa to follow him. He took up the water bowl, held it out and bade the youth wash his hands, which he did. Then the master threw the remains of the water into the ferns, held out the empty bowl and told him to bring fresh water. Dasa obeyed, and a feeling of sorrow nagged at his heart because he was now taking this tiny footpath to the spring for the last time, taking the light bowl with the smooth worn away edge to the little pond in which the hart's tongues and the treetops, with occasional patches of blue sky, were reflected and in which, too, he had become so used to seeing his own face looking back at him through the russet twilight. Slowly and thoughtfully he dipped the bowl in the water. He felt a strange sense of uncertainty and could not understand why his decision to depart grieved him so much and why it hurt him that the old man had not invited him to stay—perhaps for ever.

He knelt down at the water's edge and took a sip of water, rose carefully with the bowl in his hand so as not to spill any and was about to make his way back to the hut when a sound that at once delighted and terrified him reached his ear—a voice which he had heard so often in his dreams and about which he had thought during many of his waking hours with bitterest longing. It rang sweetly, childishly and lovingly through the twilight of the forest and made his heart tremble with fear and passion. It was the voice of Pravati his wife.

"Dasa!" she called enticingly.

Not believing his ears he looked around him, the bowl of water still in his hands, and saw emerging from between the tree trunks, slender and lithe with her long legs, the beloved, the unforgettable, the faithless Pravati. He let fall the bowl and ran to meet her. She stood before him smiling and somewhat abashed, looking at him out of her gazelle-like eyes, and now that she was near he saw that she was wearing scarlet leather sandals and beautiful, costly garments, a gold bracelet on her arm and glittering precious stones in her dark hair. He drew back involuntarily. Was she not still a prince's strumpet, running about in his finery? Had he not killed Nala? How could she appear before him and call his name decked in all these spangles and jewels?

She was more beautiful than ever, and before he could bring her to account he must needs take her in his arms, bury his forehead in her hair, lift her face up to his own and kiss her mouth, and as he did so he felt that everything he had ever possessed had returned to him once more—happiness, love, voluptuousness, lust for life and passion. He was soon far from this dark forest and the holy man in all his thoughts: forest, asceticism, meditation and yoga were forgotten, and forgotten, too, was the old water bowl which he should have returned. It remained lying at the spring's edge, whilst he and Pravati had already reached the outskirts of the forest. She began in all haste to tell him how she had come and how everything had transpired.

Her story was astonishing The manner in which Dasa
entered upon his new life was as incredible, charming and
fabulous as a fairy tale. It was not only that Pravati was his
own again, not only that the hated Nala was dead and that
the pursuit of the murderer had long since been abandoned,
but that Dasa, the former Prince's son who had become a
herdsman, had been publicly declared as the rightful Prince
and heir. An old Brahman and an old herdsman had revived
the almost forgotten story, bringing it to the lips of everyone,
and now the selfsame man who had been sought for so long as
Nala's murderer in order that he should be brought to the
torture and put to death was even more eagerly sought in
order to be crowned Rajah in his father's place and to enter
ceremoniously into the town.

It was like a dream, and what pleased the incredulous
youth most was the happy coincidence that of all the questing
messengers Pravati had been the one who had first found and
greeted him. They came to a tent at the edge of the forest
which smelt of smoke and venison, and Pravati was greeted
cordially by her followers. She presented and made known
Dasa, her husband, and a great feast was immediately
prepared. There was a man present who had been one of
Dasa's companions among the herdsmen, and it had been he
who had led Pravati and the company to this spot which he
had visited as a boy. He laughed with pleasure at seeing
Dasa and would have given him a friendly slap on the shoulder or perhaps embraced him had he not suddenly realized
that he was now Rajah and therefore no longer a comrade.
He stopped short as though suddenly maimed, walked up to
him more slowly and made a low obeisance. Dasa beckoned
him to arise and embraced him, spoke to him tenderly and
asked how he could possibly reward him. The herdsman
asked for a heifer and was promised one from the Rajah's best
strain. More and more strange faces were led before the new
Prince—officials and high Brahmans, whose homage he
received. A meal was produced and the music of drums,
banjos and flutes blared out. All this pomp and festivity
seemed to Dasa exactly like a dream: he could not really
believe it, but the most important thing was that Pravati, his
young wife, was there in his arms.

The retinue approached the town by easy stages and

runners were sent on ahead to spread the joyous news that the young Rajah had been found and was on his way home. As they came within sight of the city the sound of gongs and trumpets could be heard: a procession of sedate and white-robed Brahmans came out to meet him, headed by the successor of Vasudeva who, twenty years before, had sent him away to the herdsmen and who had only just recently died.

They greeted him, sang hymns, and then led him to the palace, before which had been lit a great sacrificial fire in his honour. Thus Dasa was conducted into his domain where there were more greetings, blessings and speeches of welcome. Outside, the townspeople celebrated until far into the night.

Each day he received instructions from two Brahmans and very soon knew everything that seemed necessary. He thenceforward attended the sacrifices, dispensed justice and practised the arts of knighthood and war. The Brahman, Gopala, initiated him into politics, informed him of the position of his house and its laws, the claims of his future heir and the nature of his foes. First and foremost of these was Nala's mother, who had once robbed Prince Dasa of his rights, who had had designs upon his life and who now hated him more than ever as the murderer of her son. She had fled to the palace of the neighbouring prince, Govinda, and had placed herself under his protection. This Govinda and his house were also enemies and were dangerous; they had already been at war with Dasa's forbears and lay claims to a certain portion of his territory. As opposed to this his southern neighbour, the Prince of Gaipali, had been a friend of Dasa's father and had not been able to suffer Nala: it would be an important duty to visit him, to take him presents and to invite him hunting in the near future.

The lady Pravati had assumed her rôle of a Princess to perfection. She understood how to behave regally and looked magnificent in her beautiful garments and jewels; in fact she looked for all the world as though she were no less well bred than her husband. They lived in blissful happiness year after year and their happiness gave them that certain glamour and charm only possessed by those whom the gods favour, so that they were loved and venerated by all, and when, after a long period of waiting, Pravati presented him with a son, whom he christened Ravana after his own father, his cup was full and all that he possessed in the way of land, power, houses, stables, dairies, cattle and horses, assumed henceforth a double importance and meaning in his eyes, assumed an increased splendour and value: all this property had been magnificent and gratifying to the extent that he had been able to surround Pravati with luxury, clothes and jewels, but it was now doubly magnificent and gratifying in that it constituted the heritage and future happiness of his son Ravana.

If Pravati derived her pleasures mainly from feasts, outings, pomp and extravagance, from clothes, jewels and servants, Dasa's chief joy lay in his garden, which he had had planted with rare and costly trees and flowers, and in which he had installed parrots and other bright coloured birds. Their daily feeding was one of his greatest amusements. In addition to this he was attracted to learning and, as a grateful pupil of the Brahmans, learned many verses and axioms and the art of reading and writing. He understood how to prepare palm leaves for writing, and under his loving care, a little library began to accumulate. Here, among his books, in a small tasteful room with walls of precious woods upon which the lives of the gods were carved and in part gilded, he sometimes allowed his Brahman guests, the cream of the scholars and thinkers among the priests, to argue upon holy things, upon the creation of the world, upon the Maya of the great Vishnu, upon the sacred Vedas, the power of sacrifice and the might of penance, through which a mortal could make the gods fear and tremble before him. The Brahmans who had spoken best in dispute and argument received sumptuous presents and many of them would bear away a fine cow as prize for a victorious argument. It was at once ludicrous and a little touching to see one of them, who had just been declaiming and commenting upon the precepts of the Vedas and who was equally at home in all the heavens and oceans, so proud and puffed up with his gifts of honour or in defeat lapsing into a jealous bickering with the others.

Occasionally it seemed to Prince Dasa that his wealth, happiness, garden and books—in fact all and everything that belonged to life and humanity—were strange and dubious and at the same time pathetic, like those vain-wise Brahmans, alternately light and dark, enviable or despicable. Sometimes when his eyes fell upon a lotus bloom in his garden, upon the brilliant plumage of his pheasants, peacocks and egrets or upon the gilded carvings of his palace, these things would seem to him divine and glowing with eternal life, and at other times—even at the same time—he would find in them something unreliable, questionable, something transitory and ephemeral, a readiness to sink once more into the formless, into chaos. Just as he himself, Prince Dasa, had once been a prince and then become a herdsman, murderer and outlaw, only to rise to the dignity of princehood once more, led and commanded by unknown powers, uncertain of to-day or of to-morrow, so the Maya game comprised the whole of life, the exalted and the humble, eternity and death, the great and the ridiculous. Even she, even the beautiful and beloved Pravati at moments seemed to lose her magic and would appear a little ridiculous with so many bangles upon her arms, so much pride and triumph in her eyes and so studied a dignity in her gait.

More prized however than his garden and his books was his little son, Ravana, the consummation of his love and the high point of his destiny, the object of his tenderness and care, a gentle lovely child, a true prince, with the gazelle-like eyes of his mother and a trace of his father's dreamy thoughtfulness. Sometimes, when he saw the little boy standing in reverie before an ornamental tree or when he surprised him squatting on a carpet examining a stone, a carved toy or a bird's feather, in deep contemplation with somewhat raised eyebrows and a far away look in his eyes, then he would seem to be a true son of his father. How much he loved him Dasa only realised when he was forced to leave him for an unspecified period of time.

A fast-riding messenger had arrived from that neighbourhood where his lands bordered upon those of Govinda, announcing that Govinda's people had invaded, stolen cattle and borne away a number of men as prisoners. Without stopping to reflect Dasa had prepared himself, gathered together a dozen horsemen under the colonel of the bodyguard, and gone off in pursuit of the robbers. When, at the moment of departure, he had taken his little son in his arms and kissed him, he had felt a fiery pang in his heart, which had been both surprising and touching, like a warning from the unknown, and during his long ride the knowledge of his love and devotion waxed to become a realization and a certainty.

He had preoccupied himself with reflecting as to the actual reasons for his being on horseback and as to why he was riding so hastily through his lands—what power it could be that compelled him to such a deed and to such strenuous efforts. Upon deep consideration he had realised that in his heart it was not really important and did not even bring him sorrow if, somewhere on his frontiers he had been robbed of men and cattle, that this insult to his princely rights would not suffice to arouse him to anger and action and that it would have been more seemly to have received the news of the cattle theft with a compassionate smile; and yet at the same time he knew that he would be committing a bitter wrong against the messenger who had hastened, to the point of exhaustion, to bring him the news, and no less so against the men who had been robbed and against those who had been taken prisoner, who had been dragged from their homes and peaceful lives and carried off into foreign slavery. Indeed, he would have wronged all his other subjects who had remained unscathed had he renounced a warlike revenge: they would have borne it badly and would not have understood why their prince had so ill-protected their land, that none of them, were they in turn to be subjected to a deed of violence, could count upon aid and revenge. He saw therefore that it was his duty to undertake this raid of reprisal. But what is duty? How many duties are there not that we often shirk without any heart pangs? How did it happen then that this duty of revenge did not come within the category of those that were a matter of indifference, that he could not shirk it, that he could not complete it half-heartedly and wearily but had to go through with it with zeal and passion? Hardly had the question arisen in his mind than his heart had already found the answer, inasmuch as it was still trembling from the pain of taking leave of Ravana, his little son. Were the Prince to allow his cattle and his people to be stolen without offering resistance, then robbery and violence would spread inwards from the frontiers of his land until at last the enemy would be able to attack him where he was capable of the greatest hurt—in the capital. They would rob him of his son, his successor. They would take him and kill him, perhaps with torture, and this was the utmost suffering that he could imagine, far worse even than the death of Pravati. He therefore rode zealously and played the dutiful prince, not because he was chagrined at the loss of cattle and land, not out of goodwill to his subjects and not out of pride in his paternal princely name, but because of a robust and insane love for his child, and because of a robust fear of the pain that the loss of this child would cause him. These were the conclusions he came to during his ride.

He did not, as a matter of fact, succeed in catching Govinda's men and punishing them for they had all escaped after their raid. In order to show his resolution he was obliged himself to violate the frontier in turn, to lay waste a village and carry off a few cattle and villagers. He had remained absent for many days and during the homeward ride had given way once more to deep thought. On his return to the palace he was very quiet and sorrowful for he had realized in the course of these reflections how completely and inextricably he had been caught up and ensnared in a cunning net, without hope of escape, as a result of his actions and his whole attitude. While on the one hand his preference for thought and his need for quiet observation, for an actionless and innocent life, increased day by day, his love for Ravana on the other hand, grew proportionately, and out of care for his existence and future arose the compulsion to action with the inevitable entanglements: out of tenderness grew conflict and out of love, war. No sooner had he robbed a herd or sacked a village and carried off poor and innocent men with violence, even though he were justified in doing so, then it would naturally be followed by new revenge and ever more violence until his whole life and the whole of his country would be involved in war, violence and the clash of arms. This was the vision that he had seen on his homeward ride and which had made him appear so quiet and sorrowful.

It transpired that his hostile neighbour from then onwards gave him no peace. He renewed his raids and attacks, and Dasa was forced to resort to defence measures and raids of reprisal: if the enemy slipped through his hands he had

perforce to allow his soldiers and huntsmen to inflict new
damage upon his neighbours. In the city more and more
armed men and horsemen were to be seen, and in many of the
frontier villages soldiers were now stationed permanently on
guard. War councils and preparations for new forays made
the days restless. Dasa could not see the use of this guerilla
warfare, and grieved for the sufferings of the victims, for the
lives of the killed, pined for his garden and his books which he
was forced more and more to forego and for the peace of his
days and heart. He spoke frequently with Gopala, the
Brahman, and sometimes even with his wife, Pravati. He
insisted that they should summon one of the respected
neighbouring princes to act as arbitrator and to strive to
make peace terms. He for his part, would willingly relinquish
a few meadows and villages in order to reach a peaceful
settlement. When he saw that neither the Brahmans nor
Pravati would hear of such a thing he was disappointed and
also somewhat indignant.

The difference of opinion with Pravati led to a serious
dispute, even to a rift. He presented his reasons and thoughts
lucidly and imploringly but she received each word as though
it had been directed not against war and useless slaughter but
against herself personally. It was, she informed him in an
impassioned speech, exactly the enemy's object to exploit
Dasa's tolerance and love of peace, not to mention his fear of
war, to his advantage. He would bring him to sign peace
treaties one after another and to pay each time with a greater
sacrifice of territory and lives, and in the end, far from being
satisfied, and as soon as he considered Dasa to be weak
enough he would declare open war on him and rob him of
everything. It was a question not of herds and villages, of
profits and losses, but of the whole: it was a question of
survival or of destruction, and if Dasa did not know wherein
lay his duty and his honour, which he owed to his wife and
child, then she must teach him. Her eyes flamed and her voice
quavered, and although he had not seen her so beautiful and
passionate for a long time he experienced only a profound
sense of grief.

In the meantime the frontier incidents and breaches of the
peace continued, and only the rainy season put an end to them.
In Dasa's court, there were now two parties. The one, the

peaceful party, was very small for, apart from Dasa himself, only a few of the older Brahmans and scholarly men who were almost completely preoccupied with their meditations belonged to it. The war party, however, Pravati's and Gopala's party, had the majority of the priests and officers on its side. They eagerly gave orders to arm, and knew that their hostile neighbour was doing the same. The boy Ravana was taught the use of the bow by the chief huntsman, and his mother often took him with her to review the troops.

Dasa frequently thought of his sojourn in the forest when, as a wretched fugitive, he had rested a while, and of the white haired sage who lived in meditation. Time and again his thoughts turned to this old man, and he felt a longing to seek him out, to see him once more and ask his counsel. He did not know whether the Yogi was still alive, but even if he were, and condescended to give him his advice, he wondered whether everything would not take its natural course and whether nothing at all would come of it. Contemplation and wisdom were good and noble things, it seemed, but they were things apart and applied only to the fringes of life. Whoever swam in life's stream and struggled with the waves, where deeds and sufferings had nothing to do with wisdom, had to surrender himself to his destiny which had to be suffered and accomplished. Nor did the gods live in eternal peace and wisdom: they too were familiar with danger and fear, struggle and slaughter, as he knew from many stories. So Dasa surrendered, no longer quarrelled with Pravati and rode to all the reviews. He distinctly saw the approach of war, felt it in his disturbing nightly dreams, and as his figure grew more haggard and his face grew darker, saw the happiness and pleasure of his life fading and growing pale. There remained only his love for the boy, which increased with his sorrow, increased with the arming and the exercising of the troops and became the one burning, scarlet blossom in his garden. He was amazed to find how much emptiness and lack of joy one can bear, how inured one can become to care and aversion and how, in a heart which was now apparently devoid of passion, such a timorous and anxious love could bloom into something burning and imperious. Even though his life were perhaps meaningless, it was nevertheless not without a core and a nucleus, for it turned about the love for

his son. On account of him he would rise betimes from his
couch and pass his days in occupations and energies whose
goal was war and which were repulsive to him. On account of
him he would listen patiently to the counsels of the leader
and only oppose the resolutions of the majority when they
were too hasty and threatened to plunge them all into some
uncalculated adventure.

Just as his joy of life, his garden and his books gradually
became estranged and of no solace to him, so also he found
that she who for so many years had been the happiness and
pleasure of his life was becoming more and more inconstant.
It had started with politics, and on the day when Pravati had
made that passionate speech in which, with undignified scorn,
she had treated his horror of transgression and love of peace
as cowardice, when she had spoken with burning cheeks and
fiery words about princely honour, heroism and insults
received, he had been struck and had felt with a sudden sense
of giddiness how far apart his wife and he had grown. Since
then the rift between them had widened and grown ever wider
each day without either of them lifting a finger to repair it.
Furthermore, it was Dasa who had decided to pursue this
course and it became more and more an example of the rift of
all rifts, of the world abyss between man and woman,
between yea and nay, between soul and body. When he
looked back, he thought he could see it all quite clearly: how
once Pravati, with her magical beauty, had trifled with him
and enflamed his feelings until he had cut loose from his
comrades and friends, the herdsmen, and from the life which
had hitherto been so peaceful; how, on her account he had
gone to live in service among strangers, had become a
son-in-law in a house of worthless people who had exploited
his love for Pravati in order that he might work for them.
Then Nala had appeared on the scene and his misfortunes had
begun. Nala, the rich dazzling Rajah, had seduced his wife,
had seduced the poor girl so unused to luxury, with beautiful
clothes and tents, with horses and servants—a conquest
which could have cost him very little effort. But could he have
seduced her so easily had she been inwardly constant and
disciplined? No. The Rajah had seduced her, or abducted her,
and had caused him a hateful pain such as he had never
suffered before. He had taken his revenge, however: he had

struck down the thief who had stolen his happiness, and that had been a moment of great triumph. Yet, hardly had he committed this deed than he had been forced to take to flight, to live for days, weeks and months on end in the jungle and the swamps, outlawed and trusting in no man.

What had Pravati done during that time? They had never referred to that period. In any case, he reflected, she had not fled to join him but only when his princely birth had been announced and his people were clamouring for him to mount the throne and occupy the palace had she come to seek him out: she had simply appeared out of the forest in the neighbourhood of the worthy hermit and led him away. He had been decked in fine raiment, had been proclaimed Rajah and all had been splendour and happiness—but in truth, what had he abandoned at that time and for what had he exchanged it? He had exchanged it for magnificence and the duties of a prince, duties which in the beginning had not been easy and which had grown more and more onerous; he had exchanged it for the repossession of a beautiful wife, for sweet hours of dalliance with her; and then there had been the son, his growing love for him and the ever increasing anxiety for his menaced life and happiness, until at last war stood at the gates. This was what Pravati had brought to him when she had discovered him in the forest at the spring's edge. What he had abandoned was the peace of the forest and a pious solitude. He had given up the neighbourship and example of a holy Yogi, had given up the hope of his instruction and perhaps his succession, the deep, radiant and imperturbable tranquility of the sage and a release from the conflicts and passions of life. Seduced by Pravati's beauty, strangled by woman and tainted with her ambition, he had abandoned the only path along which freedom and peace could be won. This is how his life history appeared to him that day. It was a plausible enough interpretation, and in actual fact it required but few omissions and suppressions for it to appear true. He had however omitted to recall, among other things, the fact that he had by no means been the hermit's pupil and had intended to leave him again voluntarily. So distorted do things become when they are viewed at some later date.

Pravati saw these things quite differently, although she devoted far less time to such speculations. She never thought of Nala at all. On the contrary, if her memory did not deceive her, it had been she who had been responsible for Dasa's happiness; it had been she who had raised him to the status of Rajah again and had presented him with a son, only ultimately to find that he was not her equal in greatness and unworthy of her great pride. It was clear to her that the impending war could lead to no less than to Govinda's destruction and to the doubling of her own power and possessions. Instead of being glad of this and instead of being anxious to co-operate, Dasa, it seemed to her, strove on the contrary in a most unprincely manner against war and conquest and would have preferred to grow old and inactive among his flowers, trees, parrots and books. Now Vishwamitra, the commander-in-chief of the cavalry, and after herself the most ardent supporter and planner of the coming war and victory, was a very different species of man. Every comparison between the two men was obviously to the soldier's advantage.

Dasa saw quite clearly how friendly his wife had become with Vishwamitra, how much she admired him and allowed herself to be admired in turn by this cool and courageous though perhaps somewhat superficial and not over-intelligent soldier, with his healthy laugh, strong white teeth and well trimmed beard. He watched all this with bitterness and at the same time contempt, deceiving himself behind a mask of scornful indifference. He did not spy upon them and desired to remain in ignorance as to whether their friendship had surpassed the limits of decency and the permissible or not. He observed that Pravati was in love with the handsome cavalier, and treated the gestures which made it obvious that she preferred him to her all too unheroic husband with the same outward indifference and inner bitter weariness with which he had now accustomed himself to look upon every event.

It was all the same to him whether it were an inconstancy or a betrayal that she seemed so determined to play upon him or merely an expression of her lack of esteem. It was a fact, and it waxed and developed against him like the war and destiny. There was no corrective and therefore no behaviour possible other than an acceptance, a weary tolerance, which was now Dasa's brand of male heroism as opposed to war and conquest.

Whether their admiration for each other remained within the bounds of morality or not, Dasa realized in any case that it was less Pravati's fault than his own. He, Dasa, the thinker and doubter, was inclined to seek in her the cause of his waning happiness, to make her jointly responsible for the fact that he had become inveigled into everything and entangled in it—in love, ambition and in acts of revenge and plunder. He made woman and the love and lust in his thoughts responsible for everything upon earth, for the whole fandango, the whole chase for passion and desire, adultery, death, murder and war. At the same time he knew full well that Pravati was not guilty or the cause, but was herself the sacrifice; that she had neither created nor was responsible for her beauty or her love but was only a mote of dust in a sunbeam, a wave in the stream, and that he ought to have fled from woman, love, ambition and the hunger for happiness, to have remained a contented herdsman or to have overcome his own shortcomings through the mysterious path of yoga. He had either missed his opportunity or he had failed. Either he had not been called to the great ones or else he had been untrue to his vocation, and his wife was right in the last analysis if she took him for a coward. On the other hand he had obtained this son from her, this pretty, tender boy on whose account he was so fearful and whose existence still justified the meaning and value of life and who was even a great source of happiness, a painful and anxious happiness, but nevertheless happiness—his happiness. This boon he was now paying for with the sorrow and bitterness in his heart, with the preparations for war and death, with the knowledge of going forward to meet his fate. Some distance away in his own country sat Govinda, advised and cajoled by the murdered Nala's mother—an evil reminder of that seducer. His invasions and provocations grew ever more frequent and impertinent, and only an alliance with the mighty Rajah of Gaipali would have made Dasa strong enough to compel him to keep the peace and to respect neighbourly treaties. But this Rajah, although well disposed towards Dasa, was related to Govinda and had refused even the politest attempts to win him over for such an alliance.

There was no way out, no hope of understanding or humanity: the fateful day approached and had to be endured.

After this outbreak of concentrated attacks and a speeding up of incidents which could no longer be tolerated, Dasa almost began to long for the war. He visited the Rajah of Gaipali once more and exchanged fruitless courtesies with him; in his councils he insisted upon moderation and patience, but had long since adopted a perfunctory attitude and was without hope. In addition to this he was arming. The differences of opinion in the council now centred around the question as to whether the next invasion by the enemy was to be countered by a march into his territory with a declaration of war or whether to await a major attack on the part of the enemy in order that he should be guilty of a breach of peace before the people and in the eyes of the whole world.

The enemy, who did not bother himself with such questions, at last put an end to discussion, councils and delays by striking. Govinda this time staged a rather larger expedition than usual, which enticed Dasa along with his commander and his best troops to the border, and while they were on the way launched his main forces upon the interior and particularly upon Dasa's capital, captured the gates and laid siege to the palace. No sooner had Dasa learned of this than he returned home immediately, as he knew that his wife and son would be imprisoned in the palace. Bloody fighting was in progress in the streets, and his heart bled when he thought of his near ones and their peril. He was now no longer the unwilling warrior for he burned with pain and rage, and rode home with his soldiers at breakneck speed. He found the battle raging in every street, cut his way through to the palace, engaged the enemy and fought like a fanatic until, as night fell, he collapsed exhausted and with several wounds.

When he recovered consciousness he found himself a prisoner in the palace. The battle had been lost and the palace was in the hands of the enemy. He was put in chains and brought before Govinda, who greeted him with scorn and led him into a nearby room—it was his own study, with the carved and gilded walls and the papyrus scrolls. On a carpet sat his wife, Pravati, surrounded by armed guards, and in her lap lay her son. The tender figure lay like a broken blossom—

dead, grey of face and his garments saturated with blood. The woman did not turn her head when her husband was led into the room: she merely stared with expressionless eyes at the little dead body. She seemed curiously changed to Dasa, and only after some minutes did he notice that her hair, which a few days previously had been jet black, was now flecked with grey. She must have been sitting there for a long time with the boy on her knee, staring into space with her mask-like face.

"Ravana!" cried Dasa, "Ravana, my child, my flower!"

He knelt down, and his face sank on to the dead child's head, knelt as though in prayer before his speechless wife and child, lamenting for both of them, protecting them. He smelt the odour of blood and death mingled with the scent of flower oil on the child's hair. Pravati looked down at them both with a face of stone.

He felt someone touch his shoulder. It was one of Govinda's men commanding him to stand up. He was led away. Neither he nor Pravati had spoken a single word to each other.

Dasa was laid upon a wagon and brought to Govinda's city, where his fetters were partially loosened. A soldier brought him a jug of water which he placed on the stone floor of the prison cell, and he was left alone behind barred doors. A wound in his shoulder burned like fire. He reached for the water jug and sprinkled water over his face and hands. He would have liked to drink but forbore: he would rather die, he thought. How long would it last—how long? He yearned for death as his parched throat yearned for water —only with death would the torture in his heart have an end, only then would the picture of the mother with her dead son fade—but in the midst of his torment weakness and weariness took compassion upon him and he sank to the floor and fell asleep.

When he came out of this short sleep he tried to rub his eyes in his drowsiness but was unable to do so: his hands were busied with something held firmly between them, and when at last he had the courage to open his eyes there were no longer prison walls around him but a greenish light which shone bright and strong upon the moss and

foliage. He blinked his eyes for a long time as the light struck
them with a silent but sturdy blow, and a trembling shudder
of terror ran through his spine. He blinked again, screwed up
his face almost with a whimper and opened his eyes wide.

He was standing in a forest and in his two hands he was
holding a bowl filled with water. At his feet the basin of a
spring gleamed like a brown and green mirror: somewhere
behind him he knew stood the hut in the fern thicket and the
Yogi who had sent him to fetch water—he who had laughed
so strangely and whom he had begged to teach him something
of Maya. He had neither lost a battle nor a son, was neither a
prince nor a father, but the Yogi had granted his wish and
taught him Maya or illusion. Palace, garden, library and
aviary, princely cares and parental love, war and jealousy,
love for Pravati and deep-rooted distrust, all were nothing—
no, not quite, but simply Maya!

Dasa stood there completely bewildered. Tears streamed
down his cheeks, his hands trembled and a little of the water
flowed over the rim of the bowl on to his feet. It felt as
though a limb had been cut from his body, as though something had been removed from his head: he felt empty, and
suddenly the long years, the pleasures enjoyed, the pain
suffered, the fear undergone and the desperation nigh unto
death had all been removed, had been extinguished and
brought to nothing, and yet not altogether to nothing for the
memory was still there, the pictures still remained with him.
He could see Pravati sitting erect and frozen and in her lap
her son lying as though she herself had suffocated him, lying
there like a trophy, his limbs hanging lifeless across her knees.

Oh, how rapidly, gruesomely and profoundly had he been
taught Maya! Everything had been displaced in time and
everything had been telescoped within the twinkling of an
eye: everything was a dream, even that which had seemed
dire truth and perhaps also all that which had happened
previously—the story of the prince's son Dasa, his cowherd's
life, his marriage, his revenge upon Nala and his sojourn with
the Yogi. They were all pictures such as one may admire on a
carved palace wall, where flowers, stars, birds, apes and gods
can be seen portrayed in bas-relief. Was not all that which he
had most recently experienced and now had before his eyes—
this awakening out of his dream of princehood, war and

prison, this standing by the spring, this water bowl which he had just shaken, along with the thoughts he was now thinking —ultimately woven of the same stuff? Was it not dream, illusion, Maya? And what he was about to live in the future, see with his eyes and feel with his hands until death should come—was that of other stuff, of some other fashion? It was a game and a delusion, foam and dream, it was Maya, the whole beautiful, dreadful, enchanting and desperate kaleidoscope of life with its burning joys and sorrows.

Numbed and paralysed, Dasa stood there. Once more the bowl trembled in his hands and the water overflowed, splashed cool upon his toes and into the soil. What should he do? Fill the bowl again and take it back to the Yogi? Submit for ever to his laughter for all that he had suffered in his dream? It was not an alluring thought. He emptied the water from the bowl and threw it down on the moss. Then he sat down and began to reflect earnestly. He had had enough and more than enough of this dreaming, of this demonic patchwork quilt of events, joys and sufferings, which strangled the heart and made the blood stand still simply to become Maya and to leave one behind like a fool. He had had enough of it all. He desired no more wife or child, neither throne nor victory nor revenge, neither happiness nor cleverness, neither might nor virtue: he desired nothing but peace, nothing except an end, wanted nothing except to bring this eternally revolving wheel, this endless picture-show to a standstill and to extinguish it. He wished to bring himself to an end, to find peace as he had once desired it when, in that last battle, he had flung himself against the enemy, striking all about him only to be struck in turn until he collapsed with his wounds. But what then? Then there would be a pause of unconsciousness, slumber or death, and immediately one would be awake once more, would be obliged to let in the stream of life into one's heart again, and the beautiful, terrifying flood of pictures—endless and inescapable—would ensue until the next consciousness, until the next death. Yes, there would perhaps be a pause, a short insignificant respite, a moment for breathing space, but then it would continue and once more one would be one of the thousand figures in the savage, intoxicating, desperate dance of life. Ah, there was no extinction, no end!

Restlessness brought him to his feet again. If there really were no rest in this infernal roundelay, if his solitary yearning desire were not to be fulfilled, then he might just as well refill the water bowl and take it to the old man as he had ordered, although he had no right to command him at all. It was a service which had been asked of him, a task that one could obey and fulfil. It was infinitely better to obey and to serve than to sit merely thinking out ways of suicide, far more innocent and seemly than to rule and take responsibility. This much he knew. Good. Dasa, take your bowl then, fill it well with water and take it to your master!

When he arrived at the hut the master received him with a remarkable look, a slightly questioning, half commiserating half merry look of complicity such as an older boy might give to a junior upon his returning from a rather tiring and somewhat shameful adventure, some test of courage that had been allotted him. This herdsman prince, this poor wight who had fled to him, who had just returned from the spring with water, had not been absent longer than a quarter-of-an-hour but had nevertheless come out of a prison cell, had lost a wife, a son and a kingdom, had taken a human life and had had a glimpse of the spinning wheel. This young man had presumably once in an earlier life been awakened and had breathed a mouthful of reality, otherwise he would not have come to this spot and remained so long. Now he seemed to be truly awake and ripe for the entrance to the long way. It would take many years to teach him the correct procedure and breathing.

Only by this look, which contained a trace of benevolent sympathy and the hint of a relationship between them—the relationship between master and pupil—did the Yogi indicate that he had accepted the youth. It banished the useless thoughts from his head and received him in discipline and service. Nothing more can be told of Dasa's life for from then onwards it took a path beyond pictures and stories.

He never left the forest again.

THE   END